OTHER
DIMENSIONS

Other Fiction by Robert Silverberg

OTHER DIMENSIONS

THE MAN IN THE MAZE
NIGHTWINGS
UP THE LINE
DYING INSIDE

ROBERT SILVERBERG

50 YEARS SFBC

First SFBC Science Fiction Printing: September 2003

Published by arrangement with:
ibooks, inc.
24 West 25th Street
New York, NY 10010

Visit us online at http://www.sfbc.com

ISBN 0-7394-3637-6

Printed in the United States of America.

CONTENTS

INTRODUCTION

by Robert Silverberg

I wrote the four novels collected in this omnibus between the autumn of 1967 and the autumn of 1971—a four-year span that marked the most fertile period of my career. At the beginning of those four years I was brimming with ideas and writing with almost freakish ease, pouring forth books and stories at a rate that even I find hard to believe by this time. By the end of that period, though, I was approaching creative exhaustion, heading toward a burnout state that would last through much of the following decade. It was, I guess, an inevitable trajectory.

I had been a full-time professional writer for a dozen years when I wrote *The Man In The Maze*, but I was still only 32. It is very much a young man's book, full of inventive concepts and intricate narrative complications. The snarling, alienated man about whom the action revolves, caught in a tragic and hopeless predicament, was then a fairly uncommon sort of figure for science fiction (Alfred Bester's Gully Foyle is the only other example that comes readily to mind), though not at all unfamiliar to readers accustomed, as I had been during my college years a little more than a decade before, to the protagonists of Kafka, Joyce, Faulkner, and Thomas Mann. The underlying plot, indeed, came straight out of Sophocles' tragedy *Philoctetes*, which I had studied as an undergraduate at Columbia. (I learned much of what I know about constructing plots from a careful study of Greek tragedy in my college days.) But note that the moral focus of the story is youthful Ned Rawlins, not the embittered Richard Muller, and note also that the book ends in Rawlins' viewpoint, and with a manifestation of his youthful impatience.

Nightwings was begun less than six months after I delivered *Man In The Maze* to my publisher, and I had written two lengthy works of non-fiction, one on voyages of circumnavigation and one on the influence of climate on the development of civilization, in between. That was how I worked in those days: at an unrelenting pace, without a break between major projects. But a close inspection of the text shows that a significant diminution of youthful exuberance had occurred in me between *Maze* and *Nightwings*.

It wasn't just the constant overwork that had done it, either. In 1961 I had used the proceeds of my early books to buy myself a grand mansion in the Riverdale section of New York City, and on a bitterly cold night in February, 1968, that magnificent house was wrecked by a fire that began in the attic and swept downward through the third floor, where my writing office was located. So I began *Nightwings* in improvised rented quarters, working on an unfamiliar typewriter in a strange and uncomfortable place, numb with the exhaustion of coping for weeks with a major catastrophe. Somehow I found the energy to invent and set on paper the romantic and colorful opening section in just a few days—a bizarre and by now implausible summoning of mysterious strength. When I wrote it, I had no idea that I was beginning a novel; sleepwalker that I was in those terrible days, I was happy enough just to have been able to write 20,000 coherent words. (Which went on to win a Hugo the following year.)

Later in 1968, while the rebuilding of my house went slowly onward, I added the second and third sections to form the novel that is republished here. There are signs everywhere in it of the chaos that that year imposed on me. (And 1968, you may recall, was a chaotic year for the entire country: I was working against a background of assassinations of great public figures, student and racial riots, an unpopular and incomprehensible war, steeply rising inflation, and all manner of other ugly distractions.) So I killed off a major character midway through the book simply because I didn't have the vitality required to handle him, and was duly taken to task for it by that shrewd old pro, my friend Lester del Rey. And the final chapters embody an overt quest for rest, peace, an end to travail, that mirrored my own feelings at the time.

The rebuilding of the house was still incomplete when I began writing *Up The Line* in October of 1968. In it I set myself the task of producing, of all crazy things, a comic novel, this at a time when my mood was anything but lighthearted; and I constructed a time-travel plot for it so complex that I needed to draw a vast chart of its switchbacks, loops, and paradoxical twists. Worse yet, midway through the book I realized that the time-paradoxes I had invented would, when carried through to their logical ends, make it impossible for me to resolve the plot of the story that I had begun to tell. So it was necessary to halt and redraw my charts, and reposition some of the earlier scenes so that I could get to the outcome I wanted.

This was in 1968, I remind you, back when writers did their work on primitive machines known as *typewriters*, which did not permit the easy rewriting and rearrangement of huge blocks of text. I was required, rather, to go back and retype page after page. I was a tired man before I began the book; I was groggy with fatigue by the end of it. Yet *Up The Line*—I re-read it only last year—somehow *is* a funny book, and an inventive one too, managing to be both a parody of time-travel fiction and an original contribution to that sub-genre. When it was done, though, I swore a mighty oath that I would never again demand as much productivity from myself as I had in 1967 and 1968, and took myself off for a holiday among the elephants and lions of Kenya and Tanzania before starting the next book.

Indeed I never did return to the old frantic pace, even after the restoration of my house was completed in the spring of 1969, fourteen months after the fire. 1969 saw plenty of work done—the novels *Downward To The Earth, Tower Of Glass*, and *Son Of Man*, a good year's production for any writer, plus a bunch of short stories and some non-fiction works—but the total output was only two thirds of what it had been a couple of years previously, and in 1970, when I allowed myself a three-month summer vacation, the total was even lower.

Not only had the fire and its exhausting consequences left me very weary, but I was beginning to feel the first normal inroads of middle age, and by the summer of 1971 I was experiencing some marital turbulence too, with terminal strain starting to manifest itself in my 15-year-old marriage. Though the house now looked more splendid than ever, I felt the need for major changes in my life—including something that once would have been unthinkable for me, departure from my native New York City for the exotic, mysterious wilds of Northern California.

Against this background of personal upheaval I began to write *Dying Inside*, my most intimate and self-revealing novel, in the autumn of 1971.

Self-revealing, yes, but not (as many people seem to think) autobiographical. In creating David Selig I used various aspects of my own life—he and I were the same age, both Jewish, we both went to Columbia, both were solitary, introverted men. Even the term papers that David ghost-wrote for other Columbia students were my own actual papers, surviving from my college days. It was simply convenient, since the book took place only a couple of years in the future, to use all that familiar material instead of making my character's history up from scratch. But most aspects of David's life were sheer invention. (I am, for example, not a telepath, although one woman who read the book seemed to think I was, and came up to me at a science-fiction convention to say, "I never realized you were one of us!" To which I replied, "If I were, you'd have known it by now." Nor do I have a troubled relationship with my sister, since I have no sister, nor have I ever written term papers for a livelihood, though I've written just about everything else, nor did I live in a scruffy little one-room flat near the Columbia campus except during my undergraduate days. Et cetera.)

There was enough autobiographical material in the book, apparently, that even my publisher, Betty Ballantine, responded worriedly to the manuscript, saying, "It's a wonderful novel, Bob, but are you all right?" In fact I wasn't entirely all right—I was busy just then putting my beloved house on sale despite great interior conflict over leaving New York, and at the same time trying to figure out what, if anything, could be done to salvage my marriage—but I still felt, correctly, as it turned out, that the chaos of 1971 would ultimately bring me to some kind of stable new existence once I had finished all the transitions I was going through.

Of course there was plenty more transitioning to do. I moved to California, where very quickly my marriage finished coming apart. I encountered problems in my professional career, brought on largely because, in writing books like *Dying Inside*, I was moving rapidly away from the expectations of the basic science-fiction readership, and the readers of that era resented that. And the ongoing weariness that the past four or five chaotic years had engendered in me left me without the reserves of energy that an intense writing career demanded. I wrote two more novels and the novella "Born with the Dead," and then, in 1974, I threw up my hands and announced I was retiring "forever" from writing. No one took me seriously, of course, after such a prolific career, but I did manage close to five years of rest and rehabilitation before returning to my métier in 1979 with the long novel *Lord Valentine's Castle*.

And there you have it: these four novels, written within the space of five years, marking a period of vast and turbulent evolution in my life and in my career. The turbulence, thank God, is over. But the books remain.

—Robert Silverberg
May, 2003

THE MAN IN THE MAZE

1.

Muller knew the maze quite well by this time. He understood its snares and its delusions, its pitfalls, its deadly traps. He had lived within it for nine years. That was long enough to come to terms with the maze, if not with the situation that had driven him to take refuge within it.

He still moved warily. Three or four times already he had learned that his knowledge of the maze, although adequate and workable, was not wholly complete. At least once he had come right to the edge of destruction, pulling back only by some improbable bit of luck just before the unexpected fountaining of an energy flare sent a stream of raw power boiling across his path. Muller had charted that flare, and fifty others much like it; but as he moved through the city-sized labyrinth he knew there was no guarantee that he would not meet an uncharted one.

Overhead the sky was darkening; the deep, rich green of late afternoon was giving way to the black of night. Muller paused a moment in his hunting to look up at the pattern of the stars. Even that was becoming familiar now. He had chosen his own constellations on this desolate world, searching the heavens for arrangements of brightness that suited his peculiarly harsh and bitter taste. Now they appeared: the Dagger, the Back, the Shaft, the Ape, the Toad. In the forehead of the Ape flickered the small grubby star that Muller believed was the sun of Earth. He was not sure, because he had destroyed his chart tank after landing here. Somehow, though, he felt that that minor fireball must be Sol. The same dim star formed the left eye of the Toad. There were times when Muller told himself that Sol would not be visible in the sky of this world ninety light-years from Earth, but at other times he was quite convinced. Beyond the Toad lay the constellation that Muller had named

Libra, the Scales. Of course, this set of scales was badly out of balance.

Three small moons glittered here. The air was thin but breathable; Muller had long ago ceased to notice that it had too much nitrogen, not enough oxygen. It was a little short on carbon dioxide, too, and one effect of that was that he hardly ever seemed to yawn. That did not trouble him. Gripping the butt of his gun tightly, he walked slowly through the alien city in search of his dinner. This too was part of a fixed routine. He had six months' supply of food stored in a radiation locker half a kilometer away, but yet each night he went hunting so that he could replace at once whatever he drew from his cache. It was a way of devouring the time. And he needed that cache, undepleted, against the day when the maze might cripple or paralyze him. His keen eyes scanned the angled streets ahead. About him rose the walls, screens, traps, and confusions of the maze within which he lived. He breathed deeply. He put each foot firmly down before lifting the other. He looked in all directions. The triple moonlight analyzed and dissected his shadow, splitting it into reduplicated images that danced and sprawled before him.

The mass detector mounted over his left ear emitted a high-pitched sound. That told Muller that it had picked up the thermals of an animal in the 50–100 kilogram range. He had the detector programmed to scan in three horizons, of which this was the middle one, the food-beast range. The detector would also report to him on the proximity of 10–20 kilogram creatures—the teeth-beast range—and on the emanations of beasts over 500 kilograms—the big-beast range. The small ones had a way of going quickly for the throat, and the great ones were careless tramplers; Muller hunted those in between and avoided the others.

Now he crouched, readying his weapon. The animals that wandered the maze here on Lemnos could be slain without stratagem; they kept watch on one another, but even after all the years of Muller's presence among them they had not learned that he was predatory. Not in several million years had an intelligent life-form done any hunting on this planet, evidently, and Muller had been potting them nightly without teaching them a thing about the nature of mankind. His only concern in hunting was to strike from a secure, well-surveyed point so that in his concentration on his prey he would not fall victim to some more dangerous creature. With the kickstaff mounted on the heel of his left boot he probed the wall behind him, making certain that it would not open and engulf him. It was solid. Good. Muller edged himself backward until his back touched the cool, polished stone. His left knee rested on the faintly yielding pavement. He sighted along the barrel of his gun. He was safe. He could wait. Perhaps three minutes went by. The mass detector continued to whine, indicating that the beast was remaining within a hundred-meter radius; the pitch rose slightly from moment to moment as the thermals grew stronger. Muller was in no hurry. He was at one side of a vast plaza bordered by glassy curving partitions, and anything that emerged from those gleaming crescents would be an easy shot. Muller was hunting tonight in Zone E of the maze, the fifth sector out from the heart, and one of the most dangerous. He rarely went past the relatively innocuous Zone D, but some daredevil mood had prodded him into E this evening. Since finding his way into the maze he had never risked G or H again at all, and had been as far out as F only twice. He came to E perhaps five times a year.

To his right the converging lines of a shadow appeared, jutting from one of the curving glassy walls. The song of the mass detector reached into the upper end of the pitch spectrum for an animal of this size. The smallest moon, Atropos, swinging giddily through the sky, changed the shadow pattern; the lines no longer converged, but now one bar of blackness cut across the other two. The shadow of a snout, Miller knew. An instant later he saw his victim. The animal was the size of a large dog, gray of muzzle and tawny of body, hump-shouldered, ugly, spectacularly carnivorous. For his first few years here Muller had avoided hunting the carnivores, thinking that their meat would not be tasty. He had gone instead after the local equivalent of cows and sheep—mild-mannered ungulates which drifted blithely through the maze cropping the grasses in the garden places. Only when that bland meat palled had he begun to go after one of the fanged, clawed creatures that harvested the herbivores, and to his surprise their flesh was excellent. He watched the animal emerge into the plaza. Its long snout twitched. Muller could hear the sniffing sounds from where he crouched. But the scent of man meant nothing to this beast.

Confidently, swaggeringly, the carnivore strode across the sleek pavement of the plaza, its unretracted claws clicking and scraping. Muller fined his beam down to needle aperture and took thoughtful aim, sighting now on the hump, now on the hindquarters. The gun was proximity-responsive and would score a hit automatically, but Muller always keyed in the manual sighting. He and the gun had different goals—the gun was concerned with killing, Muller with eating; and it was easier to do his own aiming than to try to convince the weapon that a bolt through the tender, juicy hump would deprive him of the tastiest cut. The gun, seeking the simplest target, would lance through that hump to the spine and bring the beast down: Muller favored more finesse.

He chose a target six inches forward from the hump: the place where the spine entered the skull. One shot did it. The animal toppled heavily. Muller went toward it as rapidly as he dared, checking every footfall. Quickly he carved away the inessentials—limbs, head, belly—and sprayed a seal around the raw slab of flesh he cut from the hump. He sliced a hefty steak from the hindquarters, too, and strapped both parcels to his shoulders. Then he swung around, searching for the zigzagging road that was the only safe entry to the core of the maze. In less than an hour he could be at his lair in the heart of Zone A.

He was halfway across the plaza when he heard an unfamiliar sound.

Pausing, he looked back. Three small loping creatures were heading toward the carcass he had abandoned. But the scrabbling of the scavengers was not what he had heard. Was the maze preparing some new deviltry? It had been a low rumbling sound overlaid by a hoarse throb in the middle frequencies, too prolonged to be the roaring of one of the large animals. It was a sound Muller had not heard before.

No: a sound he had not heard *here* before. It registered somewhere in his memory banks. He searched. The sound was familiar. That double boom, slowly dopplering into the distance—what was it?

He placed its position. The sound had come from over his right shoulder, so it seemed. Muller looked there and saw only the triple cascade of the maze's secondary wall, rising in tier upon glittering amber tier. Above that wall? He saw the star-brightened sky: the Ape, the Toad, the Scales.

Muller remembered the sound now.

A ship; a starship, cutting out of warp onto ion drive to make a planetary landing. The boom of the expellers, the throb of the deceleration tubes, passing over the city. It was a sound he had not heard in nine years, since his self-exile on Lemnos had begun. So he was having visitors. Casual intruders, or had he been traced? What did they want? Anger blazed through him. He had had enough of them and their world. Why did they have to trouble him here? Muller stood braced, legs apart, a segment of his mind searching as always for perils even while he glared toward the probable landing point of the ship. He wanted nothing to do with Earth or Earthmen. He glowered at the faint point of light in the eye of the Toad, in the forehead of the Ape.

They would not reach him, he decided.

They would die in the maze, and their bones would join the million-year accumulation that lay strewn in the outer corridors.

And if they succeeded in entering, as he had done—

Well, then they would have to contend with him. They would not find that pleasant. Muller smiled grimly, adjusted the meat on his back, and returned his full concentration to the job of penetrating the maze. Soon he was within Zone C, and safe. He reached his lair. He stowed his meat. He prepared his dinner. Pain hammered at his skull. After nine years he was no longer alone on this world. They had soiled his solitude. Once again, Muller felt betrayed. He wanted nothing more from Earth than privacy, now; and even that they would not give him. But they would suffer if they managed to reach him within the maze. If.

2

The ship had erupted from warp a little late, almost in the outer fringes of Lemnos' atmosphere. Charles Boardman disliked that. He demanded the highest possible standards of performance from himself, and expected everyone about him to keep to the same standards. Especially pilots.

Concealing his irritation, Boardman thumbed the screen to life and the cabin wall blossomed with a vivid image of the planet below. Scarcely any clouds swathed its surface; he had a clear view through the atmosphere. In the midst of a broad plain was a series of corrugations that were sharply outlined even at a height of a hundred kilometers. Boardman turned to the young man beside him and said, "There you are, Ned. The labyrinth of Lemnos. And Dick Muller right in the middle of it!"

Ned Rawlins pursed his lips. "So big? It must be hundreds of kilometers across!"

"What you're seeing is the outer embankment. The maze itself is surrounded by a concentric ring of earthen walls five meters high and nearly a thousand kilometers in outer circumference. But—"

"Yes, I know," Rawlins burst in. Almost immediately he turned bright red, with that appealing innocence that Boardman found so charming and soon would be trying to put to use. "I'm sorry, Charles, I didn't mean to interrupt."

"Quite all right. What did you want to ask?"

"That dark spot within the outer walls—is that the city itself?"

Boardman nodded. "That's the inner maze. Twenty, thirty kilometers in diameter—and God knows how many millions of years old. That's where we'll find Muller."

"If we can get inside."

"*When* we get inside."

"Yes. Yes. Of course. *When* we get inside," Rawlins corrected, reddening again. He flashed a quick, earnest smile. "There's no chance we won't find the entrance, is there?"

"Muller did," said Boardman quietly. "He's in there."

"But he's the first who got inside. Everyone else who tried has failed. So why will we—"

"There weren't many who tried," Boardman said. "Those who did weren't equipped for the problem. We'll manage, Ned. We'll manage. We have to. Relax, now, and enjoy the landing."

The ship swung toward the planet—going down much too rapidly, Boardman thought, oppressed by the strains of deceleration. He hated travel, and he hated the moment of landing worst of all. But this was a trip he could not have avoided. He eased back in the webfoam cradle and blanked out the screen. Ned Rawlins was still upright, eyes glowing with excitement. How wonderful to be young, Boardman thought, not sure whether he meant to be sarcastic or not. Certainly the boy was strong and healthy—and cleverer than he sometimes seemed. A likely lad, as they would have said a few centuries ago. Boardman could not remember having been that sort of young man himself. He had the feeling of having always been on the brink of middle age—shrewd, calculating, well organized. He was eighty, now, with almost half his lifetime behind him, and yet in honest self-appraisal he could not bring himself to believe that his personality had changed in any essential way since he had turned twenty. He had learned techniques, the craft of managing men; he was wiser now; but he was not qualitatively different. Young Ned Rawlins, though, was going to be another person entirely sixty-odd years from now, and very little of the callow boy in the next cradle would survive. Boardman suspected, not happily, that this very mission would be the crucible in which Ned's innocence was blasted from him.

Boardman closed his eyes as the ship entered its final landing maneuvers. He felt gravity clawing at his aging flesh. Down. Down. Down. How many planetfalls had he made, loathing every one? The diplomatic life was a restless one. Christmas on Mars, Easter on one of the Centaurine worlds, the midyear feast celebrated on a stinking planet of Rigel—and now this trip, the most complex of all. Man was not made to flash from star to star like this, Boardman thought. I have lost my sense of a universe. They say this is the richest era of human existence; but I think a man can be richer in knowing every atom of a single golden island in a blue sea than by spending his days striding among all the worlds.

He knew that his face was distorted by the pull of Lemnos as the ship plunged planetward. There were heavy fleshy jowls about his throat, and pockets of extra meat here and there about his body, giving him a soft, pampered look. With little effort Boardman could have had himself streamlined to the fashionably sleek appearance of a modern man; this was an era when men a century and a quarter old could look like striplings, if they cared to. Early in his career Boardman had chosen to simulate authentic aging. Call it an investment; what he forfeited in chic he gained in status. His business was selling advice to governments, and governments preferred not to buy their counsel from men who looked like boys. Boardman had looked fifty-five years old for the last forty years, and he expected to retain that look of strong, vigorous early middle age at least another half a century. Later, he would allow time to work on him again when he entered the final phase of his career. He would take on the whitened hair and shrunken cheek of a man of eighty, and pose as Nestor rather than as Ulysses. At the moment it was professionally useful to look only slightly out of trim, as he did.

He was a short man, though he was so stocky that he easily dominated any group at a conference table. His powerful shoulders, deep chest, and long arms would have been better suited to a giant. When he stood up Boardman revealed himself as of less than middle height, but sitting down he was awesome. He found that feature useful too, and had never considered altering it. An extremely tall man is better suited to command than to advise, and Boardman had never had the wish to command; he preferred a more subtle exercise of power. But a short man who looks big at a table can control empires. The business of empires is transacted sitting down.

He had the look of authority. His chin was strong, his nose thick and blunt and forceful, his lips both firm and sensuous, his eyebrows immense and shaggy, black strips of fur sprouting from a massive forehead that might have awed a Neanderthal. He wore his hair long and coarse. Three rings gleamed on his fingers, one a gyroscope of platinum and rubies with dull-hued inlays of U-238. His taste in clothing was severe and conservative, running to heavy fabrics and almost medieval cuts. In another epoch he might have been well cast as a worldly cardinal or as an ambitious prime minister; he would have been important in any court at any time. He was important now. The price of Boardman's importance, though, was the turmoil of travel. Soon he would land on another strange planet, where the air would smell wrong, the gravity would be just a shade too strong, and the sun's hue would not be right. Boardman scowled. How much longer would the landing take?

He looked at Ned Rawlins. Twenty-two, twenty-three years old, something like that: the picture of naive young manhood, although Boardman knew that Ned was old enough to have learned more than he seemed to show. Tall, conventionally handsome without the aid of cosmetic surgery; fair hair, blue eyes, wide, mobile lips, flawless teeth. He was the son of a communications theorist, now dead, who had been one of Richard Muller's closest friends. Boardman was counting on that connection to carry them a good distance in the delicate transactions ahead.

Rawlins said, "Are you uncomfortable, Charles?"

"I'll live. We'll be down soon."

"The landing seems so slow, doesn't it?"

"Another minute now," Boardman said.

The boy's face looked scarcely stretched by the forces acting upon them. His left cheek was drawn down slightly, that was all. It was weird to see the semblance of a sneer on that shining visage.

"Here we come now," Boardman muttered, and closed his eyes again.

The ship closed the last gap between itself and the ground. The expellers cut out; the deceleration tubes snarled their last. There was the final awkward moment of uncertainty, then steadiness, the landing jacks gripping firmly, the roar of landing silenced. We are here, Boardman thought. Now for the maze. Now for Mr. Richard Muller. Now to see if he's become any less horrible in the past nine years. Maybe he's just like everyone else, by now. If he is, Boardman told himself, God help us all.

3

Ned Rawlins had not traveled much. He had visited only five worlds, and three of them were in the mother system. When he was ten, his father had taken him on a summer tour of Mars. Two years later he had seen Venus and Mercury. As his graduation present at sixteen he had gone extrasolar as far as Alpha Centauri IV, and three years after that he had made the melancholy trip to the Rigel system to bring home his father's body after the accident.

It wasn't much of a travel record at a time when the warp drive made getting from one cluster to another not much more difficult than going from Europe to Australia, Rawlins knew. But he had time to do his jaunting later on, when he began getting his diplomatic assignments. To hear Charles Boardman tell it, the joys of travel palled pretty fast, anyway, and running around the universe became just another chore. Rawlins made allowances for the jaded attitude of a man nearly four times his own age, but he suspected that Boardman was telling the truth.

Let the jadedness come. Right now Ned Rawlins was walking an alien world for the sixth time in his life, and he loved it. The ship was docked on the big plain that surrounded Muller's maze; the outer embankments of the maze itself lay a hundred kilometers to the southeast. It was the middle of the night on this side of Lemnos. The planet had a thirty-hour day and a twenty-month year; it was early autumn in this hemisphere, and the air was chilly. Rawlins stepped away from the ship. The crewmen were unloading the extruders that would build their camp. Charles Boardman stood to one side, wrapped in a thick fur garment and buried in an introspective mood so deep that Rawlins did not dare go near him. Rawlins' attitude toward Boardman was one of mingled awe and terror. He knew that the man was a cynical old bastard, but despite that it was impossible to feel anything but admiration for him. Boardman, Rawlins knew, was an authentic great man. He hadn't met many. His own father had been one, perhaps. Dick Muller had been another; but of course Rawlins hadn't been much more than twelve years old when Muller got into the hideous mess that had shattered his life. Well, to have known three such men in one short lifetime was a privilege indeed, Rawlins told himself. He wished that his own career would turn out half as impressively as Boardman's had. Of course he didn't have Boardman's foxiness, and hoped he never would. But he had other characteristics—a nobility of soul, in a way—which Boardman lacked. I can be of service in my own style, Rawlins thought, and then wondered if that was a naive hope.

He filled his lungs with alien air. He stared at a sky swarming with strange stars, and looked futilely for some familiar pattern. A frosty wind ripped across the plain. This planet seemed forlorn, desolate, empty. He had read about Lemnos in school: one of the abandoned ancient planets of an unknown alien race, lifeless for a thousand centuries. Nothing remained of its people except fossilized bones and shreds of artifacts—and the maze. Their deadly labyrinth ringed a city of the dead that seemed almost untouched by time.

Archaeologists had scanned the city from the air, probing it with sensors and curdling in frustration, unable to enter it safely. The first dozen expeditions to Lemnos had failed to find a way into the maze; every man who entered had perished, a victim of the hidden traps so cleverly planted in the outer zones. The last attempt to get inside had been made some fifty years ago. Then Richard Muller had come here, looking for a place to hide from mankind, and somehow he had found the route.

Rawlins wondered if they would succeed in making contact with Muller. He wondered, too, how many of the men he had journeyed with would die before they got into the maze. He did not consider the possibility of his own death. At his age, death was still something that happened to other people. But some of the men now working to set up their camp would be dead in a few days.

While he thought about that an animal appeared, padding out from behind a sandy hummock a short distance from him. Rawlins regarded the alien beast curiously. It looked a little like a big cat, but its claws did not retract and its mouth was full of greenish fangs. Luminous stripes gave its lean sides a gaudy hue. Rawlins couldn't see what use such a glowing hide would be to a predator, unless it used the radiance as a kind of bait.

The animal came within a dozen meters of Rawlins, peered at him without any sign of real interest, then turned gracefully and trotted toward the ship. The combination of strange beauty, power, and menace that the animal presented was an attractive one.

It was approaching Boardman now. And Boardman was drawing a weapon.

"No!" Rawlins found himself yelling. "Don't kill it, Charles! It only wants to look at us—!"

Boardman fired.

The animal leaped, convulsed in mid-air, and fell back with its limbs outspread. Rawlins rushed up, numb with shock. There hadn't been any need for the killing, he thought. The beast was just scouting us out. What a filthy thing to do!

He blurted angrily, "Couldn't you have waited a minute, Charles? Maybe it would have gone away by itself! Why—"

Boardman smiled. He beckoned to a crewman, who squirted a spray net over the fallen animal. The beast stirred groggily as the crewman hauled it toward the ship. Softly Boardman said, "All I did was stun it, Ned. We're going to write off part of the budget for this trip against the account of the federal zoo. Did you think I was all that trigger-happy?"

Rawlins suddenly felt very small and foolish. "Well—not really. That is—"

"Forget it. No, don't forget it. Don't forget anything. Take a lesson from it: collect all the data before shouting nonsense."

"But if I had waited, and you really had killed it—"

"Then you'd have learned something ugly about me at the expense of one animal life. You'd have the useful fact that I'm provoked to murderousness by anything strange with sharp teeth. Instead all you did was make a loud noise. If I had meant to kill, your shout wouldn't have changed my intention. It might have ruined my aim, that's all, and left me at the mercy of an angry wounded beast. So bide your time, Ned. Evaluate. It's better sometimes to let a thing happen than to play your own hand too quickly." Boardman winked. "Am I offending you, Ned? Making you feel like an idiot with my little lecture?"

"Of course not, Charles. I wouldn't pretend that I don't have plenty to learn."

"And you're willing to learn it from me, even if I'm an infuriating old scoundrel?"

"Charles, I—"

"I'm sorry, Ned. I shouldn't be teasing you. You were right to try to stop me from killing that animal. It wasn't your fault that you misunderstood what I was doing. In your place I'd have acted just the way you did."

"You mean I shouldn't have bided my time and collected all the data when you pulled the stungun?" Rawlins asked, baffled.

"Probably not."

"You're contradicting yourself, Charles."

"It's my privilege to be inconsistent," Boardman said. "My stock in trade, even." He laughed heartily. "Get a good night's sleep tonight. Tomorrow we'll fly over the maze and map it a little, and then we'll start sending men in. I figure we'll be talking to Muller within a week."

"Do you think he'll be willing to cooperate?"

A cloud passed over Boardman's heavy features. "He won't be at first. He'll be so full of bitterness that he'll be spitting poison. After all, we're the ones who cast him out. Why should he want to help Earth now? But he'll come around, Ned, because fundamentally he's a man of honor, and that's something that never changes no matter how sick and lonely and anguished a man gets. Not even hatred can corrode real honor. You know that, Ned, because you're that sort of person yourself. Even I am, in my own way. A man of honor. We'll work on Muller. We'll get him to come out of that damned maze and help us."

"I hope you're right, Charles." Rawlins hesitated. "And what will it be like for us, confronting him? I mean, considering his sickness— the way he affects others—"

"It'll be bad. Very bad."

"You saw him, didn't you, after it happened?"

"Yes. Many times."

Rawlins said, "I can't really imagine what it's like to be next to a man and feel his whole soul spilling out over you. That's what happens when you're with Muller, isn't it?"

"It's like stepping into a bath of acid," said Boardman heavily. "You can get used to it, but you never like it. You feel fire all over your skin. The ugliness, the terrors, the greeds, the sicknesses—they spout from him like a fountain of muck."

"And Muller's a man of honor . . . a decent man."

"He was, yes." Boardman looked toward the distant maze. "Thank

God for that. But it's a sobering thought, isn't it, Ned? If a first-rate man like Dick Muller has all that garbage inside his brain, what do you think ordinary people are like in there? The squashed-down people with the squashed-down lives? Give them the same kind of curse Muller has and they'd be like beacons of flame, burning up every mind within light-years."

"But Muller's had nine years to stew in his misery," Rawlins said. "What if it's impossible to get near him now? What if the stuff he radiates is so strong that we won't be able to stand it?"

"We'll stand it," Boardman said.

2.

Within the maze, Muller studied his situation and contemplated his options. In the milky green recesses of the viewing tank he could see the ship and the plastic domes that had sprouted beside it, and the tiny figures of men moving about. He wished now that he had been able to find the fine control on the viewing tank; the images he received were badly out of focus. But he considered himself lucky to have the use of the tank at all. Many of the ancient instruments in this city had become useless long ago through the decay of some vital part. A surprising number had endured the eons unharmed, a tribute to the technical skill of their makers; but of these, Muller had been able to discover the function of only a few, and he operated those imperfectly.

He watched the blurred figures of his fellow humans working busily and wondered what new torment they were preparing for him.

He had tried to leave no clues to his whereabouts when he fled from Earth. He had come here in a rented ship, filing a deceptive flight plan by way of Sigma Draconis. During his warp trip, of course, he had had to pass six monitor stations; but he had given each one a simulated great-circle galactic route record, carefully designed to be as misleading as possible.

A routine comparison check of all the monitor stations would reveal that Muller's successive announcements of location added up to nonsense, but he had gambled that he would manage to complete his flight and vanish before they ran one of the regular checks. Evidently he had won that gamble, for no interceptor ships had come after him.

Emerging from warp in the vicinity of Lemnos, he had carried out one final evasive maneuver by leaving his ship in a parking orbit and descending by drop-capsule. A disruptor bomb, preprogrammed, had blasted the ship to molecules and sent the fragments traveling on a billion conflicting orbits through the universe. It would take a fancy computer indeed to calculate a probable nexus of source for those! The bomb was designed to provide fifty false vectors per square meter of explosion surface, a virtual guarantee that no tracer could possibly be effective within a finite span of time. Muller needed only a very short finite span—say, sixty years. He had been close to sixty when he left Earth. Normally, he could expect at least another century of vigorous life; but, cut off from medical service, doctoring himself with a cheap diagnostat, he'd be doing well to last into his eleventh or twelfth decade. Sixty years of solitude and a peaceful, private death, that was all he asked. But now his privacy was interrupted after only nine years.

Had they really traced him somehow?

Muller decided that they had not. For one thing, he had taken every conceivable antitracking precaution. For another, they had no motive for following him. He was no fugitive who had to be brought back to justice. He was simply a man with a loathsome affliction, an abomination in the sight of his fellow mortals, and doubtless Earth felt itself well rid of him. He was a shame and a reproach to them, a welling fount of guilt and grief, a prod to the planetary conscience. The kindest thing he could do for his own kind was to remove himself from their midst, and he had done that as thoroughly as he could. They would hardly make an effort to come looking for someone so odious to them.

Who were these intruders, then?

Archaeologists, he suspected. The ruined city of Lemnos still held a magnetic, fatal fascination for them—for everyone. Muller had hoped that the risks of the maze would continue to keep men away. It had been discovered over a century earlier, but before his arrival there had been a period of many years in which Lemnos was shunned. For good reason: Muller had many times seen the corpses of those who had tried and failed to enter the maze. He himself had come here partly out of a suicidal wish to join the roster of victims, partly out of overriding curiosity to get within and solve the secret of the labyrinth, and partly out of the knowledge that if he did penetrate he was not likely to suffer many invasions of his privacy. Now he was within; but intruders had come.

They will not enter, Muller told himself.

Snugly established at the core of the maze, he had command of enough sensing devices to follow, however vaguely, the progress of any living creatures outside. Thus he could trace the wanderings from zone to zone of the animals that were his prey, and also those of the great beasts who offered danger. To a limited degree he could control the snares of the maze, which normally were nothing more than passive traps but which could be employed aggressively, under the right conditions, against some enemy. More than once Muller had dumped an elephantine carnivore into a subterranean pit as it charged inward through Zone D. He asked himself if he would use those defenses against human beings if they penetrated that far, and had no answer. He did not really hate his own species; he just preferred to be left alone, in what passed for peace.

He eyed the screens. He occupied a squat hexagonal cell—apparently one of the housing units in the inner city—which was equipped with a wall of viewing tanks. It had taken him more than a year to find out which parts of the maze corresponded to the images on the screens; but by patiently posting markers he had matched the dim images to the glossy reality. The six lowest screens along the wall showed him pictures of areas in Zones A through F; the cameras, or whatever they were, swiveled through 180° arcs, enabling the hidden mysterious eyes to patrol the entire region around each of the zone entrances. Since only one entrance provided safe access to the zone within, all others being lethal, the screens effectively allowed Muller to watch the inward progress of any prowler. It did not matter what was taking place at any of the false entrances. Those who persisted there would die.

Screens seven through ten, in the upper bank, relayed images that apparently came from Zones G and H, the outermost, largest and deadliest zones of the maze. Muller had not wanted to go to the trouble of returning to those zones to check his theory in detail; he was satisfied that the screens were pickups from points in the outer zones, and it was not worth risking those zones again to find out more accurately where the pickups were mounted. As for the eleventh and twelfth screens, they obviously showed views of the plain outside the maze altogether—the plain now occupied by a newly-arrived starship from Earth.

Few of the other devices left by the ancient builders of the maze were as informative. Mounted on a dais in the center of the city's central plaza, shielded by a crystal vault, was a twelve-sided stone the color of ruby, in whose depths a mechanism like an intricate shutter ticked and pulsed. Muller suspected it was some sort of clock, keyed to a nuclear oscillation and sounding out the units of time its makers employed. Periodically the stone underwent temporary changes: its face turned cloudy, deepened in hue to blue or even black, swung on its mounting. Muller's careful record-keeping had not yet told him the meaning of those changes. He could not even analyze the periodicity. The metamorphoses were not random, but the pattern they followed was beyond his comprehension.

At the eight corners of the plaza were metallic spikes, smoothly tapering to heights of some twenty feet. Throughout the cycle of the year these spikes revolved, so they were calendars, it seemed, moving on hidden bearings. Muller knew that they made one complete revolution in each thirty-month turning of Lemnos about its somber orange primary, but he suspected some deeper purpose for these gleaming pylons. Searching for it occupied much of his time.

Spaced neatly in the streets of Zone A were cages with bars hewn from an alabaster-like rock. Muller could see no way of opening these cages; yet twice during his years here he had awakened to find the bars withdrawn into the stone pavement, and the cages gaping wide. The first time they had remained open for three days; then the bars had returned to their positions while he slept, sliding into place and showing no seam where they could have parted. When the cages opened again, a few years later, Muller watched them constantly to find the secret of their mechanism. But on the fourth night he dozed just long enough to miss the closing again.

Equally mysterious was the aqueduct. Around the length of Zone B ran a closed trough, perhaps of onyx, with angular spigots placed at fifty-meter intervals. When any sort of vessel, even a cupped hand, was placed beneath a spigot it yielded pure water. But when he attempted to poke a finger into one of the spigots he found no opening, nor could he see any even while the water was coming forth; it was as though the fluid issued through a permeable plug of stone, and Muller found it hard to accept that. He welcomed the water, though.

It surprised him that so much of the city should have survived. Archaeologists had concluded, from a study of the artifacts and skeletons found on Lemnos outside the maze, that there had been no intelligent life here for upward of a million years—perhaps five or six million. Muller was only an amateur archaeologist, but he had had enough field experience to know the effects of the passing of time. The fossils in the plain were clearly ancient, and the stratification of the city's outer walls showed that the labyrinth was contemporary with those fossils.

Yet most of the city, supposedly built before the evolution of mankind on Earth, appeared untouched by the ages. The dry weather could account in part for that; there were no storms here, and rain had not fallen since Muller's arrival. But wind and wind-blown sand could carve walls and pavements over a million years, and there was no sign of such carving here. Nor had sand accumulated in the open streets of the city.

Muller knew why. Hidden pumps collected all debris, keeping everything spotless. He had gathered handfuls of soil from the garden plots,
scattering little trails here and there. Within minutes the driblets of soil
had begun to slither across the polished pavement, vanishing into slots
that opened briefly and closed again at the intersection of buildings and
ground.

Evidently a network of inconceivable machinery lay beneath the
city—imperishable caretaker devices that guarded the city against the
tooth of time. Muller had not been able to reach that network, though.
He lacked the equipment for breaching the pavement; it seemed invulnerable at all points. With improvised tools he had begun to dig in the
garden areas, hoping to reach the subcity that way, but though he had
driven one pit more than a dozen feet and another even deeper he had
come upon no signs of anything below but more soil. The hidden guardians had to be there, however: the instruments that operated the viewing
tanks, swept the streets, repaired the masonry, and controlled the murderous traps that studded the outer zones of the labyrinth.

It was hard to imagine a race that could build a city of this sort—
a city designed to last millions of years. It was harder still to imagine
how they could have vanished. Assuming that the fossils found in the
burial yards outside the walls were those of the builders—not necessarily a safe assumption—this city had been put together by burly hu-
manoids a meter and a half tall, immensely thick through the chest and
shoulders, with long cunning fingers, eight to the hand, and short
double-jointed legs.

They were gone from the known worlds of the universe, and nothing
like them had been found in any other system; perhaps they had withdrawn to some far galaxy yet unvisited by man. Or, possibly, they had
been a nonspacegoing race that evolved and perished right here on Lemnos, leaving this city as their only monument.

The rest of the planet was without trace of habitation although burial
grounds had been discovered in a diminishing series radiating outward
a thousand kilometers from the maze. Maybe the years had eroded all
their cities except this one. Maybe this, which could have sheltered
perhaps a million beings, had been their only city. There was no clue
to their disappearance. The devilish ingenuity of the maze argued that
in their last days they had been harassed by enemies and had retreated
within this tricky fortress; but Muller knew that this hypothesis too was
a speculation. For all he was aware, the maze represented nothing more
than an outburst of cultural paranoia and had no relation to the actual
existence of an external threat.

Had they been invaded by beings for whom the maze posed no

problems, and had they been slaughtered in their own sleek streets, and had the mechanical wardens swept away the bones? No way of knowing. They were gone. Muller, entering their city, had found it silent, desolate, as if it had never sheltered life; an automatic city, sterile, flawless. Only beasts occupied it. They had had a million years to find their way through the maze and take possession. Muller had counted some two dozen species of mammals in all sizes from rat-equivalent to elephant-equivalent. There were grazers who munched on the city's gardens, and hunters who fed on the herbivores, and the ecological balance seemed perfect. The city in the maze was like unto Isaiah's Babylon: wild beasts of the desert shall lie there; and their houses shall be full of doleful creatures; and owls shall dwell there, and satyrs shall dance there.

The city was his now. He had the rest of his lifetime to probe its mysteries.

There had been others who had come here, and not all of them had been human. Entering the maze, Muller had been treated to the sight of those who had failed to go the route. He had sighted a score of human skeletons in Zones H, G, and F. Three men had made it to E, and one to D. Muller had expected to see their bones; but what took him off guard was the collection of alien bones. In H and G he had seen the remains of great dragon-like creatures, still clad in the shreds of space-suits. Some day curiosity might triumph over fear and he might go back out there for a second look at them. Closer to the core lay an assortment of life-forms, mostly humanoid but veering from the standard structure. How long ago they had come here, Muller could not guess; even in this dry climate, would exposed skeletons last more than a few centuries? The galactic litter was a sobering reminder of something Muller already adequately knew: that despite the experience of man's first two centuries of extrasolar travel, in which no living intelligent alien race was encountered, the universe was full of other forms of life, and sooner or later man would meet them. The boneyard on Lemnos contained relics of at least a dozen different races. It flattered Muller's ego to know that he alone, apparently, had reached the heart of the maze; but it did not cheer him to think of the diversity of peoples in the universe. He had already had his fill of galactics.

The inconsistency of finding the litter of bones within the maze did not strike him for several years. The mechanisms of the city, he knew, cleaned relentlessly, tidying up everything from particles of dust to the bones of the animals on whom he fed. Yet the skeletons of would-be invaders of the maze were allowed to remain where they lay. Why the violation of neatness? Why cart away the corpse of a dead elephant-like beast that had blundered into a power snare, and leave the remains of

a dead dragon killed by the same snare? Because the dragon wore protective clothing, and so was sapient? Sapient corpses were deliberately
allowed to remain, Muller realized.

As warnings. ABANDON ALL HOPE, YE WHO ENTER HERE.

Those skeletons were part of the psychological warfare waged
against all intruders by this mindless, deathless, diabolical city. They
were reminders of the perils that lurked everywhere. How the guardian
drew the subtle distinction between bodies that should be left in situ
and those that should be swept away, Muller did not know; but he was
convinced that the distinction was real.

He watched his screens. He eyed the tiny figures moving about the
ship on the plain.

Let them come in, he thought. The city hasn't had a victim in years.
It'll take care of them. I'm safe where I am.

And, he knew, that even if by some miracle they managed to reach
him, they would not remain long. His own special malady would drive
them away. They might be clever enough to defeat the maze, but they
could not endure the affliction that made Richard Muller intolerable to
his own species.

"Go away," Muller said aloud.

He heard the whirr of rotors, and stepped from his dwelling to see
a dark shadow traverse the plaza. They were scouting the maze from
the air. Quickly he went indoors, then smiled at his own impulse to
hide. They could detect him, of course, wherever he was. Their screens
would tell them that a human being inhabited the labyrinth. And then,
naturally, they would in their astonishment try to make contact with him
although they would not be aware of his identity. After that—

Muller stiffened as a sudden overwhelming desire blazed through
him. To have them come to him. To talk to men again. To break his
isolation.

He *wanted* them here.

Only for an instant. After the momentary breakthrough of loneliness
came the return of rationality—the chilling awareness of what it would
be like to face his kind again. No, he thought. Keep out! Or die in the
maze. Keep out. Keep out. Keep out.

2

"Right down there," Boardman said. "That's where he must be, eh, Ned?
You can see the glow on the face of the tank. We're picking up the
right mass, the right density, the right everything. One live man, and
it's got to be Muller."

"At the heart of the maze," said Rawlins. "So he really did it!"

"Somehow." Boardman peered into the viewing tank. From a height of a couple of kilometers the structure of the inner city was clear. He could make out eight distinct zones, each with its characteristic style of architecture; its plazas and promenades; its angling walls; its tangle of streets swirling in dizzyingly alien patterns. The zones were concentric, fanning out from a broad plaza at the heart of it all, and the scoutplane's mass detector had located Muller in a row of low buildings just to the east of the plaza. What Boardman failed to make out was any obvious passage linking zone to zone. There was no shortage of blind alleys, but even from the air the true route was not apparent; what was it like trying to work inward on the ground?

It was all but impossible, Boardman knew. The master data banks in the ship held the accounts of those early explorers who had tried it and failed. Boardman had brought with him every scrap of information on the penetration of the maze, and none of it was very encouraging except the one puzzling but incontrovertible datum that Richard Muller had managed to get inside.

Rawlins said, "This is going to sound naive, I know, Charles. But why don't we just come down from here and land the scoutplane in the middle of that central plaza?"

"Let me show you," said Boardman.

He spoke a command. A robot drone probe detached itself from the belly of the plane and streaked toward the city. Boardman and Rawlins followed the flight of the blunt gray metal projectile until it was only a few score meters above the tops of the buildings. Through its faceted eye they had a sharp view of the city, revealing the intricate texture of much of the stonework. Suddenly the drone probe vanished. There was a burst of incandescence, a puff of greenish smoke—and then nothing at all.

Boardman nodded. "Nothing's changed. There's still a protective field over the whole thing. It volatilizes anything that tries to get through."

"So even a bird that comes too close—"

"There are no birds on Lemnos."

"Raindrops, then. Whatever falls on the city—"

"Lemnos gets no rain," said Boardman sourly. "At least not on this continent. The only thing that field keeps out is strangers. We've known it since the first expedition. Some brave men found out about that field the hard way."

"Didn't they try a drone probe first?"

Smiling, Boardman said, "When you find a dead city in the middle of a desert on a dead world you don't expect to be blown up if you land inside it. It's a forgivable sort of mistake—except that Lemnos doesn't forgive mistakes." He gestured, and the plane dropped lower, following the orbit of the outer walls for a moment. Then it rose and hovered over the heart of the city while photographs were being taken. The wrong-colored sunlight glistened off a hall of mirrors. Boardman felt curdled weariness in his chest. They overflew the city again and again, marking off a preprogrammed observation pattern, and he discovered he was wishing irritably that a shaft of sudden light would rise from those mirrors and incinerate them on the next pass to save him the trouble of carrying out this assignment. He had lost his taste for detailwork, and too many fine details stood between him and his purpose here. They said that impatience was a mark of youth, that old men could craftily spin their webs and plot their schemes in serenity, but somehow Boardman found himself longing rashly for a quick consummation to this job. Send some sort of drone scuttling through the maze on metal tracks to seize Muller and drag him out. Tell the man what was wanted of him and make him agree to do it. Then take off for Earth, quickly, quickly. The mood passed. Boardman felt foxy again.

Captain Hosteen, who would be conducting the actual entry attempt, came aft to pay his respects. Hosteen was a short, thick-framed man with a flat nose and coppery skin; he wore his uniform as though he felt it was all going to slip off his left shoulder at any moment. But he was a good man, Boardman knew, and ready to sacrifice a score of lives, including his own, to get into that maze.

Hosteen flicked a glance from the screen to Boardman's face and said, "Learning anything?"

"Nothing new. We have a job."

"Want to go down again?"

"Might as well," Boardman said. He looked at Rawlins. "Unless you have anything else you'd like to check, Ned?"

"Me? Oh, no—no. That is—well, I wonder if we need to go into the maze at all. I mean, if we could lure Muller out somehow, talk to him outside the city—"

"No."

"Wouldn't it work?"

"No," said Boardman emphatically. "Item one, Muller wouldn't come out if we asked him. He's a misanthrope. Remember? He buried himself here to get away from humanity. Why should he socialize with us? Item two, we couldn't invite him outside without letting him know too much about what we want from him. In this deal, Ned, we need to hoard our resources of strategy, not toss them away in our first move."

"I don't understand what you mean."

Patiently Boardman said, "Suppose we used your approach. What would you say to Muller to make him come out?"

"Why—that we're here from Earth to ask him if he'll help us in a time of system-wide crisis. That we've encountered a race of alien beings with whom we're unable to communicate, and that it's absolutely necessary that we break through to them in a hurry, and that he alone can do the trick. We—" Rawlins stopped, as though the fatuity of his own words had broken through to him. Color mounted in his cheeks. He said in a hoarse voice, "Muller isn't going to give a damn for those arguments, is he?"

"No, Ned. Earth sent him to talk to a bunch of aliens once before, and they ruined him. He isn't about to try it again."

"Then how are we going to make him help us?"

"By playing on his sense of honor. But at the moment that's not the problem we're talking about. We're discussing how to get him out of his sanctuary in there. Now, you were suggesting that we set up a speaker and tell him exactly what we want from him, and then wait for him to waltz out and pledge to do his best for good old Earth. Right?"

"I guess so."

"But it won't work. Therefore we've got to get inside the maze ourselves, win Muller's trust, and persuade him to cooperate. And to do that we have to keep quiet about the real situation until we've eased him out of his suspicions."

A look of newborn wariness appeared on Rawlins' face. "What are we going to tell him, then, Charles?"

"Not *we*. You."

"What am I going to tell him, then?"

Boardman sighed. "Lies, Ned. A pack of lies."

3

They had come equipped for solving the problem of the maze. The ship's brain, of course, was a first-class computer, and it carried the details of all previous Earth-based attempts to enter the city. Except one, and unfortunately that had been the only successful one. But records of past failures have their uses. The ship's data banks had plenty of mobile extensions: airborne and groundborne drone probes, spy-eyes, sensor batteries, and more. Before any human life was risked on the maze Boardman and Hosteen would try the whole mechanical array. Mechanicals were expendable, anyway; the ship carried a set of templates, and it would be no trouble to replicate all devices destroyed. But a point would come at which the drone probes had to give way to men: the aim was to gather as much information as possible for those men to use.

Never before had anyone tried to crack the maze this way. The early explorers had simply gone walking in, unsuspecting, and had perished. Their successors had known enough of the story to avoid the more obvious traps, and to some extent had been aided by sophisticated sensory devices, but this was the first attempt to run a detailed survey before entering. No one was overly confident that the technique would let them in unscathed, but it was the best way to approach the problem.

The overflights on the first day had given everybody a good visual image of the maze. Strictly speaking, it hadn't been necessary for them to leave the ground; they could have watched big-screen relays from the comfort of their camp and gained a decent idea of the conformation below, letting airborne probes do all the work. But Boardman had insisted. The mind registers things one way when it picks them off a relay screen, and another when the sensory impressions are flooding in straight from the source. Now they all had seen the city from the air, and had seen what the guardians of the maze could do to a drone probe that ventured into the protective field overlying the city.

Rawlins had suggested the possibility that there might be a null spot in that protective field. Toward late afternoon they checked it out by loading a probe with metal pellets and stationing it fifty meters above the highest point of the maze. Scanner eyes recorded the action as the drone slowly turned, spewing the pellets one at a time into preselected one-square-meter boxes above the city. Each in turn was incinerated as it fell. They were able to calculate that the thickness of the safety field varied with distance from the center of the maze; it was only about two meters deep above the inner zones, much deeper at the outer rim, forming an invisible cup over the city. But there were no null spots; the field was continuous. Hosteen tested the notion that the field was capable of overstrain by having the probe reloaded with pellets which were catapulted simultaneously into each of the test rectangles. The field dealt with them all, creating for a moment a single pucker of flame above the city.

At the expense of a few mole probes they found out that reaching the city through a tunnel was equally impossible. The moles burrowed into the coarse sandy soil outside the outer walls, chewed themselves passageways fifty meters down, and nosed upward again when they were beneath the maze. They were destroyed by the safety field while still twenty meters below ground level. A try at burrowing in right at the base of the embankments also failed; the field went straight down, apparently, all around the city.

A power technician offered to rig an interference pylon to drain the energy of the field. It didn't work. The pylon, a hundred meters tall, sucked in power from all over the planet; blue lightning leaped and hissed along its accumulator bank, but it had no effect on the safety field. They reversed the pylon and sent a million kilowatts shooting into the city, hoping to short the field. The field drank everything and seemed ready for more. No one had any rational theory to explain the field's power source. "It must tap the planet's own energy of rotation," the technician who had rigged the pylon said, and then, realizing he hadn't contributed anything useful, he looked away and began to snap orders into the handmike he carried.

Three days of similar researches demonstrated that the city was invulnerable to intrusion from above or below.

"There's only one way in," said Hosteen, "and that's on foot, through the main gate."

"If the people in the city really wanted to be safe," Rawlins asked, "why did they leave even a gate open?"

"Maybe they wanted to go in and out themselves, Ned," said Boardman quietly. "Or maybe they wanted to give invaders a sporting chance. Hosteen, shall we send some probes inside?"

The morning was gray. Clouds the color of wood smoke stained the sky; it looked almost as if rain were on the way. A harsh wind knifed the soil from the plain and sent it slicing into their faces. Behind the veil of clouds lay the sun, a flat orange disk that seemed to have been pasted into the sky. It seemed only slightly larger than Sol as seen from Earth, though it was less than half as distant. Lemnos' sun was a gloomy M dwarf, cool and weary, an old star circled by a dozen old planets. Lemnos, the innermost, was the only one that had ever sustained life; the others were frigid and dead, beyond the range of the sun's feeble rays, frozen from core to atmosphere. It was a sleepy system with so little angular momentum that even the innermost planet dawdled along in a thirty-month orbit; the three zippy moons of Lemnos, darting on crisscrossing tracks a few thousand kilometers overhead, were flagrantly out of keeping with the prevailing mood of these worlds.

Ned Rawlins felt a chill at his heart as he stood beside the data terminal a thousand meters from the outer embankment of the maze, watching his shipmates marshalling their probes and instruments. Not even dead pockmarked Mars had depressed him like this, for Mars was a world that had never lived at all, while here life had been and had moved onward. This world was a house of the dead. In Thebes, once, he had entered the tomb of Pharaoh's vizier, five thousand years gone, and while the others in his group had eyed the gay murals with their glowing scenes of white-garbed figures punting on the Nile, he had looked toward the cool stone floor where a dead beetle lay, clawed feet upraised on a tiny mound of dust. For him Egypt would always be that stiffened beetle in the dust; for him Lemnos was likely to be autumn winds and scoured plains and a silent city. He wondered how anyone as gifted, as full of life and energy and human warmth as Dick Muller, could ever have been willing to maroon himself inside that dismal maze.

Then he remembered what had happened to Muller on Beta Hydri IV, and conceded that even a man like Muller might very well have good reasons for coming to rest on a world like this, in a city like this. Lemnos offered the perfect escape: an Earthlike world, uninhabited, where he was almost guaranteed freedom from human company. And we're here to flush him out and drag him away. Rawlins scowled. Dirty dirty dirty, he thought. The old thing about the ends and the means. Across the way Rawlins could see the blocky figure of Charles Boardman standing in front of the big data terminal, waving his arms this way and that to direct the men fanning out near the walls of the city. He began to understand that he had let Boardman dragoon him into a nasty adventure. The glib old devil hadn't gone into details, back on Earth, about the exact methods by which they were going to win Muller's cooperation. Boardman had made it sound like some kind of shining crusade. Instead it was going to be a dirty trick. Boardman never went into the details of anything before he had to, as Rawlins was beginning to see. Rule one: hoard your resources of strategy. Never tip your hand. And so here I am, part of the conspiracy.

Hosteen and Boardman had deployed a dozen drones at the various entrances to the inner part of the maze. It was already clear that the only safe way into the city was through the northeastern gate; but they had drones to spare, and they wanted all the data they could gather. The terminal Rawlins was watching flashed a partial diagram of the maze on the screen—the section immediately in front of him—and gave him a good long time to study its loops and coils, its zigzags and twists. It was his special responsibility to follow the progress of the drone through this sector. Each of the other drones was being monitored both by computer and by human observer, while Boardman and Hosteen were at the master terminal watching the progress of the entire operation all at once.

"Send them in," Boardman said.

Hosteen gave the command, and the drones rolled forward through the city's gates. Looking now through the eyes of the squat mobile probe, Rawlins got his first view of what lay in Zone H of the maze. He saw a scalloped wall of what looked like puckered blue porcelain undulating away to the left, and a barrier of metallic threads dangling from a thick stone slab to the other side. The drone skirted the threads, which tinkled and quivered in delicate response to the disturbance of the thin air; it moved to the base of the porcelain wall, and followed it at an inward-sloping angle for perhaps twenty meters. There the wall curved abruptly back on itself, forming a sort of chamber open at the top. The last time anyone had entered the maze this way—on the fourth expedition—two men had passed that open chamber; one had remained outside and was destroyed, the other had gone inside and was spared. The drone entered the chamber. A moment later a beam of pure red light lanced from the center of a mosaic decoration on the wall and swept over the area immediately outside the chamber.

Boardman's voice came to Rawlins through the speaker taped to his ear. "We lost four of the probes the moment they went through their gates. That's exactly as expected. How's yours doing?"

"Following the plan," said Rawlins. "So far, it's okay."

"You ought to lose it within six minutes of entry. What's your elapsed time now?"

"Two minutes fifteen."

The drone was out of the chamber now and shuttling quickly through the place where the light-beam had flashed. Rawlins keyed in olfactory and got the smell of scorched air, lots of ozone. The path divided ahead. To one side was a single-span bridge of stone, arching over what looked like a pit of flame; to the other was a jumbled pile of cyclopean blocks resting precariously edge to edge. The bridge seemed far more inviting, but the drone immediately turned away from it and began to pick its way over the jumbled blocks. Rawlins asked it why, and it relayed the information that the "bridge" wasn't there at all; it was a projection beamed from scanners mounted beneath the facing piers. Requesting a simulation of an approach anyway, Rawlins got a picture of the probe walking out onto the pier and stepping unsuspectingly through the solid-looking bridge to lose its balance; and as the simulated probe struggled to regain its equilibrium, the pier tipped forward and shucked it into the fiery pit. Cute, Rawlins thought, and shuddered.

Meanwhile the real probe had clambered over the blocks and was coming down the other side, unharmed. Three minutes and eight seconds had gone by. A stretch of straight road here turned out to be as safe as it looked. It was flanked on both sides by windowless towers a hundred meters high, made of some iridescent mineral, sleek and oily-surfaced, that flashed shimmering moire patterns as the drone hurried along. At the beginning of the fourth minute the probe skirted bright grillwork like interlocking teeth, and sidestepped an umbrella-shaped piledriver that descended with crushing force. Eighty seconds later it stepped around a tiltblock that opened into a yawning abyss, deftly eluded a quintet of tetrahedal blades that sheared upward out of the pavement, and emerged onto a sliding walkway that carried it quickly forward for exactly forty seconds more.

All this had been traversed long ago by a Terran explorer named Cartissant, since deceased. He had dictated a detailed record of his experiences within the maze. He had lasted five minutes and thirty seconds, and his mistake had come in not getting off the walkway by the forty-first second. Those who had been monitoring him outside, back then, could not say what had happened to him after that.

As his drone left the walkway, Rawlins asked for another simulation and saw a quick dramatization of the computer's best guess: the walkway opened to engulf its passenger at that point. The probe, meanwhile, was going swiftly toward what looked like the exit from this outermost zone of the maze. Beyond lay a well-lit, cheerful-looking plaza ringed with drifting blobs of a pearly glowing substance.

Rawlins said, "I'm into the seventh minute, and we're still going, Charles. There seems to be a door into Zone G just ahead. Maybe you ought to cut in and monitor my screen."

"If you last two more minutes, I will," Boardman said.

The probe paused just outside the inner gate. Warily it switched on its gravitron and accumulated a ball of energy with a mass equivalent to its own. It thrust the energy ball through the doorway. Nothing happened. The probe, satisfied, trundled toward the door itself. As it passed through, the sides of the door abruptly crashed together like the jaws of a mighty press, destroying the probe. Rawlins' screen went dark. Quickly he cut in one of the overhead probes; it beamed him a shot of his probe lying on the far side of the door, flattened into a two-dimensional mock-up of itself. A human being caught in that same trap would have been crushed to powder, Rawlins realized.

"My probe's been knocked out," he reported to Boardman. "Six minutes and forty seconds."

"As expected," came the reply. "We've got only two probes left. Switch over and watch."

The master diagram appeared on Rawlins' screen: a simplified and stylized light-pen picture of the entire maze as viewed from above. A small X had been placed wherever a probe had been destroyed. Rawlins found, after some searching, the path his own drone had taken, with the X marked between the zone boundaries at the place of the clashing door. It seemed to him that the drone had penetrated farther than most of the others, but he had to smile at the childish pride the discovery brought him. Anyhow, two of the probes were still moving inward. One was actually inside the second zone of the maze, and the other was cruising through a passageway that gave access to that inner ring.

The diagram vanished and Rawlins saw the maze as it looked through the pickup of one of the drones. Almost daintily, the man-high pillar of metal made its way through the baroque intricacies of the maze, past a golden pillar that beamed a twanging melody in a strange key, past a pool of light, past a web of glittering metal spokes, past spiky heaps of bleached bones. Rawlins had only glancing views of the bones as the drone moved on, but he was sure that few were human relics. This place was a galactic graveyard for the bold.

Excitement built in him as the probe went on and on. He was so thoroughly wedded to it now that it was as if he were inside the maze, avoiding one deathtrap after another, and he felt a sense of triumph as minutes mounted. Fourteen had elapsed now. This second level of the maze was not so cluttered as the first; there were spacious avenues here, handsome colonnades, long radiating passages leading from the main path. He relaxed; he felt pride in the drone's agility and in the keenness of its sensory devices. The shock was immense and stinging when a paving-block upended itself unexpectedly and dumped the probe down a long chute to a place where the gears of a giant mill turned eagerly.

They had not expected that probe to get so far, anyway. The probe the others were watching was the one that had come in via the main gate—the safe gate. The slim fund of information accumulated at the price of many lives had guided that probe past all its perils, and now it was well within Zone G, and almost to the edge of F. Thus far, everything had gone as expected; the drone's experiences had matched those of them who had tackled this route on earlier expeditions. It followed their way exactly, turning here, dodging there, and it was eighteen minutes into the maze without incident.

"All right," Boardman said. "This is where Mortenson died, isn't it?"

"Yes," Hosteen answered. "The last thing he said was that he was standing by that little pyramid, and then he was cut off."

"This is where we start gaining new information, then. All we've learned so far is that our records are accurate. This is the way in. But from here on—"

The probe, lacking a guidance pattern, now moved much more slowly, hesitating at every step to extend its network of data-gathering devices in all directions. It looked for hidden doors, for concealed openings in the pavement, for projectors, lasers, mass-detectors, power sources. It fed back to the central data banks all that it learned, thus adding to the store of information with each centimeter conquered.

It conquered, altogether, twenty-three meters. As the probe passed the small pyramid it scanned the broken body of the explorer Mortenson, lost at this point 72 years earlier. It relayed the news that Mortenson had been seized by a pressure-sensitive mangle activated by an unwary footstep too close to the pyramid. Beyond, it avoided two minor traps before failing to safeguard itself from a distortion screen that baffled its sensors and left it vulnerable to the descent of a pulverizing piston.

"The next one through will have to cut off all its inputs until it's past that point," Hosteen muttered. "Running through blindfolded— well, we'll manage."

"Maybe a man would do better than a machine there," said Boardman. "We don't know if that screen would muddle a man the way it did a batch of sensors."

"We're not yet ready to run a man in there," Hosteen pointed out.

Boardman agreed—none too graciously, Rawlins thought, listening to the interchange. The screen brightened again; a new drone probe was coming through. Hosteen had ordered a second wave of the machines to pick through the labyrinth, following what was now known to be the one safe access route, and several of them were at the eighteen-minute point where the deadly pyramid was located. Hosteen sent one ahead, and posted the others to keep watch. The lead probe came within range of the distortion screen and cut out its sensors; it heaved tipsily for a moment, lacking any way to get its bearings, but in a moment it was stable. It was deprived now of contact with its surroundings, and so it paid no heed to the siren song of the distortion screen, which had misled its predecessor into coming within range of the pulverizing piston. The phalanx of drones watching the scene was all outside the reach of the distorter's mischief, and fed a clear, true picture to the computer, which matched it with the fatal path of the last probe and plotted a route that skirted the dangerous piston. Moments later the blind probe began to move, guided now by inner impulses. Lacking all environmental feedback it was entirely a captive of the computer, which nudged it along in a series of tiny prods until it was safely around the hazard. On the far side, the sensors were switched on again. To check the procedure, Hosteen sent a second drone through, likewise blinded and moving entirely on internal guidance. It made it. Then he tried a third probe with its sensors on and under the influence of the distortion screen. The computer attempted to direct it along the safe path, but the probe, bedeviled by the faulty information coming through the distorter, tugged itself furiously to the side and was smashed.

"All right," Hosteen said. "If we can get a machine past it, we can get a man past it. He closes his eyes, and the computer calculates his motions step by step. We'll manage."

The lead probe began to move again. It got seventeen meters past the place of the distorter before it was nailed by a silvery grillwork that abruptly thrust up a pair of electrodes and cut loose with a bath of flame. Rawlins watched bleakly as the next probe avoided that obstacle and shortly fell victim to another. Plenty of probes waited patiently for their turn to press forward.

And soon men will be going in there too, Rawlins thought. *We'll* be going in there.

He shut off his data terminal and walked across to Boardman.

"How does it look so far?" he asked.

"Rough, but not impossible," Boardman said. "It can't be this tough all the way in."

"And if it is?"

"We won't run out of probes. We'll chart the whole maze until we know where all the danger points are, and then we'll start trying it ourselves."

Rawlins said, "Are *you* going to go in there, Charles?"

"Of course. So are you."

"With what odds on coming out?"

"Good ones," said Boardman. "Otherwise I doubt that I'd tackle it. Oh, it's a dangerous trip, Ned, but don't overestimate it. We've just begun to test that maze. We'll know it well enough in a few days more."

Rawlins considered that a moment. "Muller didn't have any probes," he said finally. "How did he survive that stuff?"

"I'm not sure," Boardman murmured. "I suppose he's just a naturally lucky man."

3.

Within the maze Muller watched the proceedings on his dim screens. They were sending some sort of robots in, he saw. The robots were getting chewed up quite badly, but each successive wave of them seemed to reach deeper into the labyrinth. Trial and error had led the intruders to the correct route through Zone H and well onward into G. Muller was prepared to defend himself if the robots reached the inner zones. Meanwhile he remained calm at the center of it all, going about his daily pursuits.

In the mornings he spent a good deal of the time thinking over his past. There had been other worlds in other years, springtimes, warmer seasons than this; soft eyes looking into his eyes, hands against his hands, smiles, laughter, shining floors, and elegant figures moving through arched doorways. He had married twice. Both times the arrangements had been terminated peacefully after a decent span of years. He had traveled widely. He had dealt with ministers and kings. In his nostrils was the scent of a hundred planets strung across the sky. We make only a small blaze, and then we go out; but in his springtime and his summer he had burned brightly enough, and he did not feel he had earned this sullen, joyless autumn.

The city took care of him, after its fashion. He had a place to dwell—thousands of places; he moved from time to time for the sake of changing the view. All the houses were empty boxes. He had made a bed for himself of animal hides stuffed with scraped fur; he had fashioned a chair from sinews and skin; he needed little else. The city gave him water. Wild animals roamed here in such quantity that he would never lack for food so long as he was strong enough to hunt. From Earth he had brought with him certain basic items. He had three cubes of books and one of music; they made a stack less than a meter high and could nourish his soul for all the years that remained to him. He had some woman cubes. He had a small recorder into which he sometimes dictated memoirs. He had a sketchpad. He had weapons and a mass detector. He had a diagnostat with a regenerating medical supply. It was enough.

He ate regularly. He slept well. He had no quarrels with his conscience. He had come almost to be content with his fate. One nurses bitterness only so long before one grows a cyst around the place from which the poison spews.

He blamed no one now for what had happened to him. His own hungers had brought him to this. He had tried to devour the universe; he had aspired to the condition of a god; and some implacable guiding force had hurled him down from his high place, hurled him down and smashed him, left him to crawl off to this dead world to knit his broken soul as best he could.

The way stations on his journey to this place were well known to him. At eighteen, lying naked under the stars with warmth against him, he had boasted of his lofty ambitions. At twenty-five he had begun to realize them. Before he was forty he had visited a hundred worlds, and was famous in thirty systems. A decade later he had had his delusions of statesmanship. And at the age of fifty-three he had let Charles Boardman talk him into undertaking the mission to Beta Hydri IV.

That year he was on holiday in the Tau Ceti system, a dozen lightyears from home. Marduk, the fourth world, had been designed as a pleasure planet for the mining men who were engaged in stripping her sister worlds of a fortune in reactive metals. Muller had no liking for the way those planets were being plundered, but that did not prevent him from seeking relaxation on Marduk. It was nearly a seasonless world, which rode upright in its orbital plane; four continents of unending springtime bathed by a tranquil shallow sea. The sea was green, the land vegetation had a faint bluish tinge, and the air had a little of the sparkle of young champagne. They had somehow made the planet into a counterfeit of Earth—Earth as it might have been in a more innocent time—all parks and meadows and cheery inns; it was a restful world whose challenges were purely synthetic. The giant fish in the seas always wearied and let themselves be played. The snowcapped mountains looked treacherous, even for climbers in gravitron boots, but no one had been lost on them yet. The beasts with which the forests were stocked were tall at the withers and snorted as they charged, but they were not as fierce as they looked. In principle, Muller disapproved of such places. But he had had enough adventure for a while, and he had come to

Marduk for a few weeks of phony peace, accompanied by a girl he had met the year before and twenty light-years away.

Her name was Marta. She was tall, slim, with large dark eyes fashionably rimmed with red, and lustrous blue hair that brushed her smooth shoulders. She looked about twenty, but of course she might just as well have been ninety and on her third shape-up; you never could tell about anyone, and especially not about a woman. But somehow Muller suspected that she was genuinely young. It wasn't her litheness, her coltish agility—those are commodities that can be purchased—but some subtle quality of enthusiasm, of true girlishness that, he liked to think, was no surgical product. Whether power-swimming or tree-floating or blowdart hunting or making love, Marta seemed so totally engaged in her pleasures that they surely were relatively new to her.

Muller did not care to investigate such things too deeply. She was wealthy, Earthborn, had no visible family ties, and went where she pleased. On a sudden impulse he had phoned her and asked her to meet him on Marduk; and she had come willingly, no questions asked. She was not awed to be sharing a hotel suite with Richard Muller. Clearly she knew who he was, but the aura of fame that surrounded him was unimportant to her. What mattered was what he said to her, how he held her, what they did together, and not the accomplishments he had accumulated at other times.

They stayed at a hotel that was a spire of brilliance a thousand meters high, thrusting needle-straight out of a valley overlooking a glassy oval lake. Their rooms were two hundred floors up, and they dined in a rooftop eyrie reached by gravitron disk, and during the day all the pleasures of Marduk lay spread out before them. He was with her for a week, uninterrupted. The weather was perfect. Her small cool breasts fit nicely into his cupped palms; her long slender legs encircled him pleasantly, and at the highest moments she drove her heels into his calves with sudden delicious fervor. On the eighth day Charles Boardman arrived on Marduk, hired a suite half a continent away, and invited Muller to pay a call on him.

"I'm on vacation," Muller told him.

"Give me half a day of it."

"I'm not alone, Charles."

"I know that. Bring her along. We'll take a ride. It's an important matter."

"I came here to escape important matters."

"There's never any escape, Dick. You know that. You are what you are, and we need you. Will you come?"

"Damn you," Muller said mildly.

In the morning he and Marta flew by quickboat to Boardman's hotel. Muller remembered the journey as vividly as though it had taken place last month and not almost fifteen years before. They soared above the continental divide, skimming the snowy summits of the mountains by so slim a margin that they could see the magnificent long-horned figure of a goatish rock-skipper capering across the gleaming rivers of ice: two metric tons of muscle and bone, an improbable colossus of the peaks, the costliest prey Marduk had to offer. Some men did not earn in a lifetime what it cost to buy a license to hunt rock-skipper. To Muller it seemed that even that price was too low.

They circled the mighty beast three times and streaked off into the lake country, the lowlands beyond the mountain range where a chain of diamond-bright pools girdled the fat waist of the continent, and by midday they were landed at the edge of a velvety forest of evergreens. Boardman had rented the hotel's master suite, all screens and trickery. He grasped Muller's wrist in salute, and embraced Marta with unabashed lechery. She seemed distant and restrained in Boardman's arms; quite obviously she regarded the visit as so much time lost.

"Are you hungry?" Boardman asked. "Lunch first, talk later!"

He served drinks in his suite: an amber wine out of goblets made from blue rock crystal mined on Ganymede. Then they boarded a dining capsule and left the hotel to tour the forests and lakes while they ate. Lunch glided from its container and rolled toward them as they lounged in pneumochairs before a wraparound window. Crisp salad, grilled native fish, imported vegetables; a grated Centaurine cheese to sprinkle; flasks of cold rice beer; a rich, thick, spicy green liqueur afterward. Completely passive, sealed in their moving capsule, they accepted food and drink and scenery, breathed the sparkling air pumped in from outside, watched gaudy birds flutter past them and lose themselves in the soft, drooping needles of the thickly-packed conifers of the woods. Boardman had carefully staged all this to create a mood, but his efforts were wasted, Muller knew. He could not be lulled this easily. He might take whatever job Boardman offered, but not because he had been fooled into false unwariness.

Marta was bored. She showed it by the detached response she gave to Boardman's inquiring lustful glances. The shimmering daywrap she wore was designed to reveal; as its long-chained molecules slid kaleidoscopically through their path of patterns they yielded quick, frank glimpses of thighs and breasts, of belly and loins, of hips and buttocks. Boardman appreciated the display and seemed ready to capitalize on Marta's apparent availability, but she ignored his unvoiced overtures entirely. Muller was amused by that. Boardman was not.

After lunch the capsule halted by the side of a jewel-like lake, deep and clear. The wall opened, and Boardman said, "Perhaps the young lady would like to swim while we get the dull business talk out of the way?"

"A fine idea," Marta said in a flat voice.

Arising, she touched the disrobing snap at her shoulder and let her garment slither to her ankles. Boardman made a great show of catching it up and putting it on a storage rack. She smiled mechanically at him, turned, walked down to the edge of the lake, a nude tawny figure whose tapering back and gently rounded rump were dappled by the sunlight slipping through the trees. For a moment she paused, shin-deep in the water; then she sprang forward and sliced the breast of the lake with strong steady strokes.

Boardman said, "She's quite lovely, Dick. Who is she?"

"A girl. Rather young, I think."

"Younger than your usual sort, I'd say. Also somewhat spoiled. Known her long?"

"Since last year, Charles. Interested?"

"Naturally."

"I'll tell her that," Muller said. "Some other time."

Boardman gave him a Buddha-smile and gestured toward the liquor console. Muller shook his head. Marta was backstroking in the lake, the rosy tips of her breasts just visible above the serene surface. The two men eyed one another. They appeared to be of the same age, mid-fifties; Boardman fleshy and graying and strong-looking, Muller lean and graying and strong-looking. Seated, they seemed of the same height, too. The appearances were deceptive: Boardman was a generation older, Muller half a foot taller. They had known each other for thirty years.

In a way, they were in the same line of work—both part of the corps of nonadministrative personnel that served to hold the structure of human society together across the sprawl of the galaxy. Neither held any official rank. They shared a readiness to serve, a desire to make their gifts useful to mankind; and Muller respected Boardman for the way he had used those gifts during a long and impressive career, though he could not say that he liked the older man. He knew that Boardman was shrewd, unscrupulous, and dedicated to human welfare—and the combination of dedication and unscrupulousness is always a dangerous one.

Boardman drew a vision cube from a pocket of his tunic and put it on the table before Muller. It rested there like a counter in some intricate game, six or seven centimeters along each face, soft yellow against the polished black marble face of the table. "Plug it in," Boardman invited, "the viewer's beside you."

Muller slipped the cube into the receptor slot. From the center of the table there arose a larger cube, nearly a meter across. Images flowered on its faces. Muller saw a cloud-wrapped planet, soft gray in tone. It could have been Venus. The view deepened and streaks of dark red appeared in the gray. Not Venus, then. The recording eye pierced the cloud layer and revealed an unfamiliar, not very Earthlike planet. The soil looked moist and spongy, and rubbery trees that looked like giant toadstools thrust upward from it. It was hard to judge relative sizes, but they looked big. Their pale trunks were coarse with shredded fibers, and curved like bows between ground and crown. Saucerlike growths shielded the trees at their bases, ringing them for about a fifth of their height. Above were neither branches nor leaves, only wide flat caps whose undersurfaces were mottled by corrugated processes. As Muller watched, three alien figures came strolling through the somber grove. They were elongated, almost spidery, with clusters of eight or ten jointed limbs depending from their narrow shoulders. Their heads were tapered and rimmed with eyes. Their nostrils were vertical slits flush against the skin. Their mouths opened at the sides. They walked upright on elegant legs that terminated in small globe-like pedestals instead of feet. Though they were nude except for probably ornamental strips of fabric tied between their first and second wrists, Muller was unable to detect signs either of reproductive apparatus or of mammalian functions. Their skins were unpigmented, sharing the prevailing grayness of this gray world, and were coarse in texture, with a scaly overlay of small diamond-shaped ridges.

With wonderful grace the three figures approached three of the giant toadstools and scaled them until each stood atop the uppermost saucer-like projection of a tree. Out of the cluster of limbs came one arm that seemed specially adapted; unlike the others, which were equipped with five tendril-shaped fingers arranged in a circlet, this limb ended in a needle-sharp organ. It plunged easily and deeply into the soft rubbery trunk of the tree on which its owner stood. A long moment passed, as if the aliens were draining sap from the trees. Then they climbed down and resumed their stroll, outwardly unchanged.

One of them paused, bent, peered closely at the ground. It scooped up the eye that had been witnessing its activities. The image grew chaotic; Muller guessed that the eye was being passed from hand to hand. Suddenly there was darkness. The eye had been destroyed. The cube was played out.

After a moment of troubled silence Muller said, "They look very convincing."

"They ought to be. They're real."

"Was this taken by some sort of extragalactic probe?"

"No," Boardman said. "In our own galaxy."

"Beta Hydri IV, then?"

"Yes."

Muller repressed a shiver. "May I play it again, Charles?"

"Of course."

He activated the cube a second time. Again the eye made the descent through the cloud layer; again it observed the rubbery trees; again the trio of aliens appeared, took nourishment from the trees, noticed the eye, destroyed it. Muller studied the images with cold fascination. He had never looked upon living sapient beings of another creation before. No one had, so far as he knew, until now.

The images faded from the cube.

Boardman said, "That was taken less than a month ago. We parked a drone ship fifty thousand kilometers up and dropped roughly a thousand eyes on Beta Hydri IV. At least half of them went straight to the bottom of the ocean. Most landed in uninhabited or uninteresting places. This is the only one that actually showed us a clear view of the aliens."

"Why has it been decided to break our quarantine of this planet?"

Boardman slowly let out his breath. "We think it's time we got in touch with them, Dick. We've been sniffing around them for ten years and we haven't said hello yet. That isn't neighborly. And since the Hydrans and ourselves are the only intelligent races in this whole damned galaxy—unless something's hiding somewhere unlikely— we've come to the belief that we ought to commence friendly relations."

"I don't find your coyness very appealing," Muller said bluntly. "A full-scale council decision was taken after close to a year of debate, and it was voted to leave the Hydrans alone for at least a century—unless they showed some sign of going into space. Who reversed that decision, and why, and when?"

Boardman smiled his crafty smile. But Muller knew that the only way to avoid being drawn into his web was to take a frontal approach. Slowly Boardman said, "I didn't mean to seem deceptive, Dick. The decision was reversed by a council session eight months ago, while you were out Rigel way."

"And the reason?"

"One of the extragalactic probes came back with convincing evidence that there's at least one highly intelligent and quite superior species in one of our neighboring clusters."

"Where?"

"It doesn't matter, Dick. Pardon me, but I won't tell you at this time."

"All right."

"Let's just say that from what we know of them now, they're much more than we can handle. They've got a galactic drive, and we can reasonably expect them to come visiting us one of these centuries—and when they do, we'll have a problem. So it's been voted to open contact with Beta Hydri IV ahead of schedule, by way of insurance against that day."

"You mean," Muller said, "that we want to make sure we're on good terms with the other race of our own galaxy before the extragalactics show up?"

"Exactly."

"I'll take that drink now," said Muller.

Boardman gestured. Muller tapped out a potent combination on the console, downed it quickly, ordered another. Suddenly he had a great deal to digest. He looked away from Boardman, picking up the vision cube and fingering it as though it were a sacred relic.

For a couple of centuries man had explored the stars without finding a trace of a rival. There were plenty of planets, and many of them were potentially habitable, and a surprising number were Earthlike to four or five places. That much had been expected. The sky is full of main-sequence suns, with a good many of the F-type and G-type stars most likely to support life. The process of planetogenesis is nothing remarkable, and most of those suns had complements of five to a dozen worlds, some of which were of the right size and mass and density slots to permit the retention of atmosphere and the convenient evolution of life, and a number of those worlds were situated within the orbital zone where they were best able to avoid extremes of temperature. So life abounded and the galaxy was a zoologist's delight.

But in his helter-skelter expansion out of his own system man had found only the traces of former intelligent species. Beasts laired in the ruins of unimaginably ancient civilizations. The most spectacular ancient site was the maze of Lemnos; but other worlds too had their stumps of cities, their weathered foundations, their burial grounds and strewn potsherds. Space became an archaeologist's delight, too. The collectors of alien animals and the collectors of alien relics were kept busy. Whole new scientific specialities burst into being. Societies that had vanished before the Pyramids had been conceived now underwent reconstruction.

A curious blight of extinction had come upon all the galaxy's other intelligent races, though. Evidently they had flourished so long ago that not even their decadent children survived; they were one with Nineveh and Tyre, blotted out, cut off. Careful scrutiny showed that the youngest of the dozen or so known extrasolar intelligent cultures had perished eighty thousand years earlier.

The galaxy is wide; and man kept on looking, drawn to find his stellar companions by some perverse mixture of curiosity and dread. Though the warp drive provided speedy transport to all points within the universe, neither available personnel nor available ships could cope with the immensity of the surveying tasks. Several centuries after his intrusion into the galaxy, man was still making discoveries, some of them quite close to home. The star Beta Hydri had seven planets; and on the fourth was another sapient species.

There were no landings. The possibility of such a discovery had been examined well in advance, and plans had been drawn to avoid a blundering trespass of unpredictable consequences. The survey of Beta Hydri IV had been carried out from beyond its cloud layer. Cunning devices had measured the activity behind that tantalizing gray mask. Hydran energy production was known to a tolerance of a few million kilowatt hours; Hydran urban districts had been mapped, and their population density estimated; the level of Hydran industrial development had been calculated by a study of thermal radiations. There was an aggressive, growing, potent civilization down there, probably comparable in technical level to late twentieth-century Earth. There was only one significant difference: the Hydrans had not begun to enter space. That was the fault of the cloud layer. A race that never has seen the stars is not likely to show much desire to reach them.

Muller had been privy to the frantic conferences that followed the discovery of the Hydrans. He knew the reasons why they had been placed under quarantine, and he realized that only much more urgent reasons had resulted in the lifting of that quarantine. Unsure of its ability to handle a relationship with nonhuman beings, Earth had wisely chosen to keep away from the Hydrans for a while longer; but now all that was changed.

"What happens now?" Muller asked. "An expedition?"

"Yes."

"How soon?"

"Within the next year, I'd say."

Muller tensed. "Under whose leadership?"

"Perhaps yours, Dick."

"Why 'perhaps'?"

"You might not want it."

"When I was eighteen," Muller said, "I was with a girl out in the woods on Earth, in the California forest preserve, and we made love, and it wasn't exactly my first time but the first time it worked out in any kind of proper way, and afterward we were lying on our backs looking up at the stars and I told her I was going to go out and walk around among them. And she said, Oh, Dick, how wonderful, but of course it wasn't anything special I was saying. Any kid that age says it when he looks up at the stars. And I told her that I was going to discover things out in space, that men were going to remember me the way they remember Columbus and Magellan and the early astronauts and all. I said I was going to be right in the front of whatever was happening, that I was going to move through the stars like a god. I was very eloquent. I went on like that for about ten minutes, until we were both carried away by the wonder of it all, and I turned to her and she pulled me down on top of her and I turned my backside to the stars and worked hard to nail her to the Earth, and that was the night I grew my ambitions." He laughed. "There are things we can say at eighteen that we can't say again."

"There are things we can do at eighteen that we can't do again either," said Boardman. "Well, Dick? You're past fifty now, right? You've walked in the stars. Do you feel like a god?"

"Sometimes."

"Do you want to go to Beta Hydri IV?"

"You know I do."

"Alone?"

Muller felt the ground give way before him, and abruptly it seemed to him that he was taking his first spacewalk again, falling freely toward all the universe. *"Alone?"*

"We've programmed the whole thing and concluded that to send a bunch of men down there at this point would be a mistake. The Hydrans haven't responded very well to our eye probes. You saw that: they picked the eye up and smashed it. We can't begin to fathom their psychologies, because we've never been up against alien minds before. But we feel that the safest thing—both in terms of potential manpower loss and in terms of impact on their society—is to send a single ambassador down there to them—one man, coming in peace, a shrewd, strong man who has been tested under a variety of stress situations and who will develop ways of initiating contact. That man may find himself chopped to shreds thirty seconds after making contact. On the other hand, if he survives he'll have accomplished something utterly unique in human history. It's your option."

It was irresistible. Mankind's ambassador to the Hydrans! To go alone, to walk alien soil and extend humanity's first greeting to cosmic neighbors—

It was his ticket to immortality. It would write his name forever on the stars.

"How do you figure the chances of survival?" Muller asked.

"The computation is one chance in sixty-five of coming out whole, Dick. Considering that it's not an Earth-type planet to any great degree, you'll need a life-support system. And you may get a chilly reception. One in sixty-five."

"Not too bad."

"I'd never accept such odds myself," Boardman said, grinning.

"No, but I might." He drained his glass. To carry it off meant imperishable fame. To fail, to be slain by the Hydrans, even that was not so dreadful. He had lived well. There were worse fates than to die bearing mankind's banner to a strange world. That throbbing pride of his, that hunger for glory, that childlike craving for renown that he had never outgrown, drove him to it. The odds were not too bad.

Marta reappeared. She was wet from her swim, her nude body glossy, her hair plastered to the slender column of her neck. Her breasts were heaving rapidly, little cones of flesh tipped by puckered pink nipples. She might have been a leggy fourteen-year-old, Muller thought, looking at her narrow hips, her lean thighs. Boardman tossed her a drier. She thumbed it and stepped into its yellow field, making one complete turn. Taking her garment from the rack she covered herself unhurriedly. "That was great," she said. Her eyes met Muller's for the first time since her return. "Dick, what's the matter with you? You look wide open— stunned. Are you all right?"

"Fine."

"What happened?"

"Mr. Boardman's made a proposition."

"You can tell her about it, Dick. We don't plan to keep it a secret. There'll be a galaxy-wide announcement right away."

"There's going to be a landing on Beta Hydri IV," Muller said in a thick voice. "One man. Me. How will it work, Charles? A ship in a parking orbit, and then I go down in a powered drop-capsule equipped for return?"

"Yes."

Marta said. "It's insane, Dick. Don't do it. You'll regret it forever."

"It's a quick death if things don't work out, Marta. I've taken worse risks before."

"No. Look, sometimes I think I've got a little precog. I see things ahead, Dick." She laughed nervously, her pose of cool sophistication abruptly shattering. "If you go there, I don't think you'll die. But I don't exactly think you'll live, either. Say you won't go. Say it, Dick!"

"You never officially accepted the proposition," Boardman pointed out.

"I know," Muller said. He got to his feet, nearly reaching the low roof of the dining capsule, and walked toward Marta, and put his arms around her, remembering that other girl so long ago under the California sky, remembering that wild surge of power that had come upon him as he swung over from the blaze of the stars to the warm, yielding flesh and the parting thighs beneath him. He held Marta firmly. She looked at him in horror. He kissed the tip of her nose and the lobe of her left ear. She shrank away from him, stumbled, nearly plunged into Boardman's lap. Boardman caught her and held her. Muller said, "You know what the answer has to be."

That afternoon one of the robot probes reached Zone F. They still had a distance to go; but it would not be long, Muller knew, before they were at the heart of the maze.

4.

There he is," Rawlins said. "At last!"

Via the drone probe's eyes he stared at the man in the maze. Muller leaned casually against a wall, arms folded; a big weather-beaten man with a harsh chin and a massive wedge-shaped nose. He did not seem at all alarmed by the presence of the drone.

Rawlins cut in the audio pickup and heard Muller say, "Hello, robot. Why are you bothering me?"

The probe, of course, did not reply. Neither did Rawlins, who could have piped a message through the drone. He stood by the data terminal, crouching a little for a better view. His weary eyes throbbed. It had taken them nine local-time days to get one of their probes all the way through the maze to the center. The effort had cost them close to a hundred probes; each inward extension of the safe route by twenty meters or so had required the expenditure of one of the robots. Still, that wasn't too bad, considering that the number of wrong choices in the maze was close to infinite. Through luck, the inspired use of the ship's brain, and a sturdy battery of sensory devices, they had managed to avoid all the obvious traps and most of the cleverer ones. And now they were in the center.

Rawlins felt exhausted. He had been up all night monitoring this critical phase, the penetration of Zone A. Hosteen had gone to sleep. So, finally, had Boardman. A few of the crewmen were still on duty here and aboard the ship, but Rawlins was the only member of the civilian complement still awake.

He wondered if the discovery of Muller had been supposed to take place during his stint. Probably not. Boardman wouldn't want to risk blowing things by letting a novice handle the big moment. Well, too bad. They had left him on duty, and he had moved his probe a few meters inward, and now he was looking right at Muller.

He searched for signs of the man's inner torment.

They weren't obvious. Muller had lived here alone for so many years—wouldn't that have done something to his soul? And that other thing, the prank the Hydrans had played on him—surely that too would have registered on his face. So far as Rawlins could tell, it hadn't.

Oh, he looked sad around the eyes, and his lips were compressed in a taut, tense line. But Rawlins had been expecting something more dramatic, something romantic, some mirror of agony on that face. Instead he saw only the craggy, indifferent, almost insensitive-looking features of a tough, durable man in late middle age. Muller had gone gray, and his clothing was a little ragged; he looked worn and frayed himself. But that was only to be expected of a man who had been living this kind of exile for nine years. Rawlins wanted something more, something picturesque, a gaunt, bitter face, eyes dark with misery.

"What do you want?" Muller asked the probe. "Who sent you? Why don't you go away?"

Rawlins did not dare to answer. He had no idea of the gambit Boardman had in mind at this point. Brusquely he keyed the probe to freeze and sped away toward the dome where Boardman slept.

Boardman was sleeping under a canopy of life-sustaining devices. He was, after all, at least eighty years old—though he certainly didn't look it—and one way to keep from looking it was to plug oneself into one's sustainers every night. Rawlins was a trifle embarrassed to intrude on the old man when he was enmeshed in his paraphernalia this way. Strapped to Boardman's forehead were a couple of meningeal electrodes that guaranteed a proper and healthy progression through the levels of sleep, thus washing the mind of the day's fatigue poisons. An ultrasonic drawcock filtered dregs and debris from Boardman's arteries. Hormone flow was regulated by the ornate webwork hovering above his chest. The whole business was linked to and directed by the ship's brain. Within the elaborate life system Boardman looked unreal and waxy. His breathing was slow and regular; his soft lips were slack; his cheeks seemed puffy and loose-fleshed. Boardman's eyeballs were moving rapidly beneath the lids; a sign of dreaming, of upper sleep. Could he be awakened safely now?

Rawlins feared to risk it. Not directly, anyway. He ducked out of the room and activated the terminal just outside. "Take a dream to Charles Boardman," Rawlins said. "Tell him we found Muller. Tell him he's got to wake up right away. Say, Charles, Charles, wake up, we need you. Got it?"

"Acknowledged," said the ship's brain.

The impulse leaped from dome to ship, was translated into response-directed form, and returned to the dome. Rawlins' message seeped into Boardman's mind through the electrodes on his forehead. Feeling pleased with himself, Rawlins entered the old man's sleeproom once again and waited.

Boardman stirred. His hands formed claws and scraped gently at the machinery in whose embrace he lay.

"Muller—" he muttered.

His eyes opened. For a moment he did not see. But the waking process had begun, and the life system jolted his metabolism sufficiently to get him functioning again. "Ned?" he said hoarsely. "What are you doing here? I dreamed that—"

"It wasn't a dream, Charles. I programmed it for you. We got through to Zone A. We found Muller."

Boardman undid the life system and sat up instantly, alert, aware. "What time is it?"

"Dawn's just breaking."

"And how long ago did you find him?"

"Perhaps fifteen minutes. I froze the probe, and came right to you. But I didn't want to rush you awake, so—"

"All right. All right." Boardman had swung out of bed, now. He staggered a little as he got to his feet. He wasn't yet at his daytime vigor, Rawlins realized; his real age was showing. He found an excuse to look away, studying the life system to avoid having to see the meaty folds of Boardman's body.

When I'm his age, Rawlins thought, I'll make sure I get regular shape-ups. It isn't a matter of vanity, really. It's just courtesy to other people. We don't have to look old if we don't want to look old. Why offend?

"Let's go," Boardman said. "Unfreeze that probe. I want to see him right away."

Using the terminal in the hall, Rawlins brought the probe back to life. The screen showed them Zone A of the maze, cozier-looking than the outer reaches. Muller was not in view. "Turn the audio on one way," Boardman said.

"It is."

"Where'd he go?"

"Must have walked out of sight range," Rawlins said. He moved the probe in a standing circle, taking in a broad sweep of low cubical houses, high-rising archways, and tiered walls. A small cat-like animal scampered by, but there was no sign of Muller.

"He was right over there," Rawlins insisted unhappily. "He—"

"All right. He didn't have to stay in one place while you were waking me up. Walk the probe around."

Rawlins activated the drone and started it in a slow cruising exploration of the street. Instinctively he was cautious, expecting to find more traps at any moment, though he told himself a couple of times that the builders of the maze would surely not have loaded their own inner quarters with perils. Muller abruptly stepped out of a windowless building and planted himself in front of the probe.

"Again," he said. "Back to life, are you? Why don't you speak up? What's your ship? Who sent you?"

"Should we answer?" Rawlins asked.

"No."

Boardman's face was pressed almost against the screen. He pushed Rawlins' hands from the controls and went to work on the fine tuning until Muller was sharply in focus. Boardman kept the probe moving, sliding around in front of Muller, as though trying to hold the man's attention and prevent him from wandering off again.

In a low voice Boardman said, "That's frightening. The look on his face—"

"I thought he looked pretty calm."

"What do you know? I *remember* that man. Ned, that's a face out of hell. His cheekbones are twice as sharp as they used to be. His eyes are awful. You see the way his mouth turns down—on the left side? He might even have had a light stroke. But he's lasted well enough, I suppose."

Baffled, Rawlins searched for the signs of Muller's passion. He had missed them before, and he missed them now. But of course he had no real recollection of the way Muller was supposed to look. And Boardman, naturally, would be far more expert than he at reading character.

"It won't be simple, getting him out of there," Boardman said. "He'll want to stay. But we need him, Ned. We need him."

Muller, keeping pace with the drone, said in a deep gruff voice, "You've got thirty seconds to state your purpose here. Then you'd better turn around and get going back the way you came."

"Won't you talk to him?" Rawlins asked. "He'll wreck the probe!"

"Let him," said Boardman. "The first person who talks to him is going to be flesh and blood, and he's going to be standing face to face with him. That's the only way it can be. This has to be a courtship, Ned. We can't do it through the speakers of a probe."

"Ten seconds," said Muller.

He reached into his pocket and came out with a glossy black metal globe the size of an apple, with a small square window on one side. Rawlins had never seen anything like it before. Perhaps it was some alien weapon Muller had found in this city, he decided, for swiftly Muller raised the globe and aimed the window at the face of the drone probe.

The screen went dark.

"Looks like we've lost another probe," Rawlins said.

Boardman nodded. "Yes. The last probe we're going to lose. Now we start losing men."

2

The time had come to risk human lives in the maze. It was inevitable, and Boardman regretted it, the way he regretted paying taxes or growing old or voiding waste matter or feeling the pull of strong gravity. Taxes, aging, excretion, and gravity were all permanent aspects of the human condition, though, however much all four had been alleviated by modern scientific progress. So was the risk of death. They had made good use of the drone probes here, and had probably saved a dozen lives that way; but now lives were almost surely going to be lost anyhow. Boardman grieved over that, but not for long and not very deeply. He had been asking men to risk their lives for decades, and many of them had died. He was ready to risk his own, at the right time and in the right cause.

The maze now was thoroughly mapped. The ship's brain held a detailed picture of the inward route, with all the known pitfalls charted, and Boardman was confident that he could send drones in with a ninety-five per cent probability of getting them to Zone A unharmed. Whether a man could cover that same route with equal safety was what remained to be seen. Even with the computer whispering hints to him every step of the way, a man filtering information through a fallible, fatigue-prone human brain might not quite see things the same way as a lathe-turned probe, and perhaps would make compensations of his own in the course that would prove fatal. So the data they had gathered had to be tested carefully before he or Ned Rawlins ventured inside.

There were volunteers to take care of that.

They knew they were likely to die. No one had tried to pretend otherwise to them, and they would have it no other way. It had been put to them that it was important for humanity to bring Richard Muller voluntarily out of that maze, and that it could best be accomplished by having specific human beings—Charles Boardman and Ned Rawlins—speak to Muller in person, and that since Boardman and Rawlins were nonreplaceable units it was necessary for others to explore the route ahead of them. Very well. The explorers were ready, knowing that they were expendable. They also knew that it might even be helpful for the first few of them to die. Each death brought new information; successful traversals of the inward route brought none, at this point.

They drew lots for the job.

The man chosen to go first was a lieutenant named Burke, who looked fairly young and probably was, since military men rarely went in for shape-ups until they were in the top echelons. He was a short, sturdy, dark-haired man who acted as if he could be replaced from a template aboard the ship, which was not the case.

"When I find Muller," Burke said—he did not say *if*—"I tell him I'm an archaeologist. Right? And that if he doesn't mind, I'd like some of my friends to come inside also?"

"Yes," said Boardman. "And remember, the less you say to him in the way of professional-sounding noises, the less suspicious he's going to be."

Burke was not going to live long enough to say anything to Richard Muller, and all of them knew it. But he waved goodbye jauntily, somewhat stagily, and strode into the maze. Through a backpack he was connected with the ship's brain. The computer would relay his marching orders to him, and would show the watchers in the camp exactly what was happening to him.

He moved smartly and smoothly past the terrors of Zone H. He lacked the array of detection devices that had helped the probes find the pivot-mounted slabs and the deathpits beneath, the hidden energy flares, the clashing teeth set in doorways, and all the other nightmares; but he had something much more useful riding with him: the accumulated knowledge of those nightmares, gathered through the expenditure of a lot of probes that had failed to notice them. Boardman, watching his screen, saw the by now familiar pillars and spokes and escarpments, the airy bridges, the heaps of bones, the occasional debris of a drone probe. Silently he urged Burke on, knowing that in not too many days he would have to travel this route himself. Boardman wondered how much Burke's life meant to Burke.

Burke took nearly forty minutes to pass from Zone H to Zone G. He showed no sign of elation as he negotiated the passageway; G, they all knew, was nearly as tough as H. But so far the guidance system was working well. Burke was executing a sort of grim ballet, dancing around the obstacles, counting his steps, now leaping, now turning sideways, now straining to step over some treacherous strip of pavement. He was progressing nicely. But the computer was unable to warn him about the small toothy creature awaiting atop a gilded ledge forty meters inside Zone G. It was no part of the maze's design.

It was a random menace, transacting business on its own account. Burke carried only a record of past experiences in this realm.

The animal was no bigger than a very large cat, but its fangs were long and its claws were quick. The eye in Burke's backpack saw it as it leaped—but by then it was too late. Burke, half-warned, half-turned and reached for his weapon with the beast already on his shoulders and scrambling for his throat.

The jaws opened astonishingly wide. The computer's eye relayed an anatomical touch Boardman could well have done without: within the outer row of needle-sharp teeth was an inner one, and a third one inside that, perhaps for better chewing of the prey or perhaps just a couple of sets of replacements in case outer teeth were broken off. The effect was one of a forest of jagged fangs. A moment later the jaws closed.

Burke tumbled to the ground, clutching at his attacker. A trickle of blood spurted. Man and beast rolled over twice, tripped some secret waiting relay, and were engulfed in a gust of oily smoke. When the air was clear again neither of them was in view.

Boardman said a little later, "There's something to keep in mind. The animals wouldn't bother attacking a probe. We'll have to carry mass detectors and travel in teams."

That was how they worked it the next time. It was a stiff price to pay for the knowledge, but now they realized they had to deal with the wild beasts as well as with the cunning of ancient engineers. Two men named Marshall and Petrocelli, armed, went together into the maze, looking in all directions. No animal could come near them without tell-taling its thermal output into the infrared pickups of the mass detectors they carried. They shot four animals, one of them immense, and had no trouble otherwise.

Deep within Zone G they came to the place where the distortion screen made a mockery of all information-gathering devices.

How did the screen work, Boardman wondered? He knew of Earth-made distorters that operated directly on the senses, taking perfectly proper sensory messages and scrambling them within the brain to destroy all one-to-one correlations. But this screen had to be different. It could not attack the nervous system of a drone probe, for the drones had no nervous systems in any meaningful sense of that term, and their eyes gave accurate reports of what they saw. Somehow what the drones had seen—and what they had reported to the computer—bore no relation to the real geometry of the maze at that point. Other drones, posted beyond the range of the screen, had given entirely different and much more reliable accounts of the terrain. So the thing must work on some direct optical principle, operating on the environment itself, rearranging it, blurring perspective, subtly shifting and concealing the outlines of things, transforming normal configurations into bafflement. Any sight organ within reach of the screen's effect would obtain a wholly convincing and perfectly incorrect image of the area, whether or not it had a mind to be tinkered with. That was quite interesting, Boardman thought. Perhaps later the mechanisms of this place could be studied and mastered. Later.

It was impossible for him to know what shape the maze had taken for Marshall and Petrocelli as they succumbed to the screen. Unlike the drone probes, which relayed exact accounts of everything that passed through their eyes, the two men were not directly hooked to the computer and could not transmit their visual images to the screen. The best they could do was describe what they saw. It did not match the images sent back by the probe eyes mounted on their backpacks, nor did it match the genuine configurations apparent from outside the screen's range.

They did as the computer said. They walked forward even where their own eyes told them that vast abysses lay in their path. They crouched to wriggle through a tunnel whose roof was bright with the suspended blades of guillotines. The tunnel did not exist. "Any minute I expect one of those blades to fall and chop me in half," Petrocelli said. There were no blades. At the end of the tunnel they obediently moved to the left, toward a massive flail that lashed the ground in vicious swipes. There was no flail. Reluctantly they did not set foot on a plumply upholstered walkway that appeared to lead out of the region of the screen. The walkway was imaginary; they had no way of seeing the pit of acid that actually was there.

"It would be better if they simply closed their eyes," Boardman said. "The way the drones went through—minus all visuals."

"They claim it's too scary to do it like that," said Hosteen.

"Which is better—to have no visual information, or to have the wrong information?" Boardman asked. "They could follow the computer's orders just as well with their eyes closed. And there'd be no chance that—"

Petrocelli screamed. On the split screen Boardman saw the real configuration—a flat, innocuous strip of road—and the screen-distorted one relayed by the backpack eyes—a sudden geyser of flame erupting at their feet.

"Stand where you are!" Hosteen bellowed. "It isn't real!"

Petrocelli, one foot high in the air, brought it back into place with a wrenching effort. Marshall's reaction time was slower. He had been whirling to escape the eruption when Hosteen had called to him, and he turned to the left before he halted. He was a dozen centimeters too far out of the safe road. A coil of bright metal flicked out of a block of stone and wrapped itself about his ankles. It cut through the bone without difficulty. Marshall toppled and a flashing golden bar stapled him to a wall.

Without looking back, Petrocelli passed through the column of flame unharmed, stumbled forward ten paces, and came to a halt, safe beyond the effective range of the distortion screen. "Dave?" he said hoarsely. "Dave, are you all right?"

"He stepped off the path," said Boardman. "It was a quick finish."

"What do you want me to do?"

"Stay put, Petrocelli. Get calm and don't try to go anywhere. I'm sending Chesterfield and Walker in after you. Wait right where you are."

Petrocelli was trembling. Boardman asked the ship's brain to give him a needle, and the backpack swiftly eased him with a soothing injection. Still rigid, unwilling to turn toward his impaled companion, Petrocelli stood quite still, awaiting the others.

It took Chesterfield and Walker close to an hour to reach the place of the distortion screen, and nearly fifteen minutes to shuffle through the few square meters the screen controlled. They did it with their eyes closed, and they didn't like that at all: but the phantoms of the maze could not frighten blind men, and in time Chesterfield and Walker were beyond their grasp. Petrocelli was much calmer by then. Warily, the three continued toward the heart of the maze.

Something would have to be done, Boardman thought, about recovering Marshall's body. Some other time, though.

3

The longest days of Ned Rawlins' life had been those spent on the journey to Rigel, four years before, to fetch his father's body. These days now were longer. To stand before a screen, to watch brave men die, to feel every nerve screaming for relief hour after hour after hour—

But they were winning the battle of the maze. Fourteen men had entered it so far. Four were dead. Walker and Petrocelli had made camp in Zone E; five more men had set up a relief base in F; three others were currently edging past the distortion screen in G and soon would join them. The worst was over for these. It was clear from the probe work that the curve of danger dropped off sharply past Zone F, and that there were practically no hazards at all in the three inner zones. With

E and F virtually conquered, it should not be difficult to break through
to those central zones where Muller, impassive and uncommunicating,
lurked and waited.

Rawlins thought that he knew the maze completely by now. Vicariously he had entered it more than a hundred times; first through the
eyes of the probes, then through the relays from the crewmen. At night
in feverish dreams he saw its dark patterns, its curving walls and sinuous
towers. Locked in his own skull he somehow made the circuit of that
labyrinth, kissing death a thousand times. He and Boardman would be
the beneficiaries of hard-won experience when their turns came to go
inside.

Their turns were coming near.

On a chill morning under an iron sky he stood with Boardman just
outside the maze, by the upsloping embankment of soil that rimmed the
outer flange of the city. In the short weeks they had been here, the year
had dimmed almost startlingly toward whatever winter this planet had.
Sunlight lasted only six hours a day now, out of the twenty; two hours
of pale twilight followed, and dawns were thin and prolonged. The
whirling moons danced constantly in the sky, playing twisting games
with shadows.

Rawlins, by this time, was almost eager to test the dangers of the
maze. There was a hollowness in his gut, a yearning born of impatience
and embarrassment. He had waited, peering into screens, while other
men, some hardly older than himself, gambled their lives to get inside.
It seemed to him that he had spent all his life waiting for the cue to
take the center of the stage.

On the screen, they watched Muller moving at the heart of the maze.
The hovering probes kept constant check on him, marking his peregri-
nations with a shifting line on the master chart. Muller had not left Zone
A since the time he encountered the drone; but he changed positions
daily in the labyrinth, migrating from house to house as though he feared
to sleep in the same one twice. Boardman had taken care not to let him
have any contact with them since the encounter with the drone. It often
seemed to Rawlins that Boardman was stalking some rare and fragile
beast.

Tapping the screen, Boardman said, "This afternoon we go inside,
Ned. We'll spend the night in the main camp. Tomorrow you move
forward to join Walker and Petrocelli in E. The day after that you go
on alone toward the middle and find Muller."

"Why are you going inside the maze, Charles?"

"To help you."

"You could keep in touch with me from out here," said Rawlins. "You don't need to risk yourself."

Boardman tugged thoughtfully at his dewlap. "What I'm doing is calculated for minimum risk this way."

"How?"

"If you get into problems," Boardman said, "I'll need to go to you and give you assistance. I'd rather wait in Zone F, if I'm needed, than have to come rushing in suddenly from the outside through the most dangerous part of the maze. You see what I'm telling you? I can get to you quickly from F without much danger. But not from here."

"What kind of problems?"

"Stubbornness from Muller. He's got no reason to cooperate with us, and he's not an easy man to deal with. I remember him in those months after he came back from Beta Hydri IV. We had no peace with him. He was never actually level-tempered before, but afterward he was a volcano. Mind you, Ned, I don't judge him for it. He's got a right to be furious with the universe. But he's troublesome. He's a bird of ill omen. Just to go near him brings bad luck. You'll have your hands full."

"Why don't you come with me, then?"

"Impossible," Boardman said. "It would ruin everything if he even knew I was on this planet. I'm the man who sent him to the Hydrans, don't forget. I'm the one who in effect marooned him on Lemnos. I think he might kill me if he saw me again."

Rawlins recoiled from that idea. "No. He hasn't become that barbaric."

"You don't know him. What he was. What he's become."

"If he's as full of demons as you say, how am I ever going to win his trust?"

"Go to him. Look guileless and trustworthy. You don't have to practice that, Ned. You've got a naturally innocent face. Tell him you're here on an archaeological mission. Don't let him know that we realized he was here all along. Say that the first you knew was when our probe stumbled into him—that you recognized him, from the days when he and your father were friends."

"I'm to mention my father, then?"

"By all means. Tell him who you are. It's the only way. Tell him that your father's dead, and that this is your first expedition to space. Work on his sympathies, Ned. Dig for the paternal in him."

Rawlins shook his head. "Don't get angry with me, Charles, but I've got to tell you that I don't like any of this. These lies."

"Lies?" Boardman's eyes blazed. "Lies to say that you're your father's son? That this is your first expedition?"

"That I'm an archaeologist?"

Boardman shrugged. "Would you rather tell him that you came here as part of a search mission looking for Richard Muller? Will that help win his trust? Think about our purpose, Ned."

"Yes. Ends and means. I know."

"Do you, really?"

"We're here to win Muller's cooperation because we think that he alone can save us from a terrible menace," Rawlins said stolidly, unfeelingly, flatly. "Therefore we must take any approach necessary to gain that cooperation."

"Yes. And I wish you wouldn't smirk when you say it."

"I'm sorry, Charles. But I feel so damned queasy about deceiving him."

"We need him."

"Yes. But a man who's suffered so much already—"

"We need him."

"All right, Charles."

"I need you, too," Boardman said. "If I could do this myself, I would. But if he saw me, he'd finish me. In his eyes I'm a monster. It's the same with anyone else connected with his past career. But you're different. He might be able to trust you. You're young, you look so damned virtuous, and you're the son of a good friend of his. You can get through to him."

"And fill him up with lies so we can trick him."

Boardman closed his eyes. He seemed to be containing himself with an effort.

"Stop it, Ned."

"Go on. Tell me what I do after I've introduced myself."

"Build a friendship with him. Take your time about it. Make him come to depend on your visits."

"What if I can't stand being with him?"

"Conceal it. That's the hardest part, I know."

"The hardest part is the lying, Charles."

"Whatever you say. Anyhow, show that you can tolerate his company. Make the effort. Chat with him. Make it clear to him that you're stealing time from your scientific work—that the villainous bastards who are running your expedition don't want you to have anything to do with him, but that you're drawn to him by love and pity and won't let him interfere. Tell him all about yourself, your ambitions, your love life, your hobbies, whatever you want. Run off at the mouth. It'll reinforce the image of the naive kid."

"Do I mention the galactics?" Rawlins asked.

"Not obtrusively. Work them in somewhere by way of bringing him up to date on current events. But don't tell him too much. Certainly don't tell him of the threat they pose. Or a word about the need we have for him, you understand. If he gets the idea that he's being used, we're finished."

"How will I get him to leave the maze, if I don't tell him why we want him?"

"Let that part pass for now," Boardman said. "I'll coach you in the next phase after you've succeeded in getting him to trust you."

"The translation," Rawlins said, "is that you're going to put such a whopper in my mouth that you don't even dare tell me now what it is for fear I'll throw up my hands and quit."

"Ned—"

"I'm sorry. But—look, Charles, why do we have to *trick* him out? Why can't we just say that humanity needs him, and force him to come out?"

"Do you think that's morally superior to tricking him out?"

"It's cleaner, somehow. I hate all this dirty plotting and scheming. I'd much rather help knock him cold and haul him from the maze than have to go through what you've planned. I'd be willing to help take him by force—because we really do need him. We've got enough men to do it."

"We don't," Boardman said. "We can't force him out. That's the whole point. It's too risky. He might find some way to kill himself the moment we tried to grab him."

"A stungun," said Rawlins. "I could do it, even. Just get within range and gun him down, and then we carry him out of the maze, and when he wakes up we explain—"

Boardman vehemently shook his head. "He's had nine years to figure out that maze. We don't know what tricks he's learned or what defensive traps he's planted. While he's in there I don't dare take any kind of offensive action against him. He's too valuable to risk. For all we know he's programmed the whole place to blow up if someone pulls a gun on him. He's got to come out of that labyrinth of his own free will, Ned, and that means we have to trick him with false promises. I know it stinks. The whole universe stinks, sometimes. Haven't you discovered that yet?"

"It doesn't *have* to stink!" Rawlins said sharply, his voice rising. "Is that the lesson you've learned in all those years? The universe doesn't stink. Man stinks! And he does it by voluntary choice because he'd rather stink than smell sweet! We don't *have* to lie. We don't *have* to cheat. We could opt for honor and decency and—" Rawlins stopped abruptly. In a different tone he said, "I sound young as hell to you, don't I, Charles?"

"You're entitled to make mistakes," Boardman said. "That's what being young is for."

"You genuinely believe and know that there's a cosmic malevolence in the workings of the universe?"

Boardman touched the tips of his thick, short fingers together. "I wouldn't put it that way. There's no personal power of darkness running things, any more than there's a personal power of good. The universe is a big impersonal machine. As it functions it tends to put stress on some of its minor parts, and those parts wear out, and the universe doesn't give a damn about that, because it can generate replacements. There's nothing immoral about wearing out parts, but you have to admit that from the point of view of the part under stress it's a stinking deal. It happened that two small parts of the universe clashed when we dropped Dick Muller onto the planet of the Hydrans. We had to put him there because it's our nature to find out things, and they did what they did to him because the universe puts stress on its parts, and the result was that Dick Muller came away from Beta Hydri IV in bad shape. He was drawn into the machinery of the universe and got ground up. Now we're having a second clash of parts, equally inevitable, and we have to feed Muller through the machine a second time. He's likely to be chewed again—which stinks—and in order to push him into a position where that can happen, you and I have to stain our souls a little—which also stinks—and yet we have absolutely no choice in the matter. If we don't compromise ourselves and trick Dick Muller, we may be setting in motion a new spin of the machine that will destroy all of humanity—and that would stink even worse. I'm asking you to do an unpleasant thing for a decent motive. You don't want to do it, and I understand how you feel, but I'm trying to get you to see that your personal moral code isn't always the highest factor. In wartime, a soldier shoots to kill because the universe imposes that situation on him. It may be an unjust war, and that might be his brother in the ship he's aiming at, but the war is real and he has his role."

"Where's the room for free will in this mechanical universe of yours, Charles?"

"There isn't any. That's why I say the universe stinks."

"We have no freedom at all?"

"The freedom to wriggle a little on the hook."

"Have you felt this way all your life?"

"Most of it," Boardman said.

"When you were my age?"

"Even earlier."

Rawlins looked away. "I think you're all wrong, but I'm not going to waste breath trying to tell you so. I don't have the words. I don't have the arguments. And you wouldn't listen anyway."

"I'm afraid I wouldn't, Ned. But we can discuss this some other time. Say, twenty years from now. Is it a date?"

Trying to grin, Rawlins said, "Sure. If I haven't killed myself from guilt over this."

"You won't."

"How am I suppose to live with myself after I've pulled Dick Muller out of his shell?"

"Wait and see. You'll discover that you did the right thing, in context. Or the least wrong thing, anyhow. Believe me, Ned. Just now you may feel that your soul will forever be corroded by this job, but it won't happen that way."

"We'll see," said Rawlins quietly. Boardman seemed more slippery than ever when he was in this avuncular mood. To die in the maze, Rawlins thought, was the only way to avoid getting trapped in these moral ambiguities; and the moment he hatched the thought, he abolished it in horror. He stared at the screen. "Let's go inside," he said. "I'm tired of waiting."

5.

Muller saw them coming closer, and did not understand why he was so calm about it. He had destroyed that robot, yes, and after that they had stopped sending in robots. But his viewing tanks showed him the men camping in the outer levels. He could not see their faces clearly. He could not see what they were doing out there. He counted about a dozen of them, give or take two or three; some were settled in Zone E, and a somewhat larger group in F. Muller had seen a few of them die in the outer zones.

He had ways of attacking. He could, if he cared to, flood Zone E with backup from the aqueduct. He had done that once, by accident, and it had taken the city almost a full day to clean things up. He recalled how, during the flood, Zone E had been sealed off, bulkheaded to keep the water from spilling out. If the intruders did not drown in the first rush, they would certainly blunder in alarm into some of the traps. Muller could do other things, too, to keep them from getting to the inner city.

Yet he did nothing. He knew that at the heart of his inaction was a hunger to break his years of isolation. Much as he hated them, much as he feared them, much as he dreaded the puncturing of his privacy, Muller allowed the men to work their way toward him. A meeting now was inevitable. They knew he was here. (Did they know who he was?) They would find him, to their sorrow and to his. He would learn whether in his long exile he had been purged of his affliction so that he was fit for human company again. But Muller already was sure of the answer to that.

He had spent part of a year among the Hydrans; and then, seeing that he was accomplishing nothing, he entered his powered drop-capsule, rode it into the heavens, and, repossessed his orbiting ship. If the Hydrans had a mythology, he would become part of it.

Within his ship Muller went through the operations that would return him to Earth. As he notified the ship's brain of his presence, he caught sight of himself in the burnished metal plate of the input bank and it frightened him, a little. The Hydrans did not use mirrors. Muller saw deep new lines etched on his face, which did not bother him, and he saw a strangeness in his eyes, which did. The muscles are tense, he told himself. He finished programming his return and then went to the medic chamber and ordered a forty-db drop in his neural level along with a hot bath and a thorough massage. When he came out, his eyes still looked strange; and he had sprouted a facial tic, besides. He got rid of the tic easily enough, but he could do nothing about his eyes.

The eyes have no expression, Muller told himself. It's the lids that do the work. My eyelids are strained from living in the breathing suit so long. I'll be all right. It was a rough few months, but now I'll be all right.

The ship gulped power from the nearest designated donor star. The ship's rotors whirled along the axes of warp, and Muller, along with his plastic and metal container, was hurled out of the universe on one of the shortcut routes. Even in warp, a certain amount of absolute time loss is experienced as the ship zips through the stitch in the continuum. Muller read, slept, listened to music, and played a woman cube when the need got great. He told himself that the stiffness was going out of his facial expression, but he might need a mild shape-up when he got to Earth. This jaunt had put a few years on him.

He had no work to do. The ship duly popped from warp within the prescribed limits, 100,000 kilometers out from Earth, and colored lights flashed on his communications board as the nearest traffic station signalled for his bearings. Muller instructed the ship to deal with the traffic station.

"Match velocities with us, Mr. Muller, and we'll send a pilot aboard to get you to Earth," the traffic controller said.

Muller's ship took care of it. The coppery globe of the traffic station appeared in sight. It floated just ahead of Muller for a while, but gradually his ship drew abreast of it.

"We have a relay message for you from Earth," the controller said. "Charles Boardman calling."

"Go ahead," said Muller.

Boardman's face filled the screen. He looked pink and newly-buffed, quite healthy, well rested. He smiled and put his hand forward. "Dick," he said. "God, it's great to see you!"

Muller activated tactile and put his hand on Boardman's wrist through the screen. "Hello, Charles. One in sixty-five, eh? Well, I'm back."

"Should I tell Marta?"

"Marta," Muller said, thinking for a moment. Yes. The blue-haired wench with the swivel hips and the sharp heels. "Yes. Tell Marta. It would be nice if she met me when I landed. Woman cubes aren't all that thrilling."

Boardman gave him a you-said-a-mouthful-boy kind of laugh. Then he changed gears abruptly and said, "How did it go?"

"Poorly."

"You made contact, though?"

"I found the Hydrans, yes. They didn't kill me."

"Were they hostile?"

"They didn't kill me."

"Yes, but—"

"I'm alive, Charles." Muller felt the tic beginning again. "I didn't learn their language. I can't tell you if they approved of me. They seemed quite interested. They studied me closely for a long time. They didn't say a word."

"What are they, telepaths?"

"I can't tell you that, Charles."

Boardman was silent for a while. "What did they do to you, Dick?"

"Nothing."

"That isn't so."

"What you're seeing is travel fatigue," Muller said. "I'm in good shape, just a little stretched in the nerve. I want to breathe real air and drink some real beer and taste real meat, and I'd like to have some company in bed, and I'll be as good as ever. And then maybe I'll suggest some ways of making contact with the Hydrans."

"How's the gain on your broadcast system, Dick?"

"Huh?"

"You're coming across too loud," said Boardman.

"Blame it on the relay station. Jesus, Charles. What does the gain on my system have to do with anything?"

"I'm not sure," Boardman said. "I'm just trying to find out why you're shouting at me."

"I'm not shouting," Muller shouted.

Soon after that they broke contact. Muller had word from the traffic station that they were ready to send a pilot aboard. He got the hatch ready, and let the man in. The pilot was a very blond young man with hawklike features and pale skin. As soon as he unhelmeted he said, "My name is Les Christiansen, Mr. Muller, and I want to tell you that it's an honor and a privilege for me to be the pilot for the first man to visit an alien race. I hope I'm not breaking security when I say that I'd love to know a little about it while we're descending. I mean, this is sort of a moment in history, me being the first to see you in person since you're back, and if it's not an intrusion I'd be grateful if you'd tell me just some of the—highlights—of your—of—"

"I guess I can tell you a little," Muller said affably. "First, did you see the cube of the Hydrans? I know it was supposed to be shown, and—"

"You mind if I sit down a second, Mr. Muller?"

"Go ahead. You saw them, then, the tall skinny things with all the arms—"

"I feel very woozy," said Christiansen. "I don't know what's happening." His face was crimson, suddenly, and beads of sweat glistened on his forehead. "I think I must be getting sick. I—you know, this shouldn't be happening—" The pilot crumpled into a webfoam cradle and huddled there, shivering, covering his head with his hands. Muller, his voice still rusty from the long silences of his mission, hesitated helplessly. Finally he reached down to take the man's elbow and guide him toward the medic chamber. Christiansen whirled away as if touched by fiery metal. The motion pulled him off balance and sent him into a heap on the cabin floor. He rose to his knees and wriggled until he was as far away from Muller as it was possible to get. In a strangled voice he said, "Where is it?"

"That door here."

Christiansen rushed for it, sealed himself in, and rattled the door to make sure of it. Muller, astonished, heard retching sounds, and then something that could have been a series of dry sobs. He was about to signal the traffic station that the pilot was sick, when the door opened a little and Christiansen said in a muffled voice, "Would you hand me my helmet, Mr. Muller?"

Muller gave it to him.

"I'm going to have to go back to my station, Mr. Muller."

"I'm sorry you reacted this way. Christ, I hope I'm not carrying some kind of contagion."

"I'm not sick. I just feel—lousy." Christiansen fastened the helmet in place. "I don't understand. But I want to curl up and cry. Please let me go, Mr. Muller. It—I—that is—it's terrible. That's what I feel!" He rushed into the hatch. In bewilderment Muller watched him cross the void to the nearby traffic station.

He got on the radio. "You better not send another pilot over just yet," Muller told the controller. "Christiansen folded up with instant plague as soon as he took his helmet off. I may be carrying something. Let's check it out."

The controller, looking troubled, agreed. He asked Muller to go to his medic chamber, set up the diagnostat, and transmit its report. A little while later the solemn chocolate-hued face of the station's medical officer appeared on Muller's screen and said, "This is very odd, Mr. Muller."

"What is?"

"I've run your diagnostat transmission through our machine. No unusual symptoms. I've also put Christiansen through the works without learning anything. He feels fine now, he says. He told me that an acute depression hit him the moment he saw you, and it deepened in a hurry to a sort of metabolic paralysis. That is, he felt so gloomy that he could hardly function."

"Is he prone to these attacks?"

"Never," the medic replied. "I'd like to check this out myself. May I come over?"

The medic didn't curl up with the miseries as Christiansen had done. But he didn't stay long, either, and when he left his face was glossy with tears. He looked as baffled as Muller. When the new pilot appeared twenty minutes later, he kept his suit on as he programmed the ship for planetary descent. Sitting rigidly upright at his controls, his back turned to Muller, he said nothing, scarcely acknowledged Muller's presence. As required by law, he brought the ship down until its drive system was in the grip of a groundside landing regulator, and took his leave. Muller saw the man's face, tense, sweat-shiny, tightlipped. The pilot nodded curtly, and went through the hatch. I must have a very bad smell, Muller thought, if he could smell it through his suit like that.

The landing was routine.

At the starport he cleared Immigration quickly. It took only half an hour for Earth to decide that he was acceptable; and Muller, who had passed through these computer banks hundreds of times before, figured that that was close to the record. He had feared that the giant starport diagnostat would detect whatever malady he carried that his own equipment and the traffic station medic had failed to find; but he passed through the bowels of the machine, letting it bounce sonics off his kidneys, and extract some molecules of his various bodily fluids, and at length he emerged without the ringing of bells and the flashing of warning lights. *Approved.* He spoke to the Customs machine. Where from, traveler? Where bound? *Approved.* His papers were in order. A slit in the wall widened into a doorway and he stepped through, to confront another human being for the first time since his landing.

Boardman had come to meet him. Marta was with him. A thick brown robe shot through with dull metal enfolded Boardman; he seemed weighted down with rings, and his brooding eyebrows were thick as dark tropical moss. Marta's hair was short and sea-green; she had silvered her eyes and gilded the slender column of her throat, so that she looked like some jeweled statuette of herself. Remembering her wet and naked from the crystalline lake, Muller disapproved of these changes. He doubted that they had been made for his benefit. Boardman, he knew, liked his women ornate; it was probable that they had been bedding in his absence. Muller would have been surprised and even a little shaken if they had not.

Boardman's hand encircled Muller's wrist in a firm greeting that incredibly turned flabby within seconds. The hand slipped away even before Muller could return the embrace. "It's good to see you, Dick," Boardman said without conviction, stepping back a couple of paces. His cheeks seemed to sag as though under heavy gravitational stress. Marta slipped between them and pressed herself against him. Muller seized her, touching her shoulderblades and running his hands swiftly down to her lean buttocks. He did not kiss her. Her eyes were dazzling as he looked within them and felt himself lost in rebounding mirror images. Her nostrils flared. Through her thin flesh he felt muscles bridling. She was trying to get free of him. "Dick," she whispered. "I've prayed for you every night. You don't know how I've missed you." She struggled harder. He moved his hands to her haunches and pushed inward so fiercely that he could imagine her pelvic cage yielding and flexing. His legs were trembling, and he feared that if he let go of her, she would fall. She turned her head to one side. He put his cheek against her delicate ear. "Dick," she murmured, "I feel so strange—so glad to see you that I'm all tangled up inside—let go, Dick, I feel queasy somehow—"

Yes. Yes. Of course. He released her.

Boardman, sweating, nervous, mopped at his face, jabbed himself with some soothing drug, fidgeted, paced. Muller had never seen him look this way before. "Suppose I let the two of you have some time together, eh?" Boardman suggested, his voice coming out half an octave too high. "The weather's been getting to me, Dick. I'll talk with you tomorrow. Your accommodations are all arranged." Boardman fled. Now Muller felt panic rising.

"Where do we go?" he asked.

"There's a transport pod outside. We have a room at the Starport Inn. Do you have luggage?"

"It's still aboard the ship," Muller answered. "It can wait."

Marta was chewing at the corner of her lower lip. He took her by the hand and they rode the slidewalk out of the terminal room to the transportation pods. Go on, he thought. Tell me that you don't feel well. Tell me that mysteriously you've come down with something in the last ten minutes.

"Why did you cut your hair?" he asked.

"It's a woman's right. Don't you like it this way?"

"Not as much." They entered the pod. "Longer, bluer, it was like the sea on a stormy day." The pod shot off on a bath of quicksilver. She kept far to her side, hunched against the hatch. "And the makeup, too. I'm sorry, Marta. I wish I could like it."

"I was prettying for your homecoming."

"Why are you doing that with your lip?"

"What am I doing?"

"Nothing," he said. "Here we are. The room is booked already?"

"In your name, yes."

They went in. He put his hand on the registration plate. It flashed green and they headed for the liftshaft. The inn began in the fifth sublevel of the starport and went down for fifty levels; their room was near the bottom. Choice location, he thought. The bridal suite, maybe. They stepped into a room with kaleidoscopic hangings and a wide bed with all accessories. The roomglow was tactfully dim. Muller thought of months of woman cubes and a savage throbbing rose in his groin. He knew he had no need to explain any of that to Marta. She moved past him, into the personal room, and was in there a long while. Muller undressed.

She came out nude. All the tricky makeup was gone, and her hair was blue again.

"Like the sea," she said. "I'm sorry I couldn't grow it back in there. The room wasn't programmed for it."

"It's much better now," he told her.

They were ten meters apart. She stood at an angle to him, and he studied the contours of her frail but tough form, the small upjutting breasts, the boyish buttocks, the elegant thighs.

"The Hydrans," he said, "have either five sexes or none, I'm not sure which. That's a measure of how well I got to know them while I was there. However they do it, I think people have more fun. Why are you standing over there, Marta?"

Silently she came toward him. He put one arm around her shoulders and cupped his other hand over one of her breasts. At other times when he did that he felt the nipple pebble-hard with desire against his hand. Not now. She quivered a little, like a shy mare wanting to bolt. He put his lips to her lips, and they were dry, taut, hostile. When he ran his hand along the fine line of her jaw she seemed to shudder. He drew her down and they sat side by side on the bed. Her hand reached for him, almost unwillingly.

He saw the pain in her eyes.

She rolled away from him, her head snapping back hard onto the pillow, and he watched her face writhe with some barely suppressed agony. Then she took his hands in hers and tugged him toward her. Her knees came up and her thighs opened.

"Take me, Dick," she said stagily. "Right now!"

"What's the hurry?"

She tried to force him onto her, into her. He wasn't having it that way. He pulled free of her and sat up. She was crimson to the shoulders, and tears glistened on her face. He knew as much of the truth now as he needed to know, but he had to ask.

"Tell me what's wrong, Marta."

"I don't know."

"You're acting like you're sick."

"I think I am."

"When did you start feeling ill?"

"I—oh, Dick, why all these questions? Please, love, come close."

"You don't want me to. Not really. You're being kind."

"I'm—trying to make you happy, Dick. It—it hurts so much—so—much."

"What does?"

She wouldn't answer. She gestured wantonly and tugged at him again. He sprang from the bed.

"Dick, Dick, I warned you not to go! I said I had some precog. And that other things could happen to you there besides getting killed."

"Tell me what hurts you."

"I can't. I—don't know."

"That's a lie."

"When did it start?"

"This morning. When I got up."

"That's another lie. I have to have the truth!"

"Make love to me, Dick. I can't wait much longer. I—"

"You what?"

"Can't—stand—"

"Can't stand what?"

"Nothing. Nothing." She was off the bed too, rubbing against him, a cat in heat, shivering, muscles leaping in her face, eyes wild.

He caught her wrists and ground the bones together.

"Tell me what it is you can't stand much longer, Marta."

She gasped. He squeezed harder. She swung back, head lolling, breasts thrust toward the ceiling. Her body was oiled now with sweat. Her nakedness maddened and inflamed him.

"Tell me," he said. "You can't stand—"

"—being near you," she said.

6.

Within the maze the air was somehow warmer and sweeter. The walls must cut off the winds, Rawlins thought. He walked carefully, listening to the voice at his ear.

Turn left . . . three paces . . . put your right foot beside the black stripe on the pavement . . . pivot . . . turn left . . . four paces . . . ninety-degree turn to the right . . . immediately make a ninety-degree turn to the right again.

It was like a children's street game—step on a crack, break your mother's back. The stakes were higher here, though. He moved cautiously, feeling death nipping at his heels. What sort of people would build a place like this? Ahead an energy flare spurted across the path. The computer called off the timing for him. *One, two, three, four, five, GO!* Rawlins went.

Safe.

On the far side he halted flatfooted, and looked back. Boardman was keeping pace with him, unslowed by age. Boardman waved and winked. He went through the patterns, too. *One, two, three, four, five, GO!* Boardman crossed the place of the energy flare.

"Should we stop here for a while?" Rawlins asked.

"Don't be patronizing to the old man, Ned. Keep moving. I'm not tired yet."

"We have a tough one up ahead."

"Let's take it, then."

Rawlins could not help looking at the bones. Dry skeletons ages old, and some bodies that were not old at all. Beings of many races had perished here.

What if I die in the next ten minutes?

Bright lights were flashing now, on and off many times a second. Boardman, five meters behind him, became an eerie figure moving in disconnected strides. Rawlins passed his own hand before his face to see the jerky movements. It was as though every other fraction of a second had simply been punched out of his awareness.

The computer told him: *Walk ten paces and halt. One. Two. Three. Walk ten paces and halt. One. Two. Three. Walk ten paces and halt. One. Two. Three. Proceed quickly to end of ramp.*

Rawlins could not remember what would happen to him if he failed to keep to the proper timing. Here in Zone H the nightmares were so thick that he could not keep them straight in his mind. Was this the place where a ton of stone fell on the unwary? Where the walls came together? Where a cobweb-dainty bridge delivered victims to a lake of fire?

His estimated lifespan at this point was two hundred five years. He wanted to have most of those years. I am too uncomplicated to die yet, Ned Rawlins thought.

He danced to the computer's tune, past the lake of fire, past the clashing walls.

2

Something with long teeth perched on the lintel of the door ahead. Carefully Charles Boardman unslung the gun from his backpack and cut in the proximity-responsive target finder. He keyed it for thirty kilograms of mass and downward, at fifty meters. "I've got it," he told Rawlins, and fired.

The energy bolt splashed against the wall. Streaks of shimmering green sprouted along the rich purple. The beast leaped, limbs outstretched in a final agony, and fell. From somewhere came three small scavengers that began to rip it to pieces.

Boardman chuckled. It didn't take much skill to hunt with proximity-responsives, he had to admit. But it was a long time since he had hunted at all. When he was thirty, he had spent a long week in the Sahara Preserve as the youngest of a party of eight businessmen and government consultants on a hunt. He had done it for the political usefulness of making the trip. He had hated it all: the steaming air in his nostrils, the blaze of the sun, the tawny beasts dead against the sand, the boasting, the wanton slaughter. At thirty, one is not very tolerant of the mindless sports of the middle-aged. Yet he had stayed, because he thought it would be useful to him to become friendly with these men.

It *had* been useful. He had never gone hunting again. But this was different, even with proximity-responsives. This was no sport.

3

Images played on a golden screen bracketed to a wall near the inner end of Zone H. Rawlins saw his father's face take form, coalesce with an underlying pattern of bars and crosses, burst into flame. The screen was externally primed; what it showed was in the eye of the beholder. The drones, passing this point, had seen only the blank screen. Rawlins watched the image of a girl appear. Maribeth Chambers, sixteen years old, sophomore in Our Lady of Mercies High School, Rockford, Illinois. Maribeth Chambers smiled shyly and began to remove her clothes. Her hair was silken and soft, a cloud of gold; her eyes were blue, her lips were full and moist. She unhinged her breast-binders and revealed two firm upthrust white globes tipped with dots of flame. They were high and close together, as though no gravity worked on them, and the valley between them was six inches deep and a sixteenth of an inch in breadth. Maribeth Chambers blushed and bared the lower half of her body. She wore small garnets set in the dimples just above her plump pink buttocks. A crucifix of ivory dangled from a golden chain around her hips. Rawlins tried not to look at the screen. The computer directed his feet; he shuffled along obediently.

"I am the Resurrection and the Life," said Maribeth Chambers in a husky, passionate voice.

She beckoned with the tips of three fingers. She gave him a bedroom wink. She crooned sweet obscenities.

Step around in back here, big boy! Let me show you a good time.

She giggled. She wriggled. She heaved her shoulders and made her breasts ring like tolling bells.

Her skin turned deep green. Her eyes slid about in her face. Her lower lip stretched forth like a shovel. Her thighs began to melt. Patterns of flame danced on the screen. Rawlins heard deep throbbing ponderous chords from an invisible organ. He listened to the whispering of the brain that guided him and went past the screen unharmed.

4

The screen showed abstract patterns: a geometry of power, rigid marching lines and frozen figures. Charles Boardman paused to admire it for a moment. Then he moved on.

5

A forest of whirling knives near the inner border of Zone H.

6

The heat grew strangely intense. One had to tiptoe over the pavement. This was troublesome because none who had passed this way before had experienced it. Did the route vary? Could the city introduce variations? How hot would it get? Where would the zone of warmth end? Did cold lie beyond? Would they live to reach Zone E? Was Richard Muller doing this to prevent them from entering?

7

Maybe he recognizes Boardman and is trying to kill him. There is that possibility. Muller has every reason to hate Boardman, and he has had no chance to undergo social adjustment. Maybe I should move faster and open some space between Boardman and myself. It seems to be getting hotter. On the other hand, he would accuse me of being cowardly. And disloyal.

Maribeth Chambers would never have done those things.

Do nuns still shave their heads?

8

Boardman found the distortion screen deep inside Zone G perhaps the worst of all. He was not afraid of the dangers; Marshall was the only man who had failed to get past the screen safely. He was afraid of entering a place where the evidence of his senses did not correspond to the real universe. Boardman depended on his senses. He was wearing his third set of retinas. You can make no meaningful evaluations of the universe without the confidence that you are seeing it clearly.

Now he was within the field of the distortion screen.

Parallel lines met here. The triangular figures emblazoned on the moist, quivering walls were constructed entirely of obtuse angles. A river ran sideways through the valley. The stars were quite close, and the moons orbited one another.

What we now must do is close our eyes and not be deceived.

Left foot. Right foot. Left foot. Right foot. Move to the left slightly— slide your foot. More. More. A trifle more. Back toward the right. That's it. Start walking again.

Forbidden fruit tempted him. All his life he had tried hard to see clearly. The lure of distortions was irresistible. Boardman halted, planting each foot firmly. If you hope to get out of this, he told himself, you will keep your eyes closed. If you open your eyes you will be misled

and go to your death. You have no right to die foolishly here after so
many men have struggled so hard to teach you how to survive.

Boardman remained quite still. The silent voice of the computer,
sounding a little waspish, tried to prod him on.

"Wait," said Boardman quietly. "I can look around a little if I don't
move. That's the important thing, *not to move*. You can't get into trouble
if you don't move."

The ship's brain reminded him of the geyser of flame that had sent
Marshall to his death.

Boardman opened his eyes.

He was careful not to move. All about him he saw the negation of
geometry. This was the inside of the Klein bottle, looking out. Disgust
rose like a green column within him.

You are eighty years old and you know how the universe should
look. Close your eyes now, C.B. Close your eyes and move along.
You're taking undue risks.

First he sought Ned Rawlins. The boy was twenty meters ahead of
him, shuffling slowly past the screen. Eyes closed? Of course. All of
them. Ned was an obedient boy. Or a frightened one. He wants to live
through this, and he'd rather not see how the universe looks through a
distortion screen. I'd like to have had a son like that. But I'd have
changed him by this time.

Boardman began to lift his right leg, checked himself, reimplanted
it on the pavement. Just ahead, pulsations of golden light leaped in the
air, taking now the form of a swan, now the form of a tree. Ned Rawlins'
left shoulder rose too high. His back was humped. One leg moved forward and the other moved backward. Through golden mists Boardman
saw the corpse of Marshall stapled to the wall. Marshall's eyes were
wide open. Were there no bacteria of decay on Lemnos? Looking into
those eyes Boardman saw his own curving reflection, all nose, no mouth.
He closed his eyes.

The computer, relieved, directed him onward.

9

A sea of blood. A cup of lymph.

10

To die, not having loved—

11

This is the gateway to Zone F. I am now leaving death's other kingdom.
Where is my passport? Do I need a visa? I have nothing to declare.
Nothing. Nothing. Nothing.

3

A chill wind blowing out of tomorrow.

7

The boys camped in F were supposed to come out and meet us and lead us through. I hope they don't bother. We can make it without them. We just have to get past the screen, and we're all right.

5

I've dreamed this route so often. And now I hate it, even though it's beautiful. You have to admit that: it's beautiful. And probably it looks most beautiful just before it kills you.

3

Maribeth's thighs have small puckers in the flesh. She will be fat before she's thirty.

10

You do all sorts of things in a career. I could have stopped long ago. I have never read Rousseau. I have not had time for Donne. I know nothing of Kant. If I live I will read them now. I make this vow, being of sound mind and body and eighty years of age, I Ned Rawlins will I Richard Muller will read I will I I I will read I Charles Boardman.

13

14

On the far side of the gateway Rawlins stopped short and asked the computer if it was safe for him to squat down and rest. The brain said that it was. Gingerly, Rawlins lowered himself, rocked on his heels a moment, touched his knee to the cool pebble-textured pavement. He looked back. Behind him, colossal blocks of stone, set without mortar and fitted to a perfect truing, were piled fifty meters high, flanking a tall narrow aperture through which the solid form of Charles Boardman now was passing. Boardman looked sweaty and flustered. Rawlins found that fascinating. He had never seen the old man's smugness pierced before. But they had never come through this maze before, either.

Rawlins himself was none too steady. Metabolic poisons boiled in the tubes and channels of his body. He was drenched with perspiration so thoroughly that his clothing was working overtime to get rid of it, distilling the moisture and volatilizing the substratum of chemical compounds. It was too early to rejoice. Brewster had died here in Zone F, thinking that his troubles were over once he got past the dangers of G. Well, they were.

"Resting?" Boardman asked. His voice came out thin and unfocussed.

"Why not? I've been working hard, Charles." Rawlins grinned unconvincingly. "So have you. The computer says it's safe to stay here a while. I'll make room."

Boardman came alongside and squatted. Rawlins had to steady him as he balanced before kneeling.

Rawlins said, "Muller came this way alone and made it."

"Muller was always an extraordinary man."

"How do you think he did it?"

"Why don't you ask him?"

"I mean to," Rawlins said. "Perhaps by this time tomorrow I'll be talking to him."

"Perhaps. We should go on now."

"If you say so."

"They'll be coming out to meet us soon. They should have fixes on us by now. We must be showing up on their mass detectors. Up, Ned. Up."

They stood. Once again Rawlins led the way.

In Zone F things were less cluttered but also less attractive. The prevailing mood of the architecture was taut, with a fussy line that generated a tension of mismatched objects. Though he knew that traps were fewer here, Rawlins still had the sensation that the ground was likely to open beneath him at any given moment. The air was cooler here. It had the same sharp taste as the air on the open plain. At each of the street intersections rose immense concrete tubs in which jugged, feathery plants were standing.

"Which is the worst part for you so far?" Rawlins asked.

"The distortion screen," said Boardman.

"That wasn't so bad—unless you feel peculiar about walking through stuff this dangerous with your eyes closed. You know, one of those little tigers could have jumped us then, and we wouldn't have known about it until we felt the teeth in us."

"I peeked," said Boardman.

"In the distortion zone?"

"Just for a moment. I couldn't resist it, Ned. I won't try to describe what I saw, but it was one of the strangest experiences of my life."

Rawlins smiled. He wanted to congratulate Boardman on having done something silly and dangerous and human, but he didn't dare. He said, "What did you do? Just stand still and peek and then move on? Did you have any close escapes?"

"Once. I forgot myself and started to take a step, but I didn't follow through. I kept my feet planted and looked around."

"Maybe I'll try that on the way out," Rawlins said. "Just one little look can't hurt."

"How do you know the screen's effective in the other direction?"

Rawlins frowned. "I never considered that. We haven't tried to go *outward* through the maze yet. Suppose it's altogether different coming out? We don't have charts for that direction. What if we all get clipped coming out?"

"We'll use the probes again," said Boardman. "Don't worry about that. When we're ready to go out, we'll bring a bunch of drones to the camp in Zone F here and check the exit route the same way we checked the entry route."

After a while Rawlins said, "Why should there be any traps on the outward route, anyway? That means the builders of the maze were locking themselves in as well as locking enemies out. Why would they do that?"

"Who knows, Ned? They were aliens."

"Aliens. Yes."

15

Boardman remembered that the conversation was incomplete. He tried to be affable. They were comrades in the face of danger. He said, "And which has been the worst place for you so far?"

"That other screen farther back," Rawlins said. "The one that shows you all the nasty, crawling stuff inside your own mind."

"Which screen is that?"

"Toward the inside of Zone H. It was a golden screen, fastened to a high wall with metal strips. I looked at it and saw my father, for a couple of seconds. And then I saw a girl I once knew, a girl who became a nun. On the screen she was taking her clothes off. I guess that reveals something about my unconscious, eh? Like a pit of snakes. But whose isn't?"

"I didn't see any such things."

"You couldn't miss it. It was—oh, about fifty meters after the place where you shot the first animal. A little to your left, halfway up the wall, a rectangular screen—a trapezoidal screen, really, with bright white metal borders, and colors moving on it, shapes—"

"Yes. That one. Geometrical shapes."

"I saw Maribeth getting undressed," Rawlins said, sounding confused. "And you saw geometrical shapes?"

16

Zone F could be deadly too. A small pearly blister in the ground opened and a stream of gleaming pellets rolled out. They flowed toward Rawlins. They moved with the malevolent determination of a stream of hungry soldier ants. They stung the flesh. He trampled a number of them, but in his annoyance and fervor he almost came too close to a suddenly flashing blue light. He kicked three pellets toward the light and they melted.

17

Boardman had already had much more than enough.

18

Their elapsed time out from the entrance to the maze was only one hour and forty-eight minutes, although it seemed much longer than that. The route through Zone F led into a pink-walled room where jets of steam blew up from concealed vents. At the far end of the room was an irising slot. If you did not step through it with perfect timing, you would be crushed. The slot gave access to a long low-vaulted passageway, oppressively warm and close, whose walls were blood-red in color and pulsated sickeningly. Beyond the passageway was an open plaza in which six slabs of white metal stood on end like waiting swords. A fountain hurled water a hundred meters into the air. Flanking the plaza were three towers with many windows, all of different sizes. Prismatic spotlights played against the windows. No windows were broken. On the steps of one of the towers lay the articulated skeleton of a creature close to ten meters long. The bubble of what was undoubtedly a space helmet covered its skull.

19

Alton, Antonelli, Cameron, Greenfield, and Stein constituted the Zone F camp, the relief base for the forward group. Antonelli and Stein went back to the plaza in the middle of F and found Rawlins and Boardman there.

"It's just a short way on," Stein said. "Would you like to rest a few minutes, Mr. Boardman?"

Boardman glowered. They went on.

Antonelli said, "Davis, Ottavio, and Reynolds passed on to E this morning when Alton, Cameron, and Greenfield reached us. Petrocelli and Walker are reconnoitering along the inner edge of E and looking a little way into D. They say it looks a lot better in there."

"I'll flay them if they go in," Boardman said.

Antonelli smiled worriedly.

The relief base consisted of a pair of extrusion domes side by side in a little open spot at the edge of a garden. The site had been thoroughly researched and no surprises were expected. Rawlins entered one of the domes and took his shoes off. Cameron handed him a cleanser. Greenfield gave him a food pack. Rawlins felt ill at ease among these men. They had not had the opportunities in life that had been given him. They did not have proper educations. They would not live as long, even if they avoided all of the dangers to which they were exposed. None of them had blond hair or blue eyes, and probably they could not afford to get shape-ups that would give them those qualifications. And yet they seemed happy. Perhaps it was because they never had to stop to confront the moral implications of luring Richard Muller out of the maze.

Boardman came into the dome. It amazed Rawlins how durable and tireless the old man was. Boardman said, laughing, "Tell Captain Hosteen he lost his bet. We made it."

"What bet?" asked Antonelli.

Greenfield said, "We think that Muller must be tracking us somehow. His movements have been very regular. He's occupying the back quadrant of Zone A, as far from the entrance as possible—if the entrance is the one he uses—and he swings around in a little arc balancing the advance party."

Boardman said, "Hosteen gave three to one we wouldn't get here. I heard him." To Cameron, who was a communications technician, Boardman said, "Do you think it's possible that Muller is using some kind of scanning system?"

"It's altogether likely."

"Good enough to see faces?"

"Maybe some of the time. We really can't be sure. He's had a lot of time to learn how to use this maze, sir."

"If he sees my face," said Boardman, "we might as well just go home without bothering. I never thought he might be scanning us. Who's got the thermoplastics? I need a new face fast."

20

He did not try to explain. But when he was finished he had a long sharp nose, lean, downcurving lips, and a witch's chin. It was not an attractive face. But it was not the face of Charles Boardman either.

21

After a night of unsound sleep Rawlins prepared himself to go on to the advance camp in Zone E. Boardman would not be going with him, but they would be in direct contact at all times now. Boardman would see what Rawlins saw, and hear what Rawlins heard. And in a tiny voice Boardman would be able to convey instructions to him.

The morning was dry and wintry. They tested the communications circuits. Rawlins stepped out of the dome and walked ten paces, standing alone looking inward and watching the orange glow of daylight on the pockmarked porcelain-like walls before him. The walls were deep black against the lustrous green of the sky.

Boardman said, "Lift your right hand if you hear me, Ned."

Rawlins lifted his right hand.

"Now speak to me."

"Where did you say Richard Muller was born?"

"On Earth. I hear you very well."

"Where on Earth?"

"The North American Directorate, somewhere."

"I'm from there," Rawlins said.

"Yes, I know. I think Muller is from the western part of the continent. I can't be sure." I've spent only a very little time on Earth, Ned, and I can't remember the geography. If it's important, I can have the ship look it up.

"Maybe later," said Rawlins. "Should I get started now?"

"Listen to me, first. We've been very busy getting ourselves inside this place, and I don't want you to forget that everything we've done up to this point has been a preliminary to our real purpose. We're here for Muller, remember."

"Would I forget?"

"We've been preoccupied with matters of personal survival. That can tend to blur your perspective: whether you yourself, individually, live or die. Now we take a larger view. What Richard Muller has, whether it's a gift or a curse, is of high potential value and it's your job to gain use of it, Ned. The fate of galaxies lies on what happens in the next few days between you and Muller. Eons will be reshaped. Billions yet unborn will have their lives altered for good or ill by the events at hand."

"You sound absolutely serious, Charles."

"I absolutely am. Sometimes there comes a moment when all the booming foolish inflated words mean something, and this is one of those moments. You're standing at a crossroads in galactic history. And therefore, Ned, you're going to go in there and lie and cheat and perjure and connive, and I expect that your conscience is going to be very sore for a while, and you'll hate yourself extravagantly for it, and eventually you'll realize that you've done a deed of heroism. The test of your communications equipment is now ended. Get back inside here and let's ready you to march."

22

He went alone only a short distance this time. Stein and Alton accompanied him as far as the gateway to Zone E. There were no incidents. They pointed in the right direction, and he passed through a pinwheeling shower of coruscating azure sparks to enter the austere funereal zone beyond. As he negotiated the uphill ramp of the entrance, he caught sight of a socket mounted in an upright stone column. Within the darkness of the socket was something mobile and gleaming that could have been an eye.

"I think I've found part of Muller's scanning system," Rawlins reported. "There's a thing watching me in the wall."

"Cover it with your spray," Boardman suggested.

"I think he'd interpret that as a hostile act. Why would an archaeologist mutilate a feature like that?"

"Yes. A point. Proceed."

There was less of an air of menace about Zone E. It was made up of dark, tightly-compacted low buildings which clung together like bothered turtles. Rawlins could see different topography ahead, high walls, and a shining tower. Each of the zones was so different from all the others that he began to think they had been built at different times: a core of residential sectors, and then a gradual accretion of trap-laden outer rings as the enemies grew more troublesome. It was the sort of thought an archaeologist might have; he filed it for use.

He walked a little way, and saw the shadowy figure of Walker coming toward him. Walker was lean, dour, cool. He claimed to have been married several times to the same wife. He was about forty, a career man.

"Glad you made it, Rawlins. Go easy there on your left. That wall is hinged."

"Everything all right here?"

"More or less. We lost Petrocelli about an hour ago."

Rawlins stiffened. "This zone is supposed to be safe!"

"It isn't. It's riskier than F, and nearly as bad as G. We underestimated it when we were using the probes. There's no real reason why the zones *have* to get safer toward the middle, is there? This is one of the worst."

"To lull us," Rawlins suggested. "False security."

"You bet. Come on, now. Follow me and don't use your brain too much. There's no value in originality in here. You go the way the path goes, or you don't go anywhere."

Rawlins followed. He saw no apparent danger, but he jumped where Walker jumped, and detoured where Walker detoured. Not too far on lay the inner camp. He found Davis, Ottavio, and Reynolds there, and also the upper half of Petrocelli. "We're awaiting burial orders," said Ottavio. Below the waist there was nothing left. "Hosteen's going to tell us to bring him out, I bet."

"Cover him, at least," Rawlins told him.

"You going on into D today?" Walker asked.

"I may as well."

"We'll tell you what to avoid. It's new. That's where Petrocelli got it, right near the entrance to D, maybe five meters this side. You trip a field of some kind and it cuts you in half. The drones didn't trip it at all."

"Suppose it cuts everything in half that goes by?" Rawlins asked. "Except drones."

"It didn't cut Muller," Walker said. "It won't cut you if you step around it. We'll show you how."

"And beyond?"

"That's all up to you."

23

Boardman said, "If you're tired, stay here for the night."

"I'd rather go on."

"You'll be going alone, Ned. Why not be rested?"

"Ask the brain for a reading on me. See where my fatigue level is. I'm ready to go onward."

Boardman checked. They were doing full telemetry on Rawlins; they knew his pulse rate, respiration count, hormone levels, and many more intimate things. The computer saw no reason why Rawlins could not continue without pausing.

"All right," said Boardman, "go on."

"I'm about to enter Zone D, Charles. This is where Petrocelli got it. I see the tripline—very subtle, very well hidden. Here I go past it. Yes. Ye-es. This is Zone D. I'm stopping and letting the brain get my bearings for me. Zone D looks a little cozier than E. The crossing shouldn't take long."

24
The auburn flames that guarded Zone C were frauds.

25
Rawlins said softly, "Tell the galaxies that their fate is in good hands. I should find Muller in fifteen minutes."

7.

Muller had often been alone for long periods. In drawing up the contract for his first marriage he had insisted on a withdrawal clause, the standard one; and Lorayn had not objected, for she knew that his work might occasionally take him to places where she would not or could not go. During the eight years of that marriage he had enforced the clause three times for a total of four years.

When they let the contract run out, Muller's absences were not really a contributing factor. He had learned in those years that he could stand solitude, and even that he thrived on it in a strange way. We develop everything in solitude except character, Stendhal had written; Muller was not sure of that but, in any case, his character had been fully formed before he began accepting assignments that took him unaccompanied to empty dangerous worlds. He had volunteered for those assignments. In a different sense he had volunteered to immure himself on Lemnos, and this exile was more painful to him than those other absences. Yet he got along. His own adaptability astonished and frightened him. He had not thought he could shed his social nature so easily. The sexual part was difficult, but not as difficult as he had imagined it would be; and the rest—the stimulation of debate, the change of surroundings, the interplay of personalities—had somehow ceased quickly to matter. He had enough cubes to keep him diverted, and enough challenges surviving in this maze. And memories.

He could summon remembered scenes from a hundred worlds. Man sprawled everywhere, planting the seed of Earth on colonies of a thousand stars. Delta Pavonis VI, for example: twenty light-years out, and rapidly going strange. They called the planet Loki, which struck Muller as a whopping misnomer, for Loki was agile, shrewd, slight of build, and the settlers on Loki, fifty years isolated from Earth, went in for a cult of artificial obesity through glucostatic regulation. Muller had visited them a decade before his ill-starred Beta Hydri journey. It was essentially a troubleshooting mission to a planet that had lost touch with its mother world. He remembered a warm planet, habitable only in a narrow temperate belt. Passing through walls of green jungle bordering a black river; watching beasts with jeweled eyes jostling on the swampy banks; coming at last to the settlement, where sweaty Buddhas weighing a few hundred kilograms apiece sat in stately meditation before thatched huts. He had never seen so much flesh per cubic meter before. The Lokites meddled with their peripheral glucoreceptors to induce accumulation of body fat. It was a useless adaptation, unrelated to any problem of their environment; they simply liked to be huge. Muller recalled arms that looked like thighs, thighs that looked like pillars, bellies that curved and recurved in triumphant excess.

They had hospitably offered a woman to the spy from Earth. For Muller, it was a lesson in cultural relativity; for there were in the village two or three women who, although bulky enough, were scrawny by local standards and so approximated the norm of Muller's own background. The Lokites did not give him any of these women, these pitiful underdeveloped hundred-kilogram wrecks, for it would have been a breach of manners to let a guest have a subpar companion. Instead they treated him to a blonde colossus with breasts like cannonballs and buttocks that were continents of quivering meat.

It was, at any rate, unforgettable.

There were so many other worlds. He had been a tireless voyager. To such men as Boardman he left the subtleties of political manipulation; Muller could be subtle enough, almost statesmanlike when he had to be, but he thought of himself more as an explorer than as a diplomat. He had shivered in methane lakes, had fried in post-Saharan deserts, had followed nomadic settlers across a purple plain in quest of their strayed arthropodic cattle. He had been shipwrecked by computer failure on airless worlds. He had seen the coppery cliffs of Damballa, ninety kilometers high. He had taken a swim in the gravity lake of Mordred. He had slept beside a multicolored brook under a sky blazing with a trio of suns, and he had walked the crystal bridges of Procyon XIV. He had few regrets.

Now, huddled at the heart of his maze, he watched the screens and waited for the stranger to find him. A weapon, small and cool, nestled in his hand.

2

The afternoon unrolled swiftly. Rawlins began to think that he would have done better to listen to Boardman and spend a night in camp before going on to seek Muller. At least three hours of deepsleep to comb his mind of tension—a quick dip under the sleep wire, always useful. Well, he hadn't bothered. Now there was no opportunity. His sensors told him that Muller was just ahead.

Questions of morality and questions of ordinary courage suddenly troubled him.

He had never done anything significant before. He had studied, he had performed routine tasks in Boardman's office, he had now and then handled a slightly sensitive matter. But he had always believed that his real career still was yet to open; that all this was preliminary. That sense of a future beginning was still with him, but it was time to admit that he was on the spot. This was no training simulation. Here he stood, tall and blond and young and stubborn and ambitious, at the verge of an action which—and Charles Boardman had not been altogether hypo critical about that—might well influence the course of coming history.

Ping.

He looked about. The sensors had spoken. Out of the shadows ahead emerged the figure of a man. Muller.

They faced each other across a gap of twenty meters. Rawlins had remembered Muller as a giant and was surprised to see now that they were about the same height, both of them just over two meters high. Muller was dressed in a dark glossy wrap, and in this light at this hour his face was a study in conflicting planes and jutting prominences, all peaks and valleys.

In Muller's hand lay the apple-sized device with which he had destroyed the probe.

Boardman's voice buzzed in Rawlins' ear. "Get closer to him. Smile. Look shy and uncertain and friendly, and *very* concerned. And keep your hands where he can see them at all times."

Rawlins obeyed. He wondered when he would begin to feel the effects of being this close to Muller. He found it hard to take his eyes from the shiny globe that rested like a grenade in Muller's hand. When he was ten meters away he started to pick up the emanation from Muller. Yes. That must certainly be it. He decided that he would be able to tolerate it if he came no closer.

Muller said, *"What do you—"*

The words came out as a raucous shriek. Muller stopped, cheeks flaming, and seemed to be adjusting the gears of his larynx. Rawlins chewed the corner of his lip. He felt an uncontrollable twitching in one eyelid. Harsh breathing was coming over the audio line from Boardman.

Muller began again. "What do you want from me?" he said, this time in his true voice, deep, crackling with suppressed rage.

"Just to talk. Honestly. I don't want to cause any trouble for you, Mr. Muller."

"You know me!"

"Of course I do. Everyone knows Richard Muller. I mean, you were *the* galactic hero when I was going to school. We did reports on you. Essays about you. We—"

"Get out of here!" The shriek again.

"—and Stephen Rawlins was my father. I knew you, Mr. Muller."

The dark apple was rising. The small square window was facing him. Rawlins remembered how the relay from the drone probe had suddenly ceased.

"Stephen Rawlins?" The apple descended.

"My father." Rawlins' left leg seemed to be turning to water. Volatilized sweat drifted in a cloud about his shoulders. He was getting the outpouring from Muller more strongly now, as though it took a few minutes to tune to his wavelength. Now Rawlins felt the torrent of anguish, the sadness, the sense of yawning abysses sundering calm meadows. "I met you long ago," Rawlins said. "You had just come back from—let's see, it was 82 Eridani, I think, you were all tanned and windburned—I think I was eight years old, and you picked me up and threw me, only you weren't used to Earthnorm gravity and you threw me too hard, and I hit the ceiling and began to cry, and you gave me something to make me stop, a little bead that changed colors—"

Muller's hands were limp at his sides. The apple had disappeared into his garment.

He said tautly, "What was your name? Fred, Ted, Ed—that's it. Yes. Ed. Edward Rawlins."

"They started calling me Ned a little later on. So you remember me, then?"

"A little. I remember your father a lot better." Muller turned away and coughed. His hand slipped into his pocket. He raised his head and the descending sun glittered weirdly against his face, staining it deep orange. He made a quick edgy gesture with one finger. "Go away, Ned. Tell your friends that I don't want to be bothered. I'm a very sick man, and I want to be alone."

"Sick?"

"Sick with a mysterious inward rot of the soul. Look, Ned, you're a fine handsome boy, and I love your father dearly, if any of this is true, and I don't want you hanging around me. You'll regret it. I don't mean that as a threat, just as a statement of fact. Go away. Far away."

"Stand your ground," Boardman told him. "Get closer. Right in, where it hurts."

Rawlins took a wary step, thinking of the globe in Muller's pocket and seeing from those eyes that the man was not necessarily rational. He diminished the distance between them by ten per cent. The impact of the emanation seemed to double.

He said, "Please don't chase me away, Mr. Muller. I just want to be friendly. My father would never have forgiven me if he could have found out that I met you here, like this, and didn't try to help you at all."

"*Would* have? *Could* have found out? What happened to your father?"

"Dead."

"Whcn? Where?"

"Four years ago, Rigel XXII. He was helping to set up a tight beam network connecting the Rigel worlds. There was an amplifier accident. The focus was inverted. He got the whole bcam."

"Jesus. He was still young!"

"He would have been fifty in a month. We were going to come out and visit him and give him a surprise party. Instead I came out by myself to bring his body back."

Muller's face softened. Some of the torment ebbed from his eyes. His lips became more mobile. It was as though someone else's grief had momentarily taken him from his own.

"Get closer to him," Boardman ordered.

Another step; and then, since Muller did not seem to notice, another. Rawlins sensed heat: not real but psychical, a furnace-blast of directionless emotion. He shivered in awe. He had never really believed in any essential way that the story of what the Hydrans had done to Richard Muller was true. He was too sharply limited by his father's heritage of pragmatism. If you can't duplicate it in the laboratory, it isn't real. If you can't graph it, it isn't real. If there's no circuitry, it isn't real. How could a human being possibly be redesigned to broadcast his own emotions? No circuitry could handle such a function. But Rawlins felt the fringes of that broadcast.

Muller said, "What are you doing on Lemnos, boy?"

"I'm an archaeologist." The lie came awkwardly. "This is my first field trip. We're trying to carry out a thorough examination of the maze."

"The maze happens to be someone's home. You're intruding."

Rawlins faltered.

"Tell him you didn't know he was here," Boardman prompted.

"We didn't realize that anyone was here," said Rawlins. "We had no way of knowing that—"

"You sent your damned robots in, didn't you? Once you found someone here—someone you knew damned well wouldn't want to have any company—"

"I don't understand," Rawlins said. "We had the impression you were wrecked here. We wanted to offer our help."

How easily I do this, he told himself!

Muller scowled. "You don't know why I'm here?"

"I'm afraid not."

"You wouldn't, I guess. You were too young. But the others—once they saw my face, they should have known. Why didn't they tell you? Your robot relayed my face, didn't it? You knew who it was in here. And they didn't tell you a thing?"

"I really don't understand—"

"Come close!" Muller bellowed.

Rawlins felt himself gliding forward, though he was unaware of taking individual steps. Abruptly he was face to face with Muller, conscious of the man's massive frame, his furrowed brow, his fixed, staring, angry eyes. Muller's immense hand pounced on Rawlins' wrist. Rawlins rocked, stunned by the impact, drenched with a despair so vast that it seemed to engulf whole universes. He tried not to stagger.

"Now get away from me!" Muller cried harshly. "Go on! Out of here! *Out!*"

Rawlins did not move.

Muller howled a curse and ran ponderously into a low glassy-walled building whose windows, opaque, were like blind eyes. The door closed, sealing without a perceptible opening. Rawlins sucked in breath and fought for his balance. His forehead throbbed as if something behind it were struggling to burst free.

"Stay where you are," said Boardman. "Let him get over his tantrum. Everything's going well."

3

Muller crouched behind the door. Sweat rolled down his sides. A chill swept him. He wrapped his arms about himself so tightly that his ribs complained.

He had not meant to handle the intruder that way at all.

A few words of conversation; a blunt request for privacy; then, if the man would not go away, the destructor globe. So Muller had planned. But he had hesitated. He had spoken too much and learned too much. Stephen Rawlins' son? A party of archaeologists out there? The boy had hardly seemed affected by the radiation except at very close range. Was it losing its power with the years?

Muller fought to collect himself and to analyze his hostility. Why so fearful? Why so eager to cling to solitude? He had nothing to fear from Earthmen; they, not he, were the sufferers in any contact he had with them. It was understandable that they would recoil from his presence. But there was no reason for him to withdraw like this except out of some paralyzing diffidence, the encrusted inflexibilities of nine years of isolation. Had it come to that—a love of solitude for its own sake? Was he a hermit? His original pretense was that he had come here out of consideration for his fellow men, that he was unwilling to inflict the painful ugliness that was himself upon them. But the boy had wanted to be friendly and helpful. Why flee? Why react so churlishly?

Slowly Muller rose and undid the door. He stepped outside. Night had fallen with winter's swiftness; the sky was black, and the moons scared across it. The boy was still standing in the plaza, looking a little dazed. The biggest moon, Clotho, bathed him in golden light so that his curling hair seemed to sparkle with inner flame. His face was very pale, with sharply accentuated cheekbones. His blue eyes gleamed in shock, like those of one who has been slapped.

Muller advanced, uncertain of his tactics. He felt like some great half-rusted machine called into action after too many years of neglect. "Ned?" he said. "Look, Ned, I want to tell you that I'm sorry. You've got to understand, I'm not used to people. Not—used—to—*people.*"

"It's all right, Mr. Muller. I realize it's been rough for you."

"Dick. Call me Dick." Muller raised both hands and spread them as if trying to cup moonbeams. He felt terribly cold. On the wall beyond the plaza small animal shapes leaped and danced. Muller said, "I've come to love my privacy. You can even cherish cancer if you get into the right frame of mind. Look, you ought to realize something. I came here deliberately. It wasn't any shipwreck. I picked out the one place in the universe where I was least likely to be disturbed, and hid myself inside it. But, of course, you had to come with your tricky robots and find the way in."

"If you don't want me here, I'll go," Rawlins said.

"Maybe that's best for both of us. No. Wait. Stay. Is it very bad, being this close to me?"

"It isn't exactly comfortable," said Rawlins. "But it isn't as bad as—as—well, I don't know. From this distance I just feel a little depressed."

"You know why?" Muller asked. "From the way you talk, I think you do, Ned. You're only pretending not to know what happened to me on Beta Hydri IV."

Rawlins colored. "Well, I remember a little bit, I guess. They operated on your mind?"

"Yes, that's right. What you're feeling, Ned, that's me, my goddam soul leaking into the air. You're picking up the flow of neural current, straight from the top of my skull. Isn't it lovely? Try coming a little closer . . . that's it." Rawlins halted. "There," Muller said, "now it's stronger. You're getting a better dose. Now recall what it was like when you were standing right here. That wasn't so pleasant, was it? From ten meters away you can take it. From one meter away it's intolerable. Can you imagine holding a woman in your arms while you give off a mental stink like that? You can't make love from ten meters away. At least, *I* can't. Let's sit down, Ned. It's safe here. I've got detectors rigged in case any of the nastier animals come in, and there aren't any traps in this zone. Sit." He lowered himself to the smooth milky-white stone floor, the alien marble that made this plaza so sleek. Rawlins, after an instant of deliberation, slipped lithely into the lotus position a dozen meters away.

Muller said, "How old are you, Ned?"

"Twenty-three."

"Married?"

A shy grin. "Afraid not."

"Got a girl?"

"There was one, a liaison contract. We voided it when I took on this job."

"Ah. Any girls in this expedition?"

"Only woman cubes," said Rawlins.

"They aren't much good, are they, Ned?"

"Not really. We could have brought a few women along, but—"

"But what?"

"Too dangerous. The maze—"

"How many men have you lost so far?" Muller asked.

"Five, I think. I'd like to know the sort of people who'd build a thing like this. It must have taken five hundred years of planning to make it so devilish."

Muller said, "More. This was the grand creative triumph of their race, I believe. Their masterpiece, their monument. They must have been proud of this murderous place. It summed up the whole essence of their philosophy—kill the stranger."

"Are you just speculating, or have you found some clues to their cultural outlook?"

"The only clue I have to their cultural outlook is all around us. But I'm an expert on alien psychology, Ned. I know more about it than any other human being, because I'm the only one who ever said hello to an alien race. Kill the stranger: it's the law of the universe. And if you don't kill him, at least screw him up a little."

"We aren't like that," Rawlins said. "We don't show instinctive hostility to—"

"Crap."

"But—"

Muller said, "If an alien starship ever landed on one of our planets we'd quarantine it and imprison the crew and interrogate them to destruction. Whatever good manners we may have learned grow out of decadence and complacency. We pretend that we're too noble to hate strangers, but we have the politeness of weakness. Take the Hydrans. A substantial faction within our government was in favor of generating fusion in their cloud layer and giving their system an extra sun—*before* sending an emissary to scout them."

"No."

"They were overruled, and an emissary was sent, and the Hydrans wasted him. Me." An idea struck Muller suddenly. Appalled, he said, "What's happened between us and the Hydrans in the last nine years? Any contact? War?"

"Nothing," said Rawlins. "We've kept away."

"Are you telling me the truth, or did we wipe the bastards out? God knows I wouldn't mind that, but yet it wasn't their fault they did this to me. They were reacting in a standard xenophobic way. Ned, has there been a war with them?"

"No. I swear it."

Muller relaxed. After a moment he said, "All right. I won't ask you to fill me in on all the other news developments. I don't really give a damn. How long are you people staying on Lemnos?"

"We don't know yet. A few weeks, I suppose. We haven't even really begun to explore the maze. And then there's the area outside. We want to run correlations on the work of earlier archaeologists, and—"

"And you'll be here for a while. Are the others going to come into the center of the maze?"

Rawlins moistened his lips. "They sent me ahead to establish a working relationship with you. We don't have any plan yet. It all depends on you. We don't want to impose on you. So if you don't want us to work here—"

"I don't," Muller told him crisply. "Tell that to your friends. In fifty or sixty years I'll be dead, and they can sniff around here then. But while I'm here I don't want them bothering me. Let them work in the outer four or five zones. If any of them sets foot in A, B, or C, I'll kill him. I can do that, Ned."

"What about me—am I welcome?"

"Occasionally. I can't predict my moods. If you want to talk to me, come around and see. And if I tell you to get the hell out, Ned, then get the hell out. Clear?"

Rawlins grinned sunnily. "Clear." He got to his feet. Muller, unwilling to have the boy standing over him, rose also. Rawlins took a few steps toward him.

Muller said, "Where are you going?"

"I hate having to talk at this distance, to shout like this. I can get a little closer to you, can't I?"

Instantly suspicious, Muller replied, "Are you some kind of masochist?"

"Sorry, no."

"Well, I'm no sadist either. I don't want you near me."

"It's really not that unpleasant—Dick."

"You're lying. You hate it like all the others. I'm like a leper, boy, and if you're queer for leprosy I feel sorry for you, but don't come any closer. It embarrasses me to see other people suffer on my account."

Rawlins stopped. "Whatever you say. Look, Dick, I don't want to cause troubles for you. I'm just trying to be friendly and helpful. If doing that in some way makes you uncomfortable—well, just say so, and I'll do something else. It doesn't do me any good to make things worse for you."

"That came out pretty muddled, boy. What is it you want from me, anyhow?"

"Nothing."

"Why not leave me alone?"

"You're a human being, and you've been alone here for a long time. It's my natural impulse to offer companionship. Does that sound too dumb?"

Muller shrugged. "I'm not much of a companion. Maybe you ought to take all your sweet Christian impulses and go away. There's no way you can help me, Ned. You can only hurt me by reminding me of all I can no longer have or know." Stiffening, Muller looked past the tall young man toward the shadowy figures cavorting along the walls. He was hungry, and this was the hour to begin hunting for his dinner. He said brusquely, "Son, I think my patience is running out again. Time for you to leave."

"All right. Can I come back tomorrow, though?"

"Maybe. Maybe."

The boy smiled ingenuously. "Thanks for letting me talk to you, Dick. I'll be back."

4

By troublesome moonlight Rawlins made his way out of Zone A. The voice of the ship's brain guided him back over the path he had taken inward, and now and then, in the safest spots, Boardman used the override. "You've made a good start," Boardman said. "It's a plus that he tolerated you at all. How do you feel?"

"Lousy, Charles."

"Because of the close contact with him?"

"Because I'm doing something filthy."

"Stop that, Ned. If I'm going to have to pump you full of moral reassurance every time you set out—"

"I'll do my job," said Rawlins, "but I don't have to like it." He edged over a spring-loaded stone block that was capable of hurling him from a precipice if he applied his weight the wrong way. A small toothy animal snickered at him as he crossed. On the far side, Rawlins prodded the wall in a yielding place and won admission to Zone B. He glanced at the lintel and saw the recessed slot of the visual pickup and smiled into it, just in case Muller was watching him withdraw.

He saw now why Muller had chosen to maroon himself here. Under similar circumstances he might have done the same thing. Or worse. Muller carried, thanks to the Hydrans, a deformity of the soul in an era when deformity was obsolete. It was an esthetic crime to lack a limb or an eye or a nose; these things were easily repaired, and one owed it to one's fellow man to get a shape-up and obliterate troublesome imperfections. To inflict one's flaws on society was clearly an antisocial act.

But no shape-up surgeon could do a cosmetic job on what Muller had. The only cure was separation from society. A weaker man would have chosen death: Muller had picked exile.

Rawlins still throbbed with the impact of that brief moment of direct contact. For an instant he had received from Muller a formless incoherent emanation of raw emotion, the inner self spilling out involuntarily and wordlessly. The flow of uncontrollable innerness was painful and depressing to receive.

It was not true telepathy that the Hydrans had given him. Muller could not "read" minds, nor could he communicate his thoughts to others. What came forth was this gush of self: a torrent of raw despair, a river of regrets and sorrows, all the sewage of a soul. He could not hold it back. For that eternal moment Rawlins had been bathed in it; the rest of the time he had merely picked up a vague and general sense of distress.

He could generate his own concretenesses out of that raw flow. Muller's sorrows were not unique to himself; what he offered was nothing more than an awareness of the punishments the universe devises for its inhabitants. At that moment Rawlins had felt that he was tuned to every discord in creation: the missed chances, the failed loves, the hasty words, the unfair griefs, the hungers, the greeds, the lusts, the knife of envy, the acid of frustration, the fang of time, the death of small insects in winter, the tears of things. He had known aging, loss, impotence, fury, helplessness, loneliness, desolation, self-contempt, and madness. It was a silent shriek of cosmic anger.

Are we all like that? He wondered. Is the same broadcast coming from me, and from Boardman, and from my mother, and from the girl I used to love? Do we walk about like beacons fixed to a frequency we can't receive? Thank God, then. That's a song too painful to hear.

Boardman said, "Wake up, Ned. Stop brooding and watch out for trouble. You're almost in Zone C now."

"Charles, how did you feel the first time you came close to Muller?"

"We'll discuss that later."

"Did you feel as if you knew what human beings were all about for the first time?"

"I said we'll discuss—"

"Let me say what I want to say, Charles. I'm not in any danger here. I just looked into a man's soul, and I'm shaken by it. But—listen, Charles—he isn't really like that. He's a *good* man. That stuff he radiates, it's just noise. It's a kind of sludge that doesn't tell you a real thing about Dick Muller. It's noise we aren't meant to hear, and the signal's altogether different—like when you open an amplifier up to the stars, full blast, and you get that rasping of the spectrum, you know, and some of the most beautiful stars give you the most terrible noises, but that's just an amplifier response, it has nothing to do with the quality of the star itself, it—it—"

"*Ned.*"

"I'm sorry, Charles."

"Get back to camp. We all agree that Dick Muller's a fine human being. That's why we need him. We need you, too, so shut your mouth and watch your step. Easy, now. Calm. Calm. Calm. What's that animal on your left? Hurry along, Ned. But stay calm. That's the way, son. Calm."

8.

When they met again the next morning it was easier for both of them. Rawlins, having slept well under the sleep wire, went to the heart of the maze and found Muller standing beside a tall flat-sided spike of dark metal at the edge of the great plaza.

"What do you make of this?" Muller asked conversationally as Rawlins approached. "There are eight of these, one at each corner. I've been watching them for years. They turn. Look here." Muller pointed to one face of the pylon. Rawlins came close, and when he was ten meters away he picked up Muller's emanation. Nevertheless, he forced himself to go closer. He had not been so close yesterday except in that one chilling moment when Muller had seized him and pulled him near.

"You see this?" Muller asked, tapping the spike.

"A mark."

"It took me close to six months to cut it. I used a sliver from the crystalline outcropping set in that wall yonder. Every day for an hour or two I'd scrape away, until there was a visible mark in the metal. I've been watching that mark. In the course of one local year it turns all the way around. So the spikes are moving. You can't see it, but they do. They're some kind of calendars."

"Do they—can you—have you ever—"

"You aren't making sense, boy."

"I'm sorry." Rawlins backed away, trying hard to hide the impact of Muller's nearness. He was flushed and shaken. At five meters the effect was not so agonizing, and he stayed there, making an effort, telling himself that he was developing a tolerance for it.

"You were saying?"

"Is this the only one you've been watching?"

"I've scratched a few of the others. I'm convinced that they all turn. I haven't found the mechanism. Underneath this city, you know, there's some kind of fantastic brain. It's millions of years old, but it still works. Perhaps it's some sort of liquid metal with cognition elements floating in it. It turns these pylons and runs the water supply and cleans the streets."

"And operates the traps."

"And operates the traps," Muller said. "But I haven't been able to find a sign of it. I've done some digging here and there, but I find only dirt below. Maybe you archaeologist bastards will locate the city's brain. Eh? Any clues?"

"I don't think so," said Rawlins.

"You don't sound very definite."

"I'm not. I haven't taken part in any of the work within the city." Rawlins smiled shyly. The quick facial movement annoyed him and drew reproof from Boardman, who pointed out over the monitor circuit that the shy smile always announced an upcoming lie and that it wouldn't be long before Muller caught on. Rawlins said, "Most of the time I was outside the city, directing the entry operations. And then when I got in, I came right in here. So I don't know what the others may have discovered so far. If anything."

"Are they going to rip up the streets?" Muller asked.

"I don't think so. We don't dig so much any more. We use scanners and sensors and probe beams." Glibly, impressed with his own improvisations, he went on headlong. "Archaeology used to be destructive, of course. To find out what was under a pyramid we had to take the pyramid apart. But now we can do a lot with probes. That's the new school, you understand, looking into the ground without digging, and thus preserving the monuments of the past for—"

"On one of the planets of Epsilon Indi," said Muller, "a team of archaeologists completely dismantled an ancient alien burial pavilion about fifteen years ago, and then found it impossible to put the thing back together because they couldn't comprehend the structural integrity of the building. When they tried, it fell apart and was a total loss. I happened to see the ruins a few months later. You know the case, of course."

Rawlins didn't. He said, reddening, "Well, there are always bunglers in any discipline—"

"I hope there are none here. I don't want the maze damaged. Not that there's much chance of that. The maze defends itself quite well." Muller strolled casually away from the pylon. Rawlins eased as the distance between them grew, but Boardman warned him to follow. The tactics for damping Muller's mistrust included a deliberate and rigorous self-exposure to the emotion field. Muller was not looking back, and said, half to himself, "The cages are closed again."

"Cages?"

"Look down there—into that street branching out of the plaza."

Rawlins saw an alcove against a building wall. Rising from the ground were a dozen or more curving bars of white stone that disappeared into the wall at a height of about four meters, forming a kind of cage. He could see a second such cage farther down the street.

Muller said, "There are about twenty of them, arranged symmetrically in the streets off the plaza. Three times since I've been here the cages have opened. Those bars slide into the street, somehow, and disappear. The third time was two nights ago. I've never seen the cages either open or close, and I've missed it again."

"What do you think the cages were used for?" Rawlins asked.

"To hold dangerous beasts. Or captured enemies. What else would you use a cage for?"

"And when they open now—"

"The city's still trying to serve its people. There are enemies in the outer zones. The cages are ready in case any of the enemies are captured."

"You mean us?"

"Yes. Enemies." Muller's eyes glittered with sudden paranoid fury; it was alarming how easily he slipped from rational discourse to that cold blaze. "*Homo sapiens*. The most dangerous, the most ruthless, the most despicable beast in the universe!"

"You say it as if you believe it."

"I do."

"Come on," Rawlins said. "You devoted your life to serving mankind. You can't possibly believe—"

"I devoted my life," said Muller slowly, "to serving Richard Muller." He swung around so that he faced Rawlins squarely. They were only six or seven meters apart. The emanation seemed almost as strong as though they were nose to nose. Muller said, "I gave less of a damn for humanity than you might think, boy. I saw the stars, and I wanted them. I aspired after the condition of a deity. One world wasn't enough for me. I was hungry to have them all. So I built a career that would take me to the stars. I risked my life a thousand times. I endured fantastic extremes of temperature. I rotted my lungs with crazy gases, and had to be rebuilt from the inside out. I ate foods that would sicken you to hear about. Kids like you worshipped me and wrote essays about my selfless dedication to man, my tireless quest for knowledge. Let me get you straight on that. I'm about as selfless as Columbus and Magellan and Marco Polo. They were great explorers, yes, but they also looked for a fat profit. The profit I wanted was in here. I wanted to stand a hundred kilometers high. I wanted golden statues of me on a thousand worlds. You know poetry? Fame is the spur. That last infirmity of noble mind. Milton. Do you know your Greeks, too? When a man overreaches himself, the gods cast him down. It's called *hybris*. I had a bad case of it. When I dropped through the clouds to visit the Hydrans, I felt like a god. Christ, I *was* a god. And when I left, up through the clouds again. To the Hydrans I'm a god, all right. I thought it then: I'm in their myths, they'll always tell my story. The mutilated god. The martyred god. The being who came down among them and made them so uncomfortable that they had to fix him. But—"

"The cage—"

"Let me finish!" Muller rapped. "You see, the truth is, I wasn't a god, only a rotten mortal human being who had delusions of godhood, and the real gods saw to it that I learned my lesson. They decided to remind me of the hairy beast inside the plastic clothing. To call my attention to the animal brain under the lofty cranium. So they arranged it for the Hydrans to perform a clever little surgical trick on my brain, one of their specialties, I guess. I don't know if the Hydrans were being malicious for the hell of it or whether they were genuinely trying to cure me of a defect, my inability to let my emotions get out to them. Aliens. You figure them out. But they did their little job. And then I came back to Earth. Hero and leper all at once. Stand near me and you get sick. Why? It reminds you that *you're* an animal too, because you get a full dose of me. So we go round and round in our endless feedback. You hate me because you learn things about your own soul by getting near me. And I hate you because you must draw back from me. What I am, you see, is a plague carrier, and the plague I carry is the truth. My message is that it's a lucky thing for humanity that we're shut up each in his own skull. Because if we had even a little drop of telepathy, even the blurry nonverbal thing I've got, we'd be unable to stand each other. Human society would be impossible. The Hydrans can reach right into each other's mind, and they seem to like it. But we can't. And that's why I say that man must be the most despicable beast in the whole universe. He can't even take the reek of his own kind, soul to soul!"

Rawlins said, "The cage seems to be opening."

"What? Let me look!" Muller came jostling forward. Unable to step aside rapidly enough, Rawlins received the brunt of the emanation. It was not as painful this time. Images of autumn came to him: withered leaves, dying flowers, a dusty wind, early twilight. More regret than anguish over the shortness of life, the necessity of the condition. Meanwhile Muller, oblivious, was peering intently at the alabaster bars of the cage.

"It's withdrawn by several centimeters already. Why didn't you tell me?"

"I tried to. But you weren't listening."

"No. No. My damned soliloquizing." Muller chuckled. "Ned, I've been waiting years to see this. The cage actually in motion! Look how smoothly it moves, gliding into the ground. This is strange, Ned. It's never opened twice the same year before, and here it's opening for the second time this week."

"Maybe you've just failed to notice a lot of the other openings," Rawlins suggested. "While you slept, maybe—"

"I doubt it. Look at that!"

"Why do you think it's doing it right now?"

"Enemies all around," said Muller. "The city accepts me as a native by now. I've been here so long. But it must be trying to get you into a cage. The enemy. Man."

The cage was fully open now. There was no sign of the bars except the row of small openings in the pavement.

Rawlins said, "Have you ever tried to put anything in the cages? Animals?"

"Yes. I dragged a big dead beast inside one. Nothing happened. Then I caught some live little ones. Nothing happened." He frowned. "I once thought of stepping into the cage myself to see if it would close automatically when it sensed a live human being. But I didn't. When you're alone, you don't try experiments like that." He paused a moment, "How would *you* like to help me in a little experiment right now, eh, Ned?"

Rawlins caught his breath. The thin air abruptly seemed like fire in his lungs.

Muller said quietly, "Just step across into the alcove and wait a minute or so. See if the cage closes on you. That would be important to know."

"And if it does," Rawlins said, not taking him seriously, "do you have a key to let me out?"

"I have a few weapons. We can always blast you out by lasing the bars."

"That's destructive. You warned me not to destroy anything here."

"Sometimes you destroy in order to learn. Go on, Ned. Step into the alcove."

Muller's voice grew flat and strange. He was standing in an odd expectant half-crouch, hands at his sides, fingertips bent inward toward his thighs. As though he's going to throw me into the cage himself, Rawlins thought.

Boardman said quietly in Rawlins' ear, "Do as he says, Ned. Get into the cage. Show him that you trust him."

I trust *him*, Rawlins told himself, but I don't trust that cage.

He had uncomfortable visions of the floor of the cage dropping out as soon as the bars were in place: of himself dumped into some underground vat of acid or lake of fire. The disposal pit for trapped enemies. What assurance do I have that it isn't like that?

"Do it, Ned," Boardman murmured.

It was a grand, crazy gesture. Rawlins stepped over the row of small openings and stood with his back to the wall. Almost at once the curving bars rose from the ground and locked themselves seamlessly into place above his head. The floor seemed stable. No death-rays lashed out at him. His worst fears were not realized; but he was a prisoner.

"Fascinating," Muller said. "It must scan for intelligence. When I tried with animals, nothing happened. Dead or alive. What do you make of that, Ned?"

"I'm very glad to have helped your resarch. I'd be happier if you'd let me out now."

"I can't control the movements of the bars."

"You said you'd lase them open."

"But why be destructive so fast? Let's wait, shall we? Perhaps the bars will open again of their own accord. You're perfectly safe in there. I'll bring you food, if you have to eat. Will your people miss you if you're not back by nightfall?"

"I'll send a message to them," said Rawlins glumly. "But I hope that I'm out by then."

"Stay cool," Boardman advised. "If necessary, we can get you out of that ourselves. It's important to humor Muller in everything you can until you've got real rapport with him. If you hear me, touch your right hand to your chin."

Rawlins touched his right hand to his chin.

Muller said, "That was pretty brave of you, Ned. Or stupid. I'm sometimes not sure if there's a distinction. But I'm grateful, anyway. I had to know about those cages."

"Glad to have been of assistance. You see, human beings aren't all that monstrous."

"Not consciously. It's the sludge inside that's ugly. Here, let me remind you." He approached the cage and put his hands on the smooth bars, white as bone. Rawlins felt the emanation intensify. "That's what's under the skull. I've never really felt it myself, of course. I extrapolate it from the responses of others. It must be foul."

"I could get used to it," Rawlins said. He sat down crosslegged. "Did you make any attempt to have it undone when you returned to Earth from Beta Hydri IV?"

"I talked to the shape-up boys. They couldn't begin to figure out what changes had been made in my neural flow, and so they couldn't begin to figure out how to fix things. Nice?"

"How long did you stay?"

"A few months. Long enough to discover that there wasn't one human being I knew who didn't turn green after a few minutes of close exposure to me. I started to stew in self-pity, and in self-loathing, which is about the same thing. I was going to kill myself, you know, to put the world out of its misery."

Rawlins said, "I don't believe that. Some men just aren't capable of suicide. You're one who isn't."

"So I discovered, and thank you. I didn't kill myself, you notice. I tried some fancy drugs, and then I tried drink, and then I tried living dangerously. And at the end of it I was still alive. I was in and out of four neuropsychiatric wards in a single month. I tried wearing a padded lead helmet to shield the thought radiations. It was like trying to catch neutrinos in a bucket. I caused a panic in a licensed house on Venus. All the girls stampeded out stark naked once the screaming began." Muller spat. "You know, I could always take society or leave it. When I was among people I was happy, I was cordial, I had the social graces. I wasn't a slick sunny article like you, all overflowing with kindness and nobility, but I interacted with others. I related, I got along. Then I could go on a trip for a year and a half and not see or speak to anyone, and that was all right too. But once I found out that I was shut off from society for good, I discovered that I had needed it after all. But that's over. I outgrew the need, boy. I can spend a hundred years alone and never miss one soul. I've trained myself to see humanity as humanity sees me—something sickening, a damp hunkering crippled thing best avoided. To hell with you all. I don't owe any of you anything, love included. I have no obligations. I could leave you to rot in that cage, Ned, and never feel upset about it. I could pass that cage twice a day and smile at your skull. It isn't that I hate you, either you personally or the whole galaxy full of your kind. It's simply that I despise you. You're nothing to me. Less than nothing. You're dirt. I know you now, and you know me."

"You speak as if you belong to an alien race," Rawlins said in wonder.

"No. I belong to the human race. I'm the most human being there is, because I'm the only one who can't hide his humanity. You feel it? You pick up the ugliness? What's inside me is also inside you. Go to the Hydrans and they'll help you liberate it, and then people will run from you as they run from me. I speak for man. I tell the truth. I'm the skull beneath the face, boy. I'm the hidden intestines. I'm all the garbage we pretend isn't there, all the filthy animal stuff, the lusts, the little hates, the sicknesses, the envies. And I'm the one who posed as a god. *Hybris*. I was reminded of what I really am."

Rawlins said quietly, "Why did you decide to come to Lemnos?"

"A man named Charles Boardman put the idea into my head."

Rawlins recoiled in surprise at the mention of the name.

Muller said, "You know him?"

"Well, yes. Of course. He—he's a very important man in the government."

"You might say that. It was Boardman who sent me to Beta Hydri IV, you know? Oh, he didn't trick me into it, he didn't have to persuade me in any of his slippery ways. He knew me well enough. He simply played on my ambitions. There's a world there with aliens on it, he said, and we want a man to visit it. Probably a suicide mission, but it would be man's first contact with another intelligent species, and are you interested? So of course I went. He knew I couldn't resist something like that. And afterward, when I came back *this* way, he tried to duck me a while—either because he couldn't abide being near me or because he couldn't abide his own guilt. And finally I caught up with him and I said, look at me, Charles, this is how I am now, where can I go, what shall I do? I got up close to him. This far away. His face changed color. He had to take pills. I could see the nausea in his eyes. And he reminded me about the maze on Lemnos."

"Why?"

"He offered it as a place to hide. I don't know if he was being kind or cruel. I suppose he thought I'd be killed on my way into the maze—a decent finish for my sort of chap, or at any rate better than taking a gulp of carniphage and melting down a sewer. But of course I told Boardman I wouldn't think of it. I wanted to cover my trail. I blew up and insisted that the last thing in the world I'd do was come here. Then I spent a month on the skids in Under New Orleans, and when I surfaced again I rented a ship and came here. Using maximum diversionary tactics to insure that nobody found out my true destination. Boardman was right. This was the place to come."

Rawlins said, "How did you get inside the maze?"

"Through sheer bad luck."

"*Bad* luck?"

"I was trying to die in a blaze of glory," said Muller. "I didn't give a damn if I survived the maze or not. I just plunged right in and headed for the middle."

"I can't believe that!"

"Well, it's true, more or less. The trouble was, Ned, I'm a survival type. It's an innate gift, maybe even something paranormal. I have unusual reflexes. I have a kind of sixth sense, as they say. Also my urge to stay alive is well developed. Besides that, I had mass detectors and some other useful equipment. So I came into the maze, and whenever I saw a corpse lying about I looked a little sharper than usual, and I stopped and rested when I felt my visualization of the place beginning to waver. I fully expected to be killed in Zone H. I *wanted* it. But it was my luck to make it where everybody else failed because I didn't care one way or the other, I suppose. The element of tension was removed. I moved like a cat, everything twitching at once, and I got past the tough parts of the maze somehow, much to my disappointment, and here I am."

"Have you ever gone outside it?"

"No. Now and then I go as far as Zone E, where your friends are. Twice I've been to F. Mostly I remain in the three inner zones. I've furnished things quite nicely for myself. I have a radiation locker for my meat supply, and a building I use as my library, and a place where I keep my woman cubes, and I do some taxidermy in one of the other buildings. I hunt quite a lot, also. And I examine the maze and try to analyze its workings. I've dictated several cubes of memoirs on my findings. I bet you archaeologist fellows would love to run through those cubes."

"I'm sure we'd learn a great deal from them," Rawlins said.

"I know you would. I'd destroy them before I'd let any of you see them. Are you getting hungry, boy?"

"A little."

"Don't go away. I'll bring you some lunch."

Muller strode toward the nearby buildings and disappeared. Rawlins said quietly, "This is awful, Charles. He's obviously out of his mind."

"Don't be sure of it," Boardman replied. "No doubt nine years of isolation can have effects on a man's stability, and Muller wasn't all that stable the last time I saw him. But he may be playing a game with you—pretending to be crazy to test your good faith."

"And if he isn't?"

"In terms of what we want from him, it doesn't matter in the slightest if he's insane. It might even help."

"I don't understand that."

"You don't need to," said Boardman evenly. "Just relax. You're doing fine so far."

Muller returned, carrying a platter of meat and a handsome crystal beaker of water. "Best I can offer," he said, pushing a chunk of meat between the bars. "A local beast. You eat solid food, don't you?"

"Yes."

"At your age, I guess you would. What did you say you were, twenty-five?"

"Twenty-three."

"That's even worse." Muller gave him the water. It had an agreeable flavor, or lack of flavor. Muller sat quietly before the cage, eating. Rawlins noticed that the effect of his emanation no longer seemed so disturbing, even at a range of less than five meters. Obviously one builds a tolerance to it, he thought. If one wants to make the attempt.

Rawlins said, after a while, "Would you come out and meet my companions in a few days?"

"Absolutely not."

"They'd be eager to talk to you."

"I have no interest in talking to them. I'd sooner talk to wild beasts."

"You talk to me," Rawlins pointed out.

"For the novelty of it. And because your father was a good friend. And because, as human beings go, boy, you're reasonably acceptable. But I don't want to be thrust into any miscellaneous mass of bug-eyed archaeologists."

"Possibly meet two or three of them," Rawlins suggested. "Get used to the idea of being among people again."

"*No.*"

"I don't see—"

Muller cut him off. "Wait a minute. *Why* should I get used to the idea of being among people again?"

Rawlins said uneasily, "Well, because there are people here, because it's not a good idea to get too isolated from—"

"Are you planning some sort of trick? Are you going to catch me and pull me out of this maze? Come on, come on, boy, what's in back of that little mind of yours? What motive do you have for softening me up for human contact?"

Rawlins faltered. In the awkward silence Boardman spoke quickly, supplying the guile he lacked, prompting him. Rawlins listened and did his best.

He said, "You're making me out to be a real schemer, Dick. But I swear to you I've got nothing sinister in mind. I admit I've been softening you up a little, jollying you, trying to make friends with you, and I guess I'd better tell you why."

"I guess you'd better!"

"It's for the archaeological survey's sake. We can spend only a few weeks here. You've been here—what is it, nine years? You know so much about this place, Dick, and I think it's unfair of you to keep it to yourself. So what I was hoping, I guess, was that I could get you to ease up, first become friendly with me, and then maybe come to Zone E, talk to the others, answer their questions, explain what you know about the maze—"

"*Unfair* to keep it to myself?"

"Well, yes. To hide knowledge is a sin."

"Is it fair of mankind to call me unclean, and run away from me?"

"That's a different matter," Rawlins said. "It's beyond all fairness. It's a condition you have—an unfortunate condition that you didn't deserve, and everyone is quite sorry that it came upon you, but on the other hand, you surely must realize that from the viewpoint of other human beings it's rather difficult to take a detached attitude toward your—your—"

"Toward my stink," Muller supplied. "All right. It's rather difficult to stand my presence. Therefore I willingly refrain from inflicting it upon your friends. Get it out of your head that I'm going to speak to them or sip tea with them or have anything at all to do with them. I have separated myself from the human race and I stay separated. And it's irrelevant that I've granted you the privilege of bothering me. Also, while I'm instructing you, I want to remind you that my unfortunate condition was not undeserved. I earned it by poking my nose into places where I didn't belong, and by thinking I was superhuman for being able to go to such places. *Hybris.* I told you the word."

Boardman continued to instruct him. Rawlins, with the sour taste of lies on his tongue, went on, "I can't blame you for being bitter, Dick. But I still think it isn't right for you to withhold information from us. I mean, look back on your own exploring days. If you landed on a planet, and someone had vital information you had come to find, wouldn't you make every effort to get that information—even though the other person had certain private problems which—"

"I'm sorry," said Muller frostily, "I'm beyond caring," and he walked away, leaving Rawlins alone in the cage with two chunks of meat and the nearly empty beaker of water.

When Muller was out of sight Boardman said, "He's a touchy one, all right. But I didn't expect sweetness from him. You're getting to him, Ned. You're just the right mixture of guile and naivete."

"And I'm in a cage."

"That's no problem. We can send a drone to release you if the cage doesn't open by itself soon."

"Muller isn't going to work out," Rawlins murmured. "He's full of hate. It trickles out of him everywhere. We'll never get him to cooperate. I've never seen such hate in one man."

"You don't know what hate is," said Boardman. "And neither does he. I tell you everything is moving well. There are bound to be some setbacks, but the fact that he's talking to you at all is the important thing. He doesn't *want* to be full of hate. Give him half a chance to get off his frozen position and he will."

"When will you send the probe to release me?"

"Later," said Boardman. "If we have to."

Muller did not return. The afternoon grew darker and the air became chilly. Rawlins huddled uncomfortably in the cage. He tried to imagine this city when it had been alive, when this cage had been used to display prisoners captured in the maze. In the eye of his mind he saw a throng of the city-builders, short and thick, with dense coppery fur and greenish skin, swinging their long arms and pointing toward the cage. And in the cage huddled a thing like a giant scorpion, with waxy claws that scratched at the stone paving blocks, and fiery eyes, and a savage tail that awaited anyone who came too close. Harsh music sounded through the city. Alien laughter. The warm musky reek of the city-builders. Children spitting at the thing in the cage. Their spittle like flame. Bright moonlight, dancing shadows. A trapped creature, hideous and malevolent, lonely for its own kind, its hive on a world of Alphecca or Markab, where tailed waxy things moved in shining tunnels. For days the city-builders came, mocked, reproached. The creature in the cage grew sick of their massive bodies and their intertwining spidery fingers, of their flat faces and ugly tusks. And a day came when the floor of the maze gave way, for they were tired of the outworlder captive, and down he went, tail lashing furiously, down into a pit of knives.

It was night. Rawlins had not heard from Boardman for several hours. He had not seen Muller since early afternoon. Animals were prowling the plaza, mostly small ones, all teeth and claws. Rawlins had come unarmed today. He was ready to trample on any beast that slipped between the bars of his cage.

Hunger and cold assailed him. He searched the darkness for Muller. This had ceased to be a joke.

"Can you hear me?" he said to Boardman.

"We're going to get you out soon."

"Yes, but *when?*"

"We sent a probe in, Ned."

"It shouldn't take more than fifteen minutes for a probe to reach me. These zones aren't hazardous."

Boardman paused. "Muller intercepted the probe and destroyed it an hour ago."

"Why didn't you tell me that?"

"We're sending several drones at once," Boardman told him. "Muller's bound to overlook at least one of them. Everything's perfectly all right, Ned. You're in no danger."

"Until something happens," Rawlins said gloomily.

But he did not press the point. Cold, hungry, he slouched against the wall and waited. He saw a small lithe beast stalk and kill a much bigger animal a hundred meters away in the plaza. He watched scavengers scurrying in to rip away slabs of bloody meat. He listened to the sounds of rending and tearing. His view was partially obstructed, and he craned his neck to search for the drone probe that would set him free. No probe appeared.

He felt like a sacrificial victim, staked out for the kill.

The scavengers had finished their work. They came padding across the plaza toward him—little weasel-shaped beasts with big tapering heads and paddle-shaped paws from which yellow recurving claws protruded. Their eyes were red in yellow fields. They studied him with interest, solemnly, thoughtfully. Blood, thick and purplish, was smeared over their muzzles.

They drew nearer. A long narrow snout intruded between two bars of his cage. Rawlins kicked at it. The snout withdrew. To his left, another jutted through. Then there were three snouts.

And then the scavengers began slipping into the cage on all sides.

9.

Boardman had established a comfortable little nest for himself in the Zone F camp. At his age he offered no apologies. He had never been a Spartan, and now, as the price he exacted for making these strenuous and risky journeys, he carried his pleasures around with him. Drones had fetched his belongings from the ship. Under the milky-white curve of the extrusion dome he had carved a private sector with radiant heating, glow-drapes, a gravity suppressor, even a liquor console. Brandy and other delights were never far away. He slept on a soft inflatable mattress covered with a thick red quilt inlaid with heater strands. He knew that the other men in the camp, getting along on far less, bore him no resentment. They expected Charles Boardman to live well wherever he was.

Greenfield entered. "We've lost another drone, sir," he said crisply. "That leaves three in the inner zones."

Boardman flipped the ignition cap on a cigar. He sucked fumes a moment, crossed and uncrossed his legs, exhaled, smiled. "Is Muller going to get those too?"

"I'm afraid so. He knows the access routes better than we do. He's covering them all."

"And you haven't sent any drones in through routes we haven't charted?"

"Two, sir. Lost them both."

"Umm. We'd better send out a great many probes at once, then, and hope we can slip at least one of them past Muller. That boy is getting annoyed at being caged. Change the program, will you? The brain can manage diversionary tactics, if it's told. Say, twenty probes entering simultaneously."

"We have only three left," Greenfield said.

Boardman bit convulsively into his cigar. "Three here in the camp, or three altogether?"

"Three in camp. Five more outside the maze. They're working their way inward now."

"Who allowed this to happen? Call Hosteen! Get those templates working! I want fifty drones built by morning! No, make it eighty! Of all the stupidity, Greenfield!"

"Yes, sir."

"Get out!"

"Yes, sir."

Boardman puffed furiously. He dialed for brandy, the thick, rich, viscous stuff made by the Prolepticalist Fathers on Deneb XIII. The situation was growing infuriating. He knocked back half a snifter of the brandy, gasped, filled the glass again. He knew that he was in danger of losing his perspective—the worst of sins. The delicacy of this assignment was getting to him. All these mincing steps, the tiny complications, the painstaking edgings toward and away from the goal. Rawlins in the cage. Rawlins and his moral qualms. Muller and his neurotic world-outlook. The little beasts that nipped at your heels here and thoughtfully eyed your throat. The traps these demons had built. And the waiting extragalactics, saucer-eyed, radio-sensed, to whom even a Charles Boardman was no more than an insensate vegetable. Doom overhanging all. Irritably Boardman stubbed out his cigar, and immediately stared at its unfinished length in astonishment. The ignition cap would not work a second time. He leaned forward, got a beam of infrared from the room generator, and kindled it once more, puffing energetically until it was lit. With a petulant gesture of his hand Boardman reactivated his communication link with Ned Rawlins.

The screen showed him moonlight, curving bars, and small furry snouts bristling with teeth.

"Ned?" he said. "Charles here. We're getting you those drones, boy. We'll have you out of that stupid cage in five minutes, do you hear, five minutes!"

2

Rawlins was very busy.

It seemed almost funny. There was no end to the supply of the little beasts. They came nosing through the bars two and three at a time, weasels, ferrets, minks, stoats, whatever they were, all teeth and eyes. But they were scavengers, not killers. God knew what drew them to the cage. They clustered about him, brushing his ankles with their coarse fur, pawing him, slicing through his skin with their claws, biting his shins.

He trampled them. He learned very quickly that a booted foot placed just behind the head could snap a spinal column quickly and effectively. Then, with a swift kick, he could sweep his victim into a corner of the cage, where others would pounce upon it at once. Cannibals, too. Rawlins developed a rhythm of it. Turn, stomp, kick. Turn, stomp, kick. Turn, stomp, kick. Crunch. Crunch. Crunch.

They were cutting him up badly, though.

For the first five minutes he scarcely had time to pause for breath. Turn. Stomp. Kick. He took care of at least twenty of them in that time. Against the far side of the cage a heap of ragged little corpses had risen, with their comrades nosing around hunting for the tender morsels. At last a moment came when all the scavengers currently inside the cage were busy with their fallen cohorts, and no more lurked outside. Rawlins had a momentary respite. He seized a bar with one hand and lifted his left leg to examine the miscellany of cuts, scratches, and bites. Do they give a posthumous Stellar Cross if you die of galactic rabies, he wondered? His leg was bloody from the knee down, and the wounds, though not deep, were hot and painful. Suddenly he discovered why the scavengers had come to him. While he paused he had time to inhale, and he smelled the ripe fragrance of rotting meat. He could almost visualize it: a great bestial corpse, split open at the belly to expose red sticky organs, big black flies circling overhead, perhaps a maggot or two circumnavigating the mound of flesh—

Nothing was rotting in here. The dead scavengers hadn't had time to go bad; little was left of most of them but picked bones by now anyway.

Rawlins realized that it must be some sensory delusion: an olfactory trap touched off by the cage, evidently. The cage was broadcasting the stink of decay. Why? Obviously to lure that pack of little weasels inside. A refined form of torture. He wondered if Muller had somehow been behind it, going off to a nearby control center to set up the scent.

He had no further time for contemplation. A fresh battalion of beasts was scurrying across the plaza toward the cage. These looked slightly larger, although not so large that they would not fit between the bars, and their fangs had an ugly gleam in the moonlight. Rawlins hastily stomped three of the snuffling, gorging cannibals still alive in his cage and, in a wondrous burst of inspiration, stuffed them through the bars, giving them a wristflip that tossed them eight or ten meters outside the cage. Good. The newcomers halted, skidding, and began at once to pounce on the twitching and not quite dead bodies that landed before them. Only a few of the scavengers bothered to enter the cage, and these came spaced widely enough so that Rawlins had a chance to trample each in turn and toss it out to feed the onrushing horde. At that rate, he thought, if only new ones would stop coming he could get rid of them all.

New ones finally did stop coming. He had killed seventy or eighty by this time. The stink of raw blood overlaid the synthetic stench of rot; his legs ached from all the carnage, and his brain was orbiting dizzyingly. But at length the night grew peaceful once more. Bodies, some clad in fur, some just a framework of bone, lay strewn in a wide arc before the cage. A thick, deep-hued puddle of mingled bloods spread over a dozen square meters. The last few survivors, stuffed on their gluttony, had gone slinking away without even trying to harass the occupant of the cage. Weary, drained, close to laughter and close to tears, Rawlins clung to the bars and did not look down at his throbbing blood-soaked legs. He felt the fire rising in them. He imagined alien micro-organisms launching their argosies in his bloodstream. A bloated purpling corpse by morning, a martyr to Charles Boardman's over-reaching deviousness. What an idiot's move to step into the cage! What a doltish way to win Muller's trust!

Yet the cage had its uses, Rawlins realized suddenly.

Three bulky brutes paraded toward him from different directions. They had the stride of lions, but the swinishness of boars: low-slung sharp-backed creatures, 100 kilograms or so, with long pyramidal heads, slavering thin-lipped mouths, and tiny squinting eyes arranged in two sets of two on either side just in front of their ragged droopy ears. Curving tusks jutted down and intersected smaller and sharper canine teeth that rose from powerful jaws.

The trio of uglies inspected one another suspiciously, and performed a complex series of loping movements which neatly demonstrated the three-body problem as they executed circular interlocking trots by way of staking out territory. They rooted about a bit in the heap of scavenger corpses, but clearly they were no scavengers themselves; they were looking for living meat, and their disdain for the broken cannibalized little bodies was evident. When they had completed their inspection they swung about to stare at Rawlins, standing at a three-quarters-profile angle so that each of them had one pair of eyes looking at him straight on. Rawlins was grateful for the security of his cage. He would not care to be outside, unprotected and exhausted, with these three cruising the city for their dinner.

At that moment, of course, the bars of the cage silently began to retract.

3

Muller, arriving just then, took in the whole scene. He paused only briefly to admire the seductive vanishing of the cage into the recessed slots. He contemplated the three hungry pigs and the dazed, bloody form of Rawlins standing suddenly exposed before them. "Get down!" Muller yelled.

Rawlins got down by taking four running steps to the left, slipping on the blood-slicked pavement, and skidding into a heap of small cadavers at the edge of the street. In the same moment Muller fired, not bothering with keying in the manual sighting since these were not edible animals. Three quick bolts brought the pigs down. They did not move again. Muller started to go to Rawlins, but then one of the robots from the camp in Zone F appeared, gliding cheerfully toward them. Muller cursed softly. He pulled the destructor globe from his pocket and aimed the window at the robot. The probe turned a mindless blank face at him as he fired.

The robot disintegrated. Rawlins had managed to get up. "You shouldn't have blasted it," he said woozily. "It was just coming to help."

"No help was needed," said Muller. "Can you walk?"

"I think so."

"How badly are you hurt?"

"I've been chewed on, that's all. It isn't as bad as it looks."

"Come with me," Muller said. Already more scavengers were filing through the plaza, drawn by the mysterious telegraphy of blood. Small, toothy things were getting down to serious work on the trio of fallen boars. Rawlins looked unsteady; he seemed to be talking to himself. Forgetting his own emanation, Muller seized him by the arm. Rawlins winced and twitched away, and then, as if repenting the appearance of rudeness, gave Muller his arm again. They crossed the plaza together. Rawlins was shaking, and Muller did not know whether he was more disturbed by his narrow escape or by the jangling propinquity of an unshielded mind.

"In here," Muller said roughly.

They stepped into the hexagonal cell where he kept his diagnostat. Muller sealed the door, and Rawlins sank down limply on the bare floor. His blond hair was pasted by perspiration to his forehead. His eyes were moving jerkily, the pupils dilated.

Muller said, "How long were you under attack?"

"Fifteen, twenty minutes. I don't know. There must have been fifty or a hundred of them. I kept breaking their backs. A quick crunching sound, you know, like splitting twigs. And then the cage went away." Rawlins laughed wildly. "That was the best part. I had just finished smashing up all those little bastards and was catching my breath, and then the three big monsters came along, and so naturally the cage vanished and—"

"Easy," Muller said, "you're talking so fast I can't follow everything. Can you get those boots off?"

"What's left of them."

"Yes. Get them off and we'll patch those legs of yours. Lemnos has no shortage of infectious bacteria. And protozoa, and for all I know algae and trypanosomes, and more."

Rawlins picked at the catches. "Can you help me? I'm afraid that I can't—"

"You won't like it if I come any closer," Muller warned.

"To hell with that!"

Muller shrugged. He approached Rawlins and manipulated the broken and bent snaps of the boots. The metal chasing was scarred by tiny teeth; so were the boots themselves, and so were the legs. In a few moments Rawlins was out of his boots and leggings. He lay stretched out on the floor, grimacing and trying to look heroic. His legs were in bad shape, though none of the wounds seemed really serious; it was just that there were so many of them. Muller got the diagnostat going. The lamps glowed and the receptor slot beckoned.

"It's an old model," Rawlins said. "I'm not sure what to do."

"Stick your legs in front of the scanner."

Rawlins swiveled about. A blue light played on his wounds. In the bowels of the diagnostat things chuttered and clicked. A swab came forth on a jointed arm and ran deftly and lightly up his left leg to a point just above the knee. The machine engulfed the bloody swab and began to digest it back to its component molecules while a second swab emerged to clean Rawlins' other leg. Rawlins bit his lip. He was getting a coagulant as well as a cleanser so that when the swabs had done their work all blood was gone and the shallow gouges and rips were revealed. It still looked pretty bad, Muller thought, though not as grim as before.

The diagnostat produced an ultrasonic node and injected a golden fluid into Rawlins' rump. Pain-damper, Muller guessed. A second injection, deep amber, was probably some kind of all-purpose antibiotic to ward off infection. Rawlins grew visibly less tense. Now a variety of arms sprang forward from various sectors of the device, inspecting Rawlins' lesions in detail and scanning them for necessary repairs. There was a humming sound and three sharp clicks. Then the diagnostat began to seal the wounds, clamping them firmly.

"Lie still," Muller told him. "You'll be all right in a couple of minutes."

"You shouldn't be doing this," said Rawlins. "We have our own medical supplies back in camp. You must be running short on necessities. All you had to do was let the drone probe take me back to my camp, and—"

"I don't want those robots crawling around in here. And the diagnostat has at least a fifty-year supply of usefuls. I don't get sick often. It can synthesize most of what it's ever going to need for me. So long as I feed it protoplasm from time to time, it can do the rest."

"At least let us send you replacements for some of the rare drugs."

"Not necessary. No charity wanted. Ah! There, it's done with you. Probably you won't even have scars."

The machine released Rawlins, who swung away from it and looked up at Muller. The wildness was gone from the boy's face now. Muller lounged against the wall, rubbing his shoulderblades against the angle where two faces of the hexagon met, and said, "I didn't think that you'd be attacked by beasts or I wouldn't have left you alone so long. You aren't armed?"

"No."

"Scavengers don't bother living things. What made them go after you?"

"The cage did," Rawlins said. "It began to broadcast the smell of rotting flesh. A lure. Suddenly they were crawling all over me. I thought they'd eat me alive."

Muller grinned. "Interesting. So the cage is programmed as a trap too. We get some useful information out of your little predicament, then. I can't tell you how interested I am in those cages. In every part of this weird environment of mine. The aqueduct. The calendar pylons. The streetcleaning apparatus. I'm grateful to you for helping me learn a little."

"I know someone else who has that attitude," said Rawlins. "That it doesn't matter what the risk or cost so long as you collect some useful data out of the experience. Board—"

He cut the word short with a crisp biting gesture.

"Who?"

"Bordoni," Rawlins said. "Emilio Bordoni, my epistemology professor at college. He gave this marvelous course. Actually it was applied hermeneutics, a course in how to learn."

"That's heuristics," said Muller.

"Are you sure? I have a distinct impression—"

"It's wrong," said Muller. "You're talking to an authority. Hermeneutics is the art of interpretation. Originally Scriptural interpretation but now applying to all communications functions. Your father would have known that. My mission to the Hydrans was an experiment in applied hermeneutics. It wasn't successful."

"Heuristics. Hermeneutics." Rawlins laughed. "Well, anyway, I'm glad to have helped you learn something about the cages. My heuristic good deed. Am I excused from the next round?"

"I suppose," Muller said. Somehow an odd feeling of good will had come over him. He had almost forgotten how pleasant it was to be able to help another person. Or to enjoy lazy, irrelevant conversation. He said, "Do you drink, Ned?"

"Alcoholic beverages?"

"So I mean."

"In moderation."

"This is our local liqueur," said Muller. "It's produced by gnomes somewhere in the bowels of the planet." He produced a delicate flask and two wide-mouthed goblets. Carefully he tipped about twenty centiliters into each goblet. "I get this in Zone C," he explained, handing Rawlins his drink. "It rises from a fountain. It really ought to be labeled DRINK ME, I guess."

Gingerly Rawlins tasted it. "Strong!"

"About sixty per cent alcohol, yes. Lord knows what the rest of it is, or how it's synthesized or why. I simply accept it. I like the way it manages to be both sweet and gingery at the same time. Its terribly intoxicating, of course. It's intended as another trap, I suppose. You get happily drunk—and then the maze gets you." He raised his goblet amiably. "Cheers!"

"Cheers!"

They laughed at the archaic toast and drank.

Careful, Dickie, Muller told himself. You're getting downright sociable with this boy. Remember where you are. And why. What kind of ogre are you, acting this way?

"May I take some of this back to camp with me?" Rawlins asked.

"I suppose so. Why?"

"There's a man there who'd appreciate it. He's a gourmet of sorts. He's traveling with a liquor console that dispenses a hundred different drinks, I imagine, from about forty different worlds. I can't even remember the names."

"Anything from Marduk?" Muller asked. "The Deneb worlds? Rigel?"

"I really can't be sure. I mean, I enjoy drinking, but I'm no connoisseur."

"Perhaps this friend of yours would be willing to exchange—" Muller stopped. "No. No. Forget I said that. I'm not getting into any deals."

"You could come back to camp with me," said Rawlins. "He'd give you the run of the console, I'm sure."

"Very subtle of you. No." Muller glowered at his liqueur. "I won't be eased into it, Ned. I don't want anything to do with the others." ·

"I'm sorry you feel that way."

"Another drink?"

"No. I'll have to start getting back to camp now. It's late. I wasn't supposed to spend the whole day here, and I'll catch hell for not doing my share of the work."

"You were in the cage most of the day. They can't blame you for that."

"They might. They were complaining a little yesterday. I don't think they want me to visit you."

Muller felt a sudden tightness within.

Rawlins went on, "After the way I kicked away a day's work today I wouldn't be surprised if they refused to let me come in here again. They'll be pretty stuffy about it. I mean, considering that you don't seem very cooperative, they'll regard it as wasted time for me to be paying calls on you when I could be manning the equipment in Zone E or F." Rawlins finished his drink and got to his feet, grunting a little. He looked down at his bare legs. The diagnostat had covered the wounds with a nutrient spray, flesh-colored; it was almost impossible to tell that his skin had been broken anywhere. Stiffly, he pulled his tattered leggings on. "I won't bother with the boots," he said. "They're in bad shape, and it won't be pleasant trying to get them on. I suppose I can get back to camp barefoot."

"The pavement is very smooth," Muller said.

"You'll give me some of that liqueur for my friend?"

Silently Muller extended the flask, half full.

Rawlins clipped it to his belt. "It was an interesting day. I hope I can come again."

4

Boardman said, as Rawlins limped back toward Zone E, "How are your legs?"

"Tired. They're healing fast. I'll be all right."

"Be careful not to drop that flask."

"Don't worry, Charles. I have it well fastened. I wouldn't deprive you of the experience."

"Ned, listen to me, we did try to get the drones to you. I was watching every terrible minute of it when those animals were attacking you. But there was nothing we could do. Muller was intercepting our probes and knocking them out."

"All right," Rawlins said.

"He's clearly unstable. He wasn't going to let one of those drones into the inner zones."

"All right, Charles, I survived."

Boardman could not let go of it. "It occurred to me that if we hadn't tried to send the drones at all, you would have been better off, Ned. The drones kept Muller busy for a long while. He might have gone back to your cage instead. Let you out. Or killed the animals. He—" Halting, Boardman quirked his lips and denounced himself inwardly for maundering. A sign of age. He felt the folds of flesh at his belly. He needed another shape-up. Bring his age forward to an apparent sixty or so, while actually cutting the physiological deterioration back to biological fifty. Older outside than within. A façade of shrewdness to hide shrewdness.

He said, after a long while, "It seems you and Muller are quite good friends now. I'm pleased. It's coming to be time for you to tempt him out."

"How do I do that?"

"Promise him a cure," Boardman said.

10.

They met again on the third day afterward, at midday in Zone B. Muller seemed relieved to see him, which was the idea. Rawlins came diagonally across the oval ball-court, or whatever it was, that lay between two snub-nosed dark blue towers, and Muller nodded. "How are your legs?"

"Doing fine."

"And your friend—he liked the liqueur?"

"He loved it," Rawlins said, thinking of the glow in Boardman's foxy eyes. "He sends back your flask with some special brandy in it and hopes you'll treat him to a second round."

Muller eyed the flask as Rawlins held it forth. "He can go to hell," Muller said coolly. "I won't get into any trades. If you give me that flask I'll smash it."

"Why?"

"Give it here, and I'll show you. No. Wait. Wait. I won't. Here, let me have it."

Rawlins surrendered it. Muller cradled the lovely flask tenderly in both hands, activated the cap, and put it to his lips. "You devils," he said in a soft voice. "What is this, from the monastery on Deneb XIII?"

"He didn't say. He just said you'd like it."

"Devils. Temptations. It's a trade, damn you! But only this once. If you show up here again with more liqueur—anything—the elixir of the gods—anything, I'll refuse it. Where have you been all week, anyway?"

"Working. I told you they frowned on my coming to see you."

He missed me, Rawlins thought. Charles is right: I'm getting to him. Why does he have to be such a difficult character?

"Where are they excavating?" Muller asked.

"They aren't excavating at all. They're using sonic probes at the border between Zones E and F, trying to determine the chronology—whether the whole maze was built at once, or in accretive layers out from the middle. What's your opinion, Dick?"

"Go to hell. No free archaeology out of me!" Muller sipped the brandy again. "You're standing pretty close to me, aren't you?"

"Four or five meters, I guess."

"You were closer when you gave me the brandy. Why didn't you look sick? Didn't you feel the effect?"

"I felt it, yes."

"And hid your feelings like the good stoic you are?"

Shrugging, Rawlins said genially, "I guess the effect loses impact on repeated exposure. It's still pretty strong, but not the way it was for me the first day. Have you ever noticed that happening with someone else?"

"There were no repeated exposures with anyone else," said Muller. "Come over here, boy. See the sights. This is my water supply. Quite elegant. This black pipe runs right around Zone B. Onyx, I guess. Semi-precious. Handsome, at any rate." Muller knelt and stroked the aqueduct. "There's a pumping system. Brings up water from some underground aquifer, maybe a thousand kilometers down, I don't know. This planet doesn't have any surface water, does it?"

"It has oceans."

"Aside from—well, whatever. Over here, you see, here's one of the spigots. Every fifty meters. As far as I can tell it's the water supply for the entire city, right here, so perhaps the builders didn't need much water. It couldn't have been very important if they set things up like this. No conduits that I've found. No real plumbing. Thirsty?"

"Not really."

Muller cupped his hand under the ornately engraved spigot, a thing of concentric ridges. Water gushed. Muller took a few quick gulps; the flow ceased the moment the hand was removed from the area below the spigot. A scanning system of some kind, Rawlins thought. Clever. How had it lasted all these millions of years?

"Drink," Muller said. "You may get thirsty later on."

"I can't stay long." But he drank anyway. Afterward they walked into Zone A, an easy stroll. The cages had closed again; Rawlins saw several of them, and shuddered. He would try no such experiments today. They found benches, slabs of polished stone that curled at the ends into facing seats intended for some species very much broader in the buttock than the usual *H. sapiens*. Sitting like this they could talk

at a distance, Rawlins feeling only mild discomfort from Muller's emanation, and yet there was no sensation of separation.

Muller was in a talkative mood.

The conversation was fitful, dissolving every now and then into an
acid spray of anger or self-pity, but most of the time Muller remained
calm and even charming—an older man clearly enjoying the company
of a younger one, the two of them exchanging opinions, experiences,
scraps of philosophy. Muller spoke a good deal about his early career,
the planets he had seen, the delicate negotiations on behalf of Earth with
the frequently prickly colony-worlds. He mentioned Boardman's name
quite often; Rawlins kept his face studiously blank. Muller's attitude
toward Boardman seemed to be one of deep admiration shot through
with furious loathing. He could not forgive Boardman, apparently, for
having played on his own weaknesses in getting him to go to the Hydrans. Not a rational attitude, Rawlins thought. Given Muller's trait of
overweening curiosity, he would have fought for that assignment,
Boardman or no, risks or no.

"And what about you?" Muller asked finally. "You're brighter than
you pretend to be. Hampered a little by your shyness, but plenty of
brains, carefully hidden behind college-boy virtues. What do you want
for yourself, Ned? What does archaeology give you?"

Rawlins looked him straight in the eyes. "A chance to recapture a
million pasts. I'm as greedy as you are. I want to know how things
happened, how they got this way. Not just on Earth or in the System.
Everywhere."

"Well spoken!"

I thought so too, Rawlins thought, hoping Boardman was pleased
by his newfound eloquence.

He said, "I suppose I could have gone in for diplomatic service, the
way you did. Instead I chose this. I think it'll work out. There's so much
to discover, here and everywhere else. We've only begun to look."

"The ring of dedication is in your voice."

"I suppose."

"I like to hear that sound. It reminds me of the way I used to talk."

Rawlins said, "Just so you don't think I'm hopelessly pure I ought
to say that it's personal curiosity that moves me on, more than abstract
love of knowledge."

"Understandable. Forgivable. We're not too different, really. Allowing for forty-odd years between us. Don't worry so much about your
motives, Ned. Go to the stars, see, do. Enjoy. Eventually life will smash
you, the way it's smashed me, but that's far off. Sometime, never, who
knows? Forget about that."

"I'll try," Rawlins said.

He felt the warmth of the man now, the reaching out of genuine sympathies. There was still that carrier wave of nightmare, though, the unending broadcast out of the mucky depths of the soul, attenuated at this distance but unmistakable. Imprisoned by his pity, Rawlins hesitated to say what it now was time to say. Boardman prodded him irritably. "Go *on*, boy! Slip it in!"

"You look very far away," Muller said.

"Just thinking how—how sad it is that you won't trust us at all, that you have such a negative attitude toward humanity."

"I come by it honestly."

"You don't need to spend the rest of your life in this maze, though. There's a way out."

"Garbage."

"Listen to me," Rawlins said. He took a deep breath and flashed his quick, transparent grin. "I talked about your case to our expedition medic. He's studied neurosurgery. He knew all about you. He says there's now a way to fix what you have. Recently developed, the last couple of years. It—shuts off the broadcast, Dick. He said I should tell you. We'll take you back to Earth. For the operation, Dick. The operation. The cure."

2

The sharp glittering barbed word came swimming along on the breast of a torrent of bland sounds and speared him in the gut. *Cure!* He stared. There was reverberation from the looming dark buildings. *Cure. Cure. Cure.* Muller felt the poisonous temptation gnawing at his liver. "No," he said. "That's garbage. A cure's impossible."

"How can you be so sure?"

"I know."

"Science progresses in nine years. They understand how the brain works, now. Its electrical nature. What they did, they built a tremendous simulation in one of the lunar labs—oh, a few years ago, and they ran it all through from start to finish. As a matter of fact I'm sure they're desperate to have you back, because you prove all their theories. In your present condition. And by operating on you, reversing your broadcast, they'll demonstrate that they were right. All you have to do is come back with us."

Muller methodically popped his knuckles. "Why didn't you mention this earlier?"

"I didn't know a thing about it."

"Of course."

"Really. We didn't expect to be finding you here, you realize. At first nobody was too sure who you were, why you were here. I explained it. And then the medic remembered that there was this treatment. What's wrong—don't you believe me?"

"You look so angelic," Muller said. "Those sweet blue eyes and that golden hair. What's your game, Ned? Why are you reeling off all this nonsense?"

Rawlins reddened. "It isn't nonsense!"

"I don't believe you. And I don't believe in your cure."

"It's your privilege. But you'll be the loser if—"

"Don't threaten me!"

"I'm sorry."

There was a long, sticky silence.

Muller revolved a maze of thoughts. To leave Lemnos? To have the curse lifted? To hold a woman in his arms again? Breasts like fire against his skin? Lips? Thighs? To rebuild his career. To reach across the heavens once more? To shuck nine years of anguish? To believe? To go? To submit?

"No," he said carefully. "There is no cure for what I have."

"You keep saying that. But you can't know."

"It doesn't fit the pattern. I believe in destiny, boy. In compensating tragedy. In the overthrow of the proud. The gods don't deal out temporary tragedies. They don't take back their punishments after a few years. Oedipus didn't get his eyes back. Or his mother. They didn't let Prometheus off his rock. They—"

"You aren't living a Greek play," Rawlins told him. "This is the real world. The patterns don't always fall neatly. Maybe the gods have decided that you've suffered enough. And so long as we're having a literary discussion—they forgave Orestes, didn't they? So why isn't nine years here enough for you?"

"*Is* there a cure?"

"The medic says there is."

"I think you're lying to me, boy."

Rawlins glanced away. "What do I have to gain by lying?"

"I can't guess."

"All right, I'm lying," Rawlins said brusquely. "There's no way to help you. Let's talk about something else. Why don't you show me the fountain where that liqueur rises?"

"It's in Zone C," said Muller. "I don't feel like going there just now. Why did you tell me that story if it wasn't true?"

"I said we'd change the subject."

"Let's assume for the moment that it *is* true," Muller persisted.

"That if I go back to Earth I can be cured. I want to let you know that I'm not interested, not even with a guarantee. I've seen Earthmen in their true nature. They kicked me when I was down. Not sporting, Ned. They stink. They reek. They gloried in what had happened to me."

"That isn't so!"

"What do you know? You were a child. Even more then than now. They treated me as filth because I showed them what was inside themselves. A mirror for their dirty souls. Why should I go back to them now? Why do I need them? Worms. Pigs. I saw them as they really are, those few months I was on Earth after Beta Hydri IV. The look in the eyes, the nervous smile as they back away from me. Yes, Mr. Muller. Of course, Mr. Muller. Just don't come too close, Mr. Muller. Boy, come by here some time at night and let me show you the constellations as seen from Lemnos. I've given them my own names. There's the Dagger, a long keen one. It's about to be thrust into the Back. Then there's the Shaft. And you can see the Ape, too, and the Toad. They interlock. The same star is in the forehead of the Ape and the left eye of the Toad. That star is Sol, my friend. An ugly little yellow star, the color of thin vomit. Whose planets are populated by ugly little people who have spread like trickling urine over the whole universe."

"Can I say something that might offend you?" Rawlins asked.

"You can't offend me. But you can try."

"I think your outlook is distorted. You've lost your perspective, all these years here."

"No. I've learned how to see for the first time."

"You're blaming humanity for being human. It's not easy to accept someone like you. If you were sitting here in my place, and I in yours, you'd understand that. It hurts to be near you. *It hurts*. Right now I feel pain in every nerve. If I came closer I'd feel like crying. You can't expect people to adjust quickly to somebody like that. Not even your loved ones could—"

"I had no loved ones."

"You were married."

"Terminated."

"Liaisons, then."

"They couldn't stand me when I came back."

"Friends?"

"They ran," Muller said. "On all six legs they scuttled away from me."

"You didn't give them time."

"Time enough."

"No," Rawlins persisted. He shifted about uneasily on the chair.

"Now I'm going to say something that will really hurt you, Dick. I'm sorry, but I have to. What you're telling me is the kind of stuff I heard in college. Sophomore cynicism. The world is despicable, you say. Evil, evil, evil. You've seen the true nature of mankind, and you don't want to have anything to do with mankind ever again. Everybody talks that way at eighteen. But it's a phase that passes. We get over the confusions of being eighteen, and we see that the world is a pretty decent place, that people try to do their best, that we're imperfect but not loathsome—"

"An eighteen-year-old has no right to those opinions. I do. I come by my hatreds the hard way."

"But why cling to them? You seem to be glorying in your own misery. Break loose! Shake it off! Come back to Earth with us and forget the past. Or at least forgive."

"No forgetting. No forgiving." Muller scowled. A tremor of fear shook him, and he shivered. What if this were true? A genuine cure? Leave Lemnos? He was a trifle embarrassed. The boy had scored a palpable hit with that line about sophomore cynicism. It was. Am I really such a misanthrope? A pose. He forced me to adopt it. Polemic reasons. Now I choke on my own stubbornness. But there's no cure. The boy's transparent; he's lying, though I don't know why. He wants to trap me, to get me aboard that ship of theirs. What if it's true? Why not go back? Muller could supply his own answers. It was the fear that held him. To see Earth's billions. To enter the stream of life. Nine years on a desert island and he dreaded to return. He slipped into a pit of depression, recognizing hard truths. The man who would be a god was just a pitiful neurotic now, clinging to his isolation, spitting defiance at a possible rescuer. Sad, Muller thought. Very sad.

Rawlins said, "I can feel the flavor of your thoughts changing."

"You *can?*"

"Nothing specific. But you were angry and bitter before. Now I'm getting something—wistful."

"No one ever told me he could detect meanings," Muller said in wonder. "No one ever said much. Only that it was painful to be near me. Disgusting."

"Why did you go wistful just then, though? If you did. Thinking of Earth?"

"Maybe I was." Muller hastily patched the sudden gap in his armor. His face darkened. He clenched his jaws. He stood up and deliberately approached Rawlins, watching the young man struggling to hide his real feelings of discomfort. Muller said, "I think you'd better get about your archaeologizing now, Ned. Your friends will be angry again."

"I still have some time."

"No, you don't. Go!"

3

Against Charles Boardman's express orders, Rawlins insisted on returning all the way to the Zone F camp that evening. The pretext was that Rawlins had to deliver the new flask of liqueur which he had finally been able to wheedle out of Muller. Boardman wanted one of the other men to pick up the flask, sparing Rawlins from the risks of Zone F's snares. Rawlins needed the direct contact, though. He was badly shaken. His resolve was sagging.

He found Boardman at dinner. A polished dining-board of dark wood mortised with light woods sat before him. Out of elegant stoneware he ate candied fruits, brandied vegetables, meat extracts, pungent juices. A carafe of wine of a deep olive hue was near his fleshy hand. Mysterious pills of several types rested in the shallow pits of an oblong block of black glass; from time to time Boardman popped one into his mouth. Rawlins stood at the sector opening for a long while before Boardman appeared to notice him.

"I told you not to come here, Ned," the old man said finally.

"Muller sends you this." Rawlins put the flask down beside the carafe of wine.

"We could have talked without this visit."

"I'm tired of that. I needed to see you." Boardman left him standing and did not interrupt his meal. "Charles, I don't think I can keep up the pretense with him."

"You did an excellent job today," said Boardman, sipping his wine. "Quite convincing."

"Yes, I'm learning how to tell lies. But what's the use? You heard him. Mankind disgusts him. He's not going to cooperate once we get him out of the maze."

"He isn't sincere. You said it yourself, Ned. Cheap sophomore cynicism. The man loves mankind. That's why he's so bitter—because his love has turned sour in his mouth. But it hasn't turned to hate. Not really."

"You weren't there, Charles. You weren't talking to him."

"I watched. I listened. And I've known Dick Muller for forty-odd years."

"The last nine years are the ones that count. They've twisted him." Rawlins bent into a crouch to get on Boardman's level. Boardman nudged a candied pear onto his fork, equalized gravity, and flipped it idly toward his mouth. He's intentionally ignoring me, Rawlins thought.

He said, "Charles, be serious. I've gone in there and told Muller some monstrous lies. I've offered him a completely fraudulent cure, and he threw it back in my face."

"Saying he didn't believe it existed. But he *does* believe, Ned. He's simply afraid to come out of hiding."

"Please. Listen. Assume he does come to believe me. Assume he leaves the maze and puts himself in our hands. Then what? Who gets the job of telling him that there isn't any cure, that we've tricked him shamelessly, that we merely want him to be our ambassador again, to visit a bunch of aliens twenty times as strange and fifty times as deadly as the ones that ruined his life? *I'm* not going to break that news to him!"

"You won't have to, Ned. I'll be the one."

"And how will he react? Are you simply expecting him to smile and bow and say, very clever, Charles, you've done it again? To yield and do whatever you want? No. He couldn't possibly. You can get him out of the maze, maybe, but the very methods you use for getting him out make it inconceivable that he can be of any use to you once he *is* out."

"That isn't necessarily true," said Boardman calmly.

"Will you explain the tactics you propose to use, then, once you've informed him that the cure is a lie and that there's a dangerous new job he has to undertake?"

"I prefer not to discuss future strategy now."

"I resign," Rawlins said.

4

Boardman had been expecting something like that. A noble gesture; a moment of headstrong defiance; a rush of virtue to the brain. Abandoning now his studied detachment, he looked up, his eyes locking firmly on Rawlins'. Yes, there was strength there. Yes, determination. But not guile. Not yet.

Quietly Boardman said, "You resign? After all your talk of service to mankind? We need you, Ned. You're the indispensable man, our link to Muller."

"My dedication to mankind includes a dedication to Dick Muller," Rawlins said stiffly. "He's part of mankind, whether he thinks so or not. I've already committed a considerable crime against him. If you won't let me in on the rest of this scheme, I'm damned if I'll have any part in it."

"I admire your convictions."

"My resignation still stands."

"I even agree with your position," said Boardman. "I'm not proud of what we must do here. I see it as part of historical necessity—the need for an occasional betrayal for the greater good. I have a conscience too, Ned, an eighty-year-old conscience, very well developed. It doesn't atrophy with age. We just learn to live with its complaints, that's all."

"How are you going to get Muller to cooperate? Drug him? Torture him? Brainblast him?"

"None of those."

"What, then? I'm serious, Charles. My role in this job ends right here unless I know what's ahead."

Boardman coughed, drained his wine, ate a peach, took three pills in quick succession. Rawlins' rebellion had been inevitable, and he was prepared for it, and yet he was annoyed that it had come. Now was the time for calculated risks. He said, "I see that it's time to drop the pretenses, then, Ned. I'll tell you what's in store for Dick Muller—but I want you to consider it within the framework of the larger position. Don't forget that the little game we've been playing on this planet isn't simply a matter of private moral postures. At the risk of sounding pretentious, I have to remind you that mankind's fate is at stake."

"I'm listening, Charles."

"Very well. Dick Muller must go to our extragalactic friends and convince them that human beings are indeed an intelligent species. Agreed? He alone is capable of doing this, because of his unique inability to cloak his thoughts."

"Agreed."

"Now, it isn't necessary to convince the aliens that we're good people, or that we're honorable people, or that we're lovable people. Simply that we have minds and can think. That we feel, that we sense, that we are something other than clever machines. For our purposes, it doesn't matter *what* emotions Dick Muller is radiating so long as he's radiating something."

"I begin to see."

"Therefore, once he's out of the maze we can tell him what his assignment is to be. No doubt he'll get angry at our trickery. But beyond his anger he may see where his duty lies. I hope so. You seem to think he won't. But it makes no difference, Ned. He won't be given an option once he leaves his sanctuary. He'll be taken to the aliens and handed over to them to make contact. It's brutal, I know. But necessary."

"His cooperation is irrelevant, then," said Rawlins slowly. "He'll just be dumped. Like a sack."

"A *thinking* sack. As our friends out there will learn."

"I—"

"No, Ned. Don't say anything now. I know what you're thinking. You hate the scheme. You have to. I hate it myself. Just go off, now, and think it over. Examine it from all sides before you come to a decision. If you want out tomorrow, let me know and we'll carry on somehow without you, but promise me you'll sleep on it, first. Yes? This is no time for a snap judgment."

Rawlins' face was pale a moment. Then color flooded into it. He clamped his lips. Boardman smiled benignly. Rawlins clenched his fists, squinted, turned, hastily went out.

A calculated risk.

Boardman took another pill. Then he reached for the flask Muller had sent him. He poured a little. Sweet, gingery, strong. An excellent liqueur. He let it rest a while on his tongue.

11.

Muller had almost come to like the Hydrans. What he remembered most clearly and most favorably about them was their grace of motion. They seemed virtually to float. The strangeness of their bodies had never bothered him much; he was fond of saying that one did not need to go far from Earth to find the grotesque. Giraffes. Lobsters. Sea anemones. Squids. Pelicans. Camels. Look objectively at a camel and ask yourself what is less strange about its body than about a Hydran's.

He had landed in a damp, dreary part of the planet, a little to the north of its equator, on an amoeboid continent occupied by a dozen large quasi-cities, each spread out over several thousand square kilometers. His life-support system, specially designed for this mission, was little more than a thin filtration sheet that clung to him like a second skin. It fed air to him through a thousand dialysis plaques. He moved easily if not comfortably within it.

He walked for an hour through a forest of the giant toadstool-like trees before he came upon any of the natives. The trees ran to heights of several hundred meters; perhaps the gravity, five-eighths Earthnorm, had something to do with that. Their curving trunks did not look sturdy. He suspected that an external woody layer no thicker than a fingertip surrounded a broad core of soggy pulp. The cap-like crowns of the trees met in a nearly continuous canopy overhead, cutting almost all light from the forest floor. Since the planet's cloud layer permitted only a hazy pearl-colored glow to come through, and even that was intercepted by the trees, a maroon darkness prevailed below.

When he encountered the aliens he was surprised to find that they were about three meters tall. Not since childhood had he felt so diminished; he stood ringed by them, straining upward to meet their eyes. Now it was time for his exercise in applied hermeneutics. In a quiet voice he said, "My name is Richard Muller. I come in friendship from the peoples of the Terran Cultural Sphere."

Of course they could not understand that. But they remained motionless. He imagined that their expressions were not unfriendly.

Dropping to his knees, Muller traced the Pythagorean Theorem in the soft moist soil.

He looked up. He smiled. "A basic concept of geometry. A universal pattern of thought."

Their vertical slitlike nostrils flickered slightly. They inclined their heads. He imagined that they were exchanging thoughtful glances. With eyes in a circlet entirely around their heads, they did not need to change posture to do that.

"Let me display some further tokens of our kinship," Muller said to them.

He sketched a line on the ground. A short distance from it he sketched a pair of lines. At a greater distance he drew three lines. He filled in the signs. $1 + 11 = 111$.

"Yes?" he said. "We call it addition."

The jointed limbs swayed. Two of his listeners touched arms. Muller remembered how they had obliterated the spying eye as soon as they had discovered it, not hesitating even to examine it. He had been prepared for the same reaction. Instead they were listening. A promising sign. He stood up and pointed to his marks on the ground.

"Your turn," he said. He spoke quite loudly. He smiled quite broadly. "Show me that you understand. Speak to me in the universal language of mathematics."

No response at first.

He pointed again. He gestured at his symbols, then extended his hand, palm upraised, to the nearest Hydran.

After a long pause one of the other Hydrans moved fluidly forward and let one of its globe-like foot-pedestals hover over the lines in the soil. The leg moved lightly and the lines vanished as the alien smoothed the soil.

"All right," said Muller. "Now you draw something."

The Hydran returned to its place in the circle.

"Very well," Muller said. "There's another universal language. I hope this doesn't offend your ears." He drew a soprano recorder from his pocket and put it between his lips. Playing through the filtration sheet was cumbersome. He caught breath and played a diatonic scale. Their limbs fluttered a bit. They could hear, then, or at any rate could sense vibrations. He shifted to the minor, and gave them another diatonic scale. He tried a chromatic scale. They looked a trifle more agitated. Good for you, he thought. Connoisseurs. Perhaps the whole-tone scale is more in keeping with the cloudiness of this planet, he decided. He played both of them, and gave them a bit of Debussy for good measure.

"Does that get to you?" he asked.

They appeared to be conferring.

They walked away from him.

He tried to follow. He was unable to keep up, and soon he lost sight of them in the dark, misty forest; but he persevered, and found them clustered, as if waiting for him, farther on. When he neared them they began to move again. In this way they led him, by fits and starts, into their city.

He subsisted on synthetics. Chemical analysis showed that it would be unwise to try local foods.

He drew the Pythagorean Theorem many times. He sketched a variety of arithmetical processes. He played Schönberg and Bach. He constructed equilateral triangles. He ventured into solid geometry. He sang. He spoke French, Russian, and Mandarin, as well as English, to show them the diversity of human tongues. He displayed a chart of the periodic table. After six months he still knew nothing more about the workings of their minds than he had an hour before landing. They tolerated his presence, but they said nothing to him; and when they communicated with one another it was mainly in quick, evanescent gestures, touches of the hand, flickers of the nostrils. They had a spoken language, it seemed, but it was so soft and breathy that he could not begin to distinguish words or even syllables. He recorded whatever he heard, of course.

Eventually they wearied of him and came for him.

He slept.

He did not discover until much later what had been done to him while he slept.

2

He was eighteen years old, naked under the California stars. The sky was ablaze. He felt he could reach for the stars and pluck them from the heavens.

To be a god. To possess the universe.

He turned to her. Her body was cool and slender, slightly tense. He cupped her breasts. He let his hand move across her flat belly. She shivered a little. "Dick," she said. "Oh." To be a god, he thought. He kissed her lightly, and then not lightly. "Wait," she said. "I'm not ready." He waited. He helped her get ready, or did the things he thought would help her get ready, and shortly she began to gasp. She spoke his name again. How many stars can a man visit in one lifetime? If each star has an average of twelve planets, and there are one hundred million stars within a galactic globe X light-years in diameter. . . . Her thighs opened. His eyes closed. He felt soft old pine needles against his knees and elbows. She was not his first, but the first that counted. As the lightning ripped through his brain he was dimly aware of her response, tentative, halting, then suddenly vigorous. The intensity of it frightened him, but only for a moment, and he rode with her to the end.

To be a god must be something like this.

They rolled over. He pointed to the stars and called off their names for her, getting half of them wrong, but she did not need to know that. He shared his dreams with her. Later they made love a second time, and it was even better.

He hoped it would rain at midnight, so they could dance in the rain, but the sky was clear. They went swimming instead, and came out shivering, laughing. When he took her home she washed down her pill with Chartreuse. He told her that he loved her.

They exchanged Christmas cards for several years.

3

The eighth world of Alpha Centauri B was a gas giant, with a low-density core and gravity not much more troublesome than that of Earth. Muller had honeymooned there the second time. It was partly a business trip, for there were troubles with the colonists on the sixth planet; they were talking of setting up a whirlpool effect that would suck away most of the eighth world's highly useful atmosphere to use as raw materials.

Muller's conferences with the locals went fairly well. He persuaded them to accept a quota system for their atmospheric grabs, and even won their praise for the little lesson in interplanetary morality he had administered. Afterward he and Nola were government guests for a holiday on the eighth world. Nola, unlike Lorayn, was the traveling sort. She would be accompanying him on many of his voyages.

Wearing support suits, they swam in an icy methane lake. They ran laughing along ammonia coasts. Nola was as tall as he, with powerful legs, dark red hair, green eyes. They embraced in a warm room of one-way windows overhanging a forlorn sea that stretched for hundreds of thousands of kilometers.

"For always," she said.

"Yes. For always."

Before the week ended they quarreled bitterly. But it was only a game; for the more fiercely they quarreled, the more passionate was the reconciliation. For a while. Later they stopped bothering to quarrel. When the option in the marriage contract came up, neither of them wanted to renew. Afterward, as his reputation grew, he sometimes received friendly letters from her. He had tried to see her when he returned from Beta Hydri IV to Earth. Nola, he thought, would help him in his troubles. She of all people would not turn away from him. For old times' sake.

But she was vacationing on Vesta with her seventh husband. Muller found that out from her fifth husband. He had been her third. He did not call her. He began to see there was no point in it.

4

The surgeon said, "I'm sorry, Mr. Muller. There's nothing we can do for you. I wouldn't want to raise false hopes. We've graphed your whole neural network. We can't find the sites of alteration. I'm terribly sorry."

5

He had had nine years to sharpen his memories. He had filled a few cubes with reminiscences, but that had mainly been in the early years of his exile, when he worried about having his past drift away to be lost in fog. He discovered that the memories grew keener with age. Perhaps it was training. He could summon sights, sounds, tastes, odors. He could reconstruct whole conversations convincingly. He was able to quote the full texts of several treaties he had negotiated. He could name England's kings in sequence from first to last, William I through William VII. He remembered the names of the girls whose bodies he had known.

He admitted to himself that, given the chance, he would go back. Everything else had been pretense and bluster. He had fooled neither Ned Rawlins nor himself, he knew. The contempt he felt for mankind was real, but not the wish to remain isolated. He waited eagerly for Rawlins to return. While he waited he drank several goblets of the city's liqueur; he went on a killing spree, nervously gunning down animals he could not possibly consume in a year's time; he conducted intricate dialogues with himself; he dreamed of Earth.

6

Rawlins was running. Muller, standing a hundred meters deep in Zone C, saw him come striding through the entrance, breathless, flushed.

"You shouldn't run in here," Muller said, "not even in the safer zones. There's absolutely no telling—"

Rawlins sprawled down beside a flanged limestone tub, gripping its sides and sucking air. "Get me a drink, will you?" he gasped. "That liqueur of yours—"

"Are you all right?"

"No."

Muller went to the fountain nearby and filled a handy flask with the sharp liqueur. Rawlins did not wince at all as Muller drew near to give it to him. He seemed altogether unaware of Muller's emanation. Greedily, sloppily, he emptied the flask, letting driblets of the gleaming fluid roll down his chin and on his clothes. Then he closed his eyes a moment.

"You look awful," Muller said. "As though you've just been raped, I'd say."

"I have."

"What's the trouble?"

"Wait. Let me get my breath. I ran all the way from Zone F."

"You're lucky to be alive, then."

"Perhaps."

"Another drink?"

"No," said Rawlins. "Not just yet."

Muller studied him, perplexed. The change was striking and unsettling, and mere fatigue could not account for it all. Rawlins was bloodshot, flushed, puffy-faced; his facial muscles were tightly knit; his eyes moved randomly, seeking and not finding. Drunk? Sick? Drugged?

Rawlins said nothing.

After a long moment Muller said, just to fill the vacuum of silence, "I've done a lot of thinking about our last conversation. I've decided that I was acting like a damned fool. All that cheap misanthropy I was dishing up." Muller knelt and tried to peer into the younger man's shifting eyes. "Look here, Ned, I want to take it all back. I'm willing to return to Earth for treatment. Even if the treatment's experimental, I'll chance it. I mean, the worst that can happen is that it won't cure me, and—"

"There's no treatment," said Rawlins dully.

"No—treatment . . ."

"No treatment. None. It was all a lie."

"Yes. Of course."

"You said so yourself," Rawlins reminded him. "You didn't believe a word of what I was saying. Remember?"

"A lie."

"You didn't understand why I was saying it, but you said it was nonsense. You told me I was lying. You wondered what I had to gain by lying. I *was* lying, Dick."

"Lying."

"Yes."

"But I've changed my mind," said Muller softly. "I was ready to go back to Earth."

"There's no hope of a cure," Rawlins told him.

He slowly rose to his feet and ran his hand through his long golden hair. He arranged his disarrayed clothing. He picked up the flask, went to the liqueur fountain and filled it. Returning, he handed the flask to Muller, who drank from it. Rawlins finished the flask. Something small and voracious-looking ran past them and slipped through the gate leading to Zone D.

Finally Muller said, "Do you want to explain some of this?"

"We aren't archaeologists."

"Go on."

"We came here looking especially for you. It wasn't any accident. We knew all along where you were. You were tracked from the time you left Earth nine years ago."

"I took precautions."

"They weren't any use. Boardman knew where you were going, and he had you tracked. He left you in peace because he had no use for you. But when a need developed he had to come after you. He was holding you in reserve, so to speak."

"Charles Boardman sent you to fetch me?" Muller asked.

"That's why we're here, yes. That's the whole purpose of this expedition," Rawlins replied tonelessly. "I was picked to make contact with you because you once knew my father and might trust me. And because I have an innocent face. All the time Boardman was directing me, telling me what to say, coaching me, even telling me what mistakes to make, how to blunder successfully. He told me to get into that cage, for instance. He thought it would help win your sympathy."

"Boardman is *here?* Here on Lemnos?"

"In Zone F. He's got a camp there."

"*Charles* Boardman?"

"He's here, yes. Yes."

Muller's face was stony. Within, all was turmoil. "Why did he do all this? What does he want with me?"

Rawlins said, "You know that there's a third intelligent race in the universe, beside us and the Hydrans."

"Yes. They had just been discovered when I left. That was why I went to visit the Hydrans. I was supposed to arrange a defensive alliance with them, before these other people, these extragalactics, came in contact with us. It didn't work. But what does this have to—"

"How much do you know about these extragalactics?"

"Very little," Muller admitted. "Essentially, nothing but what I've just told you. The day I agreed to go to Beta Hydri IV was the first time I had heard about them. Boardman told me, but he wouldn't say anything else. All he said was that they were extremely intelligent—a superior species, he said—and that they lived in a neighboring cluster. And that they had a galactic drive and might visit us some day."

"We know more about them now," Rawlins said.

"First tell me what Boardman wants with me."

"Everything in order, and it'll be easier." Rawlins grinned, perhaps a bit tipsily. He leaned against the stone tub and stretched his legs far out in front of himself. He said, "We don't actually know a great deal about the extragalactics. What we did was send out a ramjet, throw it into warp, and bring it out a few thousand light-years away. Or a few million light-years. I don't know the details. Anyway, it was a drone ship with all sorts of eyes. The place it went to was one of the X-ray galaxies, classified information, but I've heard it was either in Cygnus A or Scorpius II. We found that one planet of the galactic system was inhabited by an advanced race of very alien aliens."

"How alien?"

"They can see all up and down the spectrum," Rawlins said. "Their basic visual range is in the high frequencies. They see by the light of X-rays. They also seem to be able to make use of the radio frequencies to see, or at least to get some kind of sensory information. And they pick up most wavelengths in between, except that they don't have a great deal of interest in the stuff between infrared and ultraviolet. What we like to call the visible spectrum."

"Wait a minute. Radio senses? Do you have any idea how long radio waves are? If they're going to get any information out of a single wave, they'll need eyes or receptors or whatever of gigantic size. How big are these beings supposed to be?"

"They could eat elephants for breakfast," said Rawlins.

"Intelligent life doesn't come that big."

"What's the limitation? This is a gas giant planet, all ocean, no gravity to speak of. They float. They have no square-cube problems."

"And a bunch of superwhales has developed a technological culture?" Muller asked. "You won't get me to believe—"

"They have," said Rawlins. "I've told you, these are very alien aliens. They can't build machinery themselves. But they have slaves."

"Oh," said Muller quietly.

"We're only beginning to understand this, and of course I don't have much of the inside information myself, but as I piece it together it seems that these beings make use of lower life-forms, turning them essentially into radio-controlled robots. They'll use anything with limbs and mobility. They started with certain animals of their own planet, a small dolphin-like form perhaps on the threshold of intelligence, and worked through them to achieve a space drive. Then they got to neighboring planets—land planets—and took control of pseudoprimates, protochimps of some kind. They look for fingers. Manual dexterity counts a great deal with them. At present their sphere of influence covers some eighty light-years and appears to be spreading at an exponential rate."

Muller shook his head. "This is worse nonsense than the stuff you were handing me about a cure. Look, there's a limiting velocity for radio transmission, right? If they're controlling flunkeys from eighty light-years away, it'll take eighty years for any command to reach its destination. Every twitch of a muscle, every trifling movement—"

"They can leave their home world," said Rawlins.

"But if they're so big—"

"They've used their slave beings to build gravity tanks. They also have a star drive. All their colonies are run by overseers in orbit a few thousand kilometers up, floating in a simulated home-world environment. It takes one overseer to run one planet. I suppose they rotate tours of duty."

Muller closed his eyes a moment. The image came to him of these colossal, unimaginable beasts spreading through their distant galaxy, impressing animals of all sorts into service, forging a captive society, vicariously technological, and drifting in orbit like spaceborne whales to direct and coordinate the grandiose improbable enterprise while themselves remaining incapable of the smallest physical act. Monstrous masses of glossy pink protoplasm, fresh from the sea, bristling with perceptors functioning at both ends of the spectrum. Whispering to one another in pulses of X-rays. Sending out orders via radio. No, he thought. No.

"Well," he said at length, "what of it? They're in another galaxy."

"Not any longer. They've impinged on a few of our outlying colonies. Do you know what they do when they find a human world? They station an orbiting overseer above it and take control of the colonists. They find that humans make outstanding slaves, which isn't very surprising. At the moment they have six of our worlds. They had a seventh, but we shot up their overseer. Now they make it much harder to do that. They just take control of our missiles as they home in, and throw them back."

"If you're inventing this," said Muller, "I'll kill you!"

"It's true. I swear."

"When did this begin?"

"Within the past year."

"And what happens? Do they just march right through our galaxy and turn us all into zombies?"

"Boardman thinks we have one chance to prevent that."

"Which is?"

Rawlins said, "The aliens don't appear to realize that we're intelligent beings. We can't communicate with them, you see. They function on a completely nonverbal level, some kind of telepathic system. We've tried all sorts of ways to reach them, bombarding them with messages at every wavelength, without any flicker of a sign that they're receiving us. Boardman believes that if we could persuade them that we have— well, souls—they might leave us alone. God knows why he thinks so. It's some kind of computer prediction. He feels that these aliens work on a consistent moral scheme, that they're willing to grab any animals which look useful, but that they wouldn't touch a species that's on the same side of the intelligence boundary as they are. And if we could show them somehow—"

"They see that we have cities. That we have a star drive. Doesn't that prove intelligence?"

"Beavers make dams," said Rawlins. "But we don't make treaties with beavers. We don't pay reparations when we drain their marshes. We know that in some way a beaver's feelings don't count."

"Do we? Or have we simply decided arbitrarily that beavers are expendable? And what's this talk of an intelligence boundary? There's a continuous spectrum of intelligence, from the protozoa up through the primates. We're a little smarter than the chimps, sure, but is it a *qualitative* difference? Does the mere fact that we can record our knowledge and use it again make that much of a change?"

"I don't want to argue philosophy with you," Rawlins said hoarsely. "I'm trying to tell you what the situation is—and how it affects you."

"Yes. How it affects me."

"Boardman thinks that we really can get the radio beasts to leave our galaxy alone if we show them that we're closer to them in intelligence than we are to their other slaves. If we get across to them that we have emotions, needs, ambitions, dreams."

Muller spat. "Hath not a Jew eyes? Hath not a Jew hands, organs, dimensions, senses, affections, passions? If you prick us, do we not bleed?"

"Like that, yes."

"How do we get this across to them if they don't speak a verbal language?"

"Don't you see?" Rawlins asked.

"No, I—*yes*. Yes. God, yes!"

"We have one man, out of all our billions, who doesn't need words to communicate. He broadcasts his inner feelings. His soul. We don't know what frequency he uses, but *they* might."

"Yes. Yes."

"And so Boardman wanted to ask you to do one more thing for mankind. To go to these aliens. To allow them to pick up your broadcast. To show them what we are, that we're something more than beasts."

"Why the talk of taking me to Earth to be cured, then?"

"A trick. A trap. We had to get you out of the maze somehow. Once you were out, we could tell you the story and ask you to help."

"Admitting that there was no cure?"

"Yes."

"What makes you think I would lift a finger to keep all of man's worlds from being swallowed up?"

"Your help wouldn't have to be voluntary," Rawlins said.

7

Now it came flooding forth, the hatred, the anguish, the fear, the jealousy, the torment, the bitterness, the mockery, the loathing, the contempt, the despair, the viciousness, the fury, the desperation, the vehemence, the agitation, the grief, the pangs, the agony, the furor, the fire. Rawlins pulled back as though singed. Now Muller cruised the depths of desolation. A trick, a trick, all a trick! Used again. Boardman's tool. Muller blazed. He spoke only a few words aloud; the rest came from within, pouring out, the gates wide, nothing penned back, a torrent of anger.

When the wild spasm passed Muller said, standing braced between two jutting façades, "Boardman would dump me onto the aliens whether I was willing to go or not?"

"Yes. He said this was too important to allow you free choice. Your wishes are irrelevant. The many against the one."

With deadly calm Muller said, "You're part of this conspiracy. Why have you been telling me all this?"

"I resigned."

"Of course."

"No, I mean it. Oh, I was part of it. I was going along with Boardman, yes, I was lying in everything I said to you. But I didn't know the last part—that you wouldn't be given any choice. I had to pull out there. I couldn't let them do this to you. I had to tell you the truth."

"Very thoughtful. I now have two options, eh, Ned? I can let myself be dragged out of here to play catspaw for Boardman again—or I can kill myself a minute from now and let mankind go to hell. Yes?"

"Don't talk like that," Rawlins said edgily.

"Why not? Those are my options. You were kind enough to tell me the real situation, and now I can react as I choose. You've handed me a death sentence, Ned."

"No."

"What else is there? Let myself be used again?"

"You could—cooperate with Boardman," Rawlins said. He licked his lips. "I know it sounds crazy. But you could show him what you're made of. Forget all this bitterness. Turn the other cheek. Remember that Boardman isn't all of humanity. There are billions of innocent people—"

"Father, forgive them, for they know not what they do."

"Yes!"

"Every one of those billions would run from me if I came near."

"What of it? They can't help that! But they're your own people!"

"And I'm one of theirs. They didn't think of that when they cast me out."

"You aren't being rational."

"No I'm not. And I don't intend to start now. Assuming that it could affect humanity's destiny in the slightest if I became ambassador to these radio people—and I don't buy that idea at all—it would give me great pleasure to shirk my duty. I'm grateful to you for your warning. Now that at last I know what's going on here, I have the excuse I've been looking for all along. I know a thousand places here where death is quick and probably not painful. Then let Charles Boardman talk to the aliens himself. I—"

"Please don't move, Dick," said Boardman from a point about thirty meters behind him.

12.

Boardman found all this distasteful. But it was also necessary, and he was not surprised that events had taken this turn. In his original analysis he had forecast two events of equal probability: that Rawlins would succeed in winning Muller out of the maze, and that Rawlins would ultimately rebel and blurt out the truth. He was prepared for either.

Now Boardman had advanced into the center of the maze, coming from Zone F to follow Rawlins before the damage became irreparable. He could predict one of Muller's likely responses: suicide. Muller would never commit suicide out of despair, but he might do it by way of vengeance. With Boardman were Ottavio, Davis, Reynolds, and Greenfield. Hosteen and the others were monitoring from outer zones. All were armed.

Muller turned. The look on his face was not easy to behold.

"I'm sorry, Dick," Boardman said. "We had to do this."

"You have no shame at all, do you?" Muller asked.

"Not where Earth is concerned."

"I realized that a long time ago. But I thought you were human, Charles. I didn't comprehend your depths."

"I wish we didn't have to do any of this, Dick. But we do. Come with us."

"No."

"You can't refuse. The boy's told you what's at stake. We already owe you more than we can ever repay, Dick, but run the debt a little higher. Please."

"I'm not leaving Lemnos. I feel no sense of obligation to humanity. I won't do your work."

"Dick—"

Muller said, "Fifty meters to the northwest of where I stand is a flame pit. I'm going to walk over and step into it. Within ten seconds there will be no more Richard Muller. One unfortunate calamity will cancel out another, and Earth will be no worse off than it was before I acquired my special ability. Since you people didn't appreciate that ability before, I can't see any reason for letting you make use of it now."

"If you want to kill yourself," Boardman said, "why not wait a few months?"

"Because I don't care to be of service."

"That's childish. The last sin I'd ever imagine *you* committing."

"It was childish of me to dream of stars," Muller said. "I'm simply being consistent. The galactics can eat you alive, Charles. I don't care if they do. Won't you fancy being a slave? Somewhere under your skull you'll still be there, screaming to be released, and the radio messages will tell you which arm to lift, which leg to move. I wish I could last long enough to see that. But I'm going to walk into that flame pit. Do you want to wish me a good journey? Come close, let me touch your arm. Get a good dose of me first. Your last. I'll cease to give offense." Muller was trembling. His face was sweaty. His upper lip quivered.

Boardman said, "At least come out to Zone F with me. Let's sit down quietly and discuss this over brandy."

"Side by side?" Muller laughed. "You'd vomit. You couldn't bear it."

"I'm willing to talk."

"I'm not," Muller said. He took a shaky step toward the northwest. His big powerful body seemed shrunken and withered, nothing but sinews stretching tighter over a yielding armature. He took another step. Boardman watched. Ottavio and Davis stood beside him to the left; Reynolds and Greenfield on the other side, between Muller and the flame pit. Rawlins, like an afterthought, was alone at the far side of the group.

Boardman felt a throbbing in his larynx, a stirring and a tickle of tension in his loins. A great weariness possessed him, and at the same time a fierce soaring excitement of a kind he had not known since he had been a young man. He allowed Muller to take a third step toward self-destruction. Then, casually, Boardman gestured with two flicking fingers.

Greenfield and Reynolds pounced.

Catlike they darted forth, ready for this, and caught Muller by the inner forearms. Boardman saw the grayness sweep over their faces as the impact of Muller's field got to them. Muller struggled, heaved, tried to break loose. Davis and Ottavio were upon him now too. In the gathering darkness the group formed a surging Laocoon, Muller only half visible as the smaller men coiled and wound about his flexed battling body. A stungun would have been easier, Boardman reflected. But stunguns were risky, sometimes, on humans. Stunguns had been known to send hearts into wild runaways. They had no defibrillator here.

A moment more, and Muller was forced to his knees.

"Disarm him," Boardman said.

Ottavio and Davis held him. Reynolds and Greenfield searched him. From a pocket Greenfield pulled forth the deadly little windowed globe. "That's all he seems to be carrying," Greenfield said.

"Check carefully."

They checked. Meanwhile Muller remained motionless, his face frozen, his eyes stony. It was the posture and the expression of a man at the headsman's block. At length Greenfield looked up again. "Nothing," he said.

Muller said, "One of my left upper molars contains a secret compartment full of carniphage. I'll count to ten and bite hard, and I'll melt away before your eyes."

Greenfield swung around and grabbed for Muller's jaws.

Boardman said, "Leave him alone. He's joking."

"But how do we know—" Greenfield began.

"Let him be. Step back." Boardman gestured. "Stand five meters away from him. Don't go near him unless he moves."

They stepped away, obviously grateful to get back from the full thrust of Muller's field. Boardman, fifteen meters from him, could feel faint strands of pain. He went no closer.

"You can stand up now," Boardman said. "But please don't try to move. I regret this, Dick."

Muller got to his feet. His face was black with hatred. But he said nothing, nor did he move.

"If we have to," Boardman said, "we'll tape you in a webfoam cradle and carry you out of the maze to the ship. We'll keep you in foam from then on. You'll be in foam when you meet the aliens. You'll be absolutely helpless. I would hate to do that to you, Dick. The other choice is willing cooperation. Go with us of your own free will to the ship. Do what we ask of you. Help us this last time."

"May your intestines rust," said Muller almost casually. "May you live a thousand years with worms eating you. May you choke on your own smugness and never die."

"Help us. Willingly."

"Put me in the webfoam, Charles. Otherwise I'll kill myself the first chance I get."

"What a villain I must seem, eh?" Boardman said. "But I don't want to do it this way. Come willingly, Dick."

Muller's reply was close to a snarl.

Boardman sighed. This was an embarrassment. He looked toward Ottavio.

"The webfoam," he said.

Rawlins, who had been standing as though in a trance, burst into sudden activity. He darted forward, seized Reynolds' gun from its holster, ran toward Muller and pressed the weapon into his hand. "There," he said thickly. "Now you're in charge!"

2

Muller studied the gun as though he had never seen one before, but his surprise lasted only a fraction of a second. He slipped his hand around its comfortable butt and fingered the firing stud. It was a familiar model, only slightly changed from those he had known. In a quick flaring burst he could kill them all. Or himself. He stepped back so they could not come upon him from the rear. Probing with his kickstaff, he checked the wall, found it trustworthy, and planted his shoulderblades against it. Then he moved the gun in an arc of some 270°, taking them all in.

"Stand close together," he said. "The six of you. Stand one meter apart in a straight row, and keep your hands out where I can see them at all times."

He enjoyed the black, glowering look that Boardman threw at Ned Rawlins. The boy seemed dazed, flushed, confused, a figure in a dream. Muller waited patiently as the six men arranged themselves according to his orders. He was surprised at his own calmness.

"You look unhappy, Charles," he said. "How old are you now, eighty years? You'd like to live that other seventy, eighty, ninety, I guess. You have your career planned, and the plan doesn't include dying on Lemnos. Stand still, Charles. And stand straight. You won't win any pity from me by trying to look old and sagging. I know that dodge. You're as healthy as I am, beneath the phony flab. Healthier. Straight, Charles!"

Boardman said raggedly, "If it'll make you feel better, Dick, kill me. And then go aboard the ship and do what we want you to do. I'm expendable."

"Do you mean that?"

"Yes."

"I almost think you do," Muller said wonderingly. "You crafty old bastard, you're offering a trade! Your life for my cooperation! But where's the *quid pro quo?* I don't enjoy killing. It won't soothe me at all to burn you down. I'll still have my curse."

"The offer stands."

"Rejected," Muller said. "If I kill you, it won't be as part of any deal. But I'm much more likely to kill myself. You know, I'm a decent man at heart. Somewhat unstable, yes, and who's to blame me for that? But decent. I'd rather use this gun on me than on you. I'm the one who's suffering. I can end it."

"You could have ended it at any time in the past nine years," Boardman pointed out. "But you survived. You devoted all your ingenuity to staying alive in this murderous place."

"Ah. Yes. But that was different! An abstract challenge, man against the maze. A test of my skills. Ingenuity. But if I kill myself now, I thwart you. I put the thumb to the nose, with all of mankind watching. I'm the indispensable man, you say? What better way then, to pay mankind back for my pain?"

"We regretted your suffering," said Boardman.

"I'm sure you wept bitterly for me. But that was all you did. You let me go creeping away, diseased, corrupt, unclean. Now comes the release. Not really suicide, but revenge." Muller smiled. He turned the gun to finest beam and let its muzzle rest against his chest. A touch of the finger, now. His eyes raked their faces. The four soldiers did not seem to care. Rawlins appeared deep in shock. Only Boardman was animated with concern and fright. "I could kill you first, I suppose, Charles. As a lesson to our young friend—the wages of deceit is death. But no. That would spoil everything. You have to live, Charles. To go back to Earth and admit that you let the indispensable man slip through your grasp. What a blotch on your career! To fail your most important assignment! Yes. Yes. My pleasure. Falling dead here, leaving you to pick up the pieces."

His finger tightened on the stud.

"Now," he said. "Quickly."

"No!" Boardman screamed. "For the love of—"

"Man," said Muller, and laughed, and did not fire. His arm relaxed. He tossed the weapon contemptuously toward Boardman. It landed almost at his feet.

"Foam!" Boardman cried. "Quick!"

"Don't bother," said Muller. "I'm yours."

3

Rawlins took a long while to understand it. First they had the problem of getting out of the maze. Even with Muller as their leader, it was a taxing job. As they had suspected, coming upon the traps from the inner side was not the same as working through them from without. Warily Muller took them through Zone E; they could manage F well enough by now; and after they had dismantled their camp, they pressed on into G. Rawlins kept expecting Muller to bolt suddenly and hurl himself into some fearful snare. But he seemed as eager to come alive out of the maze as any of them. Boardman, oddly, appeared to recognize that. Though he watched Muller closely, he left him unconfined.

Feeling that he was in disgrace, Rawlins kept away from the others on the nearly silent outward march. He considered his career in ruins. He had jeopardized the lives of his companions and the success of the mission. Yet it had been worth it, he felt. A time comes when a man takes his stand against what he believes to be wrong.

The simple moral pleasure that he took in that was balanced and overbalanced by the knowledge that he had acted naively, romantically, foolishly. He could not bear to face Boardman now. He thought more than once of letting one of the deadly traps of these outer zones have him; but that too, he decided, would be naive, romantic, and foolish.

He watched Muller striding ahead—tall, proud, all tensions resolved, all doubts crystallized. And he wondered a thousand times why Muller had given back the gun.

Boardman finally explained it to him when they camped for the night in a precarious plaza near the outward side of Zone G.

"Look at me," Boardman said. "What's the matter? Why can't you look at me?"

"Don't toy with me, Charles. Get it over with."

"Get what over with?"

"The tonguelashing. The sentence."

"It's all right, Ned. You helped us get what we wanted. Why should I be angry?"

"But the gun—I gave him the gun—"

"Confusion of ends and means again. He's coming with us. He's doing what we wanted him to do. That's what counts."

Floundering, Rawlins asked, "And if he had killed himself—or us?"

"He wouldn't have done either."

"You can say that, now. But for the first moment, when he held the gun—"

"No," Boardman said. "I told you earlier, we'd work on his sense of honor. Which we had to reawaken. You did that. Look, here I am, the brutal agent of a brutal and amoral society, right? And I confirm all of Muller's worst thoughts about mankind. Why should he help a tribe of wolves? And here you are, young and innocent, full of hope and dreams. You remind him of the mankind he once served, before the cynicism corroded him. In your blundering way you try to be moral in a world that shows no trace of morality or meaning. You demonstrate sympathy, love for a fellow man, the willingness to make a dramatic gesture for the sake of righteousness. You show Muller that there's still hope in humanity. See? You defy me, and give him a gun and make him master of the situation. He could do the obvious, and burn us down. He could do the slightly less obvious, and burn himself. Or he could match your gesture with one of his own, top it, commit a deliberate act of renunciation, express his revived sense of moral superiority. He does it. He tosses away the gun. You were vital, Ned. You were the instrument through which we won him."

"You make it sound so ugly when you spell it out that way, Charles. As if you had planned even this. Pushing me so far that I'd give him the gun, knowing that he—"

Boardman smiled.

"Did you?" Rawlins demanded suddenly. "No. You couldn't have calculated all those twists and turns. Now, after the fact, you're trying to claim credit for having engineered it all. But I saw you in the moment I handed him the gun. There was fear on your face, and anger. You weren't at all sure what he was going to do. Only when everything worked out could you claim it went according to plan. I see through you, Charles!"

"How delightful to be transparent," Boardman said gaily.

4

The maze seemed uninterested in holding them. Carefully they traced their outward path, but they met few challenges and no serious dangers. Quickly they went toward the ship.

They gave Muller a forward cabin, well apart from the quarters of the crew. He seemed to accept that as a necessity of his condition, and showed no offense. He was withdrawn, subdued, self-contained; an ironic smile often played on his lips, and much of the time his eyes displayed a glint of contempt. But he was willing to do as they directed. He had had his moment of supremacy; now he was theirs.

Hosteen and his men bustled through the liftoff preparations. Muller remained in his cabin. Boardman went to him, alone, unarmed. He could make noble gestures too.

They faced each other across a low table. Muller waited, silent, his face cleansed of emotion. Boardman said after a long moment, "I'm grateful to you, Dick."

"Save it."

"I don't mind if you despise me. I did what I had to do. So did the boy. And now so will you. You couldn't forget that you were an Earthman, after all."

"I wish I could."

"Don't say that. It's easy, glib, cheap bitterness, Dick. We're both too old for glibness. The universe is a perilous place. We do our best. Everything else is unimportant."

He sat quite close to Muller. The emanation hit him broadside, but he deliberately remained in place. That wave of despair welling out to him made him feel a thousand years old. The decay of the body, the crumbling of the soul, the heat-death of the galaxy . . . the coming of winter . . . emptiness . . . ashes. . . .

"When we reach Earth," said Boardman crisply, "I'll put you through a detailed briefing. You'll come out of it knowing as much about the radio people as we do, which isn't saying a great deal. After that you'll be on your own. But I'm sure you'll realize, Dick, that the hearts and souls of billions of Earthmen will be praying for your success and safety."

"Who's being glib now?" Muller asked.

"Is there anyone you'd like me to have waiting for you when we dock Earthside?"

"No."

"I can send word ahead. There are people who've never stopped loving you, Dick. They'll be there if I ask them."

Muller said slowly, "I see the strain in your eyes, Charles. You feel the nearness of me, and it's ripping you apart. You feel it in your gut. In your forehead. Back of your breastbone. Your face is going gray. Your cheeks are sagging. You'll sit here if it kills you, yes, because that's your style. But it's hell for you. If there's anyone on Earth who never stopped loving me, Charles, the least I can do is spare her from hell. I don't want to meet anyone. I don't want to see anyone. I don't want to talk to anyone."

"As you wish," said Boardman. Beads of sweat hung from his bushy brows and dropped to his cheeks. "Perhaps you'll change your mind when you're close to Earth."

"I'll never be close to Earth again," Muller said.

13.

He spent three weeks absorbing all that was known of the giant extragalactic beings. At his insistence he did not set foot on Earth during that time, nor was his return from Lemnos made known to the public. They gave him quarters in a bunker on Luna and he lived quietly beneath Copernicus, moving like a robot through steely gray corridors lit by warm glowing torches. They showed him all the cubes. They ran off a variety of reconstructs in every sensory mode. Muller listened. He absorbed. He said very little.

They kept well away from him, as they had on the voyage from Lemnos. Whole days passed in which he saw no human being. When they came to him they remained at a distance of ten meters and more.

He did not object.

The exception was Boardman, who visited him three times a week and made a point always of coming well within the pain range. Muller found that contemptible. Boardman seemed to be patronizing him with this voluntary and wholly unnecessary submission to discomfort. "I wish you'd keep away," Muller told him on the fifth visit. "We can talk by screen. Or you could stay by the door."

"I don't mind the close contact."

"I do," said Muller. "Has it ever occurred to you that I've begun to find mankind as odious as mankind finds me? The reek of your meaty body, Charles—it goes into my nostrils like a spike. Not just you; all the others too. Sickening. Hideous. Even the look of your faces. The pores. The stupid gaping mouths. The ears. Look at a human ear closely some time, Charles. Have you ever seen anything more repulsive than that pink wrinkled cup? You all disgust me!"

"I'm sorry you feel that way," Boardman said.

The briefing went on and on. Muller was ready after the first week to undertake his assignment, but no, first they had to feed him all the data in the bank. He absorbed the information with twitchy impatience. A shadow of his old self remained to find it fascinating, a challenge worth accepting. He would go. He would serve as before. He would honor his obligation.

At last they said he could depart.

From Luna they took him by iondrive to a point outside the orbit of Mars, where they transferred him to a warp-drive ship already programmed to kick him to the edge of the galaxy. Alone. He would not, on this voyage, have to take care not to distress the crew by his presence. There were several reasons for this, the most important being that the mission was officially considered close to suicidal; and, since a ship could make the voyage without the use of a crew, it would have been rash to risk lives—other than his, of course. But he was a volunteer. Besides, Muller had requested a solo flight.

He did not see Boardman during the five days prior to his departure, nor had he seen Ned Rawlins at all since their return from Lemnos. Muller did not regret the absence of Boardman, but he sometimes wished he could have another hour with Rawlins. There was promise in that boy. Behind all the confusion and the foggy innocence, Muller thought, lay the seeds of manhood.

From the cabin of his small sleek ship he watched the technicians drifting in space, getting ready to sever the transfer line. Then they were returning to their own ship. Now he heard from Boardman, a final message, a Boardman special, inspirational, go forth and do your duty for mankind, et cetera, et cetera. Muller thanked him graciously for his words.

The communications channel was cut.

Moments later Muller entered warp.

2

The aliens had taken possession of three solar systems on the fringes of the galactic lens, each star having two Earth-settled planets. Muller's ship was aimed at a greenish-gold star whose worlds had been colonized only forty years before. The fifth planet, dry as iron, belonged to a Central Asian colonization society which was trying to establish a series of pastoral cultures where nomad virtues could be practiced. The sixth, with a more typically Earthlike mixture of climates and environments, was occupied by representatives of half a dozen colonization societies, each on its own continent. The relations between these groups, often intricate and touchy, had ceased to matter within the past twelve months, for both planets now were under control of extragalactic overseers.

Muller emerged from warp twenty light-seconds from the sixth planet. His ship automatically went into an observation orbit, and the scanners began to report. Screens showed him the surface picture; via template overlay he was able to compare the configurations of the outposts below with the pattern as it had been prior to alien conquest. The amplified images were quite interesting. The original settlements appeared on his screen in violet, and the recent extensions in red. Muller observed that about each of the colonies, regardless of its original ground plan, there had sprouted a network of angular streets and jagged avenues. Instinctively he recognized the geometries as alien. There sprang to mind the vivid memory of the maze; and though the patterns here bore no resemblance to those of the maze, they were alike in their lack of recognizable symmetries. He rejected the possibility that the labyrinth of Lemnos had been built long ago by direction of the radio beings. What he saw here was only the similarity of total difference. Aliens built in alien ways.

In orbit, seven thousand kilometers above the sixth planet, was a glistening capsule, slightly longer on one axis than on the other, which had about the mass of a large interstellar transport ship. Muller found a similar capsule in orbit about the fifth world. The overseers.

It was impossible for him to open communications with either of these capsules or with the planets beyond. All channels were blocked. He twisted dials fitfully for more than an hour, ignoring the irritable responses of the ship's brain which kept telling him to give up the idea. At last he conceded.

He brought his ship close to the nearer orbiting capsule. To his surprise the ship remained under his control. Destructive missiles that had come this close to alien overseers had been commandeered, but he was able to navigate. A hopeful sign? Was he under scan, and was the alien able to distinguish him from a hostile weapon? Or was he being ignored?

At a distance of one million kilometers he matched velocities with the alien satellite and put his ship in a parking orbit around it. He entered his drop-capsule. He ejected himself and slid from his ship into darkness.

3

Now the alien seized him. There was no doubt. The drop-capsule was programmed for a minimum-expenditure orbit that would bring it skimming past the alien in due time, but Muller swiftly discovered that he was deviating from that orbit. Deviations are never accidental. His capsule was accelerating beyond the program, which meant that it had been grasped and was being drawn forward. He accepted that. He was icily calm, expecting nothing and prepared for everything. The drop-capsule eased down. He saw the gleaming bulk of the alien satellite now.

Skin to metal skin, the vehicles met and touched and joined.

A hatch slid open.

He drifted within.

His capsule came to rest on a board platform in an immense cavernous room hundreds of meters long, high, and broad. Fully suited, Muller stepped from it. He activated his gravity pads; for, as he had anticipated, gravity in here was so close to null that the pull was imperceptible. In the blackness he saw only a faint purplish glow. Against a backdrop of utter silence he heard a resonant booming sound, like an enormously amplified sigh, shuddering through the struts and trusses of the satellite. Despite his gravity pads he felt dizzy; beneath him the floor rolled. Through his mind went a sensation like the throbbing of the sea; great waves slammed against ragged beaches; a mass of water stirred and groaned in its global cavity; the world shivered beneath the burden. Muller felt a chill that his suit could not counteract. An irresistible force drew him. Hesitantly he moved, relieved and surprised to see that his limbs still obeyed his commands though he was not entirely their master. The awareness of something vast nearby, something heaving and pulsating and sighing, remained with him.

He walked down a night-drowned boulevard. He came to a low railing—a dull red line against the deep darkness—and pressed his leg against it, keeping contact with it as he moved forward. At one point he slipped and as he hit the railing with his elbow he heard the clang of metal traveling through the entire structure. Blurred echoes drifted back to him. As though walking the maze he passed through corridors and hatches, across interlocking compartments, over bridges that spanned dark abysses, down sloping ramplike debouchments into lofty chambers whose ceilings were dimly visible. Here he moved in blind confidence, fearing nothing. He could barely see. He had no vision of the total structure of this satellite. He could scarcely imagine the purpose of these inner partitions.

From that hidden giant presence came silent waves, an ever-intensifying pressure. He trembled in its grip. Still he moved on, until now he was in some central gallery, and by a thin blue glow he was able to discern levels dwindling below him, and far beneath his balcony a broad tank, and within the tank something sparkling, something huge.

"Here I am," he said. "Richard Muller. Earthman."

He gripped the railing and peered downward, expecting anything. Did the great beast stir and shift? Did it grunt? Did it call to him in a language he understood? He heard nothing. But he felt a great deal: slowly, subtly, he became aware of a contact, of a mingling, of an engulfment.

He felt his soul escaping through his pores.

The drain was unrelenting. Yet Muller chose not to resist; he yielded, he welcomed, he gave freely. Down in the pit the monster tapped his spirit, opened petcocks of neural energy, drew forth from him, demanded more, drew that too.

"Go on," Muller said, and the echoes of his voice danced around him, chiming, reverberating. "Drink! What's it like? A bitter brew, eh? Drink! Drink!" His knees buckled, and he sagged forward, and he pressed his forehead to the cold railing as his last reservoirs were plumbed.

He surrendered himself gladly, in glittering droplets. He gave up first love and first disappointment, April rain, fever and ache. Pride and hope, warmth and cold, sweet and sour. The scent of sweat and the touch of flesh, the thunder of music, the music of thunder, silken hair knotted between his fingers, lines scratched in spongy soil. Snorting stallions; glittering schools of tiny fish; the towers of Newer Chicago; the brothels of Under New Orleans. Snow. Milk. Wine. Hunger. Fire. Pain. Sleep. Sorrow. Apples. Dawn. Tears. Bach. Sizzling grease. The laughter of old men. The sun on the horizon, the moon on the sea, the light of other stars, the fumes of rocket fuel, summer flowers on a glacier's flank. Father. Mother. Jesus. Mornings. Sadness. Joy. He gave it all, and much more, and he waited for an answer. None came to him. And when he was wholly empty he lay face downward, drained, hollow, staring blindly into the abyss.

4

When he was able to leave, he left. The hatch opened to pass his drop-capsule, and it rose toward his ship. Shortly he was in warp. He slept most of the way. In the vicinity of Antares he cut in the override, took command of the ship, and filed for a change of course. There was no need to return to Earth. The monitor station recorded his request, checked routinely to see that the channel was clear, and allowed him to proceed at once to Lemnos. Muller entered warp again instantly.

When he emerged, not far from Lemnos, he found another ship already in orbit and waiting for him. He started to go about his business anyway, but the other ship insisted on making contact. Muller accepted the communication.

"This is Ned Rawlins," a strangely quiet voice said. "Why have you changed your flight plan?"

"Does it matter? I've done my job."

"You haven't filed a report."

"I'm reporting now, then. I visited the alien. We had a pleasant, friendly chat. Then it let me go home. Now I'm almost home. I don't know what effect my visit will have on the future of human history. End of report."

"What are you going to do now?"

"Go home, I said. This is home."

"Lemnos?"

"Lemnos."

"Dick, let me come aboard. Give me ten minutes with you—in person. Please don't say no."

"I don't say no," Muller replied.

Soon a small craft detached itself from the other ship and matched velocities with his. Patiently, Muller allowed the rendezvous to take place. Rawlins stepped into his ship and shed his helmet. He looked pale, drawn, older. His eyes held a different expression. They faced one another for a long silent moment. Rawlins advanced and took Muller's wrist in greeting.

"I never thought I'd see you again, Dick," he began. "And I wanted to tell you—"

He stopped abruptly.

"Yes?" Muller asked.

"I don't feel it," said Rawlins. *"I don't feel it!"*

"What?"

"You. Your field. Look, I'm right next to you. I don't feel a thing. All that nastiness, the pain, the despair—it isn't coming through!"

"The alien drank it all," said Muller calmly. "I'm not surprised. My soul left my body. Not all of it was put back."

"What are you talking about?"

"I could feel it soaking up everything that was within me. I knew it was changing me. Not deliberately. It was just an incidental alteration. A byproduct."

Rawlins said slowly, "You knew it, then. Even before I came on board."

"This confirms it, though."

"And yet you want to return to the maze. Why?"

"It's home."

"Earth's your home, Dick. There's no reason why you shouldn't go back. You've been cured."

"Yes," said Muller. "A happy ending to my doleful story. I'm fit to consort with humanity again. My reward for nobly risking my life a second time among aliens. How neatly done! But is humanity fit to consort with me?"

"Don't go down there, Dick. You're being irrational now. Charles sent me to get you. He's terribly proud of you. We all are. It would be a big mistake to lock yourself away in the maze now."

"Go back to your own ship, Ned," Muller said.

"If you go into the maze, so will I."

"I'll kill you if you do. I want to be left alone, Ned, do you understand that? I've done my job. My last job. Now I retire, purged of my nightmares." Muller forced a thin smile. "Don't come after me, Ned. I trusted you, and you would have betrayed me. Everything else is incidental. Leave my ship now. We've said all that we need to say to each other, I think, except goodbye."

"Dick—"

"Goodbye, Ned. Remember me to Charles. And to all the others."

"Don't do this!"

"There's something down there I don't want to lose," Muller said. "I'm going to claim it now. Stay away. All of you. Stay away. I've learned the truth about Earthmen. Will you go now?"

Silently Rawlins suited up. He moved toward the hatch. As he stepped through it, Muller said, "Say goodbye to all of them for me, Ned. I'm glad you were the last one I saw. Somehow it was easier that way."

Rawlins vanished through the hatch.

A short while later Muller programmed his ship for a hyperbolic orbit on a twenty-minute delay, got into his drop-capsule, and readied himself for the descent to Lemnos. It was a quick drop and a good landing. He came down right in the impact area, two kilometers from the gateway to the maze. The sun was high and bright. Muller walked briskly toward the maze.

He had done what they wanted him to do.

Now he was going home.

5

"He's still making gestures," Boardman said. "He'll come out of there."

"I don't think so," replied Rawlins. "He meant that."

"You stood next to him, and you felt nothing?"

"Nothing. He doesn't have it any more."

"Which he realizes?"

"Yes."

"He'll come out, then," Boardman said. "We'll watch him, and when he asks to be taken off Lemnos, we'll take him off. Sooner or later he'll need other people again. He's been through so much that he needs to think everything through, and I guess he sees the maze as the best place for that. He isn't ready to plunge back into normal life again. Give him two years, three, four. He'll come out. The two sets of aliens have cancelled each other's work on him, and he's fit to rejoin society."

"I don't think so," Rawlins said quietly. "I don't think it cancelled out so evenly. Charles, I don't think he's human at all—any more."

Boardman laughed. "Shall we bet? I'll offer five to one that Muller comes out of the maze voluntarily within five years."

"Well—"

"It's a bet, then."

Rawlins left the older man's office. Night had fallen. He crossed the bridge outside the building. In an hour he'd be dining with someone warm and soft and willing, who was awed beyond measure by her liaison with the famous Ned Rawlins. She was a good listener, who coaxed him for tales of daring deeds and nodded gravely as he spoke of the challenges ahead. She was also good in bed.

He paused on the bridge to look upward at the stars.

A million million blazing points of light shimmered in the sky. Out there lay Lemnos, and Beta Hydri IV, and the worlds occupied by the radio beings, and all man's dominion, and even, invisible but real, the home galaxy of the others. Out there lay a labyrinth in a broad plain, and a forest of spongy trees hundreds of meters high, and a thousand planets planted with the young cities of Earthmen, and a tank of strangeness orbiting a conquered world. In the tank lay something unbearably alien. On the thousand planets lived worried men fearing the future. Under the spongy trees walked graceful silent creatures with many arms. In the maze dwelled a . . . man.

Perhaps, Rawlins thought, I'll visit Muller in a year or two.

It was too early to tell how the patterns would form. No one yet knew how the radio people were reacting, if at all, to the things they had learned from Richard Muller. The role of the Hydrans, the efforts of men in their own defense, the coming forth of Muller from the maze, these were mysteries—shifting, variable. It was exciting and a little frightening to think that he would live through the time of testing that lay ahead.

He crossed the bridge. He watched starships shattering the darkness overhead. He stood motionless, feeling the pull of the stars. All the universe tugged at him, each star exerting its finite power. The glow of the heavens dazzled him. Beckoning pathways lay open. He thought of the man in the maze. He thought too of the girl, lithe and passionate, dark-eyed, her eyes mirrors of silver, her body awaiting him.

Suddenly he was Dick Muller, once also twenty-four years old, with the galaxy his for the asking. Was it any different for you, he wondered? What did you feel when you looked up at the stars? Where did it hit you? Here. Here. Just where it hits me. And you went out there. And found. And lost. And found something else. Do you remember, Dick, the way you once felt? Tonight in your windy maze, what will you think about? Will you remember?

Why did you turn away from us, Dick?

What have you become?

He hurried to the girl who waited for him. They sipped young wine, tart, electric. They smiled through a candle's flickering glow. Later her softness yielded to him, and still later they stood close together on a balcony looking out over the greatest of all man's cities. Lights stretched toward infinity, rising to meet those other lights above. He slipped his arm around her, put his hand on her bare flank, held her against him.

She said, "How long do you stay this time?"

"Four more days."

"And when will you come back?"

"When the job's done."

"Ned, will you ever rest? Will you ever say you've had enough, that you won't go out any longer, that you'll take one planet and stick to it?"

"Yes," he said vaguely. "I suppose. After a while."

"You don't mean it. You're just saying it. None of you ever settle down."

"We can't," he murmured. "We keep going. There are always more worlds . . . new suns. . . ."

"You want too much. You want the whole universe. It's a sin, Ned. You have to accept limits."

"Yes," he said. "You're right. I know you're right." His fingers traveled over satin-smooth flesh. She trembled. He said, "We do what we have to do. We try to learn from the mistakes of others. We serve our cause. We attempt to be honest with ourselves. How else can it be?"

"The man who went back into the maze—"

"—is happy," Rawlins said. "He's following his chosen course."

"How can that be?"

"I can't explain."

"He must hate us all terribly to turn his back on the whole universe like that."

"He's beyond hate," Rawlins said. "Somehow. He's at peace. Whatever he is."

"Whatever?"

"Yes," he said gently. He felt the midnight chill and led her inside. They stood by the bed. The candle was nearly out. He kissed her solemnly, and thought of Dick Muller again, and wondered what maze was waiting for him at the end of his own path. He drew her into his arms and felt the impress of hardening flesh against his own cool skin. They lowered themselves. His hands sought, grasped, caressed. Her breath grew ragged.

When I see you again, Dick, I have much to tell you, he thought.

She said, "Why did he lock himself into the maze again, Ned?"

"For the same reason that he went among aliens in the first place. For the reason that it all happened."

"And that reason was?"

"He loved mankind," Rawlins said. It was as good an epitaph as any. He held the girl tightly. But he left before dawn.

NIGHTWINGS

For Harlan,
to remind him of open windows,
the currents of the Delaware river,
quarters with two heads,
and other pitfalls.

PART ONE
NIGHTWINGS

1.

Roum is a city built on seven hills. They say it was a capital of man in one of the earlier cycles. I knew nothing of that, for my guild was Watching, not Remembering; but yet as I had my first glimpse of Roum, coming upon it from the south at twilight, I could see that in former days it must have been of great significance. Even now it was a mighty city of many thousands of souls.

Its bony towers stood out sharply against the dusk. Lights glimmered appealingly. On my left hand the sky was ablaze with splendor as the sun relinquished possession; streaming bands of azure and violet and crimson folded and writhed about one another in the nightly dance that brings the darkness. To my right, blackness had already come. I attempted to find the seven hills, and failed, and still I knew that this must be that Roum of majesty toward which all roads are bent, and I felt awe and deep respect for the works of our bygone fathers.

We rested by the long straight road, looking up at Roum. I said, "It is a goodly city. We will find employment there."

Beside me, Avluela fluttered her lacy wings. "And food?" she asked in her high, fluty voice. "And shelter? And wine?"

"Those too," I said. "All of those."

"How long have we been walking, Watcher?" she asked.

"Two days. Three nights."

"If I had been flying, it would have been more swift."

"For you," I said. "You would have left us far behind and never seen us again. Is that your desire?"

She came close to me and rubbed the rough fabric of my sleeve, and then she pressed herself at me the way a flirting cat might do. Her wings unfolded into two broad sheets of gossamer through which I could still see the sunset and the evening lights, blurred, distorted, magical. I sensed the fragrance of her midnight hair. I put my arms to her and embraced her slender, almost boyish body.

She said, "You know it is my desire to remain with you always, Watcher. Always!"

"Yes, Avluela."

"Will we be happy in Roum?"

"We will be happy," I said, and released her.

"Shall we go into Roum now?"

"I think we should wait for Gormon," I said, shaking my head. "He'll be back soon from his explorations." I did not want to tell her of my weariness. She was only a child, seventeen summers old; what did she know of weariness or of age? And I was old. Not as old as Roum, but old enough.

"While we wait," she said, "may I fly?"

"Fly, yes."

I squatted beside our cart and warmed my hands at the throbbing generator while Avluela prepared to fly. First she removed her garments, for her wings have little strength and she cannot lift such extra baggage. Lithely, deftly, she peeled the glassy bubbles from her tiny feet and wriggled free of her crimson jacket and of her soft, furry leggings. The vanishing light in the west sparkled over her slim form. Like all Fliers, she carried no surplus body tissue: her breasts were mere bumps, her buttocks flat, her thighs so spindly that there was a span of inches between them when she stood. Could she have weighed more than a quintal? I doubt it. Looking at her, I felt, as always, gross and earthbound, a thing of loathsome flesh, and yet I am not a heavy man.

By the roadside she genuflected, knuckles to the ground, head bowed to knees, as she murmured whatever ritual words it is that the Fliers say. Her back was to me. Her delicate wings fluttered, filled with life, rose about her like a cloak whipped up by the breeze. I could not comprehend how such wings could possibly lift even so slight a form as Avluela's. They were not hawk-wings but butterfly-wings, veined and transparent, marked here and there with blotches of pigment, ebony and turquoise and scarlet. A sturdy ligament joined them to the two flat pads of muscle beneath her sharp shoulderblades; but what she did not have was the massive breastbone of a flying creature, the bands of corded muscle needed for flight. Oh, I know that the Fliers use more than muscle to get aloft, that there are mystical disciplines in their mystery. Even so, I, who was of the Watchers, remained skeptical of the more fantastic guilds.

Avluela finished her words. She rose; she caught the breeze with her wings; she ascended several feet. There she remained, suspended between earth and sky, while her wings beat frantically. It was not yet night, and Avluela's wings were merely nightwings. By day she could not fly, for the terrible pressure of the solar wind would hurl her to the ground. Now, midway between dusk and dark, it was still not the best time for her to go up. I saw her being thrust toward the east by the remnant of light in the sky. Her arms as well as her wings thrashed; her small pointed face was grim with concentration; on her thin lips were the words of her guild. She doubled her body and shot it out, head going one way, rump the other; and abruptly she hovered horizontally, looking groundward, her wings thrashing against the air. *Up, Avluela! Up!*

Up it was, as by will alone she conquered the vestige of light that still glowed.

With pleasure I surveyed her naked form against the darkness. I could see her clearly, for a Watcher's eyes are keen. She was five times her own height in the air, now, and her wings were spread to their full expanse, so that the towers of Roum were in partial eclipse for me. She waved. I threw her a kiss and offered words of love. Watchers do not marry, nor do they engender children, but yet Avluela was as a daughter to me, and I took pride in her flight. We had traveled together a year, now, since we had first met in Agupt, and it was as though I had known her all my long life. From her I drew a renewal of strength. I do not know what it was she drew from me: security, knowledge, a continuity with the days before her birth. I hoped only that she loved me as I loved her.

Now she was far aloft. She wheeled, soared, dived, pirouetted, danced. Her long black hair streamed from her scalp. Her body seemed only an incidental appendage to those two great wings that glistened and throbbed and gleamed in the night. Up she rose, glorying in her freedom from gravity, making me feel all the more leaden-footed; and like some slender rocket she shot abruptly away in the direction of Roum. I saw the soles of her feet, the tips of her wings; then I saw her no more.

I sighed. I thrust my hands into the pits of my arms to keep them warm. How is it that I felt a winter chill while the girl Avluela could soar joyously bare through the sky?

It was now the twelfth of the twenty hours, and time once again for me to do the Watching. I went to the cart, opened my cases, prepared the instruments. Some of the dial covers were yellowed and faded; the indicator needles had lost their luminous coating; sea stains defaced the instrument housings, a relic of the time that pirates had assailed me in Earth Ocean. The worn and cracked levers and nodes responded easily to my touch as I entered the preliminaries. First one prays for a pure and perceptive mind; then one creates the affinity with one's instruments; then one does the actual Watching, searching the starry heavens for the enemies of man. Such was my skill and my craft. I grasped handles and knobs, thrust things from my mind, prepared myself to become an extension of my cabinet of devices.

I was only just past my threshold and into the first phase of Watchfulness when a deep and resonant voice behind me said, "Well, Watcher, how goes it?"

I sagged against the cart. One feels a physical pain at being wrenched so unexpectedly from one's work. For a moment I felt claws clutching at my heart. My face grew hot; my eyes would not focus; the saliva drained from my throat. As soon as I could, I took the proper protective measures to ease the metabolic drain, and severed myself from my instruments. Hiding my trembling as much as possible, I turned around.

Gormon, the other member of our little band, had appeared and stood jauntily beside me. He was grinning, amused at my distress, but I could not feel angry with him. One does not show anger at a guildless person no matter what the provocation.

Tightly, with effort, I said, "Did you spend your time rewardingly?"

"Very. Where's Avluela?"

I pointed heavenward. Gormon nodded.

"What have you found?" I asked.

"That this city is definitely Roum."

"There never was doubt of that."

"For me there was. But now I have proof."

"Yes?"

"In the overpocket. Look!"

From his tunic he drew his overpocket, set it on the pavement beside me, and expanded it so that he could insert his hands into its mouth. Grunting a little, he began to pull something heavy from the pouch— something of white stone—a long marble column, I now saw, fluted, pocked with age.

"From a temple of Imperial Roum!" Gormon exulted.

"You shouldn't have taken that."

"Wait!" he cried, and reached into the overpocket once more. He took from it a handful of circular metal plaques and scattered them jingling at my feet. "Coins! Money! Look at them, Watcher! The faces of the Caesars!"

"Of whom?"

"The ancient rulers. Don't you know your history of past cycles?"

I peered at him curiously. "You claim to have no guild, Gormon. Could it be you are a Rememberer and are concealing it from me?"

"Look at my face, Watcher. Could I belong to any guild? Would a Changeling be taken?"

"True enough," I said, eyeing the golden hue of him, the thick waxen skin, the red-pupiled eyes, the jagged mouth. Gormon had been weaned on teratogenetic drugs; he was a monster, handsome in his way, but a monster nevertheless, a Changeling, outside the laws and customs of man as they are practiced in the Third Cycle of civilization. And there is no guild of Changelings.

"There's more," Gormon said. The overpocket was infinitely capacious; the contents of a world, if need be, could be stuffed into its shriveled gray maw, and still it would be no longer than a man's hand. Gormon took from it bits of machinery, reading spools, an angular thing of brown metal that might have been an ancient tool, three squares of shining glass, five slips of paper—*paper!*—and a host of other relics of antiquity. "See?" he said. "A fruitful stroll, Watcher! And not just random booty. Everything recorded, everything labeled, stratum, estimated age, position when *in situ*. Here we have many thousands of years of Roum."

"Should you have taken these things?" I asked doubtfully.

"Why not? Who is to miss them? Who of this cycle cares for the past?"

"The Rememberers."

"They don't need solid objects to help them do their work."

"Why do you want these things, though?"

"The past interests me, Watcher. In my guildless way I have my scholarly pursuits. Is that wrong? May not even a monstrosity seek knowledge?"

"Certainly, certainly. Seek what you wish. Fulfill yourself in your own way. This is Roum. At dawn we enter. I hope to find employment here."

"You may have difficulties."

"How so?"

"There are many Watchers already in Roum, no doubt. There will be little need for your services."

"I'll seek the favor of the Prince of Roum," I said.

"The Prince of Roum is a hard and cold and cruel man."

"You know of him?"

Gormon shrugged. "Somewhat." He began to stuff his artifacts back in the overpocket. "Take your chances with him, Watcher. What other choice do you have?"

"None," I said, and Gormon laughed, and I did not.

He busied himself with his ransacked loot of the past. I found myself deeply depressed by his words. He seemed so sure of himself in an uncertain world, this guildless one, this mutated monster, this man of inhuman look; how could he be so cool, so casual? He lived without concern for calamity and mocked those who admitted to fear. Gormon had been traveling with us for nine days, now, since we had met him in the ancient city beneath the volcano to the south by the edge of the sea. I had not suggested that he join us; he had invited himself along, and at Avluela's bidding I accepted. The roads are dark and cold at this time of year, and dangerous beasts of many species abound, and an old man journeying with a girl might well consider taking with him a brawny one like Gormon. Yet there were times I wished he had not come with us, and this was one.

Slowly I walked back to my equipment.

Gormon said, as though first realizing it, "Did I interrupt you at your Watching?"

I said mildly, "You did."

"Sorry. Go and start again. I'll leave you in peace." And he gave me his dazzling lopsided smile, so full of charm that it took the curse off the easy arrogance of his words.

I touched the knobs, made contact with the nodes, monitored the dials. But I did not enter Watchfulness, for I remained aware of Gormon's presence and fearful that he would break into my concentration once again at a painful moment, despite his promise. At length I looked away from the apparatus. Gormon stood at the far side of the road, craning his neck for some sight of Avluela. The moment I turned to him he became aware of me.

"Something wrong, Watcher?"

"No. The moment's not propitious for my work. I'll wait."

"Tell me," he said. "When Earth's enemies really do come from the stars, will your machines let you know it?"

"I trust they will."

"And then?"

"Then I notify the Defenders."

"After which your life's work is over?"

"Perhaps," I said.

"Why a whole guild of you, though? Why not one master center where the Watch is kept? Why a bunch of itinerant Watchers drifting from place to place?"

"The more vectors of detection," I said, "the greater the chance of early awareness of the invasion."

"Then an individual Watcher might well turn his machines on and not see anything, with an invader already here."

"It could happen. And so we practice redundancy."

"You carry it to an extreme, I sometimes think." Gormon laughed. "Do you actually believe an invasion is coming?"

"I do," I said stiffly. "Else my life was a waste."

"And why should the star people want Earth? What do we have here besides the remnants of old empires? What would they do with miserable Roum? With Perris? With Jorslem? Rotting cities! Idiot princes! Come, Watcher, admit it: the invasion's a myth, and you go through meaningless motions four times a day. Eh?"

"It is my craft and my science to Watch. It is yours to jeer. Each of us to our speciality, Gormon."

"Forgive me," he said with mock humility. "Go, then, and Watch."

"I shall."

Angrily I turned back to my cabinet of instruments, determined now to ignore any interruption, no matter how brutal. The stars were out; I gazed at the glowing constellations, and automatically my mind registered the many worlds. Let us Watch, I thought. Let us keep our vigil despite the mockers.

I entered full Watchfulness.

I clung to the grips and permitted the surge of power to rush through me. I cast my mind to the heavens and searched for hostile entities. What ecstasy! What incredible splendor! I who had never left this small planet roved the black spaces of the void, glided from star to burning star, saw the planets spinning like tops. Faces stared back at me as I journeyed, some without eyes, some with many eyes, all the complexity of the many-peopled galaxy accessible to me. I spied out possible concentrations of inimicable force. I inspected drilling-grounds and military encampments. I sought, as I had sought four times daily for all my adult life, for the invaders who had been promised us, the conquerors who at the end of days were destined to seize our tattered world.

I found nothing, and when I came up from my trance, sweaty and drained, I saw Avluela descending.

Feather-light she landed. Gormon called to her, and she ran, bare, her little breasts quivering, and he enfolded her smallness in his powerful arms, and they embraced, not passionately but joyously. When he released her she turned to me.

"Roum," she gasped. *"Roum!"*

"You saw it?"

"Everything! Thousands of people! Lights! Boulevards! A market!

Broken buildings many cycles old! Oh, Watcher, how wonderful Roum is!"

"Your flight was a good one, then," I said.

"A miracle!"

"Tomorrow we go to dwell in Roum."

"No, Watcher, tonight, tonight!" She was girlishly eager, her face bright with excitement. "It's just a short journey more! Look, it's just over there!"

"We should rest first," I said. "We would not want to arrive weary in Roum."

"We can rest when we get there," Avluela answered. "Come! Pack everything! You've done your Watching, haven't you?"

"Yes. Yes."

"Then let's go. To Roum! To Roum!"

I looked in appeal at Gormon. Night had come; it was time to make camp, to have our few hours of sleep.

For once Gormon sided with me. He said to Avluela, "The Watcher's right. We can all use some rest. We'll go on into Roum at dawn."

Avluela pouted. She looked more like a child than ever. Her wings drooped; her underdeveloped body slumped. Petulantly she closed her wings until they were mere fist-sized humps on her back, and picked up the garments she had scattered on the road. She dressed while we made camp. I distributed food tablets; we entered our receptacles; I fell into troubled sleep and dreamed of Avluela limned against the crumbling moon, and Gormon flying beside her. Two hours before dawn I arose and performed my first Watch of the new day, while they still slept. Then I aroused them, and we went onward toward the fabled imperial city, onward toward Roum.

2.

The morning's light was bright and harsh, as though this were some young world newly created. The road was all but empty; people do not travel much in these latter days unless, like me, they are wanderers by habit and profession. Occasionally we stepped aside to let a chariot of some member of the guild of Masters go by, drawn by a dozen expressionless neuters harnessed in series. Four such vehicles went by in the first two hours of the day, each shuttered and sealed to hide the Master's proud features from the gaze of such common folk as we. Several rollerwagons laden with produce passed us, and a number of floaters soared overhead. Generally we had the road to ourselves, however.

The environs of Roum showed vestiges of antiquity: isolated columns, the fragments of an aqueduct transporting nothing from nowhere to nowhere, the portals of a vanished temple. That was the oldest Roum we saw, but there were accretions of the later Roums of subsequent cycles: the huts of peasants, the domes of power drains, the hulls of dwelling-towers. Infrequently we met with the burned-out shell of some ancient airship. Gormon examined everything, taking samples from time to time. Avluela looked, wide-eyed, saying nothing. We walked on, until the walls of the city loomed before us.

They were of a blue glossy stone, neatly joined, rising to a height of perhaps eight men. Our road pierced the wall through a corbeled arch; the gate stood open. As we approached the gate, a figure came toward us; he was hooded, masked, a man of extraordinary height wearing the somber garb of the guild of Pilgrims. One does not approach such a person oneself, but one heeds him if he beckons. The Pilgrim beckoned.

Through his speaking grille he said, "Where from?"

"The south. I lived in Agupt awhile, then crossed Land Bridge to Talya," I replied.

"Where bound?"

"Roum, awhile."

"How goes the Watch?"

"As customary."

"You have a place to stay in Roum?" the Pilgrim asked.

I shook my head. "We trust to the kindness of the Will."

"The Will is not always kind," said the Pilgrim absently. "Nor is there much need of Watchers in Roum. Why do you travel with a Flier?"

"For company's sake. And because she is young and needs protection."

"Who is the other one?"

"He is guildless, a Changeling."

"So I can see. But why is he with you?"

"He is strong and I am old, and so we travel together. Where are you bound, Pilgrim?"

"Jorslem. Is there another destination for my guild?"

I conceded the point with a shrug.

The Pilgrim said, "Why do you not come to Jorslem with me?"

"My road lies north now. Jorslem is in the south, close by Agupt."

"You have been to Agupt and not to Jorslem?" he said, puzzled.

"Yes. The time was not ready for me to see Jorslem."

"Come now. We will walk together on the road, Watcher, and we will talk of the old times and of the times to come, and I will assist you in your Watching, and you will assist me in my communions with the Will. Is it agreed?"

It was a temptation. Before my eyes flashed the image of Jorslem the Golden, its holy buildings and shrines, its places of renewal where the old are made young, its spires, its tabernacles. Even though I am a man set in his ways, I was willing at the moment to abandon Roum and go with the Pilgrim to Jorslem.

I said, "And my companions—"

"Leave them. It is forbidden for me to travel with the guildless, and I do not wish to travel with a female. You and I, Watcher, will go to Jorslem together."

Avluela, who had been standing to one side frowning through all this colloquy, shot me a look of sudden terror.

"I will not abandon them," I said.

"Then I go to Jorslem alone," said the Pilgrim. Out of his robe stretched a bony hand, the fingers long and white and steady. I touched my fingers reverently to the tips of his, and the Pilgrim said, "Let the Will give you mercy, friend Watcher. And when you reach Jorslem, search for me."

He moved on down the road without further conversation.

Gormon said to me, "You would have gone with him, wouldn't you?"

"I considered it."

"What could you find in Jorslem that isn't here? That's a holy city and so is this. Here you can rest awhile. You're in no shape for more walking now."

"You may be right," I conceded, and with the last of my energy I strode toward the gate of Roum.

Watchful eyes scanned us from slots in the wall. When we were at midpoint in the gate, a fat, pockmarked Sentinel with sagging jowls halted us and asked our business in Roum. I stated my guild and purpose, and he gave a snort of disgust.

"Go elsewhere, Watcher! We need only useful men here."

"Watching has its uses," I said mildly.

"No doubt. No doubt." He squinted at Avluela. "Who's this? Watchers are celibates, no?"

"She is nothing more than a traveling companion."

The Sentinel guffawed coarsely. "It's a route you travel often, I wager! Not that there's much to her. What is she, thirteen, fourteen? Come here, child. Let me check you for contraband." He ran his hands quickly over her, scowling as he felt her breasts, then raising an eyebrow as he encountered the mounds of her wings below her shoulders. "What's this? What's this? More in back than in front! A Flier, are you? Very dirty business, Fliers consorting with foul old Watchers." He chuckled and put his hand on Avluela's body in a way that sent Gormon starting forward in fury, murder in his fire-circled eyes. I caught him in time and grasped his wrist with all my strength, holding him back lest he ruin the three of us by an attack on the Sentinel. He tugged at me, nearly pulling me over; then he grew calm and subsided, icily watching as the fat one finished checking Avluela for "contraband."

At length the Sentinel turned in distaste to Gormon and said, "What kind of thing are you?"

"Guildless, your mercy," Gormon said in sharp tones. "The humble and worthless product of teratogenesis, and yet nevertheless a free man who desires entry to Roum."

"Do we need more monsters here?"

"I eat little and work hard."

"You'd work harder still, if you were neutered," said the Sentinel.

Gormon glowered. I said, "May we have entry?"

"A moment." The Sentinel donned his thinking cap and narrowed his eyes as he transmitted a message to the memory tanks. His face tensed with the effort; then it went slack, and moments later came the reply. We could not hear the transaction at all; but from his disappointed look, it appeared evident that no reason had been found to refuse us admission to Roum.

"Go on in," he said. "The three of you. Quickly!"

We passed beyond the gate.

Gormon said, "I could have split him open with a blow."

"And be neutered by nightfall. A little patience, and we've come into Roum."

"The way he handled her—!"

"You take a very possessive attitude toward Avluela," I said. "Remember that she's a Flier, and not sexually available to the guildless."

Gormon ignored my thrust. "She arouses me no more than you do, Watcher. But it pains me to see her treated that way. I would have killed him if you hadn't held me back."

Avluela said, "Where shall we stay, now that we're in Roum?"

"First let me find the headquarters of my guild," I said. "I'll register at the Watchers' Inn. After that, perhaps we'll hunt up the Fliers' Lodge for a meal."

"And then," said Gormon drily, "we'll go to the Guildless Gutter and beg for coppers."

"I pity you because you are a Changeling," I told him, "but I find it ungraceful of you to pity yourself. Come."

We walked up a cobbled, winding street away from the gate and into Roum itself. We were in the outer ring of the city, a residential section of low, squat houses topped by the unwieldy bulk of defense installations. Within lay the shining towers we had seen from the fields the night before; the remnant of ancient Roum carefully preserved across ten thousand years or more; the market, the factory zone, the communications hump, the temples of the Will, the memory tanks, the sleepers' refuges, the outworlders' brothels, the government buildings, the headquarters of the various guilds.

At the corner, beside a Second Cycle building with walls of rubbery texture, I found a public thinking cap and slipped it on my forehead. At once my thoughts raced down the conduit until they came to the interface that gave them access to one of the storage brains of a memory tank. I pierced the interface and saw the wrinkled brain itself, pale gray against the deep green of its housing. A Rememberer once told me that, in cycles past, men built machines to do their thinking for them, although these machines were hellishly expensive and required vast amounts of space and drank power gluttonously. That was not the worst of our forefathers' follies; but why build artificial brains when death each day liberates scores of splendid natural ones to hook into the memory tanks? Was it that they lacked the knowledge to use them? I find that hard to believe.

I gave the brain my guild identification and asked the coordinates of our inn. Instantly I received them, and we set out, Avluela on one side of me, Gormon on the other, myself wheeling, as always, the cart in which my instruments resided.

The city was crowded. I had not seen such throngs in sleepy, heat-fevered Agupt, nor at any other point on my northward journey. The streets were full of Pilgrims, secretive and masked. Jostling through them went busy Rememberers and glum Merchants and now and then the litter of a Master. Avluela saw a number of Fliers, but was barred by the tenets of her guild from greeting them until she had undergone her ritual purification. I regret to say that I spied many Watchers, all of whom looked upon me disdainfully and without welcome. I noted a good many Defenders and ample representation of such lesser guilds as Vendors, Servitors, Manufactories, Scribes, Communicants, and Transporters. Naturally, a host of neuters went silently about their humble business, and numerous outworlders of all descriptions flocked the streets, most of them probably tourists, some here to do what business could be done with the sullen, poverty-blighted people of Earth. I noticed many Changelings limping furtively through the crowd, not one of them as proud of bearing as Gormon beside me. He was unique among his kind; the others, dappled and piebald and asymmetrical, limbless or overlimbed, deformed in a thousand imaginative and artistic ways, were slinkers, squinters, shufflers, hissers, creepers; they were cutpurses, brain-drainers, organ-peddlers, repentance-mongers, gleambuyers, but none held himself upright as though he thought he were a man.

The guidance of the brain was exact, and in less than an hour of walking we arrived at the Watchers' Inn. I left Gormon and Avluela outside and wheeled my cart within.

Perhaps a dozen members of my guild lounged in the main hall. I gave them the customary sign, and they returned it languidly. Were these the guardians on whom Earth's safety depended? Simpletons and weaklings!

"Where may I register?" I asked.

"New? Where from?"

"Agupt was my last place of registry."

"Should have stayed there. No need of Watchers here."

"Where may I register?" I asked again.

A foppish youngster indicated a screen in the rear of the great room. I went to it, pressed my fingertips against it, was interrogated, and gave my name, which a Watcher may utter only to another Watcher and only within the precincts of an inn. A panel shot open, and a puffy-eyed man who wore the Watcher emblem on his right cheek and not on the left, signifying his high rank in the guild, spoke my name and said, "You should have known better than to come to Roum. We're over our quota."

"I claim lodging and employment nonetheless."

"A man with your sense of humor should have been born into the guild of Clowns," he said.

"I see no joke."

"Under laws promulgated by our guild in the most recent session, an inn is under no obligation to take new lodgers once it has reached its assigned capacity. We are at our assigned capacity. Farewell, my friend."

I was aghast. "I know of no such regulation! This is incredible! For a guild to turn away a member from its own inn—when he arrives footsore and numb! A man of my age, having crossed Land Bridge out of Agupt, here as a stranger and hungry in Roum—"

"Why did you not check with us first?"

"I had no idea it would be necessary."

"The new regulations—"

"May the Will shrivel the new regulations!" I shouted. "I demand lodging! To turn away one who has Watched since before you were born—"

"Easy, brother, easy."

"Surely you have some corner where I can sleep—some crumbs to let me eat—"

Even as my tone had changed from bluster to supplication, his expression softened from indifference to mere disdain. "We have no room. We have no food. These are hard times for our guild, you know. There is talk that we will be disbanded altogether, as a useless luxury, a drain upon the Will's resources. We are very limited in our abilities. Because Roum has a surplus of Watchers, we all are on short rations as it is, and if we admit you our rations will be all the shorter."

"But where will I go? What shall I do?"

"I advise you," he said blandly, "to throw yourself upon the mercy of the Prince of Roum."

3.

Outside, I told that to Gormon, and he doubled with laughter, guffawing so furiously that the striations on his lean cheeks blazed like bloody stripes. "The mercy of the Prince of Roum!" he repeated. "The mercy—of the Prince of Roum—"

"It is customary for the unfortunate to seek the aid of the local ruler," I said coldly.

"The Prince of Roum knows no mercy," Gormon told me. "The Prince of Roum will feed you your own limbs to ease your hunger!"

"Perhaps," Avluela put in, "we should try to find the Fliers' Lodge. They'll feed us there."

"Not Gormon," I observed. "We have obligations to one another."

"We could bring food out to him," she said.

"I prefer to visit the court first," I insisted. "Let us make sure of our status. Afterward we can improvise living arrangements, if we must."

She yielded, and we made our way to the palace of the Prince of Roum, a massive building fronted by a colossal column-ringed plaza, on the far side of the river that splits the city. In the plaza we were accosted by mendicants of many sorts, some of them not even Earthborn; something with ropy tendrils and a corrugated, noseless face thrust itself at me and jabbered for alms until Gormon pushed it away, and moments later a second creature, equally strange, its skin pocked with luminescent craters and its limbs studded with eyes, embraced my knees and pleaded in the name of the Will for my mercy. "I am only a poor Watcher," I said, indicating my cart, "and am here to gain mercy myself." But the being persisted, sobbing out its misfortunes in a blurred, feathery voice, and in the end, to Gormon's immense disgust, I dropped

a few food tablets into the shelf-like pouch on its chest. Then we mus-
cled on toward the doors of the palace. At the portico a more horrid
sight presented itself: a maimed Flier, fragile limbs bent and twisted,
one wing half-unfolded and severely cropped, the other missing altogether. The Flier rushed upon Avluela, called her by a name not hers,
moistened her leggings with tears so copious that the fur of them grew
matted and stained. "Sponsor me to the lodge," he appealed. "They have
turned me away because I am crippled, but if you sponsor me—" Avluela explained that she could do nothing, that she was a stranger to
this lodge. The broken Flier would not release her, and Gormon with
great delicacy lifted him like the bundle of dry bones that he was and
set him aside. We stepped up onto the portico and at once were confronted by a trio of soft-faced neuters, who asked our business and
admitted us quickly to the next line of barrier, which was manned by a
pair of wizened Indexers. Speaking in unison, they queried us.

"We seek audience," I said. "A matter of mercy."

"The day of audience is four days hence," said the Indexer on the
right. "We will enter your request on the rolls."

"We have no place to sleep!" Avluela burst out. "We are hungry!
We—"

I hushed her. Gormon, meanwhile, was groping in the mouth of his
overpocket. Bright things glimmered in his hand: pieces of gold, the
eternal metal, stamped with hawk-nosed, bearded faces. He had found
them grubbing in the ruins. He tossed one coin to the Indexer who had
refused us. The man snapped it from the air, rubbed his thumb roughly
across its shining obverse, and dropped it instantly into a fold of his
garment. The second Indexer waited expectantly. Smiling, Gormon gave
him his coin.

"Perhaps," I said, "we can arrange for a special audience within."

"Perhaps you can," said one of the Indexers. "Go through."

And so we passed into the nave of the palace itself and stood in the
great, echoing space, looking down the central aisle toward the shielded
throne-chamber at the apse. There were more beggars in here—licensed
ones holding hereditary concessions—and also throngs of Pilgrims,
Communicants, Rememberers, Musicians, Scribes, and Indexers. I heard
muttered prayers; I smelled the scent of spicy incense; I felt the vibration
of subterranean gongs. In cycles past, this building had been a shrine
of one of the old religions—the Christers, Gormon told me, making me
suspect once more that he was a Rememberer masquerading as a
Changeling—and it still maintained something of its holy character even
though it served as Roum's seat of secular government. But how were
we to get to see the Prince? To my left I saw a small ornate chapel

which a line of prosperous-looking Merchants and Landholders was slowly entering. Peering past them, I noted three skulls mounted on an interrogation fixture—a memory-tank input—and beside them, a burly Scribe. Telling Gormon and Avluela to wait for me in the aisle, I joined the line.

It moved infrequently, and nearly an hour passed before I reached the interrogation fixture. The skulls glared sightlessly at me; within their sealed crania, nutrient fluids bubbled and gurgled, caring for the dead, yet still functional, brains whose billion billion synaptic units now served as incomparable mnemonic devices. The Scribe seemed aghast to find a Watcher in this line, but before he could challenge me I blurted, "I come as a stranger to claim the Prince's mercy. I and my companions are without lodging. My own guild has turned me away. What shall I do? How may I gain an audience?"

"Come back in four days."

"I've slept on the road for more days than that. Now I must rest more easily."

"A public inn—"

"But I am guilded!" I protested. "The public inns would not admit me while my guild maintains an inn here, and my guild refuses me because of some new regulation, and—you see my predicament?"

In a wearied voice the Scribe said, "You may have application for a special audience. It will be denied, but you may apply."

"Where?"

"Here. State your purpose."

I identified myself to the skulls by my public designation, listed the names and status of my two companions, and explained my case. All this was absorbed and transmitted to the ranks of brains mounted somewhere in the depths of the city, and when I was done the Scribe said, "If the application is approved, you will be notified."

"Meanwhile where shall I stay?"

"Close to the palace, I would suggest."

I understood. I could join that legion of unfortunates packing the plaza. How many of them had requested some special favor of the Prince and were still there, months or years later, waiting to be summoned to the Presence? Sleeping on stone, begging for crusts, living in foolish hope!

But I had exhausted my avenues. I returned to Gormon and Avluela, told them of the situation, and suggested that we now attempt to hunt whatever accommodations we could. Gormon, guildless, was welcome at any of the squalid public inns maintained for his kind; Avluela could probably find residence at her own guild's lodge; only I would have to sleep in the streets—and not for the first time. But I hoped that we would not have to separate. I had come to think of us as a family, strange thought though that was for a Watcher.

As we moved toward the exit, my timepiece told me softly that the hour of Watching had come round again. It was my obligation and my privilege to tend to my Watching wherever I might be, regardless of the circumstances, whenever my hour came round; and so I halted, opened the cart, activated the equipment. Gormon and Avluela stood beside me. I saw smirks and open mockery on the faces of those who passed in and out of the palace; Watching was not held in very high repute, for we had Watched so long, and the promised enemy had never come. Yet one has one's duties, comic though they may seem to others. What is a hollow ritual to some is a life's work to others. Doggedly I forced myself into a state of Watchfulness. The world melted away from me, and I plunged into the heavens. The familiar joy engulfed me; and I searched the familiar places, and some that were not so familiar, my amplified mind leaping through the galaxies in wild swoops. Was an armada massing? Were troops drilling for the conquest of Earth? Four times a day I Watched, and the other members of my guild did the same, each at slightly different hours, so that no moment went by without some vigilant mind on guard. I do not believe that that was a foolish calling.

When I came up from my trance, a brazen voice was crying, "—for the Prince of Roum! Make way for the Prince of Roum!"

I blinked and caught my breath and fought to shake off the last strands of my concentration. A gilded palanquin borne by a phalanx of neuters had emerged from the rear of the palace and was proceeding down the nave toward me. Four men in the elegant costumes and brilliant masks of the guild of Masters flanked the litter, and it was preceded by a trio of Changelings, squat and broad, whose throats were so modified to imitate the sounding-boxes of bullfrogs; they emitted a trumpetlike boom of majestic sound as they advanced. It struck me as most strange that a prince would admit Changelings to his service, even ones as gifted as these.

My cart was blocking the progress of this magnificent procession, and hastily I struggled to close it and move it aside before the parade swept down upon me. Age and fear made my fingers tremble, and I could not make the sealings properly; while I fumbled in increasing clumsiness, the strutting Changelings drew so close that the blare of their throats was deafening, and Gormon attempted to aid me, forcing me to hiss at him that it is forbidden for anyone not of my guild to touch the equipment. I pushed him away; and an instant later a vanguard

of neuters descended on me and prepared to scourge me from the spot
with sparkling whips. "In the Will's name," I cried, "I am a Watcher!"

And in antiphonal response came the deep, calm, enormous reply,
"Let him be. He is a watcher."

All motion ceased. The Prince of Roum had spoken.

The neuters drew back. The Changelings halted their music. The
bearers of the Palanquin eased it to the floor. All those in the nave of
the palace had pulled back, save only Gormon and Avluela and myself.
The shimmering chain-curtains of the palanquin parted. Two of the Masters hurried forward and thrust their hands through the sonic barrier
within, offering aid to their monarch. The barrier died away with a
whimpering buzz.

The Prince of Roum appeared.

He was so young! He was nothing more than a boy, his hair full
and dark, his face unlined. But he had been born to rule, and for all his
youth he was as commanding as anyone I had ever seen. His lips were
thin and tightly compressed; his aquiline nose was sharp and aggressive;
his eyes, deep and cold, were infinite pools. He wore the jeweled garments of the guild of Dominators, but incised on his cheek was the
double-barred cross of the Defenders, and around his neck he carried
the dark shawl of the Rememberers. A Dominator may enroll in as many
guilds as he pleases, and it would be a strange thing for a Dominator
not also to be a Defender; but it startled me to find this prince a Rememberer as well. That is not normally a guild for the fierce.

He looked at me with little interest and said, "You choose an odd
place to do your Watching, old man."

"The hour chose the place, sire," I replied. "I was here, and my
duty compelled me. I had no way of knowing that you were about to
come forth."

"Your Watching found no enemies?"

"None, sire."

I was about to press my luck, to take advantage of the unexpected
appearance of the Prince to beg for his aid; but his interest in me died
like a guttering candle as I stood there, and I did not dare call to him
when his head had turned. He eyed Gormon a long moment, frowning
and tugging at his chin. Then his gaze fell on Avluela. His eyes brightened. His jaw muscles flickered. His delicate nostrils widened. "Come
up here, little Flier," he said, beckoning. "Are you this Watcher's
friend?"

She nodded, terrified.

The Prince held out a hand to her and grasped; she floated up onto
the palanquin, and with a grin so evil it seemed a parody of wickedness,

the young Dominator drew her through the curtain. Instantly a pair of Masters restored the sonic barrier, but the procession did not move on. I stood mute. Gormon beside me was frozen, his powerful body rigid as a rod. I wheeled my cart to a less conspicuous place. Long moments passed. The courtiers remained silent, discreetly looking away from the palanquin.

At length the curtain parted once more. Avluela came stumbling out, her face pale, her eyes blinking rapidly. She seemed dazed. Streaks of sweat gleamed on her cheeks. She nearly fell, and a neuter caught her and swung her down to floor level. Beneath her jacket her wings were partly erect, giving her a hunchbacked look and telling me that she was in great emotional distress. In ragged, sliding steps she came to us, quivering, wordless; she darted a glance at me and flung herself against Gormon's broad chest.

The bearers lifted the palanquin. The Prince of Roum went out from his palace.

When he was gone, Avluela stammered hoarsely, "The Prince has granted us lodging in the royal hostelry!"

4.

The hostelkeepers, of course, would not believe us.

Guests of the Prince were housed in the royal hostelry, which was to the rear of the palace in a small garden of frostflowers and blossoming ferns. The usual inhabitants of such a hostelry were Masters and an occasional Dominator; sometimes a particularly important Rememberer on an errand of research would win a niche there, or some highly placed Defender visiting for purposes of strategic planning. To house a Flier in a royal hostelry was distinctly odd; to admit a Watcher was unlikely; to take in a Changeling or some other guildless person was improbable beyond comprehension. When we presented ourselves, therefore, we were met by Servitors whose attitude was at first one of high good humor at our joke, then of irritation, finally of scorn. "Get away," they told us ultimately. "Scum! Rubble!"

Avluela said in a grave voice, "The Prince has granted us lodging here, and you may not refuse us."

"Away! Away!"

One snaggle-toothed Servitor produced a neural truncheon and brandished it in Gormon's face, passing a foul remark about his guildlessness. Gormon slapped the truncheon from the man's grasp, oblivious to the painful sting, and kicked him in the gut, so that he coiled and fell over, puking. Instantly a throng of neuters came rushing from within the hostelry. Gormon seized another of the Servitors and hurled him into the midst of them, turning them into a muddled mob. Wild shouts and angry cursing cries attracted the attention of a venerable Scribe who waddled to the door, bellowed for silence, and interrogated us. "That's easily checked," he said, when Avluela had told the story. To a Servitor he said contemptuously, "Send a think to the Indexers, fast!"

In time the confusion was untangled and we were admitted. We were given separate but adjoining rooms. I had never known such luxury before, and perhaps never shall again. The rooms were long, high, and deep. One entered them through telescopic pits keyed to one's own thermal output, to assure privacy. Lights glowed at the resident's merest nod, for hanging from ceiling globes and nestling in cupolas on the walls were spicules of slavelight from one of the Brightstar worlds, trained through suffering to obey such commands. The windows came and went at the dweller's whim; when not in use, they were concealed by streamers of quasi-sentient outworld gauzes, which not only were decorative in their own right, but which functioned as monitors to produce delightful scents according to requisitioned patterns. The rooms were equipped with individual thinking caps connected to the main memory banks. They likewise had conduits that summoned Servitors, Scribes, Indexers, or Musicians as required. Of course, a man of my own humble guild would not deign to make use of other human beings that way, out of fear of their glowering resentment; but in any case I had little need of them.

I did not ask of Avluela what had occurred in the Prince's palanquin to bring us such bounty. I could well imagine, as could Gormon, whose barely suppressed inner rage was eloquent of his never-admitted love for my pale, slender little Flier.

We settled in. I placed my cart beside the window, draped it with gauzes, and left it in readiness for my next period of Watching. I cleaned my body of grime while entities mounted in the wall sang me to peace. Later I ate. Afterwards Avluela came to me, refreshed and relaxed, and sat beside me in my room as we talked of our experiences. Gormon did not appear for hours. I thought that perhaps he had left this hostelry altogether, finding the atmosphere too rarefied for him, and had sought company among his own guildless kind. But at twilight, Avluela and I walked in the cloistered courtyard of the hostelry and mounted a ramp to watch the stars emerge in Roum's sky, and Gormon was there. With him was a lanky and emaciated man in a Rememberer's shawl; they were talking in low tones.

Gormon nodded to me and said, "Watcher, meet my new friend."

The emaciated one fingered his shawl. "I am the Rememberer Basil," he intoned, in a voice as thin as a fresco that has been peeled from its wall. "I have come from Perris to delve into the mysteries of Roum. I shall be here many years."

"The Rememberer has fine stories to tell," said Gormon. "He is among the foremost of his guild. As you approached, he was describing to me the techniques by which the past is revealed. They drive a trench through the strata of Third Cycle deposits, you see, and with vacuum cores they lift the molecules of earth to lay bare the ancient layers."

"We have found," Basil said, "the catacombs of Imperial Roum, and the rubble of the Time of Sweeping, the books inscribed on slivers of white metal, written toward the close of the Second Cycle. All these go to Perris for examination and classification and decipherment; then they return. Does the past interest you, Watcher?"

"To some extent." I smiled. "This Changeling here shows much more fascination for it. I sometimes suspect his authenticity. Would you recognize a Rememberer in disguise?"

Basil scrutinized Gormon; he lingered over the bizarre features, the excessively muscular frame. "He is no Rememberer," he said at length. "But I agree that he has antiquarian interests. He has asked me many profound questions."

"Such as?"

"He wishes to know the origin of guilds. He asks the name of the genetic surgeon who crafted the first true-breeding Fliers. He wonders why there are Changelings, and if they are truly under the curse of the Will."

"And do you have answers for these?" I asked.

"For some," said Basil. "For some."

"The origin of guilds?"

"To give structure and meaning to a society that has suffered defeat and destruction," said the Rememberer. "At the end of the Second Cycle all was in flux. No man knew his rank nor his purpose. Through our world strode haughty outworlders who looked upon us all as worthless. It was necessary to establish fixed frames of reference by which one man might know his value beside another. So the first guilds appeared: Dominators, Masters, Merchants, Landholders, Vendors and Servitors. Then came Scribes, Musicians, Clowns and Transporters. Afterwards Indexers became necessary, and then Watchers and Defenders. When the Years of Magic gave us Fliers and Changelings, those guilds were added, and then the guildless ones, the neuters, were produced, so that—"

"But surely the Changelings are guildless too!" said Avluela.

The Rememberer looked at her for the first time. "Who are you, child?"

"Avluela of the Fliers. I travel with this Watcher and this Changeling."

Basil said, "As I have been telling the Changeling here, in the early days his kind was guilded. The guild was dissolved a thousand years ago by the order of the Council of Dominators after an attempt by a disreputable Changeling faction to seize control of the holy places of Jorslem, and since that time Changelings have been guildless, ranking only above neuters."

"I never knew that," I said.

"You are no Rememberer," said Basil smugly. "It is our craft to uncover the past."

"True. True."

Gormon said, "And today, how many guilds are there?"

Discomfited, Basil replied vaguely, "At least a hundred, my friend. Some are quite small; some are local. I am concerned only with the original guilds and their immediate successors; what has happened in the past few hundred years is in the province of others. Shall I requisition an information for you?"

"Never mind," Gormon said. "It was only an idle question."

"Your curiosity is well developed," said the Rememberer.

"I find the world and all it contains extremely fascinating. Is this sinful?"

"It is strange," said Basil. "The guildless rarely look beyond their own horizons."

A Servitor appeared. With a mixture of awe and contempt he genuflected before Avluela and said, "The Prince has returned. He desires your company in the palace at this time."

Terror glimmered in Avluela's eyes. But to refuse was inconceivable. "Shall I come with you?" she asked.

"Please. You must be robed and perfumed. He wishes you to come to him with your wings open, as well."

Avluela nodded. The Servitor led her away.

We remained on the ramp a while longer; the Rememberer Basil talked of the old days of Roum, and I listened, and Gormon peered into the gathering darkness. Eventually, his throat dry, the Rememberer excused himself and moved solemnly away. A few moments later, in the courtyard below us, a door opened and Avluela emerged, walking as though she were of the guild of Somnambulists, not of Fliers. She was nude under transparent draperies, and her fragile body gleamed ghostly white in the starbeams. Her wings were spread and fluttered slowly in a somber systole and diastole. One Servitor grasped each of her elbows: they seemed to be propelling her toward the palace as though she were but a dreamed facsimile of herself and not a real woman.

"Fly, Avluela, fly," Gormon growled. "Escape while you can!"

She disappeared into a side entrance of the palace.

The Changeling looked at me. "She has sold herself to the Prince to provide lodging for us."

"So it seems."

"I could smash down that palace!"

"You love her?"

"It should be obvious."

"Cure yourself," I advised. "You are an unusual man, but still a Flier is not for you. Particularly a Flier who has shared the bed of the Prince of Roum."

"She goes from my arms to his."

I was staggered. "You've known her?"

"More than once," he said, smiling sadly. "At the moment of ecstasy her wings thrash like leaves in a storm."

I gripped the railing of the ramp so that I would not tumble into the courtyard. The stars whirled overhead; the old moon and its two blank-faced consorts leaped and bobbed. I was shaken without fully understanding the cause of my emotion. Was it wrath that Gormon had dared to violate a canon of the law? Was it a manifestation of those pseudo-parental feelings I had toward Avluela? Or was it mere envy of Gormon for daring to commit a sin beyond my capacity, though not beyond my desires?

I said, "They could burn your brain for that. They could mince your soul. And now you make me an accessory."

"What of it? That Prince commands, and he gets—but others have been there before him. I had to tell someone."

"Enough. Enough."

"Will we see her again?"

"Princes tire quickly of their women. A few days, perhaps a single night—then he will throw her back to us. And perhaps then we shall have to leave this hostelry." I sighed. "At least we'll have known it a few nights more than we deserved."

"Where will you go then?" Gorman asked.

"I will stay in Roum awhile."

"Even if you sleep in the streets? There does not seem to be much demand for Watchers here."

"I'll manage," I said. "Then I may go toward Perris."

"To learn from the Rememberers?"

"To see Perris. What of you? What do you want in Roum?"

"Avluela."

"Stop that talk!"

"Very well," he said, and his smile was bitter. "But I will stay here until the Prince is through with her. Then she will be mine, and we'll find ways to survive. The guildless are resourceful. They have to be.

Maybe we'll scrounge lodgings in Roum awhile, and then follow you to Perris. If you're willing to travel with monsters and faithless Fliers."

I shrugged. "We'll see about that when the time comes."

"Have you ever been in the company of a Changeling before?"

"Not often. Not for long."

"I'm honored." He drummed on the parapet. "Don't cast me off, Watcher. I have a reason for wanting to stay with you."

"Which is?"

"To see your face on the day your machines tell you that the invasion of Earth has begun."

I let myself sag forward, shoulders drooping. "You'll stay with me a long time, then."

"Don't you believe the invasion is coming?"

"Some day. Not soon."

Gormon chuckled. "You're wrong. It's almost here."

"You don't amuse me."

"What is it, Watcher? Have you lost your faith? It's been known for a thousand years: another race covets Earth and owns it by treaty, and will some day come to collect. That much was decided at the end of the Second Cycle."

"I know all that, and I am no Rememberer." Then I turned to him and spoke words I never thought I would say aloud. "For twice your lifetime, Changeling, I've listened to the stars and done my Watching. Something done that often loses meaning. Say your own name ten thousand times and it will be an empty sound. I have Watched, and Watched well, and in the dark hours of the night I sometimes think I Watch for nothing, that I have wasted my life. There is a pleasure in Watching, but perhaps there is no real purpose."

His hand encircled my wrist. "Your confession is as shocking as mine. Keep your faith, Watcher. The invasion comes!"

"How could you possibly know?"

"The guildless also have their skills."

The conversation troubled me. I said, "Is it painful to be guildless?"

"One grows reconciled. And there are certain freedoms to compensate for the lack of status. I may speak freely to all."

"I notice."

"I move freely. I am always sure of food and lodging, though the food may be rotten and the lodging poor. Women are attracted to me despite all prohibitions. Because of them, perhaps. I am untroubled by ambitions."

"Never desire to rise above your rank?"

"Never."

"You might have been happier as a Rememberer."

"I am happy now. I can have a Rememberer's pleasures without his responsibility."

"How smug you are!" I cried. "To make a virtue of guildlessness!"

"How else does one endure the weight of the Will?" He looked toward the palace. "The humble rise. The mighty fall. Take this as prophecy, Watcher: that lusty Prince in there will know more of life before summer comes. I'll rip out his eyes for taking Avluela!"

"Strong words. You bubble with treason tonight."

"Take it as prophecy."

"You can't get close to him," I said. Then, irritated for taking his foolishness seriously, I added, "And why blame him? He only does as princes do. Blame the girl for going to him. She might have refused."

"And lost her wings. Or died. No, she had no choice. I do!" In a sudden, terrible gesture the Changeling held out thumb and forefinger, double-jointed, long-nailed, and plunged them forward into imagined eyes. "Wait," he said. "You'll see!"

In the courtyard two Chronomancers appeared, set up the apparatus of their guild, and lit tapers by which to read the shape of tomorrow. A sickly odor of pallid smoke rose to my nostrils. I had now lost further desire to speak with the Changeling.

"It grows late," I said. "I need rest, and soon I must do my Watching."

"Watch carefully," Gormon told me.

5.

At night in my chamber I performed my fourth and last Watch of that long day, and for the first time in my life I detected an anomaly. I could not interpret it. It was an obscure sensation, a mingling of tastes and sounds, a feeling of being in contact with some colossal mass. Worried, I clung to my instruments far longer than usual, but perceived no more clearly at the end of my seance than at its commencement.

Afterward I wondered about my obligations.

Watchers are trained from childhood to be swift to sound the alarm; and the alarm must be sounded when the Watcher judges the world in peril. Was I now obliged to notify the Defenders? Four times in my life the alarm had been given, on each occasion in error; and each Watcher who had thus touched off a false mobilization had suffered a fearful loss of status. One had contributed his brain to the memory banks; one had become a neuter out of shame; one had smashed his instruments and gone to live among the guildless; and one, vainly attempting to continue in his profession, had discovered himself mocked by all his comrades. I saw no virtue in scorning one who had delivered a false alarm, for was it not preferable for a Watcher to cry out too soon than not at all? But those were the customs of our guild, and I was constrained by them.

I evaluated my position and decided that I did not have valid grounds for an alarm.

I reflected that Gormon had placed suggestive ideas in my mind that evening. I might possibly be reacting only to his jeering talk of imminent invasion.

I could not act. I dared not jeopardize my standing by hasty outcry. I mistrusted my own emotional state.

I gave no alarm.

Seething, confused, my soul roiling, I closed my cart and let myself sink into a drugged sleep.

At dawn I woke and rushed to the window, expecting to find invaders in the streets. But all was still; a winter grayness hung over the courtyard, and sleepy Servitors pushed passive neuters about. Uneasily I did my first Watching of the day, and to my relief the strangenesses of the night before did not return, although I had it in mind that my sensitivity is always greater at night than upon arising.

I ate and went to the courtyard. Gormon and Avluela were already there. She looked fatigued and downcast, depleted by her night with the Prince of Roum, but I said nothing to her about it. Gormon, slouching disdainfully against a wall embellished with the shells of radiant mollusks, said to me, "Did your Watching go well?"

"Well enough."

"What of the day?"

"Out to roam Roum," I said. "Will you come? Avluela? Gormon?"

"Surely," he said, and she gave a faint nod; and, like the tourists we were, we set off to inspect the splendid city of Roum.

Gormon acted as our guide to the jumbled pasts of Roum, belying his claim never to have been here before. As well as any Rememberer he described the things we saw as we walked the winding streets. All the scattered levels of thousands of years were exposed. We saw the power domes of the Second Cycle, and the Colosseum where at an unimaginably early date man and beast contended like jungle creatures. In the broken hull of that building of horrors Gormon told us of the savagery of that unimaginably ancient time. "They fought," he said, "naked before huge throngs. With bare hands men challenged beasts called lions, great hairy cats with swollen heads; and when the lion lay in its gore, the victor turned to the Prince of Roum and asked to be pardoned for whatever crime it was that had cast him into the arena. And if he had fought well, the Prince made a gesture with his hand, and the man was freed." Gormon made the gesture for us: a thumb upraised and jerked backward over the right shoulder several times. "But if the man had shown cowardice, or if the lion had distinguished itself in the manner of its dying, the Prince made another gesture, and the man was condemned to be slain by a second beast." Gormon showed us that gesture too: the middle finger jutting upward from a clenched fist and lifted in a short sharp thrust.

"How are these things known?" Avluela asked, but Gormon pretended not to hear her.

We saw the line of fusion-pylons built early in the Third Cycle to draw energy from the world's core; they were still functioning, although stained and corroded. We saw the shattered stump of a Second Cycle weather machine, still a mighty column at least twenty men high. We saw a hill on which white marble relics of First Cycle Roum sprouted like pale clumps of winter deathflowers. Penetrating toward the inner part of the city, we came upon the embankment of defensive amplifiers waiting in readiness to hurl the full impact of the Will against invaders. We viewed a market where visitors from the stars haggled with peasants for excavated fragments of antiquity. Gormon strode into the crowd and made several purchases. We came to a flesh-house for travelers from afar, where one could buy anything from quasi-life to mounds of passion-ice. We ate at a small restaurant by the edge of the River Tver, where guildless ones were served without ceremony, and at Gormon's insistence we dined on mounds of a soft doughy substance and drank a tart yellow wine, local specialties.

Afterward we passed through a covered arcade in whose many aisles plump Vendors peddled star-goods, costly trinkets from Afreek, and the flimsy constructs of the local Manufactories. Just beyond we emerged in a plaza that contained a fountain in the shape of a boat, and to the rear of this rose a flight of cracked and battered stone stairs ascending to a zone of rubble and weeds. Gormon beckoned, and we scrambled into this dismal area, then passed rapidly through it to a place where a sumptuous palace, by its looks early Second Cycle or even First, brooded over a sloping vegetated hill.

"They say this is the center of the world," Gormon declared. "In Jorslem one finds another place that also claims the honor. They mark the spot here by a map."

"How can the world have one center," Avluela asked, "when it is round?"

Gormon laughed. We went in. Within, in wintry darkness, there stood a colossal jeweled globe lit by some inner glow.

"Here is your world," said Gormon, gesturing grandly.

"Oh!" Avluela gasped. "Everything! Everything is here!"

The map was a masterpiece of craftsmanship. It showed natural contours and elevations, its seas seemed deep liquid pools, its deserts were so parched as to make thirst spring in one's mouth, its cities swirled with vigor and life. I beheld the continents, Eyrop, Afreek, Ais, Stralya. I saw the vastness of Earth Ocean. I traversed the golden span of Land Bridge, which I had crossed so toilfully on foot not long before.

Avluela rushed forward and pointed to Roum, to Agupt, to Jorslem, to Perris. She tapped the globe at the high mountains north of Hind and said softly, "This is where I was born, where the ice lives, where the mountains touch the moons. Here is where the Fliers have their kingdom." She ran a finger westward toward Fars and beyond it into the terrible Arban Desert, and on to Agupt. "This is where I flew. By night, when I left my girlhood. We all must fly, and I flew here. A hundred times I thought I would die. Here, here in the desert, sand in my throat as I flew, sand beating against my wings—I was forced down, I lay naked on the hot sand for days, and another Flier saw me, he came down to me and pitied me, and lifted me up, and when I was aloft my strength returned, and we flew on toward Agupt. And he died over the sea, his life stopped though he was young and strong, and he fell down into the sea, and I flew down to be with him, and the water was hot even at night. I drifted, and morning came, and I saw the living stones growing like trees in the water, and the fish of many colors, and they came to him and pecked at his flesh as he floated with his wings outspread on the water, and I left him, I thrust him down to rest there, and I rose, and I flew on to Agupt, alone, frightened, and there I met you, Watcher." Timidly she smiled to me. "Show us the place where you were young, Watcher."

Painfully, for I was suddenly stiff at the knees, I hobbled to the far side of the globe. Avluela followed me; Gormon hung back, as though not interested at all. I pointed to the scattered islands rising in two long strips from Earth Ocean—the remnants of the Lost Continents.

"Here," I said, indicating my native island in the west. "I was born here."

"So far away!" Avluela cried.

"And so long ago," I said. "In the middle of the Second Cycle, it sometimes seems to me."

"No! That is not possible!" But she looked at me as though it might just be true that I was thousands of years old.

I smiled and touched her satiny cheek. "It only seems that way to me," I said.

"When did you leave your home?"

"When I was twice your age," I said. "I came first to here—" I indicated the eastern group of islands. "I spent a dozen years as a Watcher on Palash. Then the Will moved me to cross Earth Ocean to Afreek. I came. I lived awhile in the hot countries. I went on to Agupt. I met a certain small Flier." Falling silent, I looked a long while at the islands that had been my home, and within my mind my image changed from the gaunt and eroded thing I now had become, and I saw myself young and well-fleshed, climbing the green mountains and swimming in the chill sea, doing my Watching at the rim of a white beach hammered by surf.

While I brooded Avluela turned away from me to Gormon and said, "Now you. Show us where you came from, Changeling!"

Gormon shrugged. "The place does not appear to be on this globe."

"But that's *impossible!*"

"Is it?" he asked.

She pressed him, but he evaded her, and we passed through a side exit and into the streets of Roum.

I was growing tired, but Avluela hungered for this city and wished to devour it all in an afternoon, and so we went on through a maze of interlocking streets, through a zone of sparkling mansions of Masters and Merchants, and through a foul den of Servitors and Vendors that extended into subterranean catacombs, and to a place where Clowns and Musicians resorted, and to another where the guild of Somnambulists offered its doubtful wares. A bloated female Somnambulist begged us to come inside and buy the truth that comes with trances, and Avluela urged us to go, but Gormon shook his head and I smiled, and we moved on. Now we were at the edge of a park close to the city's core. Here the citizens of Roum promenaded with an energy rarely seen in hot Agupt, and we joined the parade.

"Look there!" Avluela said. "How bright it is!"

She pointed toward the shining arc of a dimensional sphere enclosing some relic of the ancient city; shading my eyes, I could make out a weathered stone wall within, and a knot of people. Gormon said, "It is the Mouth of Truth."

"What is that?" Avluela asked.

"Come. See."

A line progressed into the sphere. We joined it and soon were at the lip of the interior, peering at the timeless region just across the threshold. Why this relic and so few others had been accorded such special protection I did not know, and I asked Gormon, whose knowledge was so unaccountably as profound as any Rememberer's, and he replied, "Because this is the realm of certainty, where what one says is absolutely congruent with what actually is the case."

"I don't understand," said Avluela.

"It is impossible to lie in this place," Gormon told her. "Can you imagine any relic more worthy of protection?" He stepped across the entry duct, blurring as he did so, and I followed him quickly within. Avluela hesitated. It was a long moment before she entered; pausing a moment on the very threshold, she seemed buffeted by the wind that blew along the line of demarcation between the outer world and the pocket universe in which we stood.

An inner compartment held the Mouth of Truth itself. The line extended toward it, and a solemn Indexer was controlling the flow of entry to the tabernacle. It was a while before we three were permitted to go in. We found ourselves before the ferocious head of a monster in high relief, affixed to an ancient wall pockmarked by time. The monster's jaws gaped; the open mouth was a dark and sinister hole. Gormon nodded, inspecting it, as though he seemed pleased to find it exactly as he had thought it would be.

"What do we do?" Avluela asked.

"Gormon said, "Watcher, put your right hand into the Mouth of Truth."

Frowning, I complied.

"Now," said Gormon, "one of us asks a question. You must answer it. If you speak anything but the truth, the mouth will close and sever your hand."

"No!" Avluela cried.

I stared uneasily at the stone jaws rimming my wrist. A Watcher without both his hands is a man without a craft; in Second Cycle days one might have obtained a prosthesis more artful than one's original hand, but the Second Cycle had long ago been concluded, and such niceties were not to be purchased on Earth nowadays.

"How is such a thing possible?" I asked.

"The Will is unusually strong in these precincts," Gormon replied. "It distinguishes sternly between truth and untruth. To the rear of this wall sleeps a trio of Somnambulists through whom the Will speaks, and they control the Mouth. Do you fear the Will, Watcher?"

"I fear my own tongue."

"Be brave. Never has a lie been told before this wall. Never has a hand been lost."

"Go ahead, then," I said. "Who will ask me a question?"

"I," said Gormon. "Tell me, Watcher: all pretense aside, would you say that a life spent in Watching has been a life spent wisely?"

I was silent a long moment, rotating my thoughts, eyeing the jaws.

At length I said, "To devote oneself to vigilance on behalf of one's fellow man is perhaps the noblest purpose one can serve."

"Careful!" Gormon cried in alarm.

"I am not finished," I said.

"Go on."

"But to devote oneself to vigilance when the enemy is an imaginary one is idle, and to congratulate oneself for looking long and well for a foe that is not coming is foolish and sinful. My life has been a waste."

The jaws of the Mouth of Truth did not quiver.

I removed my hand. I stared at it as though it had newly sprouted from my wrist. I felt suddenly several cycles old. Avluela, her eyes wide, her hands to her lips, seemed shocked by what I had said. My own words appeared to hang congealed in the air before the hideous idol.

"Spoken honestly," said Gormon, "although without much mercy for yourself. You judge yourself too harshly, Watcher."

"I spoke to save my hand," I said. "Would you have had me lie?"

He smiled. To Avluela the Changeling said, "Now it's your turn."

Visibly frightened, the little Flier approached the Mouth. Her dainty hand trembled as she inserted it between the slabs of cold stone. I fought back an urge to rush toward her and pull her free of that devilish grimacing head.

"Who will question her?" I asked.

"I," said Gormon.

Avluela's wings stirred faintly beneath her garments. Her face grew pale; her nostrils flickered; her upper lip slid over the lower one. She stood slouched against the wall and stared in horror at the termination of her arm. Outside the chamber vague faces peered at us; lips moved in what no doubt were expressions of impatience over our lengthy visit to the Mouth; but we heard nothing. The atmosphere around us was warm and clammy, with a musty tang like that which would come from a well that was driven through the structure of Time.

Gormon said slowly, "This night past you allowed your body to be possessed by the Prince of Roum. Before that, you granted yourself to the Changeling Gormon, although such liaisons are forbidden by custom and law. Much prior to that you were the mate of a Flier, now deceased. You may have had other men, but I know nothing of them, and for the purposes of my question they are not relevant. Tell me this, Avluela: which of the three gave you the most intense physical pleasure, which of the three aroused your deepest emotions, and which of the three would you choose as a mate, if you were choosing a mate?"

I wanted to protest that the Changeling had asked her three questions, not one, and so had taken unfair advantage. But I had no chance to speak, because Avluela replied unfalteringly, hand wedged deep into the Mouth of Truth, "The Prince of Roum gave me greater pleasure of the body than I had ever known before, but he is cold and cruel, and I despise him. My dead Flier I loved more deeply than any person before or since, but he was weak, and I would not have wanted a weakling as a mate. You, Gormon, seem almost a stranger to me even now, and I feel that I know neither your body nor your soul, and yet, though the gulf between us is so wide, it is you with whom I would spend my days to come."

She drew her hand from the Mouth of Truth.

"Well spoken!" said Gormon, though the accuracy of her words had clearly wounded as well as pleased him. "Suddenly you find eloquence, eh, when the circumstances demand it. And now the turn is mine to risk my hand."

He neared the Mouth. I said, "You have asked the first two questions. Do you wish to finish the job and ask the third as well?"

"Hardly," he said. He made a negligent gesture with his free hand. "Put your heads together and agree on a joint question."

Avluela and I conferred. With uncharacteristic forwardness she proposed a question; and since it was the one I would have asked, I accepted it and told her to ask it.

She said, "When we stood before the globe of the world, Gormon, I asked you to show me the place where you were born, and you said you were unable to find it on the map. That seemed most strange. Tell me now: are you what you say you are, a Changeling who wanders the world?"

He replied, "I am not."

In a sense he had satisfied the question as Avluela had phrased it; but it went without saying that his reply was inadequate, and he kept his hand in the Mouth of Truth as he continued, "I did not show my birthplace to you on the globe because I was born nowhere on this globe, but on a world of a star I must not name. I am no Changeling in your meaning of the word, though by some definitions I am, for my body is somewhat disguised, and on my own world I wear a different flesh. I have lived here ten years."

"What was your purpose in coming to Earth?" I asked.

"I am obliged only to answer one question," said Gormon. Then he smiled. "But I give you an answer anyway: I was sent to Earth in the capacity of a military observer, to prepare the way for the invasion for which you have Watched so long and in which you have ceased to believe, and which will be upon you in a matter now of some hours."

"Lies!" I bellowed. *"Lies!"*

Gormon laughed. And drew his hand from the Mouth of Truth, intact, unharmed.

6.

Numb with confusion, I fled with my cart of instruments from that gleaming sphere and emerged into a street suddenly cold and dark. Night had come with winter's swiftness; it was almost the ninth hour, and almost the time for me to Watch once more.

Gormon's mockery thundered in my brain. He had arranged everything: he had maneuvered us in to the Mouth of Truth; he had wrung a confession of lost faith from me and a confession of a different sort from Avluela; he had mercilessly volunteered information he need not have revealed, spoken words calculated to split me to the core.

Was the Mouth of Truth a fraud? Could Gormon lie and emerge unscathed?

Never since I first took up my tasks had I Watched at anything but my appointed hours. This was a time of crumbling realities; I could not wait for the ninth hour to come round; crouching in the windy street, I opened my cart, readied my equipment, and sank like a diver into Watchfulness.

My amplified consciousness roared toward the stars.

Godlike I roamed infinity. I felt the rush of the solar wind, but I was no Flier to be hurled to destruction by that pressure, and I soared past it, beyond the reach of those angry particles of light, into the blackness at the edge of the sun's dominion. Down upon me there beat a different pressure.

Starships coming near.

Not the tourist lines that bring hordes of sightseers to gape at our diminished world. Not the registered mercantile transport vessels, nor the scoopships that collect the interstellar vapors, nor the resort craft on their hyperbolic orbits.

These were military craft, dark, alien, menacing. I could not tell their number; I knew only that they sped Earthward at many lights, nudging a cone of deflected energies before them; and it was that cone that I had sensed, that I had felt also the night before, booming into my mind through my instruments, engulfing me like a cube of crystal through which stress patterns play and shine.

All my life I had watched for this.

I had been trained to sense it. I had prayed that I never would sense it, and then in my emptiness I had prayed that I *would* sense it, and then I had ceased to believe in it. And then by grace of the Changeling Gormon, I had sensed it after all, Watching ahead of my hour, crouching in a cold Roumish street just outside the Mouth of Truth.

In his training, a Watcher is instructed to break from his Watchfulness as soon as his observations are confirmed by a careful check, so that he can sound the alarm. Obediently I made my check by shifting from one channel to another to another, triangulating and still picking up that foreboding sensation of titanic force rushing upon Earth at unimaginable speed.

Either I was deceived, or the invasion was come. But I could not shake from my trance to give the alarm.

Lingeringly, lovingly, I drank in the sensory data for what seemed like hours. I fondled my equipment; I drained from it the total affirmation of faith that my readings gave me. Dimly I warned myself that I was wasting vital time, that it was my duty to leave this lewd caressing of destiny to summon the Defenders.

And at last I burst free of Watchfulness and returned to the world I was guarding.

Avluela was beside me; she was dazed, terrified, her knuckles to her teeth, her eyes blank.

"Watcher! Watcher, do you hear me? What's happening? What's going to happen?"

"The invasion," I said. "How long was I under?"

"About half a minute. I don't know. Your eyes were closed. I thought you were dead."

"Gormon was speaking the truth! The invasion is almost here. Where is he? Where did he go?"

"He vanished as we came away from that place with the Mouth," Avluela whispered. "Watcher, I'm frightened. I feel everything collapsing. I have to fly—I can't stay down here now!"

"Wait," I said, clutching at her and missing her arm. "Don't go now. First I have to give the alarm, and then—"

But she was already stripping off her clothing. Bare to the waist, her pale body gleamed in the evening light, while about us people were rushing to and fro in ignorance of all that was about to occur. I wanted to keep Avluela beside me, but I could delay no longer in giving the alarm, and I turned away from her, back to my cart.

As though caught up in a dream born of overripe longings I reached for the node that I had never used, the one that would send forth a planetwide alert to the Defenders.

Had the alarm already been given? Had some other Watcher sensed what I had sensed, and, less paralyzed by bewilderment and doubt, performed a Watcher's final task?

No. No. For then I would be hearing the sirens' shriek reverberating from the orbiting loudspeakers above the city.

I touched the node. From the corner of my eye I saw Avluela, free of her encumbrances now, kneeling to say her words, filling her tender wings with strength. In a moment she would be in the air, beyond my grasp.

With a single swift tug I activated the alarm.

In that instant I became aware of a burly figure striding toward us. Gormon, I thought; and as I rose from my equipment I reached out to him; I wanted to seize him and hold him fast. But he who approached was not Gormon but some officious dough-faced Servitor who said to Avluela, "Go easy, Flier, let your wings drop. The Prince of Roum sends me to bring you to his presence."

He grappled with her. Her little breasts heaved; her eyes flashed anger at him.

"Let go of me! I'm going to fly!"

"The Prince of Roum summons you," the Servitor said, enclosing her in his heavy arms.

"The Prince of Roum will have other distractions tonight," I said. "He'll have no need of her."

As I spoke, the sirens began to sing from the skies.

The Servitor released her. His mouth worked noiselessly for an instant; he made one of the protective gestures of the Will; he looked skyward and grunted, "The alarm! Who gave the alarm? You, old Watcher?"

Figures rushed about insanely in the streets.

Avluela, freed, sped past me—on foot, her wings but half-furled—and was swallowed up in the surging throng. Over the terrifying sound of the sirens came booming messages from the public annunciators, giving instructions for defense and safety. A lanky man with the mark of the guild of Defenders upon his cheek rushed up to me, shouted words too incoherent to be understood, and sped on down the street. The world seemed to have gone mad.

Only I remained calm. I looked to the skies, half-expecting to see the invaders' black ships already hovering above the towers of Roum. But I saw nothing except the hovering nightlights and the other objects one might expect overhead.

"Gormon?" I called. "Avluela?"

I was alone.

A strange emptiness swept over me. I had given the alarm; the invaders were on their way; I had lost my occupation. There was no need of Watchers now. Almost lovingly I touched the worn cart that had been my companion for so many years. I ran my fingers over its stained and pitted instruments; and then I looked away, abandoning it, and went down the dark streets cartless, burdenless, a man whose life had found and lost meaning in the same instant. And about me raged chaos.

7.

It was understood that when the moment of Earth's final battle arrived, all guilds would be mobilized, the Watchers alone exempted. We who had manned the perimeter of defense for so long had no part in the strategy of combat; we were discharged by the giving of a true alarm. Now it was the time of the guild of Defenders to show its capabilities. They had planned for half a cycle what they would do in time of war. What plans would they call forth now? What deeds would they direct?

My only concern was to return to the royal hostelry and wait out the crisis. It was hopeless to think of finding Avluela, and I pummeled myself savagely for having let her slip away, naked and without a protector, in that confused moment. Where would she go? Who would shield her?

A fellow Watcher, pulling his cart madly along, nearly collided with me. "Careful!" I snapped. He looked up, breathless, stunned. "Is it true?" he asked. "The alarm?"

"Can't you hear?"

"But is it real?"

I pointed to his cart. "You know how to find that out."

"They say the man who gave the alarm was drunk, an old fool who was turned away from the inn yesterday."

"It could be so," I admitted.

"But if the alarm is real—!"

Smiling, I said, "If it is, now we all may rest. Good day to you, Watcher."

"Your cart! Where's your cart?" he shouted at me.

But I had moved past him, toward the mighty carven stone pillar of some relic of Imperial Roum.

Ancient images were carved on that pillar: battles and victories, foreign monarchs marched in the chains of disgrace through the streets of Roum, triumphant eagles celebrating imperial grandeur. In my strange new calmness I stood awhile before the column of stone and admired its elegant engravings. Toward me rushed a frenzied figure whom I recognized as the Rememberer Basil; I hailed him, saying, "How timely you come! Do me the kindness of explaining these images, Rememberer. They fascinate me, and my curiosity is aroused."

"Are you insane? Can't you hear the alarm?"

"I gave the alarm, Rememberer."

"Flee, then! Invaders come! We must fight!"

"Not I, Basil. Now my time is over. Tell me of these images. These beaten kings, these broken emperors. Surely a man of your years will not be doing battle."

"All are mobilized now!"

"All but Watchers," I said. "Take a moment. Yearning for the past is born in me. Gormon has vanished; be my guide to these lost cycles."

The Rememberer shook his head wildly, circled around me, and tried to get away. Hoping to seize his skinny arm and pin him to the spot, I made a lunge at him; but he eluded me and I caught only his dark shawl, which pulled free and came loose in my hands. Then he was gone, his spindly limbs pumping madly as he fled down the street and left my view. I shrugged and examined the shawl I had so unexpectedly acquired. It was shot through with glimmering threads of metal arranged in intricate patterns that teased the eye: it seemed to me that each strand disappeared into the weave of the fabric, only to reappear at some improbable point, like the lineage of dynasties unexpectedly revived in distant cities. The workmanship was superb. Idly I draped the shawl about my shoulders.

I walked on.

My legs, which had been on the verge of failing me earlier in the day, now served me well. With renewed youthfulness I made my way through the chaotic city, finding no difficulties in choosing my route. I headed for the river, then crossed it and, on the Tver's far side, sought the palace of the Prince. The night had deepened, for most lights were extinguished under the mobilization orders; and from time to time a dull boom signaled the explosion of a screening bomb overhead, liberating clouds of murk that shielded the city from most forms of long-range scrutiny. There were fewer pedestrians in the streets. The sirens still cried out. Atop the buildings the defensive installations were going into action; I heard the bleeping sounds of repellors warming up, and I saw the long spidery arms of amplification booms swinging from tower to tower as they linked for maximum output. I had no doubt now that the invasion actually was coming. My own instruments might have been fouled by inner confusion, but they would not have proceeded thus far with the mobilization if the initial report had not been confirmed by the findings of hundreds of other members of my guild.

As I neared the palace a pair of breathless Rememberers sped toward me, their shawls flapping behind them. They called to me in words I did not comprehend—some code of their guild, I realized, recollecting that I wore Basil's shawl. I could not reply, and they rushed upon me, still gabbling; and switching to the language of ordinary men they said, "What is the matter with you? To your post! We must record! We must comment! We must observe!"

"You mistake me," I said mildly. "I keep this shawl only for your brother Basil, who left it in my care. I have no post to guard at this time."

"A Watcher," they cried in unison, and cursed me separately, and ran on. I laughed and went to the palace.

Its gates stood open. The neuters who had guarded the outer portal were gone, as were the two Indexers who had stood just within the door. The beggars that had thronged the vast plaza had jostled their way into the building itself to seek shelter; this had awakened the anger of the licensed hereditary mendicants whose customary stations were in that part of the building, and they had fallen upon the inflowing refugees with fury and unexpected strength. I saw cripples lashing out with their crutches held as clubs; I saw blind men landing blows with suspicious accuracy; meek penitents were wielding a variety of weapons ranging from stilettos to sonic pistols. Holding myself aloof from this shameless spectacle, I penetrated to the inner recesses of the palace and peered into chapels where I saw Pilgrims beseeching the blessings of the Will, and Communicants desperately seeking spiritual guidance as to the outcome of the coming conflict.

Abruptly I heard the blare of trumpets and cries of, "Make way! Make way!"

A file of sturdy Servitors marched into the palace, striding toward the Prince's chambers in the apse. Several of them held a struggling, kicking, frantic figure with half-unfolded wings: Avluela! I called out to her, but my voice died in the din, nor could I reach her. The Servitors shoved me aside. The procession vanished into the princely chambers. I caught a final glimpse of the little Flier, pale and small in the grip of her captors, and then she was gone once more.

I seized a bumbling neuter who had been moving uncertainly in the wake of the Servitors.

"That Flier! Why was she brought here?"

"Ha—he—they—"

"Tell me!"

"The Prince—his woman—in his chariot—he—he—they—the invaders—"

I pushed the flabby creature aside and rushed toward the apse. A brazen wall ten times my own height confronted me. I pounded on it. "Avluela!" I shouted hoarsely. *"Av...lu...ela...!"*

I was neither thrust away nor admitted. I was ignored. The bedlam at the western doors of the palace had extended itself now to the nave and aisles, and as the ragged beggars boiled toward me I executed a quick turn and found myself passing through one of the side doors of the palace.

Suspended and passive, I stood in the courtyard that led to the royal hostelry. A strange electricity crackled in the air. I assumed it was an emanation from one of Roum's defense installations, some kind of beam designed to screen the city from attack. But an instant later I realized that it presaged the actual arrival of the invaders.

Starships blazed in the heavens.

When I had perceived them in my Watching they had appeared black against the infinite blackness, but now they burned with the radiance of suns. A stream of bright, hard, jewel-like globes bedecked the sky; they were ranged side by side, stretching from east to west in a continuous band, filling all the celestial arch, and as they erupted simultaneously into being it seemed to me that I heard the crash and throb of an invisible symphony heralding the arrival of the conquerors of Earth.

I do not know how far above me the starships were, nor how many of them hovered there, nor any of the details of their design. I know only that in sudden massive majesty they were there, and that if I had been a Defender my soul would have withered instantly at the sight.

Across the heavens shot light of many hues. The battle had been joined. I could not comprehend the actions of our warriors, and I was equally baffled by the maneuvers of those who had come to take possession of our history-crusted but time-diminished planet. To my shame I felt not only out of the struggle but above the struggle, as though this were no quarrel of mine. I wanted Avluela beside me, and she was somewhere within the depths of the palace of the Prince of Roum. Even Gormon would have been a comfort now, Gormon the Changeling, Gormon the spy, Gormon the monstrous betrayer of our world.

Gigantic amplified voices bellowed, "Make way for the Prince of

Roum! The Prince of Roum leads the Defenders in the battle for the fatherworld!"

From the palace emerged a shining vehicle the shape of a teardrop, in whose bright-metaled roof a transparent sheet had been mounted so that all the populace could see and take heart in the presence of the ruler. At the controls of the vehicle sat the Prince of Roum, proudly erect, his cruel, youthful features fixed in harsh determination; and beside him, robed like an empress, I beheld the slight figure of the Flier Avluela. She seemed in a trance.

The royal chariot soared upward and was lost in the darkness.

It seemed to me that a second vehicle appeared and followed its path, and that the Prince's reappeared, and that the two flew in tight circles, apparently locked in combat. Clouds of blue sparks wrapped both chariots now; and then they swung high and far and were lost to me behind one of the hills of Roum.

Was the battle now raging all over the planet? Was Perris in jeopardy, and holy Jorslem, and even the sleepy isles of the Lost Continents? Did starships hover everywhere? I did not know. I perceived events in only one small segment of the sky over Roum, and even there my awareness of what was taking place was dim, uncertain, and ill-informed. There were momentary flashes of light in which I saw battalions of Fliers streaming across the sky; and then darkness returned as though a velvet shroud had been hurled over the city. I saw the great machines of our defense firing in fitful bursts from the tops of our towers; and yet I saw the starships untouched, unharmed, unmoved above. The courtyard in which I stood was deserted, but in the distance I heard voices, full of fear and foreboding, shouting in tinny tones that might have been the screeching of birds. Occasionally there came a booming sound that rocked all the city. Once a platoon of Somnambulists was driven past where I was; in the plaza fronting the palace I observed what appeared to be an array of Clowns unfolding some sort of sparkling netting of a military look; by one flash of lightning I was able to see a trio of Rememberers making copious notes of all that elapsed as they soared aloft on the gravity plate. It seemed—I was not sure—that the vehicle of the Prince of Roum returned, speeding across the sky with its pursuer clinging close. "Avluela," I whispered, as the twin dots of lights left my sight. Were the starships disgorging troops? Did colossal pylons of force spiral down from those orbiting brightnesses to touch the surface of the Earth? Why had the Prince seized Avluela? Where was Gormon? What were our Defenders doing? Why were the enemy ships not blasted from the sky?

Rooted to the ancient cobbles of the courtyard, I observed the cosmic battle in total lack of understanding throughout the long night.

Dawn came. Strands of pale light looped from tower to tower. I touched fingers to my eyes, realizing that I must have slept while standing. Perhaps I should apply for membership in the guild of Somnambulists, I told myself lightly. I put my hands to the Rememberer's shawl about my shoulders and wondered how I managed to acquire it, and the answer came.

I looked toward the sky.

The alien starships were gone. I saw only the ordinary morning sky, gray with pinkness breaking through. I felt the jolt of compulsion and looked about for my cart, and reminded myself that I need do no more Watching, and I felt more empty than one would ordinarily feel at such an hour.

Was the battle over?

Had the enemy been vanquished?

Were the ships of the invaders blasted from the sky and lying in charred ruin outside Roum?

All was silent. I heard no more celestial symphonies. Then out of the eerie stillness there came a new sound, a rumbling noise as of wheeled vehicles passing through the streets of the city. And the invisible Musicians played one final note, deep and resonant, which trailed away jaggedly as though every string had been broken at once.

Over the speakers used for public announcements came quiet words.

"Roum is fallen. Roum is fallen."

8.

The royal hostelry was untended. Neuters and members of the servant guilds all had fled. Defenders, Masters, and Dominators must have perished honorably in combat. Basil the Rememberer was nowhere about; likewise none of his brethren. I went to my room, cleansed and refreshed and fed myself, gathered my few possessions, and bade farewell to the luxuries I had known so briefly. I regretted that I had had such a short time to visit Roum; but at least Gormon had been a most excellent guide, and I had seen a great deal.

Now I proposed to move on.

It did not seem prudent to remain in a conquered city. My room's thinking cap did not respond to my queries, and so I did not know what the extent of the defeat was, here or in other regions, but it was evident to me that Roum at least had passed from human control, and I wished to depart quickly. I weighed the thought of going to Jorslem, as that tall Pilgrim had suggested upon my entry into Roum; but then I reflected and chose a westward route, toward Perris, which not only was closer but held the headquarters of the Rememberers. My own occupation had been destroyed; but on this first morning of Earth's conquest I felt a sudden powerful and strange yearning to offer myself humbly to the Rememberers and seek with them knowledge of our more glittering yesterdays.

At midday I left the hostelry. I walked first to the palace, which still stood open. The beggars lay strewn about, some drugged, some sleeping, most dead; from the crude manner of their death I saw that they must have slain one another in their panic and frenzy. A despondent-looking Indexer squatted beside the three skulls of the in-

terrogation fixture in the chapel. As I entered he said, "No use. The
brains do not reply."

"How goes it with the Prince of Roum?"

"Dead. The invaders shot him from the sky."

"A young Flier rode beside him. What do you know of her?"

"Nothing. Dead, I suppose."

"And the city?"

"Fallen. Invaders are everywhere."

"Killing?"

"Not even looting," the Indexer said. "They are most gentle. They
have *collected* us."

"In Roum alone, or everywhere?"

The man shrugged. He began to rock rhythmically back and forth.
I let him be, and walked deeper into the palace. To my surprise, the
imperial chambers of the Prince were unsealed. I went within; I was
awed by the sumptuous luxury of the hangings, the draperies, the lights,
the furnishings. I passed from room to room, coming at last to the royal
bed, whose coverlet was the living flesh of a colossal bivalve of the
planet of another star, and as the shell yawned for me I touched the
infinitely soft fabric under which the Prince of Roum had lain, and I
recalled that Avluela too had lain here, and if I had been a younger man
I would have wept.

I left the palace and slowly crossed the plaza to begin my journey
toward Perris.

As I departed I had my first glimpse of our conquerors. A vehicle
of alien design drew up at the plaza's rim and perhaps a dozen figures
emerged. They might almost have been human. They were tall and
broad, deep-chested, as Gormon was, and only the extreme length of
their arms marked them instantly as alien. Their skins were of strange
texture, and if I had been closer I suspect I would have seen eyes and
lips and nostrils that were not of a human design. Taking no notice of
me, they crossed the plaza, walking in a curiously loose-jointed loping
way that reminded me irresistibly of Gormon's stride, and entered the
palace. They seemed neither swaggering nor belligerent.

Sightseers. Majestic Roum once more exerted its magnetism upon
strangers.

Leaving our new masters to their amusement, I walked off, toward
the outskirts of the city. The bleakness of eternal winter crept into my
soul. I wondered: did I feel sorrow that Roum had fallen? Or did I
mourn the loss of Avluela? Or was it only that I now had missed three
successive Watchings, and like an addict I was experiencing the pangs
of withdrawal?

It was all of these that pained me, I decided. But mostly the last.

No one was abroad in the city as I made for the gates. Fear of the new masters kept the Roumish in hiding, I supposed. From time to time one of the alien vehicles hummed past, but I was unmolested. I came to the city's western gate late in the afternoon. It was open, revealing to me a gently rising hill on whose breast rose trees with dark green crowns. I passed through and saw, a short distance beyond the gate, the figure of a Pilgrim who was shuffling slowly away from the city.

I overtook him easily.

His faltering, uncertain walk seemed strange to me, for not even his thick brown robes could hide the strength and youth of his body; he stood erect, his shoulders square and his back straight, and yet he walked with the hesitating, trembling step of an old man. When I drew abreast of him and peered under his hood I understood, for affixed to the bronze mask all Pilgrims wear was a reverberator, such as is used by blind men to warn them of obstacles and hazards. He became aware of me and said, "I am a sightless Pilgrim. I pray you do not molest me."

It was not a Pilgrim's voice. It was a strong and harsh and imperious voice.

I replied, "I molest no one. I am a Watcher who has lost his occupation this night past."

"Many occupations were lost this night past, Watcher."

"Surely not a Pilgrim's."

"No," he said. "Not a Pilgrim's."

"Where are you bound?"

"Away from Roum."

"No particular destination?"

"No," the Pilgrim said. "None. I will wander."

"Perhaps we should wander together," I said, for it is accounted good luck to travel with a Pilgrim, and, shorn of my Flier and my Changeling, I would otherwise have traveled alone. "My destination is Perris. Will you come?"

"There as well as anywhere else," he said bitterly. "Yes. We will go to Perris together. But what business does a Watcher have there?"

"A Watcher has no business anywhere. I go to Perris to offer myself in service to the Rememberers."

"Ah," he said. "I was of that guild too, but it was only honorary."

"With Earth fallen, I wish to learn more of Earth in its pride."

"Is all Earth fallen, then, and not only Roum?"

"I think it is so," I said.

"Ah," replied the Pilgrim. "Ah!"

He fell silent and we went onward. I gave him my arm, and now he shuffled no longer, but moved with a young man's brisk stride. From time to time he uttered what might have been a sigh or a smothered sob. When I asked him details of his Pilgrimage, he answered obliquely or not at all. When we were an hour's journey outside Roum, and already amid forests, he said suddenly, "This mask gives me pain. Will you help me adjust it?"

To my amazement he began to remove it. I gasped, for it is forbidden for a Pilgrim to reveal his face. Had he forgotten that I was not sightless too?

As the mask came away he said, "You will not welcome this sight."

The bronze grillwork slipped down from his forehead, and I saw first eyes that had been newly blinded, gaping holes where no surgeon's knife, but possibly thrusting fingers, had penetrated, and then the sharp regal nose, and finally the quirked, taut lips of the Prince of Roum.

"Your Majesty!" I cried.

Trails of dried blood ran down his cheeks. About the raw sockets themselves were smears of ointment. He felt little pain, I suppose, for he had killed it with those green smears, but the pain that burst through me was real and potent.

"Majesty no longer," he said. "Help me with the mask!" His hands trembled as he held it forth. "These flanges must be widened. They press cruelly at my cheeks. Here—here—"

Quickly I made the adjustments, so that I would not have to see his ruined face for long.

He replaced the mask. "I am a Pilgrim now," he said quietly. "Roum is without its Prince. Betray me if you wish, Watcher; otherwise help me to Perris; and if ever I regain my power you will be well rewarded."

"I am no betrayer," I told him.

In silence we continued. I had no way of making small talk with such a man. It would be a somber journey for us to Perris; but I was committed now to be his guide. I thought of Gormon and how well he had kept his vows. I thought too of Avluela, and a hundred times the words leaped to my tongue to ask the fallen Prince how his consort the Flier had fared in the night of defeat, and I did not ask.

Twilight gathered, but the sun still gleamed golden-red before us in the west. And suddenly I halted and made a hoarse sound of surprise deep in my throat, as a shadow passed overhead.

High above me Avluela soared. Her skin was stained by the colors of the sunset, and her wings were spread to their fullest, radiant with every hue of the spectrum. She was already at least the height of a hundred men above the ground, and still climbing, and to her I must have been only a speck among the trees.

"What is it?" the Prince asked. "What do you see?"

"Nothing."

"Tell me what you see!"

I could not deceive him. "I see a Flier, your Majesty. A slim girl far aloft."

"Then the night must have come."

"No," I said. "The sun is still above the horizon."

"How can that be? She can have only nightwings. The sun would hurl her to the ground."

I hesitated. I could not bring myself to explain how it was that this time Avluela flew by day, though she had only nightwings. I could not tell the Prince of Roum that beside her, wingless, flew the invader Gormon, effortlessly moving through the air, his arm about her thin shoulders, steadying her, supporting her, helping her resist the pressure of the solar wind. I could not tell him that his nemesis flew with the last of his consorts above his head.

"Well?" he demanded. "How does she fly by day?"

"I do not know," I said. "It is a mystery to me. There are many things nowadays I can no longer understand."

The Prince appeared to accept that. "Yes, Watcher. Many things none of us can understand."

He fell once more into silence. I yearned to call out to Avluela, but I knew she could not and would not hear me, and so I walked on toward the sunset, toward Perris, leading the blind Prince. And over us Avluela and Gormon sped onward, limned sharply against the day's last glow, until they climbed so high they were lost to my sight.

PART TWO
AMONG THE
REMEMBERERS

1.

To journey with a fallen Prince is no easy thing. His eyes were gone, but not his pride; blinding had taught him no humility. He wore the robes and mask of a Pilgrim, but there was no piety in his soul and little grace. Behind his mask he still knew himself to be the Prince of Roum.

I was all his court now, as we walked the road to Perris in early springtime. I led him along the right roads; I amused him at his command with stories of my wanderings; I nursed him through moods of sulky bitterness. In return I got very little except the assurance that I would eat regularly. No one denies food to a Pilgrim, and in each village on our way we stopped in inns, where he was fed and I, as his companion, also was given meals. Once, early in our travels, he erred and haughtily told an innkeeper, "See that you feed my servant as well!" The blinded Prince could not see that look of shocked disbelief—for what would a Pilgrim be doing with a servant?—but I smiled at the innkeeper, and winked, and tapped my forehead, and the man understood and served us both without discussion. Afterward I explained the error to the Prince, and thereafter he spoke of me as his companion. Yet I knew that to him I was nothing but a servant.

The weather was fair. Eyrop was growing warm as the year turned. Slender willows and poplars were greening beside the road, though much of the way out of Roum was planted with lavish star-trees imported during the gaudy days of the Second Cycle, and their blue-bladed leaves had resisted our puny Eyropan winter. The birds, too, were coming back from their season across the sea in Afreek. They sparkled overhead, singing, discussing among themselves the change of masters in the world. "They mock me," said the Prince one dawn. "They sing to me and defy me to see their brightness!"

Oh, he was bitter, and with good reason. He, who had had so much and lost all, had a good deal to lament. For me, the defeat of Earth meant only an end to habits. Otherwise all was the same: no longer need I keep my Watch, but I still wandered the face of the world, alone even when, as now, I had a companion.

I wondered if the Prince knew why he had been blinded. I wondered if, in the moment of his triumph, Gormon had explained to the Prince that it was as elemental a matter as jealousy over a woman that had cost him his eyes.

"You took Avluela," Gormon might have said. "You saw a little Flier, and you thought she'd amuse you. And you said, here, girl, come to my bed. Not thinking of her as a person. Not thinking she might prefer others. Thinking only as a Prince of Roum might think—imperiously. Here, Prince!"

—and the quick, forked thrust of long-tipped fingers—

But I dared not ask. That much awe remained in me for this fallen monarch. To penetrate his privacy, to strike up a conversation with him about his mishaps as though he were an ordinary companion of the road—no, I could not. I spoke when I was spoken to. I offered conversation upon command. Otherwise I kept my silence, like a good commoner in the presence of royalty.

Each day we had our reminders that the Prince of Roum was royalty no longer.

Overhead flew the invaders, sometimes in floaters or other chariots, sometimes under their own power. Traffic was heavy. They were taking inventory of their world. Their shadows passed over us, tiny eclipses, and I looked up to see our new masters and oddly felt no anger at them, only relief that Earth's long vigil was over. For the Prince it was different. He always seemed to know when some invader passed above, and he clenched his fists, and scowled, and whispered black curses. Did his optic nerves still somehow record the movements of shadows? Or were his remaining senses so sharpened by the loss of one that he could detect the imperceptible humming of a floater and sniff the skins of the soaring invaders? I did not ask. I asked so little.

Sometimes at night, when he thought I slept, he sobbed. I pitied him then. He was so young to lose what he had, after all. I learned in those dark hours that even the sobs of a Prince are not those of ordinary men. He sobbed defiantly, belligerently, angrily. But yet he sobbed.

Much of the time he seemed stoic, resigned to his losses. He put one foot before the other and walked on briskly beside me, every step taking him farther from his great city of Roum, nearer to Perris. At other times, though, it seemed I could look through the bronze grillwork of his mask to see the curdled soul within. His pent-up rage took petty outlets. He mocked me for my age, for my low rank, for the emptiness of my life's purpose now that the invasion for which I had Watched had come. He toyed with me.

"Tell me your name, Watcher!"

"It is forbidden, Majesty."

"Old laws are now repealed. Come on, man, we have months to travel together. Can I go on calling you Watcher all that time?"

"It is the custom of my guild."

"The custom of mine," he said, "is to give orders and have them obeyed. Your name!"

"Not even the guild of Dominators can have a Watcher's name without due cause and a guildmaster's writ."

He spat. "What a jackal you are, to defy me when I'm like this! If we were in my palace now, you'd never dare!"

"In your palace, Majesty, you would not make this unjust demand on me before your court. Dominators have obligations too. One of them is to respect the ways of lesser guilds."

"He lectures me," said the Prince. Irritably he threw himself down beside the road. Stretching against the grassy slope, he leaned back, touched one of the star-trees, snapped off a row of blades, clenched them in his hand so that they must have pricked his palm painfully. I stood beside him. A heavy land-vehicle rumbled by, the first we had seen on that empty road this morning. Within it were invaders. Some of them waved to us. After a long while the Prince said in a lighter, almost wheedling tone, "My name is Enric. Now tell me yours."

"I beg you to let me be, Majesty."

"But you have my name! It is just as forbidden for me to give mine as you yours!"

"I did not ask yours," I said firmly.

In the end I did not give him my name. It was a small enough victory, to refuse such information to a powerless Prince, but in a thousand little ways he made me pay for it. He nagged, chivvied, teased, cursed, and berated me. He spoke with contempt of my guild. He demanded menial services of me. I lubricated his metal mask; I sponged ointment into his ruined eyes; I did other things too humiliating to recall. And so we stumbled along the highway to Perris, the empty old man and the emptied young one, full of hatred for one another, and yet bound by the needs and the duties of wayfarers.

It was a difficult time. I had to cope with his changing moods as he soared to cosmic rapture over his plans for redeeming conquered Earth, and as he sank to abysses upon his inescapable realization that the conquest was final. I had to protect him from his own rashness in the villages, where he sometimes behaved as though he were still Prince of Roum, ordering folk about, slapping them even, in a way that was unbecoming to a holy man. Worse yet, I had to minister to his lusts, buying him women who came to him in darkness, unaware that they were dealing with one who claimed to be a Pilgrim. As a Pilgrim he was a fraud, for he did not carry the starstone with which Pilgrims make communion with the Will. Somehow I got him past all of these crises, even the time when we encountered on the road another Pilgrim, a genuine one. This was a formidable and disputatious old man full of theological quibbles. "Come and talk with me of the immanence of the Will," he said to the Prince, and the Prince, whose patience was frayed that afternoon, replied obscenely. I kicked the princely shin in a surreptitious way, and to the shocked Pilgrim I said, "Our friend is unwell today. Last night he held communion with the Will and received a revelation that unsettled his mind. I pray you, let us go on, and give him no talk of holiness until he is himself once more."

With such improvisations I managed our journey.

As the weather warmed, the Prince's attitude mellowed. Perhaps he was growing reconciled to his catastrophe, or possibly, in the prison of his lightless skull, he was teaching himself new tactics for meeting his changed existence. He talked almost idly of himself, his downfall, his humiliation. He spoke of the power that had been his in terms that said ummistakably that he had no illusions about ever recapturing it. He talked of his wealth, his women, his jewels, his strange machines, his Changelings and Musicians and Servitors, the Masters and even fellow Dominators who had knelt to him. I will not say that at any time I liked him, but at least at these times I recognized a suffering human being behind his impassive mask.

He even recognized in me a human being. I know it cost him much.

He said, "The trouble with power, Watcher, is that it cuts you off from people. People become things. Take yourself. To me, you were nothing but a machine that walked around Watching for invaders. I suppose you had dreams, ambitions, angers, all the rest, but I saw you as a dried-up old man without any independent existence outside of your guild function. Now I see much more by seeing nothing."

"What do you see?"

"You were young once, Watcher. You had a town you loved. A family. A girl, even. You chose, or had chosen for you, a guild, you went into apprenticeship, you struggled, your head ached you, your belly griped you, there were many dark moments when you wondered what it was all about, what it was for. And you saw us ride by, Masters, Dominators, and it was like comets going past. Yet here we are together, cast up by the tides on the road to Perris. And which of us is happier now?"

"I am beyond happiness or sorrow," I said.

"Is that the truth? Is that the truth? Or is it a line you hide behind? Tell me, Watcher: I know your guild forbids you to marry, but have you ever loved?"

"Sometimes."

"And are you beyond that now?"

"I am old," I said evasively.

"But you could love. You could love. You're released from your guild vows now, eh? You could take a bride."

I laughed. "Who'd have me?"

"Don't speak that way. You're not that old. You have strengths. You've seen the world, you understand it. Why, in Perris you could find yourself some wench who—" He paused. "Were you ever tempted, while you still were under your vows?"

Just then a Flier passed overhead. She was a woman of middle years, struggling a little in the sky, for some daylight remained to press on her wings. I felt a pang, and I wanted to tell the Prince: yes, yes, I was tempted, there was a little Flier not long ago, a girl, a child, Avluela; and in my way I loved her, though I never touched her; and I love her still.

I said nothing to Prince Enric.

I looked, though, at that Flier, freer than I because she had wings, and in the warmth of that spring evening I felt the chill of desolation enfolding me.

"Is it far to Perris?" the Prince asked.

"We will walk, and one day we will get there."

"And then?"

"For me an apprenticeship in the guild of Rememberers, and a new life. For you?"

"I hope to find friends there," he said.

We walked on, long hours each day. There were those who went by and offered us rides, but we refused, for at the checkpoints the invaders would be seeking such wandering members of the nobility as the Prince. We walked a tunnel miles long under sky-storming mountains sheathed in ice, and we entered a flat land of farming peasants, and we paused by awakening rivers to cool our toes. Golden summer burst upon us. We moved through the world but were not of it; we listened to no news of the conquest, although it was obvious that the invaders had taken full possession. In small vehicles they hovered everywhere, seeing our world that now was theirs.

I did the bidding of the Prince in all ways, including the unpleasant ones. I attempted to make his life less bleak. I gave him a sensation of being still a ruler—albeit of only one useless old Watcher. I taught him, too, how best to masquerade as a Pilgrim. From what little I knew I gave him postures, phrases, prayers. It was obvious that he had spent little time in contact with the Will while he reigned. Now he professed faith, but it was insincere, part of his camouflage.

In a town called Dijon, he said, "Here I will purchase eyes."

Not true eyes. The secret of making such replacements perished in the Second Cycle. Out among the more fortunate stars any miracle is available for a price, but our Earth is a neglected world in a backwater of the universe. The Prince might have gone out there in the days before conquest to purchase new sight, but now the best that was available to him was a way of distinguishing light from dark. Even that would give him a rudiment of sight; at present he had no other guidance than the reverberator that warned him of obstacles in his path. How did he know, though, that in Dijon he would find a craftsman with the necessary skills? And with what would he meet the cost?

He said, "The man here is a brother of one of my Scribes. He is of the guild of Artificers, and I often bought his work in Roum. He'll have eyes for me."

"And the cost?"

"I am not entirely without resources."

We stopped in a field of gnarled cork-trees, and the Prince undid his robes. Indicating a place in the fleshy part of his thigh, he said, "I carry a reserve here for emergencies. Give my your blade!" I handed it to him, and he seized the handle and pressed the stud that brought forth the cool, keen beam of light. With his left hand he felt his thigh, surveying for the exact place; then, stretching the flesh between two fingers, he made a surgically precise cut two inches long. He did not bleed, nor was there a sign that he felt pain. I watched in bewilderment as he slipped his fingers into the cut, spread its edges, and seemed to grope as if in a sack. He tossed my blade back to me.

Treasures tumbled from his thigh.

"Watch that nothing is lost," he ordered me.

To the grass there fell seven sparkling jewels of alien origin, a small and artful celestial globe, five golden coins of Imperial Roum of cycles past, a ring set with a glowing dab of quasi-life, a flask of some unknown perfume, a group of miniature musical instruments done in precious woods and metals, eight statuettes of regal-looking men, and more. I scooped these wonders into a dazzling heap.

"An overpocket," the Prince said coolly, "which a skilled Surgeon implanted in my flesh. I anticipated a time of crisis in which I might need to leave the palace hurriedly. Into it I stuffed what I could; there is much more where these came from. Tell me, tell me what I have taken out!"

I gave him the full inventory. He listened tensely to the end, and I knew that he had kept count of all that had poured forth, and was testing my honesty. When I was done, he nodded, pleased. "Take the globe," he said, "and the ring, and the two brightest jewels. Hide them in your pouch. The rest goes back within." He spread the lips of the incision, and one by one I dropped the glories inside, where they joined who knew what splendid things lying in another dimension, the outlet from which was embedded in the Prince. He might have half the contents of the palace tucked away in his thigh. At the end he pressed the cut together, and it healed without a trace of a mark as I watched. He robed himself.

In town we quickly located the shop of Bordo the Artificer. He was a squat man with a speckled face, a grizzled beard, a tic in one eye, and a flat coarse nose, but his fingers were as delicate as a woman's. His shop was a dark place with dusty wooden shelves and small windows; it could have been a building ten thousand years old. A few elegant items were on display. Most were not. He looked at us guardedly, obviously baffled that a Watcher and a Pilgrim should come to him.

At the Prince's prodding I said, "My friend needs eyes."

"I make a device, yes. But it is expensive, and it takes many months to prepare. Beyond the means of any Pilgrim."

I laid one jewel on the weathered counter. "We have means."

Shaken, Bordo snatched up the jewel, turned it this way and that, saw the alien fires glowing at its heart.

"If you come back when the leaves are falling—"

"You have no eyes in stock?" I asked.

He smiled. "I get few calls for such things. We keep a small inventory."

I put down the celestial globe. Bordo recognized it as the work of a master, and his jaw sagged. He put it in one palm and tugged at his beard with the other hand. I let him look at it long enough to fall in love with it, and then I took it back and said, "Autumn is too long to wait. We will have to go elsewhere. Perris, perhaps." I caught the Prince's elbow, and we shuffled toward the door.

"Stop!" Bordo cried. "At least let me check! Perhaps I have a pair somewhere—" And he began to rummage furiously in overpockets mounted in the rear wall.

He had eyes in stock, of course, and I haggled a bit on the price, and we settled for the globe, the ring, and one jewel. The Prince was silent throughout the transaction. I insisted on immediate installation and Bordo, nodding excitedly, shut his shop, slipped on a thinking cap, and summoned a sallow-faced Surgeon. Shortly the preliminaries of the operation were under way. The Prince lay on a pallet in a sealed and sterile room. He removed his reverberator and then his mask; and as those sharp features came into view, Bordo—who had been to the court of Roum—grunted in amazement and began to say something. My foot descended heavily on his. Bordo swallowed his words; and the Surgeon, unaware, began tranquilly to swab the ruined sockets.

The eyes were pearl-gray spheres, smaller than real eyes and broken by transverse slits. What mechanism was within I do not know, but from their rear projected tiny golden connections to fasten to the nerves. The Prince slept through the early part of the task, while I stood guard and Bordo assisted the Surgeon. Then it was necessary to awaken him. His face convulsed in pain, but it was so quickly mastered that Bordo muttered a prayer at this display of determination.

"Some light here," said the Surgeon.

Bordo nudged a drifting globe closer. The Prince said, "Yes, yes, I see the difference."

"We must test. We must adjust," the Surgeon said.

Bordo went outside. I followed. The man was trembling, and his face was green with fear.

"Will you kill us now?" he asked.

"Of course not."

"I recognized—"

"You recognized a poor Pilgrim," I said, "who has suffered a terrible misfortune while on his journey. No more. Nothing else."

I examined Bordo's stock awhile. Then the Surgeon and his patient emerged. The Prince now bore the pearly spheres in his sockets, with a meniscus of false flesh about them to insure a tight fit. He looked more machine than man, with those dead things beneath his brows, and as he moved his head the slits widened, narrowed, widened again, silently, stealthily. "Look," he said, and walked across the room, indicating objects, even naming them. I knew that he saw as though through a thick veil, but at least he saw, in a fashion. He masked himself again and by nightfall we were gone from Dijon.

The Prince seemed almost buoyant. But what he had in his skull was a poor substitute for what Gormon had ripped from him, and soon enough he knew it. That night, as we slept on stale cots in a Pilgrim's hostelry, the Prince cried out in wordless sounds of fury, and by the shifting light of the true moon and the two false ones I saw his arms rise, his fingers curl, his nails strike at an imagined enemy, and strike again, and again.

2.

It was summer's end when we finally reached Perris. We came into the city from the south, walking a broad, resilient highway bordered by ancient trees, amid a fine shower of rain. Gusts of wind blew shriveled leaves about us. That night of terror on which we both had fled conquered Roum now seemed almost a dream; we were toughened by a spring and summer of walking, and the gray towers of Perris seemed to hold out promise of new beginnings. I suspected that we deceived ourselves, for what did the world hold for a shattered Prince who saw only shadows, and a Watcher long past his proper years?

This was a darker city than Roum. Even in late winter, Roum had had clear skies and bright sunlight. Perris seemed perpetually clouded over, buildings and environment both somber. Even the city walls were ash-gray, and they had no sheen. The gate stood wide. Beside it there lounged a small, sullen man in the garb of the guild of Sentinels, who made no move to challenge us as we approached. I looked at him questioningly. He shook his head.

"Go in, Watcher."

"Without a check?"

"You haven't heard? All cities were declared free six nights ago. Order of the invaders. Gates are never closed now. Half the Sentinels have no work."

"I thought the invaders were searching for enemies," I said. "The former nobility."

"They have their checkpoints elsewhere, and no Sentinels are used. The city is free. Go in. Go in."

As we went in, I said, "Then why are you here?"

"It was my post for forty years," the Sentinel said. "Where should I go?"

I made the sign that told him I shared his sorrow, and the Prince and I entered Perris.

"Five times I came to Perris by the southern gate," said the Prince. "Always by chariot, with my Changelings walking before me and making music in their throats. We proceeded to the river, past the ancient buildings and monuments, on to the palace of the Comt of Perris. And by night we danced on gravity plates high above the city, and there were ballets of Fliers, and from the Tower of Perris there was performed an aurora for us. And the wine, the red wine of Perris, the women in their saucy gowns, the red-tipped breasts, the sweet thighs! We bathed in wine, Watcher." He pointed vaguely. "Is that the Tower of Perris?"

"I think it is the ruin of this city's weather machine," I said.

"A weather machine would be a vertical column. What I see rises from a wide base to a slender summit, as does the Tower of Perris."

"What I see," I said gently, "is a vertical column, at least thirty men high, ending in a rough break. The Tower would not be this close to the southern gate, would it?"

"No," said the Prince, and muttered a foulness. "The weather machine it is, then. These eyes of Bordo's don't see so clearly for me, eh? I deceive myself, Watcher. I deceive myself. Find a thinking cap and see if the Comt has fled."

I stared a moment longer at the truncated pillar of the weather machine, that fantastic device which had brought such grief upon the world in the Second Cycle. I tried to penetrate its sleek, almost oily marble sides, to see the coiling intestines of mysterious devices that had been capable of sinking whole continents, that long ago had transformed my homeland in the west from a mountainous country to a chain of islands. Then I turned away, donned a public cap, asked for the Comt, got the answer I expected, and demanded to know the locations of places where we might find lodging.

The Prince said, "Well?"

"The Comt of Perris was slain during the conquest along with all his sons. His dynasty is extinguished, his title is abolished, his palace has been transformed into a museum by the invaders. The rest of the Perrisian nobility is dead or has taken flight. I'll find a place for you at the lodge of Pilgrims."

"No. Take me with you to the Rememberers."

"Is that the guild you seek now?"

He gestured impatiently. "No, fool! But how can I stay alone in a strange city, with all my friends gone? What would I say to true Pilgrims in their hostelry? I'll stay with you. The Rememberers can hardly turn away a blind Pilgrim."

He gave me no choice. And so he accompanied me to the Hall of Rememberers.

We had to cross half the city, and it took us nearly the whole day. Perris seemed to me to be in disarray. The coming of the invaders had upset the structure of our society, liberating from their tasks great blocs of people, in some cases whole guilds. I saw dozens of my fellow Watchers in the streets, some still dragging about with them their cases of instruments, others, like me, freed of that burden and scarcely knowing what to do with their hands. My guildmates looked glum and hollow; many of them were dull-eyed with carousing, now that all discipline was shattered. Then there were Sentinels, aimless and dispirited because they had nothing to guard, and Defenders, cowed and dazed at the ending of defense. I saw no Masters and of course no Dominators, but many unemployed Clowns, Musicians, Scribes, and other court functionaries drifted randomly. Also there were hordes of dull neuters, their nearly mindless bodies slumped from unfamiliar disuse. Only Vendors and Somnambulists seemed to be carrying on business as usual.

The invaders were very much in evidence. In twos and threes they strolled on every street, long-limbed beings whose hands dangled nearly to their knees; their eyelids were heavy, their nostrils were hidden in filtration pouches, their lips were full and, when not apart, joined almost seamlessly. Most of them were dressed in identical robes of a deep, rich green, perhaps a uniform of military occupation; a few carried weapons of an oddly primitive kind, great heavy things slung across their backs, probably more for display than for self-defense. They seemed generally relaxed as they moved among us—genial conquerors, self-confident and proud, fearing no molestation from the defeated populace. Yet the fact that they never walked alone argued that they felt an inner wariness. I could not find it in me to resent their presence, nor even the implied arrogance of their possessive glances at the ancient monuments of Perris; yet the Prince of Roum, to whom all figures were merely upright bars of dark gray against a field of light gray, instinctively sensed their nearness to him and reacted with quick hostile intakes of breath.

Also there were many more outworld visitors than usual, star-beings of a hundred kinds, some able to breathe our air, others going about in hermetic globes or little pyramid-shaped breathing-boxes or contour suits. It was nothing new to see such strangers on Earth, of course, but the sheer quantity of them was astonishing. They were everywhere, prowling into the houses of Earth's old religions, buying shining models of the Tower of Perris from Vendors at street corners, clambering precariously into the upper levels of the walkways, peering into occupied dwellings, snapping images, exchanging currency with furtive hucksters, flirting with Fliers and Somnambulists, risking their lives at our restaurants, moving in shepherded groups from sight to sight. It was as though our invaders had passed the word through the galaxies: SEE OLD EARTH NOW. UNDER NEW MANAGEMENT.

At least our beggars were flourishing. The outworld ones fared poorly at the hands of the alien almsgivers, but those who were Earthborn did well, except for the Changelings, who could not be recognized as native stock. I saw several of these mutants, disgruntled at being refused, turn on other beggars who had had better luck and beat them to the ground, while image-snappers recorded the scene for the delight of galactic stay-at-homes.

We came in time to the Hall of Rememberers.

It was an imposing building, as well it might be, housing as it did all of our planet's past. It rose to an enormous height on the southern bank of the Senn, just opposite the equally massive palace of the Comt. But the dwelling of the deposed Comt was an ancient building, truly ancient, of the First Cycle even, a long, involuted structure of gray stone with a green metal roof in the traditional Perrisian style, while the Hall of Rememberers was a shaft of polished whiteness, its surface unbroken by windows, about which there coiled from summit to base a golden helix of burnished metal that bore inscribed on it the history of mankind. The upper coils of the helix were blank. At a distance I could read nothing, and I wondered whether the Rememberers had taken the trouble to inscribe upon their building the tale of Earth's final defeat. Later I learned that they had not—that the story, in fact, terminated at the end of the Second Cycle, leaving untold much for which little pleasure was felt.

Night was falling now. And Perris, which had looked so dreary in the clouded and drizzly day, came to beauty like a dowager returning from Jorslem with her youth and voluptuousness restored. The city's lights cast a soft but dazzling radiance that magically illuminated the old gray buildings, turning angles hazy, hiding antiquity's grime, blurring ugliness into poetry. The Comt's palace was transformed from a heavy thing of sprawling bulk into an airy fable. The Tower of Perris, spotlighted against the dusk, loomed above us to the east like a giant gaunt spider, but a spider of grace and charm. The whiteness of the Hall of Rememberers now was intolerably beautiful, and the helical coil of history no longer seemed to wind to the summit, but plunged directly into one's heart. The Fliers of Perris were abroad at this hour, taking their ease above us in a graceful ballet, their filmy wings spread wide to catch the light from below, their slender bodies trailing at an angle to the horizon. How they soared, these genetically altered children of Earth, these fortunate members of a guild that demands only that its members find pleasure in life! They shed beauty upon the groundlings like little moons. They were joined in their airborne dance by invaders, flying in some method unknown to me, their lengthy limbs drawn close to their bodies. I noticed that the Fliers showed no distaste for those who had come to share their sport, but rather appeared to welcome the outworlders, allowing them places in the dance.

Higher, on the backdrop of the sky itself, whirled the two false moons, blank and burnished, skimming from west to east; and blobs of disciplined light swirled in mid-atmosphere in what I supposed was a customary Perrisian diversion; and speakers floating beneath the clouds showered us with sparkling music. I heard the laughter of girls from somewhere; I scented bubbling wine. If this is Perris conquered, I wondered, what must Perris free have been like?

"Are we at the Hall of Rememberers?" asked Prince Enric testily.

"This is it, yes," I replied. "A tower of white."

"I know what it looks like, idiot! But now—I see less well after dark—that building, there?"

"You point to the palace of the Comt, Majesty."

"There, then."

"Yes."

"Why have we not gone in?"

"I am seeing Perris," I said. "I have never known such beauty. Roum is attractive too, in a different way. Roum is an emperor; Perris is a courtesan."

"You talk poetry, you shriveled old man!"

"I feel my age dropping away. I could dance in the streets now. This city sings to me."

"Go in. Go in. We are here to see the Rememberers. Let it sing to you later."

I sighed and guided him toward the entrance to the great hall. We passed up a walkway of some black glossy stone, while beams of light played down on us, scanning us and recording us. A monstrous ebon door, five men wide and ten men high, proved to be only a projected illusion, for as we neared it I sensed the depth of it, saw its vaulted interior, and knew it for a deception. I felt a vague warmth and tasted a strange perfume as we passed through it.

Within was a mammoth antechamber nearly as awesome as the grand inner space of the palace of the Prince of Roum. All was white, the stone glowing with an inner radiance that bathed everything in brilliance. To right and left, heavy doorways led to inner wings. Although night had come, many individuals were clustered about access banks mounted on the rear wall of the antechamber, where screens and caps gave them contact with the master files of the guild of Rememberers. I noticed with interest that many of those who had come here with questions about mankind's past were invaders.

Our footsteps crackled on the tiled floor as we crossed it.

I saw no actual Rememberers, and so I went to an access bank, put on a thinking cap, and notified the embalmed brain to which it was connected that I sought the Rememberer Basil, he whom I had met briefly in Roum.

"What is your business with him?"

"I bring with me his shawl, which he left in my care when he fled Roum."

"The Rememberer Basil has returned to Roum to complete his research, by permission of the conqueror. I will send to you another member of the guild to receive the shawl."

We did not have long to wait. We stood together near the rear of the antechamber, and I contemplated the spectacle of the invaders who had so much to learn, and in moments there came to us a thick-set, dour-faced man some years younger than myself, but yet not young, who wore about his broad shoulders the ceremonial shawl of his guild.

"I am the Rememberer Elegro," he announced portentously.

"I bring you Basil's shawl."

"Come. Follow."

He had emerged from an imperceptible place in the wall where a sliding block turned on pivots. Now he slid it once more and rapidly went down a passageway. I called out to him that my companion was blind and could not match his pace, and the Rememberer Elegro halted, looking visibly impatient. His downcurving mouth twitched, and he buried his short fingers in the deep black curls of his beard. When we had caught up with him he moved on less swiftly. We pursued an infinity of passageways and ended in Elegro's domicile, somewhere high in the tower.

The room was dark but amply furnished with screens, caps, scribing equipment, voice-boxes, and other aids to scholarship. The walls were hung with a purple-black fabric, evidently alive, for its marginal folds rippled in pulsating rhythms. Three drifting globes gave less than ample light.

"The shawl," he said.

I produced it from my pouch. It had amused me to wear it for a while in those first confused days of the conquest—after all, Basil had left it in my hands when he fled down the street, and I had not meant to wrest it from him, but he obviously had cared little for its loss—but shortly I had put it away, since it bred confusion for a man in Watcher's garb to wear a Rememberer's shawl. Elegro took it from me curtly and unfolded it, scrutinizing it as though looking for lice.

"How did you get this?"

"Basil and I encountered one another in the street during the actual moment of the invasion. He was highly agitated. I attempted to restrain him and he ran past me, leaving me still grasping his shawl."

"He told a different story."

"I regret it if I have compromised him," I said.

"At any rate, you have returned his shawl. I'll communicate the news to Roum tonight. Are you expecting a reward for delivering it?"

"Yes."

Displeased, Elegro said, "Which is?"

"To be allowed to come among the Rememberers as an apprentice."

He looked startled. "You have a guild!"

"To be a Watcher in these days is to be guildless. For what should I watch? I am released from my vows."

"Perhaps. But you are old to be trying a new guild."

"Not *too* old."

"Ours is a difficult one."

"I am willing to work hard. I desire to learn. In my old age curiosity is born in me."

"Become a Pilgrim like your friend here. See the world."

"I have seen the world. Now I wish to join the Rememberers and learn of the past."

"You can dial an information below. Our access banks are open to you, Watcher."

"It is not the same. Enroll me."

"Apprentice yourself to the Indexers," Elegro suggested. "The work is similar, but not so demanding."

"I claim apprenticeship here."

Elegro sighed heavily. He steepled his fingers, bowed his head, quirked his lips. This was plainly unique to him. While he pondered, an inner door opened and a female Rememberer entered the room, carrying a small turquoise music-sphere cradled in both her hands. She took four paces and halted, obviously surprised that Elegro was entertaining visitors.

She made a nod of apology and said, "I will return later."

"Stay," said the Rememberer. To myself and the Prince he said, "My wife. The Rememberer Olmayne." To his wife he said, "These are

travelers newly come from Roum. They have delivered Basil's shawl.
The Watcher now asks apprenticeship in our guild. What do you advise?"

The Rememberer Olmayne's white brow furrowed. She put down
her music-sphere in a dark crystal vase; the sphere was unintentionally
activated as she did so, and it offered us a dozen shimmering notes
before she switched it off. Then she contemplated us, and I her. She
was notably younger than her husband, who was of middle years, while
she seemed to be hardly past first bloom. Yet there was a strength about
her that argued for greater maturity. Perhaps, I thought, she had been
to Jorslem to renew her youth; but in that case it was odd that her
husband had not done the same, unless he prized his look of age. She
was surely attractive. Her face was broad, with a high forehead, pro-
nounced cheekbones, a wide, sensual mouth, a jutting chin. Her hair
was lustrous black, contrasting most vividly with the strange pallor of
her skin. Such white skin is a rarity among us, though now I know that
it was more common in ancient times, when the breed was different.
Avluela, my lovely little Flier, had displayed that same combination of
black and white, but there the resemblance ended, for Avluela was all
fragility, and the Rememberer Olmayne was strength itself. Below her
long slender neck her body blossomed into well-set shoulders, high
breasts, firm legs. Her posture was regal.

She studied us at length, until I could scarcely meet the level gaze
of her widely spaced dark eyes. Ultimately she said, "Does the Watcher
regard himself as qualified to become one of us?"

The question appeared aimed at anyone in the chamber who cared
to reply. I hesitated; Elegro did likewise; and at length it was the Prince
of Roum who replied in his voice of command, "The Watcher is qualified to enter your guild."

"And who are you?" Olmayne demanded.

Instantly the Prince adopted a more accommodating tone. "A miserable blind Pilgrim, milady, who has wandered here on foot from
Roum, in this man's company. If I am any judge, you could do worse
than admit him as an apprentice."

Elegro said, "And yourself? What plans have you?"

"I wish only refuge here," said the Prince. "I am tired of roaming
and there is much thinking I must do. Perhaps you could allow me to
carry out small tasks here. I would not want to be separated from my
companion."

To me Olmayne said, "We will confer on your case. If there is
approval, you will be given the tests. I will be your sponsor."

"Olmayne!" blurted Elegro in unmistakable amazement.

She smiled serenely at us all.

A family quarrel appeared on the verge; but it was averted, and the Rememberers offered us hospitality, juices, sharper beverages, a night's lodging. We dined apart from them in one section of their suite, while other Rememberers were summoned to consider my irregular application. The Prince seemed in strange agitation; he bolted down his food, spilled a flask of wine, fumbled with his eating utensils, put his fingers again and again to his gray metallic eyeballs as though trying to scratch an itch that troubled the lobes of his brain.

At length he said in a low, urgent voice, "Describe her to me!"

I did so, in detail, coloring and shading my words to draw him the most vivid picture I could.

"She is beautiful, you say?"

"I believe so. You know that at my age one must work from abstract notions, not from the flow of the glands."

"Her voice arouses me," said the Prince. "She has power. She is queenly. She *must* be beautiful; there'd be no justice if her body failed to match the voice."

"She is," I said heavily, "another man's wife, and the giver of hospitality."

I remembered a day in Roum when the Prince's palanquin had come forth from the palace, and the Prince had spied Avluela, and ordered her to him, drawing her through the curtain to make use of her. A Dominator may command lesser folk that way; but a Pilgrim may not, and I feared Prince Enric's schemes now. He dabbed at his eyes again. His facial muscles worked.

"Promise me you'll not start trouble with her," I said.

The corner of his mouth jerked in what must have been the beginning of an angry retort, quickly stifled. With effort he said, "You misjudge me, old man. I'll abide by the laws of hospitality here. Be a good man and get me more wine, eh?"

I thumbed the serving niche and obtained a second flask. It was strong red wine, not the golden stuff of Roum. I poured; we drank; the flask was swiftly empty. I grasped it along its lines of polarity and gave it the proper twist, and it popped and was gone like a bubble. Moments later the Rememberer Olmayne entered. She had changed her garments; earlier she had worn an afternoon gown of dull hue and coarse fabric, but now she was garbed in a sheer scarlet robe fastened between her breasts. It revealed to me the planes and shadows of her body, and it surprised me to see that she had chosen to retain a navel. The little indentation broke the smooth downward sweep of her belly in an effect so carefully calculated to arouse that it nearly incited even me.

She said complacently, "Your application has been approved under my sponsorship. The tests will be administered tonight. If you succeed, you will be pledged to our division." Her eyes twinkled in sudden mischief. "My husband, you should know, is most displeased. But my husband's displeasure is not a thing to be feared. Come with me, both of you."

She stretched forth her hands, taking mine, taking the Prince's. Her fingers were cool. I throbbed with an inner fever and marveled at this sign of new youth that arose within me—not even by virtue of the waters of the house of renewal in sacred Jorslem.

"Come," said Olmayne, and led us to the place of test.

3.

And so I passed into the guild of Rememberers.

The tests were perfunctory. Olmayne brought us to a circular room somewhere near the summit of the great tower. Its curving walls were inlaid with rare woods of many hues, and shining benches rose from the floor, and in the center of all was a helix the height of a man, inscribed with letters too small to be read. Half a dozen Rememberers lounged about, plainly there only by Olmayne's whim, and not in the slightest interested in this old and shabby Watcher whom she had so unaccountably sponsored.

A thinking cap was offered me. A scratchy voice asked me a dozen questions through the cap, probing for my typical responses, querying me on biographical details. I gave my guild identification so that they could contact the local guildmaster, check my *bona fides*, and obtain my release. Ordinarily one could not win release from a Watcher's vows, but these were not ordinary times, and I knew my guild was shattered.

Within an hour all was done. Olmayne herself placed the shawl over my shoulders.

"You'll be given sleeping quarters near our suite," she said. "You'll have to surrender your Watcher garb, though your friend may remain in Pilgrim's clothes. Your training will begin after a probationary period. Meanwhile you have full access to any of our memory tanks. You realize, of course, that it will be ten years or more before you can win full admission to the guild."

"I realize that," I said.

"Your name now will be Tomis," Olmayne told me. "Not yet the

Rememberer Tomis, but Tomis of the Rememberers. There is a difference. Your past name no longer matters."

The Prince and I were conducted to the small room we would share. It was a humble enough place, but yet it had facilities for washing, outlets for thinking caps and other information devices, and a food vent. Prince Enric went about the room, touching things, learning the geography. Cabinets, beds, chairs, storage units, and other furniture popped in and out of the walls as he blundered onto the controls. Eventually he was satisfied; not blundering now, he activated a bed, and a sheaf of brightness glided from a slot. He stretched out.

"Tell me something, Tomis of the Rememberers."

"Yes?"

"To satisfy curiosity that eats at me. What was your name in previous life?"

"It does not matter now."

"No vow binds you to secrecy. Will you thwart me still?"

"Old habit binds me," I said. "For twice your lifetime I was conditioned never to speak my name except lawfully."

"Speak it now."

"Wuellig," I said.

It was strangely liberating to commit that act. My former name seemed to hover in the air before my lips; to dart about the room like a jewelbird released from its captivity; to soar, to turn sharply, to strike a wall and shiver to pieces with a light, tinkling sound. I trembled, "Wuellig," I said again. "My name was Wuellig."

"Wuellig no more."

"Tomis of the Rememberers."

And we both laughed until it hurt, and the blinded Prince swung himself to his feet and slapped his hand against mine in high good fellowship, and we shouted my name and his and mine again and again, like small boys who suddenly have learned the words of power and have discovered at last how little power those words really have.

Thus I took up my new life among the Rememberers.

For some time to come I did not leave the Hall of Rememberers at all. My days and nights were completely occupied, and I remained a stranger to Perris without. The Prince, too, though his time was not as fully taken up, stayed in the building almost always, going out only when boredom or fury overtook him. Occasionally the Rememberer Olmayne went with him, or he with her, so that he would not be alone in his darkness; but I know that on occasion he left the building by himself, defiantly intending to show that, even sightless, he could cope with the challenges of the city.

My waking hours were divided among these activities:
+ Preliminary orientations.
+ Menial duties of an apprentice.
+ Private researches.

Not unexpectedly, I found myself much older than the other apprentices then in residence. Most were youngsters, the children of Rememberers themselves; they looked upon me in bafflement, unable to comprehend having such an ancient for a schoolmate. There were a few fairly mature apprentices, those who had found a vocation for Remembering midway in life, but none approaching my age. Hence I had little social contact with my fellows in training.

For a part of each day we learned the techniques by which the Rememberers recapture Earth's past. I was shown wide-eyed through the laboratories where analysis of field specimens is performed; I saw the detectors which, by pinpointing the decay of a few atoms, give an age to an artifact; I watched as beams of many-colored light lancing from a ringed outlet turned a sliver of wood to ash and caused it to give up its secrets; I saw the very images of past events peeled from inanimate substance. We leave our imprint where we go: the particles of light rebound from our faces, and the photonic flux nails them to the environment. From which the Rememberers strip them, categorize them, fix them. I entered a room where a phantasmagoria of faces drifted on a greasy blue mist: vanished kings and guildmasters, lost dukes, heroes of ancient days. I beheld cold-eyed technicians prodding history from handfuls of charred matter. I saw damp lumps of trash give up tales of revolutions and assassinations, of cultural change, of the discarding of mores.

Then I was instructed superficially in the techniques of the field. Through cunning simulation I was shown Rememberers at work with vacuum cores digging through the mounds of the great ruined cities of Afreek and Ais. I participated vicariously in the undersea quest for the remnants of the civilizations of the Lost Continents; teams of Rememberers entered translucent, teardrop-shaped vehicles that were like blobs of green gelatin and sped into the depths of Earth Ocean, down and down to the slime-crusted prairies of the former land and with lancing beams of violet force, they drilled through muck and girders to find buried truths. I watched the gatherers of shards, the diggers of shadows, the collectors of molecular films. One of the best of the orientation experiences they provided was a sequence in which some truly heroic Rememberers excavated a weather machine in lower Afreek, baring the base of the titanic thing, lifting it on power-pulls from the soil, an extraction so mighty that the earth itself seemed to shriek when it was done. High aloft they floated the ponderous relic of Second Cycle folly, while shawled experts prodded in its root-place to learn how the column had been erected in the first instance. My eyes throbbed at the spectacle.

I emerged from these sessions with an overwhelming awe for this guild I had chosen. Individual Rememberers whom I had known had struck me generally as pompous, disdainful, haughty, or merely aloof; I did not find them charming. Yet is the whole greater than the sum of its parts, and I saw such men as Basil and Elegro, so vacant, so absent from ordinary human concerns, so disinterested, as parts of a colossal effort to win back from eternity our brilliant yesterdays. This research into lost times was magnificent, the only proper substitute for mankind's former activities; having lost our present and our future, we had of necessity to bend all our endeavors to the past, which no one could take from us if only we were vigilant enough.

For many days I absorbed the details of this effort, every stage of the work from the collection of specks of dust in the field through their treatment and analysis in the laboratory to the highest endeavor of all, synthesis and interpretation, which was carried out by senior Rememberers on the highest level of this building. I was given but a glimpse of those sages: withered and dry, old enough to be grandfathers to me, white heads bent forward, thin lips droning comments and interpretations, quibbles and corrections. Some of them, I was told in a hushed whisper, had been renewed at Jorslem two and three times apiece, and now were beyond renewal and in their final great age.

Next we were introduced to the memory tanks where the Rememberers store their findings, and from which are dispensed informations for the benefit of the curious.

As a Watcher I had had little curiosity and less interest in visiting memory tanks. Certainly I had never seen anything like this, for the tanks of the Rememberers were no mere three-brain or five-brain storage units, but mammoth installations with a hundred brains or more hooked in series. The room to which they took us—one of dozens beneath the building, I learned—was an oblong chamber, deep but not high, in which brain-cases were arrayed in rows of nine that faded into shadowed depths. Perspective played odd tricks; I was not sure if there were ten rows or fifty, and the sight of those bleached domes was overpoweringly immense.

"Are these the brains of former Rememberers?" I asked.

The guide replied, "Some of them are. But there's no necessity to use only Rememberers. Any normal human brain will do; even a Servitor has more storage capacity than you'd believe. We have no need for redundancy in our circuits, and so we can use the full resources of each brain."

I tried to peer through the heavy block of sleekness that protected the memory tanks from harm. I said, "What is recorded in this particular room?"

"The names of dwellers in Afreek in Second Cycle times, and as much personal data about each as we have so far recovered. Also, since these cells are not yet fully charged, we have temporarily stored in them certain geographical details concerning the Lost Continents, and information pertaining to the creation of Land Bridge."

"Can such information be easily transferred from temporary storage to permanent?" I asked.

"Easily, yes. Everything is electromagnetic here. Our facts are aggregates of charges; we shift them from brain to brain by reversing polarities."

"What if there were an electrical failure?" I demanded. "You say you have no redundancy here. Is there no possibility of losing data through some accident?"

"None," said the guide smoothly. "We have a series of fallback devices to insure continuity of power. And by using organic tissue for our storage cells, we have the best assurance of safety of all: for the brains themselves will retain their data in the event of a power interruption. It would be taxing but not impossible to recapture their contents."

"During the invasion," I said, "were any difficulties experienced?"

"We are under the protection of the invaders, who regard our work as vital to their own interests."

Not long afterward, at a general convocation of the Rememberers, we apprentices were permitted to look on from a balcony of the guildhall; below us, in full majesty, were the guild members, shawls in place, Elegro and Olmayne among them. On a dais that bore the helical symbol was Chancellor Kenishal of the Rememberers, an austere and commanding figure, and beside him was an even more conspicuous personage who was of the species that had conquered Earth. Kenishal spoke briefly. The resonance of his voice did not entirely conceal the hollowness of his words; like all administrators everywhere, he gushed platitudes, praising himself by implication as he congratulated his guild for its notable work. Then he introduced the invader.

The alien stretched forth his arms until they seemed to touch the walls of the auditorium.

"I am Manrule Seven," he said quietly. "I am Procurator of Perris, with particular responsibility for the guild of Rememberers. My purpose here today is to confirm the decree of the provisional occupational government. You Rememberers are to go totally unhampered in your work. You are to have free access to all sites on this planet or on any other world that may have bearing on your mastery of the past of this planet. All files are to remain open to you, except those pertaining to the organization of the conquest itself. Chancellor Kenishal has informed me that the conquest lies outside the scope of your present research in any case, so no hardship will be worked. We of the occupying government are aware of the value of the work of your guild. The history of this planet is of great significance, and we wish your efforts continued."

"To make Earth a better tourist attraction," said the Prince of Roum bitterly at my side.

Manrule Seven went on, "The Chancellor has requested me to inform you of one administrative change that will necessarily follow from the occupied status of your planet. In the past, all disputes among you were settled by the courts of your own guild, with Chancellor Kenishal having the highest right of appeal. For the sake of efficient administration it now becomes mandatory for us to impose our jurisdiction over that of the guild. Therefore the Chancellor will transfer to us those litigations which he feels no longer fall into his sphere of authority."

The Rememberers gasped. There was a sudden shifting of postures and exchanging of glances on the floor below.

"The Chancellor's abdicating!" blurted an apprentice near me.

"What choice does he have, fool?" another whispered harshly.

The meeting broke up in some confusion. Rememberers flooded into the hallways, gesticulating, debating, expostulating. One venerable wearer of the shawl was so shaken that he crouched down and began to make the series of stabilizer responses, heedless of the throng. The tide swept over us apprentices, forcing us back. I attempted to protect the Prince, fearing that he would be thrown to the floor and trampled; but we were swept apart and I lost sight of him for minutes. When I saw him again he stood with the Rememberer Olmayne. Her face was flushed, her eyes were bright; she was speaking rapidly, and the Prince was listening. His hand clung to her elbow as if for support.

4.

After the conclusion of the early period of orientations, I was given trivial tasks. Chiefly I was asked to do things that in an earlier time would have been performed wholly by machine: for example, to monitor the feed lines that oozed nutrients into the brain-boxes of the memory tanks. For several hours each day I walked through the narrow corridor of the inspection panels, searching for clogged lines. It had been so devised that when a line became blocked, a stress pattern was created that ran the length of the clear tubing that contained it, and beams of a special polarized light illuminated that pattern for benefit of the inspector. I did my humble task, now and again finding a blockage, and I did other little jobs as befitted my status of apprenticeship.

However, I also had the opportunity to pursue my own investigations into the events of my planet's past.

Sometimes one does not learn the value of things until they are lost. For a lifetime I served as a Watcher, striving to give early warning of a promised invasion of Earth, while caring little who might wish to invade us, or why. For a lifetime I realized dimly that Earth had known grander days than those of the Third Cycle into which I had been born, and yet I sought no knowledge of what those days had been like and of the reasons for our present diminished condition. Only when the starships of the invaders blossomed in the sky did I feel a sudden hunger to know of that lost past. Now, as the most elderly of apprentices, I, Tomis of the Rememberers, rummaged through the archives of vanished time.

Any citizen has the right to go to a public thinking cap and requisition an information from the Rememberers on any given subject. Nothing is concealed. But the Rememberers volunteer no aid; you must know how to ask, which means you must know what to ask. Item by item you must seek your facts. It is useful for those who must know, say, the long-term patterns of climate in Agupt, or the symptoms of the crystallization disease, or the limitations in the charter of one of the guilds; but it is no help at all to the man who wishes knowledge of the larger questions. One would need to requisition a thousand informations merely to make a beginning. The expense would be great; few would bother.

As an apprentice Rememberer I had full access to all data. More important, I had access to the indexes. The Indexers are a guild subsidiary to the Rememberers, a donkey guild of drudges who record and classify that which they often do not understand; the end product of their toil serves the greater guild, but the indexes are not open to all. Without them one scarcely is able to cope with the problems of research.

I will not summarize the stages by which I came by my knowledge—the hours spent shuffling through interwoven corridors, the rebuffs, the bewilderments, the throbbing of the brain. As a foolish novice I was at the mercy of pranksters, and many a fellow apprentice, even a guild member or two, led me astray for the sheer wicked joy of it. But I learned which routes to follow, how to set up sequences of questions, how to follow a path of references higher and higher until the truth bursts dazzlingly upon one. With persistence rather than with great intellect I wrung from the files of the Rememberers a coherent tale of the downfall of man.

This:

There was a time in ages past when life on Earth was brutal and primitive. We call this time the First Cycle. I do not speak of the period before civilization, that time of grunting and hairiness, of caves and stone tools. We consider the First Cycle to have commenced when man first learned to record information and to control environment. This occurred in Agupt and Sumir. By our way of reckoning the First Cycle commenced some 40,000 years ago—however, we are uncertain of its true length in its own terms, since the span of the year was altered at the end of the Second Cycle, and we have been unable thus far to determine how long, in previous eras, it took for our world to circle its sun. Somewhat longer than at present, perhaps.

The First Cycle was the time of Imperial Roum and of the first flowering of Jorslem. Eyrop remained savage long after Ais and parts of Afreek were civilized. In the west, two great continents occupied much of Earth Ocean, and these too were held by savages.

It is understood that in this cycle mankind had no contact with other worlds or stars. Such solitude is difficult to comprehend; but yet so it occurred. Mankind had no way of creating light except through fire; he could not cure his ills; life was not susceptible to renewal. It was a time without comforts, a gray time, harsh in its simplicity. Death came early; one barely had time to scatter a few sons about, and one was carried off. One lived with fear, but mostly not fear of real things.

The soul recoils from such an era. But yet it is true that in the First Cycle magnificent cities were founded—Roum, Perris, Atin, Jorslem—and splendid deeds were accomplished. One stands in awe of those ancestors, foul-smelling (no doubt), illiterate, without machines, and still capable of coming to terms with their universe and to some extent of mastering it.

War and grief were constant throughout the First Cycle. Destruction and creation were nearly simultaneous. Flames ate man's most glorious cities. Chaos threatened always to engulf order. How could men have endured such conditions for thousands of years?

Towards the close of the First Cycle much of the primitivism was outgrown. At last sources of power were accessible to man; there was the beginning of true transportation; communication over distances became possible; many inventions transformed the world in a short time. Methods of making war kept pace with the technological growth in other directions; but total catastrophe was averted, although several times it appeared to have arrived. It was during this final phase of the cycle that the Lost Continents were colonized, also Stralya, and that first contact was made with the adjoining planets of our solar system.

The transition from First Cycle to Second is arbitrarily fixed at the point when man first encountered intelligent beings from distant worlds. This, the Rememberers now believe, took place less than fifty generations after the First Cycle folk had mastered electronic and nuclear energy. Thus we may rightly say that the early people of Earth stumbled headlong from savagery to galactic contact—or, perhaps, that they crossed that gap in a few quick strides.

This too is cause for pride. For if the First Cycle was great despite its handicaps, the Second Cycle knew of no handicaps and achieved miracles.

In this epoch mankind spread out to the stars, and the stars came to mankind. Earth was a market for goods of all worlds. Wonders were commonplace. One might hope to live for hundreds of years; eyes, hearts, lungs, kidneys were replaced as easily as shoes; the air was pure, no man went hungry, war was forgotten. Machines of every sort served man. But the machines were not enough, and so the Second Cycle folk bred men who were machines, or machines who were men: creatures that were genetically human, but were born artificially, and were treated with drugs that prevented the permanent storing of memories. These creatures, analogous to our neuters, were capable of performing an efficient day's work, but were unable to build up that permanent body of experiences, memories, expectations, and abilities that is the mark of a human soul. Millions of such not-quite-humans handled the duller tasks of the day, freeing others for lives of glistening fulfillment. After the creation of the subhumans came the creation of the superanimals who, through biochemical manipulation of the brain, were able to carry out tasks once beyond the capacity of their species: dogs, cats, mice, and cattle were enrolled in the labor force, while certain high primates received functions formerly reserved for humans. Through this exploitation of the environment to the fullest, man created a paradise on Earth.

The spirit of man soared to the loftiest peak it had known. Poets, scholars, and scientists made splendid contributions. Shining cities sprawled across the land. The population was enormous, and even so, there was ample room for all, with no shortage of resources. One could indulge one's whims to any extent; there was much experimentation with genetic surgery and with mutagenetic and teratogenetic drugs, so that the human species adopted many new forms. There was, however, nothing yet like the variant forms of our cycle.

Across the sky in stately procession moved space stations serving every imaginable need. It was at this time that the two new moons were built, although the Rememberers have not yet determined whether their purpose was functional or esthetic. The auroras that now appear each night in the sky may have been installed at this time, although some factions of Rememberers argue that the presence of temperate-zone auroras began with the geophysical upheavals that heralded the close of the cycle.

It was, at any rate, the finest of times to be alive.

"See earth and die," was the watchword of the outworlders. No one making the galactic grand tour dared pass up this planet of miracles. We welcomed the strangers, accepted their compliments and their money, made them comfortable in the ways they preferred, and proudly displayed our greatnesses.

The Prince of Roum can testify that it is the fate of the mighty eventually to be humbled, and also that the higher one reaches for splendor, the more catastrophic one's downfall is apt to be. After some thousands of years of glories beyond my capacity to comprehend, the fortunate ones of the Second Cycle overreached themselves and committed two misdeeds, one born of foolish arrogance, the other born of excessive confidence. Earth is paying yet for those overreachings.

The effects of the first were slow to be felt. It was a function of

Earth's attitude toward the other species of the galaxy, which had shifted during the Second Cycle from awe to matter-of-fact acceptance to contempt. At the beginning of the cycle, brash and naive Earth had erupted into a galaxy already peopled by advanced races that long had been in contact with one another. This could well have produced a soul-crushing trauma, but instead it generated an aggressive urge to excel and surpass. And so it happened that Earthmen quickly came to look upon most of the galactics as equals, and then, as progress continued on Earth, as inferiors. This bred the easy habit of contempt for the backward.

Thus it was proposed to establish "study compounds" on Earth for specimens of inferior races. These compounds would reproduce the natural habitat of the races and would be accessible to scholars wishing to observe the life-processes of these races. However, the expense of collecting and maintaining the specimens was such that it quickly became necessary to open the compounds to the public at large, for purposes of amusement. These supposedly scientific compounds were, in fact, zoos for other intelligent species.

At the outset only the truly alien beings were collected, those so remote from human biological or psychological norms that there was little danger of regarding them as "people." A many-limbed thing that dwells in a tank of methane under high pressure would not strike a sympathetic response from those likely to object to the captivity of intelligent creatures. If that methane-dweller happened to have a complex civilization of a sort uniquely fitted to its environment, it could be argued that it was all the more important to duplicate that environment on Earth so that one might study so strange a civilization. Therefore the early compounds contained only the bizarre. The collectors were limited, also, to taking creatures who had not attained the stage of galactic travel themselves. It would not have been good form to kidnap lifeforms whose relatives were among the interstellar tourists on whom our world's economy had come so heavily to depend.

The success of the first compounds led to the demand for the formation of others. Less critical standards were imposed; not merely the utterly alien and grotesque were collected, but samplings of any sort of galactic life not in a position to register diplomatic protests. And, as the audacity of our ancestors increased, so did the restrictions on collection loosen, until there were samplings from a thousand worlds on Earth, including some whose civilizations were older and more intricate than our own.

The archives of the Rememberers showed that the expansion of our compounds stirred some agitation in many parts of the universe. We were denounced as marauders, kidnapers, and pirates; committees were formed to criticize our wanton disregard for the rights of sentient beings; Earthmen traveling to other planets were occasionally beset by mobs of hostile life-forms demanding that we free the prisoners of the compounds at once. However, these protesters were only a minority—most galactics kept an uncomfortable silence about our compounds. They regretted the barbarity of them, and nevertheless made a point of touring them when they visited Earth. Where else, after all, could one see hundreds of life-forms, culled from every part of the universe, in a few days? Our compounds were a major attraction, one of the wonders of the cosmos. By silent conspiracy our neighbors in the galaxy winked at the amorality of the basic concept in order to share the pleasure of inspecting the prisoners.

There is in the archives of the Rememberers a memory-tank entry of a visit to a compound area. It is one of the oldest visual records possessed by the guild, and I obtained a look at it only with great difficulty and upon the direct intercession of the Rememberer Olmayne. Despite the use of a double filter in the cap, one sees the scene only blurredly; but yet it is clear enough. Behind a curved shield of a transparent material are fifty or more beings of an unnamed world. Their bodies are pyramidal, with dark blue surfaces and pink visual areas at each vertex; they walk upon short, thick legs; they have one pair of grasping limbs on each face. Though it is risky to attempt to interpret the inner feelings of extraterrestrial beings, one can clearly sense a mood of utter despair in these creatures. Through the murky green gases of their environment they move slowly, numbly, without animation. Several have joined tips in what must be communication. One appears newly dead. Two are bowed to the ground like tumbled toys, but their limbs move in what perhaps is prayer. It is a dismal scene. Later, I discovered other such records in neglected corners of the building. They taught me much.

For more than a thousand Second Cycle years the growth of these compounds continued unchecked, until it came to seem logical and natural to all except the victims that Earth should practice these cruelties in the name of science. Then, upon a distant world not previously visited by Earthmen, there were discovered certain beings of a primitive kind, comparable perhaps to Earthmen in early First Cycle days. These beings were roughly humanoid in form, undeniably intelligent, and fiercely savage. At the loss of several Earthborn lives, a collecting team acquired a breeding colony of these people and transported them to Earth to be placed in a compound.

This was the first of the Second Cycle's two fatal errors.

At the time of the kidnaping, the beings of this other world—which

is never named in the records, but known only by the code designation
H362—were in no position to protest or to take punitive steps. But
shortly they were visited by emissaries from certain other worlds aligned
politically against Earth. Under the guidance of these emissaries, the
beings of H362 requested the return of their people. Earth refused, citing
the long precedent of interstellar condonement of the compounds.
Lengthy diplomatic representations followed, in the course of which
Earth simply reaffirmed its right to have acted in such a fashion.

The people of H362 responded with threats. "One day," they said,
"we will cause you to regret this. We will invade and conquer your
planet, set free all the inhabitants of the compounds, and turn Earth
itself into a gigantic compound for its own people."

Under the circumstances this appeared quite amusing.

Little more was heard of the outraged inhabitants of H362 over the
next few millennia. They were progressing rapidly, in their distant part
of the universe, but since by all calculations it would take them a cosmic
period to pose any menace to Earth, they were ignored. How could one
fear spear-wielding savages?

Earth addressed itself to a new challenge: full control of the planetary climate.

Weather modification had been practiced on a small scale since late
First Cycle. Clouds holding potential rain could be induced to release
it; fogs could be dispelled; hail could be made less destructive. Certain
steps were taken toward reducing the polar ice packs and toward making
deserts more fruitful. However, these measures were strictly local and,
with few exceptions, had no lasting effects on environment.

The Second Cycle endeavor involved the erection of enormous columns at more than one hundred locations around the globe. We do not
know the heights of these columns, since none have survived intact and
the specifications are lost, but it is thought that they equaled or exceeded
the highest buildings previously constructed, and perhaps attained alti-
tudes of two miles or more. Within these columns was equipment which
was designed, among other things, to effect displacements of the poles
of Earth's magnetic field.

As we understand the aim of the weather machines, it was to modify
the planet's geography according to a carefully conceived plan arising
from the division of what we call Earth Ocean into a number of large
bodies. Although interconnected, these suboceans were considered to
have individual existences, since along most of their boundary region
they were cut off from the rest of Earth Ocean by land masses. In the
north polar region, for example, the joining of Ais to the northern Lost
Continent (known as Usa-amrik) in the west and the proximity of Usa-

amrik to Eyrop in the east left only narrow straits through which the polar waters could mingle with those of the warmer oceans flanking the Lost Continents.

Manipulation of magnetic forces produced a libration of Earth on its orbit, calculated to break up the north polar ice pack and permit the cold water trapped by this pack to come in contact with warmer water from elsewhere. By removing the northern ice pack and thus exposing the northern ocean to evaporation, precipitation would be greatly increased there. To prevent this precipitation from falling in the north as snow, additional manipulations were to be induced to change the pattern of the prevailing westerly winds which carried precipitation over temperate areas. A natural conduit was to be established that would bring the precipitation of the polar region to areas in lower latitudes lacking in proper moisture.

There was much more to the plan than this. Our knowledge of the details is hazy. We are aware of schemes to shift ocean currents by causing land subsidence or emergence, of proposals to deflect solar heat from the tropics to the poles, and of other rearrangements. The details are unimportant. What is significant to us are the consequences of this grandiose plan.

After a period of preparation lasting centuries and after absorbing more effort and wealth than any other project in human history, the weather machines were put into operation.

The result was devastation.

The disastrous experiment in planetary alteration resulted in a shifting of the geographical poles, a lengthy period of glacial conditions throughout most of the northern hemisphere, the unexpected submergence of Usa-amrik and Sud-amrik, its neighbor, the creation of Land Bridge joining Afreek and Eyrop, and the near destruction of human civilization. These upheavals did not take place with great speed. Evidently the project went smoothly for the first several centuries; the polar ice thawed, and the corresponding rise in sea levels was dealt with by constructing fusion evaporators—small suns, in effect—at selected oceanic points. Only slowly did it become clear that the weather machines were bringing about architectonic changes in the crust of Earth. These, unlike the climatic changes, proved irreversible.

It was a time of furious storms followed by unending droughts; of the loss of hundreds of millions of lives; of the disruption on all communications; of panicky mass migrations out of the doomed continents. Chaos triumphed. The splendid civilization of the Second Cycle was shattered. The compounds of alien life were destroyed.

For the sake of saving what remained of its population, several of the most powerful galactic races took command of our planet. They established energy pylons to stabilize Earth's axial wobble; they dismantled those weather machines that had not been destroyed by the planetary convulsions; they fed the hungry, clothed the naked, and offered reconstruction loans. For us it was a Time of Sweeping, when all the structures and conventions of society were expunged. No longer masters in our own world, we accepted the charity of strangers and crept pitifully about.

Yet, because we were still the same race we had been, we recovered to some extent. We had squandered our planet's capital and so could never again be anything but bankrupts and paupers, but in a humbler way we entered into our Third Cycle. Certain scientific techniques of earlier days still remained to us. Others were devised, working generally on different principles. Our guilds were formed to give order to society: Dominators, Masters, Merchants, and the rest. The Rememberers strove to salvage what could be pulled from the wreck of the past.

Our debts to our rescuers were enormous. As bankrupts, we had no way of repaying those debts; we hoped instead for a quitclaim, a statement of absolution. Negotiations to that effect were already under way when an unexpected intervention occurred. The inhabitants of H362 approached the committee of Earth's receivers and offered to reimburse them for their expenses—in return for an assignment of all rights and claims in Earth to H362.

It was done.

H362 now regarded itself the owner by treaty of our world. It served notice to the universe at large that it reserved the right to take possession at any future date. As well it might, since at that time H362 was still incapable of interstellar travel. Thereafter, though, H362 was deemed legal possessor of the assets of Earth, as purchaser in bankruptcy.

No one failed to realize that this was H362's way of fulfilling its threat to "turn Earth itself into a gigantic compound," as revenge for the injury inflicted by our collecting team long before.

On Earth, Third Cycle society constituted itself along the lines it now holds, with its rigid stratification of guilds. The threat of H362 was taken seriously, for ours was a chastened world that sneered at no menace, however slight; and a guild of Watchers was devised to scan the skies for attackers. Defenders and all the rest followed. In some small ways we demonstrated our old flair for imagination, particularly in the Years of Magic, when a fanciful impulse created the self-perpetuating mutant guild of Fliers, a parallel guild of Swimmers, of whom little is heard nowadays, and several other varieties, including a troublesome and unpredictable guild of Changelings whose genetic characteristics were highly erratic.

The Watchers watched. The Dominators ruled. The Fliers soared. Life went on, year after year, in Eyrop and in Ais, in Stralya, in Afreek, in the scattered islands that were the only remnants of the Lost Continents of Usa-amrik and Sud-amrik. The vow of H362 receded into mythology, but yet we remained vigilant. And far across the cosmos our enemies gathered strength, attaining some measure of the power that had been ours in our Second Cycle. They never forgot the day when their kinsmen had been held captive in our compounds.

In a night of terror they came to us. Now they are our masters, and their vow is fulfilled, their claim asserted.

All this, and much more, I learned as I burrowed in the accumulated knowledge of the guild of Rememberers.

5.

Meanwhile the former Prince of Roum was wantonly abusing the hospitality of our co-sponsorer, the Rememberer Elegro. I should have been aware of what was going on, for I knew the Prince and his ways better than any other man in Perris. But I was too busy in the archives, learning of the past. While I explored the details of the Second Cycle's protoplasm files and regeneration nodules, its time-wind blowers and its photonic-flux fixers, Prince Enric was seducing the Rememberer Olmayne.

I imagine that this was, like most seductions, no great contest of wills. Olmayne was a woman of sensuality, whose attitude toward her husband was affectionate but patronizing. She regarded Elegro openly as ineffectual, a bumbler; and Elegro, whose haughtiness and stern mien did not conceal his underlying weakness of purpose, seemed to merit her disdain. What kind of marriage they had was not my business to observe, but clearly she was the stronger, and just as clearly he could not meet her needs.

Then, too, why had Olmayne agreed to sponsor us into her guild?

Surely not out of any desire for a tattered old Watcher. It must have been the wish to know more of the strange and oddly commanding blind Pilgrim who was that Watcher's companion. From the very first, then, Olmayne must have been drawn to Prince Enric; and he, naturally, would need little encouragement to accept the gift she offered.

Possibly they were lovers almost from the moment of our arrival in the Hall of Rememberers.

I went my way, and Elegro went his, and Olmayne and Prince Enric went theirs, and summer gave way to autumn and autumn to winter. I excavated the records with passionate impatience. Never before had I known such involvement, such intensity of curiosity. Without benefit of a visit to Jorslem I felt renewed. I saw the Prince infrequently, and our meetings were generally silent; it was not my place to question him about his doings, and he felt no wish to volunteer information to me.

Occasionally I thought of my former life, and of my travels from place to place, and of the Flier Avluela who was now, I supposed, the consort of one of our conquerors. How did the false Changeling Gormon style himself, now that he had emerged from his disguise and owned himself to be one of those from H362? Earthking Nine? Oceanlord Five? Overman Three? Wherever he was, he must feel satisfaction, I thought, at the total success of the conquest of Earth.

Toward winter's end I learned of the affair between the Rememberer Olmayne and Prince Enric of Roum. I picked up whispered gossip in the apprentice quarters first; then I noticed the smiles on the faces of other Rememberers when Elegro and Olmayne were about; lastly, I observed the behavior of the Prince and Olmayne toward one another. It was obvious. Those touchings of hand to hand, those sly exchanges of catchwords and private phrases—what else could they mean?

Among the Rememberers the marriage vow is regarded solemnly. As with the Fliers, mating is for life, and one is not supposed to betray one's partner as Olmayne was doing. When one is married to a fellow Rememberer—a custom in the guild, but not universal—the union is all the more sacred.

What revenge would Elegro take when in time he learned the truth?

It happened that I was present when the situation at last crystallized into conflict. It was a night in earliest spring. I had worked long and hard in the deepest pits of the memory tanks, prying forth data that no one had bothered with since it had first been stored; and, with my head aswim with images of chaos, I walked through the glow of the Perris night, seeking fresh air. I strolled along the Senn and was accosted by an agent for a Somnambulist, who offered to sell me insight into the world of dreams. I came upon a lone Pilgrim at his devotions before a temple of flesh. I watched a pair of young Fliers in passage overhead, and shed a self-pitying tear or two. I was halted by a starborn tourist in breathing mask and jeweled tunic; he put his cratered red face close to mine and vented hallucinations in my nostrils. At length I returned to the Hall of Rememberers and went to the suite of my sponsors to pay my respects before retiring.

Olmayne and Elegro were there. So, too, was Prince Enric. Olmayne admitted me with a quick gesture of one fingertip, but took no further notice of me, nor did the others. Elegro was tensely pacing the floor, stomping about so vehemently that the delicate life-forms of the carpet folded and unfolded their petals in wild agitation. "A Pilgrim!" Elegro cried. "If it had been some trash of a Vendor, it would only be humiliating. But a Pilgrim? That makes it monstrous!"

Prince Enric stood with arms folded, body motionless. It was impossible to detect the expression beneath his mask of Pilgrimage, but he appeared wholly calm.

Elegro said, "Will you deny that you have been tampering with the sanctity of my pairing?"

"I deny nothing. I assert nothing."

"And you?" Elegro demanded, whirling on his lady. "Speak truth, Olmayne! For once, speak truth! What of the stories they tell of you and this Pilgrim?"

"I have heard no stories," said Olmayne sweetly.

"That he shares your bed! That you taste potions together! That you travel to ecstasy together!"

Olmayne's smile did not waver. Her broad face was tranquil. To me she looked more beautiful than ever.

Elegro tugged in anguish at the strands of his shawl. His dour, bearded face darkened in wrath and exasperation. His hand slipped within his tunic and emerged with the tiny glossy bead of a vision capsule, which he thrust forth toward the guilty pair on the palm of his hand.

"Why should I waste breath?" he asked. "Everything is here. The full record in the photonic flux. You have been under surveillance. Did either of you think anything could be hidden here, of all places? You, Olmayne, a Rememberer, how could you think so?"

Olmayne examined the capsule from a distance, as though it were a primed implosion bomb. With distaste she said, "How like you to spy on us, Elegro. Did it give you great pleasure to watch us in our joy?"

"Beast!" he cried.

Pocketing the capsule, he advanced toward the motionless Prince. Elegro's face now was contorted with righteous wrath. Standing an arm's length from the Prince he declared icily, "You will be punished to the fullest for this impiety. You will be stripped of your Pilgrim's robes and delivered up to the fate reserved for monsters. The Will shall consume your soul!"

Prince Enric replied, "Curb your tongue."

"Curb my tongue? Who are you to speak that way? A Pilgrim who lusts for the wife of his host—who doubly violates holiness—who drips lies and sanctimony at the same moment?" Elegro frothed. His iciness was gone. Now he ranted in nearly incoherent frenzy, displaying his interior weakness by his lack of self-control. We three stood frozen,

astounded by his torrent of words, and at last the stasis broke when the
Rememberer, carried away by the tide of his own indignation, seized
the Prince by the shoulders and began violently to shake him.

"Filth," Enric bellowed, "you may not put your hands to me!"

With a double thrust of his fists against Elegro's chest he hurled the
Rememberer reeling backward across the room. Elegro crashed into a
suspension cradle and sent a flank of watery artifacts tumbling; three
flasks of scintillating fluids shivered and spilled their contents; the carpet
set up a shrill cry of pained protest. Gasping, stunned, Elegro pressed
a hand to his breast and looked to us for assistance.

"Physical assault—" Elegro wheezed. "A shameful crime!"

"The first assault was your doing," Olmayne reminded her husband.

Pointing trembling fingers, Elegro muttered, "For this there can be
no forgiveness, Pilgrim!"

"Call me Pilgrim no longer," Enric said. His hands went to the
grillwork of his mask. Olmayne cried out, trying to prevent him; but in
his anger the Prince knew no check. He hurled the mask to the floor
and stood with his harsh face terribly exposed, the cruel features hawk-
lean, the gray mechanical spheres in his eyesockets masking the depths
of his fury. "I am the Prince of Roum," he announced in a voice of
thunder. "Down and abase! Down and abase! Quick, Rememberer, the
three prostrations and the five abasements!"

Elegro appeared to crumble. He peered in disbelief; then he sagged,
and in a kind of reflex of amazement he performed a ritual obeisance
before his wife's seducer. It was the first time since the fall of Roum
that the Prince had asserted his former status, and the pleasure of it was
so evident on his ravaged face that even the blank eyeballs appeared to
glow in regal pride.

"Out," the Prince ordered. "Leave us."

Elegro fled.

I remained, astounded, staggered. The Prince nodded courteously to
me. "Would you pardon us, old friend, and grant us some moments of
privacy?"

6.

A weak man can be put to rout by a surprise attack, but afterward he pauses, reconsiders, and hatches schemes. So was it with the Rememberer Elegro. Driven from his own suite by the unmasking of the Prince of Roum, he grew calm and crafty once he was out of that terrifying presence. Later that same night, as I settled into my sleeping cradle and debated aiding slumber with a drug, Elegro summoned me to his research cell on a lower level of the building.

There he sat amid the paraphernalia of his guild: reels and spools, data-flakes, capsules, caps, a quartet of series-linked skulls, a row of output screens, a small ornamental helix, all the symbology of the gatherers of information. In his hands he grasped a tension-draining crystal from one of the Cloud-worlds; its milky interior was rapidly tingeing with sepia as it pulled anxieties from his spirit. He pretended a look of stern authority, as if forgetting that I had seen him exposed in his spinelessness.

He said, "Were you aware of this man's identity when you came with him to Perris?"

"Yes."

"You said nothing about it."

"I was never asked."

"Do you know what a risk you have exposed all of us to, by causing us unknowingly to harbor a Dominator?"

"We are Earthmen," I said. "Do we not still acknowledge the authority of the Dominators?"

"Not since the conquest. By decree of the invaders all former governments are dissolved and their leaders subject to arrest."

"But surely we should resist such an order!"

The Rememberer Elegro regarded me quizzically. "Is it a Rememberer's function to meddle in politics? Tomis, we obey the government in power, whichever it may be and however it may have taken control. We conduct no resistance activities here."

"I see."

"Therefore we must rid ourselves at once of this dangerous fugitive. Tomis, I instruct you to go at once to occupation headquarters and inform Manrule Seven that we have captured the Prince of Roum and hold him here for pickup."

"*I* should go?" I blurted. "Why send an old man as a messenger in the night? An ordinary thinking-cap transmission would be enough!"

"Too risky. Strangers may intercept cap communications. It would not go well for our guild if this were spread about. This has to be a personal communication."

"But to choose an unimportant apprentice to carry it—it seems strange."

"There are only two of us who know," said Elegro. "I will not go. Therefore you must."

"With no introduction to Manrule Seven I will never be admitted."

"Inform his aides that you have information leading to the apprehension of the Prince of Roum. You'll be heard."

"Am I to mention your name?"

"If necessary. You may say that the Prince is being held prisoner in my quarters with the cooperation of my wife."

I nearly laughed at that. But I held a straight face before this cowardly Rememberer, who did not even dare to go himself to denounce the man who had cuckolded him.

"Ultimately," I said, "the Prince will become aware of what we have done. Is it right of you to ask me to betray a man who was my companion for so many months?"

"It is not a matter of betrayal. It is a matter of obligations to the government."

"I feel no obligation to this government. My loyalties are to the guild of Dominators. Which is why I gave assistance to the Prince of Roum in his moment of peril."

"For that," said Elegro, "your own life could be forfeit to our conquerors. Your only expiation is to admit your error and cooperate in bringing about his arrest. Go. Now."

In a long and tolerant life I have never despised anyone so vehemently as I did the Rememberer Elegro at that moment.

Yet I saw that I was faced with few choices, none of them palatable. Elegro wished his undoer punished, but lacked the courage to report him himself; therefore I must give over to the conquering authorities one whom I had sheltered and assisted, and for whom I felt a responsibility. If I refused, Elegro would perhaps hand me to the invaders for punishment myself, as an accessory to the Prince's escape from Roum; or he might take vengeance against me within the machinery of the guild of Rememberers. If I obliged Elegro, though, I would have a stain on my conscience forever, and in the event of a restoration of the power of the Dominators I would have much to answer for.

As I weighed the possibilities, I triply cursed the Rememberer Elegro's faithless wife and her invertebrate husband.

I hesitated a bit. Elegro offered more persuasion, threatening to arraign me before the guild on such charges as unlawfully gaining access to secret files and improperly introducing into guild precincts a proscribed fugitive. He threatened to cut me off forever from the information pool. He spoke vaguely of vengeance.

In the end I told him I would go to the invaders' headquarters and do his bidding. I had by then conceived a betrayal that would—I hoped—cancel the betrayal Elegro was enforcing on me.

Dawn was near when I left the building. The air was mild and sweet; a low mist hung over the streets of Perris, giving them a gentle shimmer. No moons were in sight. In the deserted streets I felt uneasy, although I told myself that no one would care to do harm to an aged Rememberer; but I was armed only with a small blade, and I feared bandits.

My route lay on one of the pedestrian ramps. I panted a bit at the steep incline, but when I had attained the proper level I was more secure, since here there were patrol nodes at frequent intervals, and here, too, were some other late-night strollers. I passed a spectral figure garbed in white satin through which alien features peered: a revenant, a ghostly inhabitant of a planet of the Bull, where reincarnation is the custom and no man goes about installed in his own original body. I passed three female beings of a Swan planet who giggled at me and asked if I had seen males of their species, since the time of conjugation was upon them. I passed a pair of Changelings who eyed me speculatively, decided I had nothing on me worth robbing, and moved on, their piebald dewlaps jiggling and their radiant skins flashing like beacons.

At last I came to the squat octagonal building occupied by the Procurator of Perris.

It was indifferently guarded. The invaders appeared confident that we were incapable of mounting a counter-assault against them, and quite likely they were right; a planet which can be conquered between darkness and dawn is not going to launch a plausible resistance afterwards. Around the building rose the pale glow of a protective scanner. There was a tingle of ozone in the air. In the wide plaza across the way, Merchants were setting up their market for the morning; I saw barrels of spices being unloaded by brawny Servitors, and dark sausages carried by files of neuters. I stepped through the scanner beam and an invader emerged to challenge me.

I explained that I carried urgent news for Manrule Seven, and in short order, with amazingly little consultation of intermediaries, I was ushered into the Procurator's presence.

The invader had furnished his office simply but in good style. It was decked entirely with Earthmade objects: a drapery of Afreek weave, two alabaster pots from ancient Agupt, a marble statuette that might have been early Roumish, and a dark Talyan vase in which a few wilting deathflowers languished. When I entered, he seemed preoccupied with several message-cubes; as I had heard, the invaders did most of their work in the dark hours, and it did not surprise me to find him so busy now. After a moment he looked up and said, "What is it, old man? What's this about a fugitive Dominator?"

"The Prince of Roum," I said. "I know of his location."

At once his cold eyes sparkled with interest. He ran his many-fingered hands across his desk, on which were mounted the emblems of several of our guilds, Transporters and Rememberers and Defenders and Clowns, among others. "Go on," he said.

"The Prince is in this city. He is in a specific place and has no way of escaping from it."

"And you are here to inform me of his location?"

"No," I said. "I'm here to buy his liberty."

Manrule Seven seemed perplexed. "There are times when you humans baffle me. You say you've captured this runaway Dominator, and I assume that you want to sell him to us, but you say you want to *buy* him. Why bother coming to us? Is this a joke?"

"Will you permit an explanation?"

He brooded into the mirrored top of his desk while I told him in a compressed way of my journey from Roum with the blinded Prince, of our arrival at the Hall of Rememberers, of Prince Enric's seduction of Olmayne, and of Elegro's petty, fuming desire for vengeance. I made it clear that I had come to the invaders only under duress and that it was not my intention to betray the Prince into their hands. Then I said, "I realize that all Dominators are forfeit to you. Yet this one has already paid a high price for his freedom. I ask you to notify the Rememberers that the Prince of Roum is under amnesty, and to permit him to continue on as a Pilgrim to Jorslem. In that way Elegro will lose power over him."

"What is it that you offer us," asked Manrule Seven, "in return for this amnesty for your Prince?"

"I have done research in the memory tanks of the Rememberers."

"And?"

"I have found that for which you people have been seeking."

Manrule Seven studied me with care. "How would you have any idea of what we seek?"

"There is in the deepest part of the Hall of Rememberers," I said quietly, "an image recording of the compound in which your kidnaped ancestors lived while they were prisoners on Earth. It shows their sufferings in poignant detail. It is a superb justification for the conquest of Earth by H362."

"Impossible! There's no such document!"

From the intensity of the invader's reaction, I knew that I had stung him in the vulnerable place.

He went on, "We've searched your files thoroughly. There's only one recording of compound life, and it doesn't show our people. It shows a nonhumanoid pyramid-shaped race, probably from one of the Anchor worlds."

"I have seen that one," I told him. "There are others. I spent many hours searching for them, out of hunger to know of our past injustices."

"The indexes—"

"—are sometimes incomplete. I found this recording only by accident. The Rememberers themselves have no idea it's there. I'll lead you to it—if you agree to leave the Prince of Roum unmolested."

The Procurator was silent a moment. At length he said, "You puzzle me. I am unable to make out if you are a scoundrel or a man of the highest virtue."

"I know where true loyalty lies."

"To betray the secrets of your guild, though—"

"I am no Rememberer, only an apprentice, formerly a Watcher. I would not have you harm the Prince at the wish of a cuckolded fool. The Prince is in his hands; only you can obtain his release now. And so I must offer you this document."

"Which the Rememberers have carefully deleted from their indexes, so it will not fall into our hands."

"Which the Rememberers have carelessly misplaced and forgotten."

"I doubt it," said Manrule Seven. "They are not careless folk. They hid that recording; and by giving it to us, are you not betraying all your world? Making yourself a collaborator with the hated enemy?"

I shrugged. "I am interested in having the Prince of Roum made free. Other means and ends are of no concern to me. The location of the document is yours in exchange for the grant of amnesty."

The invader displayed what might have been his equivalent of a smile. "It is not in our best interests to allow members of the former guild of Dominators to remain at large. Your position is precarious, do you see? I could extract the document's location from you by force— and still have the Prince as well."

"So you could," I agreed. "I take that risk. I assume a certain basic honor among people who came to avenge an ancient crime. I am in your power, and the whereabouts of the document is in my mind, yours for the picking."

Now he laughed in an unmistakable show of good humor.

"Wait one moment," he said. He spoke a few words of his own language into an amber communication device, and shortly a second member of his species entered the office. I recognized him instantly, although he was shorn of some of the flamboyant disguise he had worn when he traveled with me as Gormon, the supposed Changeling. He offered the ambivalent smile of his kind and said, "I greet you, Watcher."

"And I greet you, Gormon."

"My name now is Victorious Thirteen."

"I now am called Tomis of the Rememberers," I said.

Manrule Seven remarked, "When did you two become such fast friends?"

"In the time of the conquest," said Victorious Thirteen. "While performing my duties as an advance scout, I encountered this man in Talya and journeyed with him to Roum. But we were companions, in truth, and not friends."

I trembled. "Where is the Flier Avluela?"

"In Pars, I believe," he said offhandedly. "She spoke of returning to Hind, to the place of her people."

"You loved her only a short while, then?"

"We were more companions than lovers," said the invader. "It was a passing thing for us."

"For you, maybe," I said.

"For us."

"And for this passing thing you stole a man's eyes?"

He who had been Gormon shrugged. "I did that to teach a proud creature a lesson in pride."

"You said at the time that your motive was jealousy," I reminded him. "You claimed to act out of love."

Victorious Thirteen appeared to lose interest in me. To Manrule Seven he said, "Why is this man here? Why have you summoned me?"

"The Prince of Roum is in Perris," said Manrule Seven.

Victorious Thirteen registered sudden surprise.

Manrule Seven went on, "He is a prisoner of the Rememberers. This man offers a strange bargain. You know the Prince better than any of us; I ask your advice."

The Procurator sketched the outlines of the situation. He who had been Gormon listened thoughtfully, saying nothing. At the end, Manrule Seven said, "The problem is this: shall we give amnesty to a proscribed Dominator?"

"He is blind," said Victorious Thirteen. "His power is gone. His followers are scattered. His spirit may be unbroken, but he presents no danger to us. I say accept the bargain."

"There are administrative risks in exempting a Dominator from arrest," Manrule Seven pointed out. "Nevertheless, I agree. We undertake the deal." To me he said, "Tell us the location of the document we desire."

"Arrange the liberation of the Prince of Roum first," I said calmly.

Both invaders displayed amusement. "Fair enough," said Manrule Seven. "But look: how can we be certain that you'll keep your word? Anything might happen to you in the next hour while we're freeing the Prince."

"A suggestion," put in Victorious Thirteen. "This is not so much a matter of mutual mistrust as it is one of timing. Tomis, why not record the document's location on a six-hour delay cube? We'll prime the cube so that it will release its information only if within that six hours the Prince of Roum himself, and no one else, commands it to do so. If we haven't found and freed the Prince in that time, the cube will destruct. If we do release the Prince, the cube will give us the information, even if—ah—something should have happened to you in the interval."

"You cover all contingencies," I said.

"Are we agreed?" Manrule Seven asked.

"We are agreed," I said.

They brought me a cube and placed me under a privacy screen while I inscribed on its glossy surface the rack number and sequence equations of the document I had discovered. Moments passed; the cube everted itself and the information vanished into its opaque depths. I offered it to them.

Thus did I betray my Earthborn heritage and perform a service for our conquerors, out of loyalty to a blinded wife-stealing Prince.

7.

Dawn had come by this time. I did not accompany the invaders to the Hall of Rememberers; it was no business of mine to oversee the intricate events that must ensue, and I preferred to be elsewhere. A fine drizzle was falling as I turned down the gray streets that bordered the dark Senn. The timeless river, its surface stippled by the drops, swept unwearyingly against stone arches of First Cycle antiquity, bridges spanning uncountable millennia, survivors from an era when the only problems of mankind were of his own making. Morning engulfed the city. Through an old and ineradicable reflex I searched for my instruments so that I could do my Watching, and had to remind myself that that was far behind me now. The Watchers were disbanded, the enemy had come, and old Wuellig, now Tomis of the Rememberers, had sold himself to mankind's foes.

In the shadow of a twin-steepled religious house of the ancient Christers I let myself be enticed into the booth of a Somnambulist. This guild is not one with which I have often had dealings; in my way I am wary of charlatans, and charlatans are abundant in our time. The Somnambulist, in a state of trance, claims to see what has been, what is, and what will be. I know something of trances myself, for as a Watcher I entered such a state four times each day; but a Watcher with pride in his craft must necessarily despise the tawdry ethics of those who use second sight for gain, as Somnambulists do.

However, while among the Rememberers I had learned, to my surprise, that Somnambulists frequently were consulted to aid in unearthing some site of ancient times, and that they had served the Rememberers well. Though still skeptical, I was willing to be instructed. And, at the moment, I needed a shelter from the storm that was breaking over the Hall of Rememberers.

A dainty, mincing figure garbed in black greeted me with a mocking bow as I entered the low-roofed booth.

"I am Samit of the Somnambulists," he said in a high, whining voice. "I offer you welcome and good tidings. Behold my companion, the Somnambulist Murta."

The Somnambulist Murta was a robust woman in lacy robes. Her face was heavy with flesh, deep rings of darkness surrounded her eyes, a trace of mustache lined her upper lip. Somnambulists work their trade in teams, one to do the huckstering, one to perform; most teams were man and wife, as was this. My mind rebelled at the thought of the embrace of the flesh-mountain Murta and the miniature-man Samit, but it was no concern of mine. I took my seat as Samit indicated. On a table nearby I saw some food tablets of several colors; I had interrupted this family's breakfast. Murta, deep in trance, wandered the room with ponderous strides, now and again grazing some article of furniture in a gentle way. Some Somnambulists, it is said, waken only two or three hours of the twenty, simply to take meals and relieve bodily needs; there are some who ostensibly live in continuous trance and are fed and cared for by acolytes.

I scarcely listened as Samit of the Somnambulists delivered his sales-talk in rapid, feverish bursts of ritualized word-clusters. It was pitched to the ignorant; Somnambulists do much of their trade with Servitors and Clowns and other menials. At length, seemingly sensing my impatience, he cut short his extolling of the Somnambulist Murta's abilities and asked me what it was I wished to know.

"Surely the Somnambulist already is aware of that," I said.

"You wish a general analysis?"

"I want to know of the fate of those about me. I wish particularly for the Somnambulist's concentration to center on events now occurring in the Hall of Rememberers."

Samit tapped long fingernails against the smooth table and shot a glaring look at the cowlike Murta. "Are you in contact with the truth?" he asked her.

Her reply was a long feathery sigh wrenched from the core of all the quivering meat of her.

"What do you see?" he asked her.

She began to mutter thickly. Somnambulists speak in a language not otherwise used by mankind; it is a harsh thing of edgy sounds, which some claim is descended from an ancient tongue of Agupt. I know nothing of that. To me it sounded incoherent, fragmentary, impossible to hold meaning. Samit listened a while, then nodded in satisfaction and extended his palm to me.

"There is a great deal," he said.

We discussed the fee, bargained briefly, came to a settlement. "Go on," I told him. "Interpret the truth."

Cautiously he began, "There are outworlders involved in this, and also several members of the guild of Rememberers." I was silent, giving him no encouragement. "They are drawn together in a difficult quarrel. A man without eyes is at the heart of it."

I sat upright with a jolt.

Samit smiled in cool triumph. "The man without eyes has fallen from greatness. He is Earth, shall we say, broken by conquerors? Now he is near the end of his time. He seeks to restore his former condition, but he knows it is impossible. He has caused a Rememberer to violate an oath. To their guildhall have come several of the conquerors to—to chastise him? No. No. To free him from captivity. Shall I continue?"

"Quickly!"

"You have received all that you have paid for."

I scowled. This was extortion; but yet the Somnambulist had clearly seen the truth. I had learned nothing here than I did not already know, but that was sufficient to tell me I might learn more. I added to my fee.

Samit closed his fist on my coins and conferred once more with Murta. She spoke at length, in some agitation, whirling several times, colliding violently with a musty divan.

Samit said, "The man without eyes has come between a man and his wife. The outraged husband seeks punishment; the outworlders will thwart that. The outworlders seek hidden truths; they will find them, with a traitor's help. The man without eyes seeks freedom and power; he will find peace. The stained wife seeks amusement; she will find hardship."

"And I?" I said into an obstinate and expensive silence. "You say nothing of me!"

"You will leave Perris soon, in the same manner as you entered it. You will not leave alone. You will not leave in your present guild."

"What will be my destination?"

"You know that as well as we do, so why waste your money to tell you?"

He fell silent again.

"Tell me what will befall me as I journey to Jorslem," I said.

"You could not afford such information. Futures become costly. I advise you to settle for what you now know."

"I have some questions about what has already been said."

"We do not clarify at any price."

He grinned. I felt the force of his contempt. The Somnambulist Murta, still bumbling about the room, groaned and belched. The powers with whom she was in contact appeared to impart new information to her; she whimpered, shivered, made a blurred chuckling sound. Samit spoke to her in their language. She replied at length. He peered at me. "At no cost," he said, "a final information. Your life is in no danger, but your spirit is. It would be well if you made your peace with the Will as quickly as possible. Recover your moral orientation. Remember your true loyalties. Atone for well-intentioned sins. I can say no more."

Indeed, Murta stirred and seemed to wake. Great slabs of flesh jiggled in her face and body as the convulsion of leaving the trance came over her. Her eyes opened, but I saw only whites, a terrible sight. Her thick lips twitched to reveal crumbling teeth. Samit beckoned me out with quick brushing gestures of his tiny hands. I fled into a dark, rain-drenched morning.

Hurriedly I returned to the Hall of Rememberers, arriving there out of breath, with a red spike of pain behind my breastbone. I paused a while outside the superb building to recover my strength. Floaters passed overhead, leaving the guildhall from an upper level. My courage nearly failed me. But in the end I entered the hall and ascended to the level of the suite of Elegro and Olmayne.

A knot of agitated Rememberers filled the hall. A buzz of whispered comment drifted toward me. I pressed forward; and a man whom I recognized as high in the councils of the guild held up a hand and said, "What business do you have here, apprentice?"

"I am Tomis, who was sponsored by the Rememberer Olmayne. My chamber is close to here."

"Tomis!" a voice cried.

I was seized and thrust ahead into the familiar suite, now a scene of devastation.

A dozen Rememberers stood about, fingering their shawls in distress. I recognized among them the taut and elegant figure of Chancellor Kenishal, his gray eyes now dull with despair. Beneath a coverlet to the left of the entrance lay a crumpled figure in the robes of a Pilgrim: the Prince of Roum, dead in his own pooled blood. His gleaming mask, now stained, lay beside him. At the opposite side of the room, slumped against an ornate credenza containing Second Cycle artifacts of great beauty, was the Rememberer Elegro, seemingly asleep, looking furious and surprised both at once. His throat was transfixed by a single slender dart. To the rear, with burly Rememberers flanking her, stood the Rememberer Olmayne looking wild and disheveled. Her scarlet robe was torn in front and revealed high white breasts; her black hair tumbled in disorder; her satiny skin glistened with perspiration. She appeared lost in a dream, far from these present surroundings.

"What has happened here?" I asked.

"Murder twice over," said Chancellor Kenishal in a broken voice. He advanced toward me: a tall, haggard man, white-haired, an uncontrollable tic working in the lid of one eye. "When did you last see these people alive, apprentice?"

"In the night."

"How did you come to be here?"

"A visit, no more."

"Was there a disturbance?"

"A quarrel between the Rememberer Elegro and the Pilgrim, yes," I admitted.

"Over what?" asked the Chancellor thinly.

I looked uneasily at Olmayne, but she saw nothing and heard less. "Over her," I said.

I heard snickerings from the other Rememberers. They nudged each other, nodded, even smiled; I had confirmed the scandal. The Chancellor grew more solemn.

He indicated the body of the Prince.

"This was your companion when you entered Perris," he said. "Did you know of his true identity?"

I moistened my lips. "I had suspicions."

"That he was—"

"The fugitive Prince of Roum," I said. I did not dare attempt subterfuges now; my status was precarious.

More nods, more nudges. Chancellor Kenishal said, "This man was subject to arrest. It was not your place to conceal your knowledge of his identity."

I remained mute.

The Chancellor went on, "You have been absent from this hall for some hours. Tell us of your activities after leaving the suite of Elegro and Olmayne."

"I called upon the Procurator Manrule Seven," I said.

Sensation.

"For what purpose?"

"To inform the Procurator," I said, "that the Prince of Roum had been apprehended and was now in the suite of a Rememberer. I did this at the instruction of the Rememberer Elegro. After delivering my information I walked the streets several hours for no particular end, and returned here to find—to find—"

"To find everything in chaos," said Chancellor Kenishal. "The Procurator was here at dawn. He visited this suite; both Elegro and the Prince must still have been alive at that time. Then he went into our archives and removed—and removed—material of the highest sensitivity—the highest sensitivity—removed—material not believed to be accessible to—the highest sensitivity—" The Chancellor faltered. Like some intricate machine smitten with instant rust, he slowed his motions, emitted rasping sounds, appeared to be on the verge of systematic breakdown. Several high Rememberers rushed to his aid; one thrust a drug against his arm. In moments the Chancellor appeared to recover. "These murders occurred after the Procurator departed from the building," he said. "The Rememberer Olmayne has been unable to give us information concerning them. Perhaps you, apprentice, know something of value."

"I was not present. Two Somnambulists near the Senn will testify that I was with them at the time the crimes were committed."

Someone guffawed at my mention of Somnambulists. Let them; I was not seeking to retrieve dignity at a time like this. I knew that I was in peril.

The Chancellor said slowly, "You will go to your chamber, apprentice, and you will remain there to await full interrogation. Afterwards you will leave the building and be gone from Perris within twenty hours. By virtue of my authority I declare you expelled from the guild of Rememberers."

Forewarned as I had been by Samit, I was nevertheless stunned.

"*Expelled?* Why?"

"We can no longer trust you. Too many mysteries surround you. You bring us a Prince and conceal your suspicions; you are present at murderous quarrels; you visit a Procurator in the middle of the night. You may even have helped to bring about the calamitous loss suffered by our archive this morning. We have no desire for men of enigmas here. We sever our relationship with you." The Chancellor waved his hand in a grand sweep. "To your chamber now, to await interrogation, and then go!"

I was rushed from the room. As the entrance pit closed behind me, I looked back and saw the Chancellor, his face ashen, topple into the arms of his associates, while in the same instant the Rememberer Olmayne broke from her freeze and fell to the floor, screaming.

8.

A lone in my chamber, I spent a long while gathering together my possessions, though I owned little. The morning was well along before a Rememberer whom I did not know came to me; he carried interrogation equipment. I eyed it uneasily, thinking that all would be up with me if the Rememberers found proof that it was I who had betrayed the location of that compound record to the invaders. Already they suspected me of it; the Chancellor had hesitated to make the accusation only because it must have seemed odd to him that an apprentice such as myself would have cared to make a private search of the guild archive.

Fortune rode with me. My interrogator was concerned only with the details of the slaying; and once he had determined that I knew nothing on that subject, he let me be, warning me to depart from the hall within the allotted time. I told him I would do so.

But first I needed rest. I had had none that night; and so I drank a three-hour draught and settled into soothing sleep. When I awakened a figure stood beside me: the Rememberer Olmayne.

She appeared to have aged greatly since the previous evening. She was dressed in a single chaste tunic of a somber color, and she wore neither ornament nor decoration. Her features were rigidly set. I mastered my surprise at finding her there, and sat up, mumbling an apology for my delay in acknowledging her presence.

"Be at ease," she said gently. "Have I broken your sleep?"

"I had my full hours."

"I have had none. But there will be time for sleep later. We owe each other explanations, Tomis."

"Yes." I rose uncertainly. "Are you well? I saw you earlier, and you seemed lost in trance."

"They have given me medicines," she replied.

"Tell me what you can tell me about last night."

Her eyelids slid momentarily closed. "You were there when Elegro challenged us and was cast out by the Prince. Some hours later, Elegro returned. With him were the Procurator of Perris and several other invaders. Elegro appeared to be in a mood of great jubilation. The Procurator produced a cube and commanded the Prince to put his hand to it. The Prince balked, but Manrule Seven persuaded him finally to cooperate. When he had touched the cube, the Procurator and Elegro departed, leaving the Prince and myself together again, neither of us comprehending what had happened. Guards were posted to prevent the Prince from leaving. Not long afterward the Procurator and Elegro returned. Now Elegro seemed subdued and even confused, while the Procurator was clearly exhilarated. In our room the Procurator announced that amnesty had been granted to the former Prince of Roum, and that no man was to harm him. Thereupon all of the invaders departed."

"Proceed."

Olmayne spoke as though a Somnambulist. "Elegro did not appear to comprehend what had occurred. He cried out that treason had been done; he screamed that he had been betrayed. An angry scene followed. Elegro was womanish in his fury; the Prince grew more haughty; each ordered the other to leave the suite. The quarrel became so violent that the carpet itself began to die. The petals drooped; the little mouths gaped. The climax came swiftly. Elegro seized a weapon and threatened to use it if the Prince did not leave at once. The Prince misjudged Elegro's temper, thought he was bluffing, and came forward as if to throw Elegro out. Elegro slew the Prince. An instant later I grasped a dart from our rack of artifacts and hurled it into Elegro's throat. The dart bore poison; he died at once. I summoned others, and I remember no more."

"A strange night," I said.

"Too strange. Tell me now, Tomis: why did the Procurator come, and why did he not take the Prince into custody?"

I said, "The Procurator came because I asked him to, under the orders of your late husband. The Procurator did not arrest the Prince because the Prince's liberty had been purchased."

"At what price?"

"The price of a man's shame," I said.

"You speak a riddle."

"The truth dishonors me. I beg you not to press me for it."

"The Chancellor spoke of a document that had been taken by the Procurator—"

"It has to do with that," I confessed, and Olmayne looked toward the floor and asked no further questions.

I said ultimately, "You have committed a murder, then. What will your punishment be?"

"The crime was committed in passion and fear," she replied. "There will be no penalty of the civil administration. But I am expelled from my guild for my adultery and my act of violence."

"I offer my regrets."

"And I am commanded to undertake the Pilgrimage to Jorslem to purify my soul. I must leave within the day, or my life is forfeit to the guild."

"I too am expelled," I told her. "And I too am bound at last for Jorslem, though of my own choosing."

"May we travel together?"

My hesitation betrayed me. I had journeyed here with a blind Prince; I cared very little to depart with a murderous and guildless woman. Perhaps the time had come to travel alone. Yet the Somnambulist had said I would have a companion.

Olmayne said smoothly, "You lack enthusiasm. Perhaps I can create some in you." She opened her tunic. I saw mounted between the snowy hills of her breasts a gray pouch. She was tempting me not with her flesh but with an overpocket. "In this," she said, "is all that the Prince of Roum carried in his thigh. He showed me those treasures, and I removed them from his body as he lay dead in my room. Also there are certain objects of my own. I am not without resources. We will travel comfortably. Well?"

"I find it hard to refuse."

"Be ready in two hours."

"I am ready now," I said.

"Wait, then."

She left me to myself. Nearly two hours later she returned, clad now in the mask and robes of a Pilgrim. Over her arm she held a second set of Pilgrim's gear, which she offered to me. Yes: I was guildless now, and it was an unsafe way to travel. I would go, then, as a Pilgrim to Jorslem. I donned the unfamiliar gear. We gathered our possessions.

"I have notified the guild of Pilgrims," she declared as we left the Hall of Rememberers. "We are fully registered. Later today we may hope to receive our starstones. How does the mask feel, Tomis?"

"Snug."

"As it should be."

Our route out of Perris took us across the great plaza before the ancient gray holy building of the old creed. A crowd had gathered; I saw invaders at the center of the group. Beggars made the profitable orbit about it. They ignored us, for no one begs from a Pilgrim; but I collared one rascal with a gouged face and said, "What ceremony is taking place here?"

"Funeral of the Prince of Roum," he said "By order of the Procurator. State funeral with all the trimmings. They're making a real festival out of it."

"Why hold such an event in Perris?" I asked. "How did the Prince die?"

"Look, ask somebody else. I got work to do."

He wriggled free and scrambled on to work the crowd.

"Shall we attend the funeral?" I asked Olmayne.

"Best not to."

"As you wish."

We moved toward the massive stone bridge that spanned the Senn. Behind us, a brilliant blue glow arose as the pyre of the dead Prince was kindled. That pyre lit the way for us as we made our slow way through the night, eastward to Jorslem.

PART THREE
THE ROAD TO JORSLEM

1.

Our world was now truly theirs. All the way across Eyrop I could see that the invaders had taken everything, and we belonged to them as beasts in a barnyard belong to the farmer.

They were everywhere, like fleshy weeds taking root after a strange storm. They walked with cool confidence, as if telling us by the sleekness of their movements that the Will had withdrawn favor from us and conferred it upon them. They were not cruel to us, and yet they drained us of vitality by their mere presence among us. Our sun, our moons, our museums of ancient relics, our ruins of former cycles, our cities, our palaces, our future, our present, and our past had all undergone a transfer of title. Our lives now lacked meaning.

At night the blaze of the stars mocked us. All the universe looked down on our shame.

The cold wind of winter told us that for our sins our freedom had been lost. The bright heat of summer told us that for our pride we had been humbled.

Through a changed world we moved, stripped of our past selves. I, who had roved the stars each day now had lost that pleasure. Now, bound for Jorslem, I found cool comfort in the hope that as a Pilgrim I might gain redemption and renewal in that holy city. Olmayne and I repeated each night the rituals of our Pilgrimage toward that end:

"We yield to the Will."

"We yield to the Will."

"In all things great and small."

"In all things great and small."

"And ask forgiveness."

"And ask forgiveness."

"For sins actual and potential."
"For sins actual and potential."
"And pray for understanding and repose."
"And pray for understanding and repose."
"Through all our days until redemption comes."
"Through all our days until redemption comes."
Thus we spoke the words. Saying them, we clutched the cool polished spheres of starstone, icy as frostflowers, and made communion with the Will. And so we journeyed Jorslemward in this world that no longer was owned by man.

2.

It was at the Talyan approach to Land Bridge that Olmayne first used her cruelty on me. Olmayne was cruel by first nature; I had had ample proof of that in Perris; and yet we had been Pilgrims together for many months, traveling from Perris eastward over the mountains and down the length of Talya to the Bridge, and she had kept her claws sheathed. Until this place.

The occasion was our halting by a company of invaders coming north from Afreek. There were perhaps twenty of them, tall and harsh-faced, proud of being masters of conquered Earth. They rode in a gleam-ing covered vehicle of their own manufacture, long and narrow, with thick sand-colored treads and small windows. We could see the vehicle from far away, raising a cloud of dust as it neared us.

This was a hot time of year. The sky itself was the color of sand, and it was streaked with folded sheets of heat-radiation—glowing and terrible energy streams of turquoise and gold.

Perhaps fifty of us stood beside the road, with the land of Talya at our backs and the continent of Afreek before us. We were a varied group: some Pilgrims, like Olmayne and myself, making the trek toward the holy city of Jorslem, but also a random mix of the rootless, men and women who floated from continent to continent for lack of other purpose. I counted in the band five former Watchers, and also several Indexers, a Sentinel, a pair of Communicants, a Scribe, and even a few Changelings. We gathered into a straggling assembly awarding the road by default to the invaders.

Land Bridge is not wide, and the road will not allow many to use it at any time. Yet in normal times the flow of traffic had always gone in both directions at once. Here, today, we feared to go forward while invaders were this close, and so we remained clustered timidly, watching our conquerors approach.

One of the Changelings detached himself from the others of his kind and moved toward me. He was small of stature for that breed, but wide through the shoulders; his skin seemed much too tight for his frame; his eyes were large and green-rimmed; his hair grew in thick widely spaced pedestal-like clumps, and his nose was barely perceptible, so that his nostrils appeared to sprout from his upper lip. Despite this he was less grotesque than most Changelings appear. His expression was solemn, but had a hint of bizarre playfulness lurking somewhere.

He said in a voice that was little more than a feathery whisper, "Do you think we'll be delayed long, Pilgrims?"

In former times one did not address a Pilgrim unsolicited—especially if one happened to be a Changeling. Such customs meant nothing to me, but Olmayne drew back with a hiss of distaste.

I said, "We will wait here until our masters allow us to pass. Is there any choice?"

"None, friend, none."

At that *friend*, Olmayne hissed again and glowered at the little Changeling. He turned to her, and his anger showed, for suddenly six parallel bands of scarlet pigment blazed brightly beneath the glossy skin of his cheeks. But his only overt response to her was a courteous bow. He said, "I introduce myself. I am Bernalt, naturally guildless, a native of Nayrub in Deeper Afreek. I do not inquire after your names, Pilgrims. Are you bound for Jorslem?"

"Yes," I said, as Olmayne swung about to present her back. "And you? Home to Nayrub after travels?"

"No," said Bernalt. "I go to Jorslem also."

Instantly I felt cold and hostile, my initial response to the Changeling's suave charm fading at once. I had had a Changeling, false though he turned out to be, as a traveling companion before; he too had been charming, but I wanted no more like him. Edgily, distantly, I said, "May I ask what business a Changeling might have in Jorslem?"

He detected the chill in my tone, and his huge eyes registered sorrow. "We too are permitted to visit the holy city, I remind you. Even our kind. Do you fear that Changelings will once again seize the shrine of renewal, as we did a thousand years ago before we were cast down into guildlessness?" He laughed harshly. "I threaten no one, Pilgrim. I am hideous of face, but not dangerous. May the Will grant you what you seek, Pilgrim." He made a gesture of respect and went back to the other Changelings.

Furious, Olmayne spun round on me.

"Why do you talk to such beastly creatures?"

"The man approached me. He was merely being friendly. We are all cast together here, Olmayne, and—"

"*Man. Man!* You call a Changeling a man?"

"They *are* human, Olmayne."

"Just barely. Tomis, I loathe such monsters. My flesh creeps to have them near me. If I could, I'd banish them from this world!"

"Where is the serene tolerance a Rememberer must cultivate?"

She flamed at the mockery in my voice. "We are not required to love Changelings, Tomis. They are one of the curses laid upon our planet—parodies of humanity, enemics of truth and beauty. I despise them!"

It was not a unique attitude. But I had no time to reproach Olmayne for her intolerance; the vehicle of the invaders was drawing near. I hoped we might resume our journey once it went by. It slowed and halted, however, and several of the invaders came out. They walked unhurriedly toward us, their long arms dangling like slack ropes.

"Who is the leader here?" asked one of them.

No one replied, for we were independent of one another in our travel.

The invader said impatiently, after a moment, "No leader? No leader? Very well, all of you, listen. The road must be cleared. A convoy is coming through. Go back to Palerm and wait until tomorrow."

"But I must be in Agupt by—" the Scribe began.

"Land Bridge is closed today," said the invader. "Go back to Palerm."

His voice was calm. The invaders are never peremptory, never overbearing. They have the poise and assurance of those who are secure possessors.

The Scribe shivered, his jowls swinging, and said no more.

Several of the others by the side of the road looked as if they wished to protest. The Sentinel turned away and spat. A man who boldly wore the mark of the shattered guild of Defenders in his cheek clenched his fists and plainly fought back a surge of fury. The Changelings whispered to one another. Bernalt smiled bitterly at me and shrugged.

Go back to Palerm? Waste a day's march in this heat? For what? For what?

The invader gestured casually, telling us to disperse.

Now it was that Olmayne was unkind to me. In a low voice she said, "Explain to them, Tomis, that you are in the pay of the Procurator of Perris, and they will let the two of us pass."

Her dark eyes glittered with mockery and contempt.

My shoulders sagged as if she had loaded ten years on me. "Why did you say such a thing?" I asked.

"It's hot. I'm tired. It's idiotic of them to send us back to Palerm."

"I agree. But I can do nothing. Why try to hurt me?"

"Does the truth hurt that much?"

"I am no collaborator, Olmayne."

She laughed. "You say that so well! But you are, Tomis, you are! You sold them the documents."

"To save the Prince, your lover," I reminded her.

"You dealt with the invaders, though. No matter what your motive was, that fact remains."

"Stop it, Olmayne."

"Now you give me orders?"

"Olmayne—"

"Go up to them, Tomis. Tell them who you are, make them let us go ahead."

"The convoys would run us down on the road. In any case I have no influence with invaders. I am not the Procurator's man."

"I'll die before I go back to Palerm!"

"Die, then," I said wearily, and turned my back on her.

"Traitor! Treacherous old fool! Coward!"

I pretended to ignore her, but I felt the fire of her words. There was no falsehood in them, only malice. I *had* dealt with the conquerors, I *had* betrayed the guild that sheltered me, I *had* violated the code that calls for sullen passivity as our only way of protest for Earth's defeat. All true; yet it was unfair for her to reproach me with it. I had given no thought to higher matters of patriotism when I broke my trust; I was trying only to save a man to whom I felt bound, a man moreover with whom she was in love. It was loathsome of Olmayne to tax me with treason now, to torment my conscience, merely because of a petty rage at the heat and dust of the road.

But this woman had coldly slain her own husband. Why should she not be malicious in trifles as well?

The invaders had their way; we abandoned the road and straggled back to Palerm, a dismal, sizzling, sleepy town. That evening, as if to console us, five Fliers passing in formation overhead took a fancy to the town, and in the moonless night they came again and again through the sky, three men and two women, ghostly and slender and beautiful. I stood watching them for more than an hour, until my soul itself seemed lifted from me and into the air to join them. Their great shimmering wings scarcely hid the starlight; their pale angular bodies moved in graceful arcs, arms held pressed close to sides, legs together, backs gently curved. The sight of these five stirred my memories of Avluela and left me tingling with troublesome emotions.

The Fliers made their last pass and were gone. The false moons entered the sky soon afterward. I went into our hostelry then, and shortly Olmayne asked admittance to my room.

She looked contrite. She carried a squat octagonal flask of green wine, not a Talyan brew but something from an outworld, no doubt purchased at great price.

"Will you forgive me, Tomis?" she asked. "Here. I know you like these wines."

"I would rather not have had those words before, and not have the wine now," I told her.

"My temper grows short in the heat. I'm sorry, Tomis. I said a stupid and tactless thing."

I forgave her, in hope of a smoother journey thereafter, and we drank most of the wine, and then she went to her own room nearby to sleep. Pilgrims must live chaste lives—not that Olmayne would ever have bedded with such a withered old fossil as I, but the commandments of our adopted guild prevented the question from arising.

For a long while I lay awake beneath a lash of guilt. In her impatience and wrath Olmayne had stung me at my vulnerable place: I was a betrayer of mankind. I wrestled with the issue almost to dawn.

—What had I done?

I had revealed to our conquerors a certain document.

—Did the invaders have a moral right to the document?

It told of the shameful treatment they had had at the hands of our ancestors.

—What, then, was wrong about giving it to them?

One does not aid one's conquerors even when they are morally superior to one.

—Is a small treason a serious thing?

There are no small treasons.

—Perhaps the complexity of the matter should be investigated. I did not act out of love of the enemy, but to aid a friend.

Nevertheless I collaborated with our foes.

—This obstinate self-laceration smacks of sinful pride.

But I feel my guilt. I drown in shame.

In this unprofitable way I consumed the night. When the day brightened, I rose and looked skyward and begged the Will to help me find redemption in the waters of the house of renewal in Jorslem, at the end of my Pilgrimage. Then I went to awaken Olmayne.

3.

L and Bridge was open on this day, and we joined the throng that was crossing over out of Talya into Afreek. It was the second time I had traveled Land Bridge, for the year before—it seemed so much farther in the past—I had come the other way, out of Agupt and bound for Roum.

There are two main routes for Pilgrims from Eyrop to Jorslem. The northern route involves going through the Dark Lands east of Talya, taking the ferry at Stanbool, and skirting the western coast of the continent of Ais to Jorslem. It was the route I would have preferred since, of all the world's great cities, old Stanbool is the one I have never visited. But Olmayne had been there to do research in the days when she was a Rememberer, and disliked the place; and so we took the southern route—across Land Bridge into Afreek and along the shore of the great Lake Medit, through Agupt and the fringes of the Arban Desert and up to Jorslem.

A true Pilgrim travels only by foot. It was not an idea that had much appeal to Olmayne, and though we walked a great deal, we rode whenever we could. She was shameless in commandeering transportation. On only the second day of our journey she had gotten us a ride from a rich Merchant bound for the coast; the man had no intention of sharing his sumptuous vehicle with anyone, but he could not resist the sensuality of Olmayne's deep, musical voice, even though it issued from the sexless grillwork of a Pilgrim's mask.

The Merchant traveled in style. For him the conquest of Earth might never have happened, nor even all the long centuries of Third Cycle decline. His self-primed landcar was four times the length of a man and wide enough to house five people in comfort; and it shielded its riders against the outer world as effectively as a womb. There was no direct vision, only a series of screens revealing upon command what lay outside. The temperature never varied from a chosen norm. Spigots supplied liqueurs and stronger things; food tablets were available; pressure couches insulated travelers against the irregularities of the road. For illumination, there was slavelight keyed to the Merchant's whims. Beside the main couch sat a thinking cap, but I never learned whether the Merchant carried a pickled brain for his private use in the depths of the landcar, or enjoyed some sort of remote contact with the memory tanks of the cities through which he passed.

He was a man of pomp and bulk, clearly a savorer of his own flesh. Deep olive of skin, with a thick pompadour of well-oiled black hair and somber, scrutinizing eyes, he rejoiced in his solidity and in his control of an uncertain environment. He dealt, we learned, in foodstuffs of other worlds; he bartered our poor manufactures for the delicacies of the starborn ones. Now he was en route to Marsay to examine a cargo of hallucinatory insects newly come in from one of the Belt planets.

"You like the car?" he asked, seeing our awe. Olmayne, no stranger to ease herself, was peering at the dense inner mantle of diamonded brocade in obvious amazement. "It was owned by the Comt of Perris," he went on. "Yes, I mean it, the Comt himself. They turned his palace into a museum, you know."

"I know," Olmayne said softly.

"This was his chariot. It was supposed to be part of the museum, but I bought it off a crooked invader. You didn't know they had crooked ones too, eh?" The Merchant's robust laughter caused the sensitive mantle on the walls of the car to recoil in disdain. "This one was the Procurator's boy friend. Yes, they've got those, too. He was looking for a certain fancy root that grows on a planet of the Fishes, something to give his virility a little boost, you know, and he learned that I controlled the whole supply here, and so we were able to work out a little deal Of course, I had to have the car adapted, a little. The Comt kept four neuters up front and powered the engine right off their metabolisms, you understand, running the thing on thermal differentials. Well, that's a fine way to power a car, if you're a Comt, but it uses up a lot of neuters through the year, and I felt I'd be overreaching my status if I tried anything like that. It might get me into trouble with the invaders, too. So I had the drive compartment stripped down and replaced with a standard heavy-duty roller-wagon engine—a really subtle job—and there you are. You're lucky to be in here. It's only that you're Pilgrims. Ordinarily I don't let folks come inside, on account of them feeling envy, and envious folks are dangerous to a man who's made something out of his life. Yet the Will brought you two to me. Heading for Jorslem, eh?"

"Yes," Olmayne said.

"Me too, but not yet! Not just yet, thank you!" He patted his middle. "I'll be there, you can bet on it, when I feel ready for renewal, but that's a good way off, the Will willing! You two been Pilgriming long?"

"No," Olmayne said.

"A lot of folks went Pilgrim after the conquest, I guess. Well, I won't blame 'em. We each adapt in our own ways to changing times. Say, you carrying those little stones the Pilgrims carry?"

"Yes," Olmayne said.

"Mind if I see one? Always been fascinated by the things. There was this trader from one of the Darkstar worlds—little skinny bastard with skin like oozing tar—he offered me ten quintals of the things. Said they were genuine, gave you the real communion, just like the Pilgrims had. I told him no, I wasn't going to fool with the Will. Some things you don't do, even for profit. But afterward I wished I'd kept one as a souvenir. I never even touched one." He stretched a hand toward Olmayne. "Can I see?"

"We may not let others handle the starstone," I said.

"I wouldn't tell anybody you let me!"

"It is forbidden."

"Look, it's private in here, the most private place on Earth, and—"

"Please. What you ask is impossible."

His face darkened, and I thought for a moment he would halt the car and order us out, which would have caused me no grief. My hand slipped into my pouch to finger the frigid starstone sphere that I had been given at the outset of my Pilgrimage. The touch of my fingertips brought faint resonances of the communion-trance to me, and I shivered in pleasure. He must not have it, I swore. But the crisis passed without incident. The Merchant, having tested us and found resistance, did not choose to press the matter.

We sped onward toward Marsay.

He was not a likable man, but he had a certain gross charm, and we were rarely offended by his words. Olmayne, who after all was a fastidious woman and had lived most of her years in the glossy seclusion of the Hall of Rememberers, found him harder to take than I; my intolerances have been well blunted by a lifetime of wandering. But even Olmayne seemed to find him amusing when he boasted of his wealth and influence, when he told of the women who waited for him on many worlds, when he catalogued his homes and his trophies and the guildmasters who sought his counsel, when he bragged of his friendships with former Masters and Dominators. He talked almost wholly of himself and rarely of us, for which we were thankful; once he asked how it was that a male Pilgrim and a female Pilgrim were traveling together, implying that we must be lovers; we admitted that the arrangement was slightly irregular and went on to another theme, and I think he remained persuaded of our unchastity. His bawdy guesses mattered not at all to me nor, I believe, to Olmayne. We had more serious guilts as our burdens.

Our Merchant's life seemed enviably undisrupted by the fall of our planet: he was as rich as ever, as comfortable, as free to move about. But even he felt occasionally irked by the presence of the invaders, as we found out by night not far from Marsay, when we were stopped at a checkpoint on the road.

Spy-eye scanners saw us coming, gave a signal to the spinnerets, and a golden spiderweb spurted into being from one shoulder of the highway to the other. The land-car's sensors detected it and instantly signaled us to a halt. The screens showed a dozen pale human figures clustered outside.

"Bandits?" Olmayne asked.

"Worse," said the Merchant. "Traitors." He scowled and turned to his communicator horn. "What is it?" he demanded.

"Get out for inspection."

"By whose writ?"

"The Procurator of Marsay," came the reply.

It was an ugly thing to behold: human beings acting as road-agents for the invaders. But it was inevitable that we should have begun to drift into their civil service, since work was scarce, especially for those who had been in the defensive guilds. The Merchant began the complicated process of unsealing his car. He was stormy-faced with rage, but he was stymied, unable to pass the checkpoint's web. "I go armed," he whispered to us. "Wait inside and fear nothing."

He got out and engaged in a lengthy discussion, of which we could hear nothing, with the highway guards. At length some impasse must have forced recourse to higher authority, for three invaders abruptly appeared, waved their hired collaborators away, and surrounded the Merchant. His demeanor changed; his face grew oily and sly, his hands moved rapidly in eloquent gestures, his eyes glistened. He led the three interrogators to the car, opened it, and showed them his two passengers, ourselves. The invaders appeared puzzled by the sight of Pilgrims amid such opulence, but they did not ask us to step out. After some further conversation the Merchant rejoined us and sealed the car; the web was dissolved; we sped onward toward Marsay.

As we gained velocity he muttered curses and said, "Do you know how I'd handle that long-armed filth? All we need is a coordinated plan. A night of knives: every ten Earthmen make themselves responsible for taking out one invader. We'd get them all."

"Why has no one organized such a movement?" I asked.

"It's the job of the Defenders, and half of them are dead, and the other half's in the pay of *them*. It's not my place to set up a resistance movement. But that's how it should be done. Guerrilla action: sneak up behind 'em, give 'em the knife. Quick. Good old First Cycle methods; they've never lost their value."

"More invaders would come," Olmayne said morosely.

"Treat 'em the same way!"

"They would retaliate with fire. They would destroy our world," she said.

"These invaders pretend to be civilized, more civilized than ourselves," the Merchant replied. "Such barbarity would give them a bad name on a million worlds. No, they wouldn't come with fire. They'd just get tired of having to conquer us over and over, of losing so many men. And they'd go away, and we'd be free again."

"Without having won redemption for our ancient sins," I said.

"What's that, old man? What's that?"

"Never mind."

"I suppose you wouldn't join in, either of you, if we struck back at them?"

I said, "In former life I was a Watcher, and I devoted myself to the protection of this planet against them. I am no more fond of our masters than you are, and no less eager to see them depart. But your plan is not only impractical: it is also morally valueless. Mere bloody resistance would thwart the scheme the Will has devised for us. We must earn our freedom in a nobler way. We were not given this ordeal simply so that we might have practice in slitting throats."

He looked at me with contempt and snorted. "I should have remembered. I'm talking to Pilgrims. All right. Forget it all. I wasn't serious, anyway. Maybe you like the world the way it is, for all I know."

"I do not," I said.

He glanced at Olmayne. So did I, for I half expected her to tell the Merchant that I had already done my bit of collaborating with our conquerors. But Olmayne fortunately was silent on that topic, as she would be for some months more, until that unhappy day by the approach to

Land Bridge when, in her impatience, she taunted me with my sole fall from grace.

We left our benefactor in Marsay, spent the night in a Pilgrim hostelry, and set out on foot along the coast the next morning. And so we traveled, Olmayne and I, through pleasant lands swarming with invaders; now we walked, now we rode some peasant's rollerwagon, once even we were the guests of touring conquerors. We gave Roum a wide berth when we entered Talya, and turned south. And so we came to Land Bridge, and met delay, and had our frosty moment of bickering, and then were permitted to go on across that narrow tongue of sandy ground that links the lake-sundered continents. And so we crossed into Afreek, at last.

4.

Our first night on the other side, after our long and dusty crossing, we tumbled into a grimy inn near the lake's edge. It was a square whitewashed stone building, practically windowless and arranged around a cool inner courtyard. Most of its clientele appeared to be Pilgrims, but there were some members of other guilds, chiefly Vendors and Transporters. At a room near the turning of the building there stayed a Rememberer, whom Olmayne avoided even though she did not know him; she simply did not wish to be reminded of her former guild.

Among those who took lodging there was the Changeling Bernalt. Under the new laws of the invaders, Changelings might stay at any public inn, not merely those set aside for their special use; yet it seemed a little strange to see him here. We passed in the corridor. Bernalt gave me a tentative smile, as though about to speak again, but the smile died and the glow left his eyes. He appeared to realize I was not ready to accept his friendship. Or perhaps he merely recalled that Pilgrims, by the laws of their guild, were not supposed to have much to do with guildless ones. That law still stood.

Olmayne and I had a greasy meal of soups and stews. Afterward I saw her to her room and began to wish her good night when she said, "Wait. We'll do our communion together."

"I've been seen coming into your room," I pointed out. "There will be whispering if I stay long."

"We'll go to yours, then!"

Olmayne peered into the hall. All clear: she seized my wrist, and we rushed toward my chamber, across the way. Closing and sealing the warped door, she said, "Your starstone, now!"

I took the stone from its hiding place in my robe, and she produced hers, and our hands closed upon them.

During this time of Pilgrimage I had found the starstone a great comfort. Many seasons now had passed since I had last entered a Watcher's trance, but I was not yet reconciled entirely to the breaking of my old habit; the starstone provided a kind of substitute for the swooping ecstasy I had known in Watching.

Starstones come from one of the outer worlds—I could not tell you which—and may be had only by application to the guild. The stone itself determines whether one may be a Pilgrim, for it will burn the hand of one whom it considers unworthy to don the robe. They say that without exception every person who has enrolled in the guild of Pilgrims has shown uneasiness as the stone was offered to him for the first time.

"When they gave you yours," Olmayne asked, "were you worried?"

"Of course."

"So was I."

We waited for the stones to overwhelm us. I gripped mine tightly. Dark, shining, more smooth than glass, it glowed in my grasp like a pellet of ice, and I felt myself becoming attuned to the power of the Will.

First came a heightened perception of my surroundings. Every crack in the walls of this ancient inn seemed now a valley. The soft wail of the wind outside rose to a keen pitch. In the dim glow of the room's lamp I saw colors beyond the spectrum.

The quality of the experience the starstone offered was altogether different from that given by my instruments of Watching. That, too, was a transcending of self. When in a state of Watchfulness I was capable of leaving my Earthbound identity and soaring at infinite speed over infinite range, perceiving all, and this is as close to godhood as a man is likely to come. The starstone provided none of the highly specific data that a Watcher's trance yielded. In the full spell I could see nothing, nor could I identify my surroundings. I knew only that when I let myself be drawn into the stone's effect, I was engulfed by something far larger than myself, that I was in direct contact with the matrix of the universe.

Call it communion with the Will.

From a great distance I heard Olmayne say, "Do you believe what some people say of these stones? That there is no communion, that it's all an electrical deception?"

"I have no theory about that," I said. "I am less interested in causes than in effects."

Skeptics say that the starstones are nothing more than amplifying loops that bounce a man's own brain-waves back into his mind; the awesome oceanic entity with which one comes in contact, these scoffers hold, is merely the thunderous recycling oscillation of a single shuttling electrical pulse beneath the roof of the Pilgrim's own skull. Perhaps. Perhaps.

Olmayne extended the hand that gripped her stone. She said, "When you were among the Rememberers, Tomis, did you study the history of early religion? All through time, man has sought union with the infinite. Many religions—not all!—have held forth the hope of such a divine merging."

"And there were drugs, too," I murmured.

"Certain drugs, yes, cherished for their ability to bring the taker momentarily to a sensation of oneness with the universe. These star-stones, Tomis, are only the latest in a long sequence of devices for overcoming the greatest of human curses, that is, the confinement of each individual soul within a single body. Our terrible isolation from one another and from the Will itself is more than most races of the universe would be able to bear. It seems unique to humanity."

Her voice grew feathery and vague. She said much more, speaking to me out of the wisdom she had learned with the Rememberers, but her meaning eluded me; I was always quicker to enter communion than she, because of my training as a Watcher, and often her final words did not register.

That night as on other nights I seized my stone and felt the chill and closed my eyes, and heard the distant tolling of a mighty gong, the lapping of waves on an unknown beach, the whisper of the wind in an alien forest. And felt a summons. And yielded. And entered the state of communion. And gave myself up to the Will.

And slipped down through the layers of my life, through my youth and middle years, my wanderings, my old loves, my torments, my joys, my troubled later years, my treasons, my insufficiencies, my griefs, my imperfections.

And freed myself of myself. And shed my selfness. And merged. And became one of thousands of Pilgrims, not merely Olmayne nearby, but others trekking the mountains of Hind and the sands of Arba, Pilgrims at their devotions in Ais and Palash and Stralya, Pilgrims moving toward Jorslem on the journey that some complete in months, some in years, and some never at all. And shared with all of them the instant of submergence into the Will. And saw in the darkness a deep purple glow on the horizon—which grew in intensity until it became an all-encompassing red brilliance. And went into it, though unworthy, unclean, flesh-trapped, accepting fully the communion offered and wishing no other state of being than this divorce from self.

And was purified.

And awakened alone.

5.

I knew Afreek well. When still a young man I had settled in the continent's dark heart for many years. Out of restlessness I had left, finally, going as far north as Agupt, where the antique relics of First Cycle days have survived better than anywhere else. In those days antiquity held no interest for me, however. I did my Watching and went about from place to place, since a Watcher does not need to have a fixed station; and chance brought me in contact with Avluela just as I was ready to roam again, and so I left Agupt for Roum and then Perris.

Now I had come back with Olmayne. We kept close to the coast and avoided the sandy inland wastes. As Pilgrims we were immune from most of the hazards of travel: we would never go hungry or without shelter, even in a place where no lodge for our guild existed, and all owed us respect. Olmayne's great beauty might have been a hazard to her, traveling as she was with no escort other than a shriveled old man, but behind the mask and robe of a Pilgrim she was safe. We unmasked only rarely, and never where we might be seen.

I had no illusions about my importance to Olmayne. To her I was merely part of the equipment of a journey—someone to help her in her communions and rituals, to arrange for lodgings, to smooth her way for her. That role suited me. She was, I knew, a dangerous woman, given to strange whims and unpredictable fancies. I wanted no entanglements with her.

She lacked a Pilgrim's purity. Even though she had passed the test of the starstone, she had not triumphed—as a Pilgrim must—over her own flesh. She slipped off, sometimes, for half a night or longer, and I pictured her lying maskless in some alley gasping in a Servitor's arms.

That was her affair entirely; I never spoke of her absences upon her return.

Within our lodgings, too, she was careless of her virtue. We never shared a room—no Pilgrim hostelry would permit it—but we usually had adjoining ones, and she summoned me to hers or came to mine whenever the mood took her. Often as not she was unclothed; she attained the height of the grotesque one night in Agupt when I found her wearing only her mask, all her gleaming white flesh belying the intent of the bronze grillwork that hid her face. Only once did it seem to occur to her that I might ever have been young enough to feel desire. She looked my scrawny, shrunken body over and said, "How will you look, I wonder, when you've been renewed in Jorslem? I'm trying to picture you young, Tomis. Will you give me pleasure then?"

"I gave pleasure in my time," I said obliquely.

Olmayne disliked the heat and dryness of Agupt. We traveled mainly by night and clung to our hostelries by day. The roads were crowded at all hours. The press of Pilgrims towards Jorslem was extraordinarily heavy, it appeared. Olmayne and I speculated on how long it might take us to gain access to the waters of renewal at such a time.

"You've never been renewed before?" she asked.

"Never."

"Nor I. They say they don't admit all who come."

"Renewal is a privilege, not a right," I said. "Many are turned away."

"I understand also," said Olmayne, "that not all who enter the waters are successfully renewed."

"I know little of this."

"Some grow older instead of younger. Some grow young too fast, and perish. There are risks."

"Would you not take those risks?"

She laughed. "Only a fool would hesitate."

"You are in no need of renewal at this time," I pointed out. "You were sent to Jorslem for the good of your soul, not that of your body, as I recall."

"I'll tend to my soul as well, when I'm in Jorslem."

"But you talk as if the house of renewal is the only shrine you mean to visit."

"It's the important one," she said. She rose, flexing her supple body voluptuously. "True, I have atoning to do. But do you think I've come all the way to Jorslem just for the sake of my spirit?"

"I have," I pointed out.

"*You!* You're old and withered! You'd better look after your spirit—

and your flesh as well. I wouldn't mind shedding some age, though. I won't have them take off much. Eight, ten years, that's all. The years I wasted with that fool Elegro. I don't need a full renewal. You're right: I'm still in my prime." Her face clouded. "If the city is full of Pilgrims, maybe they won't let me into the house of renewal at all! They'll say I'm too young—tell me to come back in forty or fifty years—Tomis, would they do that to me?"

"It is hard for me to say."

She trembled. "They'll let *you* in. You're a walking corpse already—they have to renew you! But me—Tomis, I won't let them turn me away! If I have to pull Jorslem down stone by stone, I'll get in somehow!"

I wondered privately if her soul were in fit condition for one who poses as a candidate for renewal. Humility is recommended when one becomes a Pilgrim. But I had no wish to feel Olmayne's fury, and I kept my silence. Perhaps they would admit her to renewal despite her flaws. I had concerns of my own. It was vanity that drove Olmayne; my goals were different. I had wandered long and done much, not all of it virtuous; I needed a cleansing of my conscience in the holy city more, perhaps, than I did a lessening of my years.

Or was it only vanity for me to think so?

6.

Several days castward of that place, as Olmayne and I walked through a parched countryside, village children chattering in fear and excitement rushed upon us.

"Please, come, come!" they cried. "Pilgrims, come!"

Olmayne looked bewildered and irritated as they plucked at her robes. "What are they saying, Tomis? I can't get through their damnable Aguptan accents!"

"They want us to help," I said. I listened to their shouts. "In their village," I told Olmaync, "there is an outbreak of the crystallization disease. They wish us to seek the mercies of the Will upon the sufferers."

Olmayne drew back. I imagined the disdainful wince behind her mask. She flicked out her hands, trying to keep the children from touching her. To me she said, "We can't go there!"

"We must."

"We're in a hurry! Jorslem's crowded; I don't want to waste time in some dreary village."

"They need us, Olmayne."

"Are we Surgeons?"

"We are Pilgrims," I said quietly. "The benefits we gain from that carry certain obligations. If we are entitled to the hospitality of all we meet, we must also place our souls at the free disposal of the humble. Come."

"I won't go!"

"How will that sound in Jorslem, when you give an accounting of yourself, Olmayne?"

"It's a hideous disease. What if we get it?"

"Is that what troubles you? Trust in the Will! How can you expect renewal if your soul is so deficient in grace?"

"May you rot, Tomis," she said in a low voice. "When did you become so pious? You're doing this deliberately, because of what I said to you by Land Bridge. In a stupid moment I taunted you, and now you're willing to expose us both to a ghastly affliction for your revenge. Don't do it, Tomis!"

I ignored her accusation. "The children are growing agitated, Olmayne. Will you wait here for me, or will you go on to the next village and wait in the hostelry there?"

"Don't leave me alone in the middle of nowhere!"

"I have to go to the sick ones," I said.

In the end she accompanied me—I think not out of any suddenly conceived desire to be of help, but rather out of fear that her selfish refusal might somehow be held against her in Jorslem. We came shortly to the village, which was small and decayed, for Agupt lies in a terrible hot sleep and changes little with the millennia. The contrast with the busy cities farther to the south in Afreek—cities that prosper on the output of luxuries from their great Manufactories—is vast.

Shivering with heat, we followed the children to the houses of sickness.

The crystallization disease is an unlovely gift from the stars. Not many afflictions of outworlders affect the Earthborn; but from the worlds of the Spear came this ailment, carried by alien tourists, and the disease has settled among us. If it had come during the glorious days of the Second Cycle we might have eradicated it in a day; but our skills are dulled now, and no year has been without its outbreak. Olmayne was plainly terrified as we entered the first of the clay huts where the victims were kept.

There is no hope for one who has contracted this disease. One merely hopes that the healthy will be spared; and fortunately it is not a highly contagious disease. It works insidiously, transmitted in an unknown way, often failing to pass from husband to wife and leaping instead to the far side of a city, to another land entirely, perhaps. The first symptom is a scaliness of the skin; itch, flakes upon the clothing, inflammation. There follows a weakness in the bones as the calcium is dissolved. One grows limp and rubbery, but this is still an early phase. Soon the outer tissues harden. Thick, opaque membranes form on the surface of the eyes; the nostrils may close and seal; the skin grows coarse and pebbled. In this phase prophecy is common. The sufferer partakes of the skills of a Somnambulist, and utters oracles. The soul may wander, separating from the body for hours at a time, although the life-processes continue. Next, within twenty days after the onset of the disease, the crystallization occurs. While the skeletal structure dissolves, the skin splits and cracks, forming shining crystals in rigid geometrical patterns. The victim is quite beautiful at this time and takes on the appearance of a replica of himself in precious gems. The crystals glow with rich inner lights, violet and green and red; their sharp facets adopt new alignments from hour to hour; the slightest illumination in the room causes the sufferer to give off brilliant glittering reflections that dazzle and delight the eye. All this time the internal body is changing, as if some strange chrysalis is forming. Miraculously the organs sustain life throughout every transformation, although in the crystalline phase the victim is no longer able to communicate with others and possibly is unaware of the changes in himself. Ultimately the metamorphosis reaches the vital organs, and the process fails. The alien infestation is unable to reshape those organs without killing its host. The crisis is swift: a brief convulsion, a final discharge of energy along the nervous system of the crystallized one, and there is a quick arching of the body, accompanied by the delicate tinkling sounds of shivering glass, and then all is over. On the planet to which this is native, crystallization is not a disease but an actual metamorphosis, the result of thousands of years of evolution toward a symbiotic relationship. Unfortunately, among the Earthborn, the evolutionary preparation did not take place, and the agent of change invariably brings its subject to a fatal outcome.

Since the process is irreversible, Olmayne and I could do nothing of real value here except offer consolation to these ignorant and frightened people. I saw at once that the disease had seized this village some time ago. There were people in all stages, from the first rash to the ultimate crystallization. They were arranged in the hut according to the intensity of their infestation. To my left was a somber row of new victims, fully conscious and morbidly scratching their arms as they contemplated the horrors that awaited them. Along the rear wall were five pallets on which lay villagers in the coarse-skinned and prophetic phase. To my right were those in varying degrees of crystallization, and up front, the diadem of the lot, was one who clearly was in his last hours of life. His body, encrusted with false emeralds and rubies and opals, shimmered in almost painful beauty; he scarcely moved; within that shell of wondrous color he was lost in some dream of ecstasy, finding at the end of his days more passion, more delight, than he could ever have known in all his harsh peasant years.

Olmayne shied back from the door.

"It's horrible," she whispered. "I won't go in!"

"We must. We are under an obligation."

"I never wanted to be a Pilgrim!"

"You wanted atonement," I reminded her. "It must be earned."

"We'll catch the disease!"

"The Will can reach us anywhere to infect us with this, Olmayne. It strikes at random. The danger is no greater for us inside this building than it is in Perris."

"Why, then, are so many in this one village smitten?"

"This village has earned the displeasure of the Will."

"How neatly you serve up the mysticism, Tomis," she said bitterly. "I misjudged you. I thought you were a sensible man. This fatalism of yours is ugly."

"I watched my world conquered," I said. "I beheld the Prince of Roum destroyed. Calamities breed such attitudes as I now have. Let us go in, Olmayne."

We entered, Olmayne still reluctant. Now fear assailed me, but I concealed it. I had been almost smug in my piety while arguing with the lovely Rememberer woman who was my companion, but I could not deny the sudden seething of fright.

I forced myself to be tranquil.

There are redemptions and redemptions, I told myself. If this disease is to be the source of mine, I will abide by the Will.

Perhaps Olmayne came to some such decision too, as we went in, or maybe her own sense of the dramatic forced her into the unwanted role of the lady of mercy. She made the rounds with me. We passed from pallet to pallet, heads bowed, starstones in our hands. We said words. We smiled when the newly sick begged for reassurance. We offered prayers. Olmayne paused before one girl in the secondary phase, whose eyes already were filming over with horny tissue, and knelt and touched her starstone to the girl's scaly cheek. The girl spoke in oracles, but unhappily not in any language we understood.

At last we came to the terminal case, he who had grown his own superb sarcophagus. Somehow I felt purged of fear, and so too was Olmayne, for we stood a long while before this grotesque sight, silent, and then she whispered, "How terrible! How wonderful! How beautiful!"

Three more huts similar to this one awaited us.

The villagers clustered at the doorways. As we emerged from each building in turn, the healthy ones fell down about us, clutching at the hems of our robes, stridently demanding that we intercede for them with the Will. We spoke such words as seemed appropriate and not too insincere. Those within the huts received our words blankly, as if they already realized there was no chance for them; those outside, still untouched by the disease, clung to every syllable. The headman of the village—only an acting headman; the true chief lay crystallized—thanked us again and again, as though we had done something real. At least we had given comfort, which is not to be despised.

When we came forth from the last of the sickhouses, we saw a slight figure watching us from a distance: the Changeling Bernalt. Olmayne nudged me.

"That creature has been following us, Tomis. All the way from Land Bridge!"

"He travels to Jorslem also."

"Yes, but why should he stop here? Why in this awful place?"

"Hush, Olmayne. Be civil to him now."

"To a *Changeling?*"

Bernalt approached. The mutated one was clad in a soft white robe that blunted the strangeness of his appearance. He nodded sadly toward the village and said, "A great tragedy. The Will lies heavy on this place."

He explained that he had arrived here several days ago and had met a friend from his native city of Nayrub. I assumed he meant a Changeling, but no, Bernalt's friend was a Surgeon, he said, who had halted here to do what he could for the afflicted villagers. The idea of a friendship between a Changeling and a Surgeon seemed a bit odd to me, and positively contemptible to Olmayne, who did not trouble to hide her loathing of Bernalt.

A partly crystallized figure staggered from one of the huts, gnarled hands clutching. Bernalt went forward and gently guided it back within. Returning to us, he said, "There are times one is actually glad one is a Changeling. That disease does not affect us, you know." His eyes acquired a sudden glitter. "Am I forcing myself on you, Pilgrims? You seem like stone behind your masks. I mean no harm; shall I withdraw?"

"Of course not," I said, meaning the opposite. His company disturbed me; perhaps the ordinary disdain for Changelings was a contagion that had at last reached me. "Stay awhile. I would ask you to travel with us to Jorslem, but you know it is forbidden for us."

"Certainly. I quite understand." He was coolly polite, but the seething bitterness in him was close to the surface. Most Changelings are such degraded bestial things that they are incapable of knowing how detested they are by normal guilded men and women; but Bernalt clearly was gifted with the torment of comprehension. He smiled, and then he pointed. "My friend is here."

Three figures approached. One was Bernalt's Surgeon, a slender man, dark-skinned, soft-voiced, with weary eyes and sparse yellow hair.

With him were an official of the invaders and another outworlder from a different planet. "I had heard that two Pilgrims were summoned to this place," said the invader. "I am grateful for the comfort you may have brought these sufferers. I am Earthclaim Nineteen; this district is under my administration. Will you be my guests at dinner this night?"

I was doubtful of taking an invader's hospitality, and Olmayne's sudden clenching of her fist over her starstone told me that she also hesitated. Earthclaim Nineteen seemed eager for our acceptance. He was not as tall as most of his kind, and his malproportioned arms reached below his knees. Under the blazing Aguptan sun his thick waxy skin acquired a high gloss, although he did not perspire.

Into a long, tense, and awkward silence the Surgeon inserted: "No need to hold back. In this village we all are brothers. Join us tonight, will you?"

We did. Earthclaim Nineteen occupied a villa by the shore of Lake Medit; in the clear light of late afternoon I thought I could detect Land Bridge jutting forward to my left, and even Eyrop at the far side of the lake. We were waited upon by members of the guild of Servitors who brought us cool drinks on the patio. The invader had a large staff, all Earthborn; to me it was another sign that our conquest had become institutionalized and was wholly accepted by the bulk of the populace. Until long after dusk we talked, lingering over drinks even as the writhing auroras danced into view to herald the night. Bernalt the Changeling remained apart, though, perhaps ill at ease in our presence. Olmayne too was moody and withdrawn; a mingled depression and exaltation had settled over her in the stricken village, and the presence of Bernalt at the dinner party had reinforced her silence, for she had no idea how to be polite in the presence of a Changeling. The invader, our host, was charming and attentive, and tried to bring her forth from her bleakness. I had seen charming conquerors before. I had traveled with one who had posed as the Earthborn Changeling Gormon in the days just before the conquest. This one, Earthclaim Nineteen, had been a poet on his native world in those days. I said, "It seems unlikely that one of your inclinations would care to be part of a military occupation."

"All experiences strengthen the art," said Earthclaim Nineteen. "I seek to expand myself. In any case I am not a warrior but an administrator. Is it so strange that a poet can be an administrator, or an administrator a poet?" He laughed. "Among your many guilds, there is no guild of Poets. Why?"

"There are Communicants," I said. "They serve your muse."

"But in a religious way. They are interpreters of the Will, not of their own souls."

"The two are indistinguishable. The verses they make are divinely inspired, but rise from the hearts of their makers," I said.

Earthclaim Nineteen looked unconvinced. "You may argue that all poetry is at bottom religious, I suppose. But this stuff of your Communicants is too limited in scope. It deals only with acquiescence to the Will."

"A paradox," said Olmayne. "The Will encompasses everything, and yet you say that our Communicants' scope is limited."

"There are other themes for poetry besides immersion in the Will, my friends. The love of person for person, the joy of defending one's home, the wonder of standing naked beneath the fiery stars—" The invader laughed. "Can it be that Earth fell so swiftly because its only poets were poets of acquiescence to destiny?"

"Earth fell," said the Surgeon, "because the Will required us to atone for the sin our ancestors committed when they treated your ancestors like beasts. The quality of our poetry had nothing to do with it."

"The Will decreed that you would lose to us by way of punishment, eh? But if the Will is omnipotent, it must have decreed the sin of your ancestors that made the punishment necessary. Eh? Eh? The Will playing games with itself? You see the difficulty of believing in a divine force that determines all events? Where is the element of choice that makes suffering meaningful? To force you into a sin, and then to require you to endure defeat as atonement, seems to me an empty exercise. Forgive my blasphemy."

The Surgeon said, "You misunderstand. All that has happened on this planet is part of a process of moral instruction. The Will does not shape every event great or small; it provides the raw material of events, and allows us to follow such patterns as we desire."

"Example?"

"The Will imbued the Earthborn with skills and knowledge. During the First Cycle we rose from savagery in little time; in the Second Cycle we attained greatness. In our moment of greatness we grew swollen with pride, choosing to exceed our limitations. We imprisoned intelligent creatures of other worlds under the pretense of 'study,' when we were acting really out of an arrogant desire for amusement; and we toyed with our world's climate until oceans joined and continents sank and our old civilization was destroyed. Thus the Will instructed us in the boundaries of human ambition."

"I dislike that dark philosophy even more," said Earthclaim Nineteen. "I—"

"Let me finish," said the Surgeon. "The collapse of Second Cycle Earth was our punishment. The defeat of Third Cycle Earth by you folk from the stars is a completion of that earlier punishment, but also the beginning of a new phase. You are the instruments of our redemption. By inflicting on us the final humiliation of conquest, you bring us to the bottom of our trough; now we renew our souls, now we begin to rise, tested by adversities."

I stared in sudden amazement at this Surgeon, who was uttering ideas that had been stirring in me all along the road to Jorslem, ideas of redemption both personal and planetary. I had paid little attention to the Surgeon before.

"Permit me a statement," Bernalt said suddenly, his first words in hours.

We looked at him. The pigmented bands in his face were ablaze, marking his emotion.

He said, nodding to the Surgeon, "My friend, you speak of redemption for the Earthborn. Do you mean *all* Earthborn, or only the guilded ones?"

"All Earthborn, of course," said the Surgeon mildly. "Are we not all equally conquered?"

"We are not equal in other things, though. Can there be redemption for a planet that keeps millions of its people thrust into guildlessness? I speak of my own folk, of course. We sinned long ago when we thought we were striking out against those who had created us as monsters. We strove to take Jorslem from you; and for this we were punished, and our punishment has lasted for a thousand years. We are still outcasts, are we not? Where has our hope of redemption been? Can you guilded ones consider yourself purified and made virtuous by your recent suffering, when you still step on us?"

The Surgeon looked dismayed. "You speak rashly, Bernalt. I know the Changelings have a grievance. But you know as well as I that your time of deliverance is at hand. In the days to come no Earthborn one will scorn you, and you will stand beside us when we regain our freedom."

Bernalt peered at the floor. "Forgive me, my friend. Of course, of course, you speak the truth. I was carried away. The heat—this splendid wine—how foolishly I spoke!"

Earthclaim Nineteen said, "Are you telling me that a resistance movement is forming that will shortly drive us from your planet?"

"I speak only in abstract terms," said the Surgeon.

"I think your resistance movement will be purely abstract, too," the invader replied easily. "Forgive me, but I see little strength in a planet that could be conquered in a single night. We expect our occupation of Earth to be a long one and to meet little opposition. In the months that we have been here there has been no sign of increasing hostility to us. Quite the contrary: we are increasingly accepted among you."

"It is part of a process," said the Surgeon. "As a poet, you should understand that words carry meanings of many kinds. We do not need to overthrow our alien masters in order to be free of them. Is that poetic enough for you?"

"Splendid," said Earthclaim Nineteen, getting to his feet. "Shall we go to dinner now?"

7.

There was no way to return to the subject. A philosophical discussion at the dinner table is difficult to sustain; and our host did not seem comfortable with this analysis of Earth's destinies. Swiftly he discovered that Olmayne had been a Rememberer before turning Pilgrim, and thereafter directed his words to her, questioning her on our history and on our early poetry. Like most invaders he had a fierce curiosity concerning our past. Olmayne gradually came out of the silence that gripped her, and spoke at length about her researches in Perris. She talked with great familiarity of our hidden past, with Earthclaim Nineteen occasionally inserting an intelligent and informed question; meanwhile we dined on delicacies of a number of worlds, perhaps imported by that same fat, insensitive Merchant who had driven us from Perris to Marsay; the villa was cool and the Servitors attentive; that miserable plague-stricken peasant village half an hour's walk away might well have been in some other galaxy, so remote was it from our discourse now.

When we left the villa in the morning, the Surgeon asked permission to join our Pilgrimage. "There is nothing further I can do here," he explained. "At the outbreak of the disease I came up from my home in Nayrub, and I've been here many days, more to console than to cure, of course. Now I am called to Jorslem. However, if it violates your vows to have company on the road—"

"By all means come with us," I said.

"There will be one other companion," the Surgeon told us.

He meant the third person who had met us at the village: the outworlder, an enigma, yet to say a word in our presence. This being was a flattened spike-shaped creature somewhat taller than a man and mounted on a jointed tripod of angular legs; its place of origin was in the Golden Spiral; its skin was rough and bright red in hue, and vertical rows of glassy oval eyes descended on three sides from the top of its tapered head. I had never seen such a creature before. It had come to Earth, according to the Surgeon, on a data-gathering mission, and had already roamed much of Ais and Stralya. Now it was touring the lands on the margin of Lake Medit; and after seeing Jorslem it would depart for the great cities of Eyrop. Solemn, unsettling in its perpetual watch-fulness, never blinking its many eyes nor offering a comment on what those eyes beheld, it seemed more like some odd machine, some information-intake for a memory tank, than a living creature. But it was harmless enough to let it come with us to the holy city.

The Surgeon bade farewell to his Changeling friend, who went on alone ahead of us, and paid a final call on the crystallized village. We stayed back, since there was no point in our going. When he returned, his face was somber. "Four new cases," he said. "This entire village will perish. There has never been an outbreak of this kind before on Earth—so concentrated an epidemic."

"Something new, then?" I asked. "Will it spread everywhere?"

"Who knows? No one in the adjoining villages has caught it. The pattern is unfamiliar: a single village wholly devastated, and nowhere else besides. These people see it as divine retribution for unknown sins."

"What could peasants have done," I asked, "that would bring the wrath of the Will so harshly upon them?"

"They are asking that too," said the Surgeon.

Olmayne said, "If there are new cases, our visit yesterday was use-less. We risked ourselves and did them no good."

"Wrong," the Surgeon told her. "These cases were already incubat-ing when you arrived. We may hope that the disease will not spread to those who still were in full health."

He did not seem confident of that.

Olmayne examined herself from day to day for symptoms of the disease, but none appeared. She gave the Surgeon much trouble on that score, bothering him for opinions concerning real or fancied blemishes of her skin, embarrassing him by removing her mask in his presence so that he could determine that some speck on her cheek was not the first trace of crystallization.

The Surgeon took all this in good grace, for, while the outworld being was merely a cipher plodding alongside us, the Surgeon was a man of depth, patience, and sophistication. He was native to Afreek, and had been dedicated to his guild at birth by his father, since healing was the family tradition. Traveling widely, he had seen most of our world and had forgotten little of what he had seen. He spoke to us of Roum and Perris, of the frostflower fields of Stralya, of my own birthplace in the western island group of the Lost Continents. He questioned us tactfully about our starstones and the effects they produced—I could see he hungered to try the stone himself, but that of course was forbidden to one who had not declared himself a Pilgrim—and when he learned that in former life I had been a Watcher, he asked me a great deal concerning the instruments by which I had scanned the heavens, wishing to know what it was I perceived and how I imagined the perception was accomplished. I spoke to him as fully as I could on these matters, though in truth I knew little.

Usually we kept to the green strip of fertile land bordering the lake, but once, at the Surgeon's insistence, we detoured into the choking desert to see something that he promised would be of interest. He would not tell us what it was. We were at this point traveling in hired rollerwagons, open on top, and sharp winds blew gusts of sand in our faces. Sand adhered briefly to the outworlder's eyes, I saw; and I saw how efficiently it flushed each eye with a flood of blue tears every few moments. The rest of us huddled in our garments, heads down, whenever the wind arose.

"We are here," the Surgeon announced finally. "When I traveled with my father I first visited this place long ago. We will go inside—and then you, the former Rememberer, will tell us where we are."

It was a building two stories high made of bricks of white glass. The doors appeared sealed, but they gave at the slightest pressure. Lights glowed into life the moment we entered.

In long aisles, lightly strewn with sand, were tables on which instruments were mounted. Nothing was comprehensible to me. There were devices shaped like hands, into which one's own hands could be inserted; conduits led from the strange metal gloves to shining closed cabinets, and arrangements of mirrors transmitted images from the interiors of those cabinets to giant screens overhead. The Surgeon placed his hands in the gloves and moved his fingers; the screens brightened, and I saw images of tiny needles moving through shallow arcs. He went to other machines that released dribbles of unknown fluids; he touched small buttons that produced musical sounds; he moved freely through a laboratory of wonders, clearly ancient, which seemed still in order and awaiting the return of its users.

Olmayne was ecstatic. She followed the Surgeon from aisle to aisle, handling everything.

"Well, Rememberer?" he asked finally. "What is this?"

"A Surgery," she said in lowered voice. "A Surgery of the Years of Magic!"

"Exactly! Splendid!" He seemed in an oddly excited state. "We could make dazzling monsters here! We could work miracles! Fliers, Swimmers, Changelings, Twiners, Burners, Climbers—invent your own guilds, shape men to your whims! This was the place!"

Olmayne said, "These Surgeries have been described to me. There are six of them left, are there not, one in northern Eyrop, one on Palash, one here, one far to the south in Deeper Afreek, one in western Ais—" She faltered.

"And one in Hind, the greatest of all!" said the Surgeon.

"Yes, of course, Hind! The home of the Fliers!"

Their awe was contagious. I said, "This was where the shapes of men were changed? How was it done?"

The Surgeon shrugged. "The art is lost. The Years of Magic were long ago, old man.

"Yes, yes, I know. But surely if the equipment survives, we could guess how—"

"With these knives," said the Surgeon, "we cut into the fabric of the unborn, editing the human seed. The Surgeon placed his hands here—he manipulated—and within that incubator the knives did their work. Out of this came Fliers and all the rest. The forms bred true. Some are extinct today, but our Fliers and our Changelings owe their heritage to some such building as this. The Changelings, of course, were the Surgeons' mistakes. They should not have been permitted to live."

"I thought that these monsters were the products of teratogenic drugs given to them when they still were within the womb," I said. "You tell me now that Changelings were made by Surgeons. Which is so?"

"Both," he replied. "All Changelings today are descended from the flaws and errors committed by the Surgeons of the Years of Magic. Yet mothers in that unhappy group often enhance the monstrousness of their children with drugs, so that they will be more marketable. It is an ugly tribe not merely in looks. Small wonder that their guild was dissolved and they were thrust outside society. We—"

Something bright flew through the air, missing his face by less than a hand's breadth. He dropped to the floor and shouted to us to take cover. As I fell I saw a second missile fly toward us. The outworld being, still observing all phenomena, studied it impassively in the moment of life that remained to it. Then the weapon struck two thirds of the way up the outworlder's body and severed it instantly. Other missiles followed, clattering against the wall behind us. I saw our attackers: a band of Changelings, fierce, hideous. We were unarmed. They moved toward us. I readied myself to die.

From the doorway a voice cried out: a familiar voice, using the thick and unfamiliar words of the language Changelings speak among themselves. Instantly the assault ceased. Those who menaced us turned toward the door. The Changeling Bernalt entered.

"I saw your vehicle," he said. "I thought you might be here, and perhaps in trouble. It seems I came in time."

"Not altogether," said the Surgeon. He indicated the fallen outworlder, which was beyond all aid. "But why this attack?"

Bernalt gestured. "*They* will tell you."

We looked at the five Changelings who had ambushed us. They were not of the educated, civilized sort such as Bernalt, nor were any two of them of the same styles; each was a twisted, hunched mockery of the human form, one with ropy tendrils descending from his chin, one with a face that was a featureless void, another whose ears were giant cups, and so forth. From the one closest to us, a creature with small platforms jutting from his skin in a thousand places, we learned why we had been assaulted. In a brutal Aguptan dialect he told us that we had profaned a temple sacred to Changelings. "We keep out of Jorslem," he told us. "Why must you come here?"

Of course he was right. We asked forgiveness as sincerely as we could, and the Surgeon explained that he had visited this place long ago and it had not been a temple then. That seemed to soothe the Changeling, who admitted that only in recent years had his kind used it as a shrine. He was soothed even more when Olmayne opened the overpocket fastened between her breasts and offered a few glittering gold coins, part of the treasure she had brought with her from Perris. The bizarre and deformed beings were satisfied at that and allowed us to leave the building. We would have taken the dead outworlder with us, but during our parley with the Changelings the body had nearly vanished, nothing but a faint gray streak remaining on the sandy floor to tell us where it had fallen. "A mortuary enzyme," the Surgeon explained. "Triggered by interruption of the life processes."

Others of this community of desert-dwelling Changelings were lurking about outside the building as we came forth. They were a tribe of nightmares, with skin of every texture and color, facial features arranged at random, all kinds of genetic improvisations of organs and bodily accessories. Bernalt himself, although their brother, seemed appalled by their monstrousness. They looked to him with awe. At the sight of us some of them fondled the throwing weapons at their hips, but a sharp command from Bernalt prevented any trouble.

He said, "I regret the treatment you received and the death of the outworlder. But of course it is risky to enter a place that is sacred to backward and violent people."

"We had no idea," the Surgeon said. "We never would have gone in if we had realized—"

"Of course. Of course." Was there something patronizing about Bernalt's soft, civilized tones? "Well, again I bid you farewell."

I blurted suddenly, "No. Travel with us to Jorslem! It's ridiculous for us to go separately to the same place."

Olmayne gasped. Even the Surgeon seemed amazed. Only Bernalt remained calm. He said, "You forget, friend, that it is improper for Pilgrims to journey with the guildless. Besides, I am here to worship at this shrine, and it will take me a while. I would not wish to delay you." His hand reached out to mine. Then he moved away, entering the ancient Surgery. Scores of his fellow Changelings rushed in after him. I was grateful to Bernalt for his tact; my impulsive offer of companionship, though sincerely meant, had been impossible for him to accept.

We boarded our rollerwagons. In a moment we heard a dreadful sound: a discordant Changeling hymn in praise of I dare not think what deity, a scraping, grinding, screeching song as misshapen as those who uttered it.

"The beasts," Olmayne muttered. "A sacred shrine! A Changeling temple! How loathsome! They might have killed us all, Tomis. How can such monsters have a religion?"

I made no reply. The Surgeon looked at Olmayne sadly and shook his head as though distressed by so little charity on the part of one who claimed to be a Pilgrim.

"They also are human," he said.

At the next town along our route we reported the starborn being's death to the occupying authorities. Then, saddened and silent, we three survivors continued onward, to the place where the coastline trends north rather than east. We were leaving sleepy Agupt behind and entering now into the borders of the land in which holy Jorslem lies.

8.

The city of Jorslem sits some good distance inland from Lake Medit on a cool plateau guarded by a ring of low, barren, rock-strewn mountains. All my life, it seemed, had been but a preparation for my first glimpse of this golden city, whose image I knew so well. Hence when I saw its spires and parapets rising in the east, I felt not so much awe as a sense of a homecoming.

A winding road took us down through the encircling hills to the city, whose wall was made of squared blocks of a fine stone, dark pink-gold in color. The houses and shrines, too, were of this stone. Groves of trees bordered the road, nor were they star-trees, but native products of Earth, as was fitting to this, the oldest of man's cities, older than Roum, older than Perris, its roots deep in the First Cycle.

The invaders, shrewdly, had not meddled with Jorslem's administration. The city remained under the governorship of the Guildmaster of Pilgrims, and even an invader was required to seek the Guildmaster's permission to enter. Of course, this was strictly a matter of form; the Pilgrim Guildmaster, like the Chancellor of the Rememberers and other such officials, was in truth a puppet subject to our conquerors' wishes. But that harsh fact was kept concealed. The invaders had left our holy city as a city apart, and we would not see them swaggering in armed teams through Jorslem's streets.

At the outer wall we formally requested entry from the Sentinel guarding the gate. Though elsewhere most Sentinels now were unemployed—since cities stood open by command of our masters—this man was in full guild array and calmly insisted on thorough procedure. Olmayne and I, as Pilgrims, were entitled to automatic access to Jorslem; yet he made us produce our starstones as evidence that we came by our

robes and masks honestly, and then donned a thinking cap to check our
names with the archives of our guild. In time we met approval. The
Surgeon our companion had an easier time; he had applied in advance
for entry while in Afreek, and after a moment to check his identity he
was admitted.

Within the walls everything had the aspect of great antiquity. Jorslem alone of the world's cities still preserves much of its First Cycle
architecture: not merely broken columns and ruined aqueducts, as in
Roum, but whole streets, covered arcades, towers, boulevards, that have
lasted through every upheaval our world has seen. And so once we
passed into the city we wandered in wonder through its strangeness,
down streets paved with cobbled stones, into narrow alleys cluttered
with children and beggars, across markets fragrant with spices. After an
hour of this we felt it was time to seek lodgings, and here it was necessary for us to part company with the Surgeon, since he was ineligible
to stay at a Pilgrim hostelry, and it would have been costly and foolish
for us to stay anywhere else. We saw him to the inn where he had
previously booked a room. I thanked him for his good companionship
on our journey, and he thanked us just as gravely and expressed the
hope that he would see us again in Jorslem in the days to come. Then
Olmayne and I took leave of him and rented quarters in one of the
numerous places catering to the Pilgrim trade.

The city exists solely to serve Pilgrims and casual tourists, and so
it is really one vast hostelry; robed Pilgrims are as common in Jorslem's
streets as Fliers in Hind. We settled and rested awhile; then we dined
and afterward walked along a broad street from which we could see, to
the east, Jorslem's inner and most sacred district. There is a city within
a city here. The most ancient part, so small it can be traversed in less
than an hour on foot, is wrapped in a high wall of its own. Therein lie
shrines revered by Earth's former religions: the Christers, the Hebers,
the Mislams. The place where the god of the Christers died is said to
be there, but this may be a distortion wrought by time, since what kind
of god is it that dies? On a high place in one corner of the Old City
stands a gilded dome once sacred to the Mislams, which is carefully
tended by the common folk of Jorslem. And to the fore part of that high
place are the huge gray blocks of a stone wall that had been worshiped
by the Hebers. These things remain, but the ideas behind them are lost;
never while I was among the Rememberers did I meet any scholar who
could explain the merit of worshiping a wall or a gilded dome. Yet the
old records assure us that these three First Cycle creeds were of great
depth and richness.

In the Old City, also, is a Second Cycle place that was of much more immediate interest to Olmayne and myself. As we stared through the darkness at the holy precincts Olmayne said, "We should make application tomorrow at the house of renewal."

"I agree. I long now to give up some of my years."

"Will they accept me, Tomis?"

"Speculating on it is idle," I told her. "We will go, and we will apply, and your question will be answered."

She said something further, but I did not hear her words, for at that moment three Fliers passed above me, heading east. One was male, two female; they flew naked, according to the custom of their guild; and the Flier in the center of the group was a slim, fragile girl, mere bones and wings, moving with a grace that was exceptional even for her airy kind.

"*Avluela!*" I gasped.

The trio of Fliers disappeared beyond the parapets of the Old City. Stunned, shaken, I clung to a tree for support and struggled for breath.

"Tomis?" Olmayne said. "Tomis, are you ill?"

"I know it was Avluela. They said she had gone back to Hind, but no, that was Avluela! How could I mistake her?"

"You've said that about every Flier you've seen since leaving Perris," said Olmayne coldly.

"But this time I'm certain! Where is a thinking cap? I must check with the Fliers' Lodge at once!"

Olmayne's hand rested on my arm. "It's late, Tomis. You act feverish. Why this excitement over your skinny Flier, anyway? What did she mean to you?"

"She—"

I halted, unable to put my meaning in words. Olmayne knew the story of my journey up out of Agupt with the girl, how as a celibate old Watcher I had conceived a kind of paternal fondness for her, how I had perhaps felt something more powerful than that, how I had lost her to the false Changeling Gormon, and how he in turn had lost her to the Prince of Roum. But yet what was Avluela to me? Why did a glimpse of someone who merely might have been Avluela send me into this paroxysm of confusion? I chased symbols in my turbulent mind and found no answers.

"Come back to the inn and rest," Olmayne said. "Tomorrow we must seek renewal."

First, though, I donned a cap and made contact with the Fliers' Lodge. My thoughts slipped through the shielding interface to the storage brain of the guild registry; I asked and received the answer I had sought. Avluela of the Fliers was indeed now a resident in Jorslem. "Take this message for her," I said. "The Watcher she knew in Roum now is here as a Pilgrim, and wishes to meet her outside the house of renewal at midday tomorrow."

With that done, I accompanied Olmayne to our lodgings. She seemed sullen and aloof; and when she unmasked in my room her face appeared rigid with—jealousy? Yes. To Olmayne all men were vassals, even one so shriveled and worn as I; and she loathed it that another woman could kindle such a flame in me. When I drew forth my starstone, Olmayne at first would not join me in communion. Only when I began the rituals did she submit. But I was so tense that night that I was unable to make the merging with the Will, nor could she achieve it; and thus we faced one another glumly for half an hour, and abandoned the attempt, and parted for the night.

9.

One must go by one's self to the house of renewal. At dawn I awoke, made a brief and more successful communion, and set out unbreakfasted, without Olmayne. In half an hour I stood before the golden wall of the Old City; in half an hour more I had finished my crossing of the inner city's tangled lanes. Passing before that gray wall so dear to the ancient Hebers, I went up onto the high place; I passed near the gilded dome of the vanished Mislams and, turning to the left, followed the stream of Pilgrims which already at this early hour was proceeding to the house of renewal.

This house is a Second Cycle building, for it was then that the renewal process was conceived; and of all that era's science, only renewal has come down to us approximately as it must have been practiced in that time. Like those other few Second Cycle structures that survive, the house of renewal is supple and sleek, architecturally understated, with deft curves and smooth textures; it is without windows; it bears no external ornament whatever. There are many doors. I placed myself before the easternmost entrance, and in an hour's time I was admitted.

Just inside the entrance I was greeted by a green-robed member of the guild of Renewers—the first member of this guild I had ever seen. Renewers are recruited entirely from Pilgrims who are willing to make it their life's work to remain in Jorslem and aid others toward renewal. Their guild is under the same administration as the Pilgrims; a single guildmaster directs the destinies of both; even the garb is the same except for color. In effect Pilgrims and Renewers are of one guild and represent different phases of the same affiliation. But a distinction is always drawn.

The Renewer's voice was light and cheerful. "Welcome to this house, Pilgrim. Who are you, where are you from?"

"I am the Pilgrim Tomis, formerly Tomis of the Rememberers, and prior to that a Watcher, born to the name Wuellig. I am native to the Lost Continents and have traveled widely both before and after beginning my Pilgrimage."

"What do you seek here?"

"Renewal. Redemption."

"May the Will grant your wishes," said the Renewer. "Come with me."

I was led through a close, dimly lit passage into a small stone cell. The Renewer instructed me to remove my mask, enter into a state of communion, and wait. I freed myself from the bronze grillwork and clasped my starstone tightly. The familiar sensations of communion stole over me, but no union with the Will took place; rather, I felt a specific link forming with the mind of another human being. Although mystified, I offered no resistance.

Something probed my soul. Everything was drawn forth and laid out as if for inspection on the floor of the cell: my acts of selfishness and of cowardice, my flaws and failings, my doubts, my despairs, above all the most shameful of my acts, the selling of the Rememberer document to the invader overlord. I beheld these things and knew that I was unworthy of renewal. In this house one might extend one's lifetime two or three times over; but why should the Renewers offer such benefits to anyone as lacking in merit as I?

I remained a long while in contemplation of my faults. Then the contact broke, and a different Renewer, a man of remarkable stature, entered the cell.

"The mercy of the Will is upon you, friend," he said, reaching forth fingers of extraordinary length to touch the tips of mine.

When I heard that deep voice and saw those white fingers, I knew that I was in the presence of a man I had met briefly before, as I stood outside the gates of Roum in the season before the conquest of Earth. He had been a Pilgrim then, and he had invited me to join him on his journey to Jorslem, but I had declined, for Roum had beckoned to me.

"Was your Pilgrimage an easy one?" I asked.

"It was a valuable one," he replied. "And you? You are a Watcher no longer, I see."

"I am in my third guild this year."

"With one more yet to come," he said.

"Am I to join you in the Renewers, then?"

"I did not mean that guild, friend Tomis. But we can talk more of that when your years are fewer. You have been approved for renewal, I rejoice to tell you."

"Despite my sins?"

"Because of your sins, such that they are. At dawn tomorrow you enter the first of the renewal tanks. I will be your guide through your second birth. I am the Renewer Talmit. Go, now, and ask for me when you return."

"One question—"

"Yes?"

"I made my Pilgrimage together with a woman, Olmayne, formerly a Rememberer of Perris. Can you tell me if she has been approved for renewal as well?"

"I know nothing of this Olmayne."

"She's not a good woman," I said. "She is vain, imperious, and cruel. But yet I think she is not beyond saving. Can you do anything to help her?"

"I have no influence in such things," Talmit said. "She must face interrogation like everyone else. I can tell you this, though: virtue is not the only criterion for renewal."

He showed me from the building. Cold sunlight illuminated the city. I was drained and depleted, too empty even to feel cheered that I had qualified for renewal. It was midday; I remembered my appointment with Avluela; I circled the house of renewal in rising anxiety. Would she come?

She was waiting by the front of the building, beside a glittering monument from Second Cycle days. Crimson jacket, furry leggings, glassy bubbles on her feet, telltale humps on her back: from afar I could make her out to be a Flier. "Avluela!" I called.

She whirled. She looked pale, thin, even younger than when I had last seen her. Her eyes searched my face, once again masked, and for a moment she was bewildered.

"Watcher?" she said. "Watcher, is that you?"

"Call me Tomis now," I told her. "But I am the same man you knew in Agupt and Roum."

"Watcher! Oh, Watcher! *Tomis.*" She clung to me. "How long it's been! So much has happened!" She sparkled now, and the paleness fled her cheeks. "Come, let's find an inn, a place to sit and talk! How did you discover me here?"

"Through your guild. I saw you overhead last night."

"I came here in the winter. I was in Fars for a while, halfway back to Hind, and then I changed my mind. There could be no going home.

Now I live near Jorslem, and I help with—" She cut her sentence sharply off. "Have you won renewal, Tomis?"

We descended from the high place into a humbler part of the inner city. "Yes," I said, "I am to be made younger. My guide is the Renewer Talmit—we met him as a Pilgrim outside Roum, do you remember?"

She had forgotten that. We seated ourselves at an open-air patio adjoining an inn, and Servitors brought us food and wine. Her gaiety was infectious; I felt renewed just to be with her. She spoke of those final cataclysmic days in Roum, when she had been taken into the palace of the Prince as a concubine; and she told me of that terrible moment when Gormon the Changeling defeated the Prince of Roum on the evening of conquest—announcing himself as no Changeling but an invader in disguise, and taking from the Prince at once his throne, his concubine, and his vision.

"Did the Prince die?" she asked.

"Yes, but not of his blinding." I told her how that proud man had fled Roum disguised as a Pilgrim, and how I had accompanied him to Perris, and how, while we were among the Rememberers, he had involved himself with Olmayne, and had been slain by Olmayne's husband, whose life was thereupon taken by his wife. "I also saw Gormon in Perris," I said. "He goes by the name of Victorious Thirteen now. He is high in the councils of the invaders."

Avleula smiled. "Gormon and I were together only a short while after the conquest. He wanted to tour Eyrop; I flew with him to Donsk and Sved, and there he lost interest in me. It was then that I felt I must go home to Hind, but later I changed my mind. When does your renewal begin?"

"At dawn."

"Oh, Tomis, how will it be when you are a young man? Did you know that I loved you? All the time we traveled, all while I was sharing Gormon's bed and consorting with the Prince, you were the one I wanted! But of course you were a Watcher, and it was impossible. Besides, you were so old. Now you no longer Watch, and soon you will no longer be old, and—" Her hand rested on mine. "I should never have left your side. We both would have been spared much suffering."

"We learn, from suffering," I said.

"Yes. Yes. I see that. How long will your renewal take?"

"The usual time, whatever that may be."

"After that, what will you do? What guild will you choose? You can't be a Watcher, not now."

"No, nor a Rememberer either. My guide Talmit spoke of some other guild, which he would not name, and assumed that I would enroll in it when I was done with renewal. I supposed he thought I'd stay here and join the Renewers, but he said it was another guild."

"Not the Renewers," said Avluela. She leaned close. "The Redeemers," she whispered.

"Redeemers? That is a guild I do not know."

"It is newly founded."

"No new guild has been established in more than a—"

"This is the guild Talmit meant. You would be a desirable member. The skills you developed when you were a Watcher make you exceptionally useful."

"Redeemers," I said, probing the mystery. "*Redeemers*. What does this guild do?"

Avluela smiled jauntily. "It rescues troubled souls and saves unhappy worlds. But this is no time to talk of it. Finish your business in Jorslem, and everything will become clear." We rose. Her lips brushed mine. "This is the last time I'll see you as an old man. It will be strange, Tomis, when you're renewed!"

She left me then.

Toward evening I returned to my lodging. Olmayne was not in her room. A Servitor told me that she had been out all day. I waited until it was late; then I made my communion and slept, and at dawn I paused outside her door. It was sealed. I hurried to the house of renewal.

10.

The Renewer Talmit met me within the entrance and conducted me down a corridor of green tile to the first renewal tank. "The Pilgrim Olmayne," he informed me, "has been accepted for renewal and will come here later this day." This was the last reference to the affairs of another human being that I was to hear for some time. Talmit showed me into a small low room, close and humid, lit by dim blobs of slave-light and smelling faintly of crushed deathflower blossoms. My robe and my mask were taken from me, and the Renewer covered my head with a fine golden-green mesh of some flimsy metal, through which he sent a current; and when he removed the mesh, my hair was gone, my head was as glossy as the tiled walls. "It makes insertion of the electrodes simpler," Talmit explained. "You may enter the tank, now."

A gentle ramp led me down into the tank, which was a tub of no great size. I felt the warm soft slipperiness of mud beneath my feet, and Talmit nodded and told me it was irradiated regenerative mud, which would stimulate the increase of cell division that was to bring about my renewal, and I accepted it. I stretched out on the floor of the tank with only my head above the shimmering dark violet fluid that it contained. The mud cradled and caressed my tired body. Talmit loomed above me, holding what seemed to be a mass of entangled copper wires, but as he pressed the wires to my bare scalp they opened as of their own accord and their tips sought my skull and burrowed down through skin and bone into the hidden wrinkled grayness. I felt nothing more than tiny prickling sensations. "The electrodes," Talmit explained, "seek out the centers of aging within your brain; we transmit signals that will induce a reversal of the normal processes of decay, and your brain will lose its perception of the direction of the flow of time. Your body thus will become more receptive to the stimulation it receives from the environment of the renewal tank. Close your eyes." Over my face he placed a breathing mask. He gave me a gentle shove, and the back of my head slipped from the edge of the tank, so that I floated out into the middle. The warmth increased. I dimly heard bubbling sounds. I imagined black sulfurous bubbles coming up from the mud and through the fluid in which I floated; I imagined that the fluid had turned the color of mud. Adrift in a tideless sea I lay, distantly aware that a current was passing over the electrodes, that something was tickling my brain, that I was engulfed in mud and in what could well have been an amniotic fluid. From far away came the deep voice of the Renewer Talmit summoning me to youth, drawing me back across the decades, unreeling time for me. There was a taste of salt in my mouth. Again I was crossing Earth Ocean, beset by pirates, defending my Watching equipment against their jeers and thrusts. Again I stood beneath the hot Aguptan sun meeting Avluela for the first time. I lived once more on Palash. I returned to the place of my birth in the western isles of the Lost Continents, in what formerly had been Usa-amrik. I watched Roum fall a second time. Fragments of memories swam through my softening brain. There was no sequence, no rational unrolling of events. I was a child. I was a weary ancient. I was among the Rememberers. I visited the Somnambulists. I saw the Prince of Roum attempt to purchase eyes from an Artificer in Dijon. I bargained with the Procurator of Perris. I gripped the handles of my instruments and entered Watchfulness. I ate sweet things from a far-off world; I drew into my nostrils the perfume of springtime on Palash; I shivered in an old man's private winter; I swam in a surging sea, buoyant and happy; I sang; I wept; I resisted temptation; I yielded to temptations; I quarreled with Olmayne; I embraced Avluela; I experienced a flickering succession of nights and days as my biological clock moved in strange rhythms of reversal and acceleration. Illusions beset me. It rained fire from the sky; time rushed in several directions; I grew small and then enormous. I heard voices speaking in shades of scarlet and turquoise. Jagged music sparkled on the mountains. The sound of my drumming heartbeats was rough and fiery. I was trapped between strokes of my brain-piston, arms pressed to my sides so that I would occupy as little space as possible as it rammed itself home again and again and again. The stars throbbed, contracted, melted. Avluela said gently, "We earn a second youthtime through the indulgent, benevolent impulses of the Will and not through the performance of individual good works." Olmayne said, "How sleek I get!" Talmit said, "These oscillations of perception signify only the dissolution of the wish toward self-destruction that lies at the heart of the aging process." Gormon said, "These perceptions of oscillation signify only the self-destruction of the wish toward dissolution that lies at the aging process of the heart." The Procurator Manrule Seven said, "We have been sent to this world as the devices of your purgation. We are instruments of the Will." Earthclaim Nineteen said, "On the other hand, permit me to disagree. The intersection of Earth's destinies and ours is purely accidental." My eyelids turned to stone. The small creatures comprising my lungs began to flower. My skin sloughed off, revealing strands of muscle clinging to bone. Olmayne said, "My pores grow smaller. My flesh grows tight. My breasts grow small." Avluela said, "Afterwards you will fly with us, Tomis." The Prince of Roum covered his eyes with his hands. The towers of Roum swayed in the winds of the sun. I snatched a shawl from a passing Rememberer. Clowns wept in the streets of Perris. Talmit said, "Awaken, now, Tomis, come up from it, open your eyes."

"I am young again," I said.

"Your renewal has only begun," he said.

I could no longer move. Attendants seized me and swathed me in porous wrappings, and placed me on a rolling car, and took me to a second tank, much larger, in which dozens of people floated, each in a dreamy seclusion from the others. Their naked skulls were festooned with electrodes; their eyes were covered with pink tape; their hands were peacefully joined on their chests. Into this tank I went, and there were no illusions here, only a long slumber unbroken by dreams. This time I awakened to the sounds of a rushing tide, and found myself passing feet first through a constricted conduit into a sealed tank, where I breathed only fluid, and where I remained something more than a minute and something less than a century, while layers of sin were peeled from my soul. It was slow, taxing work. The Surgeons worked at a distance, their hands thrust into gloves that controlled the tiny flaying-knives, and they flensed me of evil with flick after flick after flick of the little blades, cutting out guilt and sorrow, jealousy and rage, greed, lust, and impatience.

When they were done with me they opened the lid of the tank and lifted me out. I was unable to stand unaided. They attached instruments to my limbs that kneaded and massaged my muscles, restoring the tone. I walked again. I looked down at my bare body, strong and taut-fleshed and vigorous. Talmit came to me and threw a handful of mirror-dust into the air so that I could see myself; and as the tiny particles cohered, I peered at my gleaming reflection.

"No," I said. "You have the face wrong. I didn't look like that. The nose was sharper—the lips weren't so full—the hair not such a deep black—"

"We have worked from the records of the guild of Watchers, Tomis. You are more exactly a replica of your early self than your own memory realizes."

"Can that be?"

"If you prefer, we can shape you to fit your self-conceptions and not reality. But it would be a frivolous thing to do, and it would take much time."

"No," I said. "It hardly matters."

He agreed. He informed me then that I would have to remain in the house of renewal a while longer, until I was fully adapted to my new self. I was given the neutral clothes of a guildless one to wear, for I was without affiliation now; my status as Pilgrim had ended with my renewal, and I might now opt for any guild that would admit me once I left the house. "How long did my renewal last?" I asked Talmit as I dressed. He replied, "You came here in summer. Now it is winter. We do not work swiftly."

"And how fares my companion Olmayne?"

"We failed with her."

"I don't understand."

"Would you like to see her?" Talmit asked.

"Yes," I said, thinking that he would bring me to Olmayne's room. Instead he conveyed me to Olmayne's tank. I stood on a ramp looking down into a sealed container; Talmit indicated a fiber telescope, and I peered into its staring eye and beheld Olmayne. Or rather, what I was asked to believe was Olmayne. A naked girl-child of about eleven, smooth-skinned and breastless, lay curled up in the tank, knees drawn close to the flat chest, thumb thrust in mouth. At first I did not understand. Then the child stirred, and I recognized the embryonic features of the regal Olmayne I had known: the wide mouth, the strong chin, the sharp, strong cheekbones. A dull shock of horror rippled through me, and I said to Talmit, "What is this?"

"When the soul is too badly stained, Tomis, we must dig deep to cleanse it. Your Olmayne was a difficult case. We should not have attempted her; but she was insistent, and there were some indications that we might succeed with her. Those indications were in error, as you can see."

"But what happened to her?"

"The renewal entered the irreversible stage before we could achieve a purging of her poisons," Talmit said.

"You went too far? You made her too young?"

"As you can see. Yes."

"What will you do? Why don't you get her out of there and let her grow up again?"

"You should listen more carefully, Tomis. I said the renewal is irreversible."

"Irreversible?"

"She is lost in childhood's dreams. Each day she grows years younger. The inner clock whirls uncontrollably. Her body shrinks; her brain grows smooth. She enters babyhood shortly. She will never awaken."

"And at the end—" I looked away. "What then? A sperm and an egg, separating in the tank?"

"The retrogression will not go that far. She will die in infancy. Many are lost this way."

"She spoke of the risks of renewal," I said.

"Yet she insisted on our taking her. Her soul was dark, Tomis. She lived only for herself. She came to Jorslem to be cleansed, and now she has been cleansed, and she is at peace with the Will. Did you love her?"

"Never. Not for an instant."

"Then what have you lost?"

"A segment of my past, perhaps." I put my eye to the telescope again and beheld Olmayne, innocent now, restored to virginity, sexless, cleansed. At peace with the Will. I searched her oddly altered yet familiar face for insight into her dreams. Had she known what was befalling her, as she tumbled helplessly into youthfulness? Had she cried out in anguish and frustration when she felt her life slipping away? Had there been a final flare of the old imperious Olmayne, before she sank into this unwanted purity? The child in the tank was smiling. The supple little body uncoiled, then drew more tightly into a huddled ball. Olmayne was at peace with the Will. Suddenly, as though Talmit had spread another mirror in the air, I looked into my own new self, and saw what had been done for me, and knew that I had been granted another life with the proviso that I make something more of it than I had of my first one, and I felt humbled, and pledged myself to serve the Will, and I was engulfed in joy that came in mighty waves, like the surging tides of Earth Ocean, and I said farewell to Olmayne, and asked Talmit to take me to another place.

11.

And Avluela came to me in my room in the house of renewal, and we both were frightened when we met. The jacket she wore left her bunched-up wings bare; they seemed hardly under her control at all, but fluttered nervously, starting to open a short way, their gossamer tips expanding in little quivering flickers. Her eyes were large and solemn; her face looked more lean and pointed than ever. We stared in silence at one another a long while; my skin grew warm, my vision hazy; I felt the churning of inner forces that had not pulled at me in decades, and I feared them even as I welcomed them.

"Tomis?" she said finally, and I nodded.

She touched my shoulders, my arms, my lips. And I put my fingers to her wrists, her flanks, and then, hesitantly, to the shallow bowls of her breasts. Like two who had lost their sight we learned each other by touch. We were strangers. That withered old Watcher she had known and perhaps loved was gone, banished for the next fifty years or more, and in his place stood someone mysteriously transformed, unknown, unmet. The old Watcher had been a sort of father to her; what was this guildless young Tomis supposed to be? And what was she to me, a daughter no longer? I did not know myself of myself. I was alien to my sleek, taut skin. I was perplexed and delighted by the juices that now flowed, by the throbbings and swellings that I had nearly forgotten.

"Your eyes are the same," she said. "I would always know you by your eyes."

"What have you done these many months, Avluela?"

"I have been flying every night. I flew to Agupt and deep into Afreek. Then I returned and flew to Stanbool. When it gets dark, I go aloft. Do you know, Tomis, I feel truly alive only when I'm up there?"

"You are of the Fliers. It is in the nature of your guild to feel that way."

"One day we'll fly side by side, Tomis."

I laughed at that. "The old Surgeries are closed, Avluela. They work wonders here, but they can't transform me into a Flier. One must be born with wings."

"One doesn't need wings to fly."

"I know. The invaders lift themselves without the help of wings. I saw you, one day soon after Roum fell—you and Gormon in the sky together—" I shook my head. "But I am no invader either."

"You will fly with me, Tomis. We'll go aloft, and not only by night, even though my wings are merely nightwings. In bright sunlight we'll soar together."

Her fantasy pleased me. I gathered her into my arms, and she was cool and fragile against me, and my own body pulsed with new heat. For a while we talked no more of flying, though I drew back from taking what she offered at that moment, and was content merely to caress her. One does not awaken in a single lunge.

Later we walked through the corridors, passing others who were newly renewed, and we went into the great central room whose ceiling admitted the winter sunlight, and studied each other by that changing pale light, and walked, and talked again. I leaned a bit on her arm, for I did not have all my strength yet, and so in a sense it was as it had been for us in the past, the girl helping the old dodderer along. When she saw me back to my room, I said, "Before I was renewed, you told me of a new guild of Redeemers. I—"

"There is time for that later," she said, displeased.

In my room we embraced, and abruptly I felt the full fire of the renewed leap up within me, so that I feared I might consume her cool, slim body. But it is a fire that does not consume—it only kindles its counterpart in others. In her ecstasy her wings unfolded until I was wrapped in their silken softness. And as I gave myself to the violence of joy, I knew I would not need again to lean on her arm.

We ceased to be strangers; we ceased to feel fear with one another. She came to me each day at my exercise time, and I walked with her, matching her stride for stride. And the fire burned even higher and more brightly for us.

Talmit was with me frequently too. He showed me the arts of using my renewed body, and helped me successfully grow youthful. I declined his invitation to view Olmayne once more. One day he told me that her retrogression had come to its end. I felt no sorrow over that, just a curious brief emptiness that soon passed.

"You will leave here soon," the Renewer said. "Are you ready?"

"I think so."

"Have you given much thought to your destination after this house?"

"I must seek a new guild, I know."

"Many guilds would have you, Tomis. But which do you want?"

"The guild in which I would be most useful to mankind," I said. "I owe the Will a life."

Talmit said, "Has the Flier girl spoken to you of the possibilities before you?"

"She mentioned a newly founded guild."

"Did she give it a name?"

"The guild of Redeemers."

"What do you know of it?"

"Very little," I said.

"Do you wish to know more?"

"If there is more to know."

"I am of the guild of Redeemers," Talmit said. "So is the Flier Avluela."

"You both are already guilded! How can you belong to more than one guild? Only the Dominators were permitted such freedom; and they—"

"Tomis, the guild of Redeemers accepts members from all other guilds. It is the supreme guild, as the guild of Dominators once was. In its ranks are Rememberers and Scribes, Indexers, Servitors, Fliers, Landholders, Somnambulists, Surgeons, Clowns, Merchants, Vendors. There are Changelings as well, and—"

"Changelings?" I gasped. "They are outside all guilds, by law! How can a guild embrace Changelings?"

"This is the guild of Redeemers. Even Changelings may win redemption, Tomis."

Chastened, I said, "Even Changelings, yes. But how strange it is to think of such a guild!"

"Would you despise a guild that embraces Changelings?"

"I find this guild difficult to comprehend."

"Understanding will come at the proper time."

"When is the proper time?"

"The day you leave this place," said Talmit.

That day arrived shortly. Avluela came to fetch me. I stepped forth uncertainly into Jorslem's springtime to complete the ritual of renewal. Talmit had instructed her on how to guide me. She took me through the city to the holy places, so that I could worship at each of the shrines.

I knelt at the wall of the Hebers and at the gilded dome of the Mislams; then I went down into the lower part of the city, through the marketplace, to the gray, dark, illfashioned building covering the place where the god of the Christers is said to have died; then I went to the spring of knowledge and the fountain of the Will, and from there to the guildhouse of the guild of Pilgrims to surrender my mask and robes and starstone, and thence to the wall of the Old City. At each of these places I offered myself to the Will with words I had waited long to speak. Pilgrims and ordinary citizens of Jorslem gathered at a respectful distance; they knew that I had been lately renewed and hoped that some emanation from my new youthful body would bring them good fortune. At last my obligations were fulfilled. I was a free man in full health, able now to choose the quality of the life I wished to lead.

Avluela said, "Will you come with me to the Redeemers now?"

"Where will we find them? In Jorslem?"

"In Jorslem, yes. A meeting will convene in an hour's time for the purpose of welcoming you into membership."

From her tunic she drew something small and gleaming, which I recognized in bewilderment as a starstone. "What are you doing with that?" I asked. "Only Pilgrims—"

"Put your hand over mine," she said, extending a fist in which the starstone was clenched.

I obeyed. Her small pinched face grew rigid with concentration for a moment. Then she relaxed. She put the starstone away.

"Avluela, what—?"

"A signal to the guild," she said gently. "A notice to them to gather now that you are on your way."

"How did you get that stone?"

"Come with me," she said. "Oh, Tomis, if only we could fly there! But it is not far. We meet almost in the shadow of the house of renewal. Come, Tomis. Come!"

12.

There was no light in the room. Avluela led me into the subterranean blackness, and told me that I had reached the guildhall of the Redeemers, and left me standing by myself. "Don't move," she cautioned.

I sensed the presence of others in the room about me. But I heard nothing and saw nothing.

Something was thrust toward me.

Avluela said, "Put out your hands. What do you feel?"

I touched a small square cabinet resting, perhaps, on a metal framework. Along its face were familiar dials and levers. My groping hands found handles rising from the cabinet's upper surface. At once it was as though all my renewal had been undone, and the conquest of Earth canceled as well: I was a Watcher again, for surely this was a Watcher's equipment!

I said, "It is not the same cabinet I once had. But it is not greatly different."

"Have you forgotten your skills, Tomis?"

"I think they remain with me even now."

"Use the machine, then," said Avluela. "Do your Watching once more, and tell me what you see."

Easily and happily I slipped into the old attitudes. I performed the preliminary rituals quickly, clearing my mind of doubts and frictions. It was surprisingly simple to bring myself into a spirit of Watchfulness; I had not attempted it since the night Earth fell, and yet it seemed to me that I was able to enter the state more rapidly than in the old days.

Now I grasped the handles. How strange they were! They did not terminate in the grips to which I was accustomed: rather, something cool and hard was mounted at the tip of each handle. A gem of some kind, perhaps. Possibly even a starstone, I realized. My hands closed over the twin coolnesses. I felt a moment of apprehension, even of raw fear. Then I regained the necessary tranquillity, and my soul flooded into the device before me, and I began to Watch.

In my Watchfulness I did not soar to the stars, as I had in the old days. Although I perceived, my perception was limited to the immediate surroundings of my room. Eyes closed, body hunched in trance, I reached out and came first to Avluela; she was near me, almost upon me. I saw her plainly. She smiled; she nodded; her eyes were aglow.

—I love you.

—Yes, Tomis. And we will be together always.

—I have never felt so close to another person.

—In this guild we are all close, all the time. We are the Redeemers, Tomis. We are new. Nothing like this has been on Earth before.

—How am I speaking to you, Avluela?

—Your mind speaks to mine through the machine. And some day the machine will not be needed.

—And then we will fly together?

—Long before then, Tomis.

The starstones grew warm in my hands. I clearly perceived the instrument, now: a Watcher's cabinet, but with certain modifications, among them the starstones mounted on the handles. And I looked beyond Avluela and saw other faces, ones that I knew. The austere figure of the Renewer Talmit was to my left. Beside him stood the Surgeon with whom I had journeyed to Jorslem, with the Changeling Bernalt at his elbow, and now at last I knew what business it was that had brought these men of Nayrub to the holy city. The others I did not recognize; but there were two Fliers, and a Rememberer grasping his shawl, and a woman Servitor, and others. And I saw them all by an inner light, for the room was as dark as it had been when I entered it. Not only did I see them, but I touched them, mind to mind.

The mind I touched first was Bernalt's. I met it easily though fearfully, drew back, met it again. He greeted me and welcomed me. I realized then that only if I could look upon a Changeling as my brother could I, and Earth itself, win the sought-for redemption. For until we were truly one people, how could we earn an end to our punishment?

I tried to enter Bernalt's mind. But I was afraid. How could I hide those prejudices, those petty contempts, those conditioned reflexes with which we unavoidably think of Changelings?

"Hide nothing," he counseled. "Those things are no secret to me. Give them up now and join me."

I struggled. I cast out demons. I summoned up the memory of the moment outside the Changeling shrine, after Bernalt had saved us, when I had invited him to journey with us. How had I felt then toward him? Had I regarded him, at least for a moment, as a brother?

I amplified that moment of gratitude and companionship. I let it swell, and blaze, and it obliterated the encrustations of scorn and empty disdain; and I saw the human soul beneath the strange Changeling surface, and I broke through that surface and found the path to redemption. He drew me toward his mind.

I joined Bernalt, and he enrolled me in his guild. I was of the Redeemers now.

Through my mind rolled a voice, and I did not know whether I heard the resonant boom of Talmit, or the dry ironic tone of the Surgeon, or Bernalt's controlled murmur, or Avluela's soft whisper, for it was all these voices at once, and others, and they said:

"When all mankind is enrolled in our guild, we will be conquered no longer. When each of us is part of every other one of us, our sufferings will end. There is no need for us to struggle against our conquerors, for we will absorb them, once we are all Redeemed. Enter us, Tomis who was the Watcher Wuellig."

And I entered.

And I became the Surgeon and the Flier and the Renewer and the Changeling and the Servitor and the rest. And they became me. And so long as my hands gripped the starstones we were of one soul and one mind. This was not the merging of communion, in which a Pilgrim sinks anonymously into the Will, but rather a union of self and self, maintaining independence within a larger dependence. It was the keen perception one gets from Watching coupled with the submergence in a larger entity that one gets from communion, and I knew this was something wholly new on Earth, not merely the founding of a new guild but the initiation of a new cycle of human existence, the birth of the Fourth Cycle upon this defeated planet.

The voice said, "Tomis, we will Redeem those in greatest need first. We will go into Agupt, into the desert where miserable Changelings huddle in an ancient building that they worship, and we will take them into us and make them clean again. We will go on, to the west, to a pitiful village smitten by the crystallization disease, and we will reach the souls of the villagers and free them from taint, and the crystallization will cease and their bodies will be healed. And we will go on beyond Agupt, to all the lands of the world, and find those who are without guilds, and those who are without hope, and those who are without tomorrows, and we will give them life and purpose again. And a time will come when all Earth is Redeemed."

They put a vision before me of a transformed planet, and of the harsh-faced invaders yielding peacefully to us and begging to be incorporated into that new thing that had germinated in the midst of their conquest. They showed me an Earth that had been purged of its ancient sins.

Then I felt it was time to withdraw my hands from the machine I grasped, and I withdrew my hands.

The vision ebbed. The glow faded. But yet I was no longer alone in my skull, for some contact lingered, and the room ceased to be dark.

"How did this happen?" I asked. "When did this begin?"

"In the days after the conquest," said Talmit, "we asked ourselves why we had fallen so easily, and how we could lift ourselves above what we had been. We saw that our guilds had not provided enough of a structure for our lives, that some closer union was our way to redemption. We had the starstones; we had the instruments of Watching; all that remained was to fuse them."

The Surgeon said, "You will be important to us, Tomis, because you understand how to throw your mind forth. We seek former Watchers. They are the nucleus of our guild. Once your soul roved the stars to search out mankind's enemies; now it will roam the Earth to bring mankind together."

Avluela said, "You will help me to fly, Tomis, even by day. And you will fly beside me."

"When do you leave?" I asked.

"Now," she said. "I go to Agupt, to the temple of the Changelings, to offer them what we have to offer. And all of us will join to give me strength, and that strength will be focused through you, Tomis." Her hands touched mine. Her lips brushed mine. "The life of Earth begins again, now, this year, this new cycle. Oh, Tomis, we are all reborn!"

13.

I remained alone in the room. The others scattered. Avluela went above, into the street. I put my hands to the mounted starstones, and I saw her as clearly as though she stood beside me. She was preparing herself for flight. First she put off her clothing, and her bare body glistened in the afternoon sun. Her little frame seemed impossibly delicate; a strong wind would shatter her, I thought. Then she knelt, bowed, made her ritual. She spoke to herself, yet I heard her words, the words Fliers say as they ready themselves to leave the ground. All guilds are one in this new guild; we have no secrets from one another; there are no mysteries. And as she beseeched the favor of the Will and the support of all her kind, my prayers joined with hers.

She rose and let her wings unfold. Some passers-by looked oddly at her, not because there was anything unusual about the sight of a naked Flier in the streets of Jorslem, but because the sunlight was so strong and her transparent wings, so lightly stained with pigment, were evidently nightwings incapable of withstanding the pressure of the solar wind.

"I love you," we said to her, and our hands ran lightly over her satiny skin in a brief caress.

Her nostrils flickered in delight. Her small girlchild's breasts became agitated. Her wings now were fully spread, and they gleamed wondrously in the sunlight.

"Now we fly to Agupt," she murmured, "to Redeem the Changelings and make them one with us. Tomis, will you come with me?"

"I will be with you," we said, and I gripped the starstones tightly and crouched over my cabinet of instruments in the dark room beneath the place where she stood. "We will fly together, Avluela."

"Up, then," she said, and we said, "Up."

Her wings beat, curving to take the wind, and we felt her struggling in the first moment, and we gave her the strength she needed, and she took it as it poured from us through me to her, and we rose high. The spires and parapets of Jorslem the golden grew small, and the city became a pink dot in the green hills, and Avluela's throbbing wings thrust her swiftly westward, toward the setting sun, toward the land of Agupt. Her ecstasy swept through us all. "See, Tomis, how wonderful it is, far above everything? Do you feel it?"

"I feel it," I whispered. "The cool wind against bare flesh—the wind in my hair—we drift on the currents, we coast, we soar, Avluela, we soar!"

To Agupt. To the sunset.

We looked down at sparkling Lake Medit. In the distance somewhere was Land Bridge. To the north, Eyrop. To the south, Afreek. Far ahead, beyond Earth Ocean, lay my homeland. Later I would return there, flying westward with Avluela, bringing the good news of Earth's transformation.

From this height one could not tell that our world had ever been conquered. One saw only the beauty of the colors of the land and the sea, not the checkpoints of the invaders.

Those checkpoints would not long endure. We would conquer our conquerors, not with weapons but with love; and as the Redemption of Earth became universal we would welcome into our new self even the beings who had seized our planet.

"I knew that some day you would fly beside me, Tomis," said Avluela.

In my dark room I sent new surges of power through her wings.

She hovered over the desert. The old Surgery, the Changeling shrine, would soon be in sight. I grieved that we would have to come down. I wished we could stay aloft forever, Avluela and I.

"We will, Tomis, we will!" she told me. "Nothing can separate us now! You believe that, don't you, Tomis?"

"Yes," we said, "I believe that." And we guided her down through the darkening sky.

UP THE LINE

For Anne McCaffrey
a friend in deed

1.

Sam the guru was a black man, and his people up the line had been slaves—and before that, kings. I wondered about mine. Generations of sweaty peasants, dying weary? Or conspirators, rebels, great seducers, swordsmen, thieves, traitors, pimps, dukes, scholars, failed priests, translators from the Gheg and the Tosk, courtesans, dealers in used ivories, short-order cooks, butlers, stockbrokers, coin-trimmers? All those people I had never known and would never be, whose blood and lymph and genes I carry—I wanted to know them. I couldn't bear the thought of being separated from my own past. I hungered to drag my past about with me like a hump on my back, dipping into it when the dry seasons came.

"Ride the time-winds, then," said Sam the guru.

I listened to him. That was how I got into the time-traveling business.

Now I have been up the line. I have seen those who wait for me in the millennia gone by. My past hugs me as a hump.

Pulcheria!

Great-great-multi-great-grandmother!

If we had never met—

If I had stayed out of the shop of sweets and spices—

If dark eyes and olive skin and high breasts had meant nothing to me, Pulcheria—

My love. My lustful ancestress. You ache me in my dreams. You sing to me from up the line.

2.

He was really black. The family had been working at it for five or six generations now, since the Afro Revival period. The idea was to purge the gonads of the hated slave-master genes, which of course had become liberally entangled in Sam's lineage over the years. There was plenty of time for Massa to dip the wick between centuries seventeen and nineteen. Starting about 1960, though, Sam's people had begun to undo the work of the white devils by mating only with the ebony of hue and woolly of hair. Judging by the family portraits Sam showed me, the starting point was a café-au-lait great-great-grandmother. But she married an ace-of-spades exchange student from Zambia or one of those funny little temporary countries, and their eldest son picked himself a Nubian princess, whose daughter married an elegant ebony buck from Mississippi, who—

"Well, my grandfather looked decently brown as a result of all this," Sam said, "but you could see the strain of the mongrel all over him. We had darkened the family hue by three shades, but we couldn't pass for pure. Then my father was born and his genes reverted. In spite of everything. Light skin and a high-bridged nose and thin lips—a mingler, a monster. Genetics must play its little joke on an earnest family of displaced Africans. So Daddo went to a helix parlor and had the caucasoid genes edited, accomplishing in four hours what the ancestors hadn't managed to do in eighty years, and here I be. Black and beautiful."

Sam was about thirty-five years old. I was twenty-four. In the spring of '59 we shared a two-room suite in Under New Orleans. It was Sam's suite, really, but he invited me to split it with him when he found out

I had no place to stay. He was working then part time as an attendant in a sniffer palace.

I was fresh off the pod out of Newer York, where I was supposed to have been third assistant statutory law clerk to Judge Mattachine of the Manhattan County More Supreme Court, Upper. Political patronage got me the job, of course, not brains. Statutory law clerks aren't supposed to have brains; it gets the computers upset. After eight days with Judge Mattachine my patience eroded and I hopped the first pod southbound, taking with me all my earthly possessions, consisting of my toothflash and blackhead remover, my key to the master information output, my most recent thumb-account statement, two changes of clothing, and my lucky piece, a Byzantine gold coin, a nomisma of Alexius I. When I reached New Orleans I got out and wandered down through the underlevels until my feet took me into the sniffer palace on Under Bourbon Street, Level Three. I confess that what attracted me inside were the two jiggly girls who swam fully submerged in a tank of what looked like and turned out to be cognac. Their names were Helen and Betsy and for a while I got to know them quite well. They were the sniffer palace's lead-in vectors, what they used to call come-ons in the atomic days. Wearing gillmasks, they displayed their pretty nudities to the bypassers, promising but never quite delivering orgiastic frenzies. I watched them paddling in slow circles, each gripping the other's left breast, and now and then a smooth thigh slid between the thighs of Helen or Betsy as the case may have been, and they smiled beckoningly at me and finally I went in.

Sam came up to greet me. He was maybe three meters tall in his build-ups, and wore a jock and a lot of oil. Judge Mattachine would have loved him. Sam said, "Evening, white folks, want to buy a dream?"

"What do you have going?"

"Sado, maso, homo, lesbo, inter, outer, upper, downer and all the variants and deviants." He indicated the charge plate. "Take your pick and put your thumb right here."

"Can I try samples first?"

He looked closely. "What's a nice Jewish boy like you doing in a place like this?"

"Funny. I was just going to ask you the same thing."

"I'm hiding out from the Gestapo," Sam said. "In blackface. *Yisgadal v'yiskadash—*"

"*—adonai elohainu,*" I said. "I'm a Revised Episcopalian, really."

"I'm First Church of Christ Voudoun. Shall I sing a nigger hymn?"

"Spare me," I told him. "Can you introduce me to the girls in the tank?"

"We don't sell flesh here, white folks, only dreams."

"I don't buy flesh, I just borrow it a little while."

"The one with the bosom is Betsy. The one with the backside is Helen. Quite frequently they're virgins, and then the price is higher. Try a dream instead. Look at those lovely masks. You sure you don't want a sniff?"

"Sure I'm sure."

"Where'd you get that Newer York accent?"

I said, "In Vermont, on summer vacation. Where'd you get that shiny black skin?"

"My daddy bought it for me in a helix parlor. What's your name?"

"Jud Elliott. What's yours?"

"Sambo Sambo."

"Sounds repetitious. Mind if I call you Sam?"

"Many people do. You live in Under New Orleans now?"

"Just off the pod. Haven't found a place."

"I get off work at 0400. So do Helen and Betsy. Let's all go home with me," said Sam.

3.

I found out a lot later that he also worked part time in the Time Service. That was a real shocker, because I always thought of Time Servicemen as stuffy, upright, hopelessly virtuous types, square-jawed and clean-cut—overgrown Boy Scouts. And my black guru was and is anything but that. Of course, I had a lot to learn about the Time Service, as well as about Sam.

Since I had a few hours to kill in the sniffer palace he let me have a mask, free, and piped cheery hallucinations to me. When I came up and out, Sam and Helen and Betsy were dressed and ready to go. I had trouble recognizing the girls with their clothes on. Betsy for bosoms, was my mnemonic, but in their Missionary sheaths they were indistinguishable. We all went down three levels to Sam's place and plugged in As the good fumes rose and clothes dropped away, I found Betsy again and we did what you might have expected us to do, and I discovered that eight nightly hours of total immersion in a tank of cognac gave her skin a certain burnished glow and did not affect her sensory responses in any negative way.

Then we sat in a droopy circle and smoked weed and the guru drew me out.

"I am a graduate student in Byzantine history," I declared.

"Fine, fine. Been there?"

"To Istanbul? Five trips."

"Not Istanbul. Constantinople."

"Same place," I said.

"Is it?"

"Oh," I said. "*Constantinople*. Very expensive."

"Not always," said black Sam. He touched his thumb to the ignition of a new weed, leaned forward tenderly, put it between my lips. "Have you come to Under New Orleans to study Byzantine history?"

"I came to run away from my job."

"Tired of Byzantium so soon?"

"Tired of being third assistant statutory law clerk to Judge Mattachine of the Manhattan County More Supreme Court, Upper."

"You said you were—"

"I know. Byzantine is what I *study*. Law clerk is what I *do*. Did."

"Why?"

"My uncle is Justice Elliott of the U.S. Higher Supreme Court. He thought I ought to get into a decent line of work."

"You don't have to go to law school to be a law clerk?"

"Not any more," I explained. "The machines do all the data retrieval, anyway. The clerks are just courtiers. They congratulate the judge on his brilliance, procure for him, submit to him, and so forth. I stuck it for eight days and podded out."

"You have troubles," Sam said sagely.

"Yes. I've got a simultaneous attack of restlessness, Weltschmerz, tax liens, and unfocused ambition."

"Want to try for tertiary syphilis?" Helen asked.

"Not just now."

"If you had a chance to attain your heart's desire," said Sam, "would you take it?"

"I don't know what my heart's desire is."

"Is that what you mean when you say you're suffering from unfocused ambitions?"

"Part of it."

"If you knew what your heart's desire was, would you lift a finger to seize it?"

"I would," I said.

"I hope you mean that," Sam told me, "because if you don't, you'll have your bluff called. Just stick around here."

He said it very aggressively. He was going to force happiness on me whether I liked it or not.

We switched partners and I made it with Helen, who had a firm white tight backside and was a virtuoso of the interior muscles. Nevertheless she was not my heart's desire. Sam gave me a three-hour sleepo and took the girls home. In the morning, after a scrub, I inspected the suite and observed that it was decorated with artifacts of many times and places: a Sumerian clay tablet, a stirrup cup from Peru, a goblet of Roman glass, a string of Egyptian faience beads, a medieval mace and suit of chain mail, several copies of *The New-York Times* from 1852 and 1853, a shelf of books bound in blind-stamped calf, two Iroquois false-face masks, an immense array of Africana, and a good deal else, cluttering every available alcove, aperture, and orifice. In my fuddled way I assumed that Sam had antiquarian leanings and drew no deeper conclusions. A week later I noticed that everything in his collection seemed newly made. He is a forger of antiquities, I told myself. "I am a part-time employee of the Time Service," black Sam insisted.

4.

The Time Service," I said, "is populated by square-jawed Boy Scouts. Your jaw is round."

"And my nose is flat, yes. And I am no Boy Scout. However, I am a part-time employee of the Time Service."

"I don't believe it. The Time Service is staffed entirely by nice boys from Indiana and Texas. Nice white boys of all races, creeds, and colors."

"That's the Time Patrol," said Sam. "I'm a Time Courier."

"There's a difference?"

"There's a difference."

"Pardon my ignorance."

"Ignorance can't be pardoned. Only cured."

"Tell me about the Time Service."

"There are two divisions," Sam said. "The Time Patrol and the Time Couriers. The people who tell ethnic jokes end up in the Time Patrol. The people who invent ethnic jokes end up as Time Couriers. *Capisce?*"

"Not really."

"Man, if you're so dumb, why ain't you black?" Sam asked gently. "Time Patrolmen do the policing of paradoxes. Time Couriers take the tourists up the line. Couriers hate the Patrol, Patrol hates Couriers. I'm a Courier. I do the Mali-Ghana-Gao-Kush-Aksum-Kongo route in January and February, and in October and November I do Sumer, Pharaonic Egypt, and sometimes the Nazca-Mochica-Inca run. When they're short-handed I fill in on Crusades, Magna Carta, 1066, and Agincourt. Three times now I've done the Fourth Crusade taking Constantinople, and twice the Turks in 1453. Eat your heart out, white folks."

"You're making this up, Sam!"

"Sure I am, sure. You see all this stuff here? Smuggled right down the line by yours truly, out past the Time Patrol, not a thing they suspected except once. Time Patrol tried to arrest me in Istanbul, 1563, I cut his balls off and sold him to the Sultan for ten bezants. Threw his timer in the Bosphorus and left him to rot as a eunuch."

"You didn't!"

"No, I didn't," Sam said. "Would have, though."

My eyes glistened. I sensed my unknown heart's desire vibrating just beyond my grasp. "Smuggle me up the line to Byzantium, Sam!"

"Go smuggle yourself. Sign on as a Courier."

"Could I?"

"They're always hiring. Boy, where's your *sense?* A graduate student in history, you call yourself, and you've never even thought of a Time Service job?"

"I've thought of it," I said indignantly. "It's just that I never thought of it seriously. It seems—well, too *easy.* To strap on a timer and visit any era that ever was—that's cheating, Sam, do you know what I mean?"

"I know what you mean, but you don't know what you mean. I'll tell you your trouble, Jud. You're a compulsive loser."

I knew that. How did he know it so soon?

He said, "What you want most of all is to go up the line, like any other kid with two synapses and a healthy honker. So you turn your back on that, and instead of signing up you let them nail you with a fake job, which you run away from at the earliest possible opportunity. Where are you now? What's ahead. You're, what, twenty-two years old—"

"—twenty-four—"

"—and you've just unmade one career, and you haven't made move one on the other, and when I get tired of you I'll toss you out on your thumb, and what happens when the money runs dry?"

I didn't answer.

He went on, "I figure you'll run out of stash in six months, Jud. At that point you can sign up as stoker for a rich widow, pick a good one out of the Throbbing Crotch Registry—"

"Yigg."

"Or you can join the Hallucination Police and help to preserve objective reality—"

"Yech."

"Or you can return to the More Supreme Court and surrender your lily-white to Judge Mattachine—"

"Blugh."

"Or you can do what you should have done all along, which is to enroll as a Time Courier. Of course, you won't do that, because you're a loser, and losers infallibly choose the least desirable alternative. Right?"

"Wrong, Sam."

"Balls."

"Are you trying to make me angry?"

"No, love." He lit a weed for me. "I go on duty at the sniffer palace in half an hour. Would you mind oiling me?"

"Oil yourself, you anthropoid. I'm not laying a hand on your lovely black flesh."

"Ah! Aggressive heterosexuality rears its ugly head!"

He stripped to his jock and poured oil into his bath machine. The machine's arms moved in spidery circles and started to polish him to a high gloss.

"Sam," I said, "I want to join the Time Service."

5.

PLEASE ANSWER ALL QUESTIONS

Name: Judson Daniel Elliott III
Place of Birth: Newer York
Date of Birth: 11 October 2035
Sex (M or F): M
Citizen Registry Number: 070-28-3479-xx5-100089891
Academic Degrees—Bachelor: Columbia '55
               Master: Columbia '56
               Doctor: Harvard, Yale,
                        Princeton, incomplete
             Scholar Magistrate:
             Other:
Height: 1 meter (s) 88 centimeters
4 Weight: 78 kg.
Hair Color: black
Eye Color: black
Racial Index: 8.5 C+
Blood Group: BB 132
Marriages (List Temporary and Permanent Liaisons, in order of registration, and duration of each):
             none

Acknowledged Offspring: none

Reason for Entering Time Service (limit: 100 words):
To improve my knowledge of Byzantine culture, which is my special study area; to enlarge my acquaintance with human customs and behavior; to deepen my relationship to other individuals through constructive service; to offer the benefits of my education thus far to those in need of information; to satisfy certain romantic longings common to young men.

Names of Blood Relatives Currently Employed by Time Service:
none

6.

Very little of the foregoing really mattered. I was supposed to keep the application on my person, like a talisman, in case anybody in the Time Service bureaucracy really wanted to see it as I moved through the stages of enrolling; but all that was actually necessary was my Citizen Registry Number, which gave the Time Service folk full access to everything else I had put on the form except my Reason for Entering Time Service, and much more besides. At the push of a node the master data center would disgorge not only my height, weight, date of birth, hair color, eye color, racial index, blood group, and academic background, but also a full list of all illnesses I had suffered, vaccinations, my medical and psychological checkups, sperm count, mean body temperature by seasons, size of all bodily organs including penis both flaccid and erect, all my places of residence, my kin to the fifth degree and the fourth generation, current bank balance, pattern of financial behavior, tax status, voting performance, record of arrests if any, preference in pets, shoe size, et cetera. Privacy is out of fashion, they tell me.

Sam waited in the waiting room, molesting the hired help, while I was filling out my application. When I had finished my paperwork he rose and conducted me down a spiraling ramp into the depths of the Time Service building. Squat hammerheaded robots laden with equipment and documents rolled beside us on the ramp. A door in the wall opened and a secretary emerged; as she crossed our path Sam gave her a lusty tweaking of the nipples and she ran away shrieking. He goosed one of the robots, too. They call it appetite for life. "Abandon all hope, ye who enter here," Sam said. "I play the part well, don't I?"

"What part? Satan?"

"Virgil," he said. "Your friendly spade guide to the nether regions. Turn left here."

We stepped onto a dropshaft and went down a long way.

We appeared in a large steamy room at least fifty meters high and crossed a swaying rope bridge far above the floor. "How," I asked, "is a new man who doesn't have a guide supposed to find his way around in this building?"

"With difficulty," said Sam.

The bridge led us into a glossy corridor lined with gaudy doors. One door had SAMUEL HERSHKOWITZ lettered on it in cutesy psychedelic lettering, real antiquarian stuff. Sam jammed his face into the scanner slot and the door instantly opened. We peered into a long narrow room, furnished in archaic fashion with blowup plastic couches, a spindly desk, even a typewriter, for God's sake. Samuel Hershkowitz was a long, long, lean individual with a deeply tanned face, curling mustachios, sideburns, and a yard of chin. At the sight of Sam he came capering across the desk and they embraced furiously.

"Soul brother!" cried Samuel Hershkowitz.

"*Landsmann!*" yelled Sam the guru.

They kissed cheekwise. They hugged. They pounded shoulders. Then they split and Hershkowitz looked at me and said, "Who?"

"New recruit. Jud Elliott. Naive, but he'll do for the Byzantium run. Knows his stuff."

"You have an application, Elliott?" Hershkowitz asked.

I produced it. He scanned it briefly and said, "Never married, eh? You a pervo-deviant?"

"No, sir."

"Just an ordinary queer?"

"No, sir."

"Scared of girls?"

"Hardly, sir. I'm just not interested in taking on the permanent responsibilities of marriage."

"But you *are* hetero?"

"Mainly, sir," I said, wondering if I had said the wrong thing.

Samuel Hershkowitz tugged at his sideburns. "Our Byzantium Couriers have to be above reproach, you understand. The prevailing climate up that particular line is, well, steamy. You can futz around all you want in the year 2059, but when you're a Courier you need to maintain a sense of perspective. Amen. Sam, you vouch for this kid?"

"I do."

"That's good enough for me. But let's just run a check, to be sure he isn't wanted for a capital crime. We had a sweet, clean-cut kid apply last week, asking to do the Golgotha run, which of course requires real tact and saintliness, and when I looked into him I found he was wanted for causing protoplasmic decay in Indiana. And several other offenses. So, thus. We check." He activated his data outlet, fed in my identification number, and got my dossier on his screen. It must have matched what I had put on my application, because after a quick inspection he blanked it, nodded, keyed in some notations of his own, and opened his desk. He took from it a smooth flat tawny thing that looked like a truss and tossed it to me. "Drop your pants and put this on," he said. "Show him how, Sam."

I pressed the snap and my trousers fell. Sam wrapped the truss around my hips and clasped it in place; it closed seamlessly upon itself as though it had always been one piece. "This," said Sam, "is your timer. It's cued in to the master shunt system, synchronized to pick up the waves of transport impulses as they come forth. As long as you don't let it run out of phlogiston, this little device is capable of moving you to any point in time within the last seven thousand years."

"No earlier?"

"Not with this model. They aren't allowing unrestricted travel to the prehistoric yet, anyway. We've got to open this thing up era by era, with care. Attend to me, now. The operating controls are simplicity itself. Right here, just over your left-hand Fallopian tubes, is a microswitch that controls backward and forward motion. In order to travel, you merely describe a semicircle with your thumb against this pressure point: from hip toward navel to go back in time, from navel toward hip to go forward. On this side is your fine tuning, which takes some training to use. You see the laminated dial—year, month, day, hour, minute? Yes, you've got to squint a little to read it; that can't be helped. The years are calibrated in B.P.—Before Present—and the months are numbered, and so on. The trick lies in being able to make an instant calculation of your destination—843 years B.P., five months, eleven days, and so on—and setting the dials. It's mostly arithmetic, but you'd be surprised how many people can't translate February 11, 1192 into a quantity of years, months, and days ago. Naturally you'll have to master the knack if you're going to be a Courier, but don't worry about that now."

He paused and looked up at Hershkowitz, who said to me, "Sam is now going to give you your preliminary disorientation tests. If you pass, you're in."

Sam strapped on a timer also.

"Ever shunted before?" he asked.

"Never."

"We gonna have some fun, baby." He leered. "I'll set your dial for you. You wait till I give the signal, then use the left-hand switch to turn the timer on. Don't forget to pull your pants back up."

"Before or after I shunt?"

"Before," he said. "You can work the switch through your clothes. It's never a good idea to arrive in the past with your pants around your knees. You can't run fast enough that way. And sometimes you've got to be ready to run the second you get there."

7.

am set my dial. I pulled up my pants. He touched his hand lightly
to the left-hand side of his abdomen and vanished. I described an
arc from my hip to my navel on my own belly with two fingertips.
I didn't vanish. Samuel Hershkowitz did.

He went wherever candle flames go when they're snuffed, and in
the same instant Sam popped back into view beside me, and the two of
us stood looking at each other in Hershkowitz' empty office. "What
happened?" I said. "Where is he?"

"It's half-past eleven at night," said Sam. "He doesn't work overtime, you know. We left him two weeks down the line when we made
our shunt. We're riding the time-winds now, boy."

"We've gone back two weeks into the past?"

"We've gone two weeks up the line," Sam corrected. "Also half a
day, which is why it's nighttime now. Let's go take a walk around the
city."

We left the Time Service building and rose to the third level of
Under New Orleans. Sam didn't seem to have any special destination
in mind. We stopped at a bar for a dozen oysters apiece; we downed a
couple of beers; we winked at tourists. Then we reached Under Bourbon
Street and I realized suddenly why Sam had chosen to go back to this
night, and I felt the tingle of fear in my scrotum and started suddenly
to sweat. Sam laughed. "It always gets the new ones right around this
point, Jud-baby. This is where most of the washouts wash out."

"I'm going to meet myself!" I cried.

"You're going to *see* yourself," he corrected. "You better take good
care not to *meet* yourself, not ever, or it'll be all up for you. The Time
Patrol will use you up if you pull any such trick."

"Suppose my earlier self happens to see me, though?"

"Then you've had it. This is a test of your nervous system, man, and you better have the juice turned on. Here we go. You recognize that dumb-looking honky coming up the street?"

"That's Judson Daniel Elliott III."

"Yeah, man! Ever see anything so stupid in your life? Back in the shadows, man. Back in the shadows. White folks there, he ain't smart, but he ain't *blind*."

We huddled in a pool of darkness and I watched, sick-bellied, as Judson Daniel Elliott III, fresh off the pod out of Newer York, came wandering up the street toward the sniffer palace on the corner, suitcase in hand. I observed the slight slackness of his posture and the hayseed out-turning of his toes as he walked. His ears seemed amazingly large and his right shoulder was a trifle lower than his left. He looked gawky; he looked like a rube. He went past us and paused before the sniffer palace, staring intently at the two nude girls in the tank of cognac. His tongue slid forth and caressed his upper lip. He rocked on the balls of his toes. He rubbed his chin. He was wondering what his chances were of spreading the legs of one or the other of those bare beauties before the night was over. I could have told him that his chances were pretty good.

He entered the sniffer palace.

"How do you feel?" Sam asked me.

"Shaky."

"At least you're honest. It always hits them hard, the first time they go up the line and see themselves. You get used to it, after a while. How does he look to you?"

"Like a clod."

"That's standard too. Be gentle with him. He can't help not knowing all the things you know. He's younger than you are, after all."

Sam laughed softly. I didn't. I was still dazed by the impact of seeing myself come up that street. I felt like my own ghost. Preliminary disorientations, Hershkowitz had said. Yes.

"Don't worry," said Sam. "You're doing fine."

His hand slipped familiarly into the front of my pants and I felt him make a small adjustment on my timer. He did the same to himself. He said, "Let's shunt up the line."

He vanished. I followed him up the line. A blurry half instant later we stood side by side again, on the same street, at the same time of night.

"When are we?" I asked.

"Twenty-four hours previous to your arrival, in New Orleans.

There's one of you here and one of you in Newer York, getting ready to take the pod south. How does that catch you?"

"Crosswise," I said. "But I'm adapting."

"There's more to come. Let's go home now."

He took me to his flat. There was nobody there, because the Sam of this time slot was at work at the sniffer palace. We went into the bathroom and Sam adjusted my timer again, setting it 31 hours forward. "Shunt," he said, and we went down the line together and came out still in Sam's bathroom, on the next night. I heard the sound of drunken laughter coming from the next room; I heard hoarse gulping cries of lust. Swiftly Sam shut the bathroom door and palmed the seal. I realized that I was in the next room sexing with Betsy or Helen, and I felt fear return.

"Wait here," Sam said crisply, "and don't let anybody in unless he knocks two longs and a short. I'll be right back, maybe."

He went out. I locked the bathroom door after him. Two or three minutes passed. There came two long knocks and a short, and I opened up. Grinning, Sam said, "It's safe to peek. Nobody's in any shape to notice us. Come on."

"Do I have to?"

"If you want to get into the Time Service you do."

We slipped out of the bathroom and went to sightsee the orgy. I had to fight to keep from coughing as the fumes hit my unready nostrils. In Sam's living room I confronted acres of bare writhing flesh. To my left I saw Sam's huge black body pounding against Helen's sleek whiteness; all that was visible of her beneath him was her face, her arms (clasped across his broad back) and one leg (hooked around his butt). To my right I saw my own prior self down on the floor entwined with busty Betsy. We lay in a kamasutroid posture, she on her right hip, I on my left, her upper leg arched over me, my body curved and pivoted at an oblique angle to hers. In a kind of cold terror I watched myself having her. Although I've seen plenty of copulation scenes before, in the tridim shows, on the beaches, occasionally at parties, this was the first time I had ever witnessed myself in the act, and I was shattered by the grotesqueness of it, the idiot gaspings, the contorted features, the sweaty humpings. Betsy made bleating sounds of passion; our thrashing limbs rearranged themselves several times; my clutching fingers dug deep into her meaty buttocks; the mechanical thrustings went on and on and on. And my terror ebbed as I grew accustomed to the sight, and I found a cold clinical detachment stealing over me, and my fear-born perspiration dried and at last I stood there with my arms folded, coolly studying the activities on the floor. Sam smiled and nodded as if to tell me that I had passed a test. He reset my timer once more and we shunted together.

The living room was empty of fornicators and free of fumes. "When are we now?" I asked.

He said, "We're back thirty-one hours and thirty minutes. In a little while now, you and I are going to come walking into the bathroom, but we won't stay around to wait for that. Let's go up on top of the town."

We journeyed uplevel to Old New Orleans, under the starry sky.

The robot who monitors the comings and goings of the eccentrics who like to go outdoors made note of us, and we passed through, into the quiet streets. Here was the real Bourbon Street; here were the crumbling buildings of the authentic French quarter. Spy-eyes mounted on the lacy grillwork balconies watched us, for in this deserted area the innocent are at the mercy of the depraved, and tourists are protected, through constant surveillance, against the marauders who prowl the surface city. We didn't stay long enough to get into trouble, though. Sam looked around, considering things a bit, and positioned us against a building wall. As he adjusted my timer for another shunt, I said, "What happens if we materialize in space that's already occupied by somebody or something?"

"Can't," Sam said. "The automatic buffers cut in and we get kicked back instantly to our starting point. But it wastes energy, and the Time Service doesn't like that, so we always try to find a nonconflicting area before we jump. Up against a building wall is usually pretty good, provided you can be fairly sure that the wall was in the same position at the time you're shunting to."

"When are we going to now?"

"Shunt and see," he said, and jumped. I followed.

The city came to life. People in twentieth-century clothes strolled the streets: men wearing neckties, women with skirts that came down to their knees, no real flesh showing, not even a nipple. Automobiles crashing along emitting fumes that made me want to vomit. Horns honking. Drills digging up the ground. Noise, stench, ugliness. "Welcome to 1961," Sam said. "John F. Kennedy has just been sworn in as President. The very first Kennedy, dig? That thing up there is a jet airplane. That's a traffic light. It tells when it's safe for you to cross the street. Those up here are street lights. They work by electricity. There are no underlevels. This is the whole thing, the city of New Orleans, right here. How do you like it?"

"It's an interesting place to visit. I wouldn't want to live here."

"You feel dizzy? Sick? Revolted?"

"I'm not sure."

"You're allowed. You always feel a little temporal shock on your first look at the past. It somehow seems smellier and more chaotic than you expect. Some applicants cave in the moment they get into a decently distant shunt up the line."

"I'm not caving."

"Good boy."

I studied the scene, the women with their breasts and rumps encased in tight exoskeletons under their clothing, the men with their strangled, florid faces, the squalling children. Be objective, I told myself. You are a student of other times, other cultures.

Someone pointed at us and screamed, "Hey, looka the beatniks!"

"Onward," Sam said. "They've noticed us."

He adjusted my timer. We jumped.

Same city. A century earlier. Same buildings, genteel and timeless in their pastels. No traffic lights, no drills, no street lights. Instead of automobiles zooming along the streets that bordered the old quarter, there were buggies.

"We can't stay," said Sam. "It's 1858. Our clothes are too weird, and I don't feel like pretending I'm a slave. Onward."

We shunted

The city vanished. We stood in a kind of swamp. Mists rose in the south. Spanish moss clung to graceful trees. A flight of birds darkened the sky.

"The year is 1382," said the guru. "Those are passenger pigeons overhead. Columbus' grandfather is still a virgin."

Back and back we hopped. 897. 441. 97. Very little changed. A couple of naked Indians wandered by at one point. Sam bowed in a courteous way. They nodded affably to us, scratched their genitals, and sauntered on. Visitors from the future did not excite them greatly. We shunted. "This is the year A.D. 1," said Sam. We shunted. "We have gone back an additional twelve months and are now in 1 B.C. The possibilities for arithmetical confusion are great. But if you think of the year as 2059 B.P., and the coming year as 2058 B.P., you won't get into any trouble."

He took me back to 5800 B.P. I observed minor changes in climate; things were drier at some points than at others, drier and cooler. Then we came forward, hopping in easy stages, five hundred years at a time. He apologized for the unvarying nature of the environment; things are more exciting, he promised me, when you go up the line in the Old World. We reached 2058 and made our way to the Time Service building. Entering Hershkowitz' empty office, we halted for a moment while Sam made a final adjustment on our timers.

"This has to be done carefully," he explained. "I want us to land in Hershkowitz' office thirty seconds after we left it. If I'm off even a little, we'll meet our departing selves and I'll be in real trouble."

"Why not play it safe and set the dial to bring us back five minutes later, then?"

"Professional pride," Sam said.

We shunted down the line from an empty Hershkowitz office to one in which Hershkowitz sat behind his desk, peering forward at the place where we had been—for him—thirty seconds earlier.

"Well?" he said.

Sam beamed. "The kid has balls. I say hire him."

8.

And so they took me on as a novice Time Serviceman, in the Time Courier division. The pay wasn't bad; the opportunities were limitless. First, though, I had to undergo my training. They don't let novices schlep tourists around the past just like that.

For a week nothing much happened. Sam went back to work at the sniffer palace and I lounged around. Then I was called down to the Time Service headquarters to begin taking instruction.

There were eight in my class, all of us novices. We made a pretty disreputable crew. In age we ranged from early twenties to—I think— late seventies; in sex we ranged from male to female with every possible gradation between; in mental outlook we were all something on the rapacious side. Our instructor, Najeeb Dajani, wasn't much better. He was a Syrian whose family had converted to Judaism after the Israeli conquest, for business reasons, and he wore a glittering, conspicuous Star of David as an insignia of his faith; but in moments of abstraction or stress he was known to evoke Allah or swear by the Prophet's beard, and I don't know if I'd really trust him on the board of directors of my synagogue, if I had a synagogue. Dajani looked like a stage Arab, swarthy and sinister, with dark sunglasses at all times, an array of massive gold rings on twelve or thirteen of his fingers, and a quick, amiable smile that showed several rows of very white teeth. I later found out that he had been taken off the lucrative Crucifixion run and demoted to this instructorship for a period of six months, by orders of the Time Patrol, by way of punishment. It seems he had been conducting a side business in fragments of the True Cross, peddling them all up and down the time lines. The rules don't allow a Courier to take advantage of his position for private profit. What the Patrol especially objected to was not that Dajani was selling fake relics, but that he was selling authentic ones.

We began with a history lesson.

"Commercial time-travel," Dajani said, "has been functioning about twenty years now. Of course, research into the Benchley Effect began toward the end of the last century, but you understand that the government could not permit private citizens to venture into temponautics until it was ruled to be perfectly safe. In this way the government benevolently oversees the welfare of all."

Dajani emitted a broad wink, visible through the dark glasses as a corrugation of his brow.

Miss Dalessandro in the front row belched in contempt.

"You disagree?" Dajani asked.

Miss Dalessandro, who was a plump but curiously small-breasted woman with black hair, distinct Sapphic urges, and a degree in the history of the industrial revolution, began to reply, but Dajani smoothly cut her off and continued, "The Time Service, in one of whose divisions you have enrolled, performs several important functions. To us is entrusted the care and maintenance of all Benchley Effect devices. Also, our research division constantly endeavors to improve the technological substructure of time transport, and in fact the timer now in use was introduced only four years ago. To our own division—the Time Couriers—is assigned the task of escorting citizens into the past." He folded his hands complacently over his paunch and studied the interlocking patterns of his gold rings. "Much of our activity is concerned with the tourist trade. This provides our economic basis. For large fees, we take groups of eight or ten sightseers on carefully conducted trips to the past, usually accompanied by one Courier, although two may be sent in unusually complex situations. At any given moment in now-time, there may be a hundred thousand tourists scattered over the previous millennia, observing the Crucifixion, the signing of the Magna Carta, the assassination of Lincoln, and such events. Because of the paradoxes inherent in creating a cumulative audience for an event located at a fixed position in the time stream, we are faced with an increasingly difficult task, and limit our tours accordingly."

"Would you explain that, sir?" said Miss Dalessandro.

"At a later meeting," Dajani replied. He went on, "Naturally, we must not confine time travel exclusively to tourists. Historians must have access to all significant events of the past, since it is necessary to revise all existing views of history in the light of the revelation of the real story. We set aside out of the profits of our tourist business a certain number of scholarships for qualified historians, enabling them to visit periods of their research without cost. These tours, too, are conducted by Courier. However, you will not be concerned with this aspect of our work. We anticipate assigning all of you who qualify as Couriers to the tourist division.

"The other division of the Time Service is the Time Patrol, whose task it is to prevent abuses of Benchley Effect devices and to guard against the emergence of paradoxes. At our next lesson we will consider in detail the nature of these paradoxes and how they may be avoided. Dismissed."

We had a small social session after Dajani left the room. Miss Dalessandro, moving in a determined whirl of hairy armpits, closed in on blonde, delicate Miss Chambers, who promptly fled toward Mr. Chudnik, a brawny, towering gentleman with the vaguely noble look of a Roman bronze. Mr. Chudnik, however, was in the process of trying to reach an accommodation with Mr. Burlingame, a dapper young man who could not possibly have been as homosexual as he looked and acted. And so, seeking some other shelter from the predatory Miss Dalessandro, Miss Chambers turned to me and invited me to take her home. I accepted. It developed that Miss Chambers was a student of later Roman imperial history, which meant that her field of interest dovetailed with mine. We sexed in a perfunctory and mechanical way, since she was not really very interested in sex but was just doing it out of politeness, and then we talked about the conversion of Constantine to Christianity until the early hours of the morning. I think she fell in love with me. I gave her no encouragement, though, and it didn't last. I admired her scholarship but her pale little body was quite a bore.

9.

At our next lesson we considered in detail the nature of the time-travel paradoxes and how they may be avoided.

"Our greatest challenge," Dajani began, "lies in maintaining the sanctity of now-time. The development of Benchley Effect devices has opened a Pandora's Box of potential paradoxes. No longer is the past a fixed quantity, since we are free now to travel up the line to any given point and alter the so-called 'real' events. The results of such alteration would of course be catastrophic, creating a widening vector of disruption that, by the time it had reached our own era, might transform every aspect of society." Dajani yawned politely. "Consider, if you will, the consequences of permitting a time-traveler to journey to the year 600 and assassinate the youthful Mohammed. The whole dynamic movement of Islam will thus be arrested at its starting point; there will be no Arab conquest of the Near East and southern Europe; the Crusades will not have taken place; millions who died as a result of the Islamic invasions will now not have died, and numerous lines of progeny that would not otherwise have existed at all will come into being, with incalculable effects. All this stems simply from the slaying of a certain young merchant of Mecca. And therefore—"

"Perhaps," suggested Miss Dalessandro, "there's a Law of Conservation of History which would provide that if Mohammed didn't happen, some other charismatic Arab would arise and play precisely the same role?"

Dajani glowered at her.

"We do not care to risk it," he said. "We prefer to see to it that all 'past' events, as recorded in the annals of history as compiled prior to the era of time-travel, go untouched. For the past fifty years of now-time the entire previous span of history, thought to be fixed, has been potentially fluid; yet we struggle to keep it fixed. Thus we employ the Time Patrol to make certain that everything will happen in the past exactly as it *did* happen, no matter how unfortunate an event it might be. Disasters, assassinations, tragedies of all kinds must occur on schedule, for otherwise the future—our now-time—may be irreparably changed."

Miss Chambers said, "But isn't the very fact of our presence in the past a changing of the past?"

"I was about to reach that point," said Dajani, displeased. "If we assume that the past and present form a single continuum, then obviously visitors from the twenty-first century *were* present at all the great events of the past, unobtrusively enough so that no mention of them found its way into the annals of the fixed-time era. So we take great care to camouflage everyone who goes up the line in the costume of the time being visited. One must watch the past without meddling, as a silent bystander, as inconspicuous as possible. This is a rule that the Time Patrol enforces with absolute inflexibility. I will discuss the nature of that enforcement shortly.

"I spoke the other day of cumulative audience paradox. This is a severe philosophical problem which has not yet been resolved, and which I will present to you now purely as a theoretical exercise, to give you some insight into the complexities of our undertaking. Consider this: the first time-traveler to go up the line to view the Crucifixion of Jesus was the experimentalist Barney Navarre, in 2012. Over the succeeding two decades, another fifteen or twenty experimentalists made the same journey. Since the commencement of commercial excursions to Golgotha in 2041, approximately one tourist group a month—or 100 tourists a year—has viewed the scene. Thus about 1800 individuals of the twenty-first century, so far, have observed the Crucifixion. Now, then: each of these groups is leaving from a different month, but *every one of them is converging on the same day!* If tourists continue to go up the line at a rate of 100 a year to see the Crucifixion, the crowd at Golgotha will consist of at least 10,000 time-travelers by the middle of the twenty-second century, and—assuming no increase in the permissible tourist trade—by the early thirtieth century, some 100,000 time-travelers will have made the trip, all of them necessarily congregating simultaneously at the site of the Passion. Yet obviously no such crowds are present there now, only a few thousand Palestinians—when I say 'now,' I mean of course the time of the Crucifixion relative to now-time 2059—and just as obviously those crowds will continue to grow in the centuries of now-time. Taken to its ultimate, the cumulative audience paradox yields us the picture of an audience of billions of time-travelers piled up in the past to witness the Crucifixion, filling all the Holy Land and spreading out into Turkey, into Arabia, even to India and Iran. Similarly for every other significant event in human history: as commercial time-travel progresses, it must inevitably smother every event in a horde of spectators, yet at the original occurrence of those events, *no such hordes were present!* How is this paradox to be resolved?"

Miss Dalessandro had no suggestions. For once, she was stumped. So were the rest of us. So was Dajani. So are the finest minds of our era.

Meanwhile, the past fills up with time-traveling sightseers.

Dajani tossed one final twister at us before he let us go. "I may add," he said, "that I myself, as a Courier, have done the Crucifixion run twenty-two times, with twenty-two different groups. If you were to attend the Crucifixion yourselves tomorrow, you would find twenty-two Najeeb Dajanis at the hill of Golgotha simultaneously, each of me occupying a different position at the event explaining the happening to my clients. Is this multiplication of Dajanis not a fascinating thing to consider? Why are there not twenty-two Dajanis at loose in now-time? It stretches the intellect to revolve such thoughts. Dismissed, dear ladies and gentlemen, dismissed."

10.

I was troubled about those twenty-one extra Dajanis, but the smart alecks in the class quickly figured out why they hadn't all jammed up together here in now-time. It had to do with the fundamental limitations of the Benchley Effect in achieving down-the-line, or forward, travel.

My classmate Mr. Burlingame explained it all to me after class. It was his quaint way of trying to seduce me. He didn't score, but I learned a little time theory.

When you go down the line, he told me, you can come forward only as far as you had previously jumped up the line, *plus* the amount of absolute time elapsed during your stay up the line. That is, if you jump from March 20, 2059, say, to the spring of 1801, and spend three months in 1801, you can come forward again as far as June 20, 2059. But you can't jump down the line to August, 2059, nor can you jump to 2159 or 20590.

There is no way at all to get into your own future.

I don't know why this is so. Mr. Burlingame placed his pale palm on my knee and gave me the theoretical substructure for it, but I was too busy fending him off to follow it.

In fact, although Dajani later spent three sessions simply instructing us on the mechanics of the Benchley Effect, I still can't say for sure how the whole thing works, or why, or even if. At times I suspect I've dreamed it all.

Anyway, there aren't twenty-two Dajanis in now-time because whenever Dajani made the Crucifixion run, he always jumped back to now-time at a point somewhat prior to his next departure for the past. He couldn't help himself about that; if you go up the line in January,

spend a couple of weeks in an earlier era, and come back, you've got
to land in January or maybe February of the year you started from. And
if your next jump isn't scheduled until March, there's no way you can
overlap yourself.

So the Dajani who escorted tourists to Golgotha was always the
"same" one, from the point of view of people in now-time. At the other
end of the jump, though, a couple dozen Dajanis have been piling up,
since he keeps jumping from different points in now-time to the same
point in then-time. The same happens to anybody who makes repeated
jumps to one spot up the line. This is the Paradox of Temporal Accumulation. You can have it.

When not wrestling with such paradoxes I passed my time pleasantly in pleasure, as usual. There were always plenty of willing girls
hanging around Sam's place.

In those days I chased crotch quite a bit. Obsessively, even. The
pursuit of cunt occupied all my idle hours; it seemed a night wasted if
I hadn't slid down that slippery slope at least once. It never occurred
to me that it might be worthwhile for me to seek a relationship with a
member of the opposite sex that was more than six inches deep. What
they call "love."

Shallow, callow youth that I was, I wasn't interested in "love."

On the other hand, maybe I wasn't so shallow. For now I've tried
"love" and I don't see where I'm the happier for it. I'm a lot worse off
than before, as a matter of fact.

Of course, nobody told me to fall in love with someone who lived
up the line.

11.

Lieutenant Bruce Sanderson of the Time Patrol came to our class one day to explain to us the perils of daring to meddle with the fixity of past time.

The lieutenant looked his part. He was the tallest man I had ever seen, with the widest shoulders and the squarest jaw. Most of the girls in the class had instant orgasms when he entered, as did Mr. Chudnik and Mr. Burlingame. He took a spread-legged stance, back to the wall, ready for trouble. His uniform was gray. His hair was red and cut very short. His eyes were a soulless blue.

Dajani, himself guilty of transgressing, himself a victim of the Time Patrol's diligence, slithered into a corner of the classroom and yielded the floor. I saw him peering balefully at the lieutenant through his dark glasses.

"Now then," Lieutenant Sanderson said, "you know that our big job involves maintaining the sanctity of now-time. We can't let all kinds of random changes get introduced into our past, because that'll mess up our present. So we have a Time Patrol that monitors the whole territory up the line and makes sure that everything happens according to the books. And I want to say, God bless the men who legislated the Time Patrol into existence."

"Amen," said the penitent Dajani.

"Mind you, it isn't that I'm thankful for the job I have," the lieutenant continued. "Although I am because I think it's the most important job a human being can have, preserving the sanctity of his now-time. But when I say God bless the men who said we had to have a Time Patrol, it's because those men are responsible for saving everything that is true and good and precious about our existence. Do you know what might have happened without a Time Patrol? What sort of things unscrupulous villains might have done? Let me give you a few examples.

"Such as going back and killing Jesus, Mohammed, Buddha, all our great religious leaders, when they were still children and hadn't had time to formulate their wonderful and inspiring ideas.

"Such as warning the great villains of our history of trouble in store for them, and thus allowing them to cheat destiny and continue doing harm to humanity.

"Such as stealing the art treasures of the past and preventing millions of people over many centuries from enjoying them.

"Such as engaging in fraudulent financial operations resulting in the bankrupting of millions of innocent investors who happened not to have information on future stock prices.

"Such as giving false advice to great rulers and leading them into terrible traps.

"I mention all these examples, my friends, because they are things that have *actually happened*. They all come from the files of the Time Patrol, believe it or not! In April, 2052, a young man from Bucharest used an illegally obtained timer to shunt up the line to A.D. 11 and poison Jesus Christ. In October, 2043, a citizen of Berlin traveled back to the year 1945 and rescued Adolf Hitler just before the Russians entered the city. In August, 2049, a woman from Nice jumped to the era of Leonardo da Vinci, stole the unfinished *Mona Lisa*, and hid it in her beach cabaña. In September, 2055, a New York man journeyed to the summer of 1929 and netted close to a billion dollars by selling stock short. In January, 2051, a professor of military history from Quebec journeyed to 1815 and, by marketing to the British what purported to be the French strategic program, caused the defeat of the Duke of Wellington by the forces of Napoleon at the Battle of Waterloo. And therefore—"

"Wait a second!" I heard myself say. "Napoleon *didn't* win at Waterloo. Christ *wasn't* poisoned in A.D. 11. If the past was really changed as you just said, how come no effects of it have been felt in now-time?"

"*Aha!*" cried Lieutenant Sanderson. He was the best crier of *"Aha!"* I have ever heard. "The fluidity of the past, my friend, is a double-edged blade. If the past can be changed once, it can be changed many times. Now we come to the role of the Time Patrol.

"Let us consider the case of the deranged person who assassinated the young Jesus. As a result of this shocking deed, Christianity did not emerge, and much of the Roman Empire was ultimately converted to Judaism. The Jewish leaders of Rome were able to steer the empire away from its collapse of the fourth and fifth centuries A.D., turning it into a monolithic theocratic state that controlled all of western Europe. However, the Byzantine Empire did not develop in the East, which instead was ruled from Jerusalem by a schismatic Hebrew sect. In the tenth century a cataclysmic war between the forces of Rome and those of Jerusalem resulted in the annihilation of civilization and in the take-over of all of Europe and Asia by Turkish nomads, who proceeded to construct a totalitarian state that, by the twenty-first century, had become the most repressive in human history.

"You can see from this how devastating it can be to meddle with the past."

"Yes," I said, "but—"

Lieutenant Sanderson gave me a frigid smile. "You are about to observe that we do not, in fact, live under a repressive Turkish tyranny. I agree. Our present pattern of existence was saved by the following procedure:

"The murder of the young Jesus was detected by a Time Courier who went up the line late in April, 2052, escorting a party of tourists to witness the Crucifixion. When the group arrived at the time and place of the Crucifixion, they found two thieves undergoing execution; no one, however, had heard of Jesus of Nazareth. The Courier instantly notified the Time Patrol, which began a paradox search. Jesus' time line was followed from birth through boyhood and was seen to be unchanged; but no trace of him could be found after mid-adolescence, and inquiry in the neighborhood finally turned up the information that he had died suddenly and mysteriously in the year 11. It was a simple matter then to maintain surveillance until we observed the arrival of the illegal time-traveler.

"What do you think we did then?"

Hands went up. Lieutenant Sanderson recognized Mr. Chudnik, who said, "You arrested the criminal five minutes before he could give the poison to Jesus, thus preventing the changing of history, and took him back down the line for trial."

Lieutenant Sanderson smiled genially. "Wrong," he said. "We let him give the poison to Jesus."

Uproar.

The Time Patrol man said benignly, "As you surely know, the maximum penalty for unauthorized interference in past events is death—the only capital offense now recognized in law. But before so severe a penalty can be invoked, absolute proof of the crime is necessary. Therefore, whenever a crime of this kind is detected, Time Patrolmen allow it to proceed and surreptitiously make a full record of it."

"But how," Miss Dalessandro demanded, "does the past get unchanged that way?"

"Aha!" cried Lieutenant Sanderson. "Once we have a proper record of the commission of the crime, we can obtain a quick conviction and secure permission to carry out sentence. This was done. The Time Patrol investigators returned with their evidence to the night of April 4, 2052. This was the date of the departure up the line of the would-be murderer of Jesus. They presented their proof of the crime to the Time Patrol commissioners, who ordered the execution of the criminal. Time Patrol executioners were dispatched to the home of the criminal, seized his timer, and painlessly put him to death an hour before his intended trip into the past. Thus he was erased from the time-stream and the main current of the past was preserved, for in fact he did not make his trip and Jesus lived on to preach his creed. In this way—through detection of unlawful changes and eradication of the changers in advance of their departure up the line—we preserve the sanctity of now-time."

How beautiful, I thought.

I'm too easily satisfied. Miss Dalessandro, that arch-troublemaker, put up her fleshy hand, and when called on, said, "I'd like one clarification, though. Presumably when your Time Patrolmen returned to April, 2052, with the evidence of the crime, they were returning to a changed world run by Turkish dictators. Where would they find Time Patrol commissioners? Where would they even find the murderer? He might have ceased to exist as a consequence of his own crime, because by murdering Jesus he set in motion some train of events that eliminated his own ancestors. For that matter, maybe time-travel itself was never invented in that world where Jesus didn't live, and so the moment Jesus was killed all Time Patrolmen and Time Couriers and tourists would become impossibilities, and cease to exist."

Lieutenant Sanderson did not look pleased.

"You bring up," he said slowly, "a number of interesting subsidiary paradoxes. I'm afraid that the time at my disposal isn't sufficient to deal with them properly. Briefly, though: if the timecrime of 11 A.D. had not been detected relatively quickly, the focus of change would indeed have widened over the centuries and eventually transformed the entire future, possibly preventing the emergence of the Benchley Effect and the Time Patrol itself, leading to what we call the Ultimate Paradox, in which time-travel becomes its own negation. In fact, though, the vast potential consequences of the poisoning of Jesus never occurred because of the detection of the crime by the Time Courier visiting the Crucifixion. Since that event took place in A.D. 33, only the years 11 to 33 were ever affected by the timecrime, and the changes created by the absence

of Jesus from those years were insignificant, because Jesus' influence
on history emerged only long after the Crucifixion. Meanwhile the ret-
roactive deletion of the timecrime canceled even the slight changes that
had taken place in the 22-year period affected; those two decades were
pinched off into another track of time, inaccessible to us and in effect
nonexistent, and the basic and authentic track was restored in full continuity from A.D. 11 to the present."

Miss Dalessandro wasn't satisfied. "There's something circular here.
Shouldn't the Ultimate Paradox have occurred all the way down the
line, the instant Jesus was poisoned? How did any of the Couriers and
Patrolmen manage to continue to exist, let alone to remember how the
past *should* have gone? It seems to me that there ought not to be any
way of correcting a timecrime sweeping enough to bring on the Ultimate
Paradox."

"You forget, or perhaps you don't yet know," said Sanderson, "that
time-travelers currently up the line at the moment of a timecrime are
unaffected by *any* change in the past, since they're detached from their
time matrices. A time-traveler in transit is a drifting bubble of now-time
ripped loose from the matrix of the continuum, immune to the trans-
formations of paradox. This means that anyone currently up the line
may observe and correct an alteration of the true past, and will continue
to retain memories both of the temporary false condition and of his role
in correcting it. Of course, any time-traveler leaving the sanctuary of
the transit state is vulnerable once he comes back to his starting point
down the line. That is, if you go up the line and kill your grandfather
before his marriage, you won't instantaneously wink out of existence,
since you're shielded from paradox by the Benchley Effect. But the
moment you return to the present you will cease *ever to have existed*,
since as a result of your alteration of your own past you no longer have
a time-link to the present. Clear?"

No, I thought. But I kept quiet.

Miss Dalessandro pressed onward. "Those in transit are protected
by—"

"The Paradox of Transit Displacement, we call it."

"The Paradox of Transit Displacement. They're encapsulated, and
as they travel they're free to compare what they see with what they
remember true time to have been like, and if necessary they can make
changes to restore the true order if it's been changed."

"Yes."

"Why? Why *should* they be immune? I know I keep coming back
to this point, but—"

Lieutenant Sanderson sighed. "Because," he said, "if they were affected by a past-change while they were in the past themselves, this would be the Ultimate Paradox: a time-traveler changing the era that produced time-travel. This is even more paradoxical than the Paradox of Transit Displacement. By the Law of Lesser Paradoxes, the Paradox of Transit Displacement, being less improbable, holds precedence. Do you see?"

"No, but—"

"I'm afraid I can't dwell on this in greater detail," said the Patrolman. "However, no doubt Mr. Dajani will go into these matters at later instruction sessions."

He gave Dajani a sickly smile and excused himself fast.

Dajani, you can bet on it, didn't deal with Miss Dalessandro's paradoxes properly, or at all. He found cunning ways to sidetrack her every time she brought up the issue. "You can be sure," he said, "that the past *is* restored whenever it is changed. The hypothetical worlds created by unlawful change cease retroactively to exist the moment the changer is apprehended. Q.E.D."

That didn't explain a damned thing. But it was the best explanation we ever got.

12.

One thing they made clear to us was that *good* changes in the past are also forbidden. Dozens of people have been eliminated for trying to persuade Abe Lincoln to stay home from the theater that night, or for trying to tell Jack Kennedy that he should for God's sake put the bulletproof bubble on his car.

They get wiped out, just like the murderers of Jesus and the rescuers of Hitler. Because it's just as deadly to the fabric of now-time to help Kennedy serve out his term as it would be to help Hitler rebuild the Third Reich. Change is change, and even the virtuous changes can have unpredictably catastrophic results. "Just imagine," said Dajani, "that because Kennedy was not assassinated in 1963, the escalation of the Vietnamese War that in fact did take place under his successor did not occur, and so the lives of thousands of servicemen were spared. Suppose now that one of those men, who otherwise would have died in 1965 or 1966, remained alive, became President of the United States in 1992, and embarked on an atomic war that brought about the destruction of civilization. You see why even supposedly beneficial alterations of the past must be prevented?"

We saw. We saw it over and over again.

We saw it until we were scared toothless of going into the Time Service, because it seemed inevitable that we would sooner or later do something up the line that would bring down on us the fatal wrath of the Time Patrol.

"Don't worry about it," Sam said. "The way they talk, the death penalty is inflicted a million times a day. Actually I don't think there have been fifty executions for timecrime in the past ten years. And all

of those were real nuts, the kind whose mission it is to murder Mohammed."

"Then how does the Patrol keep the past from being changed?"

"They don't," said Sam. "It gets changed all the time. Despite the
Time Patrol."

"Why doesn't our world change?"

"It does. In little ways." Sam laughed. "If a Time Courier gives
Alexander the Great antibiotics and helps him live to a ripe old age,
that would be an intolerable change, and the Time Patrol would prevent
it. But a lot of other stuff goes on all the time. Couriers recovering lost
manuscripts, sleeping with Catherine the Great, collecting artifacts for
resale in other eras. Your man Dajani was peddling the True Cross,
wasn't he? They found out about him, but they didn't execute him. They
just suspended him from his profitable run for a while and stuck him in
a classroom. Most of the petty tinkering never even gets discovered."
He let his glance rove meaningfully over his collection of artifacts from
the past. "As you get into this business, Jud, you'll find out that we're
in constant intersection with past events. Every time a Time Courier
steps on an ant in 2000 B.C., he's changing the past. Somehow we
survive. The dumb bastards in the Time Patrol watch out for structural
changes in history, but they leave the little crap alone. They have to.
There aren't enough Patrolmen to handle everything."

"But that means," I said, "that we're building up a lot of tiny alterations in history, bit by bit, an ant here and a butterfly there, and the
accumulation may someday cause a major change, and nobody will then
be able to trace all the causes and put things back the way they ought
to be!"

"Exactly."

"You don't sound worried about it," I said.

"Why should I be? Do I own the world? Do I give a damn if history
gets changed?"

"You would if the change involved seeing to it that you had never
existed."

"There are bigger things to worry about, Jud. Like having a good
time from day to day."

"Doesn't it scare you that someday you might just pop out of existence?"

"Someday I will," Sam said. "No maybes about it. If not sooner,
then later. Meanwhile I enjoy myself. Eat, drink, and be merry, kid. Let
the yesterdays fall where they will."

13.

When they were finished hammering the rules into our heads, they sent us on trial runs up the line. All of us had already been into the past, of course, before beginning the instruction sessions; they had tested us to see if we had any psychological hangups about time-traveling. Now they wanted us to observe Couriers in actual service, and so they let us go along as hitchhikers with tour groups.

They split us up, so there wouldn't be more than two of us to each six or eight tourists. To save expense, they assigned us all to visit events right in New Orleans. (In order to shoot us back to the Battle of Hastings, say, they would have had to fly us to London first. Time-travel doesn't include space travel; you have to be physically present in the place you want to reach, before you jump.)

New Orleans is a fine city, but it hasn't had all that many important events in its history, and I'm not sure why anybody would want to pay *very* good money to go up the line there when for about the same fee he could witness the signing of the Declaration of Independence, the fall of Constantinople, or the assassination of Julius Caesar. But the Time Service is willing to provide transport to any major historical event whatever—within certain limits of taste, I mean—for any group of at least eight tourists who have the stash for tickets, and I suppose the patriotic residents of New Orleans have every right to sightsee their city's own past, if they prefer.

So Mr. Chudnik and Miss Dalessandro were shipped to 1815 to cheer for Andrew Jackson at the Battle of New Orleans. Mr. Burlingame and Mr. Oliveira were transported to 1877 to watch the last of the carpetbaggers thrown out. Mr. Hotchkiss and Mrs. Notabene went off to 1803 to see the United States take possession of Louisiana after

buying it from the French. And Miss Chambers and I went up the line
to 1935 to view the assassination of Huey Long.

Assassinations are usually over in a hurry, and nobody goes up the
line just to watch a quick burst of gunfire. What the Time Service was
really offering these people was a five-day tour of Louisiana in the early
twentieth century, with the gunning down of the Kingfish as its climax.
We had six fellow travelers: three well-to-do Louisiana couples in their
late fifties and early sixties. One of the men was a lawyer, one a doctor,
one a big executive of Louisiana Power & Light Company. Our
Time Courier was the right sort to shepherd these pillars of the estab-
lishment around: a sleek, bland character named Madison Jefferson
Monroe. "Call me Jeff," he invited.

We had several orientation meetings before we went anywhere.

"These are your timers," said Jeff Monroe. "You keep them next to
your skin at all times. Once you put them on in Time Service headquarters, you don't remove them again until you come back down the
line. You bathe with them, sleep with them, perform—ah—all intimate
functions while wearing them. The reason for this should be obvious.
It would be highly disruptive to history if a timer were to fall into the
hands of a twentieth-century person; therefore we don't allow the devices out of your physical possession even for an instant."

("He's lying," Sam told me when I repeated this to him. "Somebody
up the line wouldn't know what the hell to do with a timer. The real
reason is that sometimes the tourists have to get out of an area in a
hurry, maybe to avoid being lynched, and the Courier can't take the risk
that some of his people may have left their timers in the hotel room.
But he doesn't dare tell them that.")

The timers that Jeff Monroe distributed were a little different from
the one I had worn the night Sam and I went jumping up the line. The
controls were sealed, and functioned only when the Courier sounded a
master frequency. Sensible enough: the Time Service doesn't want tourists slipping away for time-jaunts on their own.

Our Courier spelled out at great length the consequences of changing the past, and begged us repetitiously not to rock any boats. "Don't
speak unless spoken to," he said, "and even then confine any conversations with strangers to a minimum of words. Don't use slang; it won't
be comprehensible. You may recognize other time-tourists; under no
condition are you to speak to them or greet them in any way, and you
should ignore any attention you may get from them. Anyone who breaks
these regulations, no matter how innocently, may have his shunting
permit revoked on the spot and may be returned at once to now-time.
Understood?"

We nodded solemnly.

Jeff Monroe added, "Think of yourselves as Christians in disguise who have been smuggled into the holy Moslem city of Mecca. You're in no danger so long as you're not discovered; but if those about you find out what you are, you're in big trouble. Therefore it's to your advantage to keep your mouths shut while you're up the line, to do a lot of seeing and a minimum of saying. You'll be all right as long as you don't call attention to yourselves."

(I learned from Sam that time-tourists very frequently get themselves into muddles with people living up the line, no matter how hard their Couriers try to avoid such incidents. Sometimes the trouble can be patched up with a few diplomatic words, often when the Courier explains apologetically to the offended party that the stranger is really a mental case. Sometimes it's not so easy, and the Courier has to order a quick evacuation of all the tourists; the Courier must remain behind until he has sent all his people safely down the line, and there have been several fatalities to Couriers in the line of duty as a result. In extreme cases of tourist bungling, the Time Patrol steps in and cancels the jump retroactively, plucking the careless traveler from the tour and thereby undoing the damage. Sam said, "It can really get one of these rich bastards furious when a Patrolman shows up at the last minute and tells him that he can't make the shunt, because if he does he'll commit some ferocious faux pas up the line. They just can't understand it. They promise to be good, and won't believe that their promise is worthless because their conduct is already a matter of record. The trouble with most of the dumb tourists is that they can't think four-dimensionally." "Neither can I, Sam," I said, baffled. "You will. You'd better," said Sam.)

Before we set out for 1935 we were given a quick hypnocourse in the social background of the era. Pumped into us were data on the Depression, the New Deal, the Long family of Louisiana, Huey Long's rise to fame, his "Share Our Wealth" program of taking from the rich and giving to the poor, his feud with President Franklin Roosevelt, his dream of taking the Presidency himself in 1936, his flamboyant disregard for traditions, his demagogic appeal to the masses. We also got enough incidental details on life in 1935—celebrities, sports developments, the stock market—so we wouldn't feel hopelessly out of context there.

Lastly, they fitted us out in 1935 wardrobes. We strutted around giggling and quipping at the sight of ourselves in those quaint rigs. Jeff Monroe, checking us out, reminded the men about zipper flies and how to use them, reminded the women that it was sternly prohibited to reveal the breasts from the nipple down, and urged us strenuously to keep in mind at all times that we were entering a staunchly puritanical era where neurotic repression was regarded as a virtue and our normal freedoms of behavior were looked upon as sinful and shameless.

Finally, we were ready.

They took us uplevel to Old New Orleans, since it wouldn't have been healthy to make our jump from one of the underlevels. They had set up a room in a boarding-house on North Rampart Street for shunting to the twentieth century.

"Here we go up the line," said Madison Jefferson Monroe, and gave the signal that activated our timers.

14.

Suddenly, it was 1935.

We didn't notice any changes in the dingy room we were in, but yet we knew we were up the line.

We wore tight shoes and funny clothes, and we carried real cash money, United States dollars, because our thumbprints weren't legal tender here. The advance man of the tour had booked us into a big New Orleans hotel on Canal just at the edge of the old French quarter, for the first part of our stay, and after Jeff Monroe had given us a final warning to be circumspect, we went out and walked around the corner to it.

The automobile traffic was fantastic for this supposedly "depressed" year. So was the din. We strolled along, two by two, Jeff leading the way. We stared at things a lot, but no one would get suspicious about that. The locals would simply guess that we were tourists just down from Indiana. Nothing about our curiosity marked us particularly as tourists just down from 2059.

Thibodeaux, the power company man, couldn't get over the sight of power lines right out in the open, dangling from post to post. "I've read about such things," he said several times, "but I never really believed them!"

The womenfolk clucked a lot about the fashions. It was a hot, sticky September day and yet everybody was all covered up. They couldn't understand that.

The weather gave us trouble. We had never been exposed to real humidity before; there isn't any in the undercities, of course, and only a lunatic goes up to surface level when the climate is sour. So we sweated and labored.

There wasn't any air-conditioning in the hotel, either. I think it may not have been invented yet.

Jeff checked us all in at the hotel. When he was through signing the register, the desk clerk, who of course was human and not a computer terminal, banged a bell and yelled, "Front!" and a platoon of friendly black bellhops came over to get our luggage.

I overheard Mrs. Bienvenu, the lawyer's wife, whisper to her husband, "Do you think they're slaves?"

"Not here!" he said fiercely. "The slaves were freed seventy years ago!"

The desk clerk must have overheard that. I wonder what he made of it.

The Courier had booked Flora Chambers and me into one room. He explained that he had registered us as Mr. and Mrs. Elliott, because it wasn't permissible to let an unmarried couple share the same hotel room even if they were part of the same tour party. Flora gave me a pale but hopeful smile and said, "We'll pretend we're on a temporary."

Monroe glared at her. "We don't talk about down-the-line customs here!"

"They don't have temporary liaisons in 1935?"

"Shut *up!*" he hissed.

We unpacked and bathed and went out to see the town. We did Basin Street and heard some respectable primitive jazz. Then we walked a few blocks over to Bourbon Street for drinks and a strip-tease. The place was full; and it amazed us all that grown men and women would sit around for a full hour, enduring a lot of indifferent music and polluted atmosphere, simply to wait for a girl to come out and take off some of her clothes.

When she got undressed, finally, she kept little shiny caps on her nipples and a triangular patch of cloth over her pubic region, too. Anybody who has a serious interest in nudity can see more than that any day at a public bathhouse. But of course this was a repressive, sexually strangled era, we reminded ourselves.

Our drinks and other nightclub charges were all put on one bill, which Jeff Monroe always paid. The Time Service didn't want us ignorant tourists handling unfamiliar currencies except when absolutely necessary. The Courier also deftly fended off drunks who kept invading our group, beggars, soliciting prostitutes, and other challenges to our ability to handle the social situations 1935 presented.

"It's hard work," Flora Chambers observed, "being a Courier."

"But think of all the free traveling you get to do," I said.

We were profoundly awed by the ugliness of the people up the line.

We realized that there were no helix parlors here, that cosmetic micro-surgery was unknown, and that esthetic genetics, if it had been heard of at all in 1935, would have been regarded as a Fascist or Communist conspiracy against the right of free men to have ugly children. Never-theless, we couldn't help registering surprise and dismay at the mis-matched ears, the pockmarked skins, the distorted teeth, the bulging noses, of these unprogrammed and unedited people. The plainest mem-ber of our group was a theatrical beauty, compared to the 1935 norm.

We pitied them for having to live in their cramped, dark little era.

When we got back to our hotel room, Flora took all her clothing off, and sprawled out wildly on the bed with legs spread. "Do me!" she shrieked. "I'm drunk!"

I was a little drunk too, so I did her.

Madison Jefferson Monroe had carefully allotted each of us one alcoholic drink during the whole evening. Despite all temptations, we weren't allowed a second, and had to stick to soft drinks the rest of the time. He couldn't take the risk that we might say something dangerous under the influence of alcohol, a substance we weren't really accus-tomed to. As it is, even that one drink was enough to loosen some tongues and melt some brains, and a few remarks slipped out which, if they had been overheard, could have caused trouble.

It astounded me to see the twentieth-century people drink so much without collapsing.

("Get used to alcohol," Sam had urged me. "It's the favorite mind-poison in most places up the line. Develop a tolerance for it or you may have problems." "No drugs?" I asked. "Well, you'll find some weed here and there, but nothing really psychedelic. No sniffer palaces any-where. Learn to drink, Jud. Learn to drink.")

Later that night Jeff Monroe came to our room. Flora lay in an exhausted heap, unconscious; Jeff and I talked for a long while about the problems of being a Courier. I rather got to like him for all his slickness and blandness.

He seemed to enjoy his work. His specialty was twentieth-century United States, and the only thing he regretted was the wearying routine of covering the assassinations. "Nobody wants to see anything else," he complained. "Dallas, Los Angeles, Memphis, New York, Chicago, Baton Rouge, Cleveland, over and over again. I can't tell you how sick I am of muscling into the crowd by that overpass, and pointing out that window on the sixth floor, and watching that poor woman crawling onto the back of that car. At least the Huey Long thing is reasonably un-touched. But there are twenty of me in Dallas by now. Don't people want to see the *happy* parts of the twentieth century?"

"Were there any?" I asked.

15.

We had breakfast at Brennan's and dinner at Antoine's, and had a tour of the Garden District, and came back to the old town to visit the cathedral in Jackson Square, and then we walked down to have a look at the Mississippi. We also went to see Clark Gable and Jean Harlow in *Red Dust* at a movie house, visited the post office and the public library, bought a lot of newspapers (which are permissible souvenirs), and spent a few hours listening to the radio. We rode the Streetcar Named Desire, and Jeff took us motoring in a hired automobile. He offered to let us drive, but we were all terrified of taking the wheel after watching him going through the intricate routines of changing gears. And we did a lot of other twentieth-century things. We really soaked up the flavor of the era.

Then we went up to Baton Rouge to watch Senator Long get killed.

We got there on Saturday, September 7, and took rooms in what Jeff swore was the finest hotel in the city. The legislature was in session, and Senator Huey had come down from Washington to run things. We hovered around town aimlessly until late Sunday afternoon. Then Jeff got us ready to see the show.

He had donned a thermoplastic disguise. His pink, regular face was now pocked and sallow, he had a mustache, and he wore dark glasses that he might have borrowed from Dajani. "This is the third time I've conducted this tour," he explained to us. "I think it might look bad if somebody noticed identical triplets standing in the corridor when Huey gets shot." He warned us to pay no attention to any of the other Jeff Monroes we might see at the assassination; he, pockmarks and mustache and glasses, was our authentic Courier and the other two were not to be approached.

Toward evening we strolled over to the colossal 34-story state capitol building and casually wandered in—sightseers, here to admire Huey's $5,000,000 edifice. Unobtrusively we entered. Jeff checked the time every few seconds.

He positioned us where we'd have a good view while still keeping out of range of the bullets.

We couldn't help noticing other groups of sightseers slouching into positions nearby. I saw a man who was unmistakably Jeff Monroe standing with one group; another group was clustered around a man of the same size and physique who, however, wore metal-rimmed glasses and had a plum-colored birthmark on one cheek. We made an elaborate show of not looking at these other people. They worked hard at not looking at us.

I worried about the Cumulative Paradox. It seemed to me that everybody who would ever come up the line to witness Huey Long's assassination should be right here now—thousands of people, maybe, all crowding round, jostling for a view. Yet there were only a few dozen, representing those who had set out from 2059 and earlier. Why weren't the others here? Was time so fluid that the same event could be played off infinitely often, for a larger audience each time?

"Here he comes," Jeff whispered.

The Kingfish hurried toward us, his bodyguard close behind. He was short and chubby, with a florid face, a snub nose, orange hair, heavy lips, a deeply cleft chin. I told myself that I could sense the power of the man, and wondered if I might be deluding myself. As he approached he scratched his left buttock, said something to a man to his left, and coughed. His suit was slightly rumpled; his hair was unruly.

Since we had been coached by our Courier, we knew where to look for the assassin. On a murmured signal from Jeff—not before!—we turned our heads and saw Dr. Carl Austin Weiss detach himself from the crowd, step up to the Senator, and push a .22 automatic pistol into his stomach. He fired one shot. Huey, surprised, fell back, mortally wounded. His bodyguards instantly drew their guns and killed the assassin. Gleaming puddles of blood began to form; people screamed; the red-faced bodyguards pushed at us, hammered at us, told us to get back, get back, get back!

That was it. The event we had come to see was over.

It had seemed unreal, a playback of ancient history, a clever but not quite convincing tridim. We were impressed with the ingenuity of the process, but we were not awed by the impact of the event.

Even while the bullets had been flying, none of it had seemed completely true to us.

Yet those bullets had been real bullets, and if they had hit us, we would have died real deaths.

And for the two men lying on the capitol's polished floor, it had been an extremely real event.

16.

I went on four more training missions before they certified me as a Time Courier. All my jumps were made in the New Orleans area. I got to know the history of that area a lot better than I ever thought I would.

The third of these trips was to 1803, the Louisiana Purchase run. I was the only trainee. There were seven tourists. Our Courier was a hard-faced little man named Sid Buonocore. When I mentioned his name to Sam, Sam guffawed and said, "That shady character!"

"What's shady about him?"

"They used to have him on the Renaissance run. Then the Time Patrol caught him pimping lady tourists to Cesare Borgia. The tourist gals paid him nicely, and so did Cesare. Buonocore claimed he was just doing his job—letting his girls get a deeper experience of the Renaissance, you know. But they pulled him back here and stuck him on Louisiana Purchase."

"Is a Courier supposed to supervise the sex life of his tourists?" I asked.

"No, but he isn't supposed to encourage transtemporal fornication, either."

I found the encourager of transtemporal fornication to be an engaging rakish sort. Buonocore was a long way from handsome, but he had an aura of omnivorous sexuality about him that I had to admire. And his high regard for his own welfare was so obvious that it had a certain rapacious charm. You can't applaud a skulking pick-pocket, but you can cheer an out-and-out brigand. That was what Sid Buonocore was.

He was a capable Courier, besides. He slipped us cunningly into 1803 New Orleans in the guise of a party of Dutch traders making a market tour; as long as we didn't meet a real Hollander we were safe, and our "Dutch" label covered the oddities of our futuristic accents. We strode around town uncomfortably garbed in early nineteenth-century clothing, feeling like refugees from a costume drama, and Sid showed us the sights in fine fashion.

On the side, I quickly discovered, he was carrying on a flourishing trade in gold doubloons and Spanish eight-real pieces. He didn't bother to conceal what he was doing from me, but he didn't talk about it, either, and I never really figured out all the intricate details. It had something to do—maybe—with taking advantage of variable exchange rates. All I know is that he swapped United States silver dollars for British gold guineas, used the guineas to buy French silver currency at a big discount, and met with Caribbean buccaneers by night on the banks of the Mississippi to trade the French coins for Spanish gold and silver. What he did with his doubloons and eight-real pieces I never knew. Nor could I see where the profit in the deal was coming from. My best theory was that he simply was trying to switch as many currencies around as possible, in order to build up a stock of coins for sale to collectors down the line; but somehow that seemed too simple-minded an operation for someone of his style. He didn't offer explanations and I was too shy to ask.

He was also a busy sexman. That isn't unusual for a Courier. ("The lady tourists are fair game," Sam said. "They fall all over themselves to submit to us. It's like the white-hunter thing in Africa.") But Sid Buonocore didn't just confine himself to plugging romance-hungry tourists, I discovered.

Late one night in our 1803 trip I was bothered with some procedural point and went to the Courier's bedroom to ask him about it. I knocked and he said, "Come in," so I went in, but he wasn't alone. A tawny maiden with long black hair was sprawled on the bed, naked, sweat-shiny, rumpled. Her breasts were hard and heavy and her nipples were chocolate-colored. "Excuse me," I said. "I didn't mean to intrude." Sid Buonocore laughed. "Crap," he said. "We're finished for now. You aren't interrupting things. This is Maria."

"Hello, Maria," I said tentatively.

She giggled drunkenly. Sid spoke to her in the Creole patois and she giggled again. Rising from the bed, she performed an elegant nude curtsy before me and murmured, *"Bon soir, m'sieu."* Then she fell on her face with a gentle swooning fall.

"She's lovely, isn't she?" Sid asked proudly. "Half Indian, half Spanish, half French. Have some rum."

I took a gulp from the flask he proffered. "That's too many halves," I said.

"Maria doesn't do anything in a petty way."

"So I see."

"I met her on my last trip through here. I'm timing things very carefully so that I can have her for a little while each night, and still not deprive my other selves of her. I mean, I can't predict how often I'll be doing this goddam run, Jud, but I might as well set myself up nicely each time I go up the line."

"Should you be saying such things in front of—"

"Doesn't speak a word of English. Absolutely safe."

Maria stirred and moaned. Sid took the rum flask from me and let some splash down onto her chest. She giggled again, and sleepily began to rub it into her breasts like a magic growth ointment. She didn't need any ointment.

Sid said, "She's quite passionate."

"I'm sure."

He said something to her and she lurched to her feet and came toward me. Her breasts swayed like bells. Fumes of rum and fumes of lust rose from her. Unsteadily she reached her hands toward me, but she lost her balance and slipped once again to the planked floor. She lay there chuckling.

"Want to try her?" Sid asked. "Let her sober up a little, and take her back to your room and have some fun."

I said something about the interesting diseases she might be carrying. Sometimes I break out all over with fastidiousness at funny moments.

Buonocore spat scornfully. "You've had your shots. What are you worrying about?"

"They immunized us against typhoid and diphtheria and yellow fever and all that," I said. "But syphilis?"

"She's clean. Believe me. Anyway, if you're nervous, you can take a thermobath the minute you go down the line." He shrugged. "If something like that scares you, maybe you better not be a Courier."

"I didn't—"

"You saw that *I* was willing to ball her, didn't you? Jud, do you think I'm an ordinary fool or a goddam fool? Would I go to bed with a syphilitic? And then offer her to you?"

"Well—"

"There's only one thing you do have to worry about," he said. "Have you had your pill?"

"My pill?"

"Your *pill*, stupid! Your monthly pill!"

"Oh. Yes. Yes, of course."

"That's vital, if you're going to go up the line. You don't want to run around fertilizing other people's ancestors. The Time Patrol will really scrape you for a thing like that. You can get away with a little fraternization with up-the-line people—you can do some business with them, you can go to bed with them—but you damned well better not plant any babies in them. Got it?"

"Sure, Sid."

"Remember, just because I fool around a little, that doesn't mean I'm willing to risk changing the past in a big way. Like fouling up the genetic flow by making babies up the line. Go you and do likewise, kid. Don't forget your pills. Now take Maria and clear out."

I took Maria and cleared out.

She sobered up fast in my room. She couldn't speak a word of any language I understood. I couldn't speak a word of any language she understood. But we made out all right anyway.

Even though she was 250 years older than me, there was nothing wrong with any aspect of her performance. Some things don't change much.

17.

After I qualified as a Time Courier, and just before I departed to go on the Byzantium run, Sam gave a farewell party for me. Just about everyone I had known in Under New Orleans was invited, and we all crammed into Sam's two rooms. The girls from the sniffer palace were there, and an unemployed oral poet named Shigemitsu who spoke only in iambic pentameter, and five or six Time Service people, and a peddler of floaters, and a wild green-haired girl who worked as a splitter in a helix parlor, and others. Sam even invited Flora Chambers, but she had shipped out the day before to fill in on the Sack of Rome run.

Everyone was given a floater as he arrived. So things turned on fast. Instants after the buzz of the floater's snout against my arm I felt my consciousness expanding like a balloon, stretching until my body could no longer contain it, bursting the confines of my skin. With a *pop!* I broke free and floated. The others were going through the same experience. Liberated from our chains of flesh, we drifted around the ceiling in an ectoplasmic haze, enjoying the slinkiness of the sensation. I sent foggy tentacles off to curl around the floating forms of Betsy and Helen, and we enjoyed a tranquil triple conjugation of the psychedelic sort. Meanwhile, music came seeping from a thousand outputs in the wall paint, and the ceiling screen was tuned to the abstraction channel to enhance the effects. It was a very sweet scene.

"We grieve that you must take your leave of us," said Shigemitsu tenderly. "Your absence here creates an aching void. Though all the world now opens to your knock—"

He went on like that for at least five minutes. The poetry got really erotic toward the end. I wish I could remember that part of it.

We floated higher and higher. Sam, hosting it to the full, saw to it that nobody wore off even for a minute. His huge black body gleamed with oil. One young couple from the Time Service had brought their own coffin along; it was a lovely job, silk-lined, with all the sanitary attachments. They climbed in and let us monitor them on the telemetry line. Afterward, the rest of us tried it, in twos or threes, and there was a great deal of laughter over some of the couplings. My partner was the floater peddler, and right in the middle of things we turned on all over again.

The sniffer palace girls danced for us, and three of the Time Couriers—two men and a fragile-looking young woman in an ermine loincloth—put on an exhibition of biological acrobatics, very charming. They had learned the steps in Knossos, where they watched Minos's dancers perform, and had simply adapted the movements to modern tastes by grafting in the copulations at the right moments. During the performance Sam distributed input scramblers to everybody. We plugged them in and beautiful synesthesia took hold. For me this time, touch became smell; I caressed Betsy's cool buttocks and the fragrance of April lilacs came to me; I squeezed a cube of ice and smelled the sea at high tide; I stroked the ribbed wall fabric and my lungs filled with the dizzying flavor of a pine forest on fire. Then we did the pivot and for me sound became texture; Helen made passion-sounds in my ear and they became furry moss; music roared from the speakers as a torrent of thick cream; Shigemitsu began to moan in blank verse and the stabbing rhythms of his voice reached me as pyramids of ice. We went on to do things with color, taste, and duration. Of all the kinds of sensory pleasures invented in the last hundred years, I think scrambling is by far my favorite.

Later Emily, the helix-parlor girl, came over. She was starvation-slim, with painfully sharp cheekbones, a scraggly mop of tangled green hair, and the most beautiful piercing green eyes I have ever seen. Though she was high on everything simultaneously, she seemed cool and self-possessed—an illusion, I quickly discovered. She was floating. "Listen carefully to what she says," Sam advised me. "She goes clairvoyant under the influence of floaters. I mean it: she's the real thing."

She toppled into my arms. I supported her uncertainly a moment while her mouth sought mine. Her teeth nipped lightly into my lips. Delicately we toppled to the carpet, which emitted little thrumming sounds when we landed. Emily wore a cloak of copper mesh strips interlaced at her throat. I searched patiently beneath it for her breasts. She said in a hollow, prophetic voice, "You will soon begin a long journey."

"Yes."

"You will go up the line."

"That's right."

"In—Byzantium."

"Byzantium, yes."

"That is no country for old men!" cried a voice from the far side of the room. "The young in one another's arms, birds in the trees—"

"Byzantium," murmured an exhausted dancer spread-eagled near my feet.

"The golden smithies of the Emperor!" Shigemitsu screamed. "Spirit after spirit! The smithies break the flood! Flames that no faggot feeds, nor steel has lit!"

"The Emperor's drunken soldiery are abed," I said.

Emily, quivering, bit my ear and said, "You will find your heart's desire in Byzantium."

"Sam said the same thing to me."

"And lose it there. And you will suffer, and regret, and repent, and you will not be the same as you were before."

"That sounds serious," I said.

"Beware love in Byzantium!" the prophetess shrilled. "Beware! Beware!"

". . . the jaws that bite, the claws that catch!" sang Shigemitsu.

I promised Emily that I would be careful.

But the light of prophecy was gone from her eyes. She sat up, blinked several times, smiled uncertainly, and said, "Who are you?" Her thighs were tightly clasped around my left hand.

"I'm the guest of honor. Jud Elliott."

"I don't know you. What do you do?"

"Time Courier. Will be. I'm leaving to start service tomorrow."

"I think I remember now. I'm Emily."

"Yes, I know. You're with a helix parlor?"

"Someone's been talking about me!"

"Not much. What do you do there?"

"I'm a splitter," she said. "I separate genes. You see, when somebody is carrying the gene for red hair, and wants to transmit that to his children, but the gene is linked to, let's say, the gene for hemophilia, I split off the unwanted gene and edit it out."

"It sounds like very difficult work," I ventured.

"Not if you know what you're doing. There's a six-month training course."

"I see."

"It's interesting work. It tells you a lot about human nature, seeing

how people want their children to come out. You know, not everybody
wants improvements edited in. We get some amazing requests."

"I guess it depends on what you mean by improvements," I said.

"Well, there *are* certain norms of appearance. We assume that it's
better to have thick, lustrous hair than none at all. Better for a man to
be two meters tall than one meter tall. Better to have straight teeth than
crooked ones. But what would you say if a woman comes in and tells
you to design a son with undescended testicles?"

"Why would anybody want a child like that?"

"She doesn't like the idea of his fooling around with girls," Emily
said.

"Did you do it?"

"The request was two full points below the mark on the genetic
deviation index. We have to refer all such requests to the Board of
Genetic Review."

"Would they approve it?" I asked.

"Oh, no, never. They don't authorize counterproductive mutations
of that sort."

"I guess the poor woman is just going to have a baby with balls,
then."

Emily smiled. "She can go to bootleg helixers, if she likes. They'll
do anything for anybody. Don't you know about them?"

"Not really."

"They produce the far-out mutations for the avant-garde set. The
children with gills and scales, the children with twenty fingers, the ones
with zebra-striped skin. The bootleggers will notch any gene at all—for
the right price. They're terribly expensive. But they're the wave of the
future."

"They are?"

"Cosmetic mutations are on the way in," Emily declared. "Don't
misunderstand—*our* parlor won't touch the things. But this is the last
generation of uniformity the human race is going to have. Variety of
genotype and phenotype—that's what's ahead!" Her eyes sparkled with
sudden lunacy, and I realized that a slow-acting floater must have exploded in her veins in the last few minutes. Drawing close to me, she
whispered, "What do you think of this idea? Let's make a baby right
now, and I'll redesign it after hours at the parlor! We'll keep up with
the trends!"

"I'm sorry," I said. "I've had my pill this month."

"Let's try anyway," she said, and slipped her eager hand into my
pants.

18.

I reached Istanbul on a murky summer afternoon and caught an express pod across the Bosphorus to the Time Service headquarters, on the Asian side. The city hadn't changed much since my last visit a year before. That was no surprise. Istanbul hasn't really changed since Kemal Ataturk's time, and that was 150 years ago. The same gray buildings, the same archaic clutter of unlabeled streets, the same overlay of grit and grime. And the same heavenly mosques floating above the dilapidation.

I admire the mosques tremendously. They show that the Turks were good for *something*. But to me, Istanbul is a black joke of a city that someone has painted over the wounded stump of my beloved Constantinople. The little pieces of the Byzantine city that remain hold more magic for me than Sultan Ahmed's mosque, the Suleimaniye, and the mosque of Beyazit, all taken together.

The thought that I would soon be seeing Constantinople as a living city, with all the Turkish excrescences swept away, almost made me stain my pants with glee.

The Time Service had set up shop in a squat, formidable building of the late twentieth century, far up the Bosphorus, practically facing the Turkish fortress of Rumeli Hisari, from which the Conqueror strangled Byzantium in 1453. I was expected; even so, I had to spend fifteen minutes milling in an anteroom, surrounded by angry tourists complaining about some foulup in scheduling. One red-faced man kept shouting, "Where's the computer input? I want all this on record in the computer!" And a tired, angelic-looking secretary kept telling him wearily that everything he was saying *was* going on record, down to the ultimate bleat. Two swaggering giants in Time Patrol uniforms cut coolly through the mêlée, their faces grimly set, their minds no doubt riveted to duty. I could almost hear them thinking, "Aha! *Aha!*" A thin woman with a wedge-shaped face rushed up to them, waved papers at their deep-cleft chins, and yelled, "Seven months ago I confirmed these reservations, yet! Right after Christmas it was! And now they tell me—" The Time Patrolmen kept walking. A robot vendor entered the waiting room and started to sell lottery tickets. Behind it came a haggard, unshaven Turk in a rumpled black jacket, peddling honeycakes from a greasy tray.

I admired the quality of the confusion. It showed genius.

Still, I wasn't unhappy to be rescued. A Levantine type who might have been a cousin of my fondly remembered instructor Najeeb Dajani appeared, introduced himself to me as Spiros Protopopolos, and led me hastily through a sphincter door I had not noticed. "You should have come through the side way," he said. "I apologize for this delay. We didn't realize you were here."

He was about thirty, plump, sleek, with sunglasses and a great many white teeth. As we shot upshaft to the Couriers' lounge he said, "You have never worked as a Courier before, yes?"

"Yes," I said. "Never. My first time."

"You will love it! The Byzantium run especially. Byzantium, it is so—how shall I express it?" He pressed his pudgy palms rapturously together. "Surely you must feel some of it. But only a Greek like myself can respond fully. Byzantium! Ah, Byzantium!"

"I'm Greek also," I said.

He halted the shaft and raised his glasses. "You are not Judson Daniel Elliott III?"

"I am."

"This is Greek?"

"My mother's name was originally Passilidis. She was born in Athens. My maternal grandfather was mayor of Sparta. On his mother's side he was descended from the Markezinis family."

"You are my brother!" cried Spiros Protopopolos.

It turned out that six of the nine other Time Couriers assigned to the Byzantium run were Greeks by nationality or descent; there were two Germans, Herschel and Melamed; while the tenth man was a slick, dark-haired Spaniard named Capistrano who later on, when deep in his cups, confided to me that his great-grandmother had been a Turk. He may have invented that so I'd despise him; Capistrano had a distinct streak of masochism.

Five of my nine colleagues were currently up the line and four were here in now-time Istanbul, thanks to the scheduling mishap that was causing so much dismay in the anteroom. Protopopolos made the introductions: Melamed, Capistrano, Pappas, meet Elliott. Melamed was fair-haired and hid behind a dense sandy beard; Pappas had hollow cheeks, sad eyes, and a drooping mustache. They were both about forty. Capistrano looked a little younger.

An illuminated board monitored the doings of the other members of the team: Herschel, Kolettis, Plastiras, Metaxas, and Gompers. "Gompers?" I said. Protopopolos replied, "His grandmother was pure Hellene." The five of them were scattered over ten centuries, according to that board, with Kolettis in 1651 B.P., and Metaxas in 606 B.P.—that is, in A.D. 408 and 1453—and the others in between. As I stared at the board, Kolettis moved down the line by more than a century. "They have gone to see the riots," Melamed said softly, and Capistrano nodded, sighing.

Pappas brewed strong coffee for me. Capistrano uncorked a bottle of Turkish brandy, which I found a little hard to ingest. He prodded me encouragingly, saying, "Drink, drink, it's the best you'll taste in the last fifteen centuries!" I remembered Sam's advice that I should learn how to drink, and forced the stuff down, longing for a weed, a floater, a fume, anything decent.

While I relaxed with my new comrades, a Time Patrolman came into the room. He didn't use the scanner to get entry permission, or even knock; he just barged in. "Can't you ever be polite?" Pappas growled.

"Up yours," said the Time Patrolman. He sank down into a web and unbuttoned his uniform shirt. He was a chunky Aryan-looking sort with a hairy chest; what looked like golden wire curled toward his clavicles. "New man?" he said, jerking his head at me.

"Jud Elliott," I said. "Courier."

"Dave Van Dam," he said. "Patrol." His huge hand enfolded mine. "Don't let me catch you screwing around up the line. Nothing personal, but I'm a tough bastard. It's so easy to hate us: we're incorruptible. Try me and see."

"This is the lounge for Couriers," said Capistrano thinly.

"You don't need to tell me that," said Van Dam. "Believe it or not, I can read."

"Are you now a Courier, then?"

"Do you mind if I relax a little with the opposition?" The Patrolman grinned, scratched his chest, and put the brandy bottle to his lips. He drank copiously and belched resonantly. "Christ, what a killer of a day! You know where I was today?"

Nobody seemed to care.

He continued anyway, "I spent the whole day in 1962! Nineteen goddam sixty-two! Checking out every floor of the Istanbul Goddam Hilton for two alleged timecrimers running an alleged artifact siphon. What we heard was they were bringing gold coins and Roman glass down from 1400 B.P. and selling them to American tourists in the Hilton, then investing the proceeds on the stock market and hiding the stash in a Swiss bank for pickup in now-time. Christ! You know, you can make *billions* that way? You buy in a bear-market year and stick it away for a century and you end up owning the world. Well, maybe so, but we didn't see a thing in the whole goddam Hilton except plenty of legitimate free enterprise based in then-time. Crap on it!" He took another pull on the brandy bottle. "Let them run a recheck upstairs. Find their own goddam timecrimers."

"This is the lounge for Couriers," Capistrano said once more.

The Patrolman took no notice. When he finally left, five minutes later, I said, "Are they all like that?"

Protopopolos said, "This was one of the refined ones. Most of the others are boors."

19.

They put me to bed with a hypnosleep course in Byzantine Greek, and when I woke up I not only could order a meal, buy a tunic, and seduce a virgin in Byzantine argot, but I knew some phrases that could make the mosaics of Haghia Sophia peel from the walls in shame. I hadn't known about those phrases when I was a graduate student at Harvard, Yale, and Princeton. Good stuff, hypnosleep.

I still wasn't ready to go out solo as a Courier. Protopopolos, who was serving as staff router this month, arranged to team me with Capistrano for my first time out. If everything went smoothly, I'd be put on my own in a few weeks.

The Byzantium run, which is one of the most popular that the Time Service offers, is pretty standard stuff. Every tour is taken to see the coronation of an emperor, a chariot race in the Hippodrome, the dedication of Haghia Sophia, the sack of the city by the Fourth Crusade, and the Turkish conquest. A tour like that stays up the line for seven days. The fourteen-day tour covers all that plus the arrival of the First Crusade in Constantinople, the riots of 532, an imperial wedding, and a couple of lesser events. The Courier has his options about which coronations, emperors, or chariot races to go to; the idea is to avoid contributing to the Cumulative Paradox by cluttering any one event with too many tourists. Just about every major period between Justinian and the Turks gets visited, although we're cautioned to avoid the years of bad earthquakes, and absolutely prohibited, under penalty of obliteration by the Time Patrol, from entering the bubonic plague years of 74547.

On my last night in now-time I was so excited I couldn't sleep. Partly I was keyed up over the fear of blundering somehow on my first assignment as a Courier; it's a big responsibility to be a Courier, even with a colleague along, and I was afraid of committing some terrible mistake. The thought of having to be rescued by the Time Patrol upset me. What a humiliation!

But mainly I was worried about Constantinople. Would it live up to my dream of it? Or *would it let me down?* All my life I had cherished an image of that golden, glittering city of the past; now, on the verge of going up the line to it, I trembled.

I got up and stumbled around the little room they had given me, feeling drawn and tense. I was off all drugs and wasn't allowed to smoke—Couriers have to taper off such things ahead of time, since it's obviously an illegal anachronism to light up a weed in a tenth-century street. Capistrano had given me the dregs of his brandy, but that was small consolation. He heard me walking into furniture, though, and came to see what the trouble was.

"Restless?" he asked.

"Very."

"I always am, before a jump. It never wears off."

He talked me into going out with him to soothe our nerves. We crossed to the European side and wandered at random through the silent streets of the new city, up from Dolmabahce Palace at the shore to the old Hilton, and down past Taksim to the Galata Bridge and into Istanbul proper. We walked tirelessly. We seemed to be the only ones awake in the city. Through the winding maze of a market we wound, emerging on one of those streets leading to Haghia Sophia, where we stood a while in front of the majestic old building. I imprinted its features on my brain—the extraneous minarets, the late buttresses—and tried to make myself believe that in the morning I'd see it in its true form, serene mistress of the city, no longer compelled to share its grand plaza with the alien loveliness of the Blue Mosque across the way.

On and on we went, scrambling over the fragments of the Hippodrome, circling Topkapi, making our way to the sea and the old sea wall. Dawn found us outside the Yedikule fortress, in the shadow of the crumbling Byzantine rampart. We were half asleep. A Turkish boy of about fifteen approached us politely and asked, first in French and then in English, if we were in the market for anything—old coins, his sister, hashish, Israeli currency, gold jewelry, his brother, a carpet. We thanked him and said we weren't. Undaunted, he summoned his sister, who may have been fourteen but looked four or five years older. "Virgin," he said. "You like her? Nice figure, eh? What are you, American, English, German? Here, you look, eh?" She unsnapped her blouse at a harsh command from him, and displayed attractive taut round breasts. Dangling on a string between them was a heavy Byzantine bronze coin, possibly a *follis*. I peered close for a better look. The boy, breathing garlic at me, realized suddenly that it was the coin and not the breasts that I was studying, and made a smooth switch, saying, "You like old coins, eh? We find plenty under wall in a pot. You wait here, I show you, yes?" He ran off. The sister sullenly closed her blouse. Capistrano and I walked away. The girl followed us, calling out to us to stay, but by the time we had gone twenty meters she lost interest. We were back at the Time Service building in an hour, by pod.

After breakfast we got into costume: long silk tunics, Roman sandals, light cloaks. Capistrano solemnly handed me my timer. By now I had been well trained in its use. I slipped it in place against my skin and felt a dazzling surge of power, knowing that now I was free to transport myself to any era, and was accountable to no one so long as I kept in mind the preservation of the sanctity of now time. Capistrano winked at me.

"Up the line," he said.

"Up the line," I said.

We went downstairs to meet our eight tourists.

20.

The jumping-off place for the Byzantium run is almost always the same: the plaza in front of Haghia Sophia. The ten of us, feeling faintly foolish in our robes, were taken there by bus, arriving about ten that morning. More conventional tourists, merely there to see Istanbul, flocked back and forth between the great cathedral and nearby Sultan Ahmed. Capistrano and I made sure that everybody's timer was in place and that the rules of time-travel had been thoroughly nagged into everyone's skull.

Our group included a pair of pretty young men from London, a couple of maidenly German schoolteachers, and two elderly American husband-and-wife outfits. Everybody had had the hypnocourse in Byzantine Greek, and for the next sixty days or so would be as fluent in that as in their native languages, but Capistrano and I had to keep reminding the Americans and one of the German girls to speak it.

We jumped.

I felt the momentary disorientation that always comes when you go up the line. Then I got my bearings and discovered that I had departed from Istanbul and had reached Constantinople.

Constantinople did not let me down.

The grime was gone. The minarets were gone. The mosques were gone. The Turks were gone.

The air was blue and sweet and clear. We stood in the great plaza, the Augusteum, in front of Haghia Sophia. To my right, where there should have been bleak gray office buildings, I saw open fields. Ahead of me, where the blue fantasy of Sultan Ahmed's mosque should have been, I saw a rambling conglomeration of low marble palaces. To the side rose the flank of the Hippodrome. Figures in colorful robes, looking like fugitives from Byzantine mosaics, sauntered through the spacious square.

I swung around for my first view of Haghia Sophia without her minarets.

Haghia Sophia was not there.

On the familiar site I saw the charred and tumbled ruins of an unfamiliar rectangular basilica. The stone walls stood but precariously; the roof was gone. There soldiers drowsed in the shadow of its facade. I was lost.

Capistrano said droningly, "We have journeyed sixteen centuries up the line. The year is 408; we have come to behold the baptismal procession of Emperor Arcadius' son, who will one day rule as Theodosius II. To our rear, on the site of the well-known cathedral of Haghia Sophia, we may see the ruins of the original basilica, built during the reign of the Emperor Constantius, son of Constantine the Great, and opened for prayer on the 15th of December, 360. This building was burned on the 20th of June, 404, during a rebellion, and as you can see, reconstruction has not yet begun. The church will be rebuilt about thirty years down the line by Emperor Theodosius II, and you will view it on our next stop. Come this way."

As though in a dream I followed, as much a tourist as our eight charges. Capistrano did all the work. He lectured us in a perfunctory but comprehensive way about the marble buildings ahead, which were the beginning of the Great Palace. I couldn't reconcile what I saw with the ground plans I had memorized at Harvard; but of course the Constantinople I had studied was the later, greater, post-Justinian city, and now I stood in the city at its dawn. We turned inland, away from the palace district, into a residential district where the houses of the rich, blank-fronted and courtyarded, mixed helter-skelter with the rush-roofed hovels of the poor. And then we emerged on the Mese, the grand processional street, lined by arcaded shops, and on this day, in honor of the baptism of the prince, decked with silk hangings adorned with gold.

All the citizens of Byzantium were here, packing the street elbow to elbow in anticipation of the grand parade. Food shops were busy; we smelled grilled ham and baked lamb, and eyed stalls laden with cheeses, nuts, unfamiliar fruits. One of the German girls said she was hungry and Capistrano laughed and bought spitted lamb for us all, paying for it with bright copper coins worth a fortune to a numismatist. A one-eyed man sold us wine out of a huge cool amphora, letting us drink right from the ladle. Once it became obvious to the other peddlers in the vicinity that we were susceptible customers, they crowded around by the dozens, offering us souvenirs, candied sweets, elderly-looking hard-boiled eggs, pans of salted nuts, trays of miscellaneous animal organs, eyeballs and other balls. This was the real thing, the genuinely archaic past; that array of vended oddities and the reek of sweat and garlic coming from the mob of vendors told us that we were a long way from 2059.

"Foreigners?" asked a bearded man who was selling little clay oil lamps. "Where from? Cyprus? Egypt?"

"Spain," said Capistrano.

The oil-lamp man eyed us in awe, as though we had claimed to come from Mars. "Spain," he repeated. "Spain! Wonderful! To travel so far, to see our city—" He gave our whole group a detailed survey, taking a quick inventory and fastening on blonde and breasty Clotilde, the more voluptuous of our two German school-teachers. "Your slave-girl is a Saxon?" he asked me, feeling the merchandise through Clotilde's loose robes. "Ah, very nice! You are a man of taste!" Clotilde gasped and pried his fingers from her thigh. Coldly Capistrano seized the man, pushing him up against the wall of a shop so roughly that a dozen of his clay lamps tumbled to the pavement and shattered. The vendor winked, but Capistrano said something chilly under his breath and gave the man a terrible glare. "I meant no harm," the vendor protested. "I thought she was a slave!" He muttered a curt apology and limped away. Clotilde was trembling—whether from outrage or excitement, it was hard to tell. Her companion, Lise, looked a little envious. No Byzantine street peddler had ever fondled *her* bare flesh!

Capistrano spat. "That could have been troublesome. We must always be on our guard; innocent pinching can turn quickly to complications and catastrophe."

The peddlers edged away from us. We found places near the front of the mob, facing the street. It seemed to me that many of the faces in the crowd were un-Byzantine, and I wondered if they were the faces of time-travelers. A time is coming, I thought, when we from down the line will throng the past to the choking point. We will fill all our yesterdays with ourselves and crowd out our own ancestors.

"Here they come!" a thousand voices shouted.

Trumpets blared in several different keys. In the distance there appeared a procession of nobles, clean-cut and close-cropped in the Roman fashion, for this was still as much a Roman city as it was a Greek one. Everyone wore white silk—imported at great cost by caravan from China, Capistrano murmured; the Byzantines had not yet stolen the secret of silk manufacture—and the late afternoon sun, striking the splendid robes at a steep angle, gave the procession such a glow of beauty that even Capistrano, who had seen it all before, was moved. Slowly, slowly, the high dignitaries advanced.

"They look like snowflakes," whispered a man behind me. "Dancing snowflakes!"

It took nearly an hour for these high ones to pass us. Twilight came. Following the priests and dukes of Byzantium were the imperial troops, carrying lighted candles that flickered in the deepening dusk like an infinity of stars. Then came more priests, bearing medallions and icons; and then a prince of the royal blood, carrying the gurgling, plump infant who would be the mighty Emperor Theodosius II; and then the reigning emperor himself, Arcadius, clad in imperial purple. The Emperor of Byzantium! I repeated that to myself a thousand times. I, Judson Daniel Elliott III, stood bareheaded under the Byzantine sky, here in A.D. 408, while the Emperor of Byzantium, robes aswish, walked past me! Even though the monarch was merely the trifling Arcadius, the insignificant interpolation between the two Theodosii, I trembled. I swayed. The pavement heaved and bucked beneath me. "Are you ill?" whispered Clotilde anxiously. I sucked breath and begged the universe to stand still. I was overwhelmed, and by Arcadius. What if this had been Justinian? Constantine? Alexius?

You know how it is. Eventually I got to see even those great ones. But by then I had seen too much up the line, and though I was impressed, I wasn't engulfed with awe. Of Justinian my clearest memory is that he sneezed; but when I think of Arcadius, I hear trumpets and see stars whirling in the sky.

21.

We stayed that night in an inn overlooking the Golden Horn; on the other side of the water, where Hiltons and countinghouses one day would rise, was only an impenetrable darkness. The inn was a substantial wooden building with a dining hall on the ground floor and huge, rough, dormitory-style rooms above. Somehow I expected to be asked to sleep on the floor in a strew of rushes, but no, there were beds of a recognizable sort, and mattresses stuffed with rags. Sanitary facilities were outside, behind the building. There were no baths; we were expected to use the public bathhouses if we craved cleanliness. The ten of us shared one room, but fortunately none of us minded that. Clotilde, when she undressed, indignantly went around showing us the purpling bruises left by the vendor's grip on her soft white thigh; her angular friend Lise looked gloomy again, for having nothing to show.

That night we did little sleeping. There was too much noise, for one thing, since the celebration of the imperial baptism went on raucously throughout the city until almost dawn. But who could sleep, anyway, knowing that the world of the early fifth century lay just beyond the door?

One night before and sixteen centuries down the line, Capistrano had kindly seen me through a siege of sleeplessness. Now he did it again. I rose and stood by the little slit of a window, peering at the bonfires in the city, and when he noticed me he came over and said, "I understand. Sleeping is hard at first."

"Yes."

"Shall I get a woman for you?"

"No."

"We'll take a walk, then?"

"Can we leave them?" I asked, looking at our eight tourists.

"We won't go far. We'll stay just outside, within reach if some trouble starts."

The air was heavy and mild. Snatches of obscene song floated up from the tavern district. We walked toward it; the taverns were still open and full of drunken soldiers. Swarthy prostitutes offered their wares. One girl, hardly sixteen, had a coin on a string between her bare breasts. Capistrano nudged me to notice it, and we laughed. "The same coin, maybe?" he asked. "But different breasts?" I shrugged. "Perhaps the same breasts, too," I said, thinking of the unborn girl who had been for sale at the Yedikule a night ago. Capistrano bought two flasks of oily Greek wine and we returned to the inn, to sit quietly downstairs and drink the darkness away.

He did most of the talking. Like many Time Couriers, his life had been a complex, jagged one full of detours, and he let his autobiography dribble out between gulps of wine. Noble Spanish ancestors, he said (he didn't tell me about the Turkish great-grandmother until months later, when he was far more thoroughly drunk); early marriage to a virgin of high family; education at the best universities of Europe. Then inexplicable decline, loss of ambition, loss of fortune, loss of wife. "My life," said Capistrano, "broke in half when I was twenty-seven years of age. I required total reintegration of personality. As you see, the effort was not a true success." He spoke of a series of temporary marriages, adventures in criminality, experiments with hallucinatory drugs that made weeds and floaters look innocent. When he enrolled as a Time Courier, it was only as an alternative to suicide. "I keyed to an output and asked for a bit at random," he said. "Positive, and I become a Courier. Negative, and I drink poison. The bit came up positive. Here I am." He drained his wine.

To me that night he seemed a wonderful mixture of the desperate, tragic romantic and the self-dramatizing charlatan. Of course, I was drunk myself, and very young. But I told him how much I admired his quest for identity, and secretly wished that I could learn the knack of seeming so appealingly destroyed, so interestingly lost.

"Come," he said, when the last of the wine was gone. "To dispose of the corpses."

We hurled our flasks into the Golden Horn. Streaks of dawn were emerging. As we walked slowly back to the inn, Capistrano said, "I have made a little hobby of tracing my ancestors, do you know? It is my own private research. Here—look at these names." He produced a small, thick notebook. "In each era I visit," he said, "I seek out my ancestors and list them here. Already I know several hundred of them,

going back to the fourteenth century. Do you realize how immense the
number of one's ancestors is? We have two parents, and each of them
has two parents, and each of them two parents—go back only four
generations and you have already thirty ancestors!"

"An interesting hobby," I said.

Capistrano's eyes blazed. "More than a hobby! More than a hobby!
A matter of death and life! Look, my friend, whenever I grow more
tired than usual of existence, all I must do is find one of these people,
one, and destroy him! Take his life when he is still a child, perhaps.
Then return to now-time. And in that moment, swiftly, without pain,
my own tiresome life ceases ever to have been!"

"But the Time Patrol—"

"Helpless," said Capistrano. "What can the Patrol do? If my crime
is discovered, I am seized and erased from history for timecrime, right?
If my crime is not discovered—and why should it be?—then I have
erased myself. Either way I am gone. Is this not the most charming way
of suicide?"

"In eliminating your own ancestor," I said, "you might be changing
now-time to a greater degree. You'd also eliminate your own brothers
and sisters—uncles—grandparents and all of *their* brothers and sisters—
all by removing one prop from the past!"

He nodded solemnly. "I am aware of this. And so I compile these
genealogies, you see, in order to determine how best to effect my own
erasure. I am not Samson; I have no wish to bring the temple crashing
down with myself. I will look for the strategic person to eliminate—
one who is himself sinful, incidentally, for I will not slay the truly
innocent—and I will remove that person and thus myself, and perhaps
the changes in now-time will not be terribly great. If they are, the Patrol
will discover and undo them, and still give me the exit I crave."

I wondered if he was crazy or just drunk. A little of both, I decided.

I felt like telling him that if he really wanted to kill himself that
badly, it would be a whole lot less trouble for everybody else if he'd
just go jump in the Bosphorus.

I felt a twinge of terror at the thought that the whole Time Service
might be permeated by Capistranos, all shopping around for the most
interestingly self-destructive way of changing the past.

Upstairs, the early light revealed eight sleepers, huddled two by two.
Our elderly married folks slept peacefully; the two pretty boys from
London looked sweaty and tousled after some busy buggery; Clotilde,
smiling, slept with her hand tucked between Lise's pale thighs, and
Lise's left hand was cupped cozily about Clotilde's maidenly but firm
right breast. I lay down on my lonely bed and slipped quickly into sleep.

Soon Capistrano woke me, and we woke the others. I felt ten thousand years old.

We had a breakfast of cold lamb and went out for a quick daylight walking tour of the city. Most of the interesting things had not yet been built, or else were still in early forms; we didn't stay long. At noon we went to the Augusteum to shunt. "Our next stop," Capistrano announced, "will be A.D. 532, where we will see the city of Justinian's time and witness the riots which destroyed it, making possible the construction of the finer and more grand city that won such eternal fame." We backed into the shadows of the ruined original Haghia Sophia, so that no passersby would be startled by the sight of ten people vanishing. I set all the timers. Capistrano produced his pitchpipe and gave the master signal. We shunted.

22.

Two weeks later we all returned down the line to 2059. I was dizzied, intoxicated, my soul full of Byzantium.

I had seen the highlights of a thousand years of greatness. The city of my dreams had come to life for me. The meat and wine of Byzantium had passed through my bowels.

From a Courier's professional point of view, the trip had been a good one, that is, uneventful. Our tourists had not entangled themselves in trouble, nor had any paradoxes been created, as far as we could tell. There had been a little friction only one night, when Capistrano, very drunk, tried to seduce Clotilde; he wasn't subtle about it, letting seduction shade into rape when she resisted, but I managed to separate them before her nails got into his eyes. In the morning he wouldn't believe it. "The blonde lesbian?" he asked. "I would stoop so low? You must dream it!" And then he insisted on going eight hours up the line to see if it had really happened. I had visions of a sober Capistrano taking his earlier sozzled self to task, and it scared me. I had to argue him out of it in a blunt and direct way, reminding him of the Time Patrol's regulation prohibiting anyone from engaging in conversation with himself of a different now-time basis, and threatening to report him if he tried it. Capistrano looked wounded, but he let the matter drop. And when we came down the line and he filed a report of his own, upon request, concerning my behavior as a Courier, he gave me the highest rating. Protopopolos told me that afterward.

"Your next trip," said Protopopolos, "will be as assistant to Metaxas, on the one-week tour."

"When do I leave?"

"In two weeks," he said. "Your layoff comes first, remember? And after you return from the trip with Metaxas, you begin soloing. Where will you spend your layoff?"

"I think I'll go down to Crete or Mykonos," I said, "and get a little rest on the beach."

The Time Service insists that Couriers take two-week vacations between trips. The Time Service doesn't believe in pushing its Couriers too hard. During layoffs, Couriers are completely at liberty. They can spend the whole time relaxing in now-time, as I proposed to do, or they can sign up with a time tour, or they can simply go hopping by themselves to any era that may interest them.

There's no charge for timer use when a Courier makes jumps up the line in his layoff periods. The Time Service wants to encourage its employees to feel at home in all periods of the past, and what better way than to allow unlimited free shunting?

Protopopolos looked a little disappointed when I said I'd spend my vacation sunning myself in the islands. "Don't you want to do some jumping?" he asked.

The idea of making time-jumps on my own at this stage of my career scared me, frankly. But I couldn't tell Protopopolos that. I also considered the point that in another month he'd be handing me the responsibility for the lives of an entire tour group. Maybe this conversation was part of the test of my qualifications. Were they trying to see if I had the guts to go jumping on my own?

Protopopolos seemed to be fishing for an answer.

I said, "On second thought, why waste a chance to do some jumping? I'll have a peek at post-Byzantine Istanbul."

"With a tour group?"

"On my own," I said.

23.

So I went jumping, smack into the Paradox of Discontinuity.

My first stop was the wardrobe department. I needed costumes suited for Istanbul of the sixteenth through nineteenth centuries. Instead of giving me a whole sequence of clothes to fit the changing fashions, they decked me out in an all-purpose Moslem rig, simple white robes of no particular era, nondescript sandals, long hair, and a straggly youthful beard. By way of pocket money they supplied me with a nice assortment of gold and silver pieces of the right eras, a little of everything that might have been circulating in medieval Turkey, including some bezants of Greek-ruled times, miscellaneous coinage of the sultans, and a good deal of Venetian gold. All this was installed in a currency belt that I wore just above my timer, the coins segregated from left to right according to centuries, so that I wouldn't get into trouble by offering an eighteenth-century dinar in a sixteenth-century market place. There was no charge for the money; the Time Service runs a continuous siphon of its own, circulating coinage between now-time and then-time for the benefit of its personnel, and a Courier going on holiday can sign out any reasonable amount to cover his expenses. To the Service it's only play money, anyway, infinitely replenishible at will. I like the system.

I took hypnosleep courses in Turkish and Arabic before I left. The Special Requests department fabricated a quick cover identity for me that would work well in any era of my intended visit: if questioned, I was supposed to identify myself as a Portuguese national who had been kidnapped on the high seas by Algerian pirates when ten years old, and raised as a Moslem in Algiers. That would account for flaws in my accent and for my vagueness about my background; if I had the misfortune to be interrogated by a real Portuguese, which wasn't likely, I could simply say that I couldn't remember much about my life in Lisbon and had forgotten the names of my forebears. So long as I kept my mouth shut, prayed toward Mecca five times a day, and watched my step, I wasn't likely to get into trouble. (Of course, if I landed in a really serious mess, I could escape by using my timer, but in the Time Service that's considered a coward's route, and also undesirable because of the implications of witchcraft that you leave behind when you vanish.)

All these preparations took a day and a half. Then they told me I was ready to jump. I set my timer for 500 B.P., picking the era at random, and jumped.

I arrived on August 14, 1559, at nine-thirty in the evening. The reigning sultan was the great Suleiman I, nearing the close of his epoch. Turkish armies threatened the peace of Europe; Istanbul was bursting with the wealth of conquest. I couldn't respond to this city as I had to the sparkling Constantinople of Justinian or Alexius, but that was a personal matter having to do with ancestry, chemistry, and historical affinity. Taken on its own merits, Suleiman's Istanbul was a city among cities.

I spent half the day roaming it. For an hour I watched a lovely mosque under construction, hoping it was the Suleimaniye, but later in the day I found the Suleimaniye, brand-new and glistening in the noon light. I made a special pilgrimage, covertly consulting a map I had smuggled with me, to find the mosque of Mehmet the Conqueror, which an earthquake would bring down in 1766. It was worth the walk. Toward midafternoon, after an inspection of the mosquified Haghia Sophia and the sad ruins of the Great Palace of Byzantium across the plaza (Sultan Ahmed's mosque would be rising there fifty years down the line), I made my way to the Covered Bazaar, thinking to buy a few small trinkets as souvenirs, and when I was no more than ten paces past the entrance I caught sight of my beloved guru Sam.

Consider the odds against that: with thousands of years in which to roam, the two of us coming on holiday to the same year and the same day and the same city, and meeting under the same roof!

He was clad in Moorish costume, straight out of *Othello*. There was no mistaking him; he was by far the tallest man in sight, and his coal-black skin glistened brilliantly against his white robes. I rushed up to him.

"Sam!" I cried. "Sam, you old black bastard, what luck to meet you *here*."

He whirled in surprise, frowned at me, looked puzzled. "I know you not," he said coldly.

"Don't let the beard fool you. It's me, Sam. Jud Elliott."

He glared. He growled. A crowd began to gather. I wondered if I had been wrong. Maybe this wasn't Sam, but Sam's multi-great-grandfather, made to look like his twin by a genetic fluke. No, I told myself, this is the authentic Sambo.

But then why is he pulling out that scimitar?

We had been talking in Turkish. I switched to English and said, "Listen, Sam, I don't know what's going on, but I'm willing to ride along with your act. Suppose we meet in half an hour outside Haghia Sophia, and we can—"

"Infidel dog!" he roared. "Beggar's spawn! Masturbator of pigs! Away from me! Away, cutpurse!"

He swished the scimitar menacingly above my head and continued to rave in Turkish. Suddenly in a lower voice he muttered, "I don't know who the hell you are, pal, but if you don't clear out of here fast I'm going to have to slice you in half." That much was in English. In Turkish again he cried, "Molester of infants! Drinker of toad's milk! Devourer of cameldung!"

This was no act. He genuinely didn't recognize me, and he genuinely didn't want anything to do with me. Baffled, I backed away from him, hustled down one of the subsidiary corridors of the bazaar, stepped out into the open, and hastily shunted myself ten years down the line. A couple of people saw me go, but faex on them; to a Turk of 1559 the world must have been full of efreets and jinni, and I was just one more phantom.

I didn't stay in 1569 more than five minutes. Sam's wild reaction to my greeting had me so mystified that I couldn't relax and see the sights. I had to have an explanation. So I hurried on down the line to 2059, materializing a block from the Covered Bazaar and nearly getting smeared by a taxi. A few latter-day Turks grinned and pointed at my medieval Turkish robes. The unsophisticated apes hadn't yet learned to take returning time-travelers for granted, I guess.

I went quickly to the nearest public communications booth, thumbed the plate, and put through a call to Sam.

"He is not at his home number," the master information output told me. "Should we trace him?"

"Yes, please," I said automatically.

A moment later I slapped myself for stupidity. Of course he won't be home, you idiot! He's up the line in 1559!

But the master communications network had already begun tracing him. Instead of doing the sensible thing and hanging up, I stood there like a moron, waiting for the inevitable news that the master communications network couldn't find him anywhere.

About three minutes went by. Then the bland voice said, "We have traced your party to Nairobi and he is standing by for your call. Please notify if you wish to proceed."

"Go ahead," I said, and Sam's ebony features blossomed on the screen.

"Is there trouble, child?" he asked.

"What are you doing in Nairobi?" I screamed.

"A little holiday among my own people. Should I not be here?"

"Look," I said, "I'm on my layoff between Courier jobs, and I've just been up the line to 1559 Istanbul, and I met you there."

"So?"

"How can you be there if you're in Nairobi?"

"The same way that there can be twenty-two specimens of your Arab instructor back there watching the Romans nail up Jesus," Sam said. "Sheet, man, when will you learn to think four-dimensionally?"

"So that's a different you up the line in 1559?"

"It better be, buster! He's there and I'm here!" Sam laughed. "A little thing like that shouldn't upset you, man. You're a Courier now, remember?"

"Wait. Wait. Here's what happened. I walked into the Covered Bazaar, see, and there you were in Moorish robes, and I let out this big whoop and ran up to you to say hello. And you didn't know me, Sam! You started waving your scimitar, and cursing me out, and you told me in English to get the hell away from you, and—"

"Well, hey, man, you know it's against regulations to talk to other time-travelers when you're up the line. Unless you set out from the same now-time as the other man, you're supposed to ignore him even if you see through his cover. Fraternization is prohibited because—"

"Yeah, sure, but it was *me*, Sam. I didn't think you'd pull rules on *me*. You didn't even know me, Sam!"

"That's obvious. But why are you so upset, kid?"

"It was like you had amnesia. It scared me."

"But I *couldn't* have known you."

"What are you talking about?"

Sam began to laugh. "The Paradox of Discontinuity! Don't tell me they never taught you that one!"

"They said something about it, but I never paid much attention to a lot of that stuff, Sam."

"Well, pay attention now. You know what year it was I took that Istanbul trip?"

"No."

"It was 2056, '55, someplace back there. And I didn't meet you until three or four years later—this spring, it was. So the Sam you found in 1559 never saw you before. Discontinuity, see? You were working from a now-time basis of 2059, and I was working from a basis of maybe '55, and so you were a stranger to me, but I wasn't a stranger to you. That's one reason why Couriers aren't supposed to talk to friends they run into by accident up the line."

I began to see.

"I begin to see," I said.

"To me," said Sam, "you were some dumb fresh kid trying to make trouble, maybe even a Time Patrol fink. I didn't know you and I didn't want anything to do with you. Now that I think about it a little, I remember something like that happening when I was there. Somebody from down the line bothering me in the bazaar. Funny that I never connected him with you, though!"

"I had a fake beard on, up the line."

"That must have been it. Well, listen, are you all straightened out now?"

"The Paradox of Discontinuity, Sam. Sure."

"You'll remember to keep clear of old friends when you're up the line?"

"You bet. Christ, Sam, you really terrified me with that scimitar!"

"Otherwise, how's it going?"

"Great," I said. "It's really great."

"Watch those paradoxes, kid," Sam said, and blew me a kiss.

Much relieved, I stepped out of the booth and went up the line to 1550 to watch them build the mosque of Suleiman the Magnificent.

24.

Themistoklis Metaxas was the chief Courier for my second time-tour of Byzantium. From the moment I met him I sensed that this man was going to play a major role in my destiny, and I was right.

Metaxas was bantam-sized, maybe 1.5 meters tall. His skull was triangular, flat on top and pointed at the chin. His hair, thick and curly, was going gray. I guess he was about fifty years old. He had small glossy dark eyes, heavy brows, and a big sharp slab of a nose. He kept his lips curled inward so that he didn't seem to have lips at all. There was no fat on him anywhere. He was unusually strong. His voice was low and compelling.

Metaxas had charisma. Or should I call it chutzpah?

A little of both, I think. For him the whole universe revolved around Themistoklis Metaxas; suns were born only that they might shed starlight on Themistoklis Metaxas; the Benchley Effect had been invented solely to enable Themistoklis Metaxas to walk through the ages. If he ever died, the cosmos would crumble.

He had been one of the first Time Couriers ever hired, more than fifteen years ago. If he had cared to have the job, he could have been the head of the entire Courier Service by now, with a platoon of wanton secretaries and no need to battle fleas in old Byzantium. By choice, though, Metaxas remained a Courier on active duty, doing nothing but the Byzantium run. He practically regarded himself as a Byzantine citizen, and even spent his layoffs there, in a villa he had acquired in the suburbs of the early twelfth century.

He was engaged on the side in a variety of small and large illegalities; they might be interrupted if he retired as a Courier, so he didn't retire. The Time Patrol was terrified of him and let him have his own way in everything. Of course, Metaxas had more sense than to meddle with the past in any way that might cause serious changes in now-time, but aside from that his plunderings up the line were totally uninhibited.

When I met him for the first time, he said to me, "You haven't lived until you've laid one of your own ancestors."

25.

It was a big group: twelve tourists, Metaxas, and me. They always loaded a few extras into his tours because he was such an unusually capable Courier and in such great demand. I tagged along as an assistant, soaking up experience against my first solo trip, which would be coming next time.

Our dozen included three young and pretty single girls, Princeton co-eds making the Byzantium trip on gifts from their parents, who wanted them to learn something; two of the customary well-to-do middle-aged couples, one from Indianapolis and one from Milan; two youngish interior decorators, male and queer, from Beirut; a recently divorced response manipulator from New York, around forty-five and hungry for women; a puffy-faced little high-school teacher from Milwaukee, trying to improve his mind, and his wife; in short, the customary sampling.

At the end of the first introductory session all three of the Princeton girls, both interior decorators, and the Indianapolis wife were visibly hungering to go to bed with Metaxas. Nobody paid much attention to me.

"It will be different after the tour starts," said Metaxas consolingly. "Several of the girls will become available to you. You *do* want the girls, don't you?"

He was right. On our first night up the line he picked one of the Princeton girls for himself, and the other two resigned themselves speedily to accepting the second best. For some reason, Metaxas chose a pugnosed redhead with splashy freckles and big feet. He left for me a long, cool, sleek brunette, so flawless in every way that she was obviously the product of one of the world's finest helix men, and a cute, cheerful honey-blonde with warm eyes, smooth flesh, and the breasts of a twelve-year-old. I picked the brunette and regretted it; she came on in bed like something made of plastic. Toward dawn I traded her for the blonde and had a better time.

Metaxas was a tremendous Courier. He knew everybody and everything, and maneuvered us into superb positions for the big events.

"We are now," he said, "in January, 532. The Emperor Justinian rules. His ambition is to conquer the world and govern it from Constantinople, but most of his great achievements lie ahead. The city, as you see, still looks much as it did in the last century. In front of you is the Great Palace; to the rear is the rebuilt Haghia Sophia of Theodosius II, following the old basilica plan, not yet reconstructed with the familiar domes. The city is tense; there will soon be civil disorder. Come this way."

Shivering in the cold, we followed Metaxas through the city, down byways and avenues I had not traveled when I came this way earlier with Capistrano. Never once on this trip did I catch sight of my other self or Capistrano or any of that group; one of Metaxas' legendary skills was his ability to find new approaches to the standard scenes.

Of course, he had to. At this moment there were fifty or a hundred Metaxases leading tours through Justinian's city. As a matter of professional pride he wouldn't want to intersect any of those other selves.

"There are two factions in Constantinople now," said Metaxas. "The Blues and the Greens, they are called. They consist of perhaps a thousand men on each side, all troublemakers, and far more influential than their numbers indicate. The factions are something less than political parties, something more than mere supporters of sports teams, but they have characteristics of both. The Blues are more aristocratic; the Greens have links to the lower classes and the commercial strata. Each faction backs a team in the Hippodrome games, and each backs a certain course of governmental policies. Justinian has long been sympathetic to the Blues, and the Greens mistrust him. But as emperor he has tried to appear neutral. He would actually like to suppress both factions as threats to his power. Each night now the factions run wild in the streets. Look: those are the Blues."

Metaxas nodded at a cluster of insolent-looking bravos across the way: eight or nine idling men with long tumbles of thick hair to their shoulders, and festoons of beards and mustaches. They had cut back only the hair on the front of their heads. Their tunics were drawn in tight at the wrists, but flared out enormously from there to the shoulders; they wore gaudy capes and breeches and carried short two-edged swords. They looked brutal and dangerous.

"Wait here," said Metaxas, and went over to them.

The Blues greeted him like an old friend. They clapped him on the back, laughed, shouted in glee. I couldn't hear the conversation, but I saw Metaxas grasping hands, talking quickly, articulately, confidently. One of the Blues offered him a flask of wine and he took a deep drink; then, hugging the man in mock tipsiness, Metaxas cunningly whisked the Blue's sword from its sheath and pretended to run him through. The rowdies capered and applauded. Now Metaxas pointed at us; there were nods of agreement, oglings of the girls, winks, gestures. Finally we were summoned across the street.

"Our friends invite us to the Hippodrome as their guests," said Metaxas. "The races begin next week. Tonight we are permitted to join them in their revels."

I could hardly believe it. When I'd been here with Capistrano, we skulked about, keeping out of sight, for this was a time of rape and murder by night, and all laws ceased to function after dark. How did Metaxas dare to bring us so close to the criminals?

He dared. And that night we roamed Constantinople, watching the Blues rob, ravish, and kill. For other citizens, death lay just around any corner; we were immune, privileged witnesses to the reign of terror. Metaxas presided over the nightmare prowl like a sawed-off Satan, cavorting with his Blue friends and even fingering one or two victims for them.

In the morning it seemed like a dream. The phantoms of violence vanished with the night; by pale winter sunlight we inspected the city and listened to Metaxas' historical commentary.

"Justinian," he said, "was a great conqueror, a great lawgiver, a great diplomat, and a great builder. This is history's verdict. We also have the *Secret History* of Procopius, which says that Justinian was both a knave and a fool, and that his wife Theodora was a demonic whorish villainess. I know this Procopius: a good man, a clever writer, something of a puritan, a little too gullible. But he's right about Justinian and Theodora. Justinian is a great man in the great things and a terribly evil man in the petty things. Theodora"—he spat—"is a whore among whores. She dances naked at dinners of state; she exhibits her body in public; she sleeps with her servants. I've heard she gives herself to dogs and donkeys, too. She's every bit as depraved as Procopius claims."

Metaxas' eyes twinkled. I knew without being told that he must have shared Theodora's bed.

Later that day he whispered, "I can arrange it for you. The risks are slight. Did you ever dream you could sleep with the Empress of Byzantium?"

"The risks—"

"What risks? You have your timer! You can get free! Listen to me, boy, she's an acrobat! She wraps her heels around your ears. She *consumes* you. I can fix it up for you. The Empress of Byzantium! Justinian's wife!"

"Not this trip," I blurted. "Some other time. I'm still too new at this business."

"You're afraid of her."

"I'm not ready to fuck an empress just yet," I said solemnly.

"Everybody else does it!"

"Couriers?"

"Most of them."

"On my next trip," I promised. The idea appalled me. I had to turn it off somehow. Metaxas misunderstood; I wasn't shy, or afraid of being caught by Justinian, or anything like that; but I couldn't bring myself to intersect with history that way. Traveling up the line was still fantasy for me; humping the celebrated monstress Theodora would make the fantasy all too real. Metaxas laughed at me, and for a while I think he felt contempt for me. But afterward he said, "It's okay. Don't let me rush you into things. When you're ready for her, though, don't miss her. I recommend her personally."

26.

We stayed around for a couple of days to watch the early phases of the riots. The New Year's Games were about to begin, and the Blues and Greens were growing more unruly. Their rough-necking was verging on anarchy; no one was safe in the streets after dark. Justinian worriedly ordered the factions to halt their maraudings, and various ringleaders were arrested. Seven were condemned to death, four by decapitation because they were caught carrying weapons, three by hanging on grounds of conspiracy.

Metaxas took us to see the performance. One of the Blues survived his first hanging when the rope broke under his weight. The imperial guards put him up there again, and again the gallows couldn't finish him, though the rope left fiery marks on his throat. So they put him aside for a while and strung up a Green, and bungled that job twice too; they were about to put the battered victims through a third hanging apiece when some outraged monks came boiling out of their monastery, grabbed the men in the midst of the confusion, and spirited them across the Golden Horn by rowboat to sanctuary in some church. Metaxas, who had seen all this before, cackled wildly at the fun. It seemed to me that his face peered at me from a thousand places in the crowd that had turned out for the executions.

Then the racing season began at the Hippodrome, and we went as guests of Metaxas' friendly gang of Blues. We had plenty of company; 100,000 Byzantines were in the stands. The tiers of marble seats were crowded far past capacity, but space had been saved for us.

I hunted for myself in the stands, knowing that I sat somewhere else here with Capistrano and that tour; but in the crush I couldn't catch a glimpse of myself. I saw plenty of Metaxas, though.

The blonde Princetonian gasped when we got to our seats. "Look there!" she said. "The things from Istanbul!" Down the center of the arena was a row of familiar monuments, marking the boundary between the outward and inward courses of the track. The serpent column from Delphi, brought here by Constantine, was there, and the great obelisk of Thutmose III, stolen out of Egypt by the first Theodosius. The blonde remembered them from Istanbul down the line, where they still stand, though the Hippodrome itself is gone.

"But where's the third one?" she asked.

Metaxas said softly, "The other obelisk has not yet been erected. Best not to talk about it."

It was the third day of the races—the fatal day. An ugly mood gripped this arena where emperors had been made and unmade. Yesterday and the day before, I knew, there had been nasty outcries when Justinian appeared in the imperial box; the crowd had yelled to him to free the imprisoned ringleaders of the factions, but he had ignored the shouts and let the races proceed. Today, January 13, Constantinople would erupt. Time-tourists love catastrophes; this would be a good one. I knew. I had seen it already.

Below, officials were completing the preliminary rituals. Imperial guards, standards flying, paraded grandly. Those leaders of the Blues and Greens who were not in jail exchanged chilly ceremonial greetings. Now the mob stirred, and Justinian entered his box, a man of middle height, rather plump, with a round, florid face. Empress Theodora followed. She wore clinging, diaphanous silks, and she had rouged her nipples; they blazed through the fabric like beacons.

Justinian mounted the steps of his box. The cries began: "Free them! Let them out!" Serenely he lifted a fold of his purple robe and blessed the audience with the sign of the Cross, three times, once toward the center block of seats, then to the right, then to the left. The uproar grew. He threw a white kerchief down. Let the games begin! Theodora stretched and yawned and pulled up her robe to study the contours of her thighs. The stable doors burst open. Out came the first four chariots.

They were quadrigas, four-horse vehicles; the audience forgot about politics as, wheel to wheel, the chariots went into action. Metaxas said pleasantly, "Theodora has been to bed with each of the drivers. I wonder which one is her favorite." The empress looked profoundly bored. I had been surprised to find her here, the last time: I had thought that empresses were barred from the Hippodrome. As indeed they were, but Theodora made her own rules.

The charioteers hustled down to the spina, the row of monuments, and came round and back up the course. A race ran seven rounds; seven ostrich eggs were set out on a stand, and as each round was completed one egg was removed. We watched two races. Then Metaxas said, "Let us shunt forward by one hour and get to the climax of this." Only Metaxas would pull a bit like that: we adjusted all the timers and shunted, en masse, in casual disregard of the rules for public jumping. When we reappeared in the Hippodrome, the sixth race was about to begin.

"Now starts the trouble," said Metaxas happily.

The race was run. But as the victor came forth to receive his crown, a booming voice bellowed from out of a group of Blues, "Long live the Greens and Blues!"

An instant later, from the seats of the Greens, came the answering cry: "Long live the Blues and Greens!"

"The factions are uniting against Justinian," Metaxas said, quietly, schoolmasterishly. The chaos that was engulfing the stadium didn't ruffle him.

"Long live the Greens and Blues!"

"Long live the Blues and Greens!"

"Long live the Greens and Blues!"

"Victory!"

"Victory!"

"Victory!"

And the one word, "Victory!" became a mighty cry from thousands of throats. "*Nika! Nika!* Victory!"

Theodora laughed. Justinian, scowling, conferred with officers of his imperial guard. Greens and Blues marched from the Hippodrome, followed by a happy, screaming mob bent on destruction. We hung back, keeping a judicious distance; I caught sight of other equally cautious little groups of spectators, and knew they were no Byzantines.

Torches flared in the streets. The imperial prison was aflame. The prisoners were free, the jailers were burning. Justinian's own guard, afraid to interfere, looked on soberly. The rioters piled faggots against the gate of the Great Palace, across the plaza from the Hippodrome. Soon the palace was on fire. Theodosius' Haghia Sophia was aflame; bearded priests, waving precious icons, appeared on its blazing roof and toppled back into the inferno. The senate house caught fire. It was a glorious orgy of destruction. Whenever snarling rioters approached us, we adjusted timers and shunted down the line, taking care to jump no more than ten or fifteen minutes at a hop, so that we wouldn't reappear right inside some fire that hadn't been set when we shunted.

"*Nika! Nika!*"

Constantinople's sky was black with oily smoke, and flames danced on the horizon. Metaxas, his wedge-shaped face smudged and sooty, his eyes glinting with excitement, seemed constantly on the verge of breaking away from us and going to join the destroyers.

"The firemen themselves are looting," he called to us. "And look—the Blues burn the houses of the Greens, and the Greens burn the houses of the Blues!"

A tremendous exodus was under way, as terrified citizens streamed toward the docks and begged the boatmen to ferry them to the Asian side. Unharmed, invulnerable, we moved through the holocaust, witnessing the walls of the old Haghia Sophia collapse, watching flames sweep the Great Palace, observing the behavior of the looters and the arsonists and the rapists who paused in fire-spattered alleys to pump some screaming silk-clad noblewoman full of proletarian jissom.

Metaxas skillfully edited the riots for us; he had timed everything dozens of visits ago, and he knew exactly which highlights to hit.

"Now we shunt forward six hours and forty minutes." he said.

"Now we jump three hours and eight minutes."

"Now we jump an hour and a half."

"Now we jump two days."

We saw everything that mattered. With the city still aflame, Justinian sent bishops and priests forth bearing sacred relics, a piece of the True Cross, the rod of Moses, the horn of Abraham's ram, the bones of martyrs; the frightened clerics paraded bravely about, asking for a miracle, but no miracles came, only cascades of brickbats and stones. A general led forty guardsmen out to protect the holy men. "That is the famous Belisarius," said Metaxas. Messages came from the emperor, announcing the deposing of unpopular officials; but churches were sacked, the imperial library given the torch, the baths of Zeuxippus were destroyed.

On January 18, Justinian was bold enough to appear publicly in the Hippodrome to call for peace. He was hissed down by the Greens and fled as stone-throwing began. We saw a worthless prince named Hypatius proclaimed as emperor by the rebels in the Square of Constantine; we saw General Belisarius march through the smoldering city in defense of Justinian; we saw the butchery of the insurgents.

We saw everything. I understood why Metaxas was the most coveted of Couriers. Capistrano had done his best to give his people an exciting show, but he had wasted too much time in the early phases. Metaxas, leaping brilliantly over hours and days, unveiled the entire catastrophe for us, and brought us at last to the morning when order was restored and a shaken Justinian rode through the charred ruins of Constantinople. By a red dawn we saw the clouds of ash still dancing in the air. Justinian studied the blackened hull of Haghia Sophia, and we studied Justinian.

Metaxas said, "He is planning the new cathedral. He will make it the greatest shrine since Solomon's Temple in Jerusalem. Come: we have seen enough destruction. Now let us see the birth of beauty. Down the line, all of you! Five years and ten months down the line, and behold Haghia Sophia!"

27.

On your next layoff," said Metaxas, "visit me at my villa. I live there now in 1105. It is a good time to be in Byzantium; Alexius Comnenus rules and rules wisely. I'll have a lusty wench ready for you, and plenty of wine. You'll come?"

I was lost in admiration for the sharp-faced little man. We were nearing the end of our tour, with only the Turkish Conquest yet to do, and he had revealed to me in a stunning way the difference between an inspired Courier and a merely competent one.

Only a lifetime of dedication to the task could achieve such results, could provide such a show.

Metaxas hadn't just taken us to the standard highlights. He had shown us any number of minor events, splicing us in for an hour here, two hours there, creating for us a glorious mosaic of Byzantine history that dimmed the luster of the mosaics of Haghia Sophia. Other Couriers made a dozen stops, perhaps; Metaxas made more than fifty.

He had a special fondness for the foolish emperors. We had listened to a speech of Michael II, the Stammerer, and we had watched the antics of Michael III, the Drunkard, and we had attended the baptism of the fifth Constantine, who had the misfortune to soil the font and was known for the rest of his life as Constantine Copronymus, Constantine the Pisser. Metaxas was completely at home in Byzantium in any one of a thousand years. Coolly, easily, confidently, he ranged through the eras.

The villa he maintained was a mark of his confidence and his audacity. No other Courier had ever dared to create a second identity for himself up the line, spending all his holidays as a citizen of the past. Metaxas ran his villa on a now-time basis; when he had to leave it for two weeks to run a tour, he took care to return to it two weeks after his departure. He never overlapped himself, never let himself go to it at a time when he was already in residence; there was only one Metaxas permitted to use it, and that was the now-time Metaxas. He had bought the villa ten years ago in his double now-time: 2049 down the line, 1095 in Byzantium. And he had maintained his basis with precision; it was ten years later for him in both places. I promised to visit him in 1105. It would be an honor, I said.

He grinned and said, "I'll introduce you to my great-great-multi-great-grandmother when you come, too. She's a terrific lay. You remember what I told you about screwing your own ancestors? There's nothing finer!"

I was stunned. "Does she know who you are?"

"Don't talk nonsense," said Metaxas. "Would I break the first rule of the Time Service? Would I even hint to anyone up the line that I came from the future? *Would I?* Even Themistoklis Metaxas abides by *that* rule!"

Like the moody Capistrano, Metaxas had devoted much effort to hunting out his ancestors. His motives were altogether different, though. Capistrano was plotting an elaborate suicide, but Metaxas was obsessed with transtemporal incest.

"Isn't it risky?" I asked.

"Just take your pills and you're safe, and so is she."

"I mean the Time Patrol—"

"You make sure they don't find out," said Metaxas. "That way it isn't risky."

"If you happen to get her pregnant, you might become your own ancestor."

"Groovy," said Metaxas.

"But—"

"People don't get people pregnant by accident any more, boy. Of course," he added, "some day I might want to knock her up on purpose."

I felt the time-winds blowing up a gale.

I said, "You're talking anarchy!"

"Nihilism, to be more accurate. Look here, Jud, look at this book. I've got all my female ancestors listed, hundreds of them, from the nineteenth century back to the tenth. Nobody else in the world has a book like this except maybe some snotty ex-kings and queens, and even they don't have it this complete."

"There's Capistrano," I said.

"He goes back only to the fourteenth century! Anyway, he's sick in the head. You know why he does his genealogies?"

"Yes."

"He's pretty sick, isn't he?"

"Yes," I said. "But tell me, why are you so eager to sleep with your own ancestors?"

"Do you really want to know?"

"Really."

Metaxas said, "My father was a cold, hateful man. He beat his children every morning before breakfast for exercise. *His* father was a cold, hateful man. He forced his children to live like slaves. *His* father— I come from a long line of tyrannical authoritarian dictatorial males. I despise them all. It is my form of rebellion against the father-image. I go on and on through the past, seducing the wives and sisters and daughters of these men whom I loathe. Thus I puncture their icy smugness."

"In that case, then, to be perfectly consistent, you must have—your own mother—begun with—"

"I draw the line at abominations," said Metaxas.

"I see."

"But my grandmother, yes! And several great-grandmothers! And on and on and on!" His eyes glowed. It was a divine mission with him. "I have ploughed through twenty, thirty generations already, and I will keep on for thirty more!" Metaxas laughed his shrill, satanic laugh. "Besides," he said, "I enjoy a good lay as much as the next man. Others seduce at random; Metaxas seduces *systematically!* It gives meaning and structure to my life. This interests you, eh?"

"Well—"

"It is life's most intense joy, what I do."

I pictured a row of naked women lying side by side, reaching off to infinity. Every one of them had the wedge-shaped head and sharp features of Themistoklis Metaxas. And Metaxas was moving patiently up the line, pausing to stick it into this one, and the one next to her, and the next, and the next, and in his tireless fashion he balled right up the line until the spread-legged women grew hairy and chinless, the womenfolk of Pithecanthropus erectus, and there was Metaxas erectus still jazzing his way back to the beginning of time. Bravo, Metaxas! Bravo!

"Why don't you try it sometime?" he asked.

"Well—"

"They tell me you are of Greek descent."

"On my mother's side, yes."

"Then probably your ancestors lived right here in Constantinople. No Greek worth anything would have lived in Greece itself at this time. At this very moment a luscious ancestress of yours is in this very city!"

"Well—"

"Find her!" cried Metaxas. "Fuck her! It is joy! It is ecstasy! Defy space and time! Stick your finger in God's eye!"

"I'm not sure I really want to," I said. But I did.

28.

As I say, Metaxas transformed my life. He changed my destinies in many ways, not all of them good. But one good thing he did for me was to give me confidence. His charisma and his chutzpah both rubbed off on me. I learned arrogance from Metaxas.

Up until this point I had been a modest and self-effacing young man, at least while I was around my elders. Especially in my Time Service aspect I had been unpushy and callow. I did a lot of forelock-tugging and no doubt came across even more naive than I really was. I acted this way because I was young and had a lot to learn, not only about myself, which everybody does, but also about the workings of the Time Service. So far I had met a lot of men who were older, smarter, slicker, and more corrupt than myself, and I had treated them with deference: Sam, Dajani, Jeff Monroe, Sid Buonocore, Capistrano. But now I was with Metaxas, who was the oldest, smartest, slickest and most corrupt of them all, and he imparted momentum to me, so that I stopped orbiting other men and took up a trajectory of my own.

Later I found out that this is one of Metaxas' functions in the Time Service. He takes moist-eyed young Couriers-in-training and fills them full of the swagger they need to be successful operators in their own right.

When I got back from my tour with Metaxas I no longer feared my first solo as a Courier. I was ready to go. Metaxas had showed me how a Courier can be a kind of artist, assembling a portrait of the past for his clients, and that was what I wanted to be. The risks and responsibilities didn't trouble me now.

Protopopolos said, "When you come back from your layoff, you'll take six people out on the one-week tour."

"I'll skip the layoff. I'm ready to leave right now!"

"Well, your tourists aren't. Anyway, the law says you've got to rest between trips. So rest. I'll see you back here in two weeks, Jud."

So I had a holiday against my will. I was tempted to accept Metaxas' invitation to his villa in 1105, but it occurred to me that maybe Metaxas had had enough of my company for a while. Then I toyed with the idea of signing up with a time-tour to Hastings or Waterloo or even back to the Crucifixion to count the Dajanis. But I passed that up, too. Now that I was on the threshold of leading a tour myself, I didn't want to have to be led by somebody else, not just at the moment. I needed to be more secure in my new-found confidence before I dropped down under some other Courier's leadership again.

I dithered around in now-time Istanbul for three days, doing nothing special. Mainly I hung around the Time Service headquarters, playing stochastic chess with Kolettis and Melamed, who also happened to be off duty at this time. On the fourth day I hopped a shortshot for Athens. I didn't know why I was going there until I got there.

I was up on the Acropolis when I realized what my mission was. I was wandering around the ruins, fending off the peddlers of hologram slides and the guided-tour hucksters, when an advert globe came drifting toward me. It hovered about four feet away from me at eye level, radiating a flickering green glow designed to compel my attention, and said, "Good afternoon. We hope you're enjoying your visit to twenty-first-century Athens. Now that you've seen the picturesque ruins, how would you like to see the Parthenon as it *really* looked? See the Greece of Socrates and Aristophanes? Your local Time Service office is on Aeolou Street, just opposite the Central Post Office, and—"

Half an hour later I checked in at the Aeolou Street headquarters, identified myself as a Courier on vacation, and outfitted myself for a shunt up the line.

Not to the Greece of Socrates and Aristophanes, though.

I was heading for the Greece of the prosaic year 1997, when Konstantin Passalidis was elected mayor of Sparta.

Konstantin Passalidis was my mother's father. I was about to start tracing my ancestral seed back to its sprouting place.

Dressed in the stark, itchy clothes of the late twentieth century, and carrying crisp and colorful obsolete banknotes, I shunted back sixty years and caught the first pod from Athens to Sparta. Pod service was brand new in Greece in 1997, and I was in mortal terror of a phaseout all the way down, but the alignment held true and I got to Sparta in one piece.

Sparta was remarkably hideous.

The present Sparta is not, of course, a linear descendant of the old militaristic place that caused so much trouble for Athens. That Sparta faded away gradually, and vanished altogether in medieval times. The new Sparta was founded in the early nineteenth century on the old site. In Grandfather Passilidis' heyday it was a city of about 80,000 people, having grown rapidly after the installation of Greece's first fusion-power plant there in the 1980's.

It consisted of hundreds of identical apartment houses of gray brick, arranged in perfectly straight rows. Every one of them was ten stories high, decked with lemon-colored balconies on every floor, and about as appealing as a jail. At one end of this barracks-like city was the shining dome of the power plant; at the other was a downtown section of taverns, banks, and municipal offices. It was quite charming, if you find brutality charming.

I got off the pod and walked downtown. There weren't any master information outputs to be seen on the streets—I guess the network hadn't yet gone into operation here—but I had no trouble finding Mayor Passilidis. I stopped at a tavern for a quick *ouzo* and said, "Where can I find Mayor Passilidis?" and a dozen friendly Spartans escorted me to City Hall.

His receptionist was a dark-haired girl of about twenty with big breasts and a faint mustache. Her Minoan Revival bodice was neatly calculated to distract a man's attention from the shortcomings of her face. Wiggling those pink-tipped meaty globes at me, she said huskily, "Can I help you?"

"I'd like to see Mayor Passilidis. I'm from an American newspaper. We're doing an article on Greece's ten most dynamic young men, and we feel that Mr. Passilidis—"

It didn't sound convincing even to me. I stood there studying the beads of sweat on the white mounds of her bosom, waiting for her to turn me away. But she bought the story unhesitatingly, and with a minimum of delay I was escorted into His Honor's office.

"A pleasure to have you here," my grandfather said in perfect English. "Won't you sit down? Can I get you a martini, maybe? Or if you'd prefer a weed—"

I froze. I panicked. I didn't even take his hand when he offered it to me.

The sight of Konstantin Passilidis terrified me.

I had never seen my grandfather before, of course. He was gunned down by an Abolitionist hoodlum in 2010, long before I was born—one of the many victims of the Year of Assassins.

Time-travel had never seemed so frighteningly real to me as it did right now. Justinian in the imperial box at the Hippodrome was nothing at all compared to Konstantin Passilidis greeting me in his office in Sparta.

He was in his early thirties, a boy wonder of his time. His hair was dark and curly, just beginning to gray at the fringes, and he wore a little clipped mustache and a ring in his left ear. What terrified me so much was our physical resemblance. He could have been my older brother.

After an endless moment I snapped out of my freeze. He was a little puzzled, I guess, but he courteously offered me refreshment again, and I declined, telling him I didn't indulge, and somehow I found enough poise to launch my "interview" of him.

We talked about his political career and all the wonderful things he planned to do for Sparta and for Greece. Just as I was starting to work the conversation around to the personal side, to his family background, he looked at his watch and said, "It's time for lunch. Will you be my guest?"

What he had in mind was a typical Mediterranean siesta, closing the office down for three hours and going home. We drove there in his little electric runabout, with the mayor himself at the steering rod. He lived in one of the gray apartment houses, like any ordinary citizen: four humble rooms on the fifth floor.

"I'd like you to meet my wife," Mayor Passilidis said. "Katina, this is an American newspaperman, Jud Elliott. He wants to write about my career."

I stared at my grandmother.

My grandmother stared at me.

We both gasped. We were both amazed.

29

She was beautiful, the way the girls on the Minoan murals are beautiful. Dark, very dark, with black hair, olive skin, dark eyes. Peasant strength to her. She didn't expose her breasts the way the fashionable mustachioed receptionist had done, but her thin blouse wasn't very concealing. They were high and round. Her hips were broad. She was lush, fertile, abundant. I suppose she was about twenty-three years old, perhaps twenty-four.

It was lust at first sight. Her beauty, her simplicity, her warmth, captivated me instantly. I felt a familiar tickling in the scrotum and a familiar tightening of the glutei. I longed to rip away her clothing and sink myself deep into her hot tangled black shrubbery.

This was not a Metaxian incestuous wish. It was an innocent and purely animal reaction.

In that onrushing tide of yearning I didn't even think of her as my grandmother. I thought of her only as a young and fantastically desirable woman. A couple of ticks later I realized on an emotional level who she was, and I went limp at once.

She was Grandma Passilidis. And I remembered Grandma Passilidis.

I used to visit her at the senior citizens' camp near Tampa. She died when I was fourteen, in '49, and though she was only in her seventies then, she had always seemed terribly old and decrepit to me, a withered, shrunken, palsied little woman who wore black clothing all the time. Only her eyes—my God, her dark, liquid, warm, shining eyes!—had ever given any hint that she might once have been a healthy and vital human being.

Grandma Passilidis had had all kinds of diseases, feminine things—

prolapses of the uterus or whatever it is they get—and then kidney breakdowns and the rest. She had been through a dozen or more organ transplants, but nothing had helped, and all through my childhood she had inexorably declined. I was always hearing of some new crisis on her road to the grave, the poor old lady!

Here was the same poor old lady, miraculously relieved of her burden of years. And here was I, mentally snuggling between the thighs of my mother's mother. O vile impiety, that man should travel backward through time and think such thoughts!

Young Mrs. Passilidis' reaction to me was equally potent, although not at all lustful. For her, sex began and ended with the mayoral pecker. She stared at me not in desire but in astonishment and blurted finally, "Konstantin, he looks just like you!"

"Indeed?" said Mayor Passilidis. He hadn't noticed it before.

His wife propelled us both toward the living-room mirror, giggling and excited. The soft masses of her bosom jostled up against me and I began to sweat. "Look!" she cried. "Look there? Like brothers you are!"

"Amazing," said Mayor Passilidis.

"An incredible coincidence," I said. "Your hair is thicker, and I'm a little taller, but—"

"Yes! Yes!" The mayor clapped his hands. "Can it be that we are related?"

"Impossible," I said solemnly. "My family's from Boston. Old New England stock. Nevertheless it *is* amazing. You're sure you didn't have ancestors on the Mayflower, Mr. Passilidis?"

"Not unless there was a Greek steward on board."

"I doubt that."

"So do I. I am pure Greek on both sides for many generations," he said.

"I'd like to talk about that with you a little if I could," I said casually. "For example, I'd like to know—"

Just then a sleepy and completely naked five-year-old girl came out of one of the bedrooms. She planted herself shamelessly before me and asked me who I was. How sweet, I thought. That saucy little rump, that pink little slit—how *clean* little girls always look when they're naked. Before puberty messes them up.

Passilidis said proudly, "This is my daughter Diana."

A voice of thunder said in my brain, "THE NAKEDNESS OF THY MOTHER SHALT THOU NOT UNCOVER."

I looked away, shattered, and covered my confusion with a coughing fit. Little Diana's fleeceless labia blazed in my soul. As though sensing that I saw something improper about the child's bareness, Katina Passilidis hustled a pair of panties onto her.

I was still shaking. Passilidis, puzzled, uncorked some retsina. We sat on the balcony in the bright midday light. Below, some schoolchildren waved and shouted greetings to the mayor. Little Diana toddled out to be played with, and I tousled her fluffy hair and pressed the tip of her nose and felt very, very strange about all of this.

My grandmother provided a handsome lunch of boiled lamb and pastitsio. We went through a bottle and a half of retsina. I finished pumping the mayor about politics and shifted to the topic of his ancestors. "Have your people always lived in Sparta?" I asked.

"Oh, no," he said. "My grandfather's people came here a century ago from Cyprus. That is, on my father's side. On my mother's side I am Athenian, for many generations back."

"That's the Markezinis family?" I said.

He gave me a queer look. "Why, yes! How did you—"

"Something I came across while I was reading up on you," I said hurriedly.

Passilidis let the point pass. Now that he was on the subject of his family he grew expansive—maybe it was the wine—and favored me with the genealogical details. "My father's people were on Cyprus for at least a thousand years," he said. "There was a Passilidis there when the Crusaders came. On the other hand, my mother's ancestors came to Athens only in the nineteenth century, after the defeat of the Turks. Before that they lived in Shqiperi."

"Shqiperi?"

"Albania. They settled there in the thirteenth century when the Latins seized Constantinople. And then they remained, through the Serbians, through the Turks, through the time of Skanderbeg the rebel, always retaining their Greek heritage against all difficulties."

My ears prickled. "You mentioned Constantinople? You can trace your ancestry there?"

Passilidis smiled. "Do you know Byzantine history?"

"Slightly," I said.

"Perhaps you know that in the year 1204 the Crusaders seized Constantinople and ruled it for a while as a Latin kingdom. The Byzantine nobility fled, and several new Byzantine splinter states formed—one in Asia Minor, one on the Black Sea, and one in the west, in Albania. My ancestors followed Michael Angelus Comnenus into Albania, rather than submit to the rule of the Crusaders."

"I see." I was trembling again. "And the family name? It was Markezinis even back then?"

"Oh, no, Markezinis is a late Greek name! In Byzantium we were of the Ducas family."

"You *were?*" I gasped. It was as if he had been a German claiming Hohenzollern blood, or an Englishman laying claim to Plantagenet genes. "Ducas! Really?"

I had seen the gleaming palaces of the Ducas family. I had watched forty proud Ducases march clad in cloth of gold through the streets of Constantinople, to celebrate the rise of their cousin Constantine to the imperial throne. If Passilidis was a Ducas, *I* was a Ducas.

"Of course," he said, "the family was very large, and I believe we were of a minor branch. Still, it is something to take pride in, descent from such a family."

"It certainly is. Could you give me the names of any of your Byzantine ancestors, maybe? The first names?"

I must have sounded as though I planned to look them up the next time I was in Byzantium. Which I did, but Passilidis wasn't supposed to suspect that, because time-travel hadn't been invented yet.

He frowned and said, "Do you need this for the article you are writing?"

"No, not really. I'm just curious."

"You seem to know more than a little about Byzantium." It worried him that an American barbarian would recognize the name of a famous Byzantine family.

I said, "Just casual knowledge. I studied it in school."

"Sadly, I can give you no names. This information has not come down to us. But perhaps some day, when I have retired from politics, I will search the old records—"

My grandmother poured us more wine, and I stole a quick, guilty peek at her full, swaying breasts. My mother climbed on my knee and made little trilling noises. My grandfather shook his head and said, "It is very surprising, the way you resemble me. Can I take your photograph?"

I wondered if it went against Time Patrol regulations. I decided that it probably did. But also I saw no polite way to refuse such a trifling request.

My grandmother produced a camera. Passilidis and I stood side by side and she took a picture of us for him, and then one for me. She pulled them from the camera when they were developed and we studied them intently.

"Like brothers," she said over and over. "Like brothers!"

I destroyed my print as soon as I was out of the apartment. But I suppose that somewhere in my mother's papers there is an old and faded flattie photograph showing her father as a young man, standing beside a somewhat younger man who looks very much like him, and whom my mother probably assumed was some forgotten uncle of hers. Perhaps the photograph still exists. I'd be afraid to look.

30.

Grandfather Passilidis had saved me a great deal of trouble. He had lopped almost eight centuries off what I was already starting to think of as my quest.

I jumped down the line to now-time, did some research in the Time Service headquarters at Athens, and had myself outfitted as a Byzantine noble of the late twelfth century, with a sumptuous silk tunic, black cloak, and white bonnet. Then I podded up north to Albania, getting off at the town of Gjinokaster. In the old days this town was known as Argyrokastro, in the district of Epirus.

From Gjinokaster I went up the line to the year 1205.

The peasant folk of Argyrokastro were awed by my princely garb. I told them I was seeking the court of Michael Angelus Comnenus, and they told me the way and sold me a donkey to help me get there. I found Michael and the rest of the exiled Byzantines holding a chariot race in an improvised Hippodrome at the foot of a range of jagged hills. Quietly I affiliated myself with the crowd.

"I'm looking for Ducas," I told a harmless-looking old man who was passing around some wine.

"Ducas? Which one?"

"Are there many here? I bear a message from Constantinople for a Ducas, but they did not tell me there was more than one."

The old man laughed. "Just before me," he said, "I see Nicephorus Ducas, John Ducas, Leo Ducas, George Ducas, Nicephorus Ducas the Younger, Michael Ducas, Simeon Ducas, and Dimitrios Ducas. I am unable to find at the moment Eftimios Ducas, Leontios Ducas, Simeon Ducas the Tall, Constantine Ducas, and—let me think—Andronicus Ducas. Which member of the family, pray, do you seek?"

I thanked him and moved down the line.

In sixteenth century Gjinokaster I asked about the Markezinis family. My Byzantine garb earned me some strange glances, but the Byzantine gold pieces I carried got me all the information I needed. One bezant and I was given the location of the Markezinis estate. Two bezants more and I had an introduction to the foreman of the Markezinis vineyard. Five bezants—a steep price—and I found myself nibbling grapes in the guest-hall of Gregory Markezinis, the head of the clan. He was a distinguished man of middle years with a flowing gray beard and burning eyes; he was stern but hospitable. As we talked, his daughters moved serenely about us, refilling our cups, bringing more grapes, cold legs of lamb, mounds of rice. There were three girls, possibly thirteen, fifteen, and seventeen years old. I took good care not to look too closely at them, knowing the jealous temperament of mountain chieftains.

They were beauties: olive skin, dark eyes, high breasts, full lips. They might have been sisters of my radiant grandmother Katina Passilidis. My mother Diana, I believe, looked this way in girlhood. The family genes are powerful ones.

Unless I happened to be climbing on the wrong branch of the tree, one of these girls was my great-great-multi-great-grandmother. And Gregory Markezinis was my great-great-great-multi-great-grandfather.

I introduced myself as a wealthy young Cypriote of Byzantine descent who was traveling the world in search of pleasure and adventure. Gregory, whose Greek was slightly contaminated by Albanian words (did his serfs speak Gheg or Tosk? I forget) had evidently never met a Cypriote before, since he accepted my accent as authentic. "Where have you been?" he asked.

Oh, I said, Syria and Libya and Egypt, and Rome and Paris and Lisbon, and to London to attend the coronation of Henry VIII, and Prague, and Vienna. And now I was working my way eastward again, into the Turkish domain, determined despite all risks to visit the graves of my ancestors in Constantinople.

He raised an eyebrow at the mention of ancestors. Energetically hacking off a slice of lamb with his dagger, he said, "Was your family a high one in the old days?"

"I am of the Ducas line."

"*Ducas?*"

"Ducas," I said blandly.

"I am of the Ducas line as well."

"Indeed!"

"Beyond doubt!"

"A Ducas in Epirus!" I cried. "How did it happen?"

"We came here with the Comneni, after the Latin pigs took Constantinople."

"Indeed!"

"Beyond doubt!"

He called for more wine, the best in the house. When his daughters appeared, he did a little dance, crying, "A kinsman! A kinsman! The stranger is a kinsman! Give him proper greeting!"

I found myself engulfed in Markezinis daughters, overwhelmed by taut youthful breasts and sweet musky bodies. Chastely I embraced them, as a long-lost cousin would.

Over thick, elderly wine we talked genealogy. I went first, picking a Ducas at random—Theodoros—and claiming that he had escaped to Cyprus after the debacle in Constantinople in 1204, to found my line. Markezinis had no way of disproving that, and in fact he accepted it at face value. I unreeled a long list of Ducas forebears up the line between myself and distant Theodoros, using customary Byzantine names. When I concluded I said, "And you, Gregory?"

Using his knife to scratch family trees into the table top at some of the difficult points, Markezinis traced his line back to a Nicholas Markezinis of the late fourteenth century who had married the eldest daughter of Manuel Ducas of Argyrokastro, that Ducas having had only daughters and therefore bringing his immediate line to an end. From Manuel, then, Markezinis took things back in a leisurely way to the expulsion of the Byzantines from Constantinople by the Fourth Crusade. The particular Ducas of his direct line who had fled to Albania was, he said, Simeon.

My gonads plunged in despair.

"Simeon?" I said. "Do you mean Simeon Ducas the Tall, or the other one?"

"Were there two? How could you know?"

Cheeks flaming, I improvised, "I have to confess that I am something of a student of the family. Two Simeon Ducases followed the Comneni to this land, Simeon the Tall and a man of shorter stature."

"Of this I know nothing," said Markezinis. "I have been taught that my ancestor's name was Simeon. And his father was Nicephorus, whose palace was close to the church of St. Theodosia, by the Golden Horn. The Venetians burned the palace of Nicephorus when they took the city in 1204. And the father of Nicephorus—" He hesitated, shaking his head slowly and sadly from side to side like an aging buffalo. "I do not remember the name of the father of Nicephorus. I have forgotten the name of the father of Nicephorus. Was it Leo? Michael? Basil? I forget. My head is full of wine."

"It does not matter that much," I said. With the ancestry traced into Constantinople, there would be no further difficulties.

"Romanos? John? Isaac? It is right here, inside my head, but there are so many names—so many names—"

Still muttering names, he fell asleep at the table.

A dark-eyed daughter showed me to a drafty bedroom. I could have shunted instead, having learned all here that I had come to know; but it seemed civil to spend the night under my multi-great-grandfather's roof, rather than vanishing like a thief. I stripped, snuffed the candle, got into bed.

In the darkness a soft-bodied wench joined me under the blankets.

Her breasts nicely filled my hands and her fragrance was sweetly musky. I couldn't see her, but I assumed she must be one of the Markezinis' three daughters, coming to show how hospitable the family could be.

My palm slid down her smoothly rounded belly to its base, and when I reached the junction of her thighs, her legs opened to me, and I found her ready for love.

I felt obscurely disappointed at the thought that Markezinis' daughters would give themselves so freely to strangers—even a noble stranger claiming to be a cousin. After all, these were my *ancestors*. Was my line of descent muddied by the sperm of casual wayfarers?

That thought led logically to the really troublesome one, which was, if this girl is really my great-great-multi-great-grandmother, what am *I* doing in bed with her? To hell with sleeping with strangers—should she sleep with descendants? When I began this quest at Metaxas' prodding, it wasn't really with the intent of committing transtemporal incest—but yet here I was doing it, it seemed.

Guilt blossomed in me and I became so nervous that it made me momentarily impotent.

But my bedmate slithered down to my waist and restored my virility with busy lips. A fine old Byzantine trick, I thought, and, rigid again, I slipped into her and pronged her with gusto. I soothed my conscience by telling myself that the chances were two out of three that this girl was merely my great-great-multi-great-*aunt*, in which case the incest must surely be far less serious. So far as bloodlines went, the connection between myself and any sixteenth-century aunt must be exceedingly cloudy.

My conscience let me alone after that, and the girl and I gasped our way to completion. And then she rose, and went from the room, and as she passed the window a sliver of moonlight illuminated her white buttocks and her pale thighs and her long blonde hair, and I realized what

I should have known all along, which is that the Markezinis girls would not come like Eskimo wenches to sleep with guests, but that someone had thoughtfully sent in a slave-girl for my amusement. So much for the prickings of conscience. Absolved even of the most tenuous incest, I slept soundly.

In the morning, over a breakfast of cold lamb and rice, Gregory Markezinis said, "Word reaches me that the Spaniards have found a new world beyond the Ocean Sea. Do you think there's truth in it?"

This was the year A.D. 1556.

I said, "Beyond all doubt it's true. I saw the proof in Spain, at the court of King Charles. It's a world of gold and jade and spices—of red-skinned men—"

"*Red*-skinned men? Oh, no, cousin Ducas, no, no, I can never believe that!" Markezinis roared in delight, and summoned his daughters. "The new world of the Spaniards—its men have red skins! Cousin Ducas tells us so!"

"Well, copper-colored, really," I murmured, but Markezinis scarcely heard.

"Red skins! Red skins! And no heads, but eyes and mouths in their chests! And men with a single leg, which they raise above their heads at midday to shield themselves from the sun! Yes! Yes! Oh, wonderful new world! Cousin, you amuse me!"

I told him I was glad to bring him such pleasure. I thanked him for his gracious hospitality, and chastely embraced each of his daughters, and prepared to take my leave. And suddenly it struck me that if my ancestors' name had been Markezinis from the fourteenth century through the twentieth, then none of these girls could possibly be ancestral to me. My priggish pangs of conscience had been pointless, except insofar as they taught me where my inhabitions lay. "Do you have sons?" I asked my host.

"Oh, yes," he said, "six sons!"

"May your line increase and prosper," I said, and departed, and rode my donkey a dozen kilometers out into the countryside, and tethered it to an olive tree, and shunted down the line.

31.

A t the end of my layoff I reported for duty, and set out for the first
time solo as a Time Courier.
    I had six people to take on the one-week tour. They didn't
know it was my first solo. Protopopolos didn't see any point in telling
them, and I agreed. But I didn't *feel* as though it were my first solo. I
was full of Metaxian chutzpah. I emanated charisma. I feared nothing
except fear itself.

At the preliminary meeting I told my six the rules of time-touring
in crisp, staccato phrases. I invoked the dread menace of the Time Patrol
as I warned against changing the past either carelessly or by design. I
explained how they could best keep out of trouble. Then I handed out
timers and set them.

"Here we go," I said. "Up the line."

Charisma. Chutzpah.

Jud Elliott, Time Courier, on his own!

Up the line!

"We have arrived," I said, "in 1659 B.P., better known to you as
the year 400. I've picked it as a typical early Byzantine time. The ruling
emperor is Arcadius. You remember from now-time Istanbul that
Haghia Sophia should be back there, and the mosque of Sultan Ahmed
should be there. Well, of course, Sultan Ahmed and his mosque are
currently a dozen centuries in the future, and the church behind us is
the original Haghia Sophia, constructed forty years ago when the city
was still very young. Four years from now it'll burn down during a
rebellion caused by the exiling of Bishop John Chrysostomos by Emperor Arcadius after he had criticized Arcadius' wife Eudoxia. Let's go
inside. You see that the walls are of stone but the roof is wooden—"

My six tourists included a real-estate developer from Ohio, his wife, their gawky daughter and her husband, plus a Sicilian shrink and his bowlegged temporary wife: a typical assortment of prosperous citizens. They didn't know a nave from a narthex, but I gave them a good look at the church, and then marched them through Arcadius' Constantinople to set the background for what they'd see later. After two hours of this I jumped down the line to 408 to watch the baptism of little Theodosius again.

I caught sight of myself on the far side of the street, standing close to Capistrano. I didn't wave. My other self did not appear to see me. I wondered if this present self of mine had been standing here that other time, when I was here with Capistrano. The intricacies of the Cumulative Paradox oppressed me. I banished them from mind.

"You see the ruins of the old Haghia Sophia," I said. "It will be rebuilt under the auspices of this infant, the future Theodosius II, and opened to prayer on October, 10, 445—"

We shunted down the line to 445 and watched the ceremony of dedication.

There are two schools of thought about the proper way to conduct a time-tour. The Capistrano method is to take the tourists to four or five high spots a week, letting them spend plenty of time in taverns, inns, back alleys, and marketplaces, and moving in such a leisurely way that the flavor of each period soaks in deeply. The Metaxas method is to construct an elaborate mosaic of events, hitting the same high spots but also twenty or thirty or forty lesser events, spending half an hour here and two hours there. I had experienced both methods and I preferred Metaxas' approach. The serious student of Byzantium wants depth, not breadth; but these folk were not serious students. Better to make a pageant of Byzantium for them, hurry them breathless through the eras, show them riots and coronations, chariot races, the rise and fall of monuments and kings.

And so I took my people from time to time in imitation of my idol Metaxas. I gave them a full day in early Byzantium, as Capistrano would have done, but I split it into six shunts. We ended our day's work in 537, in the city Justinian had built on the charred ruin of the one destroyed by the rioting Blues and Greens.

"We've come to December 27," I said. "Justinian will inaugurate the new Haghia Sophia today. You see how much larger the cathedral is than the ones that preceded it—a gigantic building, one of the wonders of the world. Justinian has poured the equivalent of hundreds of millions of dollars into it."

"Is this the one they have in Istanbul now?" asked Mr. Real Estate's son-in-law doubtfully.

"Basically, yes. Except that you don't see any minarets here—the Moslems tacked those on, of course, after they turned the place into a mosque—and the gothic buttresses haven't been built yet, either. Also the great dome here is not the one you're familiar with. This one is slightly flatter and wider than the present one. It turned out that the architect's calculations of thrust were wrong, and half the dome will collapse in 558 after weakening of the arches by earthquakes. You'll see that tomorrow. Look, here comes Justinian."

A little earlier that day I had shown them the harried Justinian of 532 attempting to cope with the Nika riots. The emperor who now appeared, riding in a chariot drawn by four immense black horses, looked a good deal more than five years older, far more plump and florid of face, but he also seemed vastly more sure of himself, a figure of total command. As well he should be, having surmounted the tremendous challenge to his power that the riots presented, and having rebuilt the city into something uniquely glorious.

Senators and dukes lined the approach; we remained respectfully to one side, amid the commoners. Priests, deacons, deaconesses, subdeacons, and cantors awaited the imperial procession, all in costly robes. Hymns in the ancient mode rose to heaven. The Patriarch Menos appeared at the colossal imperial door of the cathedral; Justinian dismounted; the patriarch and the emperor, hand in hand, entered the building, followed by the high officials of state.

"According to a tenth-century chronicle," I said, "Justinian was overcome by emotion when he entered his new Haghia Sophia. Rushing to the apse, he gave thanks to God who had allowed him to achieve such a building, and cried out, 'O Solomon, I have surpassed thee.' The Time Service thought it might be interesting for visitors to this era to hear this famous line, and so some years back we planted an Ear just beside the altar." I reached into my robes. "I've brought along a pickup speaker which will transmit Justinian's words to us as he nears the apse. Listen."

I switched on the speaker. At this moment, any number of other Couriers in the crowd were doing the same thing. A time will come when so many of us are clustered in this moment that Justinian's voice, amplified by a thousand tiny speakers, will boom majestically across the whole city.

From the speaker in my palm came the sound of footsteps.

"The emperor is walking down the aisle," I said.

The footsteps halted abruptly. Justinian's words came to us—his first exclamation upon entering the architectural masterpiece of the ages.

Thick-voiced with rage, the emperor bellowed, "Look up there, you sodomitic simpleton! Find me the mother-humper who left that scaffold hanging in the dome! I want his balls in an alabaster vase before mass begins!" Then he sneezed in imperial wrath.

I said to my six tourists, "The development of time-travel has made it necessary for us to revise many of our most inspiring anecdotes in the light of new evidence."

32.

That night as my tired tourists slept, I slipped away from them to carry out some private research.

This was strictly against regulations. A Courier is supposed to remain with the clients at all times, in case an emergency occurs. The clients, after all, don't know how to operate their timers, so only the Courier can help them make a quick escape from trouble.

Despite this I jumped six centuries down the line, while my tourists slept, and I visited the era of my prosperous ancestor Nicephorus Ducas.

Which took chutzpah, of course, considering that this was my first solo trip. But actually I wasn't running any serious risks.

The safe way to carry out such side trips, as Metaxas had explained to me, is to set your timer carefully and make sure that your net absence from your tourists is one minute or less. I was departing from December 27, 537, at 2345 hours. I could go up or down the line from there and spend hours, days, weeks, or months elsewhere. When I had finished with my business, all I had to do was set my timer to bring me back to December 27, 537, at 2346 hours. From the point of view of my sleeping tourists I'd have been gone only sixty seconds.

Of course, it wouldn't be proper to land at 2344 hours on the return trip, which is to say to come back a minute before I had left. There would then be two of me in the same room, which produces the Paradox of Duplication, a subspecies of the Cumulative Paradox, and is certain to bring a reprimand or worse if the Time Patrol hears of it. No: precise coordination is necessary.

Another problem is the difficulty of making an exact point-to-point shunt. The inn where my group was lodged in 537 would almost certainly no longer exist by 1175, the year of my immediate destination. I couldn't blindly shunt forward from the room, because I might find myself materializing in some awkward place later constructed on the site—a dungeon, say.

The only safe way would be to go out in the street and shunt from there, both coming and going. This, though, requires you to be away from your tourists more than sixty seconds, just figuring the time necessary to go downstairs, find a safe and quiet place for your shunt, etc. And if a Time Patrolman comes along on a routine checkup and recognizes you in the street and asks you why the hell you aren't with the clients, you're in trouble.

Nevertheless I shunted down the line and got away with it.

I hadn't been in 1175 before. It was probably the last really good year Byzantium had.

It seemed to me that an atmosphere of gathering trouble hung over Constantinople. Even the clouds looked ominous. The air had the tang of impending calamity.

Subjective garbage. Being able to move freely along the line distorts your perspective and colors your interpretation. I knew what lay ahead for these people; they didn't. Byzantium in 1175 was cocky and optimistic; I was imagining all the omens.

Manuel I Comnenus was on the throne, a good man, coming to the end of a long, brilliant career. Disaster was closing in on him. The Comnenus emperors had spent the whole twelfth century recapturing Asia Minor from the Turks, who had grabbed it the century before. I knew that one year down the line, in 1176, Manuel was going to lose his entire Asian empire in a single day, at the battle of Myriocephalon. After that it would be downhill all the way for Byzantium. But Manuel didn't know that yet. Nobody here did. Except me.

I headed up toward the Golden Horn. The upper end of town was the most important in this period; the center of things had shifted from the Haghia Sophia/Hippodrome/Augusteum section to the Blachernae quarter, in the northernmost corner of the city at the angle where the city walls met. Here, for some reason, Emperor Alexius I had moved the court at the end of the eleventh century, abandoning the jumbled old Great Palace. Now his grandson Manuel reigned here in splendor, and the big feudal families had built new palaces nearby, all along the Golden Horn.

One of the finest of these marble edifices belonged to Nicephorus Ducas, my many-times-removed-great-grandfather.

I spent half the morning prowling around the palace grounds, getting drunk on the magnificence of it all. Toward midday the palace gate opened and I saw Nicephorus himself emerge in his chariot for his noontime drive: a stately figure with a long, ornately braided black beard and elaborate gold-trimmed robes. On his breast he wore a pendant cross, gilded and studded with huge jewels; his fingers glistened with rings. A crowd had gathered to watch the noble Nicephorus leave his palace.

Gracefully he scattered coins to the multitude as he rode forth. I caught one: a thin, shabby bezant of Alexius I, nicked and filed at the edges. The Comnenus family had debased the currency badly. Still, it's no small thing to be able to toss even debased gold coins to a mob of miscellaneous onlookers.

I have that worn and oily-looking bezant to this day. I think of it as my inheritance from my Byzantine multi-great-grandfather.

Nicephorus' chariot vanished in the direction of the imperial palace. A filthy old man standing beside me sighed, crossed himself many times, and murmured, "May the Savior bless the blessed Nicephorus! Such a wonderful person!"

The old man's nose had been lopped off at the base. He had also lost his left hand. The kindly Byzantines of this latter-day era had made mutilation the penalty for many minor crimes. A step forward; the Code of Justinian called for death in such cases. Better to lose eye or tongue or nose than life.

"Twenty years I spent in the service of Nicephorus Ducas!" the old man went on. "The finest years of my life, they were."

"Why did you leave?" I asked.

He held forth the stump of his arm. "They caught me stealing books. I was a scribe, and I hungered to keep some of the books I copied. Nicephorus has so many! He would not have missed five or six! But they caught me and I lost my hand and also my employment, ten years ago."

"And your nose?"

"In that very harsh winter six years back I stole a barrel of fish. I am a very poor thief, always getting caught."

"How do you support yourself?"

He smiled. "By public charity. And by begging. Can you spare a silver nomisma for an unhappy old man?"

I inspected the coins I carried. By ill luck all my silver pieces were early ones, of the fifth and sixth centuries, long out of circulation; if the old man tried to pass one, he'd be arrested on charges of robbing some aristocratic collector, and probably would lose his other hand. So I pressed a fine gold bezant of the early eleventh century into his palm. He stared at it in amazement. "I am yours, noble sir!" he cried. "I am wholly yours!

"Come with me to the nearest tavern, then, and answer a few questions," I said.

"Gladly! Gladly!"

I bought us wine and pumped him on the Ducas genealogy. It was hard for me to look at his mutilated face, and so as we talked I kept my eyes trained on his shoulder; but he seemed accustomed to that. He had all the information I was seeking, for one of his duties while in the service of the Ducases had been to copy out the family records.

Nicephorus, he said, was then forty-five years old, having been born in 1130. The wife of Nicephorus was the former Zoe Catacalon, and they had seven children: Simeon, John, Leo, Basil, Helena, Theodosia, and Zoe. Nicephorus was the eldest son of Nicetas Ducas, born in 1106; the wife of Nicetas was the former Irene Cerularius, whom he had married in 1129. Nicetas and Irene had had five other children: Michael, Isaac, John, Romanos, and Anna. Nicetas' father had been Leo Ducas, born in 1070; Leo had married the former Pulcheria Botaniates, in 1100, and their children, other than Nicetas, included Simeon, John, Alexander—

The recitation went on and on, carrying the Ducases back through the generations of Byzantium, into the tenth century, the ninth, the eighth, names growing cloudy now, gaps appearing in the record, the old man frowning, fumbling, apologizing for scanty data. I tried a couple of times to stop him, but he would not be stopped, until finally he sputtered out with a Tiberius Ducas of the seventh century whose existence, he said, was possibly apocryphal.

"This, you understand, is merely the lineage of Nicephorus Ducas," he said. "The imperial family is a distinct branch, which I can trace back for you through the Comneni to Emperor Constantine X and his ancestors, who—"

Those Ducases didn't interest me, even though they were distantly related to me in some way. If I wanted to know the lineage of the imperial Ducases, I could find it in Gibbon. I cared only for my own humbler branch of the family, the collateral offshoot from the imperial line. Thanks to this hideous outcast scribe I was able to secure the path of those Ducases through three Byzantine centuries, down to Nicephorus. And I already knew the rest of the line, from Nicephorus's son Simeon of Albania to Simeon's several-times-grandson Manuel Ducas of Argyrokastro, whose eldest daughter married Nicholas Markezinis, and through the Markezinis line until a Markezinis daughter married a Passilidis son and produced my estimable grandfather Konstantin, whose daughter Diana wed Judson Daniel Elliott II and brought forth into the world my own ultimate self.

"For your trouble," I said, and gave the filthy scribe another gold piece, and fled from the tavern while he still was muttering dazed thanks.

I knew Metaxas would be proud of me. A little jealous, even—for in short order I had put together a lengthier family tree than his own. *His* went back to the tenth century, mine (a little shakily) to the seventh. Of course, he had an annotated list of hundreds of ancestors, and I knew details of only a few dozen, but he had started years ahead of me.

I set my timer carefully and shunted back to December 27, 537. The street was dark and silent. I hurried into the inn. Less than three minutes had elapsed since my departure, even though I had spent eight hours down the line in 1175. My tourists slept soundly. All was well.

I was pleased with myself. By candlelight I sketched the details of the Ducas line on a scrap of old vellum. I wasn't really planning to *do* anything with the genealogy. I wasn't looking for ancestors to kill, like Capistrano, or ancestors to seduce, like Metaxas. I just wanted to gloat a little over the fact that my ancestors were Ducases. Some people don't have ancestors at all.

33.

I don't think I was quite the equal of Metaxas as a Courier, but I gave my people a respectable view of Byzantium. I did a damned good job, especially for a first try.

We shunted through all the highlights and some of the lowlights. I showed them the baptism of Constantine the Pisser; the smashing of the icons under Leo III; the invasion by the Bulgars in 813; the trees of gilded bronze in the Magnaura Hall of Theophilus; the debaucheries of Michael the Drunkard; the arrival of the First Crusade in 1096 and 1097; the much more disastrous arrival of the Fourth Crusade in 1204; the reconquest of Constantinople by the Byzantines in 1261, and the coronation of Michael VIII; in short, all that counted.

My people loved it. Like most time-tourists, they particularly loved the riots, insurrections, rebellions, sieges, massacres, invasions, and fires.

"When do you show us the Turks come bustin' in?" the Ohio real-estate-man kept asking. "I want to see those goddam Turks wreck the place!"

"We're moving toward it," I told him.

First I gave them a look at Byzantium in the sunset years, under the dynasty of the Palaeologi. "Most of the empire is gone," I said, as we dropped down the line into 1275. "The Byzantines think and build on a small scale now. Intimacy is the key word. This is the little Church of St. Mary of the Mongols, built for a bastard daughter of Michael VIII who for a short while was married to a Mongol khan. See the charm? The simplicity?"

We glided on down the line to 1330 to look in on the Church of Our Savior in Chora. The tourists had already seen it down the line in

Istanbul under its Turkish name, Kariye Camii; now they saw it in its pre-mosquified condition, with all its stunning mosaics intact and new. "See, there," I said. "There's the Mary who married the Mongol. She's still there down the line. And this—the early life and miracles of Christ—that one's gone from our time, but you can see how superb it was here."

The Sicilian shrink holographed the whole church; he was carrying a palm camera that the Time Service regards as permissible, since nobody up the line is likely to notice it or comprehend its function. His bowlegged tempie waddled around oohing at everything. The Ohio people looked bored, as I knew they would. No matter. I'd give them culture if I had to shove it up them.

"When do we see the Turks?" the Ohioans asked restlessly.

We skipped lithely over the Black Death years of 1347 and 1348. "I can't take you there," I said, when the protests came. "You've got to sign up for a special plague tour if you want to see any of the great epidemics."

Mr. Ohio's son-in-law grumbled, "We've had all our vaccinations."

"But five billion people down the line in now-time are unprotected," I explained. "You might pick up some contamination and bring it back with you, and start a world-wide epidemic. And then we'd have to edit your whole time-trip out of the flow of history to keep the disaster from happening. You wouldn't want that, would you?"

Bafflement.

"Look, I'd take you there if I could," I said. "But I can't. It's the law. Nobody can enter a plague era except under special supervision, which I'm not licensed to give."

I brought them down in 1385 and showed them the withering of Constantinople, a shrunken population within the great walls, whole districts deserted, churches falling into ruins. The Turks were devouring the surrounding countryside. I took my people up on the walls back of the Blachernae quarter and showed them the horsemen of the Turkish sultan prowling in the countryside beyond the city limits. My Ohio friend shook his fist at them. "Barbarian bastards!" he cried. "Scum of the earth!"

Down the line to 1398 we came. I showed them Anadolu Hisari, Sultan Beyazit's fortress on the Asiatic side of the Bosphorus. A summer haze made it a trifle hard to see, so we shunted a few months into autumn and looked again. Surreptitiously we passed around a little pair of field glasses. Two elderly Byzantine monks appeared, saw the field glasses before I could get hold of them and hide them, and wanted to know what we were looking through.

"It helps the eyes," I said, and we got out of there fast.

In the summer of 1422 we watched Sultan Murat II's army bashing at the city walls. About 20,000 Turks had burned the villages and fields around Constantinople, massacred the inhabitants, uprooted the vines and olive trees, and now we saw them trying to get into the city. They moved siege machines up to the walls, went to work with battering rams, giant catapults, all the heavy artillery of the time. I got my people right up close to the battle line to see the fun.

The standard technique for doing this is to masquerade as holy pilgrims. Pilgrims can go anywhere, even into the front lines. I distributed crosses and icons, taught everybody how to look devout, and led them forward, chanting and intoning. There was no hope of getting them to chant genuine Byzantine hymns, of course, and so I told them to chant anything they liked, just making sure it sounded somber and pious. The Ohio people did *The Star Spangled Banner* over and over, and the shrink and his friend sang arias from Verdi and Puccini. The Byzantine defenders paused in their work to wave to us. We waved back and made the sign of the Cross.

"What if we get killed?" asked the son-in-law.

"No chance of it. Not permanently, anyway. If a stray shot gets you, I'll summon the Time Patrol, and they'll pull you out of here five minutes ago."

The son-in-law looked puzzled.

"*Celeste Aida, forma divina—*"

"*. . . so proudly we hailed—*"

The Byzantines fought like hell to keep the Turks out. They dumped Greek fire and boiling oil on them, hacked off every head that peered over the wall, withstood the fury of the artillery. Nevertheless it seemed certain that the city would fall by sunset. The evening shadows gathered.

"Watch this," I said.

Flames burst forth at several points along the wall. The Turks were burning their own siege machines and pulling back!

"Why?" I was asked. "Another hour and they'll have the city."

"Byzantine historians," I said, "later wrote that a miracle had taken place. The Virgin Mary had appeared, clad in a violet mantle, dazzlingly bright, and had walked along the walls. The Turks, in terror, withdrew."

"Where?" the son-in-law demanded. "I didn't see any miracle! I didn't see any Virgin Mary!"

"Maybe we ought to go back half an hour and look again," said his wife vaguely.

I explained that the Virgin Mary had not in fact been seen on the battlements; rather, messengers had brought word to Sultan Murad of an uprising against him in Asia Minor, and, fearing he might be cut off and besieged in Constantinople if he succeeded in taking it, the sultan had halted operations at once to deal with the rebels in the east. The Ohioans looked disappointed. I think they genuinely had wanted to see the Virgin Mary. "We saw her on last year's trip," the son-in-law muttered.

"That was different," said his wife. "That was the *real* one, not a miracle!"

I adjusted timers and we shunted down the line.

Dawn, April 5, 1453. We waited for sunrise on the rampart of Byzantium. "The city is isolated now," I said. "Sultan Mehmet the Conqueror has built the fortress of Rumeli Hisari up along the European side of the Bosphorus. The Turks are moving in. Come, look, listen to this."

Sunrise broke. We peered over the top of the wall. A deafening shout went up. "Across the Golden Horn are the tents of the Turks— 200,000 of them. In the Bosphorus are 493 Turkish ships. There are 8,000 Byzantine defenders, 15 ships. No help has come from Christian Europe for Christian Byzantium, except 700 Genoese soldiers and sailors under the command of Giovanni Giustiniani." I lingered on the name of Byzantium's last bulwark, stressing the rich echoes of the past: "Giustiniani. . . . Justinian—" No one noticed. "Byzantium is to be thrown to the wolves," I went on. "Listen to the Turks roar!"

The famous Byzantine chain-boom was stretched across the Golden Horn and anchored at each bank: great rounded logs joined by iron hooks, designed to close the harbor to invaders. It had failed once before, in 1204; now it was stronger.

We jumped down the line to April 9, and watched the Turks creep closer to the walls. We skipped to April 12, and saw the great Turkish cannon, the Royal One, go into action. A turncoat Christian named Urban of Hungary had built it for the Turks; 100 pair of oxen had dragged it to the city; its barrel, three feet across, fired 1,500-pound granite projectiles. We saw a burst of flame, a puff of smoke, and then a monstrous ball of stone rise sleepily, slowly, and slam with earth-shaking force against the wall, sending up a cloud of dust. The thud jarred the whole city; the explosion lingered in our ears. "They can fire the Royal One only seven times a day," I said. "It takes a while to load it. And now see this." We shunted forward by a week. The invaders were clustered about the giant cannon, readying it to fire. They touched it off; it exploded with a frightful blare of flame, sending huge chunks of its barrel slewing through the Turks. Bodies lay everywhere. The

Byzantines cheered from the walls. "Among the dead," I said, "is Urban of Hungary. But soon the Turks will build a new cannon."

That evening the Turks rushed the walls, and we watched, singing *America the Beautiful* and arias from *Otello*, as the brave Genoese of Giovanni Giustiniani drove them off. Arrows whistled overhead; a few of the Byzantines fired clumsy, inaccurate rifles.

I did the final siege so brilliantly that I wept at my own virtuosity. I gave my people naval battles, hand-to-hand encounters at the walls, ceremonies of prayer in Haghia Sophia. I showed them the Turks slyly hauling their ships overland on wooden rollers from the Bosphorus to the Golden Horn, in order to get around the famous chain-boom, and I showed them the terror of the Byzantines when dawn on April 23 revealed 72 Turkish warships at anchor inside the harbor, and I showed them the gallant defeat of those ships by the Genoese.

We skipped forward through the days of the siege, watching the walls diminishing but remaining unbreached, watching the fortitude of the defenders grow and the determination of the attackers lessen. On May 28 we went by night to Haghia Sophia, to attend the last Christian service ever to be held there. It seemed that all the city was in the cathedral: Emperor Constantine XI and his court, beggars and thieves, merchants, pimps, Roman Catholics from Genoa and Venice, soldiers and sailors, dukes and prelates, and also a good many disguised visitors from the future, more, perhaps, than all the rest combined. We listened to the bells tolling, and to the melancholy *Kyrie*, and we dropped to our knees, and many, even some of the time-travelers, wept for Byzantium, and when the service ended the lights were dimmed, veiling the glittering mosaics and frescoes.

And then it was May 29, and we saw a world on its last day.

At two in the morning the Turks rushed St. Romanus Gate. Giustiniani was wounded; the fighting was terrible, and I had to keep my people back from it; the rhythmic "*Allah! Allah!*" grew until it filled the universe with noise, and the defenders panicked and fled, and the Turks burst into the city.

"All is over," I said. "Emperor Constantine perishes in battle. Thousands flee the city; thousands take refuge behind the barred doors of Haghia Sophia. Look now: the pillaging, the slaughter!" We jumped frantically, vanishing and reappearing, so that we would not be run down by the horsemen galloping joyously through the streets. Probably we startled a good many Turks, but in all that frenzy the miraculous vanishing of a few pilgrims would attract no excitement. For a climax I swept them into May 30, and we watched Sultan Mehmet ride in triumph into Byzantium, flanked by viziers and pashas and janissaries.

"He halts outside Haghia Sophia," I whispered. "He scoops up dirt, drops it on his turban; it is his act of contrition before Allah, who has given him such a glorious victory. Now he goes in. It would not be safe for us to follow him there. Inside he finds a Turk hacking up the mosaic floor, which he regards as impious; the sultan will strike the man and forbid him to harm the cathedral, and then he will go to the altar and climb upon it and make his Salaam. Haghia Sophia becomes Ayasofya, the mosque. There is no more Byzantium. Come. Now we go down the line."

Dazed by what they had seen, my six tourists let me adjust their timers. I sounded the note on my pitchpipe, and down the line we went to 2059.

In the Time Service office afterward, the Ohio real-estate man approached me. He stuck out his thumb in the vulgar way that vulgar people do, when they're offering a tip. "Son," he said, "I just want to tell you, that was one hell of a job you did! Come on over with me and let me stick this thumb on the input plate and give you a little bit of appreciation, okay?"

"I'm sorry," I said. "We're not permitted to accept gratuities."

"Crap on that, son. Suppose you don't pay any attention, and I just get some stash thumbed into your account, okay? Let's say you don't know a thing about it."

"I can't prevent a transfer of funds that I don't know about," I said.

"Good deal. By damn, when those Turks came into the city, what a show! What a show!"

When I got next month's account statement I found he had thumbed a cool thousand into my credit. I didn't report myself to my superiors. I figured I had earned it, rules or not.

34.

I figured I had also earned the right to spend my layoff at Metaxas' villa in 1105. No longer a pest, a driveling apprentice, I was a full member of the brotherhood of Time Couriers. And one of the best in the business, in my opinion. I didn't have to fear that I'd be unwelcome at Metaxas' place.

Checking the assignment board, I found that Metaxas, like myself, had just finished a tour. That meant he'd be at his villa. I picked up a fresh outfit of Byzantine clothes, requisitioned a pouch of gold bezants, and got ready to jump to 1105.

Then I remembered the Paradox of Discontinuity.

I didn't know *when* in 1105 I was supposed to arrive. And I had to allow for Metaxas' now-time basis up there. In now-time for me it was currently November, 2059. Metaxas had just jumped up the line to some point in 1105 that corresponded, for him, to November of 2059. Suppose that point was in July, 1105. If, not knowing that, I shunted back to—say—March, 1105, the Metaxas I'd find wouldn't know me at all. I'd be just some uninvited snot barging in on the party. If I jumped to—say—June, 1105, I'd be the young newcomer, not yet a proven quantity, whom Metaxas had just taken out on a training trip. And if I jumped to—say—October, 1105, I'd meet a Metaxas who was three months ahead of me on a now-time basis, and who therefore knew details of my own future. That would be the Paradox of Discontinuity in the other direction, and I wasn't eager to experience it; it's dangerous and a little frightening to run into someone who has lived through a period that you haven't reached yet, and no Time Serviceman enjoys it.

I needed help.

I went to Spiros Protopopolos and said, "Metaxas invited me to visit him during my layoff, but I don't know when he is."

Cautiously Protopopolos said, "Why do you think I know? He doesn't confide in me."

"I thought he might have left some record with you of his now-time basis."

"What the hell are you talking about?"

I wondered if I had made some hideous blunder. Bulling ahead, I winked and said, "*You* know where Metaxas is now. And maybe you know when, too. Come on, Proto. I'm in on the story. You don't need to be cagey with me."

He went into the next room and consulted Plastiras and Herschel. They must have vouched for me. Protopopolos, returning, whispered in my ear, "August 17, 1105. Say hello for me."

I thanked him and got on my way.

Metaxas lived in the suburbs, outside the walls of Constantinople. Land was cheap out there in the early twelfth century, thanks to such disturbances as the invasion of the marauding Patzinak barbarians in 1090 and the arrival of the disorderly rabble of Crusaders six years later. The settlers outside the walls had suffered badly then. Many fine estates had gone on the market. Metaxas had bought in 1095, when the land-owners were still in shock over their injuries at the hands of the Patzi-naks and were starting to worry about the next set of invaders.

He had one advantage denied to the sellers: he had already looked down the line and seen how stable things would be in the years just ahead, under Alexius I Comnenus. He knew that the countryside in which his villa was set would be spared from harm all during the twelfth century.

I crossed into Old Istanbul and cabbed out to the ruins of the city wall, and beyond it for about five kilometers. Naturally, this wasn't any suburban countryside in now-time, but just a gray sprawling extension of the modern city.

When I figured I was the proper distance out of town, I thumbed the plate and dismissed my cab. Then I took up a position on the side-walk, checking things out for my jump. Some kids saw me in my By-zantine costume and came over to watch, knowing that I must be going to go back in time. They called gaily to me in Turkish, maybe asking me to take them along.

One angelically grimy little boy said in recognizable French, "I hope they cut your head off."

Children are so sweetly frank, aren't they? And so charmingly hostile, in all eras.

I set my timer, gestured obscenely at my well-wisher, and went up the line.

The gray buildings vanished. The November bleakness gave way to the sunny glow of August. The air I breathed was suddenly fresh and fragrant. I stood beside a broad cobbled road running between two green meadows. A modest chariot drawn by two horses came clopping up and halted before me.

A lean young man in simple country clothes leaned out and said, "Sir, Metaxas has sent me to fetch you to him."

"But—he wasn't expecting—"

I shut up fast, before I said something out of line. Obviously Metaxas *was* expecting me. Had I hit the Paradox of Discontinuity, somehow?

Shrugging, I climbed up into the chariot.

As we rode into the west, my driver nodded to the acres of grapevines to the left of the road and the groves of fig trees to the right. "All this," he said proudly, "belongs to Metaxas. Have you ever been here before?"

"No, never," I said.

"He is a great man, my master. He is a friend to the poor and an ally to the mighty. Everyone respects him. Emperor Alexius himself was here last month."

I felt queasy about that. Bad enough that Metaxas had carved out a now-time identity for himself ten centuries up the line; what would the Time Patrol say about his hobnobbing with emperors? Giving advice, no doubt; altering the future by his foreknowledge of events; cementing himself into the historical matrix of this era as a valued adviser to royalty! Could anyone match him for gall?

Figs and grapes gave way to fields of wheat. "This, too, belongs to Metaxas," said the driver.

I had pictured Metaxas living in some comfortable little villa on a hectare or two of land, with a garden in front and perhaps a vegetable plot in the rear. I hadn't realized that he was a major landowner on such a scale.

We passed grazing cattle, and a mill worked by plodding oxen, and a pond no doubt well stocked with fish, and then we came to a double row of cypress trees that guarded a side road branching from the main highway, and took that road, and a splendid villa appeared, and at its entrance waited Metaxas, garbed in raiment suitable for the companion of an emperor.

"Jud!" he cried, and we embraced. "My friend! My brother! Jud, they tell me about the tour you led! Magnificent! Your tourists, they never stopped praising you?"

"Who told you?"

"Kolettis and Pappas. They're here. Come in, come in, come in! Wine for my guest! A change of robes for him! Come in, Jud, come in!"

35.

The villa was classical in style, atrium-and-peristyle, with a huge central courtyard, colonnaded walkways, mosaic floors, frescoed walls, a great apsed reception room, a pond in the courtyard, a library bulging with scrolls, a dining room whose round gold-inlaid ivory table could have seated three dozen, a statuary hall, and a marble bathroom. Metaxas' slaves hustled me toward the bathroom, and Metaxas called out that he'd see me later.

I got the royal treatment.

Three dark-haired slave wenches—Persians, Metaxas said later—ministered to me in the bath. All they wore were loinstrings, and in a moment I was wearing less than that, for in a giggling jiggle of breasts they stripped me and went to work buffing and soaping me until I gleamed. Steam bath, hot bath, cold bath—my pores got the full workout. When I emerged they dried me *most* detailedly and robed me in the most elegant tunic I ever expect to wear. Then they vanished, with a saucy wigwag of bare bottoms as they disappeared through nome subterranean passageway. A middle-aged butler appeared and conveyed me to the atrium, where Metaxas awaited me with beakers of wine.

"You like it?" he asked.

"I feel I'm in a dream."

"You are. And I'm the dreamer. You saw the farms? Wheat, olives, cattle, figs, everything. I own. My tenants farm. Each year I acquire new land on the profits of last year's work."

"It's incredible," I said. "And what's even more incredible is that you get away with it."

"I have earned my invulnerability," said Metaxas simply. "The Time Patrol knows I must not be persecuted."

"They realize you're here?"

"I believe they do," he said. "They stay away, though. I take care to make no significant changes in the fabric of history. I'm no villain. I'm merely self-indulgent."

"But you *are* changing history just by being here! Some other landowner must have held these lands in the real 1105."

"This is the real 1105."

"I mean the original, before Benchley Effect visitors began coming here. You've interpolated yourself into the landowner rolls, and—my God, the chariot driver spoke of you as Metaxas! Is that the name you use here?"

"Themistoklis Metaxas. Why not? It is a good Greek name."

"Yes, but—look, it must be in all the documents, the tax records, everything! You've certainly changed the Byzantine archives that have come down to us, putting yourself in where you weren't in before. What—"

"There is no danger," Metaxas said. "So long as I take no life and create no life here, so long as I cause no one to change a previously decided course of action, all is well. You know, making a real alteration in the time flow is a difficult thing. You have to do something big, like killing a monarch. Simply being here, I introduce tiny changes, but they are damped out by ten centuries of time, and no real change results down the line. Do you follow?"

I shrugged. "Just tell me one thing, at least. How did you know I was coming?"

Laughing, he said, "I looked two days down the line and you were here. Therefore I checked for your time of arrival and arranged to have Nicholas meet you. It saved you a long walk, yes?"

Of course. I just hadn't been thinking four-dimensionally. It stood to reason that Metaxas would habitually scan his immediate future here, so he'd never be the victim of some unpleasant surprise in this sometimes unpredictable era.

"Come," Metaxas said. "Join the others."

They were lounging on divans by the courtyard pool, nibbling bits of roasted meat that slavegirls in diaphanous robes popped into their mouths. Two of my fellow Couriers were there, Kolettis and Pappas, both enjoying layoffs. Pappas, of the drooping mustache, managed to look sad even while pinching a firm Persian buttock, but Kolettis, plump and boisterous, was in high form, singing and laughing. A third man, whom I didn't know, was peering at the fish in the pool. Though dressed in twelfth-century robes, he had a face that was instantly recognizable as modern, I thought. And I was right.

"This is Scholar Magistrate Paul Speer," said Metaxas to me in English. "A visiting academic. Meet Time Courier Jud Elliott, Dr. Speer."

We touched hands formally. Speer was about fifty, somewhat desiccated, a pale little man with an angular face and quick, nervous eyes. "Pleased," he said.

"And this," said Metaxas, "is Eudocia."

I had noticed her the instant I entered the courtyard, of course. She was a slim, auburn-haired girl, fair-skinned but with dark eyes, nineteen or twenty years old. She was heavily laden with jewelry, and so obviously was not just one of the slavegirls; yet her costume was daring by Byzantine standards, consisting only of a light double winding of translucent silk. As the fabric pulled taut against her, it displayed small high breasts, boyish buttocks, a shallow navel, even a hint of the triangular tuft at her loins. I prefer my women dark of hair and complexion and voluptuous of figure, but even so this Eudocia was enormously attractive to me. She seemed tense, coiled, full of pent-up fury and fervor.

She studied me in cool boldness and indicated her approval by placing her hands at her thighs and arching her back. The movement pulled her robes closer and showed me her nakedness in greater detail. She smiled. Her eyes sparkled wantonly.

In English, Metaxas said to me, "I've told you of her. She's my great-great-multi-great-grandmother. Try her in your bed tonight. The hip action is incredible!"

Eudocia smiled more warmly. She didn't know what Metaxas was saying, but she must have known he was talking about her. I tried not to stare too intently at the exposed beauties of the fair Eudocia. Is a man supposed to ogle his host's great-great-multi-great-grandmother?

A bare and beautiful slave offered me lamb and olives en brochette. I swallowed without tasting. My nostrils were filled with the perfume of Eudocia.

Metaxas gave me wine and led me away from her. "Dr. Speer," he said, "is here on a collecting trip. He's a student of classical Greek drama, in search of lost plays."

Dr. Speer clicked his heels. He was the sort of Teutonic pedant who, you automatically know, would use his full academic title on all occasions. *Achtung! Herr Scholar Magistrate Speer!* Scholar Magistrate Speer said, "It has been most successful for me so far. Of course, my search is just beginning, yet already from Byzantine libraries I have obtained the *Nausicaa* and *Triptolemus* of Sophocles, and of Euripides the *Andromeda,* the *Peliades,* the *Phaethon,* and the *Oedipus,* and also of Aeschylus a nearly complete manuscript of *The Women of Aetna*. So you see I have done well." He clicked heels again.

I knew better than to remind him that the Time Patrol frowns on the recovery of lost masterpieces. Here in Metaxas' villa we were all ipso facto breakers of Patrol regulations, and accessories before and after the fact to any number of timecrimes.

I said, "Do you plan to bring these manuscripts down to now-time?"

"Yes, of course."

"But you can't publish them! What will you do with them?"

"Study them," said Scholar Magistrate Speer. "Increase the depth of my understanding of the Greek drama. And in time I will plant each manuscript in some place where archaeologists are likely to discover it, and so these plays will be restored to the world. It is a minor crime, is it not? Can I be called evil for wishing to enlarge our scanty stock of Sophocles?"

It seemed quite all right to me.

To me it has always seemed like numbnoggin uptightness to have made it illegal to go up the line to discover lost manuscripts or paintings. I can see where it wouldn't be desirable to let somebody go back to 1600 and make off with Michelangelo's *Pietá* or Leonardo's *Leda*. That would be timechange and timecrime, since the *Pietá* and the *Leda* must make their way year by year toward our now-time, and not leapfrog over four and a half centuries. But why not allow us to obtain works of art that we don't already have? Who's injured by it?

Kolettis said, "Doc Speer, you're absolutely right! Hell, they let historians inspect the past to make corrections in the historical record, don't they? And when they bring out their revisionist books, it goddam well alters the state of knowledge!"

"Yes," said Pappas. "As for example when it was noticed that Lady Macbeth was in fact a tender woman who struggled in vain to limit the insane ambitions of her bloodthirsty husband. Or we could consider the case of the Moses story. Or what we know now about Richard III. Or the truth about Joan of Arc. We've patched up standard history in a million places since Benchley Effect travel began, and—"

"—and so why not patch up some of the holes in literary history?" Kolettis asked. "Here's to Doc Speer! Steal every goddam play there is, Doc!"

"The risks are great," said Speer. "If I am caught I will be severely punished, perhaps stripped of my academic standing." He said it as though he'd prefer to be parted from his genitals. "The law is so foolish—they are such frightened men, these Time Patrol, worried about changes even that are virtuous."

To the Time Patrol no change is virtuous. They accept historical revisions because they can't help themselves; the enabling legislation specifically permits that kind of research. But the same law prohibits the transportation of any tangible object from up the line, except as required for the functions of the Time Service itself, and the Patrol sticks to the letter of it.

I said, "If you're looking for Greek plays, why don't you check out the Alexandria Library? You're bound to find a dozen there for every one that's survived into the Byzantine period."

Scholar Magistrate Speer gave me the smile one gives to clever but naive children.

"The Library of Alexandria," he explained ponderously, "is of course a prime target for scholars such as myself. Therefore it is guarded perpetually by a man of the Time Patrol in the guise of a scribe. He makes several arrests a month, I hear. I take no risk such as that. Here in Byzantium my goal is more hard but my exposure is not so much. I will look more. I still hope to find some ninety plays of Sophocles, and at least so many of Aeschylus, and—"

36.

Dinner that night was a gaudy feast. We gorged on soups, stews, grilled duck, fish, pork, lamb, asparagus, mushrooms, apples, figs, artichokes, hard-boiled eggs served in blue enamel egg cups, cheese, salads, and wine. Out of courtesy to Eudocia, who was at table with us, we conversed in Greek and therefore spoke not at all of time-travel or the iniquities of the Time Patrol.

After dinner, while dwarf jesters performed, I called Metaxas aside. "I have something to show you," I said, and handed him the roll of vellum on which I had inscribed my genealogy. He glanced at it and frowned.

"What is it?"

"My ancestry. Back to the seventh century."

"When did you do all this?" he asked, laughing.

"On my last layoff." I told him of my visits to Grandfather Passilidis, to Gregory Markezinis, to the time of Nicephorus Ducas.

Metaxas studied the list more carefully.

"*Ducas?* What is this, Ducas?"

"That's me. I'm a Ducas. The scribe gave me the details right back to the seventh century."

"Impossible. Nobody knows who the Ducases were, that early! It's false!"

"Maybe that part is. But from 950 on, it's legitimate. Those are my people. I followed them right out of Byzantium into Albania and on to twentieth-century Greece."

"This is the truth?"

"I swear it!"

"You clever little cockeater," Metaxas said fondly. "All in one lay-

off, you learned this. And a Ducas, no less! A Ducas!" He consulted
the list again. "Nicephorus Ducas, son of Nicetas Ducas, son of—
hmm—Leo Ducas! Pulcheria Botaniates!"

"What's wrong?"

"I know them," Metaxas cried. "They've been my guests here, and
I've stayed with them. He's one of the richest men in Byzantium, do
you know that? And his wife Pulcheria—such a beautiful girl—" He
gripped my arm fiercely. "You'd swear? These are your ancestors?"

"I'm positive."

"Wonderful," Metaxas said. "Let me tell you about Pulcheria, now.
She's—oh, seventeen years old. Leo married her when she was just a
child; they do a lot of that here. She's got a waist like *this,* but breasts
out to *here,* and a flat belly and eyes that turn you afire, and—"

I shook free of his grasp and jammed my face close to his.

"Metaxas, have you—"

I couldn't say it.

"—slept with Pulcheria? No, no, I haven't. God's truth, Jud! I've
got enough women here. But look, boy, here's *your* opportunity! I can
help you to meet her. She's ripe for seduction. Young, childless, beautiful, bored, her husband so busy with business matters that he hardly
notices her—and she's your own great-great-multi-grandmother besides!"

"That part is your clutchup, not mine," I reminded him. "For me it
might be a reason to stay away from her, in fact."

"Don't be an idiot. I'll fix it all up for you in two, three days. An
introduction to the Ducases, a night as a guest in their palace in town,
a word to Pulcheria's lady in waiting"

"No," I said.

"No?"

"No. I don't want to get mixed up in any of this."

"You're a hard man to make happy, Jud. You don't want to fuck
Empress Theodora, you don't want to lay Pulcheria Ducas, you—say,
next thing you'll tell me you don't want Eudocia either."

"I don't mind screwing one of *your* ancestors," I said. I grinned. "I
wouldn't even mind putting a baby in Eudocia's belly. How would you
feel if I turned out to be your multi-great-grandfather?"

"You can't," said Metaxas.

"Why not?"

"Because Eudocia remains unmarried and childless until 1109. Then
she weds Basil Stratiocus and has seven sons and three daughters in the
following fifteen years, including one who is ancestral to me. Christ,
does she get fat!"

"All of that can be changed," I reminded him.

"Like holy crap it can," said Metaxas. "Don't you think I guard my own line of descent? Don't you think I'd obliterate you from history if I caught you making a timechange on Eudocia's marriage? She'll stay childless until Basil Stratiocus fills her up, and that's that. But she's yours for tonight."

And she was. Giving me the highest degree of hospitality in his lexicon, Metaxas sent his ancestress Eudocia into my bedroom. Her lean, supple body was a trifle meager for me; her hard little breasts barely filled my hands. But she was a tigress. She was all energy and all passion, and she clambered on top of me and rocked herself to ecstasy in twenty quick rotations, and that was only the beginning. It was dawn before she let me sleep.

And in my dreams I saw Metaxas escort me to the palace of the Ducases, and introduce me to my multi-great-grandfather Leo, who said serenely, "This is my wife Pulcheria," and in my dream it seemed to me that she was the loveliest woman I had ever seen.

37.

I had my first troublesome moment as a Courier on my next tour. Because I was too proud to call in the Time Patrol for help, I got myself involved in the Paradox of Duplication and also caught a taste of the Paradox of Transit Displacement. But I think I came out of it looking pretty good.

I was escorting nine tourists through the arrival of the First Crusade in Byzantium when the mess happened.

"In 1095," I told my people, "Pope Urban II called for the liberation of the Holy Land from the Saracens. Very shortly, the knights of Europe began to enroll in the Crusade. Among those who welcomed such a war of liberation was Emperor Alexius of Byzantium, who saw in it a way of regaining the territories in the Near East that Byzantium had lost to the Turks and the Arabs. Alexius sent word that he wouldn't mind getting a few hundred experienced knights to help him clean the infidels out. But he got a good deal more than that, as we'll see in a moment, down the line in 1096."

We shunted to August 1, 1096.

Ascending the walls of Constantinople, we peered out into the countryside and saw it full of troops: not mailed knights but a raggle-taggle band of tattered peasants.

"This," I said, "is the People's Crusade. While the professional soldiers were working out the logistics of their march, a scrawny, foul-smelling little charismatic named Peter the Hermit rounded up thousands of paupers and farmers and led them across Europe to Byzantium. They looted and pillaged along the way, cleaned out the harvest of half of Europe, and burned Belgrade in a dispute with the Byzantine administrators. But finally they got here, 30,000 of them."

"Which one is Peter the Hermit?" asked the most obstreperous member of the group, a full-blown, fortyish bachelor lady from Des Moines named Marge Hefferin. I checked the time. "You'll see him in another minute and a half. Alexius has sent a couple of officials to invite Peter to court. He wants Peter and his rabble to wait in Constantinople until the knights and barons get here, since these people will get slaughtered by the Turks if they go over into Asia Minor without a military escort. Look: there's Peter now."

Two dandified Byzantine grandees emerged from the mob, obviously holding their breath and looking as though they'd like to hold their noses too. Between them marched a scruffy, barefoot, rag-clad, filthy, long-chinned, gnomish man with blazing eyes and a pock-marked face.

"Peter the Hermit," I said, "on his way to see the emperor."

We shunted forward three days. The People's Crusade was inside Constantinople and playing hell with Alexius' city. A good many buildings were aflame. Ten Crusaders were atop one of the churches, stripping the lead from its roof for resale. A highborn-looking Byzantine woman emerged from Haghia Sophia and was stripped bare and raped by a pack of Peter's pious pilgrims before our eyes.

I said, "Alexius has miscalculated by letting this riffraff into the city. Now he's making arrangements to get them out the other side, by offering free ferry service across the Bosphorus to Asia. On August 6 they'll start on their way. The Crusaders will begin by massacring the Byzantine settlements in western Asia Minor; then they'll attack the Turks and be wiped out almost completely. If we had time, I'd take you down to 1097 and across to see the mountain of bones along the road. That's what happened to the People's Crusade. However, the pros are on their way, so let's watch them."

I explained about the four armies of Crusaders: the army of Raymond of Toulouse, the army of Duke Robert of Normandy, the army of Bohemond and Tancred, and the army of Godfrey of Bouillon, Eustace of Boulogne, and Baldwin of Lorraine. Some of my people had read up on their Crusader history and nodded in recognition of the names.

We shunted to the final week of 1096. "Alexius," I said, "has learned his lesson from the People's Crusade. He doesn't plan to let the real Crusaders linger long in Constantinople. They all have to pass through Byzantium on their way to the Holy Land, but he's going to hustle them through in a hurry, and he'll make their leaders swear allegiance to him before he admits them."

We watched the army of Godfrey of Bouillon pitch camp outside the walls of Constantinople. We observed the envoys going back and forth, Alexius requesting the oath of allegiance, Godfrey refusing. With careful editing I covered four months in less than an hour, showing how mistrust and enmity were building up between the Christian Crusaders and the Christian Byzantines who were supposed to collaborate in the liberation of the Holy Land. Godfrey still refused to swear allegiance; Alexius not only kept the Crusaders sealed out of Constantinople, but now was blockading their camp, hoping to starve them into going away. Baldwin of Lorraine began to raid the suburbs; Godfrey captured a platoon of Byzantine soldiers and put them to death in view of the city walls. And on April 2 the Crusaders began to lay siege to the city.

"Observe how easily the Byzantines drive them off," I said. "Alexius, losing patience, has sent his best troops into battle. The Crusaders, not yet accustomed to fighting together, flee. On Easter Sunday, Godfrey and Baldwin submit, and swear allegiance to Alexius. All now is well. The emperor will give a banquet for the Crusaders in Constantinople, and then swiftly will ship them across the Bosphorus. More Crusaders, he knows, will arrive in a few days—the army of Bohemond and Tancred."

Marge Hefferin emitted a little gasping squeak at the sound of those names. I should have been warned.

We skipped forward to April 10 for a look at the next batch of Crusaders. Thousands of soldiers again camped outside Constantinople. They strolled around arrogantly in chain mail and surcoats, and playfully swatted each other with swords or maces when things got dull.

"Which one is Bohemond?" asked Marge Hefferin.

I scanned the field. "There," I said.

"Ooooh."

He *was* impressive. About two meters tall, a giant for his times, head and shoulders above everyone else around him. Broad shoulders, deep chest, close-cropped hair. Strangely white of skin. Swaggering posture. A grim customer, tough and savage.

He was cleverer than the other leaders, too. Instead of quarreling with Alexius over the business of swearing allegiance, Bohemond gave in immediately. Oaths, to him, were only words, and it was foolish to waste time bickering with the Byzantines when there were empires to be won in Asia. So Bohemond got quick entry to Constantinople. I took my people to the gate where he'd be passing into the city, so they could have a close look at him. A mistake.

The Crusaders came striding grandly in on foot, six abreast.

When Bohemond appeared, Marge Hefferin broke from the group.

She ripped open her tunic and let her big pale breasts bobble into the open. An advertisement, I suppose.

She rushed toward Bohemond, squealing, "Bohemond, Bohemond, I love you, I've always loved you, Bohemond! Take me! Make me your slave, beloved!" And other words to that effect.

Bohemond turned and peered at her in bewilderment. I guess the sight of a hefty, shrieking, half-naked female running wildly in his direction must have puzzled him. But Marge didn't get within five meters of him.

A knight just in front of Bohemond, deciding that an assassination plot was unfolding, pulled out his dagger and jammed it right between Marge's big breasts. The impact halted her mad charge, and she staggered back, frowning. Blood burbled from her lips. As she toppled, another knight swung at her with a broadsword and just about cut her in half at the waist. Entrails went spilling all over the pavement.

The whole thing took about fifteen seconds. I had no chance to move. I stood aghast, realizing that my career as a Time Courier might just have come to an end. Losing a tourist is about the worst thing a Courier can do, short of committing timecrime itself.

I had to act quickly.

I said to my tourists, "Don't any of you move from the spot! That's an order!"

It wasn't likely that they'd disobey. They were huddled together in hysteria, sobbing and puking and shivering. The shock alone would hold them in place for a few minutes—more time than I'd need.

I set my timer for a two-minute jump up the line and shunted fast.

Instantly I found myself standing right behind myself. There I was, big ears and all, watching Bohemond saunter up the street. My tourists were standing on both sides of me. Marge Hefferin, breathing hard, rearing up on tiptoes for a better view of her idol, was already starting to undo her tunic.

I moved into position in back of her.

Just as she made the first movement toward the street, my hands shot out. I clamped my left hand on her ass and got the right hand on her breast and hissed in her ear, "Stay where you are or you'll be sorriest."

She squirmed and twisted. I dug my fingertips deep into the meat of her quivering rump and hung on. She writhed around to see who her attacker was, saw it was me, and stared in amazement at the other me a few paces to her left. All the fight went out of her. She sagged, and I whispered another reminder for her to stay put, and then Bohemond was past us and well up the street.

I released her, set my timer, and shunted down the line by sixty seconds.

My net absence from my tourists had been less than a minute. I half expected to find them still gagging and retching over the bloody smiting of Marge Hefferin. But the editing had succeeded. There was no corpse in the street now. No intestines were spilled beneath the boots of the marching Crusaders. Marge stood with the group, shaking her head in confusion and rubbing her backside. Her tunic still hung open and I could see the red imprints of my fingers on the soft globe of her right breast.

Did any of them suspect what had happened? No. No. Not even a phantom memory. My tourists did not experience the Paradox of Transit Displacement, for they had not made the jump-within-a-jump that I had; and so only I remembered what now was gone from their minds, could recall clearly the bloody event that I had transformed into a nonevent.

"Down the line!" I yelled, and shunted them all into 1098.

The street was quiet. The Crusaders were long since gone, and at the moment were hung up in Syria at the siege of Antioch. It was dusk on a sticky summer day and there were no witnesses to our sudden arrival.

Marge was the only one who realized that something funny had gone on; the others had not seen anything unusual occurring, but she clearly knew that an extra Jud Elliott had materialized behind her and prevented her from rushing out into the street.

"What the hell do you think you were doing?" I asked her. "You were about to run out into the street and throw yourself at Bohemond, weren't you?"

"I couldn't help it. It was a sudden compulsion. I've always loved Bohemond, don't you see? He's been my hero, my god—I've read every word anyone's written about him—and then there he was, right in front of me—"

"Let me tell you how events really unfolded," I said, and described the way she had been killed. Then I told her how I had edited the past, how I had pinched the episode of her death into a parallel line. I said, "I want you to know that the only reason I got you unkilled was to save my own job. It looks bad for a Courier if he can't keep control of his people. Otherwise I'd have been happy to leave you disemboweled. Didn't I tell you a million times *never* to break from cover?"

I warned her to forget every shred of my admission that I had changed events to save her life.

"The next time you disobey me in any way, though," I told her, "I'll—"

I was going to say that I'd ram her head up her tail and make a Moebius strip out of her. Then I realized that a Courier can't talk to a client that way, no matter what the provocation.

"—cancel your tour and send you down the line to now-time immediately, you hear me?"

"I won't ever try that again," she murmured. "I swear it. You know, now that you've told me about it, I can almost feel it happening. That dagger going into me—"

"It never happened."

"It never happened," she said doubtfully.

"Put some conviction into it. *It never happened.*"

"*It never happened,*" she repeated. "But I can almost feel it!"

38.

We all spent the night in an inn in 1098. Feeling tense and stale after so much delicate work, I decided to jump down to 1105, while my people slept, and drop in on Metaxas. I didn't even know if he'd be at his villa, but it was worth the try. I needed desperately to unwind.

I calibrated the timing with care.

Metaxas' last layoff had begun in early November, 2059, and he had jumped to mid-August, 1105. I figured he had spent ten or twelve days there. That schedule would have returned him to 2059 toward the end of November; and then, assuming he had taken out a group on a two-week tour, he'd have been able to get back to his villa by September 15 or so, 1105.

I played it safe and shunted down to September 20.

Now I had to find a way to get to his villa.

It is one of the oddities of the era of the Benchley Effect that I would find it easier to jump across seven years of time than to get myself a few dozen kilometers into the Byzantine countryside. But I did have that problem. I had no access to a chariot, and there aren't any cabs for hire in the twelfth century.

Walk? Ridiculous idea!

I contemplated heading for the nearest inn and dangling bezants in front of freelance charioteers until I found one willing to make the trip to Metaxas' place. As I considered this I heard a familiar voice yelling, "Herr Courier Elliott! Herr Courier Elliott!"

I turned. Scholar Magistrate Speer.

"*Guten Tag*, Herr Courier Elliott!" said Scholar Magistrate Speer.

"Guten—" I scowled, cut myself short, greeted him in a more Byzantine way. He smiled indulgently at my observance of the rules.

"I have a very successful visit been having," he said. "Since last I enjoyed with you company, have I found the *Thamyras* of Sophocles and also the *Melanippe* of Euripides, and further a partial text of what I believe is the *Archelaus* of Euripides. And then there is besides the text of a play that is claiming to be of Aeschylus the *Helios*, of which there is in the records no reference for. So perhaps is a forgery or otherwise is maybe a new discovery, I will see which only upon reading. Eh? A good visit, eh, Herr Courier!"

"Splendid," I said.

"And now I am returning to the villa of our friend Metaxas, just as soon as I complete a small purchase in this shop of spices. Would you accompany me?"

"You have wheels?" I asked.

"Was meinen Sie mit 'wheels'?"

"Transportation. A chariot."

"Naturlich! Over there. It waits for me, a chariot *mit* driver, from Metaxas."

"Swell," I said. "Take care of your business in the spice shop and then we can ride out to Metaxas' place together, okay?"

The shop was dark and fragrant. In barrels, jugs, flasks, and baskets it displayed its wares: olives, nuts, dates, figs, raisins, pistachios, cheeses, and spices both ground and whole of many different sorts. Speer, apparently running some errand for Metaxas' chef, selected a few items and pulled forth a purse of bezants to pay for them. While this was going on, an ornate chariot pulled up outside the shop and three figures dismounted and entered. One was a slavegirl—to carry the merchandise to the chariot, evidently. The second was a woman of mature years and simple dress—a duenna, I supposed, just the right kind of dragon to escort a Byzantine wife on a shopping expedition. The third person was the wife herself, obviously a woman of the very highest class making a tour of the town.

She was fantastically beautiful.

I knew at once that she was no more than seventeen. She had a supple, liquid Mediterranean beauty; her eyes were dark and large and glossy, with long lashes, and her skin was light olive in hue, and her lips were full and her nose aquiline, and her bearing was elegant and aristocratic. Her robes of white silk revealed the outlines of high, sumptuous breasts, curving flanks, voluptuous buttocks. She was all the women I had ever desired, united into one ideal form.

I stared at her without shame.

She stared back. Without shame.

Our eyes met and held, and a current of pure force passed between us, and I quivered as the full surge hit me. She smiled only on the left side of her mouth, quirking the lips in, revealing two glistening teeth. It was a smile of invitation, a smile of lust.

She nodded almost imperceptibly to me.

Then she turned away, and pointed to the bins, ordering this and this and this, and I continued to stare, until the duenna, noticing it, shot me a furious look of warning.

"Come," Speer said impatiently. "The chariot is waiting—"

"Let it wait a little longer."

I made him stay in the store with me until the three women had completed their transaction. I watched them leave, my eyes riveted to the subtle sway of my beloved's silk-sheathed tail. Then I whirled and pounced on the proprietor of the shop, seizing his wrist and barking, "That woman! What's her name?"

"Milord, I—that is—"

I flipped a gold piece to the counter. "Her name!"

"That is Pulcheria Ducas," he gasped. "The wife of the well-known Leo Ducas, who—"

I groaned and rushed out of the store.

Her chariot clattered off toward the Golden Horn.

Speer emerged. "Are you in good health, Herr Courier Elliott?"

"I'm sick as a pig," I muttered. "Pulchcria Ducas—that was Pulcheria Ducas—"

"And so?"

"I love her, Speer, can you understand that?"

Looking blankfaced, he said, "The chariot is ready."

"Never mind. I'm not going with you. Give Metaxas my best regards."

In anguish I ran down the street, aimlessly, my mind and my crotch inflamed with the vision of Pulcheria. I trembled. I streamed with sweat. I sobbed. Finally I came up against the wall of some church, and pressed my cheek to the cold stone, and touched my timer and shunted back to the tourists I had left sleeping in 1098.

39.

I was a lousy Courier for the rest of that trip.

Moody, withdrawn, lovesick, confused, I shuttled my people through the standard events, the Venetian invasion of 1204 and the Turkish conquest of 1453, in a routine, mechanical way. Maybe they didn't realize they were getting a minimum job, or didn't care. Maybe they blamed it on the trouble Marge Hefferin had caused. For better or for worse I gave them their tour and delivered them safely down the line in now-time and was rid of them.

I was on layoff again, and my soul was infected by desire.

Go to 1105? Accept Metaxas' offer, let him introduce me to Pulcheria?

I recoiled at the idea.

Time Patrol rules specifically forbid any kind of fraternization between Couriers (or other time-travelers) and people who live up the line. The only contact we are supposed to have with the residents of the past is casual and incidental—buying a bag of olives, asking how to get to Haghia Sophia from here, like that. We are not permitted to strike up friendships, get into long philosophical discussions, or have sexual intercourse with inhabitants of previous eras.

Especially with our own ancestors.

The incest taboo per se didn't scare me much; like all taboos, it isn't worth a whole lot any more, and while I'd hesitate at bedding my sister or my mother, I couldn't see any very convincing reason to abstain from bedding Pulcheria. I felt a little lingering puritanism, maybe, but I knew it would fade in a minute if Pulcheria became available.

What held me back, though, was the universal deterrent, fear of retribution. If the Time Patrol caught me sexing around with my multi-great-grandmother, they'd certainly fire me from the Time Service, might imprison me, might even try to invoke the death penalty for first-degree timecrime on the grounds that I had tried to become my own ancestor. I was terrified of the possibilities.

How could they catch me?

Plenty of scenarios presented themselves. For example:

I wangle introduction to Pulcheria. Somehow get into situation of privacy with her. Reach for her fair flesh; she screams; family body-guards seize me and put me to death. Time Patrol, when I don't check in after my layoff, traces me, finds out what has happened, rescues me, then brings charges of timecrime.

Or:

I wangle introduction, etc., and seduce Pulcheria. Just at moment of mutual climax husband bursts into bedroom and impales me. Rest of scenario follows.

Or:

I fall so desperately in love with Pulcheria that I abscond with her to some distant point in time, say 400 B.C. or A.D. 1600, and we live happily ever after until Time Patrol catches us, returns her to proper moment of 1105, brings charges of timecrime against me.

Or:

A dozen other possibilities, all of them ending in the same melancholy way. So I resisted all temptation to spend my layoff in 1105 sniffing after Pulcheria. Instead, to suit the darkness of my mood in this time of unrequited lust, I signed up to do the Black Death tour.

Only the weirds, the freaks, the sickos, and the pervos would take a tour like that, which is to say the demand is always pretty heavy. But as a vacationing Courier, I was able to bump a paying customer and get into the next group leaving.

There are four regular Black Death outings. One sets out from the Crimea for 1347 and shows you the plague as it spills out of Asia. The highlight of that tour is the siege of Kaffa, a Genoese trading port on the Black Sea, by Khan Janibeg of the Kipchak Mongols. Janibeg's men were rotten with plague, and he catapulted their corpses into the town to infect the Genoese. You have to book a reservation a year in advance for that one.

The Genoese carried the Black Death westward into the Mediterranean, and the second tour takes you to Italy, autumn of 1347, to watch it spread inland. You see a mass burning of Jews, who were thought to have caused the epidemic by poisoning the wells. The third tour brings you to France in 1348, and the fourth to England in the late spring of 1349.

The booking office got me on the England trip. I made a noon hop to London and joined the group two hours before it was about to leave. Our Courier was a tall, cadaverous man named Riley, with bushy eyebrows and bad teeth. He was a little strange, as you have to be to specialize in this particular tour. He welcomed me in friendly if moody fashion and got me fitted for a plague suit.

A plague suit is more or less a spacesuit, done up in black trim. You carry a standard fourteen-day rebreathing unit, you eat via an intake pipe, and you eliminate wastes with difficulty and complexity. The idea, naturally, is to keep you totally sealed off from the infectious environment. Tourists are told that if they open their suits even for ten seconds, they'll be marooned permanently in the plague era; and although this is not true at all, there hasn't been a case yet of a tourist calling the Time Service's bluff.

This is one of the few tours that operates to and from fixed points. We don't want returning groups materializing all over the place, carrying plague on their spacesuits, and so the Service has marked off jumping areas in red paint at the medieval end of each of the four plague tours. When your group is ready to come back, you go to a jumping area and shunt down the line from there. This materializes you within a sealed sterile dome; your suit is taken from you and you are thoroughly fumigated before you're allowed to rejoin the twenty-first century.

"What you are about to see," said Riley portentously, "is neither a reconstruction nor a simulation nor an approximation. It is the real thing, exaggerated in no way."

We shunted up the line.

40.

Clad in our black plastic suits, we marched single file through a land of the dead.

Nobody paid any attention to us. At such a time as this our costume didn't even seem outlandish; the black was logical, the airtight sealing of our suits even more logical. And though the fabric was a little on the anachronistic side for the fourteenth century, no one was curious. At this time, wise men stayed indoors and kept their curiosities on tight leashes.

Those who saw us must have assumed that we were priests going on a pilgrimage of prayer. Our somber suits, our single-file array, the fearlessness with which we paraded through the worst areas of infestation, all marked us as God's men, or else Satan's, and, either way, who would dare to interfere with us?

Bells tolled a leaden dirge, donging all day and half the night. The world was a perpetual funeral. A grim haze hung over London; the sky was never anything but gray and ashen all the time we were there. Not that nature was reinforcing the dolefulness, that old pathetic fallacy; no, the haze was man-made, for thousands of small fires were burning in England, consuming the clothes and the homes and the bodies of the stricken.

We saw plague victims in all stages, from the early staggering to the later trembling and sweating and falling and convulsing. "The onset of the disease," said Riley calmly, dispassionately, "is marked by hardenings and swellings of the glands in the armpits and the groin. The swellings rapidly grow to the size of eggs or apples. See, this woman here—" She was young, haggard, terrorstricken. She clutched desperately at the sprouting buboes and lurched past us through the smoky streets.

"Next," he said, "come the black blotches, first on the arms and thighs, then all over the body. And the carbuncles which, when lanced, give no relief. And then delirium, insanity, death always on the third day after the swellings appear. Observe here—" A victim in the late stages, groaning in the street, abandoned. "And here—" Pale faces looking down from a window. "Over here—" Heaped corpses at the door of a stable.

Houses were locked. Shops were barred. The only people in the streets were those already infected, roaming desperately about searching for a doctor, a priest, a miracle-worker.

Fractured, tormented music came to us from the distance: pipes, drums, viols, lutes, sackbuts, shawms, clarions, krummhorns, all the medieval instruments at once but giving forth not the pretty buzz and tootle of the middle ages, rather a harsh, discordant, keyless whine and screech. Riley looked pleased. "A procession of flagellants is coming!" he cried, elated. "Follow me! By all means, let's not miss it!"

And through the winding streets the flagellants came, men and women, naked to the waist, grimy, bloody, some playing on instruments, most wielding knotted whips, lashing, lashing, tirelessly bringing down the lash across bare backs, breasts, cheeks, arms, foreheads. They droned toneless hymns; they groaned in agony; they stumbled forward, a few of the whippers and some of the whipped already showing the buboes of the plague, and without looking at us they went by, down some dismal alley leading to a deserted church.

And we happy time-tourists picked our way over the dead and the dying and marched on, for our Courier wished us to drink this experience to the deepest.

We saw the bonfired bodies of the dead blackening and splitting open.

We saw other heaps of the unburied left in fields to rot.

We saw ghouls searching cadavers for items of value.

We saw a plague-smitten man fall upon a half-conscious plague-smitten woman in the streets, and part her thighs for one last desperate act of lust.

We saw priests on horseback fleeing from parishioners begging for Heaven's mercy.

We entered an unguarded palace to watch terrified surgeons letting blood from some dying duke.

We saw another procession of strange black-clad beings cross our street at an angle, their faces hidden behind mirrorlike plates, and we

shivered at the grotesque sight of these nightmare marchers, these demons without faces, and we realized only slowly that we had intersected
some other party of tourists.

Riley was ready with cool statistics. "The mortality rate of the Black
Death," he announced, "was anywhere from one-eighth to two-thirds of
the population in a given area. In Europe it is estimated that twenty-
five per cent of the entire population perished; worldwide, the mortality
was about thirty-three per cent. That is to say, a similar plague today
would take the lives of more than two billion people."

We watched a woman emerge from a thatched house and, one by
one, arrange the bodies of five children in the street so that they might
be taken away by the department of sanitation.

Riley said, "The aristocracy was annihilated, causing great shifts in
patterns of inheritance. There were permanent cultural effects as a result
of the wholesale death of painters of a single school, of poets, of learned
monks. The psychological impact was long-lasting; for generations it
was thought that the mid-fourteenth century had done something to earn
the wrath of God, and a return of His wrath was momentarily expected."

We formed the audience for a mass funeral at which two young and
frightened priests muttered words over a hundred blotched and swollen
corpses, tolled their little bells, sprinkled holy water, and signaled to the
sextons to start the bonfire.

"Not until the early sixteenth century," said Riley, "will the population reach its pre-1348 level."

It was impossible for me to tell how the others were affected by
these horrors, since we all were hidden in our suits. Probably most of
my companions were fascinated and thrilled. I'm told that it's customary
for a dedicated plague aficionado to take all four Black Death tours in
succession, starting in the Crimea; many have gone through the set five
or six times. My own reaction was one of diminishing shock. You ac-
commodate to monstrous horror. I think that by the tenth time through
I'd have been as cool and dispassionate as Courier Riley, that brimming
fount of statistics.

At the end of our journey through hell we made our way to West-
minster. On the pavement outside the palace, Time Service personnel
had painted a red circle five meters in diameter. This was our jumping
point. We gathered close in the middle. I helped Riley make the timer
adjustments—on this tour, the timers are mounted on the outside of the
suits. He gave the signal and we shunted.

A couple of plague victims, shambling past the palace, were witnesses to our departure. I doubt that it troubled them much. In a time
when all the world is perishing, who can get excited over the sight of
ten black demons vanishing?

41.

Wwe emerged under a shimmering dome, yielded up our polluted suits, and came forth purged and purified and ennobled by what we had seen. But images of Pulcheria still obsessed me. Restless, tormented, I fought with temptation.

Go back to 1105? Let Metaxas insinuate me into the Ducas household? Bed Pulcheria and ease my yearnings?

No. No. No. No.

Fight temptation. Sublimate. Fuck an empress instead.

I hurried back to Istanbul and shunted up the line to 537. I went over to Haghia Sophia to look for Metaxas at the dedication ceremony.

Metaxas was there, in many parts of the throng. I spotted at least ten of him. (I also saw two Jud Elliotts, and I wasn't half trying.) On my first two approaches, though, I ran into the Paradox of Discontinuity; neither Metaxas knew me. One shook me off with a scowl of irritation, and the other simply said, "Whoever you are, we haven't met yet. Beat it." On the third try I found a Metaxas who recognized me, and we arranged to meet that evening at the inn where he was lodging his tour. He was staying down the line in 610 to show his people the coronation of Emperor Heraclius.

"Well?" he said. "What's your now-time basis, anyway?"

"Early December, 2059."

"I'm ahead of you," said Metaxas. "I'm out of the middle of February, 2060. We're discontinuous."

That scared me. This man knew two and a half months of my future. Etiquette required him to keep his knowledge to himself; it was quite possible that I would be/had been killed in January, 2060, and that this

Metaxas knew all the details, but he couldn't drop a hint of that to this me. Still, the gap frightened me.

He saw it. "Do you want to go back and find a different one?" he asked.

"No. That's all right. I think we can manage."

His face was a frozen mask. He played by the rules; neither by inflection nor expression was he going to react to anything I said in a way that might reveal my own future to me.

"You once said you'd help me get into Empress Theodora."

"I remember that, yes."

"I turned you down then. Now I'd like to try her."

"No problem," said Metaxas. "Let's jump up to 535. Justinian will be preoccupied with building Haghia Sophia. Theodora's available."

"How easily?"

"Nothing to it," he said.

We shunted. On a cool spring day in 535 I went with Metaxas to the Great Palace, where he sought and found a plump, eunuchoid individual named Anastasius and had a long, animated discussion with him. Evidently Anastasus was chief procurer to the empress this year, and had he responsibility of finding her anywhere from one to ten young men a night. The conversation was carried on in low muttered tones, punctuated by angry outbursts, but from what I could hear of it I gathered that Anastasius was offering me an hour with Theodora, and that Metaxas was holding out for a whole night. I felt edgy about that. Virile I am, yes, but would I be able to entertain one of history's most celebrated nymphomaniacs from darkness to dawn? I signaled to Metaxas to accept something less grandiose, but he persisted, and in the end Anastasius agreed to let me have four hours with the empress.

"If he qualifies," the plump one said.

The test for qualification was administered by a ferocious little wench named Photia, one of the imperial ladies in waiting. Anastasius complacently watched us in action; Metaxas at least had the good taste to leave the room. Watching, I guess, was how Anastasius got his kickies.

Photia was black-haired, thin-lipped, busty, voracious. Have you ever seen a starfish devour an oyster? No? Well, imagine it, anyway. Photia was a starfish of sex. The suction was fantastic. I stayed with her, wrestled her into submission, pronged her off to ecstasy. And—I suppose—I passed my test with something to spare, because Anastasius gave me his seal of approval and set up my assignation with Theodora. Four hours.

I thanked Metaxas and he left, jumping down to his tour in 610.

Anastasius took charge of me. I was bathed, groomed, curried, required to swallow an oily, bitter potion that he claimed was an aphrodisiac. And an hour before midnight I was ushered into the bedchambers of the Empress Theodora.

Cleopatra . . . Delilah . . . Harlow . . . Lucrezia   Borgia . . . Theodora . . .

Had any of them ever existed? Was their legendary wantonness real? Could this truly be Judson Daniel Elliott III standing before the bed of the depraved Empress of Byzantium?

I knew the tales Procopius told of her. The orgies at dinners of state. The exhibitionist performances in the theater. The repeated illegitimate pregnancies and the annual abortions. The friends and lovers betrayed and tortured. The severed ears, noses, testicles, penes, limbs, and lips of those who displeased her. The offerings on the altar of Aphrodite of every orifice she owned. If only one story out of ten were true, her vileness was unequaled.

She was pale, fair-skinned, big-breasted, narrow-waisted, and surprisingly short, the top of her head barely reaching my chest. Perfumes drenched her skin, yet unmistakable fleshy reeks came through. Her eyes were fierce, cold, hard, slightly hyperthyroid: nymphomaniacal eyes.

She didn't ask my name. She ordered me to strip, and inspected me, and nodded. A wench brought us thick greasy wine in an enormous amphora. We drank a good deal of it, and then Theodora anointed herself with the rest, coating her skin with it from forehead to toes.

"Lick it off," she said.

I obeyed. I obeyed other commands too. Her tastes were remarkably various, and in my four hours I satisfied most of them. It may not have been the kinkiest four hours I ever spent, but came close. And yet her pyrotechnics chilled me. There was something mechanical and empty about the way Theodora presented now this, now that, now the other thing, for me to deal with. It was as if she were running through a script that she had played out a million times.

It was interesting in a strenuous way. But it wasn't overwhelming. I mean, I expected more, somehow, from being in bed with one of history's most famous sinners.

When I was fourteen years old, an old man who taught me a great deal about the way of the world said to me, "Son, when you've jazzed one snatch you've jazzed them all."

I was barely out of my virginity then, but I dared to disagree with him. I still do, in a way, but less and less each year. Women do vary—in figure, in passion, in technique, in approach. But I've had the Empress of Byzantium, mind you, Theodora herself. I'm beginning to think, after Theodora, that that old man was right. When you've jazzed one snatch you've jazzed them all.

42.

I went back down to Istanbul and reported for duty, and took a party of eight out on the two-week tour.

Neither the Black Death nor Theodora had burned away my passion for Pulcheria Ducas. I hoped now that I'd shake free of that dangerous obsession by getting back to work.

My tour group included the following people:

J. Frederick Gostaman of Biloxi, Mississippi, a retail dealer in pharmaceuticals and transplant organs, along with his wife, Louise, his sixteen-year-old daughter Palmyra, and his fourteen-year-old son Bilbo.

Conrad Sauerabend of St. Louis, Missouri, a stockbroker, traveling alone.

Miss Hester Pistil of Brooklyn, New York, a young schoolteacher.

Leopold Haggins of St. Petersburg, Florida, a retired manufacturer of power cores, and his wife Chrystal.

In short, the usual batch of overcapitalized and undereducated idlers. Sauerabend, who was fat and jowly and sullen, took an immediate dislike to Gostaman, who was fat and jowly and jovial, because Gostaman made a joking remark about the way Sauerabend was peering down the neckline of Gostaman's daughter at one of our orientation sessions. I think Gostaman was joking, anyway, but Sauerabend got red-faced and furious, and Palmyra, who though sixteen was underdeveloped enough to pass for a skinny thirteen, ran out of the room in tears. I patched things up, but Sauerabend continued to glare at Gostaman. Miss Pistil, the schoolteacher, who was a vacant-eyed blonde with an augmented bosom and an expression that managed to be both tense and languid, established at our first meeting that she is the sort of girl who takes these trips in order to get laid by Couriers; even if I hadn't been preoccupied with Pulcheria, I don't think I'd have taken advantage of her availability, but as things stood I felt very little urge to explore Miss Pistil's pelvis. This was not the case with young Bilbo Gostaman, who was such a fashion-plate that he was wearing knickers with padded groin (if they can revive Cretan bodices, why not the codpiece?) and who got his hand under Miss Pistil's skirt during our second orientation session. He thought he was being surreptitious about it, but I saw him, and so did old man Gostaman, who beamed in paternal pride, and so did Mrs. Chrystal Haggins, who was shocked into catalepsy. Miss Pistil looked thrilled, and squirmed a little to afford Bilbo a better angle for groping. Mr. Leopold Haggins, who was eighty-five and pretty leathery, meanwhile winked hopefully at Mrs. Louise Gostaman, a placid and matronly sort of woman who was destined to spend most of our tour fighting off the old scoundrel's quivering advances. You can see how it was.

Off we went for two happy weeks together.

I was, again, a second-rate Courier. I couldn't summon up the divine spark. I showed them everything I was supposed to show them, but I wasn't able to do the extra things, the leaping, cavorting, charismatic, Metaxian things, that I had vowed I would do on every trip.

Part of the trouble was my edginess over the Pulcheria situation. She danced in and out of my mind a thousand times a day. I pictured myself dropping down to 1105 or thereabouts and getting to work with her; surely she'd remember me from the spice shop, and surely that was an open invitation she had given me then.

Part of the trouble was the ebbing of my own sense of wonder. I had been on the Byzantium run for almost half a year, and the thrill was gone. A gifted Courier—a Metaxas—could derive as much excitement from his thousandth imperial coronation as from his third. And transmit that excitement to his people. Maybe I just wasn't a naturally gifted Courier. I was becoming bored with the dedication of Haghia Sophia and the baptism of Theodosius II, the way an usher in a stimmo house gets weary of watching orgies.

Part of the trouble was the presence of Conrad Sauerabend in the group. That fat, sweaty, untidy man was an instant turnoff for me every time he opened his mouth.

He wasn't stupid. But he was gross and coarse and crude. He was a leerer, a gaper, a gawker. I could count on him to make some blunt and inappropriate remark anywhere.

At the Augusteum he whistled and said, "What a parking lot this would make!"

Inside Haghia Sophia he clapped a white-bearded priest on the back and said, "I just got to tell you what a swell church you got here, priesto."

During a visit to the icon-smashings of Leo the Isaurian, when Byzantium's finest works of art were being destroyed as idols, he interrupted an earnest iconoclastic fanatic and said, "Don't be such a dumb prick. You know that you're hurting this city's tourist trade?"

Sauerabend was also a molester of little girls, and proud of it. "I can't help it," he explained. "It's my particular personal clutchup. The shrink calls it the Lolita complex. I like 'em twelve, thirteen years old. You know, old enough to bleed, maybe to have a little hair on it, but still kind of unripe. Get 'em before the tits grow, that's my ideal. I can't stand all that swinging meat on a woman. Pretty sick, huh?"

Pretty sick, yes. And also pretty annoying, because we had Palmyra Gostaman with us; Sauerabend couldn't stop staring at her. The lodgings provided on a time-tour don't always give the tourists much privacy, and Sauerabend ogled the poor girl into despair. He drooled over her constantly, forcing her to dress and undress under a blanket as if this was the nineteenth or twentieth century; and when her father wasn't looking, he'd get his fat paws on her behind or the little bumps of her breasts and whisper lewd propositions in her ear. Finally I had to tell him that if he didn't stop bothering her, I'd bounce him from the tour. That settled him down for a few days. The girl's father, incidentally, thought the whole incident was very funny. "Maybe what that girl needs is a good banging," he said to me. "Get the body juices flowing, huh?" Papa Gostaman also approved of his son Bilbo's affair with Miss Pistil, which also became a nuisance, since we wasted a terrific amount of time waiting for them to finish their current copulations. I'd be giving a preliminary talk on what we were to see this morning, get me, and Bilbo would be standing behind Miss Pistil, and suddenly she'd get this transfigured look on her face and I'd know he'd done it again, up with her skirt in back, *wham!* Bilbo looked pleased as hell all the time, which I suppose was reasonable enough for a fourteen-year-old-boy having an affair with a woman ten years his senior. Miss Pistil looked guilty. Her sore conscience, though, didn't keep her from opening the gate for Bilbo three or four times a day.

I didn't find all this conducive to creative Couriering.

Then there were minor annoyances, such as the ineffectual lecheries of old Mr. Haggins, who persecuted the dim Mrs. Gostaman mercilessly. Or the insistence of Sauerabend on fiddling around with his timer. "You know," he said several times, "I bet I could ungimmick this thing so I could run it myself. Used to be an engineer, you know, before I took up stockbroking." I told him to leave his timer alone. Behind my back, he went on tinkering with it.

Still another headache was Capistrano, whom I met by chance in 1097 while Bohemond's Crusaders were entering Constantinople. He showed up while I was concentrating on the replay of the Marge Hefferin scene. I wanted to see how permanent my correction of the past had been.

This time I lined my people up on the opposite side of the street. Yes, there I was; and there was Marge, eager and impatient and hot for Bohemond; and there was the rest of the group. As the Crusaders paraded toward us, I felt almost dizzy with suspense. Would I see myself save Marge? Or would I see Marge leap toward Bohemond and be cut down? Or would some third alternative unreel? The fluidity, the mutability, of the time stream, that was what terrified me now.

Bohemond neared. Marge was undoing her tunic. Heavy creamy breasts were visible. She tensed and readied herself for the dash into the street. And a second Jud Elliott materialized out of nowhere across the way, right behind her. I saw the look of shock on Marge's face as my alter ego's steely fingers clamped tight to her ass. I saw his hand splay wide to seize her breast. I saw her whirl, struggle, sag; and as Bohemond went by, I saw myself vanish, leaving only the two of me, one on each side of the processional avenue.

I was awash with relief. Yet I was also troubled, because I knew now that my editing of this scene was embedded in the time-flow for anyone to see. Including some passing Time Patrolman, perhaps, who might happen to observe the brief presence of a doubled Courier and wonder what was going on. At any time in the next million millennia the Patrol might monitor that scene—and then, no matter if it went undiscovered until the year 8,000,000,000,008, I would be called to account for my unauthorized correction of the record. I could expect to feel the hand on my shoulder, the voice calling my name

I felt a hand on my shoulder. A voice called my name.

I spun around. "*Capistrano!*"

"Sure, Capistrano. Did you expect someone else?"

"I—I—you surprised me, that's all." I was shaking. My knees were watery.

I was so upset that it took me a few seconds to realize how awful Capistrano looked.

He was frayed and haggard; his glossy dark hair was graying and stringy; he had lost weight and looked twenty years older than the Capistrano I knew. I sensed discontinuity and felt the fear that I always felt when confronted with someone out of my own future.

"What's the trouble?" I asked.

"I'm coming apart. Breaking up. Look, there's my tour over there." He indicated a clump of time-travelers who peered intently at the Crusaders. "I can't stay with them any more. They sicken me. Everything sickens me. It's the end for me, Elliott, absolutely the end."

"Why? What's wrong?"

"I can't talk about it here. When are you staying tonight?"

"Right here in 1097. The inn by the Golden Horn."

"I'll see you at midnight," Capistrano said. He clutched my arm for a moment. "It's the end, Elliott. Really the end. God have mercy on my soul!"

43.

Capistrano appeared at the inn just before midnight. Under his cloak he carried a lopsided bottle, which he uncorked and handed to me. "Cognac," he said. "From 1825, bottled in 1775. I just brought it up the line."

I tasted it. He slumped down in front of me. He looked worse than ever: old, drained, hollow. He took the cognac from me and gulped it greedily.

"Before you say anything," I told him, "I want to know what your now-time basis is. Discontinuities scare me."

"There's no discontinuity."

"There isn't?"

"My basis is December, 2059. The same as yours."

"Impossible!"

"Impossible?" he repeated. "How can you say that?"

"Last time I saw you, you weren't even forty. Now you're easily past fifty. Don't fool me, Capistrano. Your basis is somewhere in 2070, isn't it? And if it is, for God's sake don't tell me anything about the years still ahead for me!"

"My basis is 2059," said Capistrano in a ragged voice. I realized from the thickness of his tone that this bottle of cognac was not the first for him tonight. "I am no older now than I ought to be, for you," he said. "The trouble is that I'm a dead man."

"I don't understand."

"Last month I told you of my great-grandmother, the Turk?"

"Yes."

"This morning I went down the line to Istanbul of 1955. My great-grandmother was then seventeen years old and unmarried. In a moment of wild despair I choked her and threw her into the Bosphorus. It was at night, in the rain; no one saw us. I am dead, Elliott. Dead."

"No, Capistrano!"

"I told you, long ago, that when the time came, I would make my exit that way. A Turkish slut—she who beguiled my great-grandfather into a shameful marriage—gone now. And so am I. Once I return to now-time, I have never existed. What shall I do, Elliott? You decide. Shall I jump down the line now and end the comedy?"

Sweating, I said, after a deep pull of the cognac, "Give me the exact date of your stopoff in 1955. I'll go down the line right now and keep you from harming her."

"You will not."

"Then you do it. Arrive in the nick of time and save her, Capistrano!"

He looked at me sadly. "What's the point? Sooner or later I'll kill her again. I have to. It's my destiny. I'm going to shunt down now. Will you look after my people?"

"I've got a tour of my own," I reminded him.

"Of course. Of course. You can't handle more. Just see that mine aren't stranded. I have to go—have to—"

His hand was on his timer.

"Capis—"

He took the cognac with him when he jumped.

Gone. Extinct. A victim of suicide by timecrime. Blotted out of history's pages. I didn't know how to handle the situation. Suppose I went down to 1955 and prevented him from murdering his great-grandmother. He was already a nonperson in now-time; could I retroactively restore him to existence? How did the Paradox of Transit Displacement function in reverse? This was a case I had not studied. I wanted to do whatever was best for Capistrano; I also had his stranded tourists to think about.

I brooded over it for an hour. Finally I came to a sane if not romantic conclusion: this is none of my business, I decided, and I'd better call in the Time Patrol. Reluctantly I touched the alarm stud on my timer, the signal which is supposed to summon a Patrolman at once.

Instantly a Patrolman materialized. Dave Van Dam, the belching blond boor I had met on my first day in Istanbul.

"So?" he said.

"Timecrime suicide," I told him. "Capistrano just murdered his great-grandmother and jumped back to now-time."

"Son of a goddam bitch. Why do we have to put up with these unstable motherfuckers?"

I didn't bother to tell him that his choice of obscenity was inappropriate. I said, "He also left a party of tourists marooned here. That's why I called you in."

Van Dam spat elaborately. "Son of a goddam bitch," he said again. "Okay, I'm with it." He timed out of my room.

I was sick with grief over the stupid waste of a valuable life. I thought of Capistrano's charm, his grace, his sensitivity, all squandered because in a drunken moment of misery he had to timecrime himself. I didn't weep, but I felt like kicking furniture around, and I did. The noise woke up Miss Pistil, who gasped and murmured, "Are we being attacked?"

"You are," I said, and to ease my rage and anguish I dropped down on her bed and rammed myself into her. She was a little startled, but began to cooperate once she realized what was up. I came in half a minute and left her, throbbing, to be finished off by Bilbo Gostaman. Still in a black mood, I awakened the innkeeper and demanded his best wine, and drank myself into a foggy stupor.

Much later I learned that my dramatics had all been pointless. That slippery bastard Capistrano had had a change of heart at the last minute. Instead of shunting to 2059 and obliterating himself, he clung to his Transit Displacement invulnerability and stayed up the line in 1600, marrying a Turkish pasha's daughter and fathering three kids on her. The Time Patrol didn't succeed in tracing him until 1607, at which point they picked him up for multiple timecrime, hoisted him down to 2060, and sentenced him to obliteration. So he got his exit anyway, but not in a very heroic way. The Patrol also had to unmurder Capistrano's great-grandmother, unmarry him from the pasha's daughter in 1600, and uncreate those three kids, as well as find and rescue his stranded tourists, so all in all he was a great deal of trouble for everybody. "If a man wants to commit suicide," said Dave Van Dam, "why in hell can't he just drink carniphage in nowtime and make it easier on the rest of us?" I had to agree. It was the only time in my life when the Time Patrol and I saw things the same way.

44.

The mess over Capistrano and the general unsavoriness of this batch of tourists combined to push me into abysses of gloom.

I moved grimly along from epoch to epoch, but my heart wasn't in it. And by the time, midway through the second week, that we reached 1204, I knew I was going to do something disastrous.

Doggedly I delivered the usual orientation lecture.

"The old spirit of the Crusaders is reviving," I said, scowling at Bilbo, who was fondling Miss Pistil again, and scowling at Sauerabend, who was visibly dreaming of Palmyra Gostaman's meager breasts. "Jerusalem, which the Crusaders conquered a century ago, has been recaptured by the Saracens, but various Crusader dynasties still control most of the Mediterranean coast of the Holy Land. The Arabs now are feuding among themselves, and since 1199, Pope Innocent III has been calling for a new Crusade."

I explained how various barons answered the Pope's call.

I told how the Crusaders were unwilling to make the traditional land journey across all of Europe and down through Asia Minor into Syria. I told how they preferred to go by sea, landing at one of the Palestinian ports.

I discussed how in 1202 they applied to Venice, Europe's leading naval power of the time, for transportation.

I described the terms by which the ancient and crafty Doge Enrico Dandolo of Venice agreed to provide ships.

"Dandolo," I said, "contracted to transport 4,500 knights with their horses, 9,000 squires, and 20,000 infantrymen, along with nine months' provisions. He offered to throw in fifty armed galleys to escort the convoy. For these services he asked 85,000 silver marks, or about

$20,000,000 in our money. Plus half of all the territory or treasure that the Crusaders won in battle."

I told how the Crusaders agreed to this stiff price, planning to cheat the blind old Doge.

I told how the blind old Doge, once he had the Crusaders hung up in Venice, gripped them by the throats until they paid him every mark due him.

I told how the venerable monster seized control of the Crusade and set off in command of the fleet on Easter Monday, 1203—heading not for the Holy Land but for Constantinople.

"Byzantium," I said, "is Venice's great maritime rival. Dandolo doesn't care warm spit for Jerusalem, but wants very badly to get control of Constantinople."

I explicated the dynastic situation. The Comnenus dynasty had come to a bad end. When Manuel II died in 1180, his successor was his young son Alexius II, who shortly was murdered by his father's amoral cousin, Andronicus. The elegantly depraved Andronicus was himself destroyed in a particularly ghastly way by an enraged mob, after he had ruled harshly for a few years, and in 1185 there came to the throne Isaac Angelus, an elderly and bumbling grandson of Alexius I, by the female line. Isaac ruled for ten haphazard years, until he was dethroned, blinded, and imprisoned by his brother, who became Emperor Alexius III.

"Alexius III still rules," I said, "and Isaac Angelus is still in prison. But Isaac's son, also Alexius, has escaped and is in Venice. He has promised Dandolo huge sums of money if Dandolo will restore his father to the throne. And so Dandolo is coming to Constantinople to overthrow Alexius III and make Isaac into an imperial puppet."

They didn't follow the intricacy of it. I didn't care. They'd figure it out as they saw things taking place.

I showed them the Fourth Crusade arriving at Constantinople at the end of June, 1203. I let them see Dandolo directing the capture of Scutari, Constantinople's suburb on the Asian side of the Bosphorus. I pointed out how the entrance to the port of Constantinople was guarded by a great tower and twenty Byzantine galleys, and blocked by a huge iron chain. I called their attention to the scene in which Venetian sailors boarded and took the Byzantine galleys while one of Dandolo's ships, equipped with monstrous steel shears, cut through the chain and opened the Golden Horn to the invaders. I allowed them to watch the superhuman Dandolo, ninety years old, lead the attackers over the ramparts of Constantinople. "Never before," I said, "have invaders broken into this city."

From a distance, part of a cheering mob, we watched Dandolo bring Isaac Angelus forth from his dungeon and name him Emperor of Byzantium, with his son crowned as co-emperor, by the style of Alexius IV.

"Alexius IV," I said, "now invites the Crusaders to spend the winter in Constantinople at his expense, preparing for their attack on the Holy Land. It is a rash offer. It dooms him."

We shunted down the line to the spring of 1204.

"Alexius IV," I said, "has discovered that housing thousands of Crusaders is bankrupting Byzantium. He tells Dandolo that he is out of money and will no longer underwrite their expenses. A furious dispute begins. While it proceeds, a fire starts in the city. No one knows who caused it, but Alexius suspects the Venetians. He sets seven decrepit ships on fire and lets them drift into the Venetian fleet. Look."

We saw the fire. We saw the Venetians using boat-hooks to drag the blazing hulks away from their own ships. We saw sudden revolution break out in Constantinople, the Byzantines denouncing Alexius IV as the tool of Venice, and putting him to death. "Old Isaac Angelus dies a few days later," I said. "The Byzantines find the son-in-law of the expelled Emperor Alexius III, and put him on the throne as Alexius V. This son-in-law is a member of the famous Ducas family. Dandolo has lost both his puppet emperors, and he is furious. The Venetians and the Crusaders decide now to conquer Constantinople and rule it themselves."

Once again I took a pack of tourists through scenes of battle as, on April 8, the struggle began. Fire, slaughter, rape, Alexius V in flight, the invaders plundering the city. April 13, in Haghia Sophia: Crusaders demolish the choir stalls with their twelve columns of silver, and pull apart the altar, and seize forty chalices and scores of silver candelabra. They take the Gospel, and the Crosses, and the altar cloth, and forty incense burners of pure gold. Boniface of Montferrat, the leader of the Crusade, seizes the imperial palace. Dandolo takes the four great bronze horses that the Emperor Constantine had brought from Egypt 900 years before; he will carry them to Venice and place them over the entrance to St. Mark's Cathedral, where they still are. The priests of the Crusaders scurry after relics: two chunks of the True Cross, the head of the Holy Lance, the nails that had held Christ on the Cross, and many similar objects, long revered by the Byzantines.

From the scenes of plunder we jumped to mid-May.

"A new Emperor of Byzantium is to be elected," I said. "He will not be a Byzantine. He will be a westerner, a Frank, a Latin. The conquerors choose Count Baldwin of Flanders. We can see his coronation procession."

We waited outside Haghia Sophia. Within, Baldwin of Flanders is donning a mantle covered with jewels and embroidered with eagle figures; he is handed a scepter and a golden orb; he kneels before the altar and is anointed; he is crowned; he mounts the throne.

"Here he comes," I said.

On a white horse, clad in glittering clothes that blaze as if on fire, Emperor Baldwin of Byzantium rides forth from the cathedral to the palace. Unwillingly, sullenly, the people of Byzantium pay homage to their alien master.

"Most of the Byzantine nobility has fled," I told my tourists, who were yearning for more battles, more fires. "The aristocracy has scattered to Asia Minor, to Albania, to Bulgaria, to Greece. For fifty-seven years the Latins will rule here, though Emperor Baldwin's reign will be brief. In ten months he will lead an army against Byzantine rebels and will be captured by them, never to return."

Chrystal Haggins said, "When do the Crusaders go to Jerusalem?"

"Not these. They never bother to go. Some of them stay here, ruling pieces of the former Byzantine Empire. The rest go home stuffed with Byzantine loot."

"How fascinating," said Mrs. Haggins.

We went to our lodgings. A terrible weariness had me in its grip. I had done my job; I had shown them the Latin conquest of Byzantium, as advertised in the brochures. Suddenly I couldn't stand their faces any longer. We dined, and they went to sleep, or at least to bed. I stood a while, listening to the passionate groans of Miss Pistil and the eager snorts of Bilbo Gostaman, listening to the protests of Palmyra as Conrad Sauerabend sneakily stroked her thighs in the dark, and then I choked back tears of fury and surrendered to my temptations, and touched my timer, and shunted up the line. To 1105. To Pulcheria Ducas.

45.

Metaxas, as always, was glad to help.

"It'll take a few days," he said. "Communications are slow here. Messengers going back and forth."

"Should I wait here?"

"Why bother?" Metaxas asked. "You've got a timer. Jump down three days, and maybe by then everything will be arranged."

I jumped down the three days. Metaxas said, "Everything is arranged."

He had managed to get me invited to a soiree at the Ducas palace. Just about everyone of importance would be there, from Emperor Alexius Comnenus down. As my cover identity, I was to claim that I was Metaxas' cousin from the provinces, from Epirus. "Speak with a backwoods accent," Metaxas instructed me. "Dribble wine on your chin and make noises when you chew. Your name will be—ah—Nicetas Hyrtacenus."

I shook my head. "Too fancy. It isn't *me.*"

"Well, then, George Hyrtacenus?"

"George Markezinis," I said.

"It sounds too twentieth century."

"To them it'll sound provincial," I said, and as George Markezinis I went to the Ducas soiree.

Outside the gleaming marble walls of the Ducas palace I saw two dozen Varangian guards stationed. The presence of these yellow-bearded Norse barbarians, the core of the imperial bodyguard, told me that Alexius was already within. We entered. Metaxas had brought his fair and wanton ancestress Eudocia to the party.

Within, a dazzling scene. Musicians. Slaves. Tables heaped with food. Wine. Gorgeously dressed men and women. Superb mosaic floors; tapestried walls, heavy with cloth of gold. The tinkle of sophisticated laughter; the shimmer of female flesh beneath nearly transparent silks. I saw Pulcheria at once.

Pulcheria saw me.

Our eyes met, as they had met in the shop of sweets and spices, and she recognized me, and smiled enigmatically, and again the current surged between us. In a later era she would have fluttered her fan at me. Here, she withdrew her jeweled gloves and slapped them lightly across her left wrist. Some token of encouragement? She wore a golden circlet on her high, smooth forehead. Her lips were rouged.

"That's her husband to her left," Metaxas whispered. "Come. I'll introduce you."

I stared at Leo Ducas, my great-great-great-multi-great-grandfather, and my pride in having so distinguished an ancestor was tinged by the envy I felt for this man, who each night caressed the breasts of Pulcheria.

He was, I knew from my genealogical studies, thirty-five years old, twice the age of his wife. A tall man, graying at the temples, with unByzantine blue eyes, a neatly clipped little beard, a high-bridged, narrow nose, and thin, tightly compressed lips, he seemed austere, remote, unutterably dignified. I suspected that he might be boringly noble. He did make an impressive sight, and there was no austerity about his tunic of fine cut, nor about his jewelry, his rings and pendants and pins.

Leo presided over the gathering in serene style, befitting a man who was one of the premier nobles of the realm, and who headed his branch of the great house of Ducas. Of course, Leo's house was empty, and perhaps that accounted for the faint trace of despair that I imagined I saw on his handsome face. As Metaxas and I approached him, I picked up a stray exchange of conversation from two court ladies to my left:

"...no children, and such a pity, when all of Leo's brothers have so many. And he the eldest!"

"Pulcheria's still young, though. She looks as if she'll be a good breeder."

"If she ever gets started. Why, she's close to eighteen!"

I wanted to reassure Leo, to tell him that his seed would descend even unto the twenty-first century, to let him know that in only a year's time Pulcheria would give him a son, Nicetas, and then Simeon, John, Alexander, and more, and that Nicetas would sire six children, among them the princely Nicephorus whom I had seen seventy years down the line, and the son of Nicephorus would follow an exiled leader into Albania, and then, and then, and then—

Metaxas said, "Your grace, this is my mother's sister's third son, George Markezinis, of Epirus, now a guest at my villa during the harvest season."

"You've come a long way," said Leo Ducas. "Have you been to Constantinople before?"

"Never," I said. "A wonderful city! The churches! The palaces! The bathhouses! The food, the wine, the clothes! The women, the beautiful women!"

Pulcheria glowed. She gave me that sidewise smile of hers again, on the side away from her husband. I knew she was mine. The sweet fragrance of her drifted toward me. I began to ache and throb.

Leo said, "You know the emperor, of course?"

With a grand sweep of his arm he indicated Alexius, holding court at the far end of the room. I had seen him before: a short, stocky man of clearly imperial bearing. A circle of lords and ladies surrounded him. He seemed gracious, sophisticated, relaxed in manner, the true heir to the Caesars, the defender of civilization in these dark times. At Leo's insistence I was presented to him. He greeted me warmly, crying out that the cousin of Metaxas was as dear to him as Metaxas himself. We talked for a while, the emperor and I; I was nervous, but I carried myself well, and Leo Ducas said, finally, "You speak with emperors as though you've known a dozen of them, young man."

I smiled. I did not say that I had several times glimpsed Justinian, that I had attended the baptisms of Theodosius II, Constantine V, the yet unborn Manuel Comnenus, and many more, that I had knelt in Haghia Sophia not far from Constantine XI on Byzantium's last night, that I had watched Leo the Isaurian direct the iconoclasms. I did not say that I was one of the many pluggers of the hungry hole of the Empress Theodora, five centuries previously. I looked shy and said, "Thank you, your grace."

46.

Byzantine parties consisted of music, a dance of slave-girls, some dining, and a great deal of wine. The night wore on; the candles burned low; the assembled notables grew tipsy. In the gathering darkness I mingled easily with members of the famed families, meeting men and women named Comnenus, Phocas, Skleros, Dalassenes, Diogenes, Botaniates, Tzimisces and Ducas. I made courtly conversation and impressed myself with my glibness. I watched arrangements for adultery being made subtly, but not subtly enough, behind the backs of drunken husbands. I bade goodnight to Emperor Alexius and received an invitation to visit him at Blachernae, just up the road. I fended off Metaxas' Eudocia, who had had too much to drink and wanted a quick balling in a back room. (She finally selected one Basil Diogenes, who must have been seventy years old.) I answered, evasively, a great many questions about my "cousin" Metaxas, whom everybody knew, but whose origins were a mystery to all. And then, three hours after my arrival, I found that I was at last speaking with Pulcheria.

We stood quietly together in an angle of the great hall. Two flickering candles gave us light. She looked flushed, excited, even agitated; her breasts heaved and a line of sweat-beads stippled her upper lip. I had never beheld such beauty before.

"Look," she said. "Leo dozes. He loves his wine more than most other things."

"He must love beauty," I said. "He has surrounded himself with so much of it."

"Flatterer!"

"No. I try to speak the truth."

"You don't often succeed," she said. "Who are you?"

"Markezinis of Epirus, cousin to Metaxas."

"That tells me very little. I mean, what are you looking for in Constantinople?"

I took a deep breath. "To fulfill my destiny, by finding the one whom I am meant to find, the one whom I love."

That got through to her. Seventeen-year-old girls are susceptible to that kind of thing, even in Byzantium, where girls mature early and marry at twelve. Call me Heathcliff.

Pulcheria gasped, crossed her arms chastely over the high mounds of her breasts, and shivered. I think her pupils may have momentarily dilated.

"It's impossible," she said.

"Nothing's impossible."

"My husband—"

"Asleep," I said. "Tonight—under this roof—"

"No. We can't."

"You're trying to fight destiny, Pulcheria."

"George!"

"A bond holds us together—a bond stretching across all of time—"

"Yes, George!"

Easy, now, great-great-multi-great-grandson, don't talk too much. It's cheap timecrime to brag that you're from the future.

"This was fated," I whispered. "It had to be!"

"Yes! Yes!"

"Tonight."

"Tonight, yes."

"Here."

"Here," said Pulcheria.

"Soon."

"When the guests leave. When Leo is in bed. I'll have you hidden in a room where it's safe—I'll come to you—"

"You knew this would happen," I said, "that day when we met in the shop."

"Yes. I knew. Instantly. What magic did you work on me?"

"None, Pulcheria. The magic rules us both. Drawing us together, shaping this moment, spinning the strands of destiny toward our meeting, upsetting the boundaries of time itself—"

"You speak so strangely, George. So beautifully. You must be a poet!"

"Perhaps."

"In two hours you'll be mine."

"And you mine," I said.

"And for always."

I shivered, thinking of the Time Patrol swordlike above me. "For always, Pulcheria."

47.

She spoke to a servant, telling him that the young man from Epirus had had too much to drink, and wished to lie down in one of the guest chambers. I acted appropriately woozy. Metaxas found me and wished me well. Then I made a candlelight pilgrimage through the maze of the Ducas palace and was shown to a simple room somewhere far in the rear. A low bed was the only article of furniture. A rectangular mosaic in the center of the floor was the only decoration. The single narrow window admitted a shaft of moonlight. The servant brought me a washbasin of water, wished me a good night's rest, and let me alone.

I waited a billion years.

Sounds of distant revelry floated to me. Pulcheria did not come.

It's all a joke, I thought. A hoax. The young but sophisticated mistress of the house is having some fun with the country cousin. She'll let me fidget and fret in here alone until morning, and then send a servant to give me breakfast and show me out. Or maybe after a couple of hours she'll tell one of her slavegirls to come in here and pretend she's Pulcheria. Or send in a toothless crone, while her guests watch through concealed slots in the wall. Or—

A thousand times I considered fleeing. Just touch the timer, and shoot up the line to 1204, where Conrad Sauerabend and Palmyra Gostaman and Mr. and Mrs. Haggins and the rest of my tourists lie sleeping and unguarded.

Clear out? Now? When everything had gone so neatly so far? What would Metaxas say to me when he found out I had lost my nerve?

I remembered my guru, black Sam, asking me, "If you had a chance to attain your heart's desire, would you take it?"

Pulcheria was my heart's desire; I knew that now.

I remembered Sam Spade telling me, "You're a compulsive loser. Losers infallibly choose the least desirable alternative."

Go ahead, great-great-multi-great-grandson. Skip out of here before the luscious primordial ancestress can offer her dark musky loins to you.

I remembered Emily, the helix-parlor girl with the gift of prophecy, crying shrilly, "Beware love in Byzantium! Beware! Beware!"

I loved. In Byzantium.

Rising, I paced the room a thousand times, and stood at the door listening to the faint laughter and the far-off songs, and then I removed all of my clothing, carefully folding each garment and placing it on the floor beside my bed. I stood naked except for my timer, and I debated removing that too. What would Pulcheria say when she saw that tawny plastic band at my waist? How could I explain it?

I unfastened the timer too, separating myself from it for the first time in my career up the line. Waves of real terror burst over me. I felt more naked than naked, without it; I felt stripped down to my bones. Without my timer around my hips I was the slave of time, like all these others. I had no means of quick escape. If Pulcheria planned some cruel joke and I was caught without my timer in easy reach, I was doomed.

Hastily I put the timer back on.

Then I washed myself, meticulously, everywhere, cleansing myself for Pulcheria. And stood naked beside the bed, waiting another billion years. And thought longingly of the dark swollen tips of Pulcheria's full breasts, and the softness of the skin inside her thighs. And my manhood came to life, rising to such extravagant proportions that I was both proud and embarrassed.

I didn't want Pulcheria to walk in and find me like this, beside the bed with this tree of flesh sprouting between my legs. I looked like a tipped tripod; to greet her this way was too blunt, too direct. Quickly I dressed again, feeling foolish. And waited a billion years more. And saw dawnlight beginning to blend with moonlight in my slit of a window.

And the door opened, and Pulcheria came into the room, and bolted the door behind her.

She had wiped away her heavy makeup and had taken off all her jewelry except a single gold pectoral, and she had changed from her party clothes into a light silken wrap. Even by the dim light I saw she was nude beneath it, and the soft curves of her body inflamed me almost to insanity. She glided toward me.

I took her in my arms and tried to kiss her. She didn't understand kissing. The posture one must adopt for mouth-to-mouth contact was alien to her. I had to arrange her. I tilted her head gently. She smiled, puzzled but willing.

Our lips touched. My tongue wiggled forth.

She quivered and flattened her body tight against mine. She picked up the theory of kissing in a hurry.

My hands slid down her shoulders. I drew off her wrap; she trembled a little as I bared her.

I counted her breasts. Two. Rosy pink nipples. I measured her hind cheeks with my outspread hands. A good size. I ran fingertips over her thighs. Excellent thighs. I admired the two deep dimples in the small of her back.

She was at once shy and wanton, a superb combination.

When I undressed, she saw the timer and touched it, plucked at it, but asked for no explanation, and her hands slipped lower. We tumbled down together on the bed.

You know, sex is really a ridiculous thing. The physical act of it, I mean. What they call "making love" in twentieth-century novels; what they call "sleeping together." I mean, consider all the literary effort that has gone into writing rhapsodies to screwing. And what does it all amount to, anyway?

You take this short rigid fleshy rod and you put it into this lubricated groove, and you rub it back and forth until enough of a charge is built up so that discharge is possible. Like making a fire by twirling a stick against a plank. Really, there's nothing to it; Stick Tenon A into Mortise B. Vibrate until finished.

Look upon the act and you *know* it's preposterous. The buttocks humping up and down, the thrashing legs, the muffled groans, the speedings up and slowing down—can anything be sillier, as a central act governing human emotions?

Of course not. Yet why was this sweaty transaction with Pulcheria so important to me? (And maybe to her.)

My theory is that the real significance of sex, good sex, is a symbolic one. It's something beyond the fact that you get a tickle of "pleasure" for a short while during the ramming and butting. The same pleasure is available without the bother of finding a partner, after all, and yet it isn't the same, is it?

No, what sex is about is more than a twitch in the loins; it's a celebration of spiritual union, of mutual trust. We say to each other in bed, here, I give myself to you in the expectation that you'll give me pleasure, and I will attempt to give you pleasure too. The social contract, let's call it. And the thrill lies in the contract, not in the pleasure that is its payoff.

Also you say, here is my naked body with all its flaws, which I expose trustingly to you, knowing you will not mock it. Also you say, I accept this intimate contact with you even though I know you may transmit to me a loathsome disease. I am willing to take this risk, because you are you. And also the woman used to say—at least up until the nineteenth or early twentieth century—I will open myself to you even though there may be all sorts of biological consequences nine months from now.

All these things are much more vital than quick kickies. This is why mechanical masturbating devices have never replaced sex and never will.

This is why what happened between myself and Pulcheria Ducas on that Byzantine morning in 1105 was far more significant a transaction than what happened between myself and the Empress Theodora half a millennium earlier, and more significant than what had happened between myself and any number of girls a full millennium later. Into Theodora, into Pulcheria, and into those many girls down the line I poured roughly the same number of cubic centimeters of salty fluid; but with Pulcheria it was different. With Pulcheria, our orgasm was only the symbolic sealing of something greater. For me, Pulcheria was the embodiment of beauty and grace, and her easy surrender to me made me an emperor more mighty than Alexius, and neither the spurting of my jet nor her quiver of response mattered a tenth as much as the fact that she and I had come together in trust, in faith, in shared desire, in—love. There you have the heart of my philosophy. I stand revealed as a naked romantic. This is the profundity I've distilled from all my experience: sex with love is better than sex without love. Q.E.D. I can also show, if you like, that to be healthy is better than to be ill, and that having money is superior to being poor. My capacity for abstract thought is limitless.

48.

Nevertheless, even though we had proven the philosophical point quite adequately, we went on to prove it all over again half an hour later. Redundancy is the soul of understanding.

Afterward we lay side by side, glowing sweetly. It was the moment to offer my partner a weed and share a different sort of communion, but of course that was impossible here. I felt the lack.

"Is it very different where you come from?" Pulcheria asked. "I mean, the people, how they dress, how they talk."

"Very different."

"I sense a great strangeness about you, George. Even the way you held me in bed. Not that I am an expert on such things, you must understand. You and Leo are the only men I have ever had."

"Can this be true?"

Her eyes blazed. "You take me for a whore?"

"Well, of course not, but—" I floundered. "In my country," I said desperately, "a girl takes many men before she marries. No one objects to it. It's the custom."

"Not here. We are well sheltered. I was married at twelve; that gave me little time for liberties." She frowned, sat up, leaned across me to look in my eyes. Her breasts dangled enticingly over my face. "Are women really so loose in your country?"

"Truth, Pulcheria, they are."

"But you are Byzantines! You are not barbarians from the north! How can it be allowed, this taking of so many men?"

"It's our custom." Lamely.

"Perhaps you are not truly from Epirus," she suggested. "Perhaps you come from some more distant place. I tell you again, you are very strange to me, George."

"Don't call me George. Call me Jud," I said boldly.

"Jud?"

"Jud."

"Why should I call you this?"

"It's my inner name. My *real* name, the one I *feel*. George is just—well, a name I use."

"Jud. Jud. Such a name I have never heard. You *are* from a strange land! You *are!*"

I gave her a sphinxy smile. "I love you," I said, and nibbled her nipples to change the subject.

"So strange," she murmured. "So different. And yet I felt drawn to you from the first moment. You know, I've long dreamed of being as wicked as this, but I never dared. Oh, I've had offers, dozens of offers, but it never seemed worth the trouble. And then I saw you, and I felt this fire in me, this—this hunger. Why? Tell me why? You are neither more nor less attractive than many of the men I might have given myself to, and yet you were the one. Why?"

"It was destiny," I told her. "As I said before. An irresistible force, pulling us together, across the—"

—centuries—

"—sea," I finished lamely.

"You will come to me again?" she said.

"Again and again and again."

"I'll find ways for us to meet. Leo will never know. He spends so much of his time at the bank—you know, he's one of the directors—and in his other businesses, and with the emperor—he hardly pays attention to me. I'm one of his many pretty toys. We'll meet, Jud, and we'll know pleasure together often, and—" her dark eyes flashed "—and perhaps you'll give me a child."

I felt the heavens open and rain thunderbolts upon me.

"Five years of marriage and I have no child," she went on. "I don't understand. Perhaps I was too young, at first—I was so young—but now, nothing. Nothing. Give me a child, Jud. Leo will thank you for it—I mean, he'll be happy, he'll think it's his—you even have a Ducas look about you, in the eyes, perhaps, there'd be no trouble. Do you think we made a child tonight?"

"No," I said.

"No? How can you be sure?"

"I have ways," I said. I stroked her silkiness. Let me go twenty more days without my pill, though, and I could plant babies aplenty in you, Pulcheria! And knot the fabric of time beyond all unraveling. My own great-great-multi-great-grandfather? Am I seed of my own seed? Did time recurve on itself to produce me? No. I'd never get away with it. I'd give Pulcheria passion, but not parturition. "Dawn's here," I whispered.

"You'd better leave. Where can I send messages to you?"

"At Metaxas'."

"Good. We'll meet again two days hence, yes? I'll arrange everything."

"I'm yours, whenever you say it, Pulcheria."

"Two days. But now, go. I'll show you out."

"Too risky. Servants will be stirring. Go to your room, Pulcheria. I can get out by myself."

"But—impossible—"

"I know the way."

"Do you?"

"I swear it," I said.

She needed some convincing, but at length I persuaded her to spare herself the risk of getting me out of the palace. We kissed once more, and she donned her wrap, and I caught her by the arm and pulled her to me, and released her, and she went out of the room. I counted sixty seconds off. Then I set my timer and jumped six hours up the line. The party was going full blast. Casually I walked through the building, avoiding the room where my slightly earlier self, not yet admitted to Pulcheria's joyous body, was chatting with Emperor Alexius. I left the Ducas palace unnoticed. In the darkness outside, beside the sea wall along the Golden Horn, I set my timer again and shunted down the line to 1204. Now I hurried to the inn where I had left my sleeping tourists. I reached it less than three minutes after my departure—seemingly so many days ago—for Pulcheria's era.

All well. I had had my incandescent night of passion, my soul was purged of longings, and here I was, back at my trade once more, and no one the wiser. I checked the beds.

Mr. and Mrs. Haggins, yes.

Mr. and Mrs. Gostaman, yes.

Miss Pistil and Bilbo, yes

Palmyra Gostaman, yes.

Conrad Sauerabend, yes? No.

Conrad Sauerabend—

No Sauerabend. Sauerabend was missing. His bed was empty. In those three minutes of my absence, Sauerabend had slipped away.

Where?

I felt the early pricklings of panic.

49.

Calm. Calm. Stay calm. He went out to the *pissoir*, is all. He'll be right back.

Item One, a Courier must remain aware of the location of all of the tourists in his care at all times. The penalty—

I kindled a torch at the smoldering hearth and rushed out into the hall.

Sauerabend? Saucrabend?

Not pissing. Not downstairs rummaging in the kitchen. Not prowling in the wine cellar.

Sauerabend?

Where the devil are you, you pig?

The taste of Pulcheria's lips was still on my own. Her sweat mingled with mine. Her juices still crisped my short hairs. All the delicious forbidden joys of transtemporal incest continued to tingle in my soul.

The Time Patrol will make a nonperson out of me for this, I thought. I'll say, "I've lost a tourist," and they'll say, "How did it happen?" and I'll say, "I stepped out of the room for three minutes and he vanished," and they'll say, "Three minutes, eh? You aren't supposed to—" and I'll say, "It was only *three minutes*. Christ, you can't expect me to watch them twenty-four hours a day!" And they'll be sympathetic, but nevertheless they'll have to check the scene, and in the replay they'll discover me wantonly shunting out for some other point on the line, and they'll track me to 1105 and find me with Pulcheria, and see that not only am I guilty of negligence as a Courier, but also that I've committed incest with my great-great-multi-great—

Calm. Calm.

Into the street now. Flash the torch around. Sauerabend? Sauerabend? No Sauerabend.

If I were a Sauerabend, where would I sneak off to?

To the home of some twelve-year-old Byzantine girl? How would
he know where to find one? How to get in? No. No. He couldn't have
done that. Where is he, though? Strolling through the town? Out for
fresh air? He should be asleep. Snoring. No. I realized that when I left
he hadn't been asleep, hadn't been snoring; he'd been bothering Palmyra
Gostaman. I hurried back to the inn. There wasn't any point in roaming
Constantinople at random for him.

In mounting panic I woke up Palmyra. She rubbed her eyes, complained a little, blinked. Torchlight glittered off her flat bare chest.

"Where did Sauerabend go?" I whispered harshly.

"I told him to leave me alone. I told him if he didn't stop bothering
me I'd bite his thing off. He had his hand right here, and he—"

"Yes, but where did he *go*?"

"I don't know. He just got up and went away. It was dark in here.
I fell asleep maybe two minutes ago. Why'd you have to wake me up?"

"Some help you are," I muttered. "Go back to sleep."

Calm, Judson, calm. There's an easy solution to this. If you weren't
in such a flutter, you'd have thought about it long ago. All you have to
do is edit Sauerabend back into the room, the way you edited Marge
Hefferin back to life.

It's illegal, of course. Couriers are not supposed to engage in time
corrections. That's for the Patrol to do. But this will be such a small
correction. You can handle it quickly and no one will be the wiser. You
got away with the Hefferin revision, didn't you? Yes. Yes. It's your
only chance, Jud.

I sat down on the edge of my bed and tried to plan my actions
properly. My night with Pulcheria had dulled the edge of my intellect.
Think, Jud. Think as you never thought before.

I put great effort into my thinking.

What time was it when you shunted up to 1105?

Fourteen minutes to midnight.

What time was it when you came back down the line to 1204?

Eleven minutes to midnight.

What time is it now?

One minute to midnight.

When did Sauerabend slip out of the room, then?

Somewhere between fourteen to and eleven to.

Therefore, how far up the line must you shunt to intercept him?

About thirteen minutes.

You realize that if you jump back more than thirteen minutes, you'll encounter your prior self, who will be getting ready to depart for 1105? That's the Paradox of Duplication.

I've got to risk it. I'm in worse trouble than that already.

You'd better shunt, then, and get things fixed up.

Here I go.

I timed my shunt perfectly, going up the line thirteen minutes less a few seconds. I noticed with satisfaction that my earlier self had already departed, and that Sauerabend had not. The ugly fat bastard was still in the room, sitting up in his bed with his back to me.

It would be simplicity itself to stop him now. I simply forbid him to leave the room, and keep him here for the next three minutes, thus canceling his departure. The instant my prior self gets back—at eleven minutes to midnight—I shunt ten minutes down the line, resuming my proper place in the stream of time. Sauerabend thus will have been continuously guarded by his Courier (in one incarnation or another) throughout the whole dangerous period from fourteen minutes to midnight onward. There will be a very slight moment of duplication for me when I overlap my returning self, but I'll clear out of his time level so fast that he probably won't notice. And all will be as it should have been.

Yes. Very good.

I started across the room toward Sauerabend, meaning to block his path when he tried to leave. He pivoted, still sitting on his bed, and saw me.

"You're back?" he said.

"You bet. And I don't—"

He put his hand to his timer and vanished.

"Wait!" I yelled, waking everybody up. "You can't do that! It's impossible! A tourist's timer doesn't—"

My voice trailed away into a foolish-sounding gargle. Sauerabend was gone, time-shunting before my eyes. Yelling at the place where he had been wouldn't bring him back. The wiliness of the loathsome slob! Fooling with his timer, boasting that he could gimmick it into working for him, somehow shorting the seal and getting access to the control—

Now I was in a terrible mess of messes. One of my own tourists on the loose with an activated timer, jumping all over anywhen—what a monstrous botch! I was desperate. The Time Patrol was bound to pick him up, of course, before he could commit too many serious timecrimes, but beyond any doubt I'd be censured for letting him get away.

Unless I could catch him before he left.

Fifty-six seconds had elapsed since I had jumped here to keep Sauerabend from leaving.

Without hesitating further, I set my timer back sixty seconds, and shunted. There was Sauerabend again, sitting on his bed. There was my other self, starting across the room toward him. There were the other sleeping tourists, not yet awakened by my shout.

Okay now. We outnumber him. We've got him.

I launched myself at Sauerabend, meaning to grab his arms and keep him from shunting.

He turned as soon as I moved. With devilish swiftness he reached down to his timer.

He shunted. He was gone. I sprawled on his empty bed, numb with shock.

The other Jud glared at me and said, "Where in hell did you come from?"

"I'm fifty-six seconds ahead of you. I missed my first chance at collaring him, and jumped back to try a second time."

"And missed again, I see."

"So I did."

"And duplicated us, besides."

"At least that part can be fixed," I said. I checked the time. "In another thirty seconds, you jump back sixty seconds and get yourself into the time-flow."

"Like crap I will," said Jud B.

"What do you mean?"

"What's the point of it? Sauerabend's going to be gone, or at least on his way. I won't be able to grab him, will I?"

"But you've *got* to go," I said.

"Why?"

"Because it's what I did at that point in the flow."

"You had a reason for it," he said. "You had just missed Sauerabend, and you wanted to jump back a minute and try catching him then. But I haven't had a chance even to miss him. Besides, why worry about the time-flow? It's already been changed."

He was right. We had run out the fifty-six seconds. Now we were at the point when I had made my first try at blocking Sauerabend's exit; but Jud B, who presumably was living through the minute I had lived through just prior to Sauerabend's first disappearance, had lived through that minute in an altogether different way from me. Everything was messed up. I had spawned a duplicate who wouldn't go away and who had nowhere to go. It was now thirteen minutes to midnight. In another two minutes we'd have a third Jud here—the one who shunted down straight from Pulcheria's arms to find Sauerabend missing in the first place. *He* had a destiny of his own: to spend ten minutes in panicky dithering, and then to jump back from one-minute-to-midnight to fourteen-minutes-to-midnight, kicking off the whole process of confusions that culminated in the two of us.

"We've got to get out of here," Jud B said.

"Before *he* comes in."

"Right. Because if he sees us, he may never get around to making his shunt back to fourteen minutes to midnight, and that—"

"—might eliminate you and me from existing."

"But where do we go?" he asked.

"We could jump back to three or four minutes ago, and try to grab Sauerabend together."

"No good. We'll overlap another of us—the one who's on his way to Pulcheria."

"So what? We'll make him get on his way as soon as we've nailed down Sauerabend."

"Still no good. Because if we miss Sauerabend again, we'll induce still another change in the time-flow, and maybe bring on a third one of us. And set up a hall of mirrors effect, banging back and forth until there are a million of us in the room. He's too quick for us with that timer."

"You're right," I said, wishing Jud B had gone back when he belonged before it was too late.

It was now twelve minutes to midnight.

"We've got sixty seconds to clear out. Where do we go?"

"We don't go back and try to grab Sauerabend again. That's definite."

"Yes."

"But we *must* locate him."

"Yes."

"And he could be anywhen at all."

"Yes."

"Then two of us aren't enough. We've got to get help."

"Metaxas."

"Yes. And maybe Sam."

"Yes. And how about Capistrano?"

"Is he available?"

"Who knows? We'll try. And Buonocore. And Jeff Monroe. This is a *crisis!*"

"Yes," I said. "Listen, we've only got ten seconds now. Come on with me!"

We rushed out of the room and down the back way, missing the arrival of the eleven-minutes-to-midnight Jud by a few seconds. We crouched in a dark alcove under the stairs, thinking about the Jud who was two flights up discovering the absence of Sauerabend. I said, "This is going to call for teamwork. You shunt up the line to 1105, find Metaxas, and explain what's happened. Then call in reinforcements and get everybody busy tracing the time-line for Sauerabend."

"What about you?"

"I'm going to stay right here," I said. "Until one minute to midnight. At that point the fellow upstairs is going to shunt back a little less than thirteen minutes to look for Sauerabend—"

"—leaving his people unguarded—"

"—yes, and *somebody's* got to stay with them, so I'll go back upstairs as soon as he leaves, and slip back into the main Jud Elliott identity as their Courier. And I'll stay there, proceeding on a normal basis, until I hear from you. Okay?"

"Okay."

"Get going, then."

He got going. I huddled down in a little heap, shaking with fright. It all hit me in one mighty reaction. Sauerabend was gone, and I had spawned an alter ego by the Paradox of Duplication, and in the space of one evening I had committed more timecrimes than I could name, and—

I felt like crying.

I didn't realize it, but the mess was only beginning.

50.

A t one minute to midnight I pulled myself together and went upstairs to take over the job of being the authentic Jud Elliott. As I entered the room I allowed myself the naive hope that I'd find everything restored to the right path, with Sauerabend in his bed again. Let it have been fixed retroactively, I prayed. But Sauerabend wasn't in the room.

Did that mean that he'd never be found?

Not necessarily. Maybe, to avoid further tangles, he'd be returned to our tour slightly down the line, say in the early hours of the night, or just before dawn.

Or maybe he'd be restored to the point he jumped from—thirteen minutes or so before midnight—but I somehow wouldn't become aware of his return, through some mysterious working of the Paradox of Transit Displacement, holding me outside the whole system.

I didn't know. I didn't even *want* to know. I just wanted Conrad Sauerabend located and put back in his proper position in time, before the Patrol realized what was up and let me have it.

Sleep was out of the question. Miserably I slumped on the edge of my bed, getting up now and then to check on my tour people. The Gostamans slept on. The Hagginses slept on. Palmyra and Bilbo and Miss Pistil slept on.

At half-past two in the morning there was a light knock at the door. I leaped up and yanked it open.

Another Jud Elliott stood there.

"Who are you?" I asked morosely.

"The same one who was here before. The one who went for help. There aren't any more of us now, are there?"

"I don't think so." I stepped out into the hall with him. "Well? What's been going on?"

He was grimy and unshaven. "I've been gone for a week. We've searched all up and down the line."

"Who has?"

"Well, I went to Metaxas first, in 1105, just as you said. He's terribly concerned for our sake. What he did, first of all, was to put all his servants to work, checking to see if anybody answering to Sauerabend's description could be found in or around 1105."

"It can't hurt, I guess."

"It's worth trying," my twin agreed. "Next, Metaxas went down to now-time and phoned Sam, who came flying in from New Orleans and brought Sid Buonocore with him. Metaxas also alerted Kolettis, Gompers, Plastiras, Pappas—all the Byzantium Couriers, the whole staff. Because of discontinuity problems, we're not notifying anyone who's on an earlier now-time basis than December 2059, but that still gives us a big posse. What we're doing now, what we've been doing for the past week, is simply moving around, year by year, hunting for Sauerabend, asking questions in the marketplace, sniffing for clues. I've been at it eighteen, twenty hours a day. So have all the others. It's wonderful, how loyal they are!"

"It certainly is," I said. "What are the chances of finding him, though?"

"Well, we assume that he hasn't left the Constantinople area, although there's nothing to prevent him from going down the line to 2059, hopping off to Vienna or Moscow, and vanishing up the line again. All we can do is plug away. If he doesn't turn up in Byzantine, we'll check Turkish, and then pre-Byzantine, and then we'll pass the word to now-time so Couriers on other runs can watch for him, and—"

He sagged. He was exhausted.

"Look," I said, "you've got to get some rest. Why don't you go back to 1105 and settle down at Metaxas' place for a few days? Then come back here when you're rested, and let me join the search. We can alternate that way indefinitely. Meanwhile, let's keep this night in 1204 as our reference point. Whenever you jump to me, jump to this night, so we don't lose contact. It may take us a couple of lifetimes, but we'll get Sauerabend back into the group before morning comes."

"Right."

"All clear, then? You spend a few days at the villa resting up, and come back here half an hour from now. And then I'll go."

"Clear," he said, and went down to the street to jump.

I returned to the room and resumed my melancholy vigil. At three in the morning, Jud B was back, looking like a new man. He had shaved, taken a bath or two, changed his clothes, obviously had had plenty of sleep. "Three days of rest at Metaxas' place," he said. *"Magnifique!"*

"You look great. *Too* great. You didn't, perhaps, sneak off to fool around with Pulcheria?"

"The thought didn't occur to me. But what if I had? You bastard, are you warning me to leave her alone?"

I said, "You don't have any right to—"

"I'm *you*, remember? You can't be jealous of yourself."

"I guess you can't," I said. "Stupid of me."

"Stupider of me," he said. "I *should* have dropped in on her while I was there."

"Well, now it's my turn. I'll put in some time on searching, then stop at the villa for rest and recuperation, and maybe have some fun with our beloved. You won't object to that, will you?"

"Fair's fair," he sighed. "She's yours as much as she's mine."

"Correct. When I've taken care of everything, I'll get back here at— let's see—quarter past three tonight. Got it?"

We synchronized our timetables for the 1105 end of the line to avoid discontinuities; I didn't want to get there while he was still there, or, worse, before he had ever arrived. Then I left the inn and shunted up the line. In 1105 I hired a chariot and was taken out to the villa on a golden autumn day.

Metaxas, bleary-eyed and stubble-faced, greeted me at the porch by asking, "Which one are you, A or B?"

"A. B's taking over for me at the inn in 1204. How's the search going?"

"Lousy," said Metaxas. "But don't give up hope. We're with you all the way. Come inside and meet some old friends."

51.

I said to them, "I'm sorry as hell to be putting you through all this trouble."

The men I respected most in the world laughed and grinned and chuckled and spat and said, "Shucks, 't'ain't nothin'."

They were frayed and grimy. They had been working hard and fruitlessly for me, and it showed. I wanted to hug all of them at once. Black Sambo, and plastic-faced Jeff Monroe, and shifty-eyed Sid Buonocore. Pappas, Kolettis, Plastiras. They had rigged a chart to mark off the places where they hadn't found Conrad Sauerabend. The chart had a lot of marks on it.

Sam said, "Don't worry, boy. We'll track him down."

"I feel so awful, making you give up free time—"

"It could have happened to any one of us," Sam said. "It wasn't your fault."

"It wasn't?"

"Sauerabend gimmicked his timer behind your back, didn't he? How could you have prevented it?" Sam grinned. "We got to help you out. We don't know when same'll happen to us."

"All for one," said Madison Jefferson Monroe. "One for all."

"You think you're the first Courier to have a customer skip out?" Sid Buonocore asked. "Don't be a craphead! Those timers can be rigged for manual use by anyone who understands Benchley Effect theory."

"They never told me—"

"They don't like to advertise it. But it happens. Five, six times a year, somebody takes a private time-trip behind his Courier's back."

I said, "What happens to the Courier?"

"If the Time Patrol finds out? They fire him," said Buonocore bleakly. "What we try to do is cover for each other, before the Patrol moves in. It's a bitch of a job, but we got to do it. I mean, if you don't look after one of your own when he's in trouble, who in hell will look after you?"

"Besides," said Sam, "it makes us feel like heroes."

I studied the chart. They had looked for Sauerabend pretty thoroughly in early Byzantium—Constantine through the second Theodosius—and they had checked out the final two centuries with equal care. Searching the middle had so far been a matter of random investigations. Sam, Buonocore, and Monroe were coming off search duty now and were going to rest; Kolettis, Plastiris, and Pappas were getting ready to go out, and they were planning strategy.

Everybody went on being very nice to me during the discussion of ways to catch Sauerabend. I felt a real sentimental glow of warmth for them. My comrades in adversity. My companions. My colleagues. The Time Musketeers. My heart expanded. I made a little speech telling them how grateful I was for all their help. They looked embarrassed and told me once again that it was a simple matter of good fellowship, the golden rule in action.

The door opened and a dusty figure stumbled in, wearing anachronistic sunglasses. Najeeb Dajani, my old tutor! He scowled, slumped down on a chair, and gestured impatiently to nobody in particular, hoping for wine.

Kolettis handed him wine. Dajani poured some of it into his hand and used it to wash the dust from his sunglasses. Then he gulped the rest.

"Mr. Dajani!" I cried. "I didn't know they had called you in too! Listen, I want to thank you for helping—"

"You stupid prick," said Dajani quietly. "How did I ever let you get your Courier license?"

52.

D ajani had just returned from a survey of the city in 630650, with no luck at all. He was tired and irritated, and he obviously wasn't happy about spending his layoff searching for somebody else's runaway tourist.

He put out my sentimental glow in a hurry. I tried to foist on him my gratitude speech, and he said sourly, "Skip the grease job. I'm doing this because it'll reflect badly on my capabilities as an instructor if the Patrol finds out what kind of anthropoid I let loose as a Courier. It's my own hide I'm protecting."

There was a nasty moment of silence. A lot of shuffling of feet and clearing of throats took place.

"That's not very gratifying to hear," I said to Dajani.

Buonocore said, "Don't let him upset you, kid. Like I told you, any Courier's tourist is likely to gimmick his timer, and—"

"I don't refer to the loss of the tourist," said Dajani testily. "I refer to the fact that this idiot managed to duplicate himself while trying to edit the mistake!" He gargled wine. "I forgive him for the one, but not for the other."

"The duplication is pretty ugly," Buonocore admitted.

"It's a serious thing," said Kolettis.

"Bad karma," Sam said. "No telling how we'll cover that one up."

"I can't remember a case to match," declared Pappas.

"A messy miscalculation," Plastiras commented.

"Look," I said, "the duplication was an accident. I was so much in a sweat to find Sauerabend that I didn't stop to calculate the implications of—"

"We understand," Sam said.

"It's a natural error, when you're under pressure," said Jeff Monroe.
"Could have happened to anyone," Buonocore told me.
"A shame. A damned shame," murmured Pappas.

I started to feel less like an important member of a close-knit fraternity, and more like a pitied halfwit nephew who can't help leaving little puddles of mess wherever he goes. The halfwit's uncles were trying to clean up a particularly messy mess for him, and trying to keep the halfwit serene so he wouldn't make a worse mess.

When I realized what the real attitude of these men toward me was, I felt like calling in the Time Patrol, confessing my timecrimes, and requesting eradication. My soul shriveled. My manhood withered. I, the copulator with empresses, the seducer of secluded noblewomen, the maker of smalltalk with emperors, I, the last of the Ducases, I, the strider across millennia, I, the brilliant Courier in the style of Metaxas, I . . . I, to these veteran Couriers here, was simply an upright mass of perambulating dreck. A faex that walks like a man. Which is the singular of faeces. Which is to say, a shit.

53.

Metaxas, who had not spoken for fifteen minutes, said finally, "If those of you who are going are ready to go, I'll get a chariot to take you into town."

Kolettis shook his head. "We haven't allotted eras yet. But it'll take only a minute."

There was a buzzing consultation over the chart. It was decided that Kolettis would cover 700725, Plastiras 11501175, and I would inspect 725745. Pappas had brought a plague suit with him and was going to make a survey of the plague years 745747, just in case Sauerabend had looped into that proscribed period by accident.

I was surprised that they trusted me to make a time-jump all by myself, considering what they obviously thought of me. But I suppose they figured I couldn't get into any worse trouble. Off we went to town in one of Metaxas' chariots. Each of us carried a small but remarkably accurate portrait of Conrad Sauerabend, painted on a varnished wooden plaque by a contemporary Byzantine artist hired by Metaxas. The artist had worked from a holophoto; I wonder what he'd made of *that*.

When we reached Constantinople proper, we split up and, one by one, timed off to the eras we were supposed to search. I materialized up the line in 725 and realized the little joke that had been played on me.

This was the beginning of the era of iconoclasm, when Emperor Leo III had first denounced the worship of painted images. At that time, most of the Byzantines were fervent iconodules—image-worshippers—and Leo set out to smash the cult of icons, first by speaking and preaching against them, then by destroying an image of Christ in the chapel of the Chalke, or Brazen House, in front of the Great Palace. After that things got worse; images and image-makers were persecuted, and Leo's son issued a proclamation declaring, "There shall be rejected, removed and cursed out of the Christian Church every likeness which is made out of any material whatever by the evil art of painters."

And in such an era I was supposed to walk around town holding a little painting of Conrad Sauerabend, asking people, "Have you seen this man anywhere?"

My painting wasn't exactly an icon. Nobody who looked at it was likely to mistake Sauerabend for a saint. Even so, it caused a lot of trouble for me.

"Have you seen this man anywhere?" I asked, and took out the painting.

In the marketplace.

In the bathhouses.

On the steps of Haghia Sophia.

Outside the Great Palace.

"Have you seen this man anywhere?"

In the Hippodrome during a polo match.

At the annual distribution of free bread and fish to the poor on May 11, celebrating the anniversary of the founding of the city.

In front of the Church of Saints Sergius and Bacchus.

"I'm looking for this man whose portrait I have here."

Half the time, I didn't even manage to get the painting fully into the open. They'd see a man pulling an icon from his tunic, and they'd run away, screaming, "Iconodule dog! Worshipper of images!"

"But this isn't—I'm only looking for—you mustn't mistake this painting for—won't you come back?"

I got pushed and shoved and expectorated upon. I got bullied by imperial guards and glowered at by iconoclastic priests. Several times I was invited to attend underground ceremonies of secret iconodules.

I didn't get much information about Conrad Sauerabend.

Still, despite all the difficulties, there were always some people who looked at the painting. None of them had seen Sauerabend, although a few "thought" they had noticed someone resembling the man in the picture. I wasted two days tracking one of the supposed resemblers, and found no resemblance at all.

I kept on, jumping from year to year. I lurked at the fringes of tourist groups, thinking that Sauerabend might prefer to stick close to people of his own era.

Nothing. No clue.

Finally, footsore and discouraged, I hopped back down to 1105. At

Metaxas' place I found only Pappas, who looked even more weary and bedraggled than I did.

"It's useless," I said. "We aren't going to find him. It's like looking for—looking for—"

"A needle in a timestack," Pappas said helpfully.

54.

I had earned a little rest before I returned to that long night in 1204 and sent my alter ego here to continue the search. I bathed, slept, banged a garlicky slavegirl two or three times, and brooded. Kolettis returned: no luck. Plastiras came back: no luck. They went down the line to resume their Courier jobs. Gompers, Herschel, and Melamed, donating time from their current layoffs, appeared and immediately set out on the quest for Sauerabend. The more Couriers who volunteered to help me in my time of need, the worse I felt.

I decided to console myself in Pulcheria's arms.

I mean, as long as I happened to be in the right era, and as long as Jud B had neglected to stop in to see her, it seemed only proper. We *had* had some sort of date. Just about the last thing Pulcheria had said to me after that night of nights was, "We'll meet again two days hence, yes? I'll arrange everything."

How long ago had that been?

At least two weeks on the 1105 now-time basis, I figured. Maybe three.

She was supposed to have sent a message to me at Metaxas', telling me where and how we could have our second meeting. In my concern with Sauerabend I had forgotten about that. Now I raced all around the villa, asking Metaxas' butlers and his major domo if any messages had arrived from town for me.

"No," they said. "No messages."

"Think carefully. I'm expecting an important message from the Ducas palace. From Pulcheria Ducas."

"From whom?"

"Pulcheria Ducas."

"No messages, sir."

I clothed myself in my finest finery and clipclopped into Constantinople. Did I dare present myself at the Ducas place uninvited? I did dare. My country-bumpkin cover identity would justify my possible breach of etiquette.

At the gate of the Ducas palace I rang for the servants, and an old groom came out, the one who had shown me to the chamber that night where Pulcheria had given herself to me. I smiled in a friendly way; the groom peered blankly back. Forgotten me, I thought.

I said, "My compliments to Lord Leo and Lady Pulcheria, and would you kindly tell them that George Markezinis of Epirus is here to call upon them?"

"To Lord Leo and Lady—" the groom repeated.

"Pulcheria," I said. "They know me. I'm cousin to Themistoklis Metaxas, and—" I hesitated, feeling even more foolish than usual at giving my pedigree to a groom. "Get me the major-domo," I snapped.

The groom scuttled within.

After a long delay, an imperious-looking individual in the Byzantine equivalent of livery emerged and surveyed me.

"Yes?"

"My compliments to Lord Leo and Lady Pulcheria, and would you kindly tell them—"

"Lady *who?*"

"Lady Pulcheria, wife to Leo Ducas. I am George Markezinis of Epirus, cousin to Themistoklis Metaxas, who only several weeks ago attended the party given by—"

"The wife to Leo Ducas," said the major-domo frostily, "is named Euprepia."

"Euprepia?"

"Euprepia Ducas, the lady of this household. Man, what do you want here? If you come drunken in the middle of the day to trouble Lord Leo, I—"

"Wait," I said. "*Euprepia? Not Pulcheria?*" A golden bezant flickered into my hand and fluttered swiftly across to the waiting palm of the major-domo. "I'm not drunk, and this is important. When did Leo marry this—this Euprepia?"

"Four years ago."

"Four—years—ago. No, that's impossible. *Five* years ago he married Pulcheria, who—"

"You must be mistaken. The Lord Leo has been married only once, to Euprepia Macrembolitissa, the mother of his son Basil and of his daughter Zoe."

The hand came forth. I dropped another bezant into it.

Dizzily I murmured, "His eldest son is Nicetas, who isn't even born yet, and he isn't supposed to have a son named Basil at all, and—my God, are you playing a game with me?"

"I swear before Christ Pantocrator that I have said no word but the truth," declared the major-domo resonantly.

Tapping my pouch of bezants, I said, desperate now, "Would it be possible for me to have an audience with the Lady Euprepia?"

"Perhaps so, yes. But she is not here. For three months now she has rested at the Ducas palace on the coast at Trebizond, where she awaits her next child."

"Three months. Then there was no party here a few weeks ago?"

"No, sir."

"The Emperor Alexius wasn't here? Nor Themistoklis Metaxas? Nor George Markezinis of Epirus? Nor—"

"None of those, sir. Can I help you further?"

"I don't think so," I said, and went staggering from the gate of the Ducas palace like unto one who has been smitten by the wrath of the gods.

55.

Dismally I wandered in a southeasterly way along the Golden Horn until I came to the maze of shops, marketplaces, and taverns near the place where there would one day be the Galata Bridge, and where today there is still a maze of shops, marketplaces, and taverns. Through those narrow, interweaving, chaotic streets I marched like a zombie, having no destination. I saw not, neither did I think; I just put one foot ahead of the other one and kept going until, early in the afternoon, kismet once more seized me by the privates.

I stumbled randomly into a tavern, a two-story structure of unpainted boards. A few merchants were downing their midday wine. I dropped down heavily at a warped and wobbly table in an unoccupied corner of the room and sat staring at the wall, thinking about Leo Ducas' pregnant wife Euprepia.

A comely tavern-slut appeared and said, "Some wine?"

"Yes. The stronger the better."

"A little roast lamb too?"

"I'm not hungry, thanks."

"We make very good lamb here."

"I'm not hungry," I said. I stared somberly at her ankles. They were very good ankles. I looked up at her calves, and then her legs vanished within the folds of her simple cloth wrap. She strode away and came back with a flask of wine. As she set it before me, the front of her wrap fell away at her throat, and I peered in at the two pale, full, rosy-tipped breasts that swung freely there. Then at last I looked at her face.

She could have been Pulcheria's twin sister.

Same dark, mischievous eyes. Same flawless olive skin. Same full lips and aquiline nose. Same age, about seventeen. The differences between this girl and my Pulcheria were differences of dress, of posture, and of expression. This girl was coarsely clad; she lacked Pulcheria's aristocratic elegance of bearing; and there was a certain pouting sullenness about her, the look of a girl who is living below her station in life and is angry about it.

I said, "You could almost be Pulcheria!"

She laughed harshly. "What kind of nonsensical talk is that?"

"A girl I know, who resembles you closely—Pulcheria, her name is—"

"Are you insane, or only drunk? *I* am Pulcheria. Your little game isn't pleasing to me, stranger."

"You—Pulcheria?"

"Certainly."

"Pulcheria Ducas?"

She cackled in my face. "Ducas, you say? Now I know you're crazy. Pulcheria Photis, wife of Heracles Photis the innkeeper!"

"Pulcheria—Photis—" I repeated numbly. "Pulcheria—Photis— wife—of—Heracles—Photis—"

She leaned close over me, giving me a second view of her miraculous breasts. Not haughty now but worried, she said in a low voice, "I can tell by your clothes that you're someone important. What do you want here? Has Heracles done something wrong?"

"I'm here just for wine," I said. "But listen, tell me this one thing: are you the Pulcheria who was born Botaniates?"

She looked stunned. "You know that!"

"It's true?"

"Yes," said my adored Pulcheria, and sank down next to me on the bench. "But I am a Botaniates no longer. For five years now—ever since Heracles—the filthy Heracles—ever since he—" She took some of my wine in her agitation. "Who are you, stranger?"

"George Markezinis of Epirus."

The name meant nothing to her.

"Cousin to Themistoklis Metaxas."

She gasped. "I *knew* you were someone important! I knew!" Trembling prettily, she said, "What do you want with me?"

The other patrons in the tavern were beginning to stare at us. I said, "Can we go somewhere to talk? Someplace private?"

Her eyes took on a cool, knowing look. "Just a moment," she said, and went out of the tavern. I heard her calling to someone, shouting like any fishwife, and after a moment a ragged girl of about fifteen came into the room. Pulcheria said, "Look after things, Anna. I'm going to be busy." To me she said, "We can go upstairs."

She led me to a bedchamber on the second floor of the building and carefully bolted the door behind us.

"My husband," she said, "has gone to Galata to buy meat, and will not be back for two hours. While the loathsome pig is away, I don't mind earning a bezant or two from a handsome stranger."

Her clothing fell away and she stood incandescently nude before me. Her smile was a defiant one, a smile that said that she retained her inner self no matter what stains of degration others inflicted on her. Her eyes flashed with lusty zeal.

I stood dazzled before those high, heavy breasts, whose nipples were visibly hardening, and before that flat, taut belly with its dark, mounded bush, and before those firm muscular thighs and before those outstretched, beckoning arms.

She tumbled down onto the rough cot. She flexed her knees and drew her legs apart.

"Two bezants?" she suggested.

Pulcheria transformed into a tavern whore? My goddess? My adored one?

"Why do you hesitate?" she asked. "Come, climb aboard, give the fat dog Heracles another pair of horns. What's wrong? Do I seem ugly to you?"

"Pulcheria—Pulcheria—I love you, Pulcheria—"

She giggled, shrill in her delight. She waved her heels at me. "Come on, then!"

"You were Leo Ducas' wife," I murmured. "You lived in a marble palace, and wore silk robes, and went about the city escorted by a watchful duenna. And the emperor was at your party, and just before dawn you came to me, and gave yourself to me, and it was all a dream, Pulcheria, all a dream, eh?"

"You are a madman," she said. "But a handsome madman, and I yearn to have you between my legs, and I yearn also for your bezants. Come close. Are you shy? Look, put your hand here, feel how hot Pulcheria grows, how she throbs—"

I was rigid with desire, but I knew I couldn't touch her. Not this Pulcheria, this coarse, shameless, wanton, sluttish wench, this gorgeous creature who capered and pumped and writhed impatiently on the cot before me.

I pulled out my pouch and emptied it over her nakedness, dumping golden bezants into her navel, her loins, spilling them across her breasts. Pulcheria shrieked in astonishment. She sat up, clutching at the money, scrambling for it, her breasts heaving and swaying, her eyes bright.

I fled.

56.

At the villa I found Metaxas and said, "What's the name of Leo Ducas' wife?"

"Pulcheria."

"When did you last see her?"

"Three weeks ago, when we went to that party."

"No," I said. "You're suffering from Transit Displacement, and so am I. Leo Ducas is married to someone named Euprepia, and has two children by her, and a third on the way. And Pulcheria is the wife of a tavern-keeper named Heracles Photis."

"Have you gone spotty potty?" Metaxas asked.

"The past has been changed. I don't know how it happened, but there's been a change, right in my own ancestry, don't you see, and Pulcheria's no longer my ancestress, and God knows if I even exist any more. If I'm not descended from Leo Ducas and Pulcheria, then who am I descended from, and—"

"When did you find all this out?"

"Just now. I went to look for Pulcheria, and—Christ, Metaxas, what am I going to do?"

"Maybe there's been a mistake," he said calmly.

"No. No. Ask your own servants. *They* don't undergo Transit Displacement. Ask them if they've ever heard of a Pulcheria Ducas. They haven't. Ask them the name of Leo Ducas' wife. Or go into town and see for yourself. There's been a change in the past, don't you see, and everything's different, and—Christ, Metaxas! Christ!"

He took hold of my wrists and said in a very quiet tone, "Tell me all about this from the beginning, Jud."

But I had no chance to. For just then big black Sam came rushing into the hall, whooping and screaming.

"We found him! God damn, but we found him!"

"Who?" Metaxas said.

"Who?" I said simultaneously.

"*Who?*" Sam repeated. "Who the hell do you think? Sauerabend. Conrad F. X. Sauerabend himself!"

"You found him?" I said, limp with relief. "Where? When? How?"

"Right here in 1105," said Sam. "This morning, Melamed and I were in the marketplace, just checking around a little, and we showed the picture, and sure enough, some peddler of pig's feet recognized him. Sauerabend's been living in Constantinople for the past five or six years, running a tavern down near the water. He goes under the name of Heracles Photis—"

"No!" I bellowed. "No, you black nigger bastard, no, no, no, no, no! It isn't true!"

And I launched myself at him in blind fury.

And I drove my fists into his belly, and sent him reeling backward toward the wall.

And he looked at me strangely, and caught his breath, and came toward me and picked me up and dropped me. And picked me up and dropped me. And picked me up a third time, but Metaxas made him put me down.

Sam said gently, "It's true that I *am* a black nigger bastard, but was it really necessary to say so that loudly?"

Metaxas said, "Give him some wine, somebody. I think he's going off his head."

I said, seizing control of myself somehow, "Sam, I didn't mean to call you names, but it absolutely cannot be the case that Conrad Sauerabend is living under the name of Heracles Photis."

"Why not?"

"Because—because—"

"I saw him myself," Sam said. "I had wine in his tavern no more than five hours ago. He's big and fat and red-faced, and thinks a great deal of himself. And he's got this little hot-ass Byzantine wife, maybe sixteen, seventeen years old, who waits on table in the place, and waves her boobies at the customers, and I bet sells her tail in the upstairs rooms—"

"All right," I said in a dead man's voice. "You win. The wife's name is Pulcheria."

Metaxas made a choking sound.

Sam said, "I didn't ask about her name."

"She's seventeen years old, and she comes from the Botaniates family," I went on, "which is one of the important Byzantine families, and only Buddha knows what she's doing married to Heracles Photis Conrad Sauerabend. And the past has been changed, Sam, because up until a few weeks ago on my now-time basis she was the wife of Leo Ducas and lived in a palace near the imperial palace, and it happened that I was having a love affair with her, and it also happens that until the past got changed she and Leo Ducas were my great-great-multi-great-grandparents, and it seems to have happened that a very stinking coincidence has taken place, which I don't comprehend the details of at all, except that I'm probably a nonperson now and there's no such individual as Pulcheria Ducas. And now, if you don't mind, I'm going to go into a quiet corner and cut my throat."

"This isn't happening," said Sam. "This is all a bad dream."

57.

B ut, of course, it wasn't. It was as real as any other event in this
fluid and changeable cosmos.

   The three of us drank a great deal of wine, and Sam gave me
some of the other details. How he had asked about in the neighborhood
concerning Sauerabend/Photis, and had been told that the man had arrived mysteriously from some other part of the country, about the year
1099. How the regulars at his tavern disliked him, but came to the place
just to get a view of his beautiful wife. How there was general suspicion
that he was engaged in some kind of illegal activity.

   "He excused himself," Sam said, "and told us that he had to go
across to Galata to do some marketing. But Kolettis followed him and
found that he didn't go marketing at all. He went into some kind of
warehouse on the Galata side, and apparently he disappeared. Kolettis
went in after him and couldn't find him anywhere. He must have time-
jumped, Kolettis assumed. Then this Photis reappeared, maybe half an
hour later, and took the ferry back into Constantinople."

   "Timecrime," Metaxas suggested. "He's engaged in smuggling."

   "That's what I think," said Sam. "He's using the early twelfth century as a base of operations, under this cover identity of Photis, and
he's running artifacts or gold coins or something like that down the line
to now-time."

   "How did he get mixed up with the girl, though?" Metaxas asked.

   Sam shrugged. "That part isn't clear yet. But now that we've found
him, we can trace him back up the line until we find the point of his
arrival. And see exactly what he's been up to."

   I groaned. "How are we ever going to restore the proper sequence
of events?"

Metaxas said, "We've got to locate the precise moment to which he made his jump out of your tour. Then we station ourselves there, catch him as soon as he materializes, take away that trick timer of his, and bring him back to 1204. That extricates him from the time-flow right where he came in, and puts him back into your 1204 trip where he belongs."

"You make it sound so simple," I said. "But it isn't. What about all the changes that have been made in the past? His five years of marriage to Pulcheria Botaniates—"

"Nonevents," said Sam. "As soon as we whisk Sauerabend from 1099 or whenever back into 1204, his marriage to this Pulcheria is automatically deleted, right? The time-flow resumes its unedited shape, and she marries whoever she was supposed to marry—"

"Leo Ducas," I said. "My ancestor."

"Leo Ducas, yes," Sam went on. "And for everybody in Byzantium, this whole Heracles Photis episode will never have happened. The only ones who'll know about it are us, because we're subject to Transit Displacement."

"What about the artifacts Sauerabend's been smuggling to now-time?" I asked.

Sam said, "They won't be there. They won't ever have been smuggled. And his fences down there won't have any recollection of having received them, either. The fabric of time will have been restored, and the Patrol won't be the wiser for it, and—"

"You're overlooking one little item," I said.

"Which is?"

"In the course of these shenanigans I generated an extra Jud Elliott. Where does *he* go?"

"Christ," Sam said. "I forgot about him!"

58.

I had now been running around 1105 for quite a while, and I figured
it was time to get back to 1204 and let my alter ego know something
of what was going on. So I made the shunt down the line and got to
the inn at quarter past three on that same long night of Conrad Sauerabend's disappearance from 1204. My other self was slouched gloomily
on his bed, studying the ceiling's heavy beams.

"Well?" he said. "How goes it?"

"Catastrophic. Come out into the hall."

"What's happening?"

"Brace yourself," I said. "We finally tracked Sauerabend down. He
shunted to 1099, and took a cover identity as a tavernkeeper. A year
later he married Pulcheria."

I watched my other self crumble.

"The past has been changed," I went on. "Leo Ducas married some-
body else, Euprepia something, and has two and a half children by her.
Pulcheria's a serving wench in Sauerabend's tavern. I saw her there.
She didn't know who I was, but she offered to screw me for two bezants.
Sauerabend is smuggling goods down the line, and—"

"Don't tell me any more," he said. "I don't want to hear any more."

"I haven't told you the good part yet."

"There's a good part?"

"The good part is that we're going to unhappen all of this. Sam and
Metaxas and you are going to trace Sauerabend back from 1105 to the
moment of his arrival in 1099, and unarrive him, and shunt him back
here into this evening. Thus canceling the whole episode."

"What happens to us?" my other self asked.

"We discussed that, more or less," I said vaguely. "We aren't sure.

Apparently we're both protected by Transit Displacement, so that we'll continue to exist even if we get Sauerabend back into his proper time flow."

"But where did we come from? There can't be creation of something out of nothing! Conservation of mass—"

"One of us was here all along," I reminded him. "As a matter of fact, *I* was here all along. I brought you into being by looping back fifty-six seconds into your time-flow."

"Balls," he said. "I was in that time-flow all along, doing what I was supposed to do. You came looping in out of nowhere. You're the goddam paradox, buster."

"I've lived fifty-six seconds longer than you, absolute. Therefore I must have been created first."

"We were both created in the same instant, on October 11, 2035," he shot back at me. "The fact that our time lines got snarled because of your faulty thinking has no bearing on which of us is more real than the other. The question is not who's the real Jud Elliott, but how we're going to continue to operate without getting in each other's way."

"We'll have to work out a tight schedule," I said. "One of us working as a Courier while the other one's hiding out up the line. And the two of us never in the same time at once, up or down the line. But how—"

"I have it," he said. "We'll establish a now-time existence in 1105, the way Metaxas has done, only for us it'll be continuous. There'll always be one of us pegged to now-time in the early twelfth century as George Markezinis, living in Metaxas' villa. The other one of us will be functioning as a Courier, and he'll go through a trip-and-layoff cycle—"

"—taking his layoff anywhen but in the 1105 basis."

"Right. And when he's completed the cycle, he'll go to the villa and pick up the Markezinis identity, and the other one will go down the line and report for Courier duty—"

"—and if we keep everything coordinated, there's no reason why the Patrol should ever find out about us."

"Brilliant!"

"And the one who's being Markezinis," I finished, "can always be carrying on a full-time affair with Pulcheria, and she'll never know that we're taking turns with her."

"As soon as Pulcheria is herself again."

"As soon as Pulcheria is herself again," I agreed.

That was a sobering thought. Our whole giddy plan for alternating our identities was just so much noise until we straightened out the mess Sauerabend had caused.

I checked the time. "You get back to 1105 and help Sam and Metaxas," I said. "Shunt here again by half past three tonight."

"Right," he said, and left.

59.

He came back on time, looking disgusted, and said, "We're all waiting for you on August 9, 1100, by the land wall back of Blachernae, about a hundred meters to the right of the first gate."

"What's the story?"

"Go and see for yourself. It makes me sick to think about it. Go, and do what has to be done, and then this filthy lunacy will be over. Go on. Jump up and join us there."

"What time of day?" I asked.

He pondered a moment. "Twenty past noon, I'd say."

I went out of the inn and walked to the land wall, and set my timer with care, and jumped. The transition from late-night darkness to midday brightness left me blinded for an instant; when I stopped blinking I found myself standing before a grim-faced trio: Sam, Metaxas—and Jud B.

"Jesus," I said, "Don't tell me we've committed another duplication!"

"This time it's only the Paradox of Temporal Accumulation," my alter ego said. "Nothing serious."

I was too muddled to reason it through. "But if we're both here, who's watching our tourists down in 1204?"

"Idiot," he said fiercely, "think four-dimensionally! How can you be so stupid if you're identical to me? Look, I jumped here from one point in that night in 1204, and you jumped from another point fifteen minutes away. When we go back, we each go to our proper starting point in the sequence. I'm due to arrive at half past three, and you aren't suppose to be there until quarter to four, but that doesn't mean that neither of us is there right now. Or all these others of us."

I looked around. I saw at least five groups of Metaxas-Sam-me arranged in a wide arc near the wall. Obviously they had been monitoring this time point closely, making repeated short-run shunts to check on the sequence of events, and the Cumulative Paradox was building up a multitude of them.

"Even so," I said dimly, "it somehow seems that I'm not correctly perceiving the linear chain of—"

"*Stuff* the linear chain of!" the other Jud snarled at me. "Will you look over there? There, on the far side of the gate!"

He pointed.

I looked.

I saw a gray-haired woman in simple clothes. I recognized her as a somewhat younger version of the woman whom I had seen escorting Pulcheria Ducas into the shop of sweets and spices that day, seemingly so long ago, five years down the line in 1105. The duenna was propped up against the city wall, giggling to herself. Her eyes were closed.

A short distance from her was a girl of about twelve, who could only have been Pulcheria's younger self. The resemblance was unmistakable. This girl still had a child's unformed features, and her breasts were only gentle bumps under her tunic, but the raw materials of Pulcheria's beauty were there.

Next to the girl was Conrad Sauerabend, in Byzantine lower-middle-class clothes.

Sauerabend was cooing in the girl's ear. He was dangling before her face a little twenty-first century gimcrack, a gyroscopic pendant or something like that. His other hand was under her tunic and visibly groping in the vicinity of her thighs. Pulcheria was frowning, but yet she wasn't making any move to get the hand out of her crotch. She seemed a little uncertain about what Sauerabend was up to, but she was altogether fascinated by the toy, and perhaps didn't mind the wandering fingers, either.

Metaxas said, "He's been living in Constantinople for a little less than a year, and commuting frequently to 2059 to drop off marketable artifacts. He's been coming by the wall every day to watch the little girl and her duenna take their noontime stroll. The girl is Pulcheria Botaniates, and that's the Botaniates palace just over there. About half an hour ago Sauerabend came along and saw the two of them. He gave the duenna a floater and she's been up high ever since. Then he sat down next to the girl and began to charm her. He's really very slick with little girls."

"It's his hobby," I said.

"Watch what happens now," said Metaxas.

Sauerabend and Pulcheria rose and walked toward the gate in the wall. We faded back into the shadows to remain unobserved. Most of our paradoxical duplicates had disappeared, evidently shunting to other positions along the line to monitor the events. We watched as the fat man and the lovely little girl strolled through the gate, into the countryside just beyond the city boundary.

I started to follow.

"Wait," said Sam. "See who's coming now? That's Pulcheria's older brother Andronicus."

A young man, perhaps eighteen, was approaching. He halted and stared in broad disbelief at the giggling duenna. We saw him rush toward her, shake her, yank her to her feet. The woman tumbled down again, helpless.

"Where's Pulcheria?" he roared. *"Where is she?"*

The duenna laughed.

Young Botaniates, desperate, rushed about the deserted sunbaked street, yelling for his maiden sister. Then he hurried through the gate.

"We follow him," Metaxas said. Several other groups of us were already outside the gate, I discovered when we got there. Andronicus Botaniates ran hither and thither. I heard the sound of girlish laughter coming from, seemingly, the wall itself.

Andronicus heard it too. There was a breach in the wall, a shallow cavelike opening at ground level, perhaps five meters deep. He ran toward it. We ran toward it too, jostling with a mob that consisted entirely of our duplicated selves. There must have been fifteen of us—five of each.

Andronicus entered the breach in the wall and let out a terrible howl. A moment later I peered in.

Pulcheria, naked, her tunic down near her ankles, stood in the classic position of modesty, with one hand flung across her budding breasts and the other spread over her loins. Next to her was Sauerabend, with his clothes open. He had his tool out and ready for business. I suppose he had been in the process of maneuvering Pulcheria into a suitable position when the interruption came.

"Outrage!" cried Andronicus. "Foulness! Seduction of a virgin maiden! I call you all to witness! Look at this, this monstrosity, this criminal deed!"

And he caught Sauerabend by one hand and his sister by the other, and tugged them both out into the open.

"Bear witness!" he bellowed. We got out of the way before Sauerabend could recognize us, although I think he was too terrified to see anyone. Pitiful Pulcheria, trying to hide all of herself at once, was huddled into a ball at her brother's feet; but he kept pulling her up, exposing her, crying, "Look at the little whore! Look at her! Look, look, look!" And a considerable crowd came to look.

We moved to one side. I felt like throwing up. That vile molester of children, that Humbert of stockbrokers—exposing his swollen red thing to Pulcheria, involving her in this scandal—

Now Andronicus had drawn his sword and was trying to kill either Sauerabend or Pulcheria or both. But the onlookers prevented him, bearing him to the ground and taking away his weapon. Pulcheria, in frantic dismay at having her nakedness exposed to such a multitude, grabbed a dagger from someone else and attempted to kill herself, but was stopped in time; finally an old man threw his cloak about her. All was confusion.

Metaxas said calmly, "We followed the rest of the sequence from here before you arrived, then doubled back to wait for you. Here's what happened: The girl was engaged to Leo Ducas, but of course it was impossible for him to marry her after half of Byzantium had seen her naked like this. Besides, she was considered tainted, even though Sauerabend didn't actually have time to get into her. The marriage was called off. Her family, blaming her for letting Sauerabend charm her into taking off her clothes, disowned her. Meanwhile, Sauerabend was given the choice of marrying the girl he dishonored, or suffering the usual penalty."

"Which was?"

"Castration," said Metaxas. "And so, as Heracles Photis, Sauerabend married her, changing the pattern of history at least to the extent of depriving you of your proper ancestral line. Which we're now going to correct."

"Not me," said Jud B. "I've seen all I can stand. I'm going back to 1204. I'm due there at half past three in the morning to tell this guy to come back here and watch things."

"But—" I said.

"Never mind figuring out the paradoxes," Sam said. "We've got work to do."

"Relieve me at quarter to four," said Jud B, and shunted.

Metaxas and Sam and I coordinated our timers. "We go up the line," said Metaxas, "by exactly one hour. To finish the comedy." We shunted.

60.

And with great precision and no little relief, we finished the comedy. In this fashion:

We shunted to noon, exactly, on that hot summer day of the year 1100, and took up positions along the wall of Constantinople. And waited, trying hard to ignore the other versions of ourselves who passed briefly through our time level on snooping missions of their own.

The pretty little girl and the watchful duenna came into view.

My heart ached with love for young Pulcheria, and I ached in other places as well, out of lust for the Pulcheria who would be, the Pulcheria whom I had known.

The pretty little girl and the unsuspecting duenna, keeping close together, strolled past us.

Conrad Sauerabend/Heracles Photis appeared. Discordant sounds in the orchestra; twirling of mustaches; hisses. He studied the girl and the woman. He patted his bulging belly. He drew forth a snubby little floater and checked its snout. Leering enthusiastically, he came forward, planning to thrust the floater against the duenna's arm and, by giving her an hour of the giggling highs, to gain unimpeded access to the little girl.

Metaxas nodded to Sam.

Sam nodded to me.

We approached Sauerabend on a slanting path of approach.

"Now!" said Metaxas, and we went into action.

Huge black Sam lunged forward and clasped his right forearm across Sauerabend's throat. Metaxas seized Sauerabend's left wrist and bent his entire arm backward, far from the controls of the timer that could whiz him from our grasp. Simultaneously, I caught Sauerabend's right arm, jerking it up and back and forcing him to drop the floater.

This entire maneuver occupied perhaps an eighth of a second and resulted in the effective immobilization of Sauerabend. The duenna, meanwhile, had wisely fled with Pulcheria at the sight of this unseemly struggle.

Sam now reached under Sauerabend's clothing and deprived him of his gimmicked timer.

Then we released him. Sauerabend, who undoubtedly thought that he had been set upon by bandits, saw me and grunted a couple of shocked monosyllables.

I said, "You thought you were pretty clever, didn't you?"

He grunted some more.

I said, "Gimmicking your timer, slipping away, thinking you could set up in business for yourself as a smuggler. Eh? You didn't believe we'd catch you?"

I didn't tell him of the weeks of hard work that we had put in. I didn't tell him of the timecrimes we ourselves had committed for the sake of detecting him—the paradoxes we had left strewn all up and down the line, the needless duplications of ourselves. I didn't tell him that we had just pinched six years of his life as a Byzantine tavernkeeper into a pocket universe that, so far as he was concerned, had no existence whatever. Nor did I tell him of the chain of events that had made him the husband of Pulcheria Botaniates in that pinched-off universe, depriving me of my proper ancestry. All of those things had now unhappened. There now would be no tavernkeeper named Heracles Photis selling meat and drink to the Byzantines of the years 11001105.

Metaxas produced a spare timer, ungimmicked, that he had carried for the purpose.

"Put it on," he said.

Sullenly, Sauerabend donned it.

I said, "We're going back to 1204, more or less to the time you set out from. And then we're going to finish our tour and go back down the line to 2059. And God help you if you cause any more trouble for me, Sauerabend. I won't report you for timecrime, because I'm a merciful man, even though an unauthorized shunt like yours is very definitely a criminal act; but if you do anything whatever that displeases me in the slightest between now and the moment I'm rid of you, I'll make you roast for it. Clear?"

He nodded bleakly.

To Sam and Metaxas I said, "I can handle this from here on. Thanks for everything. I can't possibly tell you—"

"Don't try," said Metaxas, and together they shunted down the line.

I set Sauerabend's new timer and my own, and drew forth my pitchpipe. "Here we go," I said, and we shunted into 1204.

61.

At quarter to four on that very familiar night in 1204 I went once more up the stairs of the inn, this time with Sauerabend. Jud B paced restlessly just within the door of the room. He brightened at the sight of my captive. Sauerabend looked puzzled at the presence of two of me, but he didn't dare say anything.

"Get inside," I said to him. "And don't monkey with your goddam timer or you'll suffer for it."

Sauerabend went in.

I said to Jud B, "The nightmare's over. We grabbed him, took away his timer, put a regulation one on him, and here he is. The whole operation took just exactly four hours, right?"

"Plus who remembers how many weeks of running up and down the line."

"No matter now. We got him back. We start from scratch."

"And there's now an extra one of us," Jud B pointed out. "Do we work that little deal of taking turns?"

"We do. One of us stays with these clowns, takes them on down to 1453 as scheduled, and back to the twenty-first century. The other one of us goes to Metaxas' villa. Want to flip a coin?"

"Why not?" He pulled a bezant of Alexius I from his pouch, and let me inspect it for kosherness. It was okay: a standing figure of Alexius on the obverse, an image of Christ enthroned on the reverse. We stipulated that Alexius was heads and Jesus was tails. Then I flipped the coin high, caught it with a quick snap of my hand, and clapped it down on the back of my other hand. I knew, from the feel of the concave coin's edge against my skin, that it had landed heads up.

"Tails," said the other Jud.

"Tough luck, amigo." I showed him the coin. He grimaced and took it back from me.

Gloomily he said, "I've got three or four days left with this tour, right? Then two weeks of layoff, which I can't spend in 1105. That means you can expect to see me showing up at Metaxas' place in seventeen, eighteen days absolute."

"Something like that," I agreed.

"During which time you'll make it like crazy with Pulcheria."

"Naturally."

"Give her one for me," he said, and went into the room.

Downstairs, I slouched against a pillar and spent half an hour rechecking all of my comings and goings of this hectic night, to make sure I'd land in 1105 at a non-discontinuous point. The last thing I needed now was to miscalculate and show up there at a time prior to the whole Sauerabend caper, thereby finding a Metaxas to whom the entire thing was, well, Greek.

I did my calculations.

I shunted.

I wended my way once more to the lovely villa.

Everything had worked out perfectly. Metaxas embraced me in joy.

"The time-flow is intact again," he said. "I've been back from 1100 only a couple of hours, but that was enough to check up on things. Leo Ducas' wife is named Pulcheria. Someone named Angelus runs the tavern Sauerabend owned. Nobody here remembers a thing about anything. You're safe."

"I can't tell you how much I—"

"Skip it, will you?"

"I suppose. Where's Sam?"

"Down the line. He had to go back to work. And I'm about to do the same," Metaxas said. "My layoff's over, and there's a tour waiting for me in the middle of December, 2059. So I'll be gone about two weeks, and then I'll be back here on—" He considered it. "—on October 18, 1105. What about you?"

"I stay here until October 22." I said. "Then my alter ego will be finished with his post-tour layoff and will replace me here, while I go down the line to take out my next tour."

"Is that how you're going to work it? Turns?"

"It's the only way."

"You're probably right," said Metaxas, but I wasn't.

62.

Metaxas took his leave, and I took a bath. And then, really relaxed for the first time in what seemed like several geological epochs, I contemplated my immediate future.

First, a nap. Then a meal. And then a journey into town to call on Pulcheria, who would be restored to her rightful place in the Ducas household, and unaware of the strange metamorphosis that had temporarily come over her destinies.

We'd make love, and I'd come back to the villa, and in the morning I'd go into town again, and afterward—

Then I stopped hatching further plans, because Sam appeared unexpectedly and smashed everything.

He was wearing a Byzantine cloak, but it was just a hasty prop, for I could see his ordinary down-the-line clothes on underneath. He looked harried and upset.

"What the hell are you doing here?" I asked.

"A favor to you," he said.

"Huh?"

"I said I'm here as a favor to you. And I'm not going to stay long, because I don't want the Time Patrol after me too."

"Is the Time Patrol after me?"

"You bet your white ass it is!" he yelled. "Get your things together and clear out of here, fast! You've got to hide, maybe three, four thousand years back, somewhere. Hurry it up!"

He began collecting a few stray possessions of mine scattered about the room. I caught hold of him and said, "Will you tell me what's going on? Sit down and stop acting like a maniac. You come in here at a million kilometers an hour and—"

"All right," he said. "All right. I'll spell it all out for you, and if I get arrested too, so be it. I'm stained with sin. I *deserve* to be arrested. And—"

"Sam—"

"All right," he said again. He closed his eyes a moment. "My now-time basis," he said hollowly, "is December 25, 2059. Merry Christmas. Several days ago on my time-level, your other self brought your current tour back from Byzantium. Including Sauerabend and all the rest of them. Do you know what happened to your other self the instant he arrived in 2059?"

"The Time Patrol arrested him?"

"Worse."

"What could be worse?"

"He vanished, Jud. He became a nonperson. He ceased ever to have existed."

I had to laugh. "The cocksure bastard! I *told* him that I was the real one and that he was just some kind of phantom, but he wouldn't listen! Well, I can't say that I'm sorry to see—"

"No, Jud," Sam said sadly. "He was every bit as real as you, when he was back here up the line. And you're every bit as unreal as he is now."

"I don't understand."

"You're a nonperson, Jud, same as he is. You have retroactively ceased to exist. I'm sorry. You never happened. And it's our fault as much as yours. We moved so fast that we slipped up on one small detail."

He looked frighteningly somber. But how else are you supposed to look, when you come to tell somebody that he's not only dead but never was born?

"What happened, Sam? What detail?"

"It's like this, Jud. You know, when we took Sauerabend's gimmicked timer away, we got him another one. Metaxas keeps a few smuggled spares around—that tricky bastard has everything."

"So?"

"Its serial number, naturally, was different from the number of the timer Sauerabend started his tour with. Normally, nobody notices something like that, but when this tour checked back in, it just happened that the check-in man was a stickler for the rules, and he examined serial numbers. And saw there was a substitution, and yelled for the Patrol."

"Oh," I said weakly.

"They questioned Sauerabend," Sam said, "and of course he was cagey, more to protect himself than you. And since he couldn't give any explanation of the switch, the Patrol got authorization to run a recheck on the entire tour he had just taken."

"Oh-oh."

"They monitored it from every angle. They saw you leave your group, they saw Sauerabend skip out the moment you were gone, they saw you and me and Metaxas catch him and bring him back to that night in 1204."

"So all three of us are in trouble?"

Sam shook his head. "Metaxas has pull. So have I. We wiggled out of it on a sympathy line, that we were just trying to help a buddy in trouble. It took all the strings we could pull. But we couldn't do a thing for you, Jud. The Patrol is out for your head. They looked in on that little routine in 1204 by which you duplicated yourself, and they began to realize that you were guilty not only of negligence in letting Sauerabend get away from you in the first place, but also of various paradoxes caused in your unlawful attempts to correct the situation. The charges against you were so serious that we couldn't get them dropped, and we tried, man, we *tried*. The Patrol thereupon took action against you."

"What kind of action?" I asked in a dead man's voice.

"You were removed from your tour on that evening in 1204 two hours prior to your original shunt to 1105 for your tryst with Pulcheria. Another Courier replaced you in 1204; you were plucked from the time-flow and brought down the line to stand trial in 2059 for assorted time-crimes."

"Therefore—"

"Therefore," Sam swept on, "you never did slip away to 1105 to pay that call on Pulcheria. Your whole love affair with Pulcheria has become a nonevent, and if you were to visit her now, you'd find that she has no recollection of having slept with you. Next: since you didn't go to 1105, you obviously didn't return to 1204 and find Sauerabend missing, and anyway Sauerabend had never been part of your tour group. And thus there was no need for you to make that fifty-six-second shunt up the line which created the duplication. Neither you nor Jud B ever came into being, since the existence of both of you dates from a point later than your visit to Pulcheria, and you never made that visit, having been plucked out of the time-flow before you got a chance to do it. You and Jud B are nonpersons and always have been. You happen to be protected by the Paradox of Transit Displacement, as long as you stay up the line; Jud B ceased to be protected the moment he returned to now-time, and disappeared irretrievably. Got that?"

Shivering, I said, "Sam, what's happening to that other Jud, the—

the—the *real* Jud? The one they plucked, the one they've got down there in 2059?"

"He's in custody, awaiting trial on timecrime charges."

"What about me?"

"If the Patrol ever finds you, you'll be brought to now-time and thus automatically obliterated. But the Patrol doesn't know where you are. If I you stay in Byzantium, sooner or later you'll be discovered, and that'll be the end for you. When I found all this out, I shot back here to warn you. Hide in prehistory. Get away into some period earlier than the founding of the old Greek Byzantium—earlier than 700 B.C., I guess. You can manage there. We'll bring you books, tools, whatever you need. There'll be people of some sort, nomads, maybe—anyway, company. You'll be like a god to them. They'll worship you, they'll bring you a woman a day. It's your only chance, Jud."

"I don't want to be a prehistoric god! I want to be able to go down the line again! And to see Pulcheria! And—"

"There's no chance of any of that," Sam said, and his words came down like the blade of a guillotine. "You don't exist. It's suicide for you ever to try to go down the line. And if you go anywhere near Pulcheria, the Patrol will catch you and *take* you down the line. Hide or die, Jud. Hide or die."

"But I'm real, Sam! I *do* exist!"

"Only the Jud Elliott who's currently in custody in 2059 exists. You're a residual phenomenon, a paradox product, nothing more. I love you all the same, boy, and that's why I've risked my own black hide to help you, but you aren't real. Believe me. Believe me. You're your own ghost. Pack up and clear out!"

63.

I've been here for three and a half months now. By the calendar I keep, the date is March 15, 3060 B.P. I'm living a thousand years before Christ, more or less.

It's not a bad life. The people here are subsistence farmers, maybe remnants of the old Hittite empire; the Greek colonists won't be getting here for another three centuries. I'm starting to learn the language; it's Indo-European and I pick it up fast. As Sam predicted, I'm a god. They wanted to kill me when I showed up, but I did a few tricks with my timer, shunting right before their eyes, and now they don't dare offend me. I try to be a kindly god, though. Right now I'm helping spring to arrive. I went down to the shore of what will someday be called the Bosphorus and delivered a long prayer, in English, for good weather. The locals loved it.

They give me all the women I want. The first night they gave me the chief's daughter, and since then I've rotated pretty well through the whole nubile population of the village. I imagine they'll want me to marry someone eventually, but I want to complete the inspection first. The women don't smell too good, but some of them are impressively passionate.

I'm terribly lonely.

Sam has been here three times, Metaxas twice. The others don't come. I don't blame them; the risks are great. My two loyal friends have brought me floaters, books, a laser, a big box of music cubes, and plenty of other things that are going to perplex the tails off some archaeologists eventually.

I said to Sam, "Bring me Pulcheria, just for a visit."

"I can't," he said. And he's right. It would have to be a kidnapping, and there might be repercussions, leading to Time Patrol troubles for Sam and obliteration for me.

I miss Pulcheria ferociously. You know, I had sex with her only that one night, though it seems as if I knew her much better than that. I wish now that I'd had her in the tavern, while she was Pulcheria Photis, too.

My beloved. My wicked great-great-multi-great-grand-mother. Never to see you again! Never to touch your smooth skin, your—no, I won't torture myself. I'll try to forget you. Hah!

I console myself, when not busy in my duties as a deity, by dictating my memoirs. Everything now is recorded, all the details of how I maneuvered myself into this terrible fix. A cautionary tale: from promising young man to absolute nonperson in sixty-two brief chapters. I'll keep on writing too, now and then. I'll tell what it's like to be a Hittite god. Let's see, tomorrow we'll have the spring fertility festival, and the ten fairest maidens of the village will come to the god's house so that we—

Pulcheria!

Why am I here so far from you, Pulcheria?

I have too much time to think about you, here.

I also have too much time to think unpleasant thoughts about my ultimate fate. I doubt that the Time Patrol will find me here. But there's another possibility.

The Patrol knows that I'm hiding somewhere up the line, protected by displacement.

The Patrol wants to smoke me out and abolish me, because I'm a filthy spawn of paradox.

And it's in the power of the Patrol to do it. Suppose they retroactively discharge Jud Elliott from the Time Service prior to the time he set out on his ill-starred last trip? If Jud Elliott never ever got to Byzantium that time at all, the probability of my existence reaches the zero point, and I no longer am protected by the Paradox of Transit Displacement. The Law of Lesser Paradoxes prevails. Out I go—poof!

I know why they haven't done that to me yet. It's because that other Jud, God bless him, is standing trial for timecrime down the line, and they can't retroactively pluck him until they've found him guilty. They have to complete the trial. If he's found guilty, I guess they'll take some action of that sort. But court procedures are slow. Jud will stall. Sam's told him I'm here and have to be protected. It might be months, years, who knows? He's on his now-time basis, I'm on mine, and we move forward into our futures together, day by day, and so far I'm still here.

Lonely. Heartsick.

Dreaming of my forever lost Pulcheria.

Maybe they'll never take action against me.

Or maybe they'll end me tomorrow.

Who knows? There are moments when I don't even care. There's one comforting thing, at least. It'll be the most painless of deaths. Not even a flicker of pain. I'll simply go wherever the flame of the candle goes when it's snuffed. It could happen at any time, and meanwhile I live from hour to hour, playing god, listening to Bach, indulging in floaters, dictating my memoirs, and waiting for the end. Why, it could even come right in the middle of a sentence, and I'd

DYING INSIDE

For B and T and C and me—
we sweated it out

1.

So, then, I have to go downtown to the University and forage for dollars again. It doesn't take much cash to keep me going—$200 a month will do nicely—but I'm running low, and I don't dare try to borrow from my sister again. The students will shortly be needing their first term papers of the semester; that's always a steady business. The weary, eroding brain of David Selig is once more for hire. I should be able to pick up $75 worth of work on this lovely golden October morning. The air is crisp and clear. A high-pressure system covers New York City, banishing humidity and haze. In such weather my fading powers still flourish. Let us go then, you and I, when the morning is spread out against the sky. To the Broadway-IRT subway. Have your tokens ready, please.

You and I. To whom do I refer? I'm heading downtown alone, after all. *You and I.*

Why, of course I refer to myself and to that creature which lives within me, skulking in its spongy lair and spying on unsuspecting mortals. That sneaky monster within me, that ailing monster, dying even more swiftly than I. Yeats once wrote a dialogue of self and soul; why then shouldn't Selig, who is divided against himself in a way poor goofy Yeats could never have understood, speak of his unique and perishable gift as though it were some encapsulated intruder lodged in his skull? Why not? Let us go then, you and I. Down the hall. Push the button. Into the elevator. There is a stink of garlic in it. These peasants, these swarming Puerto Ricans, they leave their emphatic smells everywhere. My neighbors. I love them. Down. Down.

It is 10:43 A.M., Eastern Daylight Savings Time. The current temperature reading in Central Park is 57°. The humidity stands at 28% and the barometer is 30.30 and falling, with the wind northeast at 11 miles per hour. The forecast is for fair skies and sunny weather today, tonight, and tomorrow, with the highs in the low to middle 60's. The chance of precipitation is zero today and 10% tomorrow. Air quality level is rated good. David Selig is 41 and counting. Slightly above medium height, he has the lean figure of a bachelor accustomed to his own meager cooking, and his customary facial expression is a mild, puzzled frown. He blinks a lot. In his faded blue denim jacket, heavy-duty boots, and 1969-vintage striped bells he presents a superficially youthful appearance, at least from the neck down; but in fact he looks like some sort of refugee from an illicit research laboratory where the balding, furrowed heads of anguished middle-aged men are grafted to the reluctant bodies of adolescent boys. How did this happen to him? At what point did his face and scalp begin to grow old? The dangling cables of the elevator hurl shrieks of mocking laughter at him as he descends from his two-room refuge on the twelfth floor. He wonders if those rusty cables might be even older than he is. He is of the 1935 vintage. This housing project, he suspects, might date from 1933 or 1934. The Hon. Fiorello H. LaGuardia, Mayor. Though perhaps it's younger—just immediately pre-war, say. (Do you remember 1940, Duvid? That was the year we took you to the World's Fair. This is the trylon, that's the perisphere.) Anyway the buildings are getting old. What isn't?

The elevator halts grindingly at the 7th floor. Even before the scarred door opens I detect a quick mental flutter of female Hispanic vitality dancing through the girders. Of course, the odds are overwhelming that the summoner of the elevator is a young Puerto Rican wife—the house is full of them, the husbands are away at work at this time of day—but all the same I'm pretty certain that I'm reading her psychic emanations and not just playing the hunches. Sure enough. She is short, swarthy, maybe about 23 years old, and very pregnant. I can pick up the double neural output clearly; the quicksilver darting of her shallow, sensual mind and the furry, blurry thumpings of the fetus, about six months old, sealed within her hard bulging body. She is flat-faced and broad-hipped, with little glossy eyes and a thin, pinched mouth. A second child, a dirty girl of about two, clutches her mother's thumb. The babe giggles up at me and the woman favors me with a brief, suspicious smile as they enter the elevator.

They stand with their backs toward me. Dense silence. *Buenos dias, señora.* Nice day, isn't it, ma'am? What a lovely little child. But I remain mute. I don't know her; she looks just like all the others who live in this project, and even her cerebral output is standard stuff, unindividuated, indistinguishable: vague thoughts of plantains and rice, this week's lottery results, and tonight's television highlights. She is a dull bitch but she is human and I love her. What's her name? Maybe it's Mrs. Altagracia Morales. Mrs. Amantina Figueroa. Mrs. Filomena Mercado. I love their names. Pure poetry. I grew up with plump clumping girls named Sondra Wiener, Beverly Schwartz, Sheila Weisbard. Ma'am, can you possibly be Mrs. Inocencia Fernandez? Mrs. Clodomira Espinosa? Mrs. Bonifacia Colon? Perhaps Mrs. Esperanza Dominguez. Esperanza. Esperanza. I love you, Esperanza. Esperanza springs eternal in the human breast. (I was there last Christmas for the bullfights. Esperanza Springs, New Mexico; I stayed at the Holiday Inn. No, I'm kidding.) Ground floor. Nimbly I step forward to hold the door open. The lovely stolid pregnant chiquita doesn't smile at me as she exits.

To the subway now, hippity-hop, one long block away. This far uptown the tracks are still elevated. I sprint up the cracking, peeling staircase and arrive at the station level hardly winded at all. The results of clean living, I guess. Simple diet, no smoking, not much drinking, no acid or mesc, no speed. The station, at this hour, is practically deserted. But in a moment I hear the wailing of onrushing wheels, metal on metal, and simultaneously I pick up the blasting impact of a sudden phalanx of minds all rushing toward me at once out of the north, packed aboard the five or six cars of the oncoming train. The compressed souls of those passengers form a single inchoate mass, pressing insistently against me. They quiver like trembling jellylike bites of plankton squeezed brutally together in some oceanographer's net, creating one complex organism in which the separate identities of all are lost. As the train glides into the station I am able to pick up isolated blurts and squeaks of discrete selfhood: a fierce jab of desire, a squawk of hatred, a pang of regret, a sudden purposeful inner mumbling, rising from the confusing totality the way odd little scraps and stabs of melody rise from the murky orchestral smear of a Mahler symphony. The power is deceptively strong in me today. I'm picking up plenty. This is the strongest it's been in weeks. Surely the low humidity is a factor. But I'm not deceived into thinking that the decline in my ability has been checked. When I first began to lose my hair, there was a happy period when the process of erosion seemed to halt and reverse itself, when new patches of fine dark floss began to sprout on my denuded forehead. But after an initial freshet of hope I took a more realistic view: this was no miraculous reforestation but only a twitch of the hormones, a temporary cessation of decay, not to be relied upon. And in time my hairline resumed its retreat. So too in this instance. When you know that something is dying inside you, you learn not to put much trust in the random

vitalities of the fleeting moment. Today the power is strong yet tomorrow I may hear nothing but distant tantalizing murmurs.

I find a seat in the corner of the second car, open my book, and
wait out the ride downtown. I am reading Beckett again, *Malone Dies*;
it plays nicely to my prevailing mood, which as you have noticed is
one of self-pity. *My time is limited. It is thence that one fine day, when
all nature smiles and shines, the rack lets loose its black unforgettable
cohorts and sweeps away the blue for ever. My situation is truly delicate. What fine things, what momentous things, I am going to miss
through fear, fear of falling back into the old error, fear of not finishing
in time, fear of revelling, for the last time, in a last outpouring of misery,
impotence and hate. The forms are many in which the unchanging seeks
relief from its formlessness.* Ah yes, the good Samuel, always ready
with a word or two of bleak comfort.

Somewhere about 180th Street I look up and see a girl sitting diagonally opposite me and apparently studying me. She is in her very
early twenties, attractive in a sallow way, with long legs, decent breasts,
a bush of auburn hair. She has a book too—the paperback of *Ulysses*,
I recognize the cover—but it lies neglected on her lap. Is she interested
in me? I am not reading her mind; when I entered the train I automatically stopped my inputs down to the minimum, a trick I learned when
I was a child. If I don't insulate myself against scatter-shot crowd-noises
on trains or in other enclosed public places I can't concentrate at all.
Without attempting to detect her signals, I speculate on what she's thinking about me, playing a game I often play. *How intelligent he looks.
. . . He must have suffered a good deal, his face is so much older than
his body . . . tenderness in his eyes . . . so sad they look . . . a poet, a
scholar. . . . I bet he's very passionate . . . pouring all his pent-up love
into the physical act, into screwing . . . What's he reading? Beckett? Yes,
a poet, a novelist he must be . . . maybe somebody famous. . . . I mustn't
be too aggressive, though. He'll be turned off by pushiness. A shy smile,
that'll catch him. . . . One thing leads to another. . . . I'll invite him up
for lunch. . . .* Then, to check on the accuracy of my intuitive perceptions,
I tune in on her mind. At first there is no signal. My damnable waning
powers betraying me again! But then it comes—static, first, as I get the
low-level muzzy ruminations of all the passengers around me, and then
the clear sweet tone of her soul. She is thinking about a karate class
she will attend later this morning on 96th Street. She is in love with her
instructor, a brawny pockmarked Japanese. She will see him tonight.
Dimly through her mind swims the memory of the taste of sake and the
image of his powerful naked body rearing above her. There is nothing
in her mind about me. I am simply part of the scenery, like the map of

the subway system on the wall above my head. Selig, your egocentricity kills you every time. I note that she does indeed wear a shy smile now, but it is not for me, and when she sees me staring at her the smile vanishes abruptly. I return my attention to my book.

The train treats me to a long sweaty unscheduled halt in the tunnel between stations north of 137th Street; eventually it gets going again and deposits me at 116th Street, Columbia University. I climb toward the sunlight. I first climbed these stairs a full quarter of a century ago, October '51, a terrified high-school senior with acne and a crew-cut, coming out of Brooklyn for my college entrance interview. Under the bright lights in University Hall. The interviewer terribly poised, mature—why, he must have been 24, 25 years old. They let me into their college, anyway. And then this was my subway station every day, beginning in September '52 and continuing until I finally got away from home and moved up close to the campus. In those days there was an old cast-iron kiosk at street level marking the entrance to the depths; it was positioned between two lanes of traffic, and students, their absent minds full of Kierkegaard and Sophocles and Fitzgerald, were forever stepping in front of cars and getting killed. Now the kiosk is gone and the subway entrances are placed more rationally, on the sidewalks.

I walk along 116th Street. To my right, the broad greensward of South Field; to my left, the shallow steps rising to Low Library. I remember South Field when it was an athletic field in the middle of the campus: brown dirt, basepaths, fence. My freshman year I played softball there. We'd go to the lockers in University Hall to change, and then, wearing sneakers, polo shirts, dingy gray shorts, feeling naked amidst the other students in business suits or ROTC uniforms, we'd sprint down the endless steps to South Field for an hour of outdoor activity. I was good at softball. Not much muscle, but quick reflexes and a good eye, and I had the advantage of knowing what was on the pitcher's mind. He'd stand there thinking, *This guy's too skinny to hit, I'll give him a high fast one*, and I'd be ready for it and bust it out into left field, circling the bases before anyone knew what was happening. Or the other side would try some clumsy bit of strategy like hit-and-run, and I'd move effortlessly over to gather up the grounder and start the double play. Of course it was only softball and my classmates were mostly pudgy dubs who couldn't even run, let alone read minds, but I enjoyed the unfamiliar sensation of being an outstanding athlete and indulged in fantasies of playing shortstop for the Dodgers. The *Brooklyn* Dodgers, remember? In my sophomore year they ripped up South Field and turned it into a fine grassy showplace divided by a paved promenade, in honor of the University's 200th birthday. Which happened in

1954. Christ, so very long ago. I grow old . . . I grow old . . . I shall wear the bottoms of my trousers rolled. The mermaids singing, each to each. I do not think that they will sing to me.

I go up the steps and take a seat about fifteen feet to the left of the bronze statue of Alma Mater. This is my office in fair weather or foul. The students know where to look for me, and when I'm there the word quickly spreads. There are five or six other people who provide the service I provide—impecunious graduate students, mostly, down on their luck—but I'm the quickest and most reliable, and I have an enthusiastic following. Today, though, business gets off to a slow start. I sit for twenty minutes, fidgeting, peering into Beckett, staring at Alma Mater. Some years ago a radical bomber blew a hole in her side, but there's no sign of the damage now. I remember being shocked at the news, and then shocked at being shocked—why should I give a damn about a dumb statue symbolic of a dumb school? That was about 1969, I guess. Back in the Neolithic.

"Mr. Selig?"

Big brawny jock looming above me. Colossal shoulders, chubby innocent face. He's deeply embarrassed. He's taking Comp Lit 18 and needs a paper fast, on the novels of Kafka, which he hasn't read. (This is the football season; he's the starting halfback and he's very very busy.) I tell him the terms and he hastily agrees. While he stands there I covertly take a reading of him, getting the measure of his intelligence, his probable vocabulary, his style. He's smarter than he appears. Most of them are. They could write their own papers well enough if they only had the time. I make notes, setting down my quick impressions of him, and he goes away happy. After that, trade is brisk: he sends a fraternity brother, the brother sends a friend, the friend sends one of *his* fraternity brothers, a different fraternity, and the daisy-chain lengthens until by early afternoon I find I've taken on all the work I can handle. I know my capacity. So all is well. I'll eat regularly for two or three weeks, without having to tap my sister's grudging generosity. Judith will be pleased not to hear from me. Home, now, to begin my ghostly tasks. I'm good—glib, earnest, profound in a convincingly sophomoric way— and I can vary my styles. I know my way around literature, psychology, anthropology, philosophy, all the soft subjects. Thank God I kept my own term papers; even after twenty-odd years they can still be mined. I charge $3.50 a typed page, sometimes more if my probing reveals that the client has money. A minimum grade of B+ guaranteed or there's no fee. I've never had to make a refund.

2.

When he was seven and a half years old and causing a great deal of trouble for his third-grade teacher, they sent little David to the school psychiatrist, Dr. Hittner, for an examination. The school was an expensive private one on a quiet leafy street in the Park Slope section of Brooklyn; its orientation was socialist-progressive, with a smarmy pedagogical underpinning of warmed-over Marxism and Freudianism and John Deweyism, and the psychiatrist, a specialist in the disturbances of middle-class children, paid a call every Wednesday afternoon to peer into the soul of the current problem child. Now it was David's turn. His parents gave their consent, of course. They were deeply concerned about his behavior. Everyone agreed that he was a brilliant child: he was extraordinarily precocious, with a reading-comprehension score on the twelve-year-old level, and adults found him almost frighteningly bright. But he was uncontrollable in class, raucous, disrespectful; the schoolwork, hopelessly elementary for him, bored him to desperation; his only friends were the class misfits, whom he persecuted cruelly; most of the children hated him and the teachers feared his unpredictability. One day he had up-ended a hallway fire extinguisher simply to see if it would spray foam as promised. It did. He brought garter snakes to school and let them loose in the auditorium. He mimed classmates and even teachers with vicious accuracy. "Dr. Hittner would just like to have a little chat with you," his mother told him. "He's heard you're a very special boy and he'd like to get to know you better." David resisted, kicking up a great fuss over the psychiatrist's name. "Hitler? Hitler? I don't want to talk to Hitler!" It was the fall of 1942 and the childish pun was an inevitable one, but he clung to it with irritating stubbornness. "Dr. Hitler wants to see me. Dr. Hitler wants to get to know me." And his mother said, "No, Duvid, it's *Hittner, Hittner,* with an *n.*" He went anyway. He strutted into the psychiatrist's office, and when Dr. Hittner smiled benignly and said, "Hello, there, David," David shot forth a stiff arm and snapped: *"Heil!"*

Dr. Hittner chuckled. "You've got the wrong man," he said. "I'm *Hittner* with an *n.*" Perhaps he had heard such jokes before. He was a huge man with a long horsey face, a wide fleshy mouth, a high curving forehead. Watery blue eyes twinkled behind rimless glasses. His skin was soft and pink and he had a good tangy smell, and he was trying hard to seem friendly and amused and big-brotherly, but David couldn't help picking up the impression that Dr. Hittner's brotherliness was just an act. It was something he felt with most adults: they smiled a lot, but inside themselves they were thinking things like, *What a scary brat, what a creepy little kid.* Even his mother and father sometimes thought things like that. He didn't understand why adults said one thing with their faces and another with their minds, but he was accustomed to it. It was something he had come to expect and accept.

"Let's play some games, shall we?" Dr. Hittner said.

Out of the vest pocket of his tweed suit he produced a little plastic globe on a metal chain. He showed it to David; then he pulled on the chain and the globe came apart into eight or nine pieces of different colors. "Watch closely, now, while I put it back together," said Dr. Hittner. His thick fingers expertly reassembled the globe. Then he pulled it apart again and shoved it across the desk toward David. "Your turn. Can you put it back together too?"

David remembered that the doctor had started by taking the E-shaped white piece and fitting the D-shaped blue piece into one of its grooves. Then had come the yellow piece, but David didn't recall what to do with it; he sat there a moment, puzzled, until Dr. Hittner obligingly flashed him a mental image of the proper manipulation. David did it and the rest was easy. A couple of times he got stuck, but he was always able to pull the answer out of the doctor's mind. Why does he think he's testing me, David wondered, if he keeps giving me so many hints? What's he proving? When the globe was intact David handed it back. "Would you like to keep it?" Dr. Hittner asked.

"I don't need it," David said. But he pocketed it anyway.

They played a few more games. There was one with little cards about the size of playing cards, with drawings of animals and birds and trees and houses on them; David was supposed to arrange them so that they told a story, and then tell the doctor what the story was. He scattered them at random on the desk and made up a story as he went along. "The duck goes into the forest, you see, and he meets a wolf, so he turns into a frog and jumps over the wolf right into the elephant's mouth, only he escapes out of the elephant's tushie and falls into a lake, and when he comes out he sees the pretty princess here, who says come home and I'll give you gingerbread, but he can read her mind and he sees that she's really a wicked witch, who—" Another game involved slips of paper that had big blue ink-blots on them. "Do any of these shapes remind you of real things?" the doctor asked. "Yes," David said, "this is an elephant, see, his tail is here and here all crumpled up, and this is his tushie, and this is where he makes pee-pee." He had already discovered that Dr. Hittner became very interested when he talked about tushies or pee-pee, so he gave the doctor plenty to be interested about, finding such things in every ink-blot picture. This seemed a very silly game to David, but apparently it was important to Dr. Hittner, who scribbled notes on everything David was saying. David studied Dr. Hittner's mind while the psychiatrist wrote things down. Most of the words he picked up were incomprehensible, but he did recognize a few, the grown-up terms for the parts of the body that David's mother had taught him: *penis, vulva, buttocks, rectum*, things like that. Obviously Dr. Hittner liked those words a great deal, so David began to use them. "This is a picture of an eagle that's picking up a little sheep and flying away with it. This is the eagle's penis, down here, and over here is the sheep's rectum. And in the next one there's a man and a woman, and they're both naked, and the man is trying to put his penis inside the woman's vulva only it won't fit, and—" David watched the fountain pen flying over the paper. He grinned at Dr. Hittner and turned to the next ink-blot.

Next they played word games. The doctor spoke a word and asked David to say the first word that came into his head. David found it more amusing to say the first word that came into Dr. Hittner's head. It took only a fraction of a second to pick it up, and Dr. Hittner didn't seem to notice what was going on. The game went like this:

"Father."

"Penis."

"Mother."

"Bed."

"Baby."

"Dead."

"Water."

"Belly."

"Tunnel."

"Shovel."

"Coffin."

"Mother."

Were those the right words to say? Who was the winner in this game? Why did Dr. Hittner seem so upset?

Finally they stopped playing games and simply talked. "You're a very bright little boy," Dr. Hittner said. "I don't have to worry about spoiling you by telling you that, because you know it already. What do you want to be when you grow up?"

"Nothing."

"Nothing?"

"I just want to play and read a lot of books and swim."

"But how will you earn a living?"

"I'll get money from people when I need it."

"If you find out how, I hope you'll tell me the secret," the doctor said. "Are you happy here in school?"

"No."

"Why not?"

"The teachers are too strict. The work is too dumb. The children don't like me."

"Do you ever wonder why they don't like you?"

"Because I'm smarter than they are," David said. "Because I—" Ooops. Almost said it. *Because I can see what they're thinking.* Mustn't ever tell anyone that. Dr. Hittner was waiting for him to finish the sentence. "Because I make a lot of trouble in class."

"And why do you do that, David?"

"I don't know. It gives me something to do, I guess."

"Maybe if you didn't make so much trouble, people would like you more. Don't you want people to like you?"

"I don't care. I don't need it."

"Everybody needs friends, David."

"I've got friends."

"Mrs. Fleischer says you don't have very many, and that you hit them a lot and make them unhappy. Why do you hit your friends?"

"Because I don't like them. Because they're dumb."

"Then they aren't really friends, if that's how you feel about them."

Shrugging, David said, "I can get along without them. I have fun just being by myself."

"Are you happy at home?"

"I guess so."

"You love your mommy and daddy?"

A pause. A feeling of great tension coming out of the doctor's mind. This is an important question. Give the right answer, David. Give him the answer he wants.

"Yes," David said.

"Do you ever wish you had a baby brother or sister?"

No hesitation now. "No."

"Really, no? You like being all alone?"

David nodded. "The afternoons are the best time. When I'm home from school and there's nobody around. Am I going to have a baby brother or sister?"

Chuckles from the doctor. "I'm sure I don't know. That would be up to your mommy and daddy, wouldn't it?"

"You won't tell them to get one for me, will you? I mean, you might say to them that it would be good for me to have one, and then they'd go and get one, but I really don't want—" I'm in trouble, David realized suddenly.

"What makes you think I'd tell your parents it would be good for you to have a baby brother or sister?" the doctor asked quietly, not smiling now at all.

"I don't know. It was just an idea." Which I found inside your head, doctor. And now I want to get out of here. I don't want to talk to you any more. "Hey, your name isn't really Hittner, is it? With an *n*? I bet I know your real name. *Heil!*"

3.

I never could send my thoughts into anybody else's head. Even when the power was strongest in me, I couldn't transmit. I could only receive. Maybe there are people around who do have that power, who can transmit thoughts even to those who don't have any special receiving gift, but I wasn't ever one of them. So right there I was condemned to be society's ugliest toad, the eavesdropper, the voyeur. Old English proverb: *He who peeps through a hole may see what will vex him.* Yes. In those years when I was particularly eager to communicate with people, I'd work up fearful sweats trying to plant my thoughts in them. I'd sit in a classroom staring at the back of some girl's head, and I'd think hard at her: *Hello, Annie, this is David Selig calling, do you read me? Do you read me? I love you, Annie. Over. Over and out.* But Annie never read me, and the currents of her mind would roll on like a placid river, undisturbed by the existence of David Selig.

No way, then, for me to speak to other minds, only to spy on them. The way the power manifests itself in me has always been highly variable. I never had much conscious control over it, other than being able to stop down the intensity of input and to do a certain amount of fine tuning; basically I had to take whatever came drifting in. Most often I would pick up a person's surface thoughts, his subvocalizations of the things he's just about to say. These would come to me in a clear conversational manner, exactly as though he *had* said them, except the tone of voice was different, it was plainly not a tone produced by the vocal apparatus. I don't remember any period even in my childhood when I confused spoken communication with mental communication. This ability to read surface thoughts has been fairly consistent throughout: I still can anticipate verbal statements more often than not, especially when

I'm with someone who has the habit of rehearsing what he intends to say.

I could also and to some extent still can anticipate immediate intentions, such as the decision to throw a short right jab to the jaw. My way of knowing such things varies. I might pick up a coherent inner verbal statement—*I'm now going to throw a short right jab to his jaw*—or, if the power happens to be working on deeper levels that day, I may simply pick up a series of non-verbal instructions to the muscles, which add up in a fraction of a second to the process of bringing the right arm up for a short jab to the jaw. Call it body language on the telepathic wavelength.

Another thing I've been able to do, though never consistently, is tune in to the deepest layers of the mind—where the soul lives, if you will. Where the consciousness lies bathed in a murky soup of indistinct unconscious phenomena. Here lurk hopes, fears, perceptions, purposes, passions, memories, philosophical positions, moral policies, hungers, sorrows, the whole ragbag accumulation of events and attitudes that defines the private self. Ordinarily some of this bleeds through to me even when the most superficial mental contact is established: I can't help getting a certain amount of information about the coloration of the soul. But occasionally—hardly ever, now—I fasten my hooks into the real stuff, the whole person. There's ecstasy in that. There's an electrifying sense of contact. Coupled, of course, with a stabbing, numbing sense of guilt, because of the totality of my voyeurism: how much more of a peeping tom can a person be? Incidentally, the soul speaks a universal language. When I look into the mind of Mrs. Esperanza Dominguez, say, and I get a gabble of Spanish out of it, I don't really know what she's thinking, because I don't understand very much Spanish. But if I were to get into the depths of her soul I'd have complete comprehension of anything I picked up. The mind may think in Spanish or Basque or Hungarian or Finnish, but the soul thinks in a languageless language accessible to any prying sneaking freak who comes along to peer at its mysteries.

No matter. It's all going from me now.

4.

Paul F. Bruno
Comp Lit 18, Prof. Schmitz
October 15, 1976

The Novels of Kafka

In the nightmare world of *The Trial* and *The Castle*, only one thing is certain: that the central figure, significantly known by the initial K, is doomed to frustration. All else is dreamlike and unsure; courtrooms spring up in tenements, mysterious warders devour one's breakfast, a man thought to be Sordini is actually Sortini. The central fact is certain, though: K will fail in his attempt to attain grace.

The two novels have the same theme and approximately the same basic structure. In both, K seeks for grace and is led to the final realization that it is to be withheld from him. (*The Castle* is unfinished, but its conclusion seems plain.) Kafka brings his heroes into involvement with their situations in opposite ways: in *The Trial*, Joseph K. is passive until he is jolted into the action of the book by the unexpected arrival of the two warders; in *The Castle*, K is first shown as an active character making efforts on his own behalf to reach the mysterious Castle. To be sure, though, he has originally been summoned by the Castle; the action did not originate in himself, and thus he began as as passive a character as Joseph K. The distinction is that *The Trial* opens at a point earlier in the timestream of the action—at the earliest possible point, in fact. *The Castle* follows more closely the ancient rule of beginning *in medias res*, with K already summoned and trying to reach the Castle.

Both books get off to rapid starts. Joseph K. is arrested in the very first sentence of *The Trial*, and his counterpart K arrives at what he thinks is going to be the last stop before the Castle on the first page of that novel. From there, both K's struggle futilely toward their goals (in *The Castle*, simply to get to the top of the hill; in *The Trial*, first to understand the nature of his guilt, and then, despairing of this, to achieve acquittal without understanding). Both actually get farther from their goals with each succeeding action. *The Trial* reaches its peak in the wonderful Cathedral scene, quite likely the most terrifying single sequence in any of Kafka's work, in which K is given to realize that he is guilty and can never be acquitted; the chapter that follows, describing K's execution, is little more than an anticlimactic appendage. *The Castle*, less complete than *The Trial*, lacks the counterpart of the Cathedral scene (perhaps Kafka was unable to devise one?) and thus is artistically less satisfying than the shorter, more intense, more tightly constructed *Trial*.

Despite their surface artlessness, both novels appear to be built on the fundamental three-part structure of the tragic rhythm, labeled by the critic Kenneth Burke as "purpose, passion, perception." *The Trial* follows this scheme with greater success than does the incomplete *Castle*; the purpose, to achieve acquittal, is demonstrated through as harrowing a passion as any fictional hero has undergone. Finally, when Joseph K. has been reduced from his original defiant, self-confident attitude to a fearful, timid state of mind, and he is obviously ready to capitulate to the forces of the Court, the time is at hand for the final moment of perception.

The agent used to bring him to the scene of the climax is a classically Kafkaesque figure—the mysterious "Italian colleague who was on his first visit to the town and had influential connexions that made him important to the Bank." The theme that runs through all of Kafka's work, the impossibility of human communication, is repeated here: though Joseph has spent half the night studying Italian in preparation for the visit, and is half asleep in consequence, the stranger speaks an unknown southern dialect which Joseph cannot understand. Then—a crowning comic touch—the stranger shifts to French, but his French is just as difficult to follow, and his bushy mustache foils Joseph's attempts at lip-reading.

Once he reaches the Cathedral, which he has been asked to show to the Italian (who, as we are not surprised to find, never keeps the date), the tension mounts. Joseph wanders through the building, which is empty, dark, cold, lit only by candles flickering far in the distance, while night inexplicably begins fast to fall out-side. Then the priest calls to him, and relates the allegory of the Doorkeeper. It is only when the story is ended that we realize we did not at all understand it; far from being the simple tale it had originally seemed to be, it reveals itself as complex and difficult. Joseph and the priest discuss the story at great length, in the manner of a pair of rabbinical scholars disputing a point in the Talmud. Slowly its implications sink in, and we and Joseph see that the light streaming from the door to the Law will not be visible for him until it is too late.

Structurally the novel is over right here. Joseph has received the final perception that acquittal is impossible; his guilt is estab-lished, and he is not yet to receive grace. His quest is ended. The final element of the tragic rhythm, the perception that ends the pas-sion, has been reached.

We know that Kafka planned further chapters showing the pro-gress of Joseph's trial through various later stages, ending in his execution. Kafka's biographer Max Brod says the book could have been prolonged infinitely. This is true, of course; it is inherent in the nature of Joseph K.'s guilt that he could never get to the highest Court, just as the other K could wander for all time without ever reaching the Castle. But structurally the novel ends in the Cathedral; the rest of what Kafka intended would not have added anything essential to Joseph's self-knowledge. The Cathedral scene shows us what we have known since page one: that there is no acquittal. The action concludes with that perception.

The Castle, a much longer and more loosely constructed book, lacks the power of *The Trial*. It rambles. The passion of K is much less clearly defined, and K is a less consistent character, not as interesting psychologically as he is in *The Trial*. Whereas in the earlier book he takes active charge of his case as soon as he realizes his danger, in *The Castle* he quickly becomes the victim of the bureaucracy. The transit of character in *The Trial* is from early passivity to activity back to passive resignation after the epiphany in the Cathedral. In *The Castle* K undergoes no such clearcut changes; he is an active character as the novel opens, but soon is lost in the nightmare maze of the village below the Castle, and sinks deeper and deeper into degradation. Joseph K. is almost an heroic character, while K of *The Castle* is merely a pathetic one.

The two books represent varying attempts at telling the same story, that of the existentially disengaged man who is suddenly in-volved in a situation from which there is no escape, and who, after making attempts to achieve the grace that will release him from his predicament, succumbs. As they exist today, *The Trial* is unquestionably the greater artistic success, firmly constructed and at all times under the author's technical control. *The Castle*, or rather the fragment of it we have, is potentially the greater novel, however. Everything that was in *The Trial* would have been in *The Castle*, and a great deal more. But, one feels, Kafka abandoned work on *The Castle* because he saw he lacked the resources to carry it through. He could not handle the world of the Castle, with its sweeping background of Brueghelesque country life, with the same assurance as he did the urban world of *The Trial*. And there is a lack of urgency in *The Castle*; we are never too concerned over K's doom because it is inevitable; Joseph K., though, is fighting more tangible forces, and until the end we have the illusion that victory is possible for him. *The Castle*, also, is too ponderous. Like a Mahler symphony, it collapses of its own weight. One wonders if Kafka had in mind some structure enabling him to end *The Castle*. Perhaps he never intended to close the novel at all, but meant to have K wander in ever-widening circles, never arriving at the tragic perception that he can never reach the Castle. Perhaps this is the reason for the comparative formlessness of the later work: Kafka's discovery that the true tragedy of K, his archetypical hero-as-victim figure, lies not in his final perception of the impossibility of attaining grace, but in the fact that he will never reach even as much as that final perception. Here we have the tragic rhythm, a structure found throughout literature, truncated to depict more pointedly the contemporary human condition—a condition so abhorrent to Kafka. Joseph K., who actually reaches a form of grace, thereby attains true tragic stature; K, who simply sinks lower and lower, might symbolize for Kafka the contemporary individual, so crushed by the general tragedy of the times that he is incapable of any tragedy on an individual level. K is a pathetic figure, Joseph K. a tragic one. Joseph K. is a more interesting character, but perhaps it was K whom Kafka understood more deeply. And for K's story no ending is possible, perhaps, save the pointless one of death.

That's not so bad. Six double-spaced typed pages. At $3.50 per, it earns me a cool $21 for less than two hours work, and it'll earn the brawny halfback, Mr. Paul F. Bruno, a sure B + from Prof. Schmitz. I'm confident of that because the very same paper, differing only in a few minor stylistic flourishes, got me a B from the very demanding Prof. Dupee in May, 1955. Standards are lower today, after two decades of academic inflation Bruno may even rack up an A—for the Kafka job. It's got just the right quality of earnest intelligence, with the proper undergraduate mixture of sophisticated insight and naive dogmatism, and Dupee found the writing "clear and forceful" in '55, according to his note in the margin. All right, now. Time out for a little chow mein, with maybe a side order of eggroll. Then I'll tackle *Odysseus as a Symbol of Society* or perhaps *Aeschylus and the Aristotelian Tragedy.* I can't work from my own old term papers for those, but they shouldn't be too tough to do. Old typewriter, old humbugger, stand me now and ever in good stead.

5.

Aldous Huxley thought that evolution has designed our brains to serve as filters, screening out a lot of stuff that's of no real value to us in our daily struggle for bread. Visions, mystical experiences, psi phenomena such as telepathic messages from other brains—all sorts of things along these lines would forever be flooding into us were it not for the action of what Huxley called, in a little book entitled *Heaven and Hell,* "the cerebral reducing valve." Thank God for the cerebral reducing valve! If we hadn't evolved it, we'd be distracted all the time by scenes of incredible beauty, by spiritual insights of overwhelming grandeur, and by scaring, utterly honest mind-to-mind contact with our fellow human beings. Luckily, the workings of the valve protect us—most of us—from such things, and we are free to go about our daily lives, buying cheap and selling dear.

Of course, some of us seem to be born with defective valves. I mean the artists like Besch or El Greco, whose eyes did not see the world as it appears to thee and me; I mean the visionary philosophers, the ecstatics and the nirvana-attainers; I mean the miserable freakish flukes who can read the thoughts of others. Mutants, all of us. Genetic sports.

However, Huxley believed that the efficiency of the cerebral reducing valve could be impaired by various artificial means, thus giving ordinary mortals access to the extrasensory data customarily seen only by the chosen few. The psychedelic drugs, he thought, have this effect. Mescaline, he suggested, interferes with the enzyme system that regulates cerebral function, and by so doing "lowers the efficiency of the brain as an instrument for focusing mind on the problems of life on the surface of our planet. This . . . seems to permit the entry into consciousness of certain classes of mental events, which are normally excluded, because they possess no survival value. Similar intrusions of biologically useless, but aesthetically and sometimes spiritually valuable, material may occur as the result of illness or fatigue; or they may be induced by fasting, or a period of confinement in a place of darkness and complete silence."

Speaking for himself, David Selig can say very little about the psychedelic drugs. He had only one experience with them, and it wasn't a happy one. That was in the summer of 1968, when he was living with Toni.

Though Huxley thought highly of the psychedelics, he didn't see them as the only gateway to visionary experience. Fasting and physical mortification could get you there also. He wrote of mystics who "regularly used upon themselves the whip of knotted leather or even of iron wire. These beatings were the equivalent of fairly extensive surgery without anaesthetics, and heir effects on the body chemistry of the penitent were considerable. Large quantities of histamine and adrenalin were released while the whip was actually being plied; and when the resulting wounds began to fester (as wounds practically always did before the age of soap), various toxic substances, produced by the decomposition of protein, found their way into the bloodstream. But histamine produces shock, and shock affects the the mind no less profoundly than the body. Moreover, large quantities of adrenalin may cause hallucinations, and some of the products of its decomposition are known to induce symptoms resembling those of schizophrenia. As for toxins from wounds—these upset the enzyme systems regulating the brain, and lower its efficiency as an instrument for getting on in a world where the biologically fittest survive. This may explain why the Curé d'Ars used to say that, in the days when he was free to flagellate himself without mercy, God would refuse him nothing. In other words, when remorse, self-loathing, and the fear of hell release adrenalin, when self-inflicted surgery releases adrenalin and histamine, and when infected wounds release decomposed protein into the blood, the efficiency of the cerebral reducing valve is lowered and unfamiliar aspects of Mind-at-Large (including psi phenomena, visions, and, if he is philosophically and ethically prepared for it, mystical experiences) will flow into the ascetic's consciousness."

Remorse, self-loathing, and the fear of hell. Fasting and prayer. Whips and chains. Festering wounds. Everybody to his own trip, I suppose, and welcome to it. As the power fades in me, as the sacred gift dies, I toy with the idea of trying to revive it by artificial means. Acid, mescaline, psilocybin? I don't think I'd care to go there again. Mortification of the flesh? That seems obsolete to me, like marching off to the Crusades or wearing spats: something that simply isn't appropriate for 1976. I doubt that I could get very deep into flagellation, anyway. What does that leave? Fasting and prayer? I could fast, I suppose. Prayer? To whom? To what? I'd feel like a fool. Dear God, give me my power again. Dear Moses, please help me. Crap on that. Jews don't pray for favors, because they know nobody will answer. What's left, then? Remorse, self-loathing, and the fear of hell? I have those three already, and they do me no good. We must try some other way of goading the power back to life. Invent something new. Flagellation of the mind, perhaps? Yes. I'll try that. I'll get out the metaphorical cudgels and let myself have it. Flagellation of the aching, weakening, throbbing, dissolving mind. The treacherous, hateful mind.

6.

But why does David Selig want his power to come back? Why not let it fade? It's always been a curse to him, hasn't it? It's cut him off from his fellow men and doomed him to a loveless life. Leave well enough alone, Duvid. Let it fade. Let it fade. On the other hand, without the power, what are you? Without that one faltering unpredictable unsatisfactory means of contact with them, how will you be able to touch them at all? Your power joins you to mankind, for better or for worse, in the only joining you have: you can't bear to surrender it. Admit it. You love it and you despise it, this gift of yours. You dread losing it despite all it's done to you. You'll fight to cling to the last shreds of it, even though you know the struggle's hopeless. Fight on, then. Read Huxley again. Try acid, if you dare. Try flagellation. Try fasting, at least. All right, fasting. I'll skip the chow mein. I'll skip the eggroll. Let's slide a fresh sheet into the typewriter and think about Odysseus as a symbol of society.

7.

Hark to the silvery jangle of the telephone. The hour is late. Who calls? Is it Aldous Huxley from beyond the grave, urging me to have courage? Dr. Hittner, with some important questions about making pee-pee? Toni, to tell me she's in the neighborhood with a thousand mikes of dynamite acid and is it okay to come up? Sure. Sure. I stare at the telephone, clueless. My power even at its height was never equal to the task of penetrating the consciousness of the American Telephone & Telegraph Company. Sighing, I pick up the receiver on the fifth ring and hear the sweet contralto voice of my sister Judith.

"Am I interrupting something?" Typical Judith opening.

"A quiet night at home. I'm ghosting a term paper on *The Odyssey*. Got any bright ideas for me, Jude?"

"You haven't called in two weeks."

"I was broke. After that scene the last time I didn't want to bring up the subject of money, and lately it's been the only subject I can think of talking about, so I didn't call."

"Shit," she says, "I wasn't angry at you."

"You sounded mad as hell."

"I didn't mean any of that stuff. Why did you think I was serious? Just because I was yelling? Do you really believe that I regard you as— as—what did I call you?"

"A shiftless sponger, I think."

"A shiftless sponger. Shit. I was tense that night, Duv; I had personal problems, and my period was coming on besides. I lost control. I was just shouting the first dumb crap that came into my head, but why did you believe I meant it? You of all people shouldn't have thought I was serious. Since when do you take what people say with their mouths at face value?"

"You were saying it with your head too, Jude."

"I was?" Her voice is suddenly small and contrite. "Are you sure?"

"It came through loud and clear."

"Oh, Jesus, Duv, have a heart! In the heat of the moment I could have been thinking anything. But underneath the anger—*underneath*, Duv—you must have seen that I didn't mean it. That I love you, that I don't want to drive you away from me. You're all I've got, Duv, you and the baby."

Her love is unpalatable to me, and her sentimentality is even less to my taste. I say, "I don't read much of what's underneath any more, Jude. Not much comes through these days. Anyway, look, it isn't worth hassling over. I *am* a shiftless sponger, and I *have* borrowed more from you than you can afford to give. The black sheep big brother feels enough guilt as it is. I'm damned if I'm ever going to ask for money from you again."

"Guilt? You talk about guilt, when I—"

"No," I warn her, "don't you go on a guilt trip now, Jude. Not now." Her remorse for her past coldness toward me has a flavor even more stinking than her newfound love. "I don't feel up to assigning the ratio of blames and guilts tonight."

"All right. All right. Are you okay now for money, though?"

"I told you, I'm ghosting term papers. I'm getting by."

"Do you want to come over here for dinner tomorrow night?"

"I think I'd better work instead. I've got a lot of papers to write, Jude. It's the busy season."

"It would be just the two of us. And the kid, of course, but I'll put him to sleep early. Just you and me. We could talk. We've got so much to talk about. Why don't you come over, Duv? You don't need to work all day and all night. I'll cook up something you like. I'll do the spaghetti and hot sauce. Anything. You name it." She is pleading with me, this icy sister who gave me nothing but hatred for twenty-five years. Come over and I'll be a mama for you, Duv. Come let me be loving, brother.

"Maybe the night after next. I'll call you."

"No chance for tomorrow?"

"I don't think so," I say. There is silence. She doesn't want to beg me. Into the sudden screeching silence I say, "What have you been doing with yourself, Judith? Seeing anyone interesting?"

"Not seeing anyone at all." A flinty edge to her voice. She is two and a half years into her divorce; she sleeps around a good deal; juices are souring in her soul. She is 31 years old. "I'm between men right now. Maybe I'm off men altogether. I don't care if I never do any screwing again ever."

I throttle a somber laugh. "What happened to that travel agent you were seeing? Mickey?"

"Marty. That was just a gimmick. He got me all over Europe for 10% of the fare. Otherwise I couldn't have afforded to go. I was using him."

"So?"

"I felt shitty about it. Last month I broke off. I wasn't in love with him. I don't think I even liked him."

"But you played around with him long enough to get a trip to Europe, first."

"It didn't cost *him* anything, Duv. I had to go to bed with him; all he had to do was fill out a form. What are you saying, anyway? That I'm a whore?"

"Jude—"

"Okay, I'm a whore. At least I'm trying to go straight for a while. Lots of fresh orange juice and plenty of serious reading. I'm reading Proust now, would you believe that? I just finished *Swann's Way* and tomorrow—"

"I've still got some work to do tonight, Jude."

"I'm sorry. I didn't mean to intrude. Will you come for dinner this week?"

"I'll think about it. I'll let you know."

"Why do you hate me so much, Duv?"

"I don't hate you. And we were about to get off the phone, I think."

"Don't forget to call," she says. Clutching at straws.

8.

Toni. I should tell you about Toni now.

I lived with Toni for seven weeks, one summer eight years ago. That's as long as I've ever lived with anybody, except my parents and my sister, whom I got away from as soon as I decently could, and myself, whom I can't get away from at all. Toni was one of the two great loves of my life, the other being Kitty. I'll tell you about Kitty some other time.

Can I reconstruct Toni? Let's try it in a few swift strokes. She was 24 that year. A tall coltish girl, five feet six, five feet seven. Slender. Agile and awkward, both at once. Long legs, long arms, thin wrists, thin ankles. Glossy black hair, very straight, cascading to her shoulders. Warm, quick brown eyes, alert and quizzical. A witty, shrewd girl, not really well educated but extraordinarily wise. The face by no means conventionally pretty—too much mouth, too much nose, the cheek-bones too high—but yet producing a sexy and highly attractive effect, sufficient to make a lot of heads turn when she enters a room. Full, heavy breasts. I dig busty women: I often need a soft place to rest my tired head. So often so tired. My mother was built 32-A, no cozy pillows there. She couldn't have nursed me if she'd wanted to, which she didn't. (Will I ever forgive her for letting me escape from the womb? Ah, now, Selig, show some filial piety, for God's sake!)

I never looked into Toni's mind except twice, once on the day I met her and once a couple of weeks after that, plus a third time on the day we broke up. The third time was a sheer disastrous accident. The second was more or less an accident too, not quite. Only the first was a deliberate probe. After I realized I loved her I took care never to spy on her head. *He who peeps through a hole may see what will vex him.*

A lesson I learned very young. Besides, I didn't want Toni to suspect anything about my power. My curse. I was afraid it might frighten her away.

That summer I was working as an $85-a-week researcher, latest in my infinite series of odd jobs, for a well-known professional writer who was doing an immense book on the political machinations involved in the founding of the State of Israel. Eight hours a day I went through old newspaper files for him in the bowels of the Columbia library. Toni was a junior editor for the publishing house that was bringing out his book. I met her one afternoon in late spring at his posh apartment on East End Avenue. I went over there to deliver a bundle of notes on Harry Truman's 1948 campaign speeches and she happened to be there, discussing some cuts to be made in the early chapters. Her beauty stung me. I hadn't been with a woman in months. I automatically assumed she was the writer's mistress—screwing editors, I'm told, is standard practice on certain high levels of the literary profession—but my old peeping-tom instincts quickly gave me the true scoop. I tossed a fast probe at him and found that his mind was a cesspool of frustrated longings for her. He ached for her and she had no yen for him at all, evidently. Next I poked into *her* mind. I sank in, deep, finding myself in warm, rich loam. Quickly got oriented. Stray fragments of autobiography bombarded me, incoherent, non-linear: a divorce, some good sex and some bad sex, college days, a trip to the Caribbean, all swimming around in the usual chaotic way. I got past that fast and checked out what I was after. No, she wasn't sleeping with the writer. Physically he registered absolute zero for her. (Odd. To me he seemed attractive, a romantic and appealing figure, so far as a drearily heterosexual soul like me is able to judge such things.) She didn't even like his writing, I learned. Then, still rummaging around, I learned something else, much more surprising: *I* seemed to be turning her on. Forth from her came the explicit line: *I wonder if he's free tonight.* She looked upon the aging researcher, a venerable 33 and already going thin on top, and did not find him repellent. I was so shaken by that—her dark-eyed glamour, her leggy sexiness, aimed at *me*—that I got the hell out of her head, fast. "Here's the Truman stuff," I said to my employer. "There's more coming in from the Truman Library in Missouri." We talked a few minutes about the next assignment he had for me, and then I made as though to leave. A quick guarded look at her.

"Wait," she said. "We can ride down together. I'm just about done here."

The man of letters shot me a poisonous envious glance. Oh, God, fired again. But he bade us both civil goodbyes. In the elevator going down we stood apart. Toni in this corner, I in that one, with a quivering wall of tension and yearning separating and uniting us. I had to struggle to keep from reading her; I was afraid, terrified, not of getting the wrong answer but of getting the right one. In the street we stood apart also, dithering a moment. Finally I said I was getting a cab to take me to the Upper West Side—me, a cab, on $85 a week!—and could I drop her off anywhere? She said she lived on 105th and West End. Close enough. When the cab stopped outside her place she invited me up for a drink. Three rooms, indifferently furnished: mostly books, records, scatter-rugs, posters. She went to pour some wine for us and I caught her and pulled her around and kissed her. She trembled against me, or was I the one who was trembling?

Over a bowl of hot-and-sour soup at the Great Shanghai, a little later that evening, she said she'd be moving in a couple of days. The apartment belonged to her current roommate—male—with whom she'd split up just three days before. She had no place to stay. "I've got only one lousy room," I said, "but it has a double bed." Shy grins, hers, mine. So she moved in. I didn't think she was in love with me, not at all, but I wasn't going to ask. If what she felt for me wasn't love, it was good enough, the best I could hope for; and in the privacy of my own head I could feel love for her. She had needed a port in a storm. I had happened to offer one. If that was all I meant to her now, so be it. So be it. There was time for things to ripen.

We slept very little, our first two weeks. Not that we were screwing all the time, though there was a lot of that; but we *talked*. We were new to each other, which is the best time of any relationship, when there are whole pasts to share, when everything pours out and there's no need to search for things to say. (Not quite everything poured out. The only thing I concealed from her was the central fact of my life, the fact that had shaped my every aspect.) She talked of her marriage—young, at 20, and brief, and empty—and of how she had lived in the three years since its ending—a succession of men, a dip into occultism and Reichian therapy, a newfound dedication to her editing career. Giddy weeks.

Then, our third week. My second peep into her mind. A sweltering June night, with a full moon sending cold illumination through the slatted blinds into our room. She was sitting astride me—her favorite position—and her body, very pale, wore a white glow in the eerie darkness. Her long lean form rearing far above me. Her face half hidden in her own dangling unruly hair. Her eyes closed. Her lips slack. Her breasts, viewed from below, seeming even bigger than they really were. Cleopatra by moonlight. She was rocking and jouncing her way to a private ecstasy, and her beauty and the strangeness of her so overwhelmed me that I could not resist watching her at the moment of climax, watching on all levels, and so I opened the barrier that I had so scrupulously erected, and, just as she was coming, my mind touched a curious finger to her soul and received the full uprushing volcanic intensity of her pleasure. I found no thought of me in her mind. Only sheer animal frenzy, bursting from every nerve. I've seen that in other women, before and after Toni, as they come: they are islands, alone in the void of space, aware only of their bodies and perhaps of that intrusive rigid rod against which they thrust. When pleasure takes them it is a curiously impersonal phenomenon, no matter how titanic its impact. So it was then with Toni. I didn't object; I knew what to expect and I didn't feel cheated or rejected. In fact my joining of souls with her at that awesome moment served to trigger my own coming and to treble its intensity. I lost contact with her then. The upheavals of orgasm shatter the fragile telepathic link. Afterwards I felt a little sleazy at having spied, but not overly guilty about it. How magical a thing it was, after all, to have been with her in that moment. To be aware of her joy not just as mindless spasms of her loins but as jolts of brilliant light flaring across the dark terrain of her soul. An instant of beauty and wonder, an illumination never to be forgotten. But never to be repeated, either. I resolved, once more, to keep our relationship clean and honest. To take no unfair advantage of her. To stay out of her head forever after.

Despite which, I found myself some weeks later entering Toni's consciousness a third time. By accident. By damnable abominable accident. Oy, that third time!

That bummer—that disaster—

That catastrophe—

9.

In the early spring of 1945, when he was ten years old, his loving mother and father got him a little sister. That was exactly how they phrased it: his mother, smiling her warmest phony smile, hugging him, telling him in her best this-is-how-we-talk-to-bright-children tone, "Dad and I have a wonderful surprise for you, David. We're going to get a little sister for you."

It was no surprise, of course. They had been discussing it among themselves for months, maybe for years, always making the fallacious assumption that their son, clever as he was, didn't understand what they were talking about. Thinking that he was unable to associate one fragment of conversation with another, that he was incapable of putting the proper antecedents to their deliberately vague pronouns, their torrent of "it" and "him." And, naturally, he had been reading their minds. In those days the power was sharp and clear; lying in his bedroom, surrounded by his dog-eared books and his stamp albums, he could effortlessly tune in on everything that went on behind the closed door of theirs, fifty feet away. It was like an endless radio broadcast without commercials. He could listen to WJZ, WHN, WEAF, WOR, all the stations on the dial, but the one he listened to most was WPMS, Paul-and-Martha-Selig. They had no secrets from him. He had no shame about spying. Preternaturally adult, privy to all their privities, he meditated daily on the raw torrid stuff of married life: the financial anxieties, the moments of sweet undifferentiated lovingness, the moments of guiltily suppressed hatred for the wearisome eternal spouse, the copulatory joys and anguishes, the comings together and the fallings apart, the mysteries of failed orgasms and wilted erections, the intense and terrifyingly singleminded concentration on the growth and proper development of The Child.

Their minds poured forth a steady stream of rich yeasty foam and he lapped it all up. Reading their souls was his game, his toy, his religion, his revenge. They never suspected he was doing it. That was one point on which he constantly sought reassurance, anxiously prying for it, and constantly he was reassured: they didn't dream his gift existed. They merely thought he was abnormally intelligent, and never questioned the means by which he learned so much about so many improbable things. Perhaps if they had realized the truth, they would have choked him in his crib. But they had no inkling. He went on comfortably spying, year after year, his perceptions deepening as he came to comprehend more and more of the material his parents unwittingly offered.

He knew that Dr. Hittner—baffled, wholly out of his depth with the strange Selig child—believed it would be better for everyone if David had a sibling. That was the word he used, *sibling,* and David had to fish the meaning out of Hittner's head as though out of a dictionary. Sibling: a brother or a sister. Oh, the treacherous horse-faced bastard! The one thing young David had asked Hittner not to suggest, and naturally he had suggested it. But what else could he have expected? The desirability of siblings had been in Hittner's mind all along, lying there like a grenade. David, picking his mother's mind one night, had found the text of a letter from Hittner. *The only child is an emotionally deprived child. Without the rough-and-tumble interplay with siblings he has no way of learning the best techniques of relating to his peers, and he develops a dangerously burdensome relation with his parents, for whom he becomes a companion instead of a dependent.* Hittner's universal panacea: lots of siblings. As though there are no neurotics in big families.

David was aware of his parents' frantic attempts at filling Hittner's prescription. No time to waste; the boy grows older all the time, siblingless, lacking each day the means of learning the best techniques of relating to his peers. And so, night after night, the poor aging bodies of Paul and Martha Selig grapple with the problem. They force themselves sweatily onward to self-defeating prodigies of lustfulness, and each month the bad news comes in a rush of blood: there will be no sibling this time. But at last the seed takes root. They said nothing about that to him, ashamed, perhaps, to admit to an eight-year-old that such things as sexual intercourse occurred in their lives. But he knew. He knew why his mother's belly was beginning to bulge and why they still hesitated to explain it to him. He knew, too, that his mother's mysterious "appendicitis" attack of July, 1944, was actually a miscarriage. He knew why they both wore tragic faces for months afterward. He knew that Martha's doctor had told her that autumn that it really wasn't wise for her to be having babies at the age of 35, that if they were going to insist on a second child the best course was to adopt one. He knew his father's traumatic response to that suggestion: *What, bring into the household a bastard that some shiksa threw away?* Poor old Paul lay tossing awake every night for weeks, not even confessing to his wife why he was so upset, but unknowingly spilling the whole thing to his nosy son. The insecurities, the irrational hostilities. *Why do I have to raise a stranger's brat, just because this psychiatrist says it'll do David some good? What kind of garbage will I be taking into the house? How can I love this child that isn't mine? How can I tell it that it's a Jew when—who knows?—it may have been made by some Irish mick, some Italian boot-black, some carpenter?* All this the all-perceiving David perceives. Finally the elder Selig voices his misgivings, carefully edited, to his wife, saying, Maybe Hittner's wrong, maybe this is just a phase David's going through and another child isn't the right answer at all. Telling her to consider the expense, the changes they'd have to make in their way of life—they're not young, they've grown settled in their ways, a child at this time of their lives, the getting up at four in the morning, the crying, the diapers. And David silently cheering his father on, because who needs this intruder, this sibling, this enemy of the peace? But Martha tearfully fights back, quoting Hittner's letter, reading key passages out of her extensive library on child psychology, offering damning statistics on the incidence of neurosis, maladjustment, bed-wetting, and homosexuality among only children. The old man yields by Christmas. *Okay, okay, we'll adopt, but let's not take just anything, hear? It's got to be Jewish.* Wintry weeks of touring the adoption agencies, pretending all the while to David that these trips to Manhattan are mere innocuous shopping excursions. He wasn't fooled. How could anyone fool this omniscient child? He had only to look behind their foreheads to know that they were shopping for a sibling. His one comfort was the hope that they would fail to find one. This was still wartime: if you couldn't buy a new car, maybe you couldn't get siblings either. For many weeks that appeared to be the case. Not many babies were available, and those that were seemed to have some grave defect: insufficiently Jewish, or too fragile-looking, or too cranky, or of the wrong sex. Some boys were available but Paul and Martha had decided to get David a little sister. Already that limited things considerably, since people tended not to give girls up for adoption as readily as they did boys, but one snowy night in March David detected an ominous note of satisfaction in the mind of his mother, newly returned from yet another shopping trip, and, looking more closely, he realized that the quest was over. She had found a lovely little girl, four months old. The mother, aged 19, was not only certifiably Jewish but even a college girl, described by the agency as "extremely intelligent." Not so intelligent, evidently, as to avoid being fertilized by a handsome, young air force captain, also Jewish, while he was home on leave in February, 1944. Though he felt remorse over his carelessness he was unwilling to marry the victim of his lusts, and was now on active duty in the Pacific, where, so far as the girl's parents were concerned he should only be shot down ten times over. They had forced her to give the child out for adoption. David wondered why Martha hadn't brought the baby home with her that very afternoon, but soon he discovered that several weeks of legal formalities lay ahead, and April was well along before his mother finally announced, "Dad and I have a wonderful surprise for you, Duvid."

They named her Judith Hannah Selig, after her adoptive father's recently deceased mother. David hated her instantly. He had been afraid they were going to move her into his bedroom, but no, they set up her crib in their own room; nevertheless, her crying filled the whole apartment night after night, unending raucous wails. It was incredible how much noise she could emit. Paul and Martha spent practically all their time feeding her or playing with her or changing her diapers, and David didn't mind that very much, for it kept them busy and took some of the pressure off him. But he loathed having Judith around. He saw nothing cute about her pudgy limbs and curly hair and dimpled cheeks. Watching her while she was being changed, he found some academic interest in observing her little pink slit, so alien to his experience; but once he had seen it his curiosity was assuaged. *So they have a slit instead of a thing. Okay, but so what?* In general she was an irritating distraction. He couldn't read properly because of the noise she made, and reading was his one pleasure. The apartment was always full of relatives or friends, paying ceremonial visits to the new baby, and their stupid conventional minds flooded the place with blunt thoughts that impinged like mallets on David's vulnerable consciousness. Now and then he tried to read the baby's mind, but there was nothing in it except vague blurry formless globs of cloudy sensation; he had had more rewarding insights reading the minds of dogs and cats. She didn't appear to have any thoughts. All he could pick up were feelings of hunger, of drowsiness, and of dim orgasmic release as she wet her diaper. About ten days after she arrived, he decided to try to kill her telepathically. While his parents were busy elsewhere he went to their room, peered into his sister's bassinet, and concentrated as hard as he could on draining her unformed mind out of her skull. If only he could manage somehow to suck the spark of intellect from her, to draw her consciousness into himself, to transform her into an empty mindless shell, she would surely die. He sought to sink his hooks into her soul. He stared into her eyes and opened his power wide, taking her entire feeble output and pulling for more. *Come . . . come . . .your mind is sliding toward me. . . . I'm getting it, I'm getting all of it. . . . zam! I have your whole mind!* Unmoved by his conjurations, she continued to gurgle and wave her arms about. He stared more intensely, redoubling the vigor of his concentration. Her smile wavered and vanished. Her brows puckered into a frown. Did she know he was attacking her, or was she merely bothered by the faces he was making? *Come. . . . come. . . . your mind is sliding toward me. . . .*

For a moment he thought he might actually succeed. But then she shot him a look of frosty malevolence, incredibly fierce, truly terrifying coming from an infant, and he backed away, frightened, fearing some sudden counterattack. An instant later she was gurgling again. She had defeated him. He went on hating her, but he never again tried to harm her. She, by the time she was old enough to know what the concept of hatred meant, was well aware of how her brother felt about her. And she hated back. She proved to be a far more efficient hater than he was. Oh, was she ever an expert at hating.

10.

The subject of this composition is My Very First Acid Trip. My first and my last, eight years ago. Actually it wasn't my trip at all, but Toni's. D-lysergic acid diethlyamide has never passed through my digestive tract, if truth be told. What I did was hitchhike on Toni's trip. In a sense I'm still a hitchhiker on that trip, that very bad trip. Let me tell you.

This happened in the summer of '68. That summer was a bad trip all in itself. Do you remember '68 at all? That was the year we all woke up to the fact that the whole business was coming apart. I mean American society. That pervasive feeling of decay and imminent collapse, so familiar to us all—it really dates from '68, I think. When the world around us became a metaphor for the process of violent entropic increase that had been going on inside our souls—inside my soul, at any rate for some time.

That summer Lyndon Baines MacBird was in the White House, just barely, serving out his time after his abdication in March. Bobby Kennedy had finally met the bullet with his name on it, and so had Martin Luther King. Neither killing was any surprise; the only surprise was that they had been so long in coming. The blacks were burning down the cities—back then, it was their *own* neighborhoods they burned, remember? Ordinary everyday people were starting to wear freaky clothes to work, bells and body shirts and mini-miniskirts, and hair was getting longer even for those over 25. It was the year of sideburns and Buffalo Bill mustachios. Gene McCarthy, a Senator from—where? Minnesota? Wisconsin?—was quoting poetry at news conferences as part of his attempt to gain the Democratic presidential nomination, but it was a sure bet that the Democrats would give it to Hubert Horatio Humphrey when they got together for their convention in Chicago. (And wasn't that convention a lovely festival of American patriotism?) Over in the other camp Rockefeller was running hard to catch up with Tricky Dick, but everybody knew where that was going to get him. Babies were dying of malnutrition in a place called Biafra, which you don't remember, and the Russians were moving troops into Czechoslovakia in yet another demonstration of socialist brotherhood. In a place called Vietnam, which you probably wish you didn't remember either, we were dumping napalm on everything in sight for the sake of promoting peace and democracy, and a lieutenant named William Calley had recently coordinated the liquidation of 100-odd sinister and dangerous old men, women, and children at the town of Mylai, only we didn't know anything about that yet. The books everybody was reading were *Couples, Myra Breckinridge, The Confessions of Nat Turner*, and *The Money Game*. I forget that year's movies. *Easy Rider* hadn't happened yet and *The Graduate* was the year before. Maybe it was the year of *Rosemary's Baby*. Yes, that sounds right: 1968 was the devil's year for sure. It was also the year when a lot of middle-class middle-aged people started using, self-consciously, terms like "pot" and "grass" when they meant "marijuana." Some of them were smoking it as well as talking it. (Me. Finally turning on at the age of 33.) Let's see, what else? President Johnson nominated Abe Fortas to replace Earl Warren as Chief Justice of the Supreme Court. Where are you now, Chief Justice Fortas, when we need you? The Paris peace talks, believe it or not, had just begun that summer. In later years it came to seem that the talks had been going on since the beginning of time, as eternal and everlasting as the Grand Canyon and the Republican Party, but no, they were invented in 1968. Denny McLain was on his way toward winning 31 games that season. I guess McLain was the only human being who found 1968 a worthwhile experience. His team lost the World Series, though. (No. What am I saying? The Tigers *won*, 4 games to 3. But Mickey Lolich was the star, not McLain.) That was the sort of year it was. Oh, Christ, I've forgotten one significant chunk of history. In the spring of '68 we had the riots at Columbia, with radical students occupying the campus (*"Kirk Must Go!"*) and classes being suspended (*"Shut It Down!"*) and final exams called off and nightly confrontations with the police, in the course of which a good many undergraduate skulls were laid open and much high-quality blood leaked into the gutters. How funny it is that I pushed that event out of my mind, when of all the things I've listed here it was the only one I actually experienced at first hand. Standing at Broadway and 116th Street watching platoons of cold-eyed fuzz go racing toward Butler Library. ("Fuzz" is what we called policemen before we started calling them "pigs," which happened a little later that same year.) Holding my hand aloft in the forked V-for-Peace gesture and screaming idiotic slogans with the best of them. Cowering in the lobby of Furnald Hall as the blue-clad nightstick brigade went on its rampage. Debating tactics with a ragged-bearded SDS gauleiter who finally spat in my face and called me a stinking liberal fink. Watching sweet Barnard girls ripping open their blouses and waving their bare breasts at horny, exasperated cops, while simultaneously shrieking ferocious Anglo-Saxonisms that the Barnard girls of my own remote era hadn't ever heard. Watching a group of young shaggy Columbia men ritualistically pissing on a pile of research documents that had been liberated from the filing cabinet of some hapless instructor going for his doctorate. It was then that I knew there could be no hope for mankind, when even the best of us were capable of going berserk in the cause of love and peace and human equality. On those dark nights I looked into many minds and found only hysteria and madness, and once, in despair, realizing I was living in a world where two factions of lunatics were battling for control of the asylum, I went off to vomit in Riverside Park after a particularly bloody riot and was caught unawares (me, caught unawares!) by a lithe 14-year-old black mugger who smilingly relieved me of $22.

I was living near Columbia in '68, in a seedy residence hotel on 114th Street, where I had one medium-big room plus kitchen and bathroom privileges, cockroaches at no extra charge. It was the very same place where I had lived as an undergraduate in my junior and senior years, 1955–56. The building had been going downhill even then and was an abominable hellhole when I came back to it twelve years later— the courtyard was littered with broken hypodermic needles the way another building's courtyard might be littered with cigarette butts—but I have an odd way, maybe masochistic, of not letting go of bits of my past however ugly they may be, and when I needed a place to live I picked that one. Besides, it was cheap—$14.50 a week—and I had to be close to the University because of the work I was doing, researching that Israel book. Are you still following me? I was telling you about my first acid trip, which was really Toni's trip.

We had shared our shabby room nearly seven weeks—a bit of May, all of June, some of July—through thick and thin, heat waves and rainstorms, misunderstandings and reconciliations, and it had been a happy time, perhaps the happiest of my life. I loved her and I think she loved me. I haven't had much love in my life. That isn't intended as a grab for your pity, just as a simple statement of fact, objective and cool. The nature of my condition diminishes my capacity to love and be loved. A man in my circumstances, wide open to everyone's innermost thoughts, really isn't going to experience a great deal of love. He is poor at giving love because he doesn't much trust his fellow human beings: he knows too many of their dirty little secrets, and that kills his feelings for them. Unable to give, he cannot get. His soul, hardened by isolation and un-givingness, becomes inaccessible, and so it is not easy for others to love him. The loop closes upon itself and he is trapped within. Nevertheless I loved Toni, having taken special care not to see too deeply into her, and I didn't doubt my love was returned. What defines love, anyway? We preferred each other's company to the company of anyone else. We excited one another in every imaginable way. We never bored each other. Our bodies mirrored our souls' closeness: I never failed of erec-tion, she never lacked for lubrication, our couplings carried us both to ecstasy. I'd call these things the parameters of love.

On the Friday of our seventh week Toni came home from her office with two small squares of white blotting paper in her purse. In the center on each square was a faint blue-green stain. I studied them a moment or two, without comprehending.

"Acid," she said finally.

"Acid?"

"You know. LSD. Teddy gave them to me."

Teddy was her boss, the editor-in-chief. LSD, yes. I knew. I had read Huxley on mescaline in 1957. I was fascinated and tempted. For years I had flirted with the psychedelic experience, even once attempting to volunteer for an LSD research program at the Columbia Medical Center. I was too late signing up, though; and then, as the drug became a fad, came all the horror stories of suicides, psychoses, bad trips. Knowing my vulnerabilities, I decided it was the part of wisdom to leave acid to others. Though still I was curious about it. And now these squares of blotting paper sitting in the palm of Toni's hand.

"It's supposed to be dynamite stuff," she said. "Absolutely pure, laboratory quality. Teddy's already tripped on a tab from this batch and he says it's very smooth, very clean, no speed in it or any crap like that. I thought we could spend tomorrow tripping, and sleep it off on Sunday."

"Both of us?"

"Why not?"

"Do you think it's safe for both of us to be out of our minds at the same time?"

She gave me a peculiar look. "Do you think acid drives you out of your mind?"

"I don't know. I've heard a lot of scary stories."

"You've never tripped?"

"No," I said. "Have you?"

"Well, no. But I've watched friends of mine while they were tripping." I felt a pang at this reminder of the life she had led before I met her. "They don't go out of their minds, David. There's a kind of wild high for an hour or so when things sometimes get jumbled up, but basically somebody who's tripping sits there as lucid and as calm as— well, Aldous Huxley. Can you imagine Huxley out of his mind? Gibbering and drooling and smashing furniture?"

"What about the fellow who killed his mother-in-law while he was on acid, though? And the girl who jumped out of a window?"

Toni shrugged. "They were unstable," she said loftily. "Perhaps murder or suicide was where they were really at, and the acid just gave them the push they needed to go and do it. But that doesn't mean you would, or me. Or maybe the doses were too strong, or the stuff was cut with some other drug. Who knows? Those are one-in-a-million cases. I have friends who've tripped fifty, sixty times, and they've never had any trouble." She sounded impatient with me. There was a patronizing, lecturing tone in her voice. Her esteem for me seemed clearly diminished by these old-maid hesitations of mine; we were on the threshold of a real rift. "What's the matter, David? Are you afraid to trip?"

"I think it's unwise for both of us to trip at once, that's all. When we aren't sure where the stuff is going to take us."

"Tripping together is the most loving thing two people can do," she said.

"But it's a risky thing. We just don't know. Look, you can get more acid if you want it, can't you?"

"I suppose so."

"Okay, then. Let's do this thing in an orderly way, one step at a time. There's no hurry. You trip tomorrow and I'll watch. I'll trip on Sunday and you'll watch. If we both like what the acid does to our heads, we can trip together next time. All right, Toni? All right?"

It wasn't all right. I saw her begin to speak, begin to frame some argument, some objection; but also I saw her catch herself, back up, rethink her position, and decide not to make an issue of it. Although I at no time went into her mind while this process was going on, her facial expressions made her sequence of thoughts wholly evident to me. "All right," she said softly. "It isn't worth a hassle."

Saturday morning she skipped breakfast—she'd been told to trip on an empty stomach—and, after I had eaten, we sat for a time in the kitchen with one of the squares of blotting paper lying innocently on the table between us. We pretended it wasn't there. Toni seemed a little clutched; I didn't know whether she was bothered about my insisting that she trip without me or just troubled, here at the brink of it, by the whole idea of tripping. There wasn't much conversation. She filled an ashtray with a great dismal mound of half-smoked cigarettes. From time to time she grinned nervously. From time to time I took her hand and smiled encouragingly. During this touching scene various of the tenants with whom we shared the kitchen on this floor of the hotel drifted in and out. First Eloise, the sleek black hooker. Then Miss Theotokis, the grim-faced nurse who worked at St. Luke's. Mr. Wong, the mysterious little roly-poly Chinese who always walked around in his underwear. Aitken, the scholarly fag from Toledo, and his cadaverous mainlining roommate, Donaldson. A couple of them nodded to us but no one actually said anything, not even "Good morning." In this place it was proper to behave as though your neighbors were invisible. The fine old New York tradition. About half past ten in the morning Toni said, "Get me some orange juice, will you?" I poured a glass from the container in the refrigerator that was labeled with my name. Giving me a wink and a broad toothy smile, all false bravado, she wadded up the blotting paper and pushed it into her mouth, bolting it and gulping the orange juice as a chaser.

"How long will it take to hit?" I asked.

"About an hour and a half," she said.

In fact it was more like fifty minutes. We were back in our own room, the door locked, faint scratchy sounds of Bach coming from the portable phonograph. I was trying to read, and so was Toni; the pages weren't turning very fast. She looked up suddenly and said, "I'm starting to feel a little funny."

"Funny how?"

"Dizzy. A slight touch of nausea. There's a prickling at the back of my neck."

"Can I get you anything? Glass of water? Juice?"

"Nothing, thanks. I'm fine. Really I am." A smile, timid but genuine. She seemed a little apprehensive but not at all frightened. Eager for the voyage. I put down my book and watched her vigilantly, feeling protective, almost wishing that I'd have some occasion to be of service to her. I didn't want her to have a bad trip but I wanted her to need me.

She gave me bulletins on the progress of the acid through her nervous system. I took notes until she indicated that the scratching of pencil against paper was distracting her. Visual effects were beginning. The walls looked a trifle concave to her, and the flaws in the plaster were taking on extraordinary texture and complexity. The color of everything was unnaturally bright. The shafts of sunlight coming through the dirty window were prismatic, shattering and spewing pieces of the spectrum over the floor. The music—I had a stack of her favorite records on the changer—had acquired a curious new intensity; she was having difficulty following melodic lines, and it seemed to her that the turntable kept stopping and starting, but the sound itself, as sound, had some indescribable quality of density and tangibility that fascinated her. There was a whistling sound in her ears, too, as of air rushing past her cheeks. She spoke of a pervading sense of strangeness—"I'm on some other planet," she said twice. She looked flushed, excited, happy. Remembering the terrible tales I had heard of acid-induced descents into hell, harrowing accounts of grueling bummers lovingly recounted for the delight of the millions by the diligent anonymous journalists of *Time* and *Life*, I nearly wept in relief at this evidence that my Toni would come through her journey unscathed. I had feared the worst. But she was making out all right. Her eyes were closed, her face was serene and exultant, her breathing was deep and relaxed. Lost in transcendental realms of mystery was my Toni. She was barely speaking to me now, breaking her silences only every few minutes to murmur something indistinct and oblique. Half an hour had passed since she first had reported strange sensations. As she drifted deeper into her trip, my love for her grew deeper also. Her ability to cope with acid was proof of the basic toughness of her personality, and that delighted me. I admire capable women. Already I was planning my own trip for the next day— selecting the musical accompaniment, trying to imagine the sort of interesting distortions of reality I'd experience, looking forward to comparing notes with Toni afterward. I was regretting the cowardice that had deprived me of the pleasure of tripping with Toni this day.

But what is this, now? What's happening to my head? Why this sudden feeling of suffocation? The pounding in my chest? The dryness in my throat? The walls are flexing; the air seems close and heavy; my right arm is suddenly a foot longer than the left one. These are effects Toni had noticed and described a little while ago. Why do I feel them now? I tremble. Muscles leap about of their own accord in my thighs. Is this what they call a contact high? Merely being so close to Toni while she trips—did she breathe particles of LSD at me, have I inadvertently turned on through some contagion of the atmosphere?

"My dear Selig," says my armchair smugly, "how can you be so foolish? Obviously you're picking these phenomena right out of her mind!"

Obviously? Is it so obvious? I consider the possibility. Am I reading Toni without knowing it? Apparently I am. In the past some effort of concentration, however slight, has always been necessary in order for me to manage a fine-focus peep into another head. But it seems that the acid must intensify her outputs and bring them to me unsolicited. What other explanation can there be? She is broadcasting her trip; and somehow I have tuned to her wavelength, despite all my noble resolutions about respecting her privacy. And now the acid's strangenesses, spreading across the gap between us, infect me as well.

Shall I get out of her mind?

The acid effects distract me. I look at Toni and she seems transformed. A small dark mole on her lower cheek, near the corner of her mouth, flashes a vortex of blazing color: red, blue, violet, green. Her lips are too full, her mouth too wide. All those teeth. Row upon row upon row, like a shark. Why have I never noticed that predatory mouth before? She frightens me. Her neck elongates; her body compresses; her breasts move about like restless cats beneath her familiar red sweater, which itself has taken on an ominous, threatening purplish tinge. To escape her I glance toward the window. A pattern of cracks that I have never been aware of before runs through the soiled panes. In a moment, surely, the shattered window will implode and shower us with fiery fragments of glass. The building across the street is unnaturally squat today. There is menace in its altered form. The ceiling is coming toward me, too. I hear muffled drumbeats overhead—the footsteps of my upstairs neighbor, I tell myself—and I imagine cannibals preparing their dinner. Is this what tripping is like? Is this what the young of our nation have been doing to themselves, voluntarily, even eagerly, for the sake of amusement?

I should turn this off, before it freaks me altogether. I want out.

Well, easily done. I have my ways of stopping down the inputs, of blocking the flow. Only they don't work this time. I am helpless before the power of the acid. I try to shut myself away from these unfamiliar and unsettling sensations, and they march onward into me all the same. I am wide open to everything emanating from Toni. I am caught up in it. I go deeper and deeper. This is a trip. This is a bad trip. This is a very bad trip. How odd: Toni was having a good trip, wasn't she? So it seemed to one outside observer. Then why do I, accidentally hitchhiking on her trip, find myself having a bad one?

Whatever is in Toni's mind floods into mine. Receiving another's soul is no new experience for me, but this is a transfer such as I have never had before, for the information, modulated by the drug, comes to me in ghastly distortions. I am an unwilling spectator in Toni's soul, and what I see is a feast of demons. Can such darkness really live within her? I saw nothing like this those other two times: has the acid released some level of nightmare not accessible to me before? Her past is on parade. Gaudy images, bathed in a lurid light. Lovers. Copulations. Abominations. A torrent of menstrual blood, or is that scarlet river something more sinister? Here is a clot of pain: what is that, cruelty to others, cruelty to self? And look how she gives herself to that army of monstrous men! They advance mechanically, a thundering legion. Their rigid cocks blaze with a terrible red light. One by one they plunge into her, and I see the light streaming from her loins as they plow her. Their faces are masks. I know none of them. Why am I not on line too? Where am I? Where am I? Ah, there: off to one side, insignificant, irrelevant. Is that thing me? Is that how she really sees me? A hairy vampire bat, a crouching huddled bloodsucker? Or is that merely David Selig's own image of David Selig, bouncing between us like the reflections in a barber shop's parallel mirrors? God help me, am I laying my own bad trip on her, then reading it back from her and blaming her for harboring nightmares not of her own making?

How can I break this link?

I stumble to my feet. Staggering, splay-footed, nauseated. The room whirls. Where is the door? The doorknob retreats from me. I lunge for it.

"David?" Her voice reverberates unendingly. "David David David David David David—".

"Some fresh air," I mutter. "Just stepping outside a minute—"

It does no good. The nightmare images pursue me through the door. I lean against the sweating wall, clinging to a flickering sconce. The Chinaman drifts by me as though a ghost. Far away I hear the telephone ringing. The refrigerator door slams, and slams again, and slams again, and the Chinaman goes by me a second time from the same direction, and the doorknob retreats from me, as the universe folds back upon itself, locking me into a looped moment. Entropy decreases. The green wall sweats green blood. A voice like thistles says, "Selig? Is something wrong?" It's Donaldson, the junkie. His face is a skull's face. His hand on my shoulder is all bones. "Are you sick?" he asks. I shake my head. He leans toward me until his empty eye-sockets are inches from my face, and studies me a long moment. He says, "You're *tripping*, man! Isn't that right? Listen, if you're freaking out, come on down the hall, we've got some stuff that might help you."

"No. No problem."

I go lurching into my room. The door, suddenly flexible, will not close; I push it with both hands, holding it in place until the latch clicks. Toni is sitting where I left her. She looks baffled. Her face is a monstrous thing, pure Picasso; I turn away from her, dismayed.

"David?"

Her voice is cracked and harsh, and seems to be pitched in two octaves at once, with a filling of scratchy wool between the top tone and the bottom. I wave my hands frantically, trying to get her to stop talking, but she goes on, expressing concern for me, wanting to know what's happening, why I've been running in and out of the room. Every sound she makes is torment for me. Nor do the images cease to flow from her mind to mine. That shaggy toothy bat, wearing my face, still glowers in a corner of her skull. Toni, I thought you loved me. Toni, I thought I made you happy. I drop to my knees and explore the dirt-encrusted carpet, a million years old, a faded thinning threadbare piece of the Pleistocene. She comes to me, bending down solicitously, she who is tripping looking after the welfare of her untripping companion, who mysteriously is tripping also. "I don't understand," she whispers. "You're crying, David. Your face is all blotchy. Did I say something wrong? Please don't carry on, David. I was having such a good trip, and now—I just don't understand—"

The bat. The bat. Spreading its rubbery wings. Baring its yellow fangs.

Biting. Sucking. Drinking.

I choke a few words out: "I'm—tripping—too—"

My face pushed against the carpet. The smell of dust in my dry nostrils. Trilobites crawling through my brain. A bat crawling through hers. Shrill laughter in the hallway. The telephone. The refrigerator door: slam, slam, slam! The cannibals dancing upstairs. The ceiling pressing against my back. My hungry mind looting Toni's soul. He who peeps through a hole may see what will vex him. Toni says, "You took the other acid? When?"

"I didn't."

"Then how can you be tripping?"

I make no reply. I crouch, I huddle, I sweat, I moan. This is the descent into hell. Huxley warned me. I didn't want Toni's trip. I didn't ask to see any of this. My defenses are destroyed now. She overwhelms me. She engulfs me.

Toni says, "Are you reading my mind, David?"

"Yes." The miserable ultimate confession. "I'm reading your mind."

"What did you say?"

"I said I'm reading your mind. I can see every thought. Every experience. I see myself the way you see me. Oh, Christ, Toni, Toni, Toni, it's so awful!"

She tugs at me and tries to pull me up to look at her. Finally I rise. Her face is horribly pale; her eyes are rigid. She asks for clarifications.

What's this about reading minds? Did I really say it, or is it something her acid-blurred mind invented? I really said it, I tell her. You asked me if I was reading your mind and I said yes, I was.

"I never asked any such thing," she says.

"I heard you ask it."

"But I didn't—" Trembling, now. Both of us. Her voice is bleak. "You're trying to bum-trip me, aren't you, David? I don't understand. Why would you want to hurt me? Why are you messing me up? It was a good trip. *It was a good trip.*"

"Not for me," I say.

"You weren't tripping."

"But I was."

She gives me a look of total incomprehension and pulls away from me and throws herself on the bed, sobbing. Out of her mind, cutting through the grotesqueries of the acid images, comes a blast of raw emotion: fear, resentment, pain, anger. She thinks I've deliberately tried to injure her. Nothing I can say now will repair things. Nothing can ever repair things. She despises me. I am a vampire to her, a bloodsucker, a leech; she knows my gift for what it is. We have crossed some fatal threshold and she will never again think of me without anguish and shame. Nor I her. I rush from the room, down the hall to the room shared by Donaldson and Aitken. "Bad trip," I mutter. "Sorry to trouble you, but—"

I stayed with them the rest of the afternoon. They gave me a tranquilizer and brought me gently through the downslope of the trip. The psychedelic images still came to me out of Toni for half an hour or so, as though an inexorable umbilical chain linked us across all the length of the hallway; but then to my relief the sense of contact began to slip and fade, and suddenly, with a kind of audible click at the moment of severance, it was gone altogether. The flamboyant phantoms ceased to vex my soul. Color and dimension and texture returned to their proper states. And at last I was free from that merciless reflected self-image. Once I was fully alone in my own skull again I felt like weeping to celebrate my deliverance, but no tears would come, and I sat passively, sipping a Bromo-Seltzer. Time trickled away. Donaldson and Aitken and I talked in a peaceful, civilized, burned-out way about Bach, medieval art, Richard M. Nixon, pot, and a great many other things. I hardly knew these two, yet they were willing to surrender their time to ease a stranger's pain. Eventually I felt better. Shortly before six o'clock, thanking them gravely, I went back to my room. Toni was not there. The place seemed oddly altered. Books were gone from the shelves, prints from the walls; the closet door stood open and half the things in it were missing. In my befuddled, fatigued state it took me a moment or two to grasp what had happened. At first I imagined burglary, abduction, but then I saw the truth. She had moved out.

11.

Today there is a hint of encroaching winter in the air: it takes tentative nips at the cheeks. October is dying too quickly. The sky is mottled and unhealthy-looking, cluttered by sad, heavy, low-hanging clouds. Yesterday it rained, skinning yellow leaves from the trees, and now they lie pasted to the pavement of College Walk, their tips fluttering raggedly in the harsh breeze. There are puddles everywhere. As I settled down beside Alma Mater's massive green form I primly spread newspaper sheets, selected portions of today's issue of *The Columbia Daily Spectator*, over the cold damp stone steps. Twenty-odd years ago, when I was a foolishly ambitious sophomore dreaming of a career in journalism—how sly, a reporter who reads minds!—*Spec* seemed central to my life; now it serves only for keeping my rump dry.

Here I sit. Office hours. On my knees rests a thick manila folder, held closed by a ballsy big rubber band. Within, neatly typed, each with its own coppery paperclip, are five term papers, the products of my busy week. *The Novels of Kafka. Shaw as Tragedian. The Concept of Synthetic A Priori Statements. Odysseus as a Symbol of Society. Aeschylus and the Aristotelian Tragedy.* The old academic bullshit, confirmed in its hopeless fecality by the cheerful willingness of these bright young men to let an old grad turn the stuff out for them. This is the day appointed for delivering the goods and, perhaps, picking up some new assignments. Five minutes to eleven. My clients will be arriving soon. Meanwhile I scan the passing parade. Students hurrying by, clutching mounds of books. Hair rippling in the wind, breasts bobbling. They all look frighteningly young to me, even the bearded ones. Especially the bearded ones. Do you realize that each year there are more and more young people in the world? Their tribe ever increases as the old farts drop off the nether end of the curve and I shuttle graveward. Even the professors look young to me these days. There are people with doctorates who are fifteen years younger than I am. Isn't that a killer? Imagine a kid born in 1950 who has a doctorate already. In 1950 I was shaving three times a week, and masturbating every Wednesday and Saturday; I was a hearty pubescent *bulyak* five feet nine inches tall, with ambitions and griefs and knowledge, with an identity. In 1950 today's newly fledged Ph.D.'s were toothless infants just squirting from the womb, their faces puckered, their skins sticky with amniotic juices. How can those infants have doctorates so soon? Those infants have lapped me as I plod along the track.

I find my own company wearisome when I descend into self-pity. To divert myself I try to touch the minds of passers-by and learn what I can learn. Playing my old game, my only game. Selig the voyeur, the soul-vampire, ripping off the intimacies of innocent strangers to cheer his chilly heart. But no: my head is full of cotton today. Only muffled murmurs come to me, indistinct, content-free. No discrete words, no flashes of identity, no visions of soul's essence. This is one of the bad days. All inputs converge into unintelligibility; each bit of information is identical to all others. It is the triumph of entropy. I am reminded of Forster's Mrs. Moore, listening tensely for revelation in the echoing Marabar caves, and hearing only the same monotonous noise, the same meaningless all-dissolving sound: *Boum.* The sum and essence of mankind's earnest strivings: *Boum.* The minds flashing past me on College Walk now give me only: *Boum.* Perhaps it is all I deserve. Love, fear, faith, churlishness, hunger, self-satisfaction, every species of interior monolog, all come to me with identical content. *Boum.* I must work to correct this. It is not too late to wage war against entropy. Gradually, sweating, struggling, scrabbling for solid purchase, I widen the aperture, coaxing my perceptions to function. Yes. Yes. Come back to life. Get it up, you miserable spy! Give me my fix! Within me the power stirs. The inner murk clears a bit; stray scraps of isolated but coherent thought find their way into me. *Neurotic but not altogether psycho yet. Going to see the department head and tell him to shove it up. Tickets for the opera, but I have to. Fucking is fun, fucking is very important, but there's more. Like standing on a very high diving board about to take a plunge.* This scratchy chaotic chatter tells me nothing except that the power is not yet dead, and I take comfort enough in that. I visualize the power as a sort of worm wrapped around my cerebrum, a poor tired worm, wrinkled and shrunken, its once-glossy skin now ulcerous with shabby, flaking patches. That is a relatively recent image, but even in happier days I always thought of the gift as something apart from myself, something intrusive. An inhabitant. It and me, me and it. I used to discuss such things with Nyquist. (Has he entered these exhalations yet? Perhaps not. A person I once knew, a certain Tom Nyquist, a former friend of mine. Who carried a somewhat similar intruder within his skull.) Nyquist didn't like my outlook. "That's schizoid, man, setting up a duality like that. Your power is you. You are your power. Why try to alienate yourself from your own brain?" Probably Nyquist was right, but it's much too late. It and me is how it will be, till death do us part.

Here is my client, the bulky halfback, Paul F. Bruno. His face is swollen and purple, and he is unsmiling, as though Saturday's heroics have cost him some teeth. I flip the rubber band down, extract *The Novels of Kafka*, and offer the paper to him. "Six pages," I say. He has given me a ten-dollar advance. "You owe me another eleven bucks. Do you want to read it first?"

"How good is it?"

"You won't be sorry."

"I'll take your word for it." He manages a painful, close-mouthed grin. Pulling forth his thick wallet, he crosses my palm with greenbacks. I slip quickly into his mind, just for the hell of it now that my power is working again, a fast psychic rip-off, and pick up the surface levels: loose teeth at the football game, a sweet compensatory blow-job at the frat house Saturday night, vague plans for getting laid after next Saturday's game, etc., etc. Concerning the present transaction I detect guilt, embarrassment, even some annoyance with me for having helped him. Oh, well: the gratitude of the *goy*. I pocket his money. He favors me with a curt nod and tucks *The Novels of Kafka* under his immense forearm. Hastily, in shame, he goes hustling down the steps and off in the direction of Hamilton Hall. I watch his broad retreating back. A sudden gust of malevolent wind, rising off the Hudson, comes knifing eastward and cuts me bone-deep.

Bruno has paused at the sundial, where a slender black student close to seven feet tall has intercepted him. A basketball player, obviously. The black wears a blue varsity jacket, green sneakers, and tight tubular yellow slacks. His legs alone seem five feet long. He and Bruno talk for a moment. Bruno points toward me. The black nods. I am about to gain a new client, I realize. Bruno vanishes and the black trots spring-legged across the walk, up the steps. He is very dark, almost purple-skinned, yet his features have a Caucasian sharpness, fierce cheekbones, proud aquiline nose, thin frosty lips. He is formidably handsome, some kind of walking statuary, some sort of idol. Perhaps his genes are not Negroid at all: an Ethiopian, maybe, some tribesman of the Nile bulrushes? Yet he wears his midnight mass of kinky hair in a vast aggressive Afro halo a foot in diameter or more, fastidiously trimmed. I would not have been surprised by scarified cheeks, a bone through the nostrils. As he nears me, my mind, barely slit-wide, picks up peripheral generalized emanations of his personality. Everything is predictable, even stereotyped: I expect him to be touchy, cocky, defensive, hostile, and what comes to me is a bouillabaisse of ferocious racial pride, overwhelming physical self-satisfaction, explosive mistrust of others—especially whites. All right. Familiar patterns.

His elongated shadow falls suddenly upon me as the sun momentarily pierces the clouds. He sways bouncily on the balls of his feet. "Your name Selig?" he asks. I nod. "Yahya Lumumba," he says.

"Pardon me?"

"Yahya Lumumba." His eyes, glossy white against glossy purple, blaze with fury. From the impatience of his tone I realize that he is telling me his name, or at least the name he prefers to use. His tone indicates also that he assumes it's a name everyone on this campus will recognize. Well, what would I know of college basketball stars? He could throw the ball through the hoop fifty times a game and I'd still not have heard of him. He says, "I hear you do term papers, man."

"That's right."

"You got a good recommend from my pal Bruno there. How much you charge?"

"$3.50 a page. Typed, double-spaced."

He considers it. He shows many teeth and says, "What kind of fucking rip-off is that?"

"It's how I earn my living, Mr. Lumumba." I hate myself for that toadying, cowardly *mister*. "That's about $20 for an average-length paper. A decent job takes a fair amount of time, right?"

"Yeah. Yeah." An elaborate shrug. "Okay, I'm not hassling you, man. I got need for your work. You know anything about Europydes?"

"Euripides?"

"That's what I said." He's baiting me, coming on with exaggerated black mannerisms, talking watermelon-nigger at me with his *Europydes.* "That Greek cat who wrote plays."

"I know who you mean. What sort of paper do you need, Mr. Lumumba?"

He pulls a scrap of a notebook sheet from a breast pocket and makes a great show of consulting it. "The prof he want us to compare the 'Electra' theme in Europydes, Sophocles, and Eesk—Aysk—"

"Aeschylus?"

"Him, yeah. Five to ten pages. It due by November 10. Can you swing it?"

"I think so," I say, reaching for my pen. "It shouldn't be any trouble at all," especially since there resides in my files a paper of my own, vintage 1952, covering this very same hoary old Humanities theme. "I'll need some information about you for the heading. Exact spelling of your name, the name of your professor, the course number—" He starts to tell me these things. As I jot them down, I simultaneously open the aperture of my mind for my customary scan of the client's interior, to give me some idea of the proper tone to use in the paper. Will I be able to do a convincing job of faking the kind of essay Yahya Lumumba is likely to turn in? It will be a taxing technical challenge if I have to write in black hipster jargon, coming on all cool and jazzy and snotty, every line laughing in the ofay prof's fat face. I imagine I could do it: but does Lumumba want me to? Will he think I'm mocking *him* if I adopt the jiveass style and seem to be putting him on as he might put on the prof? I must know these things. So I slip my snaky tendrils past his woolly scalp into the hidden gray jelly. Hello, big black man. Entering, I pick up a somewhat more immediate and vivid version of the generalized persona he constantly projects: the hyped-up black pride, the mistrust of the paleface stranger, the chuckling enjoyment of his own lean long-legged muscular frame. But these are mere residual attitudes, the standard furniture of his mind. I have not yet reached the level of this-minute thought. I have not penetrated to the essential Yahya Lumumba, the unique individual whose style I must assume. I push deeper. As I sink in, I sense a distinct warming of the psychic temperature, an outflow of heat, comparable perhaps to what a miner might experience five miles down, tunneling toward the magmatic fires at the earth's core. This man Lumumba is constantly boiling within, I realize. The glow from his tumultuous soul warns me to be careful, but I have not yet gained the information I seek, and so I go onward, until abruptly the molten frenzy of his stream of consciousness hits me with terrible force. *Fucking Jew bigbrain shithead Christ how I hate the little bald mother conning me three-fifty a page I ought to jew him down I ought to bust his teeth the exploiter the oppressor he wouldn't charge a Jew that much I bet special price for niggers sure well I ought to jew him down that's a good one jew him down I ought to bust his teeth pick him up throw him into the trash what if I wrote the fucking paper myself show him but I can't shit I can't that's the whole fucking trouble mom I can't Europydes Sophocles Eeskilus who knows shit about them I got other stuff on my mind the Rutgers game one-on-one down the court gimme the ball you dumb prick that's it and it's up and in for Lumumba!*

and wait folks he was fouled in the act of shooting now he goes to the line big confident easy six feet ten inches tall holder of every Columbia scoring record bounces the ball once twice up, swish! Lumumba on his way to another big evening tonight folks Europydes Sophocles Eeskilus why the fuck do I have to know anything about them write anything about them what good is it to a black man those old dead Greek fuckers how are they relevant to the black experience relevant relevant relevant not to me just to the Jews shit what do any of them, know four hundred years of slavery we got other stuff on our minds what do any of them know especially this shithead mother here I got to pay him twenty bucks to do something I'm not good enough to do for myself who says I have to what good is any of it why why why why

A roaring furnace. The heat is overwhelming. I've been in contact with intense minds before, far more intense even than this one, but that was when I was younger, stronger, more resilient. I can't handle this volcanic blast. The force of his contempt for me is magnified factorially by the force of the self-contempt that needing my services makes him feel. He is a pillar of hatred. And my poor enfeebled power can't take it. Some sort of automatic safety device cuts in to protect me from an overload: the mental receptors shut themselves down. This is a new experience for me, a strange one, this load-shedding phenomenon. It is as though limbs are dropping off, ears, balls, anything disposable, leaving nothing but a smooth torso. The inputs fall away, the mind of Yahya Lumumba retreats and is inaccessible to me, and I find myself involuntarily reversing the process of penetration until I can feel only his most superficial emanations, then not even those, only a gray furry exudation marking the mere presence of him alongside me. All is indistinct. All is muffled. *Boum.* We are back to that again. There is a ringing in my ears: it is an artifact of the sudden silence, a silence loud as thunder. A new stage on my downward path. Never have I lost my grip and slipped from a mind like this. I look up, dazed, shattered. Yahya Lumumba's thin lips are tightly compressed; he stares down at me in distaste, having no inkling of what has occurred. I say faintly, "I'd like ten dollars now in advance. The rest you pay when I deliver the paper." He tells me coldly that he has no money to give me today. His next check from the scholarship fund isn't due until the beginning of the coming month. I'll just have to do the job on faith, he says. Take it or leave it, man. "Can you manage five?" I ask. "As a binder. Faith isn't enough. I have expenses." He glares. He draws himself to his full height; he seems nine or ten feet tall. Without a word he takes a five-dollar bill from his wallet, crumples it, scornfully tosses it into my lap. "I'll see you here the morning of November 9," I call after him, as he stalks away. Europydes, Sophocles, Eeskilus. I sit stunned, shivering, listening to the bellowing silence. *Boum. Boum. Boum.*

12.

In his more flamboyantly Dostoevskian moments, David Selig liked to think of his power as a curse, a savage penalty for some unimaginable sin. The mark of Cain, perhaps. Certainly his special ability had caused a lot of trouble for him, but in his saner moments he knew that calling it a curse was sheer self-indulgent melodramatic bullshit. The power was a divine gift. The power brought ecstasy. Without the power he was nothing, a schmendrick; with it he was a god. Is that a curse? Is that so terrible? Something funny happens when gamete meets gamete, and destiny cries, Here, Selig-baby: be a god! This you would spurn? Sophocles, age 88 or so, was heard to express his great relief at having outlived the pressures of the physical passions. I am freed at last from a tyrannical master, said the wise and happy Sophocles. Can we then assume that Sophocles, had Zeus given him a chance retroactively to alter the entire course of his days, would have opted for lifelong impotence? Don't kid yourself, Duvid: no matter how badly the telepathy stuff fucked you up, and it fucked you up pretty badly, you wouldn't have done without it for a minute. Because the power brought ecstasy.

The power brought ecstasy. That's the whole megillah in a single crisp phrase. Mortals are born into a vale of tears and they get their kicks wherever they can. Some, seeking pleasure, are compelled to turn to sex, drugs, booze, television, movies, pinochle, the stock market, the racetrack, the roulette wheel, whips and chains, collecting first editions, Caribbean cruises, Chinese snuff bottles, Anglo-Saxon poetry, rubber garments, professional football games, whatever. Not him, not the accursed David Selig. All he had to do was sit quietly with his apparatus wide open and drink in the thought-waves drifting on the telepathic breeze. With the greatest of ease he lived a hundred vicarious lives. He heaped his treasurehouse with the plunder of a thousand souls. Ecstasy. Of course, the ecstatic part was all quite some time ago.

The best years were those between the ages of fourteen and twenty-five. Younger, and he was still too naive, too unformed, to wring much appreciation from the data he took in. Older, and his growing bitterness, his sour sense of isolation, damped his capacity for joy. Fourteen to twenty-five, though. The golden years. Ah!

It was so very much more vivid then. Life was like a waking dream. There were no walls in his world; he could go anywhere and see anything. The intense flavor of existence. Steeped in the rich juices of perception. Not until Selig was past forty did he realize how much he had lost, over the years, in the way of fine focus and depth of field. The power had not begun detectibly to dim until he was well along in his thirties, but it obviously must have been fading by easy stages all through his manhood, dwindling so gradually that he remained unaware of the cumulative loss. The change had been absolute, qualitative rather than quantitative. Even on a good day, now, the inputs did not begin to approach the intensity of those he remembered from his adolescence. In those remote years the power had brought him not only bits of sub-cranial conversation and scattered snatches of soul, as now, but also a gaudy universe of colors, textures, scents, densities: the world through an infinity of other sensory intakes, the world captured and played out for his delight on the glassy radiant spherical screen within his mind.

For instance. He lies propped against an itchy August haystack in a hot Brueghelesque landscape, shortly past noon. This is 1950 and he hangs becalmed midway between his fifteenth birthday and his sixteenth. Some sound effects, Maestro: Beethoven's Sixth, bubbling up gently, sweet flutes and playful piccolos. The sun dangles in a cloudless sky. A gentle wind stirs the willows bordering the cornfield. The young corn trembles. The brook burbles. A starling circles overhead. He hears crickets. He hears the drone of a mosquito, and watches calmly as it zeroes in on his bare, hairless, sweat-shiny chest. His feet are bare too; he wears only tight, faded blue jeans. City boy, digging the country.

The farm is in the Catskills, twelve miles north of Ellenville. It is owned by the Schieles, a tribe of tawny Teutons, who produce eggs and an assortment of vegetable crops and who supplement their earnings every summer by renting out their guest house to some family of urban Yids looking for rural solace. This year the tenants are Sam and Annette Stein of Brooklyn, New York, and their daughter Barbara. The Steins have invited their close friends, Paul and Martha Selig, to spend a week on the farm with their son David and their daughter Judith. (Sam Stein and Paul Selig are hatching a scheme, destined ultimately to empty their bank accounts and destroy the friendship between the two families, to enter into a partnership and act as jobbers for replacement parts for television sets. Paul Selig is forever attempting unwise business ventures.) Today is the third day of the visit, and this afternoon, mysteriously, David finds himself utterly alone. His father has gone on an all-day hike with Sam Stein: in the serenity of the nearby hills they will plot the details of their commercial coup. Their wives have driven off, taking five-year-old Judith with them, to explore the antique shops of Ellenville. No one remains on the premises except the tightlipped Schieles, going somberly about their unending chores, and sixteen-year-old Barbara Stein, who has been David's classmate from the third grade on through high school. Willy-nilly, David and Barbara are thrown together for the day. The Steins and the Seligs evidently have some unvoiced hope that romance will blossom between their offspring. This is naive of them. Barbara, a lush and reasonably beautiful dark-haired girl, sleek-skinned and long-legged, sophisticated and smooth of manner, is six months older than David chronologically, and three or four years ahead of him in social development. She does not actually dislike him, but she regards him as strange, disturbing, alien, and repellent. She has no knowledge of his special gift—no one does; he's seen to that—but she's had seven years to observe him at close range, and she knows there's something fishy about him. She is a conventional girl, plainly destined to marry early (a doctor, a lawyer, an insurance broker) and have lots of babies, and the chances of romance flowering between her and anyone as dark-souled and odd as David Selig are slight. David knows this very well and he is not at all surprised, or even dismayed, when Barbara slips away in mid-morning. "If anyone asks," she says, "tell them I went for a stroll in the woods." She carries a paperback poetry anthology. David is not deceived by it. He knows she goes off to screw 19-year-old Hans Schiele at every chance she gets.

So he is left to his own resources. No matter. He has ways of entertaining himself. He wanders the farm for a while, peering at the hen-coop and the combine, and then settles down in a quiet corner of the fields. Time for mind-movies. Lazily he casts his net. The power rises and goes forth, looking for emanations. What shall I read, what shall I read? Ah. A sense of contact. His questing mind has snared another mind, a buzzing one, small, dim, intense. It is a bee's mind, in fact: David is not limited only to contact with humans. Of course there are no verbal outputs from the bee, nor any conceptual ones. If the bee thinks at all, David is incapable of detecting those thoughts. But he does

get into the bee's head. He experiences a strong sense of what it is like
to be tiny and compact and winged and fuzzy. How *dry* the universe of
a bee is: bloodless, desiccated, arid. He soars. He swoops. He evades a
passing bird, as monstrous as a winged elephant. He burrows deep into
a steamy, pollen-laden blossom. He goes aloft again. He sees the world
through the bee's faceted eyes. Everything breaks into a thousand fragments, as though seen through a cracked glass; the essential color of
everything is gray, but odd hues lurk at the corners of things, peripheral
blues and scarlets that do not correspond in any way to the colors he
knows. The effect, he might have said twenty years later, is an extremely
trippy one. But the mind of a bee is a limited one. David bores easily.
He abandons the insect abruptly and, zooming his perceptions barnward,
clicks into the soul of a hen. She is laying an egg! Rhythmic internal
contractions, pleasurable and painful, like the voiding of a mighty turd.
Frenzied squawks. The smarmy hen-coop odor, sharp and biting. A
sense of too much straw all about. The world looks dark and dull to
this bird. *Heave. Heave.* Oooh! Orgasmic excitement! The egg slides
through the hatch and lands safely. The hen subsides, fulfilled, exhausted. David departs from her in this moment of rapture. He plunges
deep into the adjoining woods, finds a human mind, enters it. How much
richer and more intense it is to make communion with his own species.
His identity blurs into that of his communicant who is Barbara Stein,
who is getting laid by Hans Schiele. She is naked and lying on a carpet
of last year's fallen leaves. Her legs are spread and her eyes are closed.
Her skin is damp with sweat. Hans' fingers dig into the soft flesh of her
shoulders and his cheek, rough with blond stubble, abrades her cheek.
His weight presses down on her chest, flattening her breasts and emp-
tying her lungs. With steady thrusts and unvarying tempo he penetrates
her, and as his long stiff member slowly and patiently rams into her
again and again, throbbing sensation spreads in eddying ripples outward
from her loins, growing less intense with distance. Through her mind
David observes the impact of the hard penis against the tender, slippery
internal membranes. He picks up her clamorous heartbeat. He notices
her hammering her heels against the calves of Hans' legs. He is aware
of the slickness of her own fluids on her buttocks and thighs. And now
he senses the first dizzying spasms of orgasm. David struggles to remain
with her, but he knows he won't succeed; clinging to the consciousness
of someone who's coming is like trying to ride a wild horse. Her pelvis
bucks and heaves, her fingernails desperately rake her lover's back, her
head twists to one side, she gulps for air, and, as she erupts with pleasure, she catapults David from her unsaddled mind. He travels only a
short way, into the stolid soul of Hans Schiele, who unknowingly grants

the virgin voyeur a few instants of knowledge of what it is like to be
stoking the furnace of Barbara Stein, thrust and thrust and thrust and
thrust, her inner muscles clamping fiercely against the swollen prod, and
then, almost immediately, comes the tickle of Hans' onrushing climax.
Hungry for information, David holds on with all his strength, hoping to
keep contact right through the tumult of fulfillment, but no, he is flipped
free, he tumbles uncontrollably, the world goes swinging past him in
giddy streaks of color, until—click!—he finds a new sanctuary. All is
calm here. He glides through a dark cold environment. He has no
weight; his body is long and slender and agile; his mind is nearly a
void, but through it run faint chilly flickering perceptions of a low order.
He has entered the consciousness of a fish, perhaps a brook trout. Down-
stream he moves in the swiftly rushing creek, taking delight in the
smoothness of his motions and the delicious texture of the pure icy water
flowing past his fins. He can see very little and smell even less; information comes to him in the form of minute impacts on his scales, tiny
deflections and interferences. Easily he responds to each incoming news
item, now twisting to avoid a fang of rock, now fluttering his fins to
seize some speedy subcurrent. The process is fascinating, but the trout
itself is a dull companion, and David, having extracted the troutness of
the experience in two or three minutes, leaps gladly to a more complex
mind the moment he approaches one. It is the mind of gnarled old Georg
Schiele, Hans' father, who is at work in a remote corner of the cornfield.
David has never entered the elder Schiele's mind before. The old man
is a grim and forbidding character, well past sixty, who says little and
stalks dourly through his day-long round of chores with his heavy-
jowled face perpetually locked in a frosty scowl. David occasionally
wonders whether he once might have been a concentration-camp attendant, though he knows the Schieles came to America in 1935. The
farmer gives off so unpleasant a psychic aura that David has steered
clear of him, but he is bored with the trout and he slips now into Schiele,
slides down through dense layers of unintelligible Deutsch ruminations,
and strikes bottom in the basement of the farmer's soul, the place where
his essence lives. Astonishment: old Schiele is a mystic, an ecstatic! No
dourness here. No dark Lutheran vindictiveness. This is pure Buddhism:
Schiele stands in the rich soil of his fields, leaning on his hoe, feet
firmly planted, communing with the universe. God floods his soul. He
touches the unity of all things. Sky, trees, earth, sun, plants, brook,
insects, birds—everything is one, part of a seamless whole, and Schiele
resonates in perfect harmony with it. How can this be? How can such
a bleak, inaccessible man entertain such raptures in his depths? Feel his
joy! Sensations drench him! Birdsong, sunlight, the scent of flowers and

clods of upturned earth, the rustling of the sharp-bladed green corn-
stalks, the trickle of sweat down the reddened deep-channeled neck, the
curve of the planet, the fleecy premature outline of the full moon—a
thousand delights enfold this man. David shares his pleasure. He kneels
in his mind, reverent, awed. The world is a mighty hymn. Schiele breaks
from his stasis, raises his hoe, brings it down; heavy muscles go taut
and metal digs into earth, and everything is as it should be, all conforms
to the divine plan. Is this how Schiele goes through his days? Is such
happiness possible? David is surprised to find tears bulging in his eyes.
This simple man, this narrow man, lives in daily grace. Suddenly sullen,
bitterly envious, David rips his mind free, whirls, projects it toward the
woods, drops down into Barbara Stein again. She lies back, sweat-
sticky, exhausted. Through her nostrils David receives the stink of semen already going sour. She rubs her hands over her skin, plucking
stray bits of leaf and grass from herself. Idly she touches her softening
nipples. Her mind is slow, dull, almost as empty as the trout's, just now:
sex seems to have drained her of personality. David shifts to Hans and
finds him no better. Lying by Barbara's side, still breathing hard after
his exertions, he is torpid and depressed. His wad is shot and all desire
is gone from him; peering sleepily at the girl he has just possessed, he
is conscious mainly of body odors and the untidiness of her hair.
Through the upper levels of his mind wanders a wistful thought, in
English punctuated by clumsy German, of a girl from an adjoining farm
who will do something to him with her mouth that Barbara refuses to
do. Hans will be seeing her on Saturday night. Poor Barbara, David
thinks, and wonders what she would say if she knew what Hans is
thinking. Idly he tries to bridge their two minds, entering both in the
mischievous hope that thoughts may flow from one to the other, but he
miscalculates his span and finds himself returning to old Schiele, deep
in his ecstasy, while holding contact with Hans as well. Father and son,
old and young, priest and profaner. David sustains the twin contact a
moment. He shivers. He is filled with a thundering sense of the wholeness of life.

It was like that all the time, in those years: an endless trip, a gaudy
voyage. But powers decay. Time leaches the colors from the best of
visions. The world becomes grayer. Entropy beats us down. Everything
fades. Everything goes. Everything dies.

13.

J udith's dark, rambling apartment fills with pungent smells. I hear her in the kitchen, bustling, dumping spices into the pot: hot chili, oregano, tarragon, cloves, garlic, powdered mustard, sesame oil, curry powder, God knows what else. Fire burn and cauldron bubble. Her famous fiery spaghetti sauce is in the making, a compound product of mysterious antecedents, part Mexican in inspiration, part Szechuan, part Madras, part pure Judith. My unhappy sister is not really much of a domestic type, but the few dishes she can cook she does extraordinarily well, and her spaghetti is celebrated on three continents; I'm convinced there are men who go to bed with her just to have dining-in privileges here.

I have arrived unexpectedly early, half an hour before the appointed time, catching Judith unprepared, not even dressed; so I am on my own while she readies dinner. "Fix yourself a drink," she calls to me. I go to the sideboard and pour a shot of dark rum, then into the kitchen for ice cubes. Judith, flustered, wearing housecoat and headband, flies madly about, breathlessly selecting spices. She does everything at top speed. "Be with you in another ten minutes," she gasps, reaching for the pepper mill. "Is the kid making a lot of trouble for you?"

My nephew, she means. His name is Paul, in honor of our father which art in heaven, but she never calls him that, only "the baby," "the kid." Four years old. Child of divorce, destined to be as taut-strung as his mother. "He's not bothering me at all," I assure her, and go back to the livingroom.

The apartment is one of those old, immense West Side jobs, roomy and high-ceilinged, which carries with it some sort of aura of intellectual distinction simply because so many critics, poets, playwrights, and choreographers have lived in similar apartments in this very neighborhood. Giant livingroom with many windows looking out over West End Avenue; formal dining room; big kitchen; master bedroom; child's room; maid's room; two bathrooms. All for Judith and her cub. The rent is cosmic, but Judith can manage it. She gets well over a thousand a month from her ex, and earns a modest but decent living of her own as an editor and translator; aside from that she has a small income from a portfolio of stocks, shrewdly chosen for her a few years ago by a lover from Wall Street, which she purchased with her inherited share of our parents' surprisingly robust savings. (My share went to clean up accumulated debts; the whole thing melted like June snow.) The place is furnished half in 1960 Greenwich Village and half in 1970 Urban Elegance—black pole-lamps, gray string chairs, red brick bookcases, cheap prints, and wax-encrusted Chianti bottles on the one hand; leather couches, Hopi pottery, psychedelic silkscreens, glass-topped coffee-tables, and giant potted cacti on the other. Bach harpischord sonatas tinkle from the thousand-dollar speaker system. The floor, ebony-dark and mirror-bright, gleams between the lush, thick area rugs. A pile of broken-backed paperbacks clutters one wall. Opposite it stand two rough unopened wooden crates, wine newly arrived from her vintner. A good life my sister leads here. Good and miserable.

The kid eyes me untrustingly. He sits twenty feet away, by the window, fiddling with some intricate plastic toy but keeping close watch on me. A dark child, slender and tense like his mother, aloof, cool. No love is lost between us: I've been inside his head and I know what he thinks of me. To him I'm one of the many men in his mother's life, a real uncle being not very different from the innumerable uncle-surrogates forever sleeping over; I suppose he thinks I'm just one of her lovers who shows up more often than most. An understandable error. But while he resents the others merely because they compete with him for her affection, he looks coldly upon me because he thinks I've caused his mother pain; he dislikes me for her sake. How shrewdly he's discerned the decades-old network of hostilities and tensions that shapes and defines my relationship with Judith! So I'm an enemy. He'd gut me if he could.

I sip my drink, listen to Bach, smile insincerely at the kid, and inhale the aroma of spaghetti sauce. My power is practically quiescent; I try not to use it much here, and in any case its intake is feeble today. After some time Judith emerges from the kitchen and, flashing across the livingroom, says, "Come talk to me while I get dressed, Duv." I follow her to her bedroom and sit down on the bed; she takes her clothes into the adjoining bathroom, leaving the door open only an inch or two. The

last time I saw her naked she was seven years old. She says, "I'm glad
you decided to come."

"So am I."

"You look awfully peaked though."

"Just hungry, Jude."

"I'll fix that in five minutes." Sounds of water running. She says
something else; the sink drowns her out. I look idly around the bedroom.
A man's white shirt, much too big for Judith, hangs casually from the
doorknob of the closet. On the night-table sit two fat textbooky-looking
books. *Analytical Neuroendocrinology* and *Studies in the Physiology of
Thermoregulation.* Unlikely reading for Judith. Maybe she's been hired
to translate them into French. I observe that they're brand new copies,
though one book was published in 1964 and the other in 1969. Both by
the same author: K. F. Silvestri, M.D., Ph.D.

"You going to medical school these days?" I ask.

"The books, you mean? They're Karl's."

Karl? A new name. Dr. Karl F. Silvestri. I touch her mind lightly
and extract his image: a tall hefty sober-faced man, broad shoulders,
strong dimpled chin, flowing mane of graying hair. About fifty, I'd
guess. Judith digs older men. While I raid her consciousness she tells
me about him. Her current "friend," the kid's latest "uncle." He's someone very big at Columbia Medical Center, a real authority on the human
body. Including her body, I assume. Newly divorced after a 25-year
marriage. Uh-huh: she likes getting them on the rebound. He met her
three weeks ago through a mutual friend, a psychoanalyst. They've only
seen each other four or five times; he's always busy, committee meetings at this hospital or that, seminars, consultations. It wasn't very long
ago that Judith told me she was between men, maybe off men altogether.
Evidently not. It must be a serious affair if she's trying to read his books.
They look absolutely opaque to me, all charts and statistical tables and
heavy Latinate terminology.

She comes out of the bathroom wearing a sleek purple pants-suit
and the crystal earrings I gave her for her 29th birthday. When I visit
she always tries to register some little sentimental touch to tie us together; tonight it's the earrings. There is a convalescent quality to our
friendship nowadays, as we tiptoe gently through the garden where our
old hatred lies buried: We embrace, a brother-sister hug. A pleasant
perfume. "Hello," she says. "I'm sorry I was such a mess when you
walked in."

"It's my fault. I was too early. Anyway, you weren't a mess at all."

She leads me to the livingroom. She carries herself well. Judith is
a handsome woman, tall and extremely slender, exotic-looking, with

dark hair, dark complexion, sharp cheekbones. The slim sultry type. I suppose she'd be considered very sexy, except that there is something cruel about her thin lips and her quick glistening brown eyes, and that cruelty, which grows more intense in these years of divorce and discontent, turns people off. She's had lovers by the dozen, by the gross, but not much love. You and me, sis, you and me. Chips off the old block.

She sets the table while I fix a drink for her, the usual, Pernod on the rocks. The kid, thank God, has already eaten; I hate having him at the table. He plays with his plastic thingy and favors me with occasional sour glares. Judith and I clink our cocktail glasses together, a stagy gesture. She produces a wintry smile. "Cheers," we say. Cheers.

"Why don't you move back downtown?" she asks. "We could see more of each other."

"It's cheap up there. Do we want to see more of each other?"

"Who else do we have?"

"You have Karl."

"I don't *have* him or anybody. Just my kid and my brother."

I think of the time when I tried to murder her in her bassinet. She doesn't know about that. "Are we really friends, Jude?"

"Now we are. At last."

"We haven't exactly been fond of each other all these years."

"People change, Duv. They grow up. I was dumb, a real shithead, so wrapped up in myself that I couldn't give anything but hate to anybody around me. That's over now. If you don't believe me, look into my head and see."

"You don't want me poking around in there."

"Go ahead," she says. "Take a good look and see if I haven't changed toward you."

"No. I'd rather not." I deal myself another two ounces of rum. The hand shakes a little. "Shouldn't you check the spaghetti sauce? Maybe it's boiling over."

"Let it boil. I haven't finished my drink. Duv, are you still having trouble? With your power, I mean."

"Yes. Still. Worse than ever."

"What do you think is happening?"

I shrug. Insouciant old me. "I'm losing it, that's all. It's like hair, I suppose. A lot of it when you're young, then less and less, and finally none. Fuck it. It never did me any good anyway."

"You don't mean that."

"Show me any good it did me, Jude."

"It made you someone special. It made you unique. When everything else went wrong for you, you could always fall back on that, the knowledge that you could go into minds, that you could see the unseeable, that you could get close to people's souls. A gift from God."

"A useless gift. Except if I'd gone into the sideshow business."

"It made you a richer person. More complex, more interesting. Without it you might have been someone quite ordinary."

"With it I turned out to be someone quite ordinary. A nobody, a zero. Without it I might have been a happy nobody instead of a dismal one."

"You pity yourself a lot, Duv."

"I've got a lot to pity myself for. More Pernod, Jude?"

"Thanks, no. I ought to look after dinner. Will you pour the wine?"

She goes into the kitchen. I do the wine thing; then I carry the salad bowl to the table. Behind me the kid begins to chant derisive nonsense syllables in his weirdly mature baritone. Even in my current state of dulled deceptivity I feel the pressure of the kid's cold hatred against the back of my skull. Judith returns, toting a well-laden tray: spaghetti, garlic bread, cheese. She flashes a warm smile, evidently sincere, as we sit down. We clink wine-glasses. We eat in silence a few minutes. I praise the spaghetti. She says, finally, "Can I do some mindreading on you, Duv?"

"Be my guest."

"You say you're glad the power's going. Is that snow-job directed at me or at yourself? Because you're snowing somebody. You hate the idea of losing it, don't you?"

"A little."

"A lot, Duv."

"All right, a lot. I'm of two minds. I'd like it to vanish completely. Christ, I wish I'd never had it. But on the other hand, if I lose it, who am I? Where's my identity? I'm Selig the Mindreader, right? The Amazing Mental Man. So if I stop being him—you see, Jude?"

"I see. The pain's all over your face. I'm so sorry, Duv."

"For what?"

"That you're losing it."

"You despised my guts for using it on you, didn't you?"

"That's different. That was a long time ago. I know what you must be going through, now. Do you have any idea why you're losing it?"

"No. A function of aging, I guess."

"Is there anything that might be done to stop it from going?"

"I doubt it, Jude. I don't even know why I have the gift in the first place, let alone how to nurture it now. I don't know how it works. It's just something in my head, a genetic fluke, a thing I was born with, like freckles. If your freckles start to fade, can you figure out a way of making them stay, if you want them to stay?"

"You've never let yourself be studied, have you?"

"No."

"Why not?"

"I don't like people poking in my head any more than you do," I say softly. "I don't want to be a case history. I've always kept a low profile. If the world ever found out about me, I'd become a pariah. I'd probably be lynched. Do you know how many people there are to whom I've openly admitted the truth about myself? In my whole life, how many?"

"A dozen."

"Three," I say. "And I wouldn't willingly have told any of them."

"Three?"

"You. I suppose you suspected it all along, but you didn't find out for sure till you were sixteen, remember? Then there's Tom Nyquist, who I don't see any more. And a girl named Kitty, who I don't see any more either."

"What about the tall brunette?"

"Toni? I never explicitly told her. I tried to hide it from her. She found out indirectly. A lot of people may have found out indirectly. But I've only told three. I don't want to be known as a freak. So let it fade. Let it die. Good riddance."

"You want to keep it, though."

"To keep it and lose it both."

"That's a contradiction."

"Do I contradict myself? Very well, then I contradict myself. I am large, I contain multitudes. What can I say, Jude? What can I tell you that's true?"

"Are you in pain?"

"Who isn't in pain?"

She says, "Losing it is almost like becoming impotent, isn't it, Duv? To reach into a mind and find out that you can't connect? You said there was ecstasy in it for you, once. That flood of information, that vicarious experience. And now you can't get it as much, or at all. Your mind can't get it up. Do you see it that way, as a sexual metaphor?"

"Sometimes." I give her more wine. For a few minutes we sit silently, shoveling down the spaghetti, exchanging tentative grins. I almost feel warmth toward her. Forgiveness for all the years when she treated me like a circus attraction. *You sneaky fucker, Duv, stay out of my head or I'll kill you! You voyeur. You peeper. Keep away, man, keep away.* She didn't want me to meet her fiancé. Afraid I'd tell him about

her other men, I guess. *I'd like to find you dead in the gutter some day,*
Duv, with all my secrets rotting inside you. So long ago. Maybe we
love each other a little now, Jude. Just a little, but you love me more
than I love you.

"I don't come any more," she says abruptly. "You know, I used to
come, practically every time. The original Hot Pants Kid, me. But
around five years ago something happened, around the time my marriage
was first breaking up. A short circuit down below. I started coming
every fifth time, every tenth time. Feeling the ability to respond slip
away from me. Lying there waiting for it to happen, and of course that
doused it every time. Finally I couldn't come at all. I still can't. Not in
three years. I've laid maybe a hundred men since the divorce, give or
take five or ten, and not one brought me off, and some of them were
studs, real bulls. It's one of the things Karl's going to work on with me.
So I know what it's like, Duv. What you must be going through. To
lose your best way of making contact with others. To lose contact gradually with yourself. To become a stranger in your own head." She
smiles. "Did you know that about me? About the troubles I've been
having in bed?"

I hesitate briefly. The icy glare in her eyes gives her away. The
aggressiveness. The resentment she feels. Even when she tries to be
loving she can't help hating. How fragile our relationship is! We're
locked in a kind of marriage, Judith and I, an old burned-out marriage
held together with skewers. What the hell, though. "Yes," I tell her. "I
knew about it."

"I thought so. You've never stopped probing me." Her smile is all
hateful glee now. She's glad I'm losing it. She's relieved. "I'm always
wide open to you, Duv."

"Don't worry, you won't be much longer." Oh, you sadistic bitch!
Oh, you beautiful ball-buster! And you're all I've got. "How about some
more spaghetti, Jude?" Sister. Sister. Sister.

14.

Yahya Lumumba
Humanities 2A, Dr. Katz
November 10, 1976

The "Electra" Theme in Aeschylus,
Sophocles, and Euripides

The use of the "Electra" motif by Aeschylus, Sophocles, and Euripides is a study in varying dramatic methods and modes of attack. The plot is basically the same in Aeschylus' *Choephori* and the *Electras* of Sophocles and Euripides: Orestes, exiled son of murdered Agamemnon, returns to his native Mycenae, where he discovers his sister Electra. She persuades him to avenge Agamemnon's murder by killing Clytemnestra and Aegisthus, who had slain Agamemnon on his return from Troy. The treatment of the plot varies greatly at the hands of each dramatist.

Aeschylus, unlike his later rivals, held as prime consideration the ethical and religious aspects of Orestes' crime. Characterization and motivation in *The Choephori* are simple to the point of inviting ridicule—as, indeed, can we see when the more worldly-minded Euripides ridicules Aeschylus in the recognition scene of his *Electra*. In Aeschylus' play Orestes appears accompanied by his friend Pylades and places an offering on Agamemnon's tomb: a lock of his hair. They withdraw, and lamenting Electra comes to the tomb. Noticing the lock of hair, she recognizes it as being "like unto those my father's children wear," and decides Orestes has sent it to the tomb as a token of mourning. Orestes then reappears, and identifies himself to Electra. It is this implausible means of identification which was parodied by Euripides.

Orestes reveals that Apollo's oracle had commanded him to avenge Agememnon's murder. In a long poetic passage, Electra steels Orestes' courage, and he goes forth to kill Clytemnestra and Aegisthus. He obtains entrance to the palace by deception, pretending to his mother Clytemnestra that he is a messenger from far-off Phocis, bearing news of Orestes' death. Once inside, he slays Aegisthus, and then, confronting his mother, he accuses her of the murder and kills her.

The play ends with Orestes, maddened by his crime, seeing the Furies coming to pursue him. He takes refuge in the temple of Apollo. The mystic and allegorical sequel, *The Eumenides*, sees Orestes absolved of blame.

Aeschylus, in short, was not overly concerned with the credibility of his play's action. His purpose in the *Oresteia* trilogy was a theological one: to examine the actions of the gods in placing a curse upon a house, a curse stemming from murder and leading to further murder. The keynote of his philosophy is perhaps the line, " 'Tis Zeus alone who shows the perfect way of knowledge: He hath ruled, men shall learn wisdom, by affliction schooled." Aeschylus sacrifices dramatic technique, or at least holds it in secondary importance, in order to focus attention on the religious and psychological aspects of the matricide.

The *Electra* of Euripides is virtually at an opposite pole from the concept of Aeschylus; though he uses the same plot, he elaborates and innovates to provide far richer texture. Electra and Orestes stand out in relief in Euripides: Electra a near-mad woman, banished from the court, married to a peasant, craving vengeance; Orestes a coward, sneaking into Mycenae the back way, abjectly stabbing Aegisthus from behind, luring Clytemnestra to her doom by a ruse. Euripides is concerned with dramatic credibility, whereas Aeschylus is not. After the famous parody of the Aeschylean recognition scene, Orestes makes himself known to Electra not by his hair or the size of his foot, but rather by

Oh God. Oh shit. Shit shit shit. This is deadly. This is no fucking good at all. Could Yahya Lumumba have written any of this crap? Phony from Word One. Why should Yahya Lumumba give a shit about Greek tragedy? Why should I? What's Hecuba to him or he to Hecuba, that he should weep for her? I'll tear this up and start again. I'll write it jivey, man. I'll give it dat ole watermelon rhythm. God help me to think black. But I can't. But I can't. But I can't. Christ, I'd like to throw up. I think I'm getting a fever. Wait. Maybe a joint would help some. Yeah. Let's get high and try again. A lil ole stick of mootah. Get some soul into it, man. Smartass white Jew-bastard, get some soul into it, you hear? Okay, now. There was this cat Agamemnon, he was one big important fucker, you hear, he was The Man, but he got fucked all the same. His old lady Clytemnestra, she was makin' it with this chickenshit muthafuck Aegisthus, and one day she say, Baby, let's waste old Aggie, you and me, and then you gonna be king—gwine be king?—gonna—and we have a high ole time. Aggie, he off in the Nam runnin' the show, but he come home for some R & R and before he know what happenin' they stick him good, right, they really cut him, and that all for *him.* Now there this crazy cunt Electra, dig, she the daughter of ole Aggie, and she get real uptight when they use him up, so she say to her brother, his name Orestes, she say, listen, Orestes, I want you to *get* them two muthafucks, I want you to get them real good. Now, this cat Orestes he been out of town for a while, he don't know the score, but—

Yeah, that's it, man! You're digging it! Now go on to explain about Euripides' use of the *deus ex machina* and the cathartic virtues of Sophocles' realistic dramatic technique. Sure. What a dumb schmuck you are, Selig. What a dumb schmuck.

15.

I tried to be good to Judith, I tried to be kind and loving, but our hatred kept coming between us. I said to myself, She's my kid sister, my only sibling, I must love her more. But you can't will love. You can't conjure it into existence on nothing more than good intentions. Besides, my intentions had never been that good. I saw her as a rival from the word go. I was the firstborn, I was the difficult one, the maladjusted one. I was supposed to be the center of everything. Those were the terms of my contract with God: I must suffer because I am different, but by way of compensation the entire universe will revolve about me. The girlbaby who was brought into the household was intended to be nothing more than a therapeutic aid designed to help me relate better to the human race. That was the deal: she wasn't supposed to have independent reality as a person, she wasn't supposed to have her own needs or make demands or drain away their love. Just a thing, an item of furniture. But I knew better than to believe that. I was ten years old, remember, when they adopted her. Your ten-year-old, he's no fool. I knew that my parents, no longer feeling obliged now to direct all their concern exclusively toward their mysteriously intense and troubled son, would rapidly and with great relief transfer their attention and their love—yes, particularly their love—to the cuddly, uncomplicated infant. She would take my place at the center; I'd become a quirky obsolescent artifact. I couldn't help resenting that. Do you blame me for trying to kill her in her bassinet? On the other hand you can understand the origin of her life-long coldness toward me. I offer no defense at this late date. The cycle of hatred began with me. With me, Jude, with me, with me, with me. You could have broken it with love, though, if you wanted to. You didn't want to.

On a Saturday afternoon in May, 1961, I went out to my parents' house. In those years I didn't go there often, though I lived twenty minutes away by subway. I was outside the family circle, autonomous and remote, and I felt powerful resistance to any kind of reattachment. For one thing I had free-floating hostilities toward my parents: it was their fluky genes, after all, that had sent me into the world this way. And then too there was Judith, shriveling me with her disdain: did I need more of that? So I stayed away from the three of them for weeks, months, at a time, until the melancholy maternal phonecalls became too much for me, until the weight of my guilt overcame my resistances.

I was happy to discover, when I got there, that Judith was still in her bedroom, asleep. At three in the afternoon? Well, my mother said, she was out very late last night on a date. Judith was sixteen, I imagined her going to a high school basketball game with some skinny pimply kid and sipping milkshakes afterwards. Sleep well, sister, sleep on and on. But of course her absence put me into direct and unshielded confrontation with my sad depleted parents. My mother, mild and dim; my father, weary and bitter. All my life they had steadily grown smaller. They seemed very small now. They seemed close to the vanishing point.

I had never lived in this apartment. For years Paul and Martha had struggled with the upkeep of a three-bedroom place they couldn't afford, simply because it had become impossible for Judith and me to share the same bedroom once she was past her infancy. The moment I left for college, taking a room near campus, they found a smaller and far less expensive one. Their bedroom was to the right of the entry foyer, and Judith's, down a long hall and past the kitchen, was to the left; straight ahead was the livingroom, in which my father sat dreamily leafing through the *Times*. He read nothing but the newspaper these days, though once his mind had been more active. From him came a dull sludgy emanation of fatigue. He was making some decent money for the first time in his life, actually would end up quite prosperous, yet he had conditioned himself to the poor-man psychology: poor Paul, you're a pitiful failure, you deserved so much better from life. I looked at the newspaper through his mind as he turned the pages. Yesterday Alan Shepard had made his epochal sub-orbital flight, the first manned venture into space by the United States. U.S. HURLS MAN 115 MILES INTO SPACE, cried the banner headline. SHEPARD WORKS CONTROLS IN CAPSULE, REPORTS BY RADIO IN 15-MINUTE FLIGHT. I groped for some way to connect with my father. "What did you think of the space voyage?" I asked. "Did you listen to the broadcast?" He shrugged. "Who gives a damn? It's all crazy. A mishigos. A waste of everybody's time and money." ELIZABETH VISITS POPE

IN VATICAN. Fat Pope John, looking like a well-fed rabbi. JOHNSON TO MEET LEADERS IN ASIA ON U.S. TROOP USE. He skimmed onward, skipping pages. HELP OF GOLDBERG ASKED ON ROCK-ETS. KENNEDY SIGNS WAGE-FLOOR BILL. Nothing registered on him, not even KENNEDY TO SEEK INCOME TAX CUTS. He lingered at the sports pages. A faint flicker of interest. MUD MAKES CARRY BACK STRONGER FAVORITE FOR 87th KENTUCKY DERBY TODAY. YANKS OPPOSE ANGELS IN OPENER OF 3-GAME SERIES BEFORE 21,000 ON COAST. "Who do you like in the Derby?" I asked. He shook his head. "What do I know about horses?" he said. He was, I realized, already dead, although in fact his heart would beat for another decade. He had stopped responding. The world had defeated him.

I left him to his brooding and made polite talk with my mother: her Hadassah reading group was discussing *To Kill a Mockingbird* next Thursday and she wanted to know if I had read it. I hadn't. What was I doing with myself? Had I seen any good movies? *L'Avventura*, I said. Is that a French film? she asked. Italian, I said. She wanted me to describe the plot. She listened patiently, looking troubled, not following anything. "Who did you go with?" she asked. "Are you seeing any nice girls?" My son the bachelor. Already 26 and not even engaged. I deflected the tiresome question with patient skill born of long experience. Sorry, Martha. I won't give you the grandchildren you're waiting for. You'll have to get them from Judith; it won't be all that long.

"I have to baste the chicken now," she said, and disappeared. I sat with my father for a while, until I couldn't stand that and went down the hall to the john, next to Judith's room. Her door was ajar. I glanced in. Lights off, blinds drawn, but I touched her mind and found that she was awake and thinking of getting up. All right, make a gesture, be friendly, Duvid. It won't cost you anything. I knocked lightly. "Hi, it's me," I said. "Okay if I come in?"

She was sitting up, wearing a frilly white bathrobe over dark-blue pajamas. Yawning, stretching. Her face, usually so taut, was puffy from too much sleep. Out of force of habit I went into her mind, and saw something new and surprising there. My sister's erotic inauguration. The night before. The whole thing: the scurry in the parked car, the rise of excitement, the sudden realization that this was going to be more than an interlude of petting, the panties coming down, the awkward shiftings of position, the fumble with the condom, the moment of ultimate hesitation giving way to total willingness, the hasty inexpert fingers coaxing lubrication out of the virgin crevice, the cautious clumsy poking, the thrust, the surprise of discovering that penetration was accomplished without pain, the pistoning of body against body, the boy's quick explosion, the messy aftermath, the guilt and confusion and disappointment as it ended with Judith still unsatisfied. The drive home, silent, shamefaced. Into the house, tiptoe, hoarsely greeting the vigilant, unsleeping parents. The late-night shower. Inspection and cleansing of the deflowered and slightly swollen vulva. Uneasy sleep, frequently punctured. A long stretch of wakefulness, in which the night's event is considered: she is pleased and relieved to have entered womanhood, but also frightened. Unwillingness to rise and face the world the next day, especially to face Paul and Martha. Judith, your secret is no secret to me.

"How are you?" I asked.

Stagily casual, she drawled, "Sleepy. I was out very late. How come you're here?"

"I drop in to see the family now and then."

"Nice to have seen you."

"That isn't friendly, Jude. Am I that loathsome to you?"

"Why are you bothering me, Duv?"

"I told you, I'm trying to be sociable. You're my only sister, the only one I'll ever have. I thought I'd stick my head in the door and say hello."

"You've done that. So?"

"You might tell me what you've been doing with yourself since the last time I saw you."

"Do you care?"

"If I didn't care, would I ask?"

"Sure," she said. "You don't give a crap about what I've been doing. You don't give a crap about anybody but David Selig, and why pretend otherwise? You don't need to ask me polite questions. It isn't natural coming from you."

"Hey, hold on!" Let's not be dueling so fast, sister. "What gives you the idea that—"

"Do you think of me from one week to the next? I'm just furniture to you. The drippy little sister. The brat. The inconvenience. Have you ever talked to me? About anything? Do you even know the name of the school I go to? I'm a total stranger to you."

"No, you're not."

"What the hell *do* you know about me?"

"Plenty."

"For example."

"Quit it, Jude."

"One example. Just one. One thing about me. For example—"

"For example. All right. For example, I know that you got laid last night."

We were both amazed by that. I stood in shocked silence, not believing that I had allowed those words to pass my lips; and Judith jerked as though electrified, her body stiffening and rearing, her eyes blazing with astonishment. I don't know how long we remained frozen, unable to speak.

"What?" she said finally. "What did you say, Duv?"

"You heard it."

"I heard it but I think I must have dreamed it. Say it again."

"No."

"Why not?"

"Leave me alone, Jude."

"Who told you?"

"Please, Jude—"

"Who told you?"

"Nobody," I muttered.

Her smile was terrifyingly triumphant. "You know something? I believe you. I honestly believe you. Nobody told you. You pulled it right out of my mind, didn't you, Duv?"

"I wish I had never come in here."

"Admit it. Why won't you admit it? You see into people's minds, don't you, Duvid? You're some kind of circus freak. I've suspected that a long time. All those little hunches you have, and they always turn out to be right, and the embarrassed phony way you cover up for yourself when you're right. Talking about your 'luck' at guessing things. Sure! Sure, luck! I knew the real scoop. I said to myself, This fucker is reading my mind. But I told myself it was crazy, there aren't any such people, it has to be impossible. Only it's true, isn't it? You don't guess. You look. We're wide open to you and you read us like books. Spying on us. Isn't that so?"

I heard a sound behind me. I jumped, frightened. But it was only Martha, poking her head into Judith's bedroom. A vague, dreamy grin. "Good morning, Judith. Or good afternoon, I should say. Having a nice chat, children? I'm so glad. Don't forget to have breakfast, Judith." And she drifted on her way.

Judith said sharply, "Why didn't you tell her? Describe the whole thing. Who I was with last night, what I did with him, how it felt—"

"Stop it, Jude."

"You didn't answer my other question. You've got this weird power, don't you? *Don't you?*"

"Yes."

"And you've been secretly spying on people all your life."

"Yes. Yes."

"I knew it. I didn't know, but I really did, all along. And it explains so much. Why I always felt dirty when I was a kid and you were around. Why I felt as if anything I did was likely to show up in tomorrow's newspapers. I never had any privacy, even when I was locked in the bathroom. I didn't *feel* private." She shuddered. "I hope I never see you again, Duv. Now that I know what you are. I wish I never *had* seen you. If I ever catch you poking around in my head after this, I'll cut your balls off. Got that? I'll cut your balls off. Now clear out of here so I can get dressed."

I stumbled away. In the bathroom I gripped the cold edge of the sink and leaned close to the mirror to study my flushed, flustered face. I looked stunned and dazed, my features as rigid as though I had had a stroke. *I know that you got laid last night.* Why had I told her that? An accident? The words spilling out of me because she had goaded me past the point of prudence? But I had never let anyone push me into a revelation like that before. There are no accidents, Freud said. There are never any slips of the tongue. Everything's deliberate, on one level or another. I must have said what I did to Judith because I wanted her at last to know the truth about me. But why? Why her? I had already told Nyquist, yes; there could be no risk in that; but I had never admitted it to anyone else. Always taken such great pains to conceal it, eh, Miss Mueller? And now Judith knew. I had given her a weapon with which she could destroy me.

I had given her a weapon. How strange that she never chose to use it.

16.

Nyquist said, "The real trouble with you, Selig, is that you're a deeply religious man who doesn't happen to believe in God." Nyquist was always saying things like that, and Selig never could be sure whether he meant them or was just playing verbal games. No matter how deeply Selig penetrated the other man's soul, he never could be sure of anything. Nyquist was too wily, too elusive.

Playing it safe, Selig said nothing. He stood with his back to Nyquist, looking out the window. Snow was falling. The narrow streets below were choked with it; not even the municipal snowplows could get through, and a strange serenity prevailed. High winds whipped the drifts about. Parked cars were disappearing under the white blanket. A few janitors from the apartment houses on the block were out, digging manfully. It had been snowing on and off for three days. Snow was general all over the Northeast. It was falling on every filthy city, on the arid suburbs, falling softly upon the Appalachians and, farther eastward, softly falling into the dark mutinous Atlantic waves. Nothing was moving in New York City. Everything was shut down: office buildings, schools, the concert halls, the theaters. The railroads were out of commission and the highways were blocked. There was no action at the airports. Basketball games were being canceled at Madison Square Garden. Unable to get to work, Selig had waited out most of the blizzard in Nyquist's apartment, spending so much time with him that by now he had come to find his friend's company stifling and oppressive. What earlier had seemed amusing and charming in Nyquist had become abrasive and tricksy. Nyquist's bland self-assurance conveyed itself now as smugness; his casual forays into Selig's mind were no longer affectionate gestures of intimacy, but rather, conscious acts of aggression.

His habit of repeating aloud what Selig was thinking was increasingly irritating, and there seemed to be no deterring him from that. Here he was doing it again, plucking a quotation from Selig's head and declaiming it in half-mocking tones: "Ah. How pretty. 'His soul swooned slowly as he heard the snow falling faintly through the universe and faintly falling, like the descent of their last end, upon all the living and the dead.' I like that. What is it, David?"

"James Joyce," said Selig sourly. " 'The Dead,' from *Dubliners*. I asked you yesterday not to do that."

"I envy the breadth and depth of your culture. I like to borrow fancy quotations from you."

"Fine. Do you always have to play them back at me?"

Nyquist, gesturing broadly as Selig stepped away from the window, humbly turned his palms outward. "I'm sorry. I forgot you didn't like it."

"You never forget a thing, Tom. You never do anything accidentally." Then, guilty over his peevishness: "Christ, I've had about enough snow!"

"Snow is general," said Nyquist. "It isn't ever going to stop. What are we going to do today?"

"The same as yesterday and the day before, I imagine. Sitting around watching the snowflakes fall and listening to records and getting sloshed."

"How about getting laid?"

"I don't think you're my type," Selig said.

Nyquist flashed an empty smile. "Funny man. I mean finding a couple of ladies marooned somewhere in this building and inviting them to a little party. You don't think there are two available ladies under this roof?"

"We could look, I suppose," Selig said, shrugging. "Is there any more bourbon?"

"I'll get it," Nyquist said.

He brought the bottle over. Nyquist moved with a strange slowness, like a man moving through a dense reluctant atmosphere of mercury or some other viscous fluid. Selig had never seen him hurry. He was heavy without being fat, a thick-shouldered, thick-necked man with a square head, close-cropped yellow hair, a flat wide-flanged nose, and an easy, innocent grin. Very, very Aryan: he was Scandinavian, a Swede perhaps, raised in Finland and transplanted to the United States at the age of 10. He still had the elusive traces of an accent. He said he was 28 and looked a few years older than that to Selig, who had just turned 23. This was February, 1958, in an era when Selig still had the delusion that he was going to make it in the adult world. Eisenhower was President, the stock market had gone to hell, the post-Sputnik emotional slump was troubling everybody even though the first American space satellite had just been orbited, and the latest feminine fashion was the gunny-sack chemise. Selig was living in Brooklyn Heights, on Pierrepont Street, commuting several days a week to the lower Fifth Avenue office of a publishing company for which he was doing freelance copyediting at $3 an hour. Nyquist lived in the same building, four floors higher.

He was the only other person Selig knew who had the power. Not only that, having it hadn't crippled him at all. Nyquist used his gift as simply and naturally as he did his eyes or his legs, for his own advantage, without apologies and without guilt. Perhaps he was the least neurotic person Selig had ever met. By occupation he was a predator, skimming an income by raiding the minds of others; but, like any jungle cat, he pounced only when hungry, never for sheer love of pouncing. He took what he needed, never questioning the providence that had made him so superbly fitted for taking, yet he did not take more than he needed, and his needs were moderate. He held no job and apparently never had. Whenever he wanted money he made the ten-minute subway ride to Wall Street, sauntered through the gloomy canyons of the financial district, and rummaged about freely in the minds of the moneymen cloistered in the lofty boardrooms. On any given day there was always some major development hatching that would have an impact on the market—a merger, a stock split, an ore discovery, a favorable earnings report—and Nyquist had no difficulty learning the essential details. This information he swiftly sold at handsome but reasonable fees to some twelve or fifteen private investors who had learned in the happiest possible way that Nyquist was a reliable tout. Many of the unaccountable leaks on which quick fortunes had been made in the bull market of the '50's were his doing. He earned a comfortable living this way, enough to support himself in a congenial style. His apartment was small and agreeable—black Naugahyde upholstery, Tiffany lamps, Picasso wallpaper, a well-stocked liquor closet, a superb music system that emitted a seamless flow of Monteverdi and Palestrina, Bartok and Stravinsky. He lived a gracious bachelor life, going out often, making the rounds of his favorite restaurants, all of them obscure and ethnic—Japanese, Pakistani, Syrian, Greek. His circle of friends was limited but distinguished: painters, writers, musicians, poets, mainly. He slept with many women, but Selig rarely saw him with the same one twice.

Like Selig, Nyquist could receive but was unable to send; he was, however, able to tell when his own mind was being probed. That was how they had happened to meet. Selig, newly arrived in the building, had indulged himself in his hobby, letting his consciousness rove freely from floor to floor by way of getting acquainted with his neighbors. Bouncing about, surveying this head and that, finding nothing of any special interest, and then suddenly:

—Tell me where you are.

A crystalline string of words glimmering at the periphery of a sturdy, complacent mind. The statement came through with the immediacy of an explicit message. Yet Selig realized that no act of active transmission had taken place; he had simply found the words lying passively in wait. He made quick reply:

—35 Pierrepont Street.

—No, I know that. I mean, where are you in the building?

—Fourth floor.

—I'm on the eighth. What's your name?

—Selig.

—Nyquist.

The mental contact was stunningly intimate. It was almost a sexual thing, as though he were slicing into a body, not a mind, and he was abashed by the resonant masculinity of the soul he had entered; he felt that there was something not quite permissible about such closeness with another man. But he did not draw back. That rapid interplay of verbal communication across the gap of darkness was a delicious experience, too rewarding to reject. Selig had the momentary illusion of having expanded his powers, of having learned how to send as well as to draw forth the contents of other minds. It was, he knew, only an illusion. He was sending nothing, nor was Nyquist. He and Nyquist were merely picking information out of each other's minds. Each planted phrases for the other to find, which was not quite the same thing, in terms of the situational dynamics, as sending messages to one another. It was a fine and possibly pointless distinction, though; the net effect of the juxtaposition of two wide-open receivers was an efficient send/receive circuit as reliable as a telephone. The marriage of true minds, to which let no impediments be admitted. Tentatively, self-consciously, Selig reached into the lower levels of Nyquist's consciousness, seeking the man as well as the messages, and as he did so he was vaguely aware of disquiet in the depths of his own mind, probably indicating that Nyquist was doing the same to him. For long minutes they explored each other like lovers entwined in the first discovering caresses, although there was nothing loving about Nyquist's touch, which was cool and impersonal. Nevertheless Selig quivered; he felt as if he stood at the edge of an

abyss. At last he gently withdrew, as did Nyquist. Then, from the other:
—Come upstairs. I'll meet you by the elevator.

He was bigger than Selig expected, a fullback of a man, his blue
eyes uninviting, his smile a purely formal one. He was remote without
actually being cold. They went into his apartment: soft lights, unfamiliar
music playing, an atmosphere of unostentatious elegance. Nyquist offered him a drink and they talked, keeping out of one another's minds
as much as possible. It was a subdued visit, unsentimental, no tears of
joy at having come together at last. Nyquist was affable, inaccessible,
pleased that Selig had appeared, but not at all delirious with excitement
at the discovery of a fellow freak. Possibly it was because he had discovered fellow freaks before. "There are others," he said. "You're the
third, fourth, fifth I've met since I came to the States. Let's see: one in
Chicago, one in San Francisco, one in Miami, one in Minneapolis.
You're the fifth. Two women, three men."

"Are you still in touch with the others?"

"No."

"What happened?"

"We drifted apart," Nyquist said. "What did you expect? That we'd
be clannish? Look, we talked, we played games with our minds, we got
to know each other, and after a while we got bored. I think two of them
are dead now. I don't mind being isolated from the rest of my kind. I
don't think of myself as one of a tribe."

"I never met another one," said Selig. "Until today."

"It isn't important. What's important is living your own life. How
old were you when you found out you could do it?"

"I don't know. Five, six years old, maybe. And you?"

"I didn't realize I had anything special until I was eleven. I thought
everybody could do it. It was only after I came to the States and heard
people thinking in a different language that I knew there was something
out of the ordinary about my mind."

"What kind of work do you do?" Selig asked.

"As little as I can," said Nyquist. He grinned and thrust his perceptors brusquely into Selig's mind. It seemed like an invitation of sorts;
Selig accepted it and pushed forth his own antennae. Roaming the other
man's consciousness, he quickly grasped the picture of Nyquist's Wall
Street sorties. He saw the entire balanced, rhythmic, unobsessive life of
the man. He was amazed by Nyquist's coolness, his wholeness, his
clarity of spirit. How limpid Nyquist's soul was! How unmarred by life!
Where did he keep his anguish? Where did he hide his loneliness, his
fear, his insecurity? Nyquist, withdrawing, said, "Why do you feel so
sorry for yourself?"

"Do I?"

"It's all over your head. What's the problem, Selig? I've looked into you and I don't see the problem, only the pain."

"The problem is that I feel isolated from other human beings."

"Isolated? You? You can get right inside people's heads. You can do something that 99.999% of the human race can't do. They've got to struggle along using words, approximations, semaphore signals, and you go straight to the core of meaning. How can you pretend you're isolated?"

"The information I get is useless," Selig said. "I can't act on it. I might just as well not be reading it in."

"Why?"

"Because it's just voyeurism. I'm spying on them."

"You feel guilty about that?"

"Don't you?"

"I didn't ask for my gift," Nyquist said. "I just happen to have it. Since I have it, I use it. I like it. I like the life I lead. I like myself. Why don't you like yourself, Selig?"

"You tell me."

But Nyquist had nothing to tell him, and when he finished his drink he went back downstairs. His own apartment seemed so strange to him as he re-entered it that he spent a few minutes handling familiar artifacts: his parents' photograph, his little collection of adolescent love-letters, the plastic toy that the psychiatrist had given him years ago. The presence of Nyquist continued to buzz in his mind—a residue of the visit, nothing more, for Selig was certain that Nyquist was not now probing him. He felt so jarred by their meeting, so intruded upon, that he resolved never to see him again, in fact to move somewhere else as soon as possible, to Manhattan, to Philadelphia, to Los Angeles, anywhere that might be beyond Nyquist's reach. All his life he had yearned to meet someone who shared his gift, and now that he had, he felt threatened by it. Nyquist was so much in control of his life that it was terrifying. He'll humiliate me, Selig thought. He'll devour me. But that panic faded. Two days later Nyquist came around to ask him out to dinner. They ate in a nearby Mexican restaurant and got smashed on Carta Blanca. It still appeared to Selig that Nyquist was toying with him, teasing him, holding him at arm's length and tickling him; but it was all done so amiably that Selig felt no resentment. Nyquist's charm was irresistible, and his strength was worth taking as a model of behavior. Nyquist was like an older brother who had preceded him through this same vale of traumas and had emerged unscathed long ago; now he was jollying Selig into an acceptance of the terms of his existence. The superhuman condition, Nyquist called it.

They became close friends. Two or three times a week they went out together, ate together, drank together. Selig had always imagined that a friendship with someone else of his kind would be uniquely intense, but this was not; after the first week they took their specialness for granted and rarely discussed the gift they shared, nor did they ever congratulate each other on having formed an alliance against the ungifted world around them. They communicated sometimes by words, sometimes by the direct contact of minds; it became an easy, cheerful relationship, strained only when Selig slipped into his habitual brooding mood and Nyquist mocked him for such self-indulgence. Even that was no difficulty between them until the days of the blizzard, when all tensions became exaggerated because they were spending so much time together.

"Hold out your glass," Nyquist said.

He poured an amber splash of bourbon. Selig settled back to drink while Nyquist set about finding girls for them. The project took him five minutes. He scanned the building and turned up a pair of roommates on the fifth floor. "Take a look," he said to Selig. Selig entered Nyquist's mind. Nyquist had attuned himself to the consciousness of one of the girls—sensual, sleepy, kittenish—and was looking through her eyes at the other, a tall gaunt blonde. The doubly refracted mental image nevertheless was quite clear: the blonde had a leggy voluptuousness and fashion-model poise. "That one's mine," Nyquist said. "Now tell me if you like yours." He jumped, Selig following along, to the mind of the blonde. Yes, a fashion model, more intelligent than the other girl, cold, selfish, passionate. From her mind, via Nyquist, came the image of her roommate, sprawled out on a sofa in a pink housecoat: a short plump redhead, breasty, full-faced. "Sure," Selig said. "Why not?" Nyquist, rummaging through minds, found the girls' phone number, called, worked his charm. They came up for drinks. "This awful snowstorm," the blonde said, shuddering. "It can drive you crazy!" The four of them went through a lot of liquor to a tinkling jazz accompaniment: Mingus, MJQ, Chico Hamilton. The redhead was better-looking than Selig expected, not quite so plump or coarse—the double refraction must have introduced some distortions—but she giggled too much, and he found himself disliking her to some degree. Still, there was no backing out now. Eventually, very late in the evening, they coupled off, Nyquist and the blonde in the bedroom, Selig and the redhead in the livingroom. Selig grinned selfconsciously at her when they were finally alone. He had never learned how to suppress that infantile grin, which he knew must reveal a mingling of gawky anticipation and plummeting terror. "Hello," he said. They kissed and his hands went to her breasts, and she pushed herself up against him in an unashamedly hungry way. She seemed a few years older than he was, but most women seemed that way to him. Their clothes dropped away. "I like lean men," she said, and giggled as she pinched his sparse flesh. Her breasts rose to him like pink birds. He caressed her with a virgin's timid intensity. During the months of their friendship Nyquist had occasionally supplied him with his own discarded women, but it was weeks since he had been to bed with anyone, and he was afraid that his abstinence would rush him into an embarrassing calamity. No: the liquor cooled his ardor just enough, and he held himself in check, ploughing her solemnly and energetically with no fears of going off too fast.

About the time he realized the redhead was too drunk to come, Selig felt a tickle in his skull: Nyquist was probing him! This show of curiosity, this voyeurism, seemed an odd diversion for the usually self-contained Nyquist. Spying's *my* trick, Selig thought, and for a moment he was so disturbed by being observed in the act of love that he began to soften. Through conscious effort he reconstituted himself. This has no deep significance, he told himself. Nyquist is wholly amoral and does what he pleases, peeks here and peeks there without regard for propriety, and why should I let his scanning bother me? Recovering, he reached toward Nyquist and reciprocated the probe. Nyquist welcomed him:

—How you doing, Davey?

—Fine. Just fine.

—I got me a hot one here. Take a look.

Selig envied Nyquist's cool detachment. No shame, no guilt, no hangups of any kind. No trace of exhibitionistic pride nor voyeuristic panting, either: it seemed altogether natural to him to exchange such contacts now. Selig, though, could not help feeling queasy as he watched, through closed eyes, Nyquist busily working over the blonde, and watched Nyquist similarly watching him, echoing images of their parallel copulations reverberating dizzily from mind to mind. Nyquist, pausing a moment to detect and isolate Selig's sense of uneasiness, mocked it gently. You're worried that there's some kind of latent gayness in this thing, Nyquist told him. But I think what really scares you is contact, any sort of contact. Right? Wrong, Selig said, but he had felt the point hit home. For five minutes more they monitored each other's minds, until Nyquist decided the time had come to come, and the tempestuous tremors of his nervous system flung Selig, as usual, from his consciousness. Soon after, growing bored with humping the jiggling, sweaty redhead, Selig let his own climax overwhelm him and slumped down, shivering, weary.

Nyquist came into the livingroom half an hour later, the blonde with him, both of them naked. He didn't bother to knock, which surprised the redhead a little; Selig had no way of telling her that Nyquist had known they were finished. Nyquist put some music on and they all sat quietly, Selig and the redhead working on the bourbon, Nyquist and the blonde nipping into the Scotch, and toward dawn, as the snow began to slacken, Selig tentatively suggested a second round of lovemaking with a change of partners. "No," the redhead said. "I'm all fucked out. I want to go to sleep. Some other time, okay?" She fumbled for her clothes. At the door, wobbling and staggering, making a boozy farewell, she let something slip. "I can't help thinking there's something peculiar about you two guys," she said. *In vino veritas.* "You aren't a couple of queers, by any chance, are you?"

17.

I remain on dead center. Becalmed, static, anchored. No, that's a lie, or if not a lie then at the very least a benign misstatement, a faulty cluster of metaphors. I am ebbing. Ebbing all the time. My tide is going out. I am revealed as a bare rocky shore, iron-hard, with trailing streamers of dirty brown seaweed dangling toward the absenting surf. Green crabs scuttling about. Yes, I ebb, which is to say I diminish, I attenuate. Do you know, I feel quite calm about it now? Of course my moods fluctuate but

I feel

Quite calm

About it now.

This is the third year since first I began to recede from myself. I think it started in the spring of 1974. Up till then it worked faultlessly, I mean the power, always there when I had occasion to call upon it, always dependable, doing all its customary tricks, serving me in all my dirty needs; and then without warning, without reason, it began dying. Little failures of input. Tiny episodes of psychic impotence. I associate these events with early spring, blackened wisps of late snow still clinging to the streets, and it could not have been '75 nor was it '73, which leads me to place the onset of outgo in the intermediate year. I would be snug and smug inside someone's head, scanning scandals thought to be safely hidden, and suddenly everything would blur and become uncertain. Rather like reading the *Times* and having the text abruptly turn to Joycean dream-gabble between one line and the next, so that a straightforward dreary account of the latest Presidential fact-finding commission's finding of futile facts has metamorphosed into a foggy impenetrable report on old Earwicker's borborygmi. At such times I would falter and pull out in fear. What would you do if you believed you were in bed with your heart's desire and awakened to find yourself screwing a starfish? But these unclarities and distortions were not the worst part: I think the inversions were, the total reversal of signal. Such as picking up a flash of love when what is really being radiated is frosty hatred. Or vice versa. When that happens I want to pound on walls to test reality. From Judith one day I got strong waves of sexual desire, an overpowering incestuous yearning, which cost me a fine dinner as I ran nauseated and retching to the bowl. All an error, all a deception; she was aiming spears at me and I took them for Cupid's arrows, more fool I. Well, after that I got blank spaces, tiny deaths of perception in mid-contact, and after that came mingled inputs, crossed wires, two minds coming in at once and me unable to tell the which from the which. For a time the color appercept dropped out, though that has come back, one of the many false returns. And there were other losses, barely discernible ones but cumulative in their effect. I make lists now of the things I once could do that I can no longer. Inventories of the shrinkage. Like a dying man confined to his bed, paralyzed but observant, watching his relatives pilfer his goods. This day the television set has gone, and this day the Thackeray first editions, and this day the spoons, and now they have made off with my Piranesi, and tomorrow it will be the pots and pans, the Venetian blinds, my neckties, and my trousers, and by next week they will be taking toes, intestines, corneas, testicles, lungs, and nostrils. What will they use my nostrils for? I used to fight back with long walks, cold showers, tennis, massive doses of Vitamin A, and other hopeful, implausible remedies, and more recently I experimented with fasting and pure thoughts, but such struggling now seems to me inappropriate and even blasphemous; these days I strive toward cheerful acceptance of loss, with such success as you may have already perceived. Aeschylus warns me not to kick against the pricks, also Euripides and I believe Pindar, and if I were to check the New Testament I think I would find the injunction there as well, and so I obey, I kick not, even when the pricks are fiercest. I accept, I accept. Do you see that quality of acceptance growing in me? Make no mistake, I am sincere. This morning, at least, I am well on my way to acceptance, as golden autumn sunlight floods my room and expands my tattered soul. I lie here practicing the techniques that will make me invulnerable to the knowledge that it's all fleeing from me. I search for the joy that I know lies buried in the awareness of decline. Grow old along with me! The best is yet to be, The last of life, for which the first was made. Do you believe that? I believe that. I'm getting better at believing all sorts of things. Why, sometimes I've believed as many as six impossible things before breakfast. Good old Browning! How comforting he is:

> Then welcome each rebuff
> That turns earth's smoothness rough,
> Each sting that bids not sit nor stand, but go!
>
> Be our joys three parts pain!
> Strive, and hold cheap the strain.

Yes. Of course. And be our pains three parts joy, he might have added. Such joy this morning. And it's all fleeing from me, all ebbing. Going out of me from every pore.

Silence is coming over me. I will speak to no one after it's gone. And no one will speak to me.

I stand here over the bowl patiently pissing my power away. Naturally I feel some sorrow over what's happening, I feel regret, I feel—why crap around?—I feel anger and frustration and despair, but also, strangely, I feel shame. My cheeks burn, my eyes will not meet other eyes, I can hardly face my fellow mortals for the shame of it, as if something precious has been entrusted to me and I have failed in my trusteeship. I must say to the world, I've wasted my assets, I've squandered my patrimony, I've let it slip away, going, going, I'm a bankrupt now, a bankrupt. Perhaps this is a family trait, this embarrassment when disaster comes. We Seligs like to tell the world we are orderly people, captains of our souls, and when something external downs us we are abashed. I remember when my parents briefly owned a car, a dark-green 1948 Chevrolet purchased at some absurdly low price in 1950, and we were driving somewhere deep in Queens, perhaps on our way to my grandmother's grave, the annual pilgrimage, and a car emerged from a blind alley and hit us. A schvartze at the wheel, drunk, giddy. Nobody hurt, but our fender badly crumpled and our grille broken, the distinctive T-bar that identified the 1948 model hanging loose. Though the accident was in no way his fault my father reddened and reddened, transmitting feverish embarrassment, as though he were apologizing to the universe for having done anything so thoughtless as allowing his car to be hit. How he apologized to the other driver, too, my grim bitter father! It's all right, it's all right, accidents can happen, you mustn't feel upset about it, see, we're all okay! Looka mah car, man, looka mah car, the other driver kept saying, evidently aware that he was on to a soft touch, and

I feared my father was going to give him money for the repairs, but my mother, fearing the same thing, headed him off at the pass. A week later he was still embarrassed; I popped into his mind while he was talking with a friend and heard him trying to pretend my mother had been driving, which was absurd—she never had a license—and then I felt embarrassed for him. Judith, too, when her marriage broke up, when she walked out on an impossible situation, registered enormous grief over the shameful fact that someone so purposeful and effective in life as Judith Hannah Selig should have entered into a lousy, murderous marriage which had to be terminated vulgarly in the divorce courts. Ego, ego, ego. I the miraculous mindreader, entering upon a mysterious decline, apologizing for my carelessness. I have misplaced my gift somewhere. Will you forgive me?

> Good, to forgive;
> Best, to forget!
> Living, we fret;
> Dying, we live.

Take an imaginary letter, Mr. Selig. Harrumph. Miss Kitty Holstein, Something West Sixty-something Street, New York City. Check the address later. Don't bother about the zipcode.

Dear Kitty:

I know you haven't heard from me in ages but I think now it's appropriate to try to get in touch with you again. Thirteen years have passed and a certain maturity must have come over both of us, I think, healing old wounds and making communication possible. Despite all hard feelings that may once have existed between us I never lost my fondness for you, and you remain bright in my mind.

Speaking of my mind, there's something I ought to tell you. I no longer do things very well with it. By "things" I mean the mental thing, the mindreading trick, which of course I couldn't do on you in any case, but which defined and shaped my relationship to everybody else in the world. This power seems to be slipping away from me now. It caused us so much grief, remember? It was what ultimately split us up, as I tried to explain in my last letter to you, the one you never answered. In another year or so—who knows, six months, a month, a week?—it will be totally gone and I will be just an ordinary human being, like yourself. I will be a freak no longer. Perhaps then there will be an opportunity for us to resume the relationship that was interrupted in 1963 and to reestablish it on a more realistic footing.

I know I did dumb things then. I pushed you mercilessly. I refused

*to accept you for yourself, and tried to make something else out of you,
something freakish, in fact, something just like myself. I had good reasons in theory for attempting that, I thought then, but of course they
were wrong, they had to be wrong, and I never saw that until it was
too late. To you I seemed domineering, overpowering, dictatorial—me,
mild self-effacing me! Because I was trying to transform you. And eventually I bored you. Of course you were very young then, you were—
shall I say it?—shallow, unformed, and you resisted me. But now that
we're both adults we might be able to make a go of it.*

    *I hardly know what my life will be like as an ordinary human being
unable to enter minds. Right now I'm floundering, looking for definitions
of myself, looking for structures. I'm thinking seriously of entering the
Roman Catholic Church.* (Good Christ, am I? That's the first I've heard
of that! The stink of incense, the mumble of priests, is that what I want?)
*Or perhaps the Episcopalians, I don't know. It's a matter of affiliating
myself with the human race. And also I want to fall in love again. I
want to be part of someone else. I've already begun tentatively, timidly
getting in touch with my sister Judith again, after a whole lifetime of
warfare; we're starting to relate to each other for the first time, and
that's encouraging to me. But I need more: a woman to love, not just
sexually but in all ways. I've really had that only twice in my life, once
with you, once about five years later with a girl named Toni who wasn't
very much like you, and both times this power of mine ruined things,
once because I got too close with it, once because I couldn't get close
enough. As the power slips away from me, as it dies, perhaps there's a
chance for an ordinary human relationship between us at last, of the
kind that ordinary human beings have all the time. For I will be ordinary. For I will be very ordinary.*

    *I wonder about you. You're 35 years old now, I think. That sounds
very old to me, even though I'm 41. (41 doesn't sound old, somehow!)
I still think of you as being 22. You seemed even younger than that:
sunny, open, naive. Of course that was my fantasy-image of you; I had
nothing to go by but externals, I couldn't do my usual number on your
psyche, and so I made up a Kitty who probably wasn't the real Kitty at
all. Anyway, so you're 35. I imagine you look younger than that today.
Did you marry? Of course you did. A happy marriage? Lots of kids?
Are you still married? What's your married name, then, and where do
you live, and how can I find you? If you're married, will you be able
to see me anyway? Somehow I don't think you'd be a completely faithful
wife—does that insult you?—and so there ought to be room in your life
for me, as a friend, as a lover. Do you ever see Tom Nyquist? Did you
go on seeing him for long, after you and I broke up? Were you bitter*

toward me for the things I told you about him in that letter? If your marriage has broken up, or if somehow you never married, would you live with me now? Not as a wife, not yet, just as a companion. To help me get through the last phases of what's happening to me? I need help so much. I need love. I know that's a lousy way to go about making a proposition, let alone a proposal, that is, saying, Help me, comfort me, stay with me. I'd rather reach to you in strength than in weakness. But right now I'm weak. There's this globe of silence growing in my head, expanding, expanding, filling my whole skull, creating this big empty place. I'm suffering a slow reality leakage. I can only see the edges of things, not their substance, and now the edges are getting indistinct too. Oh, Christ. Kitty I need you. Kitty how will I find you? Kitty I hardly knew you. Kitty Kitty Kitty

Twang. The plangent chord. *Twing.* The breaking string. *Twong.* The lyre untuned. Twang. Twing. Twong.

Dear children of God, my sermon this morning will be a very short one. I wish only that you should ponder and meditate the deep meaning and mystery of a few lines I intend to rip off the saintly Tom Eliot, a thoughtful guide for troubled times. Beloved, I direct you to his *Four Quartets*, to his paradoxical line, "In my beginning is my end," which he amplifies some pages later with the comment, "What we call the beginning is often the end/ And to make an end is to make a beginning." Some of us are ending right now, dear children; that is to say, aspects of their lives that once were central to them are drawing to a close. Is this an end or is it a beginning? Can the end of one thing not be the beginning of another? I think so, beloved. I think that the closing of a door does not preclude the opening of a different door. Of course, it takes courage to walk through that new door when we do not know what may lie beyond it, but one who has faith in Our Lord who died for us, who trusts fully in Him who came for the salvation of man, need have no fears. Our lives are pilgrimages toward Him. We may die small deaths every day, but we are reborn from death to death, until at last we go into the dark, into the vacant interstellar spaces where He awaits us, and why should we fear that, if He is there? And until that time comes let us live our lives without giving way to the temptation to grieve for ourselves. Remember always that the world still is full of wonders, that there are always new quests, that seeming ends are not ends in truth, but only transitions, stations of the way. Why should we mourn? Why should we give ourselves over to sorrow, though our lives be daily subtractions? If we lose *this*, do we also lose *that*? If sight goes, does love go also? If feeling grows faint, may we not return to old feelings and draw comfort from them? Much of our pain is mere confusion.

Be then of good cheer on this Our Lord's day, beloved, and spin no snares in which to catch yourselves, nor allow yourselves the self-indulgent sin of misery, and make no false distinctions between ends and beginnings, but go onward, ever searching, to new ecstasies, to new communions, to new worlds, and give no space in your soul to fear, but yield yourself up to the Peace of Christ and await that which must come. In the Name of the Father, and of the Son, and of the Holy Ghost. Amen.

Now comes a dark equinox out of its proper moment. The bleached moon glimmers like a wretched old skull. The leaves shrivel and fall. The fires die down. The dove, wearying, flutters to earth. Darkness spreads. Everything blows away. The purple blood falters in the narrowing veins; the chill impinges on the straining heart; the soul dwindles; even the feet become untrustworthy. Words fail. Our guides admit they are lost. That which has been solid grows transparent. Things pass away. Colors fade. This is a gray time, and I fear it will be grayer still, one of these days. Tenants of the house, thoughts of a dry brain in a dry season.

18.

When Toni moved out of my place on 114th Street I waited two days before I did anything. I assumed she would come back when she calmed down; I figured she'd call, contrite, from some friend's house and say she was sorry she panicked and would I come get her in a cab. Also, in those two days I was in no shape to take any sort of action, because I was still suffering the aftereffects of my vicarious trip; I felt as though someone had seized my head and pulled on it, stretching my neck like a rubber band, letting it finally snap back into place with a sharp *thwock!* that addled my brains. I spent those two days in bed, dozing mostly, occasionally reading, and rushing madly out into the hall every time the telephone rang.

But she didn't come back and she didn't call, and on the Tuesday after the acid trip I started searching for her. I phoned her office first. Teddy, her boss, a bland sweet scholarly man, very gentle, very gay. No, she hadn't been to work this week. No, she hadn't been in touch at all. Was it urgent? Would I like to have her home number? "I'm *calling* from her home number," I said. "She isn't here and I don't know where she's gone. This is David Selig, Teddy." "Oh," he said. Very faintly, with great compassion. "Oh." And I said, "If she happens to call in, will you tell her to get in touch with me?" Next I started to phone her friends, those whose numbers I could find: Alice, Doris, Helen, Pam, Grace. Most of them, I knew, didn't like me. I didn't have to be telepathic to realize that. They thought she was throwing herself away on me, wasting her life with a man without career, prospects, money, ambition, talent, or looks. All five of them told me they hadn't heard from her. Doris, Helen, and Pam sounded sincere. The other two, it seemed to me, were lying. I took a taxi over to Alice's place in the Village and shot a probe upward, *zam!* nine stories into her head, and I learned a lot of things about Alice that I hadn't really wanted to know, but I didn't find out where Toni was. I felt dirty about spying and didn't probe Grace. Instead I called my employer, the writer, whose book Toni was editing, and asked if he'd seen her. Not in weeks, he told me, all ice. Dead end. The trail had run out.

I dithered on Wednesday, wondering what to do, and finally, melodramatically, called the police. Gave a bored desk sergeant her description: tall, thin, long dark hair, brown eyes. No bodies found in Central Park lately? In subway trash cans? The basements of Amsterdam Avenue tenements? No. No. No. Look, buddy, if we hear anything we'll let you know, but it don't sound serious to me. So much for the police. Restless, hopelessly strung out, I walked down to the Great Shanghai for a miserable half-eaten dinner, good food gone to waste. (Children are starving in Europe, Duv. Eat. Eat.) Afterwards, sitting around over the sad scattered remnants of my shrimp with sizzling rice and feeling myself drop deep into bereavement, I scored a cheap pickup in a manner I've always despised: I scanned the various single girls in the big restaurant, of whom there were numerous, looking for one who was lonely, thwarted, vulnerable, sexually permissive, and in generally urgent need of ego reinforcement. It's no trick getting laid if you have a sure way of knowing who's available, but there's not much sport in the chase. She was, this fish in the barrel, a passably attractive married lady in her mid-20's, childless, whose husband, a Columbia instructor, evidently had more interest in his doctoral thesis than in her. He spent every night immured in the stacks of Butler Library doing research, creeping home late, exhausted, irritable, and generally impotent. I took her to my room, couldn't get it up either—that bothered her; she assumed it was a sign of rejection—and spent two tense hours listening to her life story. Ultimately I managed to screw her, and I came almost instantly. Not my finest hour. When I returned from walking her home—110th and Riverside Drive—the phone was ringing. Pam. "I've heard from Toni," she said, and suddenly I was slimy with guilt over my sleazy consolatory infidelity. "She's staying with Bob Larkin at his place over on East 83rd Street."

Jealousy, despair, humiliation, agony.

"Bob who?"

"Larkin. He's that high-bracket interior decorator she always talks about."

"Not to me."

"One of Toni's oldest friends. They're very close. I think he used to date her when she was in high school." A long pause. Then Pam chuckled warmly into my numb silence. "Oh, relax, relax, David! He's *gay*! He's just a kind of father-confessor for her. She goes to him when there's trouble."

"I see."

"You two have broken up, haven't you?"

"I'm not sure. I suppose we have. I don't know."

"Is there anything I can do to help?" This from Pam, who I had always thought regarded me as a destructive influence of whom Toni was well advised to be quit.

"Just give me his phone number," I said.

I phoned. It rang and rang and rang. At last Bob Larkin picked up. Gay, all right, a sweet tenor voice complete with lisp, not very different from the voice of Teddy-at-work. Who teaches them to speak with the homo accent? I asked, "Is Toni there?" A guarded response: "Who's calling, please?" I told him. He asked me to wait, and a minute or so passed while he conferred with her, hand over the mouthpiece. At last he came back and said Toni was there, yes, but she was very tired and resting and didn't want to talk to me right now. "It's urgent," I said. "Please tell her it's urgent." Another muffled conference. Same reply. He suggested vaguely that I call back in two or three days. I started to wheedle, to whine, to beg. In the middle of that unheroic performance the phone abruptly changed hands and Toni said to me, "Why did you call?"

"That ought to be obvious. I want you to come back."

"I can't."

She didn't say *I won't*. She said *I can't*.

I said, "Would you like to tell me why?"

"Not really."

"You didn't even leave a note. Not a word of explanation. You ran out so fast."

"I'm sorry, David."

"It was something you saw in me while you were tripping, wasn't it?"

"Let's not talk about it," she said. "It's over."

"I don't want it to be over."

"I do."

I do. That was like the sound of a great gate clanging shut in my face. But I wasn't going to let her throw home the bolts just yet. I told her she had left some of her things in my room, some books, some clothing. A lie; she had made a clean sweep. But I can be persuasive when I'm cornered, and she began to think it might be true. I offered to bring the stuff over right now. She didn't want me to come. She preferred never to see me again, she told me. Less painful all around, that way. But her voice lacked conviction; it was higher in pitch and much more nasal than it was when she spoke with sincerity. I knew she still loved me, more or less; even after a forest fire, some of the burned snags live on, and green new shoots spring from them. So I told myself. Fool that I was. In any case she couldn't entirely turn me away. Just as she had been unable to refrain from picking up the telephone, now she found it impossible to refuse me access to her. Talking very fast, I bludgeoned her into yielding. All right, she said. Come over. Come over. But you're wasting your time.

It was close to midnight. The summer air was clinging and clammy, with a hint of rain on the way. No stars visible. I hurried crosstown, choked with the vapors of the humid city and the bile of my shattered love. Larkin's apartment was on the nineteenth floor of an immense new terraced white-brick tower, far over on York Avenue. Admitting me, he gave me a tender, compassionate smile, as if to say, You poor bastard, you've been hurt and you're bleeding and now you're going to get ripped open again. He was about 30, a stocky, boyish-faced man with long unruly curly brown hair and large uneven teeth. He radiated warmth and sympathy and kindness. I could understand why Toni ran to him at times like this. "She's in the livingroom," he said. "To the left."

It was a big, impeccable place, somewhat freaky in decor, with jagged blurts of color dancing over the walls, pre-Columbian artifacts in spotlighted showcases, bizarre African masks, chrome-steel furniture—the kind of implausible apartment you see photographed in the Sunday *Times'* magazine section. The livingroom was the core of the spectacle, a vast white-walled room with a long curving window that revealed all the splendors of Queens across the East River. Toni sat at the far end, near the window, on an angular couch, dark blue flecked with gold. She wore old, dowdy clothes that clashed furiously with the splendor around her: a motheaten red sweater that I detested, a short frumpy black skirt, dark hose—and she was slumped down sullenly on her spine, leaning on one elbow, her legs jutting awkwardly forward. It was a posture that made her look bony and ungraceful. A cigarette drooped in her hand and there was a huge pile of butts in the ashtray beside her. Her eyes were bleak. Her long hair was tangled. She didn't move as I walked toward her. Such an aura of hostility came from her that I halted twenty feet away.

"Where's the stuff you were bringing?" she asked.

"There wasn't any. I just said that to have an excuse to see you."

"I figured that."

"What went wrong, Toni?"

"Don't ask. Just don't ask." Her voice had dropped into its lowest register, a bitter husky contralto. "You shouldn't have come here at all."

"If you'd tell me what I did—"

"You tried to hurt me," she said. "You tried to bum-trip me." She stubbed out her cigarette and immediately lit another. Her eyes, somber and hooded, refused to meet mine. "I realized finally that you were my enemy, that I had to escape from you. So I packed and got out."

"Your enemy? You know that isn't true."

"It was strange," she said. "I didn't understand what was happening, and I've talked to some people who've dropped a lot of acid and they can't understand it either. It was like our minds were linked, David. Like a telepathic channel had opened between us. And all sorts of stuff was pouring from you into me. Hateful stuff. Poisonous stuff. I was thinking your thoughts. Seeing myself as you saw me. Remember, when you said you were tripping too, even though you hadn't had any acid? And then you told me you were, like, reading my mind. That was what scared me. The way our minds seemed to blur together, to overlap. To become one. I never knew acid could do that to people."

This was my cue to tell her that it wasn't only the acid, that it hadn't been some druggy delusion, that what she had felt was the impingement of a special power granted me at birth, a gift, a curse, a freak of nature. But the words congealed in my mouth. They sounded insane to me. How could I confess such stuff? I let the moment pass. Instead I said lamely, "Okay, it was a strange moment for both of us. We were a little out of our heads. But the trip's over. You don't have to hide from me now. Come back, Toni."

"No."

"In a few days, then?"

"No."

"I don't understand this."

"Everything's changed," she said. "I couldn't ever live with you now. You scare me too much. The trip's over, but I look at you and I see demons. I see some kind of thing that's half-bat, half-man, with big rubbery wings and long yellow fangs and—oh, Jesus, David, I can't help any of this! I *still* feel as if our minds are linked. Stuff creeping out of you into my head. I should never have touched the acid." Carelessly she crushed her cigarette and found another. "You make me uncomfortable now. I wish you'd go. It gives me a headache just being this close to you. Please. Please. I'm sorry David."

I didn't dare look into her mind. I was afraid that what I'd find there would blast and shrivel me. But in those days my power was still so strong that I couldn't help picking up, whether I sought it or not, a generalized low-level mental radiation from everyone I came close to, and what I picked up now from Toni confirmed what she was saying. She hadn't stopped loving me. But the acid, though lysergic and not sulfuric, had scarred and corroded our relationship by opening that terrible gateway between us. It was torment for her to be in the same room with me. No resources of mine could deal with that. I considered strategies, looked for angles of approach, ways to reason with her, to heal her through soft earnest words. No way. No way at all. I ran a dozen trial dialogs in my head and they all ended with Toni begging me to get out of her life. So. The End. She sat there all but motionless, downcast, dark-faced, her wide mouth clapped in pain, her brilliant smile extinguished. She seemed to have aged twenty years. Her odd, exotic desert-princess beauty had wholly fled from her. Suddenly she was more real to me, in her shroud of pain, than ever before. Ablaze with suffering, alive with anguish. And no way for me to reach her. "All right," I said quietly. "I'm sorry too." Over, done with, swiftly, suddenly, no warning, the bullet singing through the air, the grenade rolling treacherously into the tent, the anvil falling from the placid sky. Done with. Alone again. Not even any tears. Cry? What shall I cry?

Bob Larkin had tactfully remained outside, in his long foyer papered with dazzling black and white optical illusions, during our brief muffled conversation. Again the gentle sorrowing smile from him as I emerged.

"Thanks for letting me bother you this late," I said.

"No trouble at all. Too bad about you and Toni."

I nodded. "Yes. Too bad."

We faced each other uncertainly, and he moved toward me, digging his fingers momentarily into the muscle of my arm, telling me without words to shape up, to ride out the storm, to get myself together. He was so open that my mind sank unexpectedly into his, and I saw him plain, his goodness, his kindness, his sorrow. Out of him an image rose to me, a sharp encapsulated memory: himself and a sobbing, demolished Toni, the night before last, lying naked together on his modish round bed, her head cradled against his muscular hairy chest, his hands fondling the pale heavy globes of her breasts. Her body trembling with need. His unwilling drooping manhood struggling to offer her the consolation of sex. His gentle spirit at war with itself, flooded with pity and love for her but dismayed by her disturbing femaleness, those breasts, that cleft, her softness. You don't have to, Bob, she keeps saying, you don't have to, you really don't have to, but he tells her he wants to, it's about time we made it after knowing each other all these years, it'll cheer you up, Toni, and anyway a man needs a little variety, right? His heart goes out to her but his body resists, and their lovemaking, when it happens, is a hurried, pathetic, fumbled thing, a butting of troubled reluctant bodies, ending in tears, tremors, shared distress, and, finally, laughter, a triumph over pain. He kisses her tears away. She thanks him gravely for his efforts. They fall into childlike sleep, side by side. How civilized, how tender. My poor Toni. Goodbye. Goodbye. "I'm glad she went to you," I said. He walked me to the elevator. What shall I cry? "If she snaps out of it I'll make sure she calls you," he told me. I put my hand to his arm as he had to mine, and gave him the best smile in my repertoire. Goodbye.

19.

This is my cave. Twelve floors high in the Marble Hill Houses, Broadway and 228th Street, formerly a middle-income municipal housing project, now a catch-all for classless and deracinated urban detritus. Two rooms plus bathroom, kitchenette, hallway. Once upon a time you couldn't get into this project unless you were married and had kids. Nowadays a few singles have slipped in, on the grounds that they're destitute. Things change as the city decays; regulations break down. Most of the building's population is Puerto Rican, with a sprinkling of Irish and Italian. In this den of papists a David Selig is a great anomaly. Sometimes he thinks he owes his neighbors a daily lusty rendition of the *Shma Yisroel*, but he doesn't know the words. *Kol Nidre*, perhaps. Or the *Kaddish*. This is the bread of affliction which our forefathers ate in the land of Egypt. He is lucky to have been led out of Egypt into the Promised Land.

Would you like the guided tour of David Selig's cave? Very well. Please come this way. No touching anything, please, and don't park your chewing gum on the furniture. The sensitive, intelligent, amiable, neurotic man who will be your guide is none other than David Selig himself. No tipping allowed. Welcome, folks, welcome to my humble abode. We'll begin our tour in the bathroom. See, this is the tub—that yellow stain in the porcelain was already there when he moved in—this is the crapper, this is the medicine chest. Selig spends a great deal of time in here; it's a room significant to any in-depth understanding of his existence. For example, he sometimes takes two or three showers a day. What is it, do you think, that he's trying to wash away? Leave that toothbrush alone, sonny. All right, come with me. Do you see these posters in the hallway? They are artifacts of the 1960's. This one shows the poet Allen Ginsberg in the costume of Uncle Sam. This one is a crude vulgarization of a subtle topological paradox by the Dutch printmaker M. C. Escher. This one shows a nude young couple making love in the Pacific surf. Eight to ten years ago, hundreds of thousands of young people decorated their rooms with such posters. Selig, although he was not exactly young even then, did the same. He often has followed current fads and modes in an attempt to affiliate himself more firmly with the structures of contemporary existence. I suppose these posters are quite valuable now; he takes them with him from one cheap rooming house to the next.

This room is the bedroom. Dark and narrow, with the low ceiling typical of municipal construction a generation ago. I keep the window closed at all times so that the elevated train, roaring through the adjacent sky late at night, doesn't awaken me. It's hard enough to get some sleep even when things are quiet around you. This is his bed, in which he dreams uneasy dreams, occasionally, even now, involuntarily reading the minds of his neighbors and incorporating their thoughts in his fantasies. On this bed he has fornicated perhaps fifteen women, one or two or occasionally three times each, during the two and a half years of his residence here. Don't look so abashed, young lady! Sex is a healthy human endeavor and it remains an essential aspect of Selig's life, even now in middle age! It may become even more important to him in the years ahead, for sex is, after all, a way of establishing communication with other human beings, and certain other channels of communication appear to be closing for him. Who are these girls? Some of them are not girls; some are women well along in life. He charms them in his diffident way and persuades them to share an hour of joy with him. He rarely invites any of them back, and those whom he does invite back often refuse the invitation, but that's all right. His needs are met. What's that? Fifteen girls in two and a half years isn't very many for a bachelor? Who are you to judge? He finds it sufficient. I assure you, he finds it sufficient. Please don't sit on his bed. It's an old one, bought secondhand at an upstairs bargain basement that the Salvation Army runs in Harlem. I picked it up for a few bucks when I moved out of my last place, a furnished room on St. Nicholas Avenue, and needed some furniture of my own. Some years before that, around 1971, 1972, I had a waterbed, another example of my following of transient fads, but I couldn't ever get used to the swooshing and gurgling and I gave it, finally, to a hip young lady who dug it the most. What else is in the bedroom? Very little of interest, I'm afraid. A chest of drawers containing commonplace clothing. A pair of worn slippers. A cracked mirror: are you superstitious? A lopsided bookcase packed tight with old magazines that he will never look at again—*Partisan Review, Evergreen, Paris Review, New York Review of Books, Encounter,* a mound of trendy literary stuff, plus a few journals of psychoanalysis and psychiatry, which Selig reads sporadically in the hope of increasing his self-knowledge; he always tosses them aside in boredom and disappointment. Let's get out of here. This room must be depressing you. We go past the kitchenette—four-burner stove, half-size refrigerator, formica-topped table—where he assembles very modest breakfasts and lunches (dinner he usually eats out) and enter the main focus of the apartment, the L-shaped blue-walled jam-packed livingroom/study.

Here you can observe the full range of David Selig's intellectual development. This is his record collection, about a hundred well-worn disks, some of them purchased as far back as 1951. (Archaic monophonic records!) Almost entirely classical music, although you will note two intrusive deposits: five or six jazz records dating from 1959 and five or six rock records dating from 1969, both groups acquired in vague, abortive efforts at expanding the horizons of his taste. Otherwise, what you will find here, in the main, is pretty austere stuff, thorny, inaccessible: Schoenberg, late Beethoven, Mahler, Berg, the Bartok quartets, Bach passacaglias. Nothing that you'd be likely to whistle after one hearing. He doesn't know a lot about music, but he knows what he likes; you wouldn't much care for it.

And these are his books, accumulated since the age of ten and hauled lovingly about with him from place to place. The archaeological strata of his reading can readily be isolated and examined. Jules Verne, H. G. Wells, Mark Twain, Dashiell Hammett at the bottom. Sabatini. Kipling. Sir Walter Scott. Van Loon, *The Story of Mankind.* Verrill, *Great Conquerors of South and Central America.* The books of a sober, earnest, alienated little boy. Suddenly, with adolescence, a quantum leap: Orwell, Fitzgerald, Hemingway, Hardy, the easier Faulkner. Look at these rare paperbacks of the 1940's and early 1950's, in odd off sized formats, with laminated plastic covers! See what you could buy then for only 25¢! Look at the prurient paintings, the garish lettering! These science-fiction books date from that era too. I gobbled the stuff whole, hoping to find some clues to my own dislocated self's nature in the fantasies of Bradbury, Heinlein, Asimov, Sturgeon, Clarke. Look, here's Stapledon's *Odd John,* here's Beresford's *Hampdenshire Wonder,* here's a whole book called *Outsiders: Children of Wonder,* full of stories of little superbrats with freaky powers. I've underlined a lot of passages in that last one, usually places where I quarreled with the writers. *Outsiders?* Those writers, gifted as they were, were the outsiders, trying to imagine powers they'd never had; and I, who was on the

inside, I the youthful mind-prowler (the book is dated 1954), had bones
to pick with them. They stressed the angst of being supernormal, forgot
about the ecstasy. Although, thinking about angst vs. ecstasy now, I
have to admit they knew whereof they writ. Fellows, I have fewer bones
to pick these days. This is rats' alley, where the dead men lost their
bones.

Observe how Selig's reading becomes more rarefied as we reach
the college years. Joyce, Proust, Mann, Eliot, Pound, the old avant-garde
hierarchy. The French period: Zola, Balzac, Montaigne, Celine, Rimbaud, Baudelaire. This thick slug of Dostoevsky occupying half a shelf.
Lawrence. Woolf. The mystical era: Augustine, Aquinas, the *Tao Te
Ching*, the *Upanishads*, the *Bhagavad-Gita*. The psychological era:
Freud, Jung, Adler, Reich, Reik. The philosophical era. The Marxist era.
All that Koestler. Back to literature: Conrad, Forster, Beckett. Moving
onward toward the fractured '60's: Bellow, Pynchon, Malamud, Mailer,
Burroughs, Barth. *Catch-22* and *The Politics of Experience*. Oh, yes,
ladies and gentlemen, you are in the presence of a well-read man!

Here we have his files. A treasure-trove of personalia, awaiting a
biographer yet unknown. Report cards, always with low marks for conduct. ("David shows little interest in his work and frequently disrupts
the class.") Crudely crayoned birthday cards for his mother and father.
Old photographs: can this fat freckled boy be the gaunt individual who
stands before you now? This man with the high forehead and the forced
rigid smile is the late Paul Selig, father of our subject, deceased (*olav
hasholom!*) 11 August 1971 of complications following surgery for a
perforated ulcer. This gray-haired woman with the hyperthyroid eyes is
the late Martha Selig, wife of Paul, mother of David, deceased (*oy, veh,
mama!*) 15 March 1973 of mysterious rot of internal organs, probably
cancerous. This grim young lady with cold knifeblade face is Judith
Hannah Selig, adopted child of P. and M., unloving sister of D. Date
on back of photo: July 1963. Judith is therefore 18 years old and in the
summertime of her hate for me. How much she looks like Toni in this
picture! I never noticed the resemblance before, but they've got the same
dusky Yemenite look, the same long black hair. But Toni's eyes were
always warm and loving, except right at the very end, and Jude's eyes
never held anything for me other than ice, ice, Plutonian ice. Let us
continue with the examination of David Selig's private effects. This is
his collection of essays and term papers, written during his college
years. ("Carew is a courtly and elegant poet, whose work reflects influ-
ences both of Jonson's precise classicism and Donne's grotesque
fancy—an interesting synthesis. His poems are neatly constructed and
sharp of diction; in a poem such as 'Ask me no more where Jove be-

stows,' he captures Jonson's harmonious austerity perfectly, while in others, such as 'Mediocrity in Love Rejected' or 'Ingrateful Beauty Threatened,' his wit is akin to that of Donne.") How fortunate for D. Selig that he kept all this literary twaddle: here in his later years these papers have become the capital on which he lives, for you know, of course, how the central figure of our investigations earns his livelihood nowadays. What else do we find in these archives? The carbon copies of innumerable letters. Some of them are quite impersonal missives. *Dear President Eisenhower. Dear Pope John. Dear Secretary-General Hammarskjold.* Quite often, once, though rarely in recent years, he launched these letters to far corners of the globe. His fitful unilateral efforts at making contact with a deaf world. His troubled futile attempts at restoring order in a universe plainly tumbling toward the ultimate thermodynamic doom. Shall we look at a few of these documents? *You say, Governor Rockefeller, that "with nuclear weapons multiplying, our security is dependent on the credibility of our willingness to resort to our deterrent. It is our heavy responsibility as public officials and as citizens to save the lives and to protect the health of our people. A lagging civil-defense effort cannot be excused by our conviction that nuclear war is a tragedy and that we must strive by all honorable means to assure peace." Permit me to disagree. Your bomb-shelter program, Governor, is the project of a morally impoverished mind. To divert energy and resources from the search for a lasting peace to this ostrich-in-the-sand scheme is, I think, a foolish and dangerous policy that....* The Governor, by way of replying, sent his thanks and an offprint of the very speech which Selig was protesting. Can one expect more? *Mr. Nixon, your entire campaign is pitched to the theory that America never had it so good under President Eisenhower, and so let's have four more years of the same. To me you sound like Faust, crying out to the passing moment, Bleibe doch, du bist so schoen! (Am I too literate for you, Mr. Vice-President?) Please bear in mind that when Faust utters those words, Mephistopheles arrives to collect his soul. Does it honestly seem to you that this instant in history is so sweet that you would stop the clocks forever? Listen to the anguish in the land. Listen to the voices of Mississippi's Negroes, listen to the cries of the hungry children of factory workers thrown out of work by a Republican recession, listen to....Dear Mrs. Hemingway: Please allow me to add my words to the thousands expressing sorrow at the death of your husband. The bravery he showed in the face of a life-situation that had become unendurable and intolerable is indeed an example for those of us who....Dear Dr. Buber....Dear Professor Toynbee....Dear President Nehru....Dear Mr. Pound: The whole civilized world rejoices with you upon your lib-*

eration from the cruel and unnatural confinement which. . . . *Dear Lord Russell.* . . . *Dear Chairman Khrushchev.* . . . *Dear M. Malraux.* . . . *dear.* . . . *dear.* . . . *.dear.* . . . A remarkable collection of correspondence, you must agree. With equally remarkable replies. See, this answer says, *You may be right,* and this one says, *I am grateful for your interest,* and this one says, *Of course time does not permit individual replies to all letters received, but nevertheless please be assured that your thoughts will receive careful consideration,* and this one says, *Send this bastard the bedbug letter.*

Unfortunately we do not have the imaginary letters which he dictates constantly to himself but never sends. *Dear Mr. Kierkegaard: I agree entirely with your celebrated dictum equating "the absurd" with "the fact that with God all things are possible," and declaring, "The absurd is not one of the factors which can be discriminated within the proper compass of the understanding: it is not identical with the improbable, the unexpected, the unforeseen." In my own experiences with the absurd.* . . . *Dear Mr. Shakespeare: How aptly you put it when you say, "Love is not love Which alters when it alteration finds, Or bends with the remover to remove." Your sonnet, however, begs the question: If love is not love, what then is it, that feeling of closeness which can be so absurdly and unexpectedly destroyed by a trifle? If you could suggest some alternate existential mode of relating to others that.* . . . Since they are transient, the product of vagrant impulses, and often incomprehensible, we have no satisfactory access to such communications, which Selig sometimes produces at a rate of hundreds per hour. *Dear Mr. Justice Holmes: In Southern Pacific Co. v. Jensen, 244 U.S. 205, 221 [1917], you ruled, "I recognize without hesitation that judges do and must legislate, but they can do so only interstitially; they are confined from molar to molecular motions." This splendid metaphor is not entirely clear to me, I must confess, and.* . . .

> Dear Mr. Selig:
> The present state of the world and the whole of life is diseased. If I were a doctor and were asked for my advice, I should reply, "Create silence."
>
> > Yours very sincerely,
> > Sören Kierkegaard
> > (1813–1855)

And then there are these three folders here, thick beige cardboard. They are not available for public inspection, since they contain letters of a rather more personal kind. Under the terms of our agreement with the David Selig Foundation, I am forbidden to quote, though I may paraphrase. These are his letters to and occasionally from the girls he has loved or has wanted to love. The earliest is dated 1950 and bears the notation at the top in large red letters, NEVER SENT. *Dear Beverly* it begins, and it is full of embarrassingly graphic sexual imagery. What can you tell us about this Beverly, Selig? Well, she was short and cute and freckled, with big headlights and a sunny disposition, and sat in front of me in my biology class, and had a creepy twin sister, Estelle, who scowled a lot and through some fluke of genetics was as flat as Beverly was bosomy. Maybe that was why she scowled so much. Estelle liked me in her bitter murky way and I think might eventually have slept with me, which would have done my 15-year-old ego a lot of good, but I despised her. She seemed like a blotchy, badly done imitation of Beverly, whom I loved. I used to wander barefoot in Beverly's mind while the teacher, Miss Mueller, droned on about mitosis and chromosomes. She had just yielded her cherry to Victor Schlitz, the big rawboned green-eyed red-haired boy who sat next to her, and I learned a lot about sex from her at one remove, with a 12-hour time-lag, as she radiated every morning her adventure of the night before with Victor. I wasn't jealous of him. He was handsome and self-confident and deserved her, and I was too shy and insecure to lay anybody anyway, then. So I rode secretly piggyback on their romance and fantasized doing with Beverly the gaudy things Victor was doing with her, until I desperately wanted to get into her myself, but my explorations of her head told me that to her I was just an amusing gnomish child, an oddity, a jester. How then to score? I wrote her this letter describing in vivid sweaty detail everything that she and Victor had been up to, and said, Don't you wonder how I know all this, heh heh heh? The implication being that I'm some kind of superman with the power to penetrate the intimacies of a woman's mind. I figured that would topple her right into my arms in a swoon of awe, but some second thoughts led me to see that she'd either think I was crazy or a peeping tom, and would in either case be wholly turned off me, so I filed the letter away undelivered. My mother found it one night but she didn't dare say anything about it to me, hopelessly blocked as she was on the entire subject of sexuality; she just put it back in my notebook. I picked her thoughts that night and discovered she'd sneaked a look. Was she shocked and disturbed? Yes, she was, but also she felt very proud that her boy was a man at last, writing smutty stuff to pretty girls. My son the pornographer.

Most of the letters in this file date between 1954 and 1968. The most recent was written in the autumn of 1974, after which time Selig began to feel less and less in touch with the rest of the human race and stopped writing letters, except in his head. I don't know how many girls are represented here, but there must have been quite a few. Generally these were all superficial affairs, for Selig, as you know, never married or even had many serious involvements with women. As in the case of Beverly, the ones he loved most deeply he usually never had actual relationships with, though he was capable of pretending he felt love for someone who was in fact a casual pickup. At times he made use of his special gifts knowingly to exploit women sexually, especially about the age of 25. He is not proud of that period. Wouldn't you like to read these letters, you stinking voyeurs? But you won't. You won't get your paws on them. Why have I invited you in here, anyway? Why do I let you peer at my books and my photographs and my unwashed dishes and my stained bathtub? It must be that my sense of self is slipping. Isolation is choking me; the windows are closed but at least I've opened the door. I need you to bolster my grip on reality by looking into my life, by incorporating parts of it into your own experience, by discovering that I'm real, I exist, I suffer, I have a past if not a future. So that you can go away from here saying, Yes, I know David Selig, actually I know him quite well. But that doesn't mean I have to show you everything. Hey, here's a letter to Amy! Amy who relieved me of my festering virginity in the spring of 1953. Wouldn't you like to know the story of how that happened? Anybody's first time has an irresistible fascination. Well, fuck you: I don't feel like discussing it. It isn't much of a story anyway. I put it in her and I came and she didn't, that's how it was, and if you want to know the rest, who she was, how I seduced her, make up the details yourself. Where's Amy now? Amy's dead. How do you like that? His first lay, and he's outlived her already. She died in an auto accident at the age of 23 and her husband, who knew me vaguely, phoned me to tell me, since I had once been a friend of hers. He was still in trauma because the police had made him come down to identify the body, and she had really been destroyed, mangled, mutilated. Like something from another planet, that's how she looked, he told me. Catapulted through the windshield and into a tree. And I told him, "Amy was the first girl I ever slept with," and he started consoling me. He, consoling me, and I had only been trying to be sadistic.

Time passes. Amy's dead and Beverly's a pudgy middle-aged housewife, I bet. Here's a letter to Jackie Newhouse, telling her I can't sleep for thinking about her. Jackie Newhouse? Who that? Oh, yes. Five feet two and a pair of boobs that would have made Marilyn Monroe feel topheavy. Sweet. Dumb. Puckered lips, baby-blue eyes. Jackie had nothing going for her at all except her bosom, but that was enough for me, 17 years old and hung up on breasts, God knows why. I loved her for her mammaries, so globular and conspicuous in the tight white polo shirts she liked to wear. Summer of 1952. She loved Frank Sinatra and Perry Como, and had FRANKIE written in lipstick down the left thigh of her jeans and PERRY on the right. She also loved her history teacher, whose name, I think, was Leon Sissinger or Zippinger or something like that, and she had LEON on her jeans too, from hip to hip. I kissed her twice but that was all, not even my tongue in her mouth; she was even more shy than I, terrified that some hideous male hand would violate the purity of those mighty knockers. I followed her around, trying not to get into her head because it depressed me to see how empty it was. How did it end? Oh, yes: her kid brother Arnie was telling me how he sees her naked at home all the time, and I, desperate for a vicarious glimpse of her bare breasts, plunged into his skull and stole a second-hand peek. I hadn't realized until then how important a bra can be. Unbound, they hung to her plump little belly, two mounds of dangling meat crisscrossed by bulging blue veins. Cured me of my fixation. So long ago, so unreal to me now, Jackie.

Here. Look. Spy on me. My fervid frenzied outpourings of love. Read them all, what do I care? Donna, Elsie, Magda, Mona, Sue, Lois, Karen. Did you think I was sexually deprived? Did you think my lame adolescence sent me stumbling into manhood incapable of finding women? I quarried for my life between their thighs. Dear Connie, what a wild night that was! Dear Chiquita, your perfume still lingers in the air. Dear Elaine, when I woke this morning the taste of you was on my lips. Dear Kitty, I—

Oh, God. Kitty. *Dear Kitty, I have so much to explain to you that I don't know where to begin. You never understood me, and I never understood you, and so the love I had for you was fated to bring us to a bad pass sooner or later. Which it now has. The failures of communication extended all up and down our relationship, but because you were different from any person I had ever known, truly and qualitatively different, I made you the center of my fantasies and could not accept you as you were, but had to keep hammering and hammering and hammering away at you, until*—Oh, God. This one's too painful. What the hell are you doing reading someone else's mail? Don't you have any decency? I can't show you this. The tour's over. Out!

Out! Everybody out! For Christ's sake, get *out!*

20.

There was always the danger of being found out. He knew he had to be on his guard. This was an era of witch-hunters, when anyone who departed from community norms was ferreted out and burned at the stake. Spies were everywhere, probing for young Selig's secret, fishing for the awful truth about him. Even Miss Mueller, his biology teacher. She was a pudgy little poodle of a woman, about 40, with a glum face and dark arcs under her eyes; like a cryptodyke of some sort she wore her hair cut brutally short, the back of her neck always showing the stubble of a recent shave, and came to class every day in a gray laboratory smock. Miss Mueller was very deep into the realm of extrasensory and occult phenomena. Of course they didn't use phrases like "very deep into" in 1949, when David Selig was in her class, but let the anachronism stand: she was ahead of her time, a hippie born too soon. She really grooved behind the irrational, the unknown. She knew her way around the high-school bio curriculum in her sleep, which was more or less the way she taught it. What turned her on, really, were things like telepathy, clairvoyance, telekinesis, astrology, the whole parapsychological bag. The most slender provocation was enough to nudge her away from the day's assignment, the study of metabolism or the circulatory system or whatever, and onto one of her hobbyhorses. She was the first on her block to own the *I Ching*. She had done time inside orgone boxes. She believed that the Great Pyramid of Gizeh held divine revelations for mankind. She had sought deeper truths by way of Zen, General Semantics, the Bates eyesight exercises, and the readings of Edgar Cayce. (How easily I can extend her quest past the year of my own exposure to her! She must have gone on to dianetics, Velikovsky, Bridey Murphy, and Timothy Leary, and ended up, in her old age, as a lady guru in some Los Angeles eyrie, heavy into psilocybin and peyote. Poor silly gullible pitiful old bitch.)

Naturally she kept up with the research into extrasensory perception that J. B. Rhine was doing down at Duke University. It terrified David whenever she spoke of this. He constantly feared that she was going to give way to the temptation to run some Rhine experiments in class, and would thereby flush him out of hiding. He had read Rhine himself, of course, *The Reach of the Mind* and *New Frontiers of the Mind*, had even peered into the opacities of *The Journal of Parapsychology*, hoping to find something that would explain him to himself, but there was nothing there except statistics and foggy conjecture. Okay, Rhine was no threat to him so long as he went on piddling around in North Carolina. But muddled Miss Mueller might just strip him naked and deliver him to the pyre.

Inevitable, the progression toward disaster. The topic for the week, suddenly, was the human brain, its functions and capabilities. See, this is the cerebrum, this is the cerebellum, this is the medulla oblongata. A child's garden of synapses. Fat-cheeked Norman Heimlich, gunning for a 99, knowing precisely which button to push, put up his hand: "Miss Mueller, do you think it'll ever be possible for people really to read minds, I mean not by tricks or anything but actual mental telepathy?" Oh, the joy of Miss Mueller! Her lumpy face glowing. This was her cue to launch into an animated discussion of ESP, parapsychology, inexplicable phenomena, supernormal modes of communication and perception, the Rhine researches, et cetera, et cetera, a torrent of metaphysical irrelevance. David wanted to hide under his desk. The word "telepathy" made him wince. He already suspected that half the class realized what he was. Now a flash of wild paranoia. Are they looking at me, are they staring and pointing and tapping their heads and nodding? Certainly these were irrational fears. He had surveyed every mind in the class again and again, desperately trying to amuse himself during the arid stretches of boredom, and he knew that his secret was safe. His classmates, plodding young Brooklynites all, would never cotton to the veiled presence of a superman in their midst. They thought he was strange, yes, but had no notion of *how* strange. Would Miss Mueller now blow his cover, though? She was talking about conducting parapsychology experiments in class to demonstrate the potential reach of the human brain. Oh where can I hide?

No escape. She had her cards with her the next day. "These are known as Zener cards," she explained solemnly, holding them up, fanning them out like Wild Bill Hickok about to deal himself a straight flush. David had never actually seen a set of the cards before, yet they were as familiar to him as the deck his parents used in their interminable canasta games. "They were devised about twenty-five years ago at Duke University by Dr. Karl E. Zener and Dr. J. B. Rhine. Another name for them is 'ESP cards.' Who can tell me what 'ESP' means?"

Norman Heimlich's stubby hand waving in the air. "Extrasensory perception, Miss Mueller!"

"Very good, Norman." Absentmindedly she began to shuffle the cards. Her eyes, normally inexpressive, gleamed with a Las Vegas intensity. She said, "The deck consists of 25 cards, divided into five 'suits' or symbols. There are five cards marked with a star, five with a circle, five with a square, five with a pattern of wavy lines, and five with a cross or plus sign. Otherwise they look just like ordinary playing cards." She handed the pack to Barbara Stein, another of her favorites, and told her to copy the five symbols on the blackboard. "The idea is for the subject being examined to look at each card in turn, face down, and try to name the symbol on the other side. The test can be run in many different ways. Sometimes the examiner looks briefly at each card first; that gives the subject a chance to pick the right answer out of the examiner's mind, if he can. Sometimes neither the subject nor the examiner sees the card in advance. Sometimes the subject is allowed to touch the card before he makes his guess. Sometimes he may be blindfolded, and other times he may be permitted to stare at the back of each card. No matter how it's done, though, the basic aim is always the same: for the subject to determine, using extrasensory powers, the design on a card that he can't see. Estelle, suppose the subject has no extrasensory powers at all, but is simply operating on pure guesswork. How many right guesses could we expect him to make, out of the 25 cards?"

Estelle, caught by surprise, reddened and blurted, "Uh—twelve and a half?"

A sour smirk from Miss Mueller, who turned to the brighter, happier twin. "Beverly?"

"Five, Miss Mueller?"

"Correct. You always have one chance out of five of guessing the right suit, so five right calls out of 25 is what luck alone ought to bring. Of course, the results are never that neat. On one run through the deck you might have four correct hits, and then next time six, and then five, and then maybe seven, and then perhaps only three—but the *average*, over a long series of trials, ought to be about five. That is, if pure chance is the only factor operating. Actually, in the Rhine experiments some groups of subjects have averaged 6½ or 7 hits out of 25 over many tests. Rhine believes that this above-average performance can only be explained as ESP. And certain subjects have done much better. There was a man once who called nine straight cards right, two days in a row. Then a few days later he hit 15 straight cards, 21 out of 25. The odds against that are fantastic. How many of you think it could have been nothing but luck?"

About a third of the hands in the class went up. Some of them belonged to dullards who failed to realize that it was shrewd politics to show sympathy for the teacher's pet enthusiasms. Some of them belonged to incorrigible skeptics who disdained such cynical manipulations. One of the hands belonged to David Selig. He was merely trying to don protective coloration.

Miss Mueller said, "Let's run a few tests today. Victor, will you be our first guinea pig? Come to the front of the room."

Grinning nervously, Victor Schlitz shambled forward. He stood stiffly beside Miss Mueller's desk as she cut the cards and cut them again. Then, peering quickly at the top card, she slid it toward him. "Which symbol?" she asked.

"Circle?"

"We'll see. Class, don't say anything." She handed the card to Barbara Stein, telling her to place a checkmark under the proper symbol on the blackboard. Barbara checked the square. Miss Mueller glanced at the next card. *Star,* David thought.

"Waves," Victor said. Barbara checked the star.

"Plus." *Square, dummy!* Square.

"Circle." *Circle.* Circle. A sudden ripple of excitement in the classroom at Victor's hit. Miss Mueller, glaring, called for silence.

"Star." *Waves.* Waves was what Barbara checked.

"Square." *Square,* David agreed. Square. Another ripple, more subdued.

Victor went through the deck. Miss Mueller had kept score: four correct hits. Not even as good as chance. She put him through a second round. Five. All right, Victor: you may be sexy, but a telepath you aren't. Miss Mueller's eyes roved the room. Another subject? Let it not be me, David prayed. God, let it not be me. It wasn't. She summoned Sheldon Feinberg. He hit five the first time, six the second. Respectable, unspectacular. Then Alice Cohen. Four and four. Stony soil, Miss Mueller. David, following each turn of the cards, had hit 25 out of 25 every time, but he was the only one who knew that.

"Next?" Miss Mueller said. David shrank into his seat. How much longer until the dismissal bell? "Norman Heimlich." Norman waddled toward the teacher's desk. She glanced at a card. David, scanning her, picked up the image of a star. Bouncing then to Norman's mind, David was amazed to detect a flicker of an image there, a star perversely rounding its points to form a circle, then reverting to being a star. What was this? Did the odious Heimlich have a shred of the power? "Circle," Norman murmured. But he hit the next one—the waves—and the one after that, the square. He did indeed seem to be picking up emanations, fuzzy and indistinct but emanations all the same, from Miss Mueller's mind. Fat Heimlich had the vestiges of the gift. But only the vestiges; David, scanning his mind and the teacher's, watched the images grow ever more cloudy and vanish altogether by the tenth card, fatigue scattering Norman's feeble strength. He scored a seven, though, the best so far. *The bell*, David prayed. *The bell, the bell, the bell!* Twenty minutes away.

A small mercy. Miss Mueller briskly distributed test paper. She would run the whole class at once. "I'll call numbers from 1 to 25," she said. "As I call each number, write down the symbol you think you see. Ready? *One.*"

David saw a circle. *Waves*, he wrote.

Star. *Square.*

Waves. *Circle.*

Star. *Waves.*

As the test neared its close, it occurred to him that he might be making a tactical error by muffing every call. He told himself to put down two or three right ones, just for camouflage. But it was too late for that. There were only four numbers left; it would look too conspicuous if he hit several of them correctly after missing all the others. He went on missing.

Miss Mueller said, "Now exchange papers with your neighbor and mark his answers. Ready? Number one: circle. Number two: star. Number three: waves. Number four. . . ."

Tensely she called for results. Had anyone scored ten hits or more? No, teacher. Nine? Eight? Seven? Norman Heimlich had seven again. He preened himself: Heimlich the mind-reader. David felt disgust at the knowledge that Heimlich had even a crumb of power. Six? Four students had six. Five? Four? Miss Mueller diligently jotted down the results. Any other figures? Sidney Goldblatt began to snicker. "Miss Mueller, how about zero?"

She looked startled. "*Zero?* Was there someone who got all 25 cards *wrong?*"

"David Selig did!"

David Selig wanted to drop through the floor. All eyes were on him. Cruel laughter assailed him. *David Selig got them all wrong.* It was like saying, David Selig wet his pants, David Selig cheated on the exam, David Selig went into the girls' toilet. By trying to conceal himself, he had made himself terribly conspicuous. Miss Mueller, looking stern and oracular, said, "A null score can be quite significant too, class. It might mean extremely strong ESP abilities, rather than the total absence of such powers, as you might think." Oh, God. Extremely strong ESP abilities. She went on, "Rhine talks of phenomena such as 'forward displacement' and 'backward displacement,' in which an unusually powerful ESP force might accidentally focus on one card ahead of the right one, or one card behind it, or even two or three cards away. So the subject would appear to get a below-average result when actually he's hitting perfectly, just off the target! David, let me see your answers."

"I wasn't getting anything, Miss Mueller. I was just putting down my guesses, and I suppose they were all wrong."

"Let me see."

As though marching to the scaffold, he brought her the sheet. She placed it beside her own list and tried to realign it, searching for some correlation, some displacement sequence. But the randomness of his deliberately wrong answers protected him. A forward displacement of one card gave him two hits; a backward displacement of one card gave him three. Nothing significant there. Nevertheless, Miss Mueller would not let go. "I'd like to test you again," she said. "We'll run several kinds of trials. A null score is fascinating." She began to shuffle the deck. God, God, God, where are you? Ah. The bell! Saved by the bell! "Can you stay after class?" she asked. In agony, he shook his head. "Got to go to geometry next, Miss Mueller." She relented. Tomorrow, then. We'll run the tests tomorrow. God! He was up all the night in a turmoil of fear, sweating, shivering; about four in the morning he vomited. He hoped his mother would make him stay home from school, but no luck: at half past seven he was aboard the bus. Would Miss Mueller forget about the test? Miss Mueller had not forgotten. The fateful cards were on her desk. There would be no escape. He found himself the center of all attention. All right, Duv, be cleverer this time. "Are you ready to begin?" she asked, tipping up the first card. He saw a plus sign in her mind.

"Square," he said.

He saw a circle. "Waves," he said.

He saw another circle. "Plus," he said.

He saw a star. "Circle," he said.

He saw a square. "Square," he said. *That's one.*

He kept careful count. Four wrong answers, then a right one. Three wrong answers, another right one. Spacing them with false randomness, he allowed himself five hits on the first test. On the second he had four.

On the third, six. On the fourth, four. Am I being too average, he wondered? Should I give her a one-hit run, now? But she was losing interest. "I still can't understand your null score, David," she told him. "But it does seem to me as if you have no ESP ability whatever." He tried to look disappointed. Apologetic, even. Sorry, teach, I ain't got no ESP. Humbly the deficient boy made his way to his seat.

In one blazing instant of revelation and communion, Miss Mueller, I could have justified your whole lifelong quest for the improbable, the inexplicable, the unknowable, the irrational. The miraculous. But I didn't have the guts to do it. I had to look after my own skin, Miss Mueller. I had to keep a low profile. Will you forgive me? Instead of giving you truth, I faked you out, Miss Mueller, and sent you spinning blindly onward to the tarot, to the signs of the zodiac, to the flying-saucer people, to a thousand surreal vibrations, to a million apocalyptic astral antiworlds, when the touch of my mind against yours might have been enough to heal your madness. One touch from me. In a moment. In the twinkling of an eye.

Wednesday. I doodle with Yahya Lumumba's half-finished term paper and other such projects, a few futile lines on each. Getting nowhere. Judith calls. "A party," she says. "You're invited. Everybody'll be there."

"A party? Who? Where? Why? When?"

"Saturday night. Near Columbia. The host is Claude Guermantes. Do you know him? Professor of French Literature." No, the name is not Guermantes. I have changed the name to protect the guilty. "He's one of those charismatic new professors. Young, dynamic, handsome, a friend of Simone de Beauvoir, of Genet. Karl and I are coming. And a lot of others. He always invites the most interesting people."

"Genet? Simone de Beauvoir? Will they be there?"

"No, silly, not them. But it'll be worth your time. Claude gives the best parties of anybody I know. Brilliant combinations of people."

"Sounds like a vampire to me."

"He gives as well as takes, Duv. He specifically asked me to invite you."

"How does he know me at all?"

"Through me," she says. "I've talked of you. He's dying to meet you."

"I don't like parties."

"*Duv—*"

I know that warning tone of voice. I have no stomach for a hassle just now. "All right," I say, sighing. "Saturday night. Give me the ad dress." Why am I so pliable? Why do I let Judith manipulate me? Is this how I build my love for her, through these surrenders?

Thursday. I do two paragraphs, a.m., for Yahya Lumumba. Very appre hensive about his reaction to the thing I'm writing for him. He might just loathe it. If I ever finish it. I *must* finish it. Never missed a deadline yet. Don't dare to. In the p.m. I walk up to the 230th St. bookstore, needing fresh air and wanting, as usual, to see if anything interesting has come out since my last visit, three days before. Compulsively buy a few paperbacks—an anthology of minor metaphysical poets, Updike's *Rabbit Redux*, and a heavy Levi-Straussian anthropological study, folk-ways of some Amazonian tribe, that I know I'll *never* get around to reading. A new clerk at the cash register: a girl, 19, 20, pale, blond, white silk blouse, short plaid skirt, impersonal smile. Attractive in a vacant-eyed way. She isn't at all interesting to me, sexually or other-wise, and as I think that I chide myself for putting her down—let nothing human be alien to me—and on a whim I invade her mind as I pay for my books, so that I won't be judging her by superficials. I

21.

These are the days of David's passion, when he writhes a lot on his bed of nails. Let's do it in short takes. It hurts less that way.

Tuesday. Election Day. For months the clamor of the campaign has fouled the air. The free world is choosing its new maximum leader. The sound-trucks rumble along Broadway, belching slogans. Our next President! The man for all America! Vote! Vote! Vote! Vote for X! Vote for Y! The hollow words merge and blur and flow. Republocrat. Demican. *Boum.* Why should I vote? I will not vote. I do not vote. I am not plugged in. I am not part of the circuit. Voting is for *them.* Once, in the late autumn of 1968, I think it was, I was standing outside Carnegie Hall, thinking of going over to the paperback bookshop on the other side of the street, when suddenly all traffic halted on 57th and scores of policemen sprang up from the pavement like the dragon's-teeth warriors sown by Cadmus, and a motorcade came rumbling out of the east, and lo! in a dark black limousine rode Richard M. Nixon, President-Elect of the United States of America, waving jovially to the assembled populace. My big chance at last, I thought. I will look into his mind and make myself privy to great secrets of state; I will discover what it is about our leaders that sets them apart from ordinary mortals. And I looked into his mind, and what I found in there I will not tell you, except to say that it was more or less what I should have expected to find. And since that day I have had nothing to do with politics or politicians. Today I stay home from the polls. Let them elect the nex President without my help.

* * *

burrow in easily, deep, down through layer after layer of trivia, mining her without hindrance, getting right to the real stuff. Oh! What a sudden blazing communion, soul to soul! She glows. She streams fire. She comes to me with a vividness and a completeness that stun me, so rare has this sort of experience became for me. No dumb pallid mannequin now. I see her full and entire, her dreams, her fantasies, her ambitions, her loves, her soaring ecstasies (last night's gasping copulation and the shame and guilt afterward), a whole churning steaming sizzling human soul. Only once in the last six months have I hit this quality of total contact, only once, that awful day with Yahya Lumumba on the steps of Low Library. And as I remember that searing, numbing experience, something is triggered in me and the same thing happens. A dark curtain falls. I am disconnected. My grip on her consciousness is severed. Silence, that terrible mental silence, rushes to enfold me. I stand there, gaping, stunned, alone again and frightened, and I start to shake and drop my change, and she says to me, worried, "Sir? *Sir?*" in that sweet fluting little-girl voice.

Friday. Wake up with aches, high fever. Undoubtedly an attack of psychosomatic ague. The angry, embittered mind mercilessly flagellating the defenseless body. Chills followed by hot sweats followed by chills. Empty-gut puking. I feel hollow. Headpiece filled with straw. Alas! Can't work. I scribble a few pseudo-Lumumbesque lines and toss the sheet away. Sick as a dog. Well, a good excuse not to go to that dumb party, anyhow. I read my minor metaphysicals. Some of them not so minor. Traherne, Crashaw, William Cartwright. As for instance, Traherne:

> Pure native Powers that Corruption loathe,
>> Did, like the fairest Glass
>> Or, spotless polished Brass,
> Themselves soon in their Object's Image clothe:
>> Divine Impressions, when they came,
>> Did quickly enter and my Soul enflame.
> 'Tis not the Object, but the Light,
> That maketh Heav'n: 'Tis a clearer Sight.
>> Felicity
> Appears to none but them that purely see.

Threw up again after that. Not to be interpreted as an expression of criticism. Felt better for a while. I should call Judith. Have her make some chicken soup for me. Oy, veh. Veh is mir.

*   *   *

Saturday. Without help of chicken soup I recover and decide to go to the party. Veh is mir, in spades. Remember, remember, the sixth of November. Why has David allowed Judith to drag him from his cave? An endless subway ride downtown; spades full of weekend wine add a special *frisson* to the ordinary adventure of Manhattan transportation. At last the familiar Columbia station. I must walk a few blocks, shivering, not dressed properly for the wintry weather, to the huge old apartment house at Riverside Drive and 112th St. where Claude Guermantes is reputed to live. I stand hesitantly outside. A cold, sour breeze ripping malevolently across the Hudson at me, bearing the windborne detritus of New Jersey. Dead leaves swirling in the park. Inside, a mahogany doorman eyes me fishily. "Professor Guermantes?" I say. He jerks a thumb. "Seventh floor, 7-G." Waving me toward the elevator. I'm late; it's almost ten o'clock. Upstairs in the weary Otis, creak creak creak creak, elevator door rolls back, silkscreen poster in the hallway proclaims the route to Guermantes' lair. Not that posters are necessary. A high-decibel roar from the left tells me where the action is. I ring the bell. Wait. Nothing. Ring again. Too loud for them to hear me. Oh, to be able to transmit thoughts instead of just to receive them! I'd announce myself in tones of thunder. Ring again, more aggressively. Ah! Yes! Door opens. Short dark-haired girl, undergraduate-looking, wearing a sort of orange sari that leaves her right breast—small—bare. Nudity a la mode. Flashes her teeth gaily. "Come in, come in, come in!"

A mob scene. Eighty, ninety, a hundred people, everyone dressed in Seventies Flamboyant, gathered in groups of eight to ten, shouting profundities at one another. Those who hold no highballs are busily passing joints, ritualistic hissing intake of breath, much coughing, passionate exhaling. Before I have my coat off someone pops an elaborate ivory-headed pipe in my mouth. "Super hash," he explains. "Just in from Damascus. Come on, man, toke up!" I suck smoke willy-nilly and feel an immediate effect. I blink. "Yeah," my benefactor shouts. "It's got the power to cloud men's minds, don't it?" In this mob my mind is already pretty well clouded, however, sans cannabis, solely from input overload. My power seems to be functioning at reasonably high intensity tonight, only without much differentiation of persons, and I am involuntarily taking in a thick soup of overlapping transmissions, a chaos of merging thoughts. Murky stuff. Pipe and passer vanish and I stumble stonedly forward into a cluttered room lined from floor to ceiling with crammed bookcases. I catch sight of Judith just as she catches sight of me, and from her on a direct line of contact comes her outflow, fiercely vivid at first, trailing off in moments into mush: *brother, pain, love, fear, shared memories, forgiveness, forgetting, hatred, hostility, murmphness, froomz, zzzhhh, mmmm. Brother. Love. Hate. Zzzhhh.* "Duv!" she cries. "Oh, here I am, Duvid!"

Judith looks sexy tonight. Her long lithe body is sheathed in a purple satiny wrap, skin-tight, throat-high, plainly showing her breasts and the little bumps of her nipples and the cleft between her buttocks. On her bosom nestles a glittering slab of gold-rimmed jade, intricately carved; her hair, unbound, tumbles gloriously. I feel pride in her beauty. She is flanked by two impressive-looking men. On one side is Dr. Karl F. Silvestri, author of *Studies in the Physiology of Thermoregulation.* He corresponds fairly closely to the image of him that I had plucked from Judith's mind at her apartment a week or two ago, though he is older than I had guessed, at least 55, maybe closer to 60. Bigger, too—perhaps six feet five. I try to envision his huge burly body atop Jude's wiry slender self, pressing down. I can't. He has florid cheeks, a stolid self-satisfied facial expression, tender intelligent eyes. He radiates something avuncular or even paternal toward her. I see why Jude is attracted to him: he is the powerful father-figure that poor beaten Paul Selig never could have been for her. On Judith's other side is a man whom I suspect to be Professor Claude Guermantes; I bounce a quick probe into him and confirm that guess. His mind is quicksilver, a glittering, shimmering pool. He thinks in three or four languages at once. His rampaging energy exhausts me at a single touch. He is about 40, just under six feet tall, muscular, athletic; he wears his elegant sandy hair done in swirling baroque waves, and his short goatee is impeccably clipped. His clothing is so advanced in style that I lack the vocabulary to describe it, being unaware of fashions myself: a kind of mantle of coarse green and gold fabric (linen? muslin?), a scarlet sash, flaring satin trousers, turned-up pointed-toed medieval boots. His dandyish appearance and mannered posture suggest that he might be gay, but he gives off a powerful aura of heterosexuality, and from Judith's stance and fond way of looking at him I begin to realize that he and she must once have been lovers. May still be. I am shy about probing that. My raids on Judith's privacy are too sore a point between us.

"I'd like you to meet my brother David," Judith says.

Silvestri beams. "I've heard so much about you, Mr. Selig."

"Have you really?" (*"I've got this freak of a brother, Karl. Would you believe it, he can actually read minds? Your thoughts are as clear as a radio broadcast to him."*) How much has Judith actually revealed about me? I'll try to probe him and see. "And call me David. You're Dr. Silvestri, right?"

"That's right. Karl. I'd prefer Karl."

"I've heard a lot about you from Jude," I say. No go on the probe. My abominable waning gifts; I get only sputtering bits of static, misty scraps of unintelligible thought. His mind is opaque to me. My head starts to throb. "She showed me two of your books. I wish I could understand things like that."

A pleased chuckle from lofty Silvestri. Judith meanwhile has begun to introduce me to Guermantes. He murmurs his delight at making any acquaintance. I half expect him to kiss my cheeks, or maybe my hand. His voice is soft, purring; it carries an accent, but not a French one. Something strange, a mixture, Franco-Italic, maybe, or Franco-Hispanic. Him at least I can probe, even now; somehow his mind, more volatile than Silvestri's, remains within my reach. I slither in and take a look, even while exchanging platitudes about the weather and the recent election. Christ! Casanova Redivivus! He's slept with everything that walks or crawls, masculine feminine neuter, including of course my accessible sister Judith, whom—according to a neatly filed surface memory—he last penetrated just five hours ago, in this very room. His semen now curdles within her. He is obscurely restless over the fact that she never has come with him; he takes it as a failure of his flawless technique. The professor is speculating in a civilized way on the possibilities of nailing me before the night is out. No hope, professor. I will not be added to your Selig collection. He asks me pleasantly about my degrees. "Just one," I say. "A B.A. in '56. I thought about doing graduate work in English literature but never got around to it." He teaches Rimbaud, Verlain, Mallarmé, Baudelaire, Lautréamont, that whole sick crew, and identifies with them spiritually; his classes are full of adoring Barnard girls whose thighs open gladly for him, although in his Rimbaud facet he is not averse to romping with hearty Columbia men on occasions. As he talks to me he fondles Judith's shoulderblades affectionately, proprietorially. Dr. Silvestri appears not to notice, or else not to care. "Your sister," Guermantes murmurs, "she is a marvel, she is an original, a splendor—a *type*, M'sieu Selig, a *type*." A compliment, in the froggish sense. I poke his mind again and learn that he is writing a novel about a bitter, voluptuous young divorcee and a French intellectual who is an incarnation of the life-force, and expects to make millions from it. He fascinates me: so blatant, so phony, so manipulative, and yet so attractive despite all his transparent failings. He offers me cocktails, highballs, liqueurs, brandies, pot, hash, cocaine, anything I crave. I feel engulfed and escape from him, in some relief, slipping away to pour a little rum.

A girl accosts me at the liquor table. One of Guermantes' students, no more than 20. Coarse black hair tumbling into ringlets; pug nose;

fierce perceptive eyes; full fleshy lips. Not beautiful but somehow interesting. Evidently I interest her, too, for she grins at me and says, "Would you like to go home with me?"

"I just got here."

"Later. Later. No hurry. You look like you're fun to fuck."

"Do you say that to everybody you've just met?"

"We haven't even met," she points out. "And no, I don't say it to everybody. To lots, though. What's wrong? Girls can take the initiative these days. Besides, it's leap year. Are you a poet?"

"Not really."

"You look like one. I bet you're sensitive and you suffer a lot." My familiar dopy fantasy, coming to life before my eyes. *Her* eyes are red-rimmed. She's stoned. An acrid smell of sweat rising from her black sweater. Her legs are too short for her torso, her hips too wide, her breasts too heavy. Probably she's got the clap. Is she putting me on? *I bet you're sensitive and you suffer a lot. Are you a poet?* I try to explore her, but it's useless; fatigue is blanking my mind, and the collective shriek of the massed mob of partygoers is drowning out all individual outputs now. "What's your name?" she asks.

"David Selig."

"Lisa Holstein. I'm a senior at Barn—"

"Holstein?" The name triggers me. Kitty, Kitty, Kitty! "Is that what you said? Holstein?"

"Holstein, yes, and spare me the cow jokes."

"Do you have a sister named Kitty? Catherine, I guess. Kitty Holstein. About 35 years old. Your sister, maybe your cousin—"

"No. Never heard of her. Someone you know?"

"Used to know," I say. "Kitty Holstein." I pick up my drink and turn away.

"Hey," she calls after me. "Did you think I was kidding? Do you want to go home with me tonight or don't you?"

A black colossus confronts me. Immense Afro nimbus, terrifying jungle face. His clothing a sunburst of clashing colors. *Him*, here? Oh, God. Just who I most need to see. I think guiltily of the unfinished term paper, lame, humpbacked, a no-ass monstrosity, sitting on my desk. What is he doing here? How has Claude Guermantes managed to draw Yahya Lumumba into his orbit? The evening's token black, perhaps. Or the delegate from the world of high-powered sports, summoned here by way of demonstrating our host's intellectual versatility, his eclectic ballsiness. Lumumba stands over me, glowering, coldly examining me from his implausible height like an ebony Zeus. A spectacular black woman has her arm through his, a goddess, a titan, well over six feet tall, skin like polished onyx, eyes like beacons. A stunning couple. They shame us all with their beauty. Lumumba says, finally, "I *know* you, man. I know you from someplace."

"Selig. David Selig."

"Sounds familiar. Where do I know you?"

"Euripides, Sophocles, and Aeschylus."

"What the fuck?" Baffled. Pausing, then. Grinning. "Oh, yeah. Yeah, baby. That fucking term paper. How you coming along on that, man?"

"Coming along."

"You gonna have it Wednesday? Wednesday when it due."

"I'll have it, Mr. Lumumba." *Doin' my best, massa.*

"You better, boy. I counting on you."

"—Tom Nyquist—"

The name leaps suddenly, startlingly, out of the white-noised background hum of party chatter. For an instant it hangs in the smoky air like a dead leaf caught by a lazy October breeze. Who said "Tom Nyquist" just then? Who was it who spoke his name? A pleasant baritone voice, no more than a dozen feet from me. I look for likely owners of that voice. Men all around. You? You? You? No way of telling. Yes, one way. When words are spoken aloud, they reverberate in the mind of the speaker for a short while. (Also in the minds of his hearers, but the reverberations are different in tonality.) I summon my slippery skill and, straining, force needles of inquiry into the nearby consciousnesses, hunting for echoes. The effort is murderously great. The skulls I enter are solid bony domes through whose few crevices I struggle to ram my limp, feeble probes. But I enter. I seek the proper reverberations. *Tom Nyquist? Tom Nyquist?* Who spoke his name? You? You? Ah. There. The echo is almost gone, just a dim hollow clangor at the far end of a cavern. A tall plump man with a comic fringe of blond beard.

"Excuse me," I say. "I didn't mean to eavesdrop, but I heard you mention the name of a very old friend of mine—"

"Oh?"

"—and I couldn't help coming over to ask you about him. Tom Nyquist. He and I were once very close. If you know where he is now, what he's doing—"

"Tom Nyquist?"

"Yes. I'm sure I heard you mention him."

A blank smile. "I'm afraid there's been a mistake. I don't know anyone by that name. Jim? Fred? Can you help?"

"But I'm positive I heard—" The echo. *Boum* in the cave. Was I mistaken? At close range I try to get inside his head, to hunt in his filing system for any knowledge of Nyquist. But I can't function at all, now. They are conferring earnestly. Nyquist? Nyquist? Did anybody hear a Nyquist mentioned? Does anyone know a Nyquist?

One of them suddenly cries: "John Leibnitz!"

"Yes," says the plump one happily. "Maybe that's who you heard me mention. I was talking about John Leibnitz a few moments ago. A mutual friend. In this racket that might very well have sounded like Nyquist to you."

Leibnitz. Nyquist. Leibnitz. Nyquist. *Boum. Boum.* "Quite possibly," I agree. "No doubt that's what happened. Silly of me." John Leibnitz. "Sorry to have bothered you."

Guermantes says, mincing and prancing at my elbow, "You really must audit my class one of these days. This Wednesday afternoon I start Rimbaud and Verlaine, the first of six lectures on them. Do come around. You'll be on campus Wednesday, won't you?"

Wednesday is the day I must deliver Yahya Lumumba's term paper on the Greek tragedians. I'll be on campus, yes. I'd better be. But how does Guermantes know that? Is he getting into my head somehow? What if he has the gift too? And I'm wide open to him, he knows everything, my poor pathetic secret, my daily increment of loss, and there he stands, patronizing me because I'm failing and he's as sharp as I ever was. Then a quick paranoiac flash: not only does he have the gift but perhaps he's some kind of telepathic leech, draining me, bleeding the power right out of my mind and into his. Perhaps he's been tapping me on the sly ever since '74.

I shake these useless idiocies away. "I expect to be around on Wednesday, yes. Perhaps I will drop in."

There is no chance whatever that I will go to hear Claude Guermantes lecture on Rimbaud or Verlaine. If he's got the power, let him put *that* in his pipe and smoke it!

"I'd love it if you came," he tells me. He leans close to me. His androgynous Mediterranean smoothness permits him casually to breach the established American code of male-to-male distancing customs. I smell hair tonic, shaving lotion, deodorant, and other perfumes. A small blessing: not all my senses are dwindling at once. "Your sister," he murmurs. "Marvelous woman! How I love her! She speaks often of you."

"Does she?"

"With great love. Also with great guilt. It seems you and she were estranged for many years."

"That's over now. We're finally becoming friends."

"How wonderful for you both." He gestures with a flick of his eyes. "That doctor. No good for her. Too old, too static. After fifty most men lose the capacity to grow. He'll bore her to death in six months."

"Maybe boredom is what she needs," I reply. "She's had an exciting life. It hasn't made her happy."

"No one ever needs boredom," Guermantes says, and winks.

"Karl and I would love to have you come for dinner next week, Duv. There's so much we three need to talk about."

"I'll see, Jude. I'm not sure about anything about next week yet. I'll call you."

Lisa Holstein. John Leibnitz. I think I need another drink.

Sunday. Greatly overhung. Hash, rum, wine, pot, God knows what else. And somebody popping amyl nitrite under my nose about two in the morning. That filthy fucking party. I should never have gone. My head, my head, my head. Where's the typewriter? I've got to get some work done. Let's go, then:

We see, thus, the difference in method of approach of these three tragedians to the same story. Aeschylus' primary concern is theological implications of the crime and the inexorable workings of the gods: Orestes is torn between the command of Apollo to slay his mother and his own fear of matricide, and goes mad as a result. Euripides dwells on the characterization, and takes a less allegorical

No damned good. Save it for later.

Silence between my ears. The echoing black void. I have nothing going for me at all today, nothing. I think it may be completely gone. I can't even pick up the clamor of the spics next door. November is the cruelest month, breeding onions out of the dead mind. I'm living an Eliot poem. I'm turning into words on a page. Shall I sit here feeling sorry for myself? No. No. No. No. I'll fight back. Spiritual exercises designed to restore my power. On your knees, Selig. Bow the head. Concentrate. Transform yourself into a fine needle of thought, a slim telepathic laser-beam, stretching from this room to the vicinity of the lovely star Betelgeuse. Got it? Good. That sharp pure mental beam piercing the universe. Hold it. Hold it firm. No spreading at the edges allowed, man. Good. Now ascend. We are climbing Jacob's ladder. This will be an out-of-the-body experience, Duvid. Up, up and away! Rise through the ceiling, through the roof, through the atmosphere, through the ionosphere, through the stratosphere, through the whatsisphere. Outward. Into the vacant interstellar spaces.

O dark dark dark. Cold the sense and lost the motive of action. No, stop that stuff! Only positive thinking is allowed on this trip. Soar! Soar! Toward the little green men of Betelgeuse IX. Reach their minds, Selig. Make contact. Make . . . contact. Soar, you lazy yid-bastard! Why aren't you soaring? *Soar!*

Well?

Nothing. *Nada. Niente.* Nowhere. *Nulla. Nicht.*

Tumbling back to earth. Into the silent funeral. All right, give up, if that's what you want. All right. Rest, for a little while. Rest and then pray, Selig. Pray.

Monday. The hangover gone. The brain once again receptive. In a glorious burst of creative frenzy I rewrite *The "Electra" Theme in Aeschylus, Sophocles, and Euripides* from gunwale to fetlock, completely recasting it, revoicing it, clarifying and strengthening the ideas while simultaneously catching what I think is just the perfect tone of offhand niggerish hipness. As I hammer out the final words the telephone rings. Nicely timed; I feel sociable now. Who calls? Judith? No. It is Lisa Holstein who calls. "You promised to take me home after the party," she says mournfully, accusingly. "What the hell did you do, sneak away?"

"How did you get my number?"

"From Claude. Professor Guermantes." That sleek devil. He knows everything. "Look, what are you doing right now?"

"Thinking about having a shower. I've been working all morning and I stink like a goat."

"What kind of work do you do?"

"I ghostwrite term papers for Columbia men."

She ponders that a moment. "You sure have a weird head, man. I mean really: what do you do?"

"I just told you."

A long digestive silence. Then: "Okay. I can dig it. You ghostwrite term papers. Look, Dave, go take your shower. How long is it on the subway from 110th Street and Broadway to your place?"

"Maybe forty minutes, if you get a train right away."

"Swell. See you in an hour, then." *Click.*

I shrug. A crazy broad. Dave, she calls me. Nobody calls me Dave. Stripping, I head for the shower, a long leisurely soaping. Afterward, sprawling out in a rare interlude of relaxation, Dave Selig re-reads this

morning's labors and finds pleasure in what he has wrought. Let's hope
Lumumba does too. Then I pick up the Updike book. I get to page four
and the phone rings again. Lisa: she's on the train platform at 225th,
wants to know how to get to my apartment. This is more than a joke,
now. Why is she pursuing me so singlemindedly? But okay. I can play
her game. I give her the instructions. Ten minutes later, a knock on the
door. Lisa in thick black sweater, the same sweaty one as Saturday night,
and tight blue jeans. A shy grin, strangely out of character for her. "Hi,"
she says. Making herself comfortable. "When I first saw you, I had this
intuitive flash on you: *This guy's got something special. Make it with
him.* If there's one thing I've learned, its that you've got to trust your
intuition. I go with the flow, Dave, I go with the flow." Her sweater is
off by now. Her breasts are heavy and round, with tiny, almost imperceptible nipples. A Jewish star nestles in the deep valley between them.
She wanders the room, examining my books, my records, my photographs. "So tell me," she says. "Now that I'm here. Was I right? *Is*
there anything special about you?"

"There once was."

"What?"

"That's for me to know and you to find out," I say, and gathering
my strength, I ram my mind into hers. It's a brutal frontal assault, a
rape, a true mindfuck. Of course she doesn't feel a thing. I say, "I used
to have a really extraordinary gift. It's mostly worn off by now, but
some of the time I still have it, and as a matter of fact I'm using it on
you right now."

"Far out," she says, and drops her jeans. No underpants. She will
be fat before she's 30. Her thighs are thick, her belly protrudes. Her
pubic hair is oddly dense and widespread, less a triangle than a sort of
diamond, a black diamond reaching past her loins to her hips, almost.
Her buttocks are deeply dimpled. While I inspect her flesh I savagely
ransack her mind, sparing her no areas of privacy, enjoying my access
while it lasts. I don't need to be polite. I owe her nothing: she forced
herself on me. I check, first, to see if she had been lying when she said
she'd never heard of Kitty. The truth: Kitty is no kin to her. A meaningless coincidence of surnames, is all. "I'm sure you're a poet, Dave,"
she says as we entwine and drop onto the unmade bed. "That's an
intuition flash too. Even if you're doing this term paper thing now,
poetry is where you're really at, right?" I run my hands over her breasts
and belly. A sharp odor comes from her skin. She hasn't washed in
three or four days, I bet. No matter. Her nipples mysteriously emerge,
tiny rigid pink nubs. She wriggles. I continue to loot her mind like a
Goth plundering the Forum. She is fully open to me; I delight in this

unexpected return of vigor. Her autobiography assembles itself for me. Born in Cambridge. Twenty years old. Father a professor. Mother a professor. One younger brother. Tomboy childhood. Measles, chicken pox, scarlet fever. Puberty at eleven, lost her virginity at twelve. Abortion at sixteen. Several Lesbian adventures. Passionate interest in French decadent poets. Acid, mescaline, psilocybin, cocaine, even a sniff of smack. Guermantes gave her that. Guermantes also took her to bed five or six times. Vivid memories of that. Her mind shows me more of Guermantes than I want to see. He's hung very impressively. Lisa comes through with a tough, aggressive self-image, captain of her soul, master of her fate, etc. Underneath that it's just the opposite, of course; she's scared as hell. Not a bad kid. I feel a little guilty about the casual way I slammed into her head, no regard for her privacy at all. But I have my needs. I continue to prowl her, and meanwhile she goes down on me. I can hardly remember the last time anyone did that. I can hardly remember my last lay, it's been so bad lately. She's an expert fellatrice. I'd like to reciprocate but I can't bring myself to do it; sometimes I'm fastidious and she's not the douching type. Oh, well, leave that stuff for the Guermanteses of this world. I lie there picking her brain and accepting the gift of her mouth. I feel virile, bouncy, cocksure, and why not, getting my kicks from two inputs at once, head and crotch? Without withdrawing from her mind I withdraw, at last, from her lips, turn around, part her thighs, slide deep into her tight narrow-mouthed harbor. Selig the stallion. Selig the stud. "Oooh," she says, flexing her knees. "Oooh." And we begin to play the beast with two backs. Covertly I feed on feedback, tapping into her pleasure-responses and thereby doubling my own; each thrust brings me a factored and deliciously exponential delight. But then a funny thing happens. Although she is nowhere close to coming—an event that I know will disrupt our mental contact when it occurs—the broadcast from her mind is already becoming erratic and indistinct, more noise than signal. The images break up in a pounding of static. What comes through is garbled and distant; I scramble to maintain my hold on her consciousness, but no use, no use, she slips away, moment by moment receding from me, until there is no communion at all. And in that moment of severance my cock suddenly softens and slips out of her. She is jolted by that, caught by surprise. "What brought you down?" she asks. I find it impossible to tell her. I remember Judith asking me, some weeks back, whether I had ever regarded my loss of mental powers as a kind of metaphor of impotence. Sometimes yes, I told her. And now here, for the first time, metaphor blends with reality; the two failures are integrated. He is impotent here and he is impotent there. Poor David. "I guess I got distracted," I tell her. Well, she has her skills; for half an hour she works me over, fingers, lips, tongue, hair, breasts, not getting a rise out of me with anything, in fact turning me off more than ever by her grim purposefulness. "I don't understand it," she says. "You were doing so well. Was there something about me that brought you down?" I reassure her. You were great, baby. Stuff like this sometimes just happens, no one knows why. I tell her, "Let's just rest and maybe I'll come back to life." We rest. Side by side, stroking her skin in an abstract way, I run a few tentative probing efforts. Not a flicker on the telepathic level. Not a flicker. The silence of the tomb. Is this it, the end, right here and now? Is this where it finally burns out? And I am like all the rest of you now. I am condemned to make do with mere words. "I have an idea," she says. "Let's take a shower together. That sometimes peps a guy up." To this I make no objection; it might just work, and in any case she'll smell better afterward. We head for the bathroom. Torrents of brisk cool water.

Success. The ministrations of her soapy hand hand revive me.

We spring toward the bed. Still stiff, I top her and take her. Gasp gasp gasp, moan moan moan. I can get nothing on the mental band. Suddenly she goes into a funny little spasm, intense but quick, and my own spurt swiftly follows. So much for sex. We curl up together, cuddly in the afterglow. I try again to probe her. Zero. Zee-ro. Is it gone? I think it's really gone. You have been present today at an historic event, young lady. The perishing of a remarkable extrasensory power. Leaving behind this merely mortal husk of mine. Alas.

"I'd love to read some of your poetry, Dave," she says.

Monday night, about seven-thirty. Lisa has left, finally. I go out for dinner, to a nearby pizzeria. I am quite calm. The impact of what has befallen me hasn't really registered yet. How strange that I can be so accepting. At any moment, I know, it's bound to come rushing in on me, crushing me, shattering me; I'll weep, I'll scream, I'll bang my head against walls. But for now I'm surprisingly cool. An oddly post-humous feeling, as of having outlived myself. And a feeling of relief: the suspense is over, the process has completed itself, the dying is done, and I've survived it. Of course I don't expect this mood to last. I've lost something central to my being, and now I await the anguish and the grief and the despair that must surely be due to erupt shortly.

But it seems that my mourning must be postponed. What I thought was all over isn't over yet. I walk into the pizzeria and the counterman gives me his flat cold New York smile of welcome, and I get this, unsolicited, from behind his greasy face: *Hey, here's the fag who always wants extra anchovies.*

Reading him clearly. So it's not dead yet! Not quite dead! Only resting a while. Only hiding.

Tuesday. Bitter cold; one of those terrible late-autumn days when every drop of moisture has been squeezed from the air and the sunlight is like knives. I finish two more term papers for delivery tomorrow. I read Updike. Judith calls after lunch. The usual dinner invitation. My usual oblique reply.

"What did you think of Karl?" she asks.

"A very substantial man."

"He wants me to marry him."

"Well?"

"It's too soon. I don't really know him, Duv. I like him, I admire him tremendously, but I don't know whether I love him."

"Then don't rush into anything with him," I say. Her soap-opera hesitations bore me. I don't understand why anybody old enough to know the score ever gets married, anyway. Why should love require a contract? Why put yourself into the clutches of the state and give it power over you? Why invite lawyers to fuck around with your assets? Marriage is for the immature and the insecure and the ignorant. We who see through such institutions should be content to live together without legal coercion, eh, Toni? Eh? I say, "Besides, if you marry him, he'd probably want you to give up Guermantes. I don't think he could dig it."

"You know about me and Claude?"

"Of course."

"You always know everything."

"This was pretty obvious, Jude."

"I thought your power was waning."

"It is, it is, it's waning faster than ever. But this was still pretty obvious. To the naked eye."

"All right. What did you think of him?"

"He's death. He's a killer."

"You misjudged him, Duv."

"I was in his head. I *saw* him, Jude. He isn't human. People are toys to him."

"If you could hear the sound of your own voice now, Duv. The hostility, the outright jealousy—"

"*Jealousy?* Am I that incestuous?"

"You always were," she says. "But let that pass. I really thought you'd enjoy meeting Claude."

"I did. He's fascinating. I think cobras are fascinating too."

"Oh, fuck you, Duv."

"You want me to pretend I liked him?"

"Don't do me any favors." The old icy Judith.

"What's Karl's reaction to Guermantes?"

She pauses. Finally: "Pretty negative. Karl's very conventional, you know. Just as you are."

"Me?"

"Oh, you're so fucking straight, Duv! You're such a puritan! You've been lecturing me on morality all my goddamned life. The very first time I got laid there you were, wagging your finger at me—"

"Why doesn't Karl like him?"

"I don't know. He thinks Claude's sinister. Exploitive." Her voice is suddenly flat and dull. "Maybe he's just jealous. He knows I'm still sleeping with Claude. Oh, Jesus, Duv, why are we fighting again? Why can't we just *talk*?"

"I'm not the one who's fighting. I'm not the one who raised his voice."

"You're challenging me. That's what you always do. You spy on me and then you challenge me and try to put me down."

"Old habits are hard to break, Jude. Really, though: I'm not angry with you."

"You sound so smug!"

"I'm *not* angry. You are. You got angry when you saw that Karl and I agree about your friend Claude. People always get angry when they're told something they don't want to hear. Listen, Jude, do whatever you want. If Guermantes is your trip, go ahead."

"I don't know. I just don't know." An unexpected concession: "Maybe there *is* something sick about my relationship with him." Her flinty self-assurance vanishes abruptly. That's the wonderful thing about her: you get a different Judith every two minutes. Now, softening, thawing, she sounds uncertain of herself. In a moment she'll turn her concern outward, away from her own troubles, toward me. "Will you come to dinner next week? We very much do want to get together with you."

"I'll try."

"I'm worried about you, Duv." Yes, here it comes. "You looked so strung out on Saturday night."

"It's been a pretty rough time for me. But I'll manage." I don't feel like talking about myself. I don't want her pity, because after I get hers, I'll start giving myself mine. "Listen, I'll call you soon, okay?"

"Are you still in so much pain, Duv?"

"I'm adapting. I'm accepting the whole thing. I mean, I'll be okay.

Keep in touch, Jude. My best to Karl." And Claude, I add, as I put down the receiver.

Wednesday morning. Downtown to deliver my latest batch of masterpieces. It's colder even than yesterday, the air clearer, the sun brighter, more remote. How dry the world seems. The humidity is minus sixteen percent, I think. The sort of weather in which I used to function with overwhelming clarity of perception. But I was picking up hardly anything at all on the subway ride down to Columbia, just muzzy little blurts and squeaks, nothing coherent. I can no longer be certain of having the power on any given day, apparently, and this is one of the days off. Unpredictable. That's what you are, you who live in my head: unpredictable. Thrashing about randomly in your death-throes. I go to the usual place and await my clients. They come, they get from me what they have come for, they cross my palm with greenbacks. David Selig, benefactor of undergraduate mankind. I see Yahya Lumumba like a black sequoia making his way across from Butler Library. Why am I trembling? It's the chill in the air, isn't it, the hint of winter, the death of the year. As the basketball star approaches he waves, nods, grins; everyone knows him, everyone calls out to him. I feel a sense of participation in his glory. When the season starts maybe I'll go watch him play.

"You got the paper, man?"

"Right here." I deal it off the stack. "Aeschylus, Sophocles, Euripides. Six pages. That's $21, minus the five you already gave me is $16 you owe me."

"Wait, man." He sits down beside me on the steps. "I got to read this fucker first, right? How I know you did a righteous job if I don't read it?"

I watch him as he reads. Somehow I expect him to be moving his lips, to be stumbling over the unfamiliar words, but no, his eyes flicker rapidly over the lines. He gnaws his lip. He reads faster and faster, impatiently turning the pages. At length he looks at me and there is death in his eyes.

"This is shit, man," he says. "I mean, this here is just shit. What kind of con you trying to pull?"

"I guarantee you'll get a B+. You don't have to pay me until you get the grade. Anything less than B+ and—"

"No, listen to me. Who talking about grades? I can't turn this fucking thing in *at all*. Look, half this thing is jive-talk, the other half it copied straight out of some book. Crazy shit, that's what. The prof he going to read it, he going to look at me, he going to say, Lumumba,

who you think I am? You think I a dummy, Lumumba? You didn't
write this crap, he going to say to me. You don't believe Word One of
this." Angrily he rises. "Here, I going to read you some of this, man. I
show you what you give me." Leafing through the pages, he scowls,
spits, shakes his head. "No. Why the hell should I? You know what you
up to here, man? You making fun of me, that's what. You playing games
with the dumb nigger, man."

"I was trying to make it look plausible that you had written—"

"Crap. You pulling a mindfuck, man. You making up a pile of
stinking Jew shit about Europydes and you hoping I get in trouble trying
to pass it off as my own stuff."

"That's a lie. I did the best possible job for you, and don't think I
didn't sweat plenty. When you hire another man to write a term paper
for you, I think you have to be prepared to expect a certain—"

"How long this take you? Fifteen minutes?"

"Eight hours, maybe ten," I say. "You know what I think you're
trying to do, Lumumba? You're pulling reverse racism on me. Jew this
and Jew that—if you dislike Jews so much, why didn't you get a black
to write your paper for you? Why didn't you write it yourself? I did an
honest job for you. I don't like hearing it put down as stinking Jew shit.
And I tell you that if you turn it in, you'll get a passing grade for sure,
you'll probably get a B+ at the very least."

"I gonna get flunked, is what."

"No. No. Maybe you just don't see what I was driving at. Let me
try to explain it to you. If you'll give it to me for a minute so I can
read you a couple of things—maybe it'll be clearer if I—" Getting to
my feet, I extend a hand toward the paper, but he grins and holds it
high above my head. I'd need a ladder to reach it. No use jumping.
"Come on, damn it, don't play games with me! Let me have it!" I snap,
and he flicks his wrist and the six sheets of paper soar into the wind
and go sailing eastward along College Walk. Dying, I watch them go.
I clench my fists; an astonishing burst of rage explodes in me. I want
to smash his mocking face in. "You shouldn't have done that." I say.
"You shouldn't have just thrown it away."

"You owe me my five bucks back, man."

"Hold on, now. I did the work you hired me to do, and—"

"You said you don't charge if the paper's no good. Okay, the paper
was shit. No charge. Give me the five."

"You aren't playing fair, Lumumba. You're trying to rip me off."

"Who ripping who off? Who set up that money-back deal anyhow?
Me? *You.* What I gonna do for a term paper now? I got to take an
incomplete and it your fault. Suppose they make me ineligible for the

team because of that. Huh? Huh? What then? Look, man, you make me want to puke. Give me the five."

Is he serious about the refund? I can't tell. The idea of paying him back disgusts me, and it isn't just on account of losing the money. I wish I could read him, but I can't get anything out of him on that level; I'm completely blocked now. I'll bluff. I say, "What is this, slavery turned upside down? I did the work. I don't give a damn what kind of crazy irrational reasons you've got for rejecting it. I'm going to keep the five. At least the five."

"Give me the money, man."

"Go to hell."

I start to walk away. He grabs me—his arm, fully outspread toward me, must be as long as one of my legs—and hauls me toward him. He starts to shake me. My teeth are rattling. His grin is broader than ever, but his eyes are demonic. I wave my fists at him, but, held at arm's length, I can't even touch him. I start to yell. A crowd is gathering. Suddenly there are three or four other men in varsity jackets surrounding us, all black, all gigantic, though not as big as he is. His teammates. Laughing, whooping, cavorting. I am a toy to them. "Hey, man, he bothering you?" one of them asks. "You need help, Yahya?" yells another. "What's the muthafuck honkie doing to you, man?" calls a third. They form a ring and Lumumba thrusts me toward the man on his left, who catches me and flings me onward around the circle. I spin; I stumble; I reel; they never let me fall. Around and around and around. An elbow explodes against my lip. I taste blood. Someone slaps me, and my head rockets backward. Fingers jabbing my ribs. I realize that I'm going to get very badly hurt, that in fact these giants are going to beat me up. A voice I barely recognize as my own offers Lumumba his refund, but no one notices. They continue to whirl me from one to the next. Not slapping now, not jabbing, but punching. Where are the campus police? Help! Help! Pigs to the rescue! But no one comes. I can't catch my breath. I'd like to drop to my knees and huddle against the ground. They're yelling at me, racial epithets, words I barely comprehend, soul-brother jargon that must have been invented last week; I don't know what they're calling me, but I can feel the hatred in every syllable. Help? Help? The world spins wildly. I know now how a basketball would feel, if a basketball could feel. The steady pounding, the blur of unending motion. Please, someone, anyone, help me, stop them. Pain in my chest: a lump of white-hot metal back of my breast-bone. I can't see. I can only feel. Where are my feet? I'm falling at last. Look how fast the steps rush toward me. The cold kiss of the stone bruises my cheek. I may already have lost consciousness; how can I tell? There's one comfort, at least. I can't get any further down than this.

22.

He was ready to fall in love when he met Kitty, overripe and eager for an emotional entanglement. Perhaps that was the whole trouble; what he felt for her was not so much love as simply satisfaction at the idea of being in love. Or perhaps not. He never understood his feelings for Kitty in any orderly way. They had their romance in the summer of 1963, which he remembers as the last summer of hope and good cheer before the long autumn of entropic chaos and philosophical despair descended on western society. Jack Kennedy was running things then, and while things weren't going especially well for him politically, he still managed to give the impression that he was going to get it all together, if not right away then in his inevitable second term. Atmospheric nuclear tests had just been banned. The Washington-to-Moscow hot line was being set up. Secretary of State Rusk announced in August that the South Vietnamese government was rapidly taking control of additional areas of the countryside. The number of Americans killed fighting in Vietnam had not yet reached 100.

Selig, who was 28 years old, had just moved from his Brooklyn Heights apartment to a small place in the West Seventies. He was working as a stockbroker then, of all unlikely things. This was Tom Nyquist's idea. After six years, Nyquist was still his closest and possibly only friend, although the friendship had waned considerably in the last year or two: Nyquist's almost arrogant self-assurance made Selig increasingly more uncomfortable, and he found it desirable to put some distance, psychological and geographical, between himself and the older man. One day Selig had said wistfully that if he could only manage to get a bundle of money together—say, $25,000 or so—he'd go off to a remote island and spend a couple of years writing a novel, a major statement about alienation in contemporary life, something like that. He had never written anything serious and wasn't sure he was sincere about wanting to. He was secretly hoping that Nyquist would simply hand him the money—Nyquist could pick up $25,000 in one afternoon's work, if he felt like it—and say, "Here, chum, go and be creative." But Nyquist didn't do things that way. Instead he said that the easiest way for someone without capital to make a lot of money in a hurry was to take a job as a customer's man with a brokerage firm. The commissions would be decent, enough to live on and something left over, but the real money would come from riding along on all the in-shop maneuvers of the experienced brokers—the short sales, the new-issue purchases, the arbitrage ploys. If you're dedicated enough, Nyquist told him, you can make just about as much as you like. Selig protested that he knew nothing about Wall Street. "I could teach you everything in three days," said Nyquist.

Actually it took less than that. Selig slipped into Nyquist's mind for a quick cram course in financial terminology. Nyquist had all the definitions beautifully arranged: common stocks and preferred, shorts and longs, puts and calls, debentures, convertibles, capital gains, special situations, closed-end versus open-end funds, secondary offerings, specialists and what they do, the over-the-counter market, the Dow-Jones averages, point-and-figure charts, and everything else. Selig memorized all of it. There was a vivid quality about mind-to-mind transferences with Nyquist that made memorizing things easy. The next step was to enroll as a trainee. Every big brokerage firm was looking for beginners—Merrill Lynch, Goodbody, Hayden Stone, Clark Dodge, scads of them. Selig picked one at random and applied. They gave him a stock-market quiz by way of preliminary screening; he knew most of the answers, and those he didn't know he picked up out of the minds of his fellow testees, most of whom had been following the market since childhood. He got a perfect score and was hired. After a brief training period he passed the licensing test, and before long he was a registered representative operating out of a fairly new brokerage office on Broadway near 72nd Street.

He was one of five brokers, all of them fairly young. The clientele was predominantly Jewish and generally geriatric: 75-year-old widows from the huge apartment houses along 72nd Street, and cigar-chomping retired garment manufacturers who lived on West End Avenue and Riverside Drive. Some of them had quite a lot of money, which they invested in the most cautious way possible. Some were practically penniless, but insisted on buying four shares of Con Edison or three shares of Telephone just to have the illusion of prosperity. Since most of the clients were elderly and didn't work, the bulk of dealings at the office were transacted in person rather than by phone; there were always ten or twelve senior citizens schmoozing in front of the stock ticker, and now and then one of them would dodder to the desk of his pet broker and place an order. On Selig's fourth day at work one venerable client suffered a fatal heart attack during a nine-point rally. Nobody seemed surprised or even dismayed, neither the brokers nor the friends of the victim: customers died in the shop about once a month, Selig learned. Kismet. You come to expect your friends to drop dead, once you reach a certain age. He quickly became a favorite, especially among the old ladies; they liked him because he was a nice Jewish boy, and several offered to introduce him to comely granddaughters. These offers he always refused, but politely; he made a point of being courteous and patient with them, of playing grandson. Most of them were ignorant, practically illiterate women, kept in a state of lifelong innocence by their hard-driving, acquisitive, coronary-prone husbands; now, having inherited more money than they could possibly spend, they had no real idea of how to manage it, and were wholly dependent on the nice young broker. Probing their minds, Selig found them almost always to be dim and sadly unformed—how could you live to the age of 75 without ever having had an idea?—but a few of the livelier ladies showed vigorous, passionate peasant rapacity, charming in its way. The men were less agreeable—loaded with dough, yet always on the lookout for more. The vulgarity and ferocity of their ambitions repelled him, and he glanced into their minds no more often than necessary, merely probing to have a better idea of their investment goals so he could serve them as they would be served. A month among such people, he decided, would be sufficient to turn a Rockefeller into a socialist.

Business was steady but unspectacular; once he had acquired his own nucleus of regulars, Selig's commissions ran to about $160 a week, which was more money than he had ever made before, but hardly the kind of income he imagined brokers pulled down. "You're lucky you came here in the spring," one of the other customer's men told him. "In the winter months all the clients go to Florida and we can choke before anybody gives us any business here." As Nyquist had predicted, he was able to turn some pleasant profits by trading for his own account; there were always nice little deals circulating in the office, hot tips with substance behind them. He started with savings of $350 and quickly pyramided his wad to a high four-figure sum, making money on Chrysler and Control Data and RCA and Sunray DX Oil, nimbly trading in and out on rumors of mergers, stock splits, or dynamic earnings gains; but he discovered that Wall Street runs in two directions, and much of his winnings melted away through badly timed trades in Brunswick, Beckman Instruments, and Martin Marietta. He came to see that he was never going to have enough of a stake to go off and write that novel. Possibly just as well: did the world need another amateur novelist? He wondered what he would do next. After three months as a broker he had some money in the bank, but not much, and he was hideously bored.

Luck delivered Kitty to him. She came in one muggy July morning at half past nine. The market hadn't opened yet, most of the customers had fled to the Catskills for the summer, and the only people in the office were Martinson, the manager, Nadel, one of the other customer's men, and Selig. Martinson was going over his totals, Nadel was on the phone to somebody downtown trying to work a complicated finagle in American Photocopy, and Selig, idle, was daydreaming of falling in love with somebody's beautiful granddaughter. Then the door opened and somebody's beautiful granddaughter came in. Not exactly beautiful, maybe, but certainly attractive: a girl in her early twenties, slim and well proportioned, perhaps five feet three or four, with fluffy light-brown hair, blue-green eyes, finely outlined features, a graceful slender figure. She seemed shy, intelligent, somehow innocent, a curious mixture of knowledge and naiveté. She wore a white silk blouse—gold chain lying on the smallish breasts—and an ankle-length brown skirt, offering a hint of excellent legs beneath. No, not a beautiful girl, but certainly pretty. Refreshing to look at. What the hell, Selig wondered, does she want in this temple of Mammon at her age? She's here fifty years too early. Curiosity led him to send a probe drilling into her forehead as she walked toward him. Seeking only surface stuff: name, age, marital status, address, telephone number, purpose of visit—what else?

He got nothing.

That shocked him. It was an incredible experience. Unique. To reach toward a mind and find it absolutely inaccessible, opaque, hidden as if behind an impenetrable wall—he had never had that happen to him before. He got no aura from her at all. She might as well have been a department store's plaster window mannequin, or a mindless robot from another planet. He sat there blinking, trying to account for his failure to make contact. He was so astounded by her total blankness that he forgot to listen to what she was saying to him, and had to ask her to repeat.

"I said, I'd like to open a brokerage account. Are you a broker?"

Sheepish, fumbling, stricken with sudden adolescent clumsiness, he gave her the new-account forms. By this time the other brokers had arrived, but too late: by the rules of the house she was his client. Sitting beside his cluttered desk, she told him of her investment needs while he studied the elegant tapered structure of her high-bridged nose, fought without success against her perplexing and enigmatic mental inaccessibility, and, despite or perhaps because of that inaccessibility, felt himself helplessly falling in love with her.

She was 22, one year out of Radcliffe, came from Long Island, and shared a West End Avenue apartment with two other girls. Unmarried— there had been a long futile love affair ending in a broken engagement not long before, he would discover later. (How strange it was for him not to be discovering everything at once, taking the information as he desired it.) Her background was in mathematics and she worked as a computer programmer, a term which, in 1963, meant very little to him; he wasn't sure whether she designed computers, operated them, or repaired them. Recently she had inherited $6500 from an aunt in Arizona, and her parents, who evidently were stern and formidable advocates of sink-or-swim education, had told her to invest the money on her own, by way of assuming adult responsibilities. So she had gone to her friendly neighborhood brokerage office, a lamb for the shearing, to invest her money. "What do you want?" Selig asked her. "To stash it away in safe blue chips, or to go for a little action, a chance for capital gains?"

"I don't know. I don't know the first thing about the market. I just don't want to do anything silly."

Another broker—Nadel, say—would have given her the Nothing Ventured, Nothing Gained speech, and, advising her to forget about such old and tired concepts as dividends, would have steered her into an action portfolio—Texas Instruments, Collins Radio, Polaroid, stuff like that. Then he would churn her account every few months, switch Polaroid into Xerox, Texas Instruments into Fairchild Camera, Collins into American Motors, American Motors back into Polaroid, running up fancy commissions for himself and, perhaps, making some money for her, or perhaps losing some. Selig had no stomach for such maneuvers. "This is going to sound stodgy," he said, "but let's play it very safe. I'll recommend some decent things that won't ever make you rich but that you won't get hurt on, either. And then you can just put them away and watch them grow, without having to check the market quotations every day to find out if you ought to sell. Because you don't really want to bother worrying about the short-term fluctuations, do you?" This was absolutely not what Martinson had instructed him to tell new clients, but to hell with that. He got her some Jersey Standard, some Telephone, a little IBM, two good electric utilities, and 30 shares of a closed-end fund called Lehman Corporation that a lot of his elderly customers owned. She didn't ask questions, didn't even want to know what a closed-end fund was. "There," he said. "Now you have a portfolio. You're a capitalist." She smiled. It was a shy, half-forced smile, but he thought he detected flirtatiousness in her eyes. It was agony for him not to be able to read her, to be compelled to depend on external signals alone in order to know where he stood with her. But he took the chance. "What are you doing this evening?" he asked. "I get out of here at four o'clock."

She was free, she said. Except that she worked from eleven to six. He arranged to pick her up at her apartment around seven. There was no mistaking the warmth of her smile as she left the office. "You lucky bastard," Nadel said. "What did you do, make a date with her? It violates the SEC rules for customer's men to go around laying the customers."

Selig only laughed. Twenty minutes after the market opened he shorted 200 Molybdenum on the Amex, and covered his sale a point and a half lower at lunchtime. That ought to take care of the cost of dinner, he figured, with some to spare. Nyquist had given him the tip yesterday: Moly's a good short, she's sure to fall out of bed. During the mid-afternoon lull, feeling satisfied with himself, he phoned Nyquist to report on his maneuver. "You covered too soon," Nyquist said immediately. "She'll drop five or six more points this week. The smart money's waiting for that."

"I'm not that greedy. I'll settle for the quick three bills."

"That's no way to get rich."

"I guess I lack the gambling instinct," Selig said. He hesitated. He hadn't really called Nyquist to talk about shorting Molybdenum. I met a girl, he wanted to say, and I have this funny problem with her. I met a girl, I met a girl. Sudden fears held him back. Nyquist's silent passive presence at the other end of the telephone line seemed somehow threatening. He'll laugh at me, Selig thought. He's always laughing at me, quietly, thinking I don't see it. But this is foolishness. He said, "Tom, something strange happened today. A girl came into the office, a very attractive girl. I'm seeing her tonight."

"Congratulations."

"Wait. The thing is, I was entirely unable to read her. I mean, I couldn't even pick up an aura. Blank, absolutely blank. I've never had that with anybody before. Have you?"

"I don't think so."

"A complete blank. I can't understand it. What could account for her having such a strong screen?"

"Maybe you're tired today," Nyquist suggested.

"No. No. I can read everybody else, same as always. Just not her."

"Does that irritate you?"

"Of course it does."

"Why do you say of course?"

It seemed obvious to Selig. He could tell that Nyquist was baiting him: the voice calm, uninflected, neutral. A game. A way of passing time. He wished he hadn't phoned. Something important seemed to be coming across on the ticker, and the other phone was lighting up. Nadel, grabbing it, shot a fierce look at him: *Come on, man, there's work to do!* Brusquely Selig said, "I'm—well, very interested in her. And it bothers me that I have no way of getting through to her real self."

Nyquist said, "You mean you're annoyed that you can't spy on her."

"I don't like that phrase."

"Whose phrase is it? Not mine. That's how you regard what we do, isn't it? As spying. You feel guilty about spying on people, right? But it seems you also feel upset when you can't spy."

"I suppose," Selig admitted sullenly.

"With this girl you find yourself forced back on the same old clumsy guesswork techniques for dealing with people that the rest of the world is condemned to use all the time, and you don't like that. Yes?"

"You make it sound so evil, Tom."

"What do you want me to say?"

"I don't want you to say anything. I'm just telling you that there's this girl I can't read, that I've never been up against this situation before, that I wonder if you have any theories to account for why she's the way she is."

"I don't," Nyquist said. "Not off the top of my head."

"All right, then. I—"

But Nyquist wasn't finished. "You realize that I have no way of telling whether she's opaque to the telepathic process in general or just opaque to you, David." That possibility had occurred to Selig a moment earlier. He found it deeply disturbing. Nyquist went on smoothly, "Suppose you bring her around one of these days and let me take a look at her. Maybe I'll be able to learn something useful about her that way."

"I'll do that," Selig said without enthusiasm. He knew such a meeting was necessary and inevitable, but the idea of exposing Kitty to Nyquist produced agitation in him. He had no clear understanding of why that should be happening. "One of these days soon," he said. "Look, all the phones are lighting up. I'll be in touch, Tom."

"Give her one for me," said Nyquist.

23.

David Selig
Selig Studies 101, Prof. Selig
November 10, 1976

Entropy As a Factor in Everyday Life

Entropy is defined in physics as a mathematical expression of the degree to which the energy of a thermo-dynamic system is so distributed as to be unavailable for conversion into work. In more general metaphorical terms, entropy may be seen as the irreversible tendency of a system, including the universe, toward increasing disorder and inertness. That is to say, things have a way of getting worse and worse all the time, until in the end they get so bad that we lack even the means of knowing how bad they really are.

The great American physicist Josiah Willard Gibbs (1839–1903) was the first to apply the second law of thermodynamics—the law that defines the increasing disorder of energy moving at random within a closed system—to chemistry. It was Gibbs who most firmly enunciated the principle that disorder spontaneously increases as the universe grows older. Among those who extended Gibbs' insights into the realm of philosophy was the brilliant mathematician Norbert Wiener (1894–1964), who declared, in his book *The Human Use of Human Beings*, "As entropy increases, the universe, and all closed systems in the universe, tend naturally to deteriorate and lose their distinctiveness, to move from the least to the most probable state, from a state of organization and differentiation in which distinctions and forms exist, to a state of chaos and same-

ness. In Gibbs' universe order is least probable, chaos most probable. But while the universe as a whole, if indeed there is a whole
universe, tends to run down, there are local enclaves whose direction seems opposed to that of the universe at large and in which
there is a limited and temporary tendency for organization to increase. Life finds its home in some of these enclaves."

Thus Wiener hails living things in general and human beings
in particular as heroes in the war against entropy—which he equates
in another passage with the war against evil: "This random element,
this organic incompleteness [that is, the fundamental element of
chance in the texture of the universe], is one which without too
violent a figure of speech we may consider evil." Human beings,
says Wiener, carry on anti-entropic processes. We have sensory receptors. We communicate with one another. We make use of what
we learn from one another. Therefore we are something more than
mere passive victims of the spontaneous spread of universal chaos.
"We, as human beings, are not isolated systems. We take in food,
which generates energy, from the outside, and are, as a result, parts
of that larger world which contains those sources of our vitality.
But even more important is the fact that we take in information
through our sense organs, and we act on information received."
There is feedback, in other words. Through communication we learn
to control our environment, and, he says, "In control and communication we are always fighting nature's tendency to degrade the
organized and to destroy the meaningful; the tendency . . . for entropy to increase." In the very long run entropy must inevitably nail
us all; in the short run we can fight back. "We are not yet spectators
at the last stages of the world's death."

But what if a human being *turns* himself, inadvertently or by
choice, into an isolated system?

A hermit, say. He lives in a dark cave. No information penetrates. He eats mushrooms.' They give him just enough energy to
keep going, but otherwise he lacks inputs. He's forced back on his
own spiritual and mental resources, which he eventually exhausts.
Gradually the chaos expands in him, gradually the forces of entropy
seize possession of this ganglion, that synapse. He takes in a de-
creasing amount of sensory data until his surrender to entropy is
complete. He ceases to move, to grow, to respire, to function in any
way. This condition is known as death.

One doesn't have to hide in a cave. One can make an interior
migration, locking oneself away from the life-giving energy sources.
Often this is done because it appears that the energy sources are

threats to the stability of the self. Indeed, inputs do threaten the self: a push usually will upset equilibrium. However, equilibrium itself is a threat to the self, though this is frequently overlooked. There are married people who strive fiercely to reach equilibrium. They seal themselves off, clinging to one another and shutting out the rest of the universe, making themselves into a two-person closed system from which all vitality is steadily and inexorably expelled by the deadly equilibrium they have established. Two can perish as well as one, if they are sufficiently isolated from everything else. I call this the monogamous fallacy. My sister Judith said she left her husband because she felt herself dying, day by day, while she was living with him. Of course, Judith's a slut.

The sensory shutdown is not always a willed event, naturally. It happens to us whether we like it or not. If we don't climb into the box ourselves, we'll get shoved in anyway. That's what I mean about entropy inevitably nailing us all in the long run. No matter how vital, how vigorous, how world-devouring we are, the inputs dwindle as time goes by. Sight, hearing, touch, smell—everything goes, as good old Will S. said, and we end up sans teeth, sans eyes, sans taste, sans everything. Sans everything. Or, as the same clever man also put it, from hour to hour we ripe and ripe, and then from hour to hour we rot and rot, and thereby hangs a tale.

I offer myself as a case in point. What does this man's sad history reveal? An inexplicable diminution of once-remarkable powers. A shrinkage of the inputs. A small death, endured while he still lives. Am I not a casualty of the entropic wars? Do I not now dwindle into stasis and silence before your very eyes? Is my distress not evident and poignant? Who will I be, when I have ceased to be myself? I am dying the heat death. A spontaneous decay. A random twitch of probability undoes me. And I am made into nothingness. I am becoming cinders and ash. I will wait here for the broom to gather me up.

That's very eloquent, Selig. Take an A. Your writing is clear and forceful and you show an excellent grasp of the underlying philosophical issues. You may go to the head of the class. Do you feel better now?

24.

It was a crazy idea, Kitty, a dumb fantasy. It could never have worked. I was asking the impossible from you. There was only one conceivable outcome, really: that is, that I would annoy you and bore you and drive you away from me. Well, blame Tom Nyquist. It was his idea. No, blame me. I didn't have to listen to his crazy ideas, did I? Blame me. Blame me.

Axiom: It's a sin against love to try to remake the soul of someone you love, even if you think you'll love her more after you've transformed her into something else.

Nyquist said, "Maybe she's a mindreader too, and the blockage is a matter of interference, of a clash between your transmissions and hers, canceling out the waves in one direction or in both. So that there's no transmission from her to you and probably none from you to her."

"I doubt that very much," I told him. This was August of 1963, two or three weeks after you and I had met. We weren't living together yet but we had already been to bed a couple of times. "She doesn't have a shred of telepathic ability," I insisted. "She's completely normal. That's the essential thing about her, Tom: she's a completely normal girl."

"Don't be so sure," Nyquist said.

He hadn't met you yet. He wanted to meet you, but I hadn't set anything up. You had never heard his name.

I said, "If there's one thing I know about her, it's that she's a sane, healthy, well-balanced, absolutely normal girl. Therefore she's no mindreader."

"Because mindreaders are insane, unhealthy, and unbalanced. Like you and like me. Q.E.D., eh? Speak for yourself, man."

"The gift tips the spirit," I said. "It darkens the soul."

"Yours, maybe. Not mine."

He was right about that. Telepathy hadn't injured him. Maybe I'd have had the problems I have even if I hadn't been born with the gift. I can't credit all my maladjustments to the presence of one unusual ability; can I? And God knows there are plenty of neurotics around who have never read a mind in their lives.

Syllogism:

    Some telepaths are not neurotic.

    Some neurotics are not telepaths.

    Therefore telepathy and neurosis aren't necessarily related.

Corollary:

    You can seem cherry-pie normal and still have the power.

I remained skeptical of this. Nyquist agreed, under pressure, that if you did have the power, you would have probably revealed it to me by now through certain unconscious mannerisms that any telepath would readily recognize; I had detected no such mannerisms. He suggested, though, that you might be a latent telepath—that the gift was there, undeveloped, unfunctional, lurking at the core of your mind and serving somehow to screen your mind from my probing. Just a hypothesis, he said. But it tickled me with temptation. "Suppose she's got this latent power," I said. "Could it be awakened, do you think?"

"Why not?" Nyquist asked.

I was willing to believe it. I had this vision of you awakened to full receptive capacity, able to pick up transmissions as easily and as sharply as Nyquist and I. How intense our love would be, then! We would be wholly open to one another, shorn of all the little pretenses and defenses that keep even the closest of lovers from truly achieving a union of souls. I had already tasted a limited form of that sort of closeness with Tom Nyquist, but of course I had no love for him, I didn't even really *like* him, and so it was a waste, a brutal irony, that our minds could have such intimate contact. But you? If I could only awaken you, Kitty! And why not? I asked Nyquist if he thought it might be possible. Try it and find out, he said. Make experiments. Hold hands, sit together in the dark, put some energy into trying to get across to her. It's worth trying, isn't it? Yes, I said, of course it's worth trying.

You seemed latent in so many other ways, Kitty: a potential human being rather than an actual one. An air of adolescence surrounded you. You seemed much younger than you actually were; if I hadn't known you were a college graduate I would have guessed you were 18 or 19.

You hadn't read much outside your fields of interest—mathematics, computers, technology—and, since those weren't my fields of interest, I thought of you as not having read anything at all. You hadn't traveled; your world was limited by the Atlantic and the Mississippi, and the big trip of your life was a summer in Illinois. You hadn't even had much sexual experience: three men, wasn't it, in your 22 years, and only one of those a serious affair? So I saw you as raw material awaiting the sculptor's hand. I would be your Pygmalion.

In September of 1963 you moved in with me. You were spending so much time at my place anyway that you agreed it didn't make sense to keep going back and forth. I felt very married: wet stockings hanging over the showercurtain rod, an extra toothbrush on the shelf, long brown hairs in the sink. The warmth of you beside me in bed every night. My belly against your smooth cool butt, yang and yin. I gave you books to read: poetry, novels, essays. How diligently you devoured them! You read Trilling on the bus going to work and Conrad in the quiet after-dinner hours and Yeats on a Sunday morning while I was out hunting for the *Times*. But nothing really seemed to stick with you; you had no natural bent for literature; I think you had trouble distinguishing Lord Jim from Lucky Jim, Malcolm Lowry from Malcolm Cowley, James Joyce from Joyce Kilmer. Your fine mind, so easily able to master COBOL and FORTRAN, could not decipher the language of poetry, and you would look up from *The Waste Land*, baffled, to ask some naive high-school-girl question that would leave me irritated for hours. A hopeless case, I sometimes thought. Although on a day when the stock market was closed you took me down to the computer center where you worked and I listened to your explanations of the equipment and your functions as though you were talking so much Sanskrit to me. Different worlds, different kinds of mind. Yet I always had hope of creating a bridge.

At strategically timed moments I spoke elliptically of my interest in extrasensory phenomena.

I made it out to be a hobby of mine, a cool dispassionate study. I was fascinated, I said, by the possibility of attaining true mind-to-mind communication between human beings. I took care not to come on like a fanatic, not to oversell my case; I kept my desperation out of sight. Because I genuinely couldn't read you, it was easier for me to pretend to a scholarly objectivity than it would have been with anyone else. And I had to pretend. My strategy didn't allow for any true confessions. I didn't want to frighten you, Kitty, I didn't want to turn you off by giving you reason to think I was a freak, or, as I probably would have seemed to you, a lunatic. Just a hobby, then. A hobby.

You couldn't bring yourself to believe in ESP. If it can't be measured with a voltmeter or recorded on an electroencephalograph, you said, it isn't real. Be tolerant, I pleaded. There *are* such things as telepathic powers. I know there are. (Be careful, Duv!) I couldn't cite EEG readings—I've never been near an EEG in my life, have no idea whether my power would register. And I had barred myself from conquering your skepticism by calling in some outsider and doing some party-game mindreading on him. But I could offer other arguments. Look at Rhine's results, look at all these series of correct readings of the Zener cards. How can you explain them, if not by ESP? And the evidence for telekinesis, teleportation, clairvoyance—

You remained skeptical, coolly putting down most of the data I cited. Your reasoning was keen and close; there was nothing fuzzy about your mind when it was on its own home territory, the scientific method. Rhine, you said, fudges his results by testing heterogeneous groups, then selecting for further testing only those subjects who show unusual runs of luck, dropping the others from his surveys. And he publishes only the scores that seem to prove his thesis. It's a statistical anomaly, not an extrasensory one, that turns up all those correct guesses of the Zener cards, you insisted. Besides, the experimenter is prejudiced in favor of belief in ESP, and that surely leads to all sorts of unconscious errors of procedure, tiny accesses of unintentional bias that inevitably skew the outcome. Cautiously I invited you to try some experiments with me, letting you set up the procedures to suit yourself. You said okay, mainly, I think, because it was something we could do together, and—this was early October—we were already searching selfconsciously for areas of closeness, your literary education having become a strain for both of us.

We agreed—how subtly I made it seem like your own idea!—to concentrate on transmitting images or ideas to one another. And right at the outset we had a cruelly deceptive success. We assembled some packets of pictures and tried to relay them mentally. I still have, here in the archives, our notes on those experiments:

Pictures Seen By Me	Your Guess
1. A rowboat	1. Oak Trees
2. Marigolds in a field	2. Bouquet of roses
3. A kangaroo	3. President Kennedy
4. Twin baby girls	4. A statue
5. The Empire State Building	5. The Pentagon
6. A snow-capped mountain	6. ? image unclear
7. Profile of old man's face	7. A pair of scissors
8. Baseball player at bat.	8. A carving knife
9. An elephant	9. A tractor
10. A locomotive	10. An airplane

You had no direct hits. But four out of ten could be considered close associations: marigolds and roses, the Empire State and the Pentagon, elephant and tractor, locomotive and airplane. (Flowers, buildings, heavy-duty equipment, means of transportation.) Enough to give us false hopes of true transmission. Followed by this:

Pictures Seen By You	My Guess
1. A butterfly	1. A railway train
2. An octopus	2. Mountains
3. Tropical beach scene	3. Landscape, bright sunlight
4. Young Negro boy	4. An automobile
5. Map of South America	5. Grapevines
6. George Washington Bridge	6. The Washington Monument
7. Bowl of apples and bananas	7. Stock market quotations
8. El Greco's *Toledo*	8. A shelf of books
9. A highway at rush hour	9. A beehive
10. An ICBM	10. Cary Grant

No direct hits for me either. But three close associations, of sorts, out of ten: tropical beach and sunny landscape, George Washington Bridge and Washington Monument, highway at rush hour and beehive, the common denominators being sunlight, George Washington, and intense tight-packed activity. At least we deceived ourselves into seeing them as close associations rather than coincidences. I confess I was stabbing in the dark at all times, guessing rather than receiving, and I had little faith even then in the quality of our responses. Nevertheless those probably random collisions of images aroused your curiosity: there's something in this stuff, maybe, you began to say. And we went onward.

We varied the conditions for thought transmission. We tried doing it in absolute darkness, one room apart. We tried it with the lights on, holding hands. We tried it during sex: I entered you and held you in my arms and thought hard at you, and you thought hard at me. We tried it drunk. We tried it fasting. We tried it under conditions of sleep-deprivation, forcing ourselves to stay up around the clock in the random hope that minds groggy with fatigue might permit mental impulses to slip through the barriers separating us. We would have tried it under the influence of pot or acid, but no one thought much about pot or acid in '63. We sought in a dozen other ways to open the telepathic conduit. Perhaps you recall the details of them even now; embarrassment drives them from my mind. I know we wrestled with our futile project night after night for more than a month, while your involvement with it swelled and peaked and dwindled again, carrying you through a series of phases from skepticism to cool neutral interest to unmistakable fascination and enthusiasm, then to an awareness of inevitable failure, a sense of the impossibility of our goal, leading then to weariness, to boredom, and to irritation. I realized none of this: I thought you were as dedicated to the work as I was. But it had ceased to be either an experiment or a game; it was, you saw, plainly an obsessive quest, and you asked several times in November if we could quit. All this mind-reading, you said, left you with woeful headaches. But I couldn't give up, Kitty. I overrode your objections and insisted we go on. I was hooked, I was impaled, I browbeat you mercilessly into cooperating, I tyrannized you in the name of love, seeing always that telepathic Kitty I would ultimately produce. Every ten days, maybe, some delusive flicker of seeming contact buoyed my idiotic optimism. We *would* break through; we *would* touch each other's minds. How could I quit now, when we were so close? But we were never close.

Early in November Nyquist gave one of his occasional dinner parties, catered by a Chinatown restaurant he favored. His parties were always brilliant events; to refuse the invitation would have been absurd. So at last I would have to expose you to him. For more than three months I had been more or less deliberately concealing you from him, avoiding the moment of confrontation, out of a cowardice I didn't fully understand. We came late: you were slow getting ready. The party was well under way, fifteen or eighteen people, many of them celebrities, although not to you, for what did you know of poets, composers, novelists? I introduced you to Nyquist. He smiled and murmured a sleek compliment and gave you a bland, impersonal kiss. You seemed shy, almost afraid of him, of his confidence and smoothness. After a moment of patter he went spinning away to answer the doorbell. A little later, as we were handed our first drinks, I planted a thought for him:

—Well? What do you think of her.

But he was too busy with his other guests to probe me, and didn't pick up on my question. I had to seek my own answers in his skull. I inserted myself—he glanced at me across the room, realizing what I was doing—and rummaged for information. Layers of hostly trivia masked his surface levels; he was simultaneously offering drinks, steering a conversation, signaling for the eggrolls to be brought from the kitchen, and inwardly going over the guest list to see who was yet to arrive. But I cut swiftly through that stuff and in a moment found his locus of Kitty-thoughts. At once I acquired the knowledge I wanted and dreaded. He could read you. Yes. To him you were as transparent as anyone else. Only to me were you opaque, for reasons none of us knew.

Nyquist had instantly penetrated you, had assessed you, had formed his judgment of you, there for me to examine: he saw you as awkward, immature, naive, but yet also attractive and charming. (That's how he really saw you. I'm not trying, for ulterior reasons of my own, to make him seem more critical of you than he really was. You were very young, you were unsophisticated, and he saw that.) The discovery numbed me. Jealousy curdled me. That I should work so ponderously for so many weeks to reach you, getting nowhere, and he could knife so easily to your depths, Kitty! I was instantly suspicious. Nyquist and his malicious games: was this yet one more? *Could* he read you? How could I be sure he hadn't planted a fiction for me? He picked up on that:

—You don't trust me? Of course I'm reading her.

—Maybe yes, maybe no.

—Do you want me to prove it?

—How?

—Watch.

Without interrupting for a moment his role of host, he entered your mind, while mine remained locked on his. And so, through him, I had my first and only glimpse of your inwardness, Kitty, reflected by way of Tom Nyquist. Oh! It was no glimpse I ever wanted. I saw myself through your eyes through his mind. Physically I looked, if anything, better than I imagined I would, my shoulders broader than they really are, my face leaner, the features more regular. No doubt that you responded to my body. But the emotional associations! You saw me as stern father, as grim schoolmaster, as grumbling tyrant. Read this, read that, improve your mind, girl! Study hard to be worthy of me! Oh! Oh! And that flaming core of resentment over our ESP experiments: worse than useless to you, a monumental bore, an excursion into insanity, a wearying, grinding drag. Night after night to be bugged by monomaniacal me. Even our screwing invaded by the foolish quest for mind-to-mind contact. How sick you were of me, Kitty! How monstrously dull you thought me!

An instant of such revelation was more than enough. Stung, I retreated, pulling away quickly from Nyquist. You looked at me in a startled way, I recall, as if you knew on some subliminal level that mental energies were flashing around the room, revealing the privacies of your soul. You blinked and your cheeks reddened and you took a hasty diving gulp of your drink. Nyquist shot me a sardonic smile. I couldn't meet his eyes. But even then I resisted what he had showed me. Had I not seen odd refraction effects before in such relays? Should I not mistrust the accuracy of his picture of your image of me? Was he not shading and coloring it? Introducing sly distortions and magnifications? Did I truly bug you all that much, Kitty, or was he not playfully exaggerating mild annoyance into vivid distaste? I chose not to believe I bored you quite so much. We tend to interpret events according to the way we prefer to see them. But I vowed to go easier on you in the future.

Later, after we had eaten, I saw you talking animatedly to Nyquist at the far side of the room. You were flirtatious and giddy, as you had been with me that first day at the brokerage office. I imagined you were discussing me and not being complimentary. I tried to pick up the conversation by way of Nyquist, but at my first tentative probe he glared at me.

—Get out of my head, will you?

I obeyed. I heard your laughter, too loud, rising above the hum of conversation. I drifted off to talk to a lithe little Japanese sculptress whose flat tawny chest sprouted untemptingly from a low-cut black sheath, and found her thinking, in French, that she would like me to ask her to go home with me. But I went home with you, Kitty, sitting sullen and graceless beside you on the empty subway train, and when I asked you what you and Nyquist had been discussing you said, "Oh, we were just kidding around. Just having a little fun."

About two weeks later, on a clear crisp autumn afternoon, President Kennedy was shot in Dallas. The stock market closed early after a calamitous slide and Martinson shut the office down, turning me out, dazed, into the street. I couldn't easily accept the reality of the progression of events. *Someone shot at the President. . . . Someone shot the President. . . . Someone shot the President in the head. . . . The President has been critically wounded. . . . The President has been rushed to Parkland Hospital. . . . The President has received the last rites. . . . The President is dead.* I was never a particularly political person, but this rupture of the commonwealth devastated me. Kennedy was the only presidential candidate I ever voted for who won, and they killed him: the story of my life in one compressed bloody parable. And now there would be a President Johnson. Could I adapt? I cling to zones of stability. When I was 10 years old and Roosevelt died, Roosevelt who had been President all my life, I tested the unfamiliar syllables of *President Truman* on my tongue and rejected them at once, telling myself that I would call him President Roosevelt too, for that was what I was accustomed to calling the President.

That November afternoon I picked up emanations of fear on all sides as I walked fearfully home. Paranoia was general everywhere. People sidled warily, one shoulder in front of the other, ready to bolt.

Pale female faces peered between parted curtains in the windows of the towering apartment houses, high above the silent streets. The drivers of cars looked in all directions at intersections, as if expecting the tanks of the storm troopers to come rumbling down Broadway. (At this time of day it was generally believed that the assassination was the first blow in a right-wing putsch.) No one lingered in the open; everyone hurried toward shelter. Anything might happen now. Packs of wolves might burst out of Riverside Drive. Maddened patriots might launch a pogrom. From my apartment—door bolted, windows locked—I tried to phone you at the computer center, thinking you might somehow not have heard the news, or perhaps I just wanted to hear your voice in this traumatic time. The telephone lines were choked. I gave up the attempt after twenty minutes. Then, wandering aimlessly from bedroom to livingroom and back, clutching my transistor, twisting the dial trying to find the one radio station whose newscaster would tell me that he was still alive after all, I detoured into the kitchen and found your note on the table, telling me that you were leaving, that you couldn't stay with me any more. The note was dated 10:30 A.M., before the assassination, in another era. I rushed to the bedroom closet and saw what I had not seen before, that your things were gone. When women leave me, Kitty, they leave suddenly and stealthily, giving no warning.

Toward evening I telephoned Nyquist. This time the lines were open. "Is Kitty there?" I asked. "Yes," he said. "Just a minute." And put you on. You explained that you were going to live with him for a while, until you got yourself sorted out. He had been very helpful. No, you had no hard feelings toward me, no bitterness at all. It was just that I seemed, well, insensitive, whereas he—he had this instinctive, intuitive grasp of your emotional needs—he was able to get onto your trip, Kitty, and I couldn't manage that. So you had gone to him for comfort and love. Goodbye, you said, and thanks for everything, and I muttered a goodbye and put down the phone. During the night the weather changed, and a weekend of black skies and cold rain saw JFK to his grave. I missed everything—the casket in the rotunda, the brave widow and the gallant children, the murder of Oswald, the funeral procession, all that instant history. Saturday and Sunday I slept late, got drunk, read six books without absorbing a word. On Monday, the day of national mourning, I wrote you that incoherent letter, Kitty, explaining everything, telling you what I had tried to make out of you and why, confessing my power to you and describing the effects it had had on my life, telling you also about Nyquist, warning you of what he was, that he had the power too, that he could read you and you would have no secrets from him, telling you not to mistake him for a real human being, telling you that he was a machine, self-programmed for maximum self-realization, telling you that the power had made him cold and cruelly strong whereas it had made me weak and jittery, insisting that essentially he was as sick as I, a manipulative man, incapable of giving love, capable only of using. I told you that he would hurt you if you made yourself vulnerable to him. You didn't answer. I never heard from you again, never saw you again, never heard from or saw him again either. Thirteen years. I have no idea what became of either of you. Probably I'll never know. But listen. Listen. I loved you, lady, in my clumsy way. I love you now. And you are lost to me forever.

25.

He wakes, feeling stiff and sore and numb, in a bleak, dreary hospital ward. Evidently this is St. Luke's, perhaps the emergency room. His lower lip is swollen, his left eye opens only reluctantly, and his nose makes an unfamiliar whistling sound at every intake of air. Did they bring him here on a stretcher after the basketball players finished with him? He has spent relatively little time in hospitals. He wonders if his clothing is stained with dried blood, but when he succeeds in looking down—his neck, oddly rigid, does not want to obey him—he sees only the dingy whiteness of a hospital gown. Each time he breathes, he imagines he can feel the ragged edges of broken ribs scraping together; slipping a hand under the gown, he touches his bare chest and finds that it has not been taped. He does not know whether to be relieved or apprehensive about that.

Carefully he sits up. A tumult of impressions strikes him. The room is crowded and noisy, with beds pushed close together. The beds have curtains but no curtains are drawn. Most of his fellow patients are black, and many of them are in serious condition, surrounded by festoons of equipment. Mutilated by knives? Lacerated by windshields? Friends and relatives, clustering around each bed, gesticulate and argue and berate; the normal tone of voice is a yelping shout. Impassive nurses drift through the room, showing much the same distant concern for the patients as museum guards do for mummies in display cases. No one is paying any attention to Selig except Selig, who returns to the examination of himself. His fingertips explore his cheeks. Without a mirror he cannot tell how battered his face is, but there are many tender places. His left clavicle aches as from a light, glancing karate chop. His right knee radiates throbbings and twinges, as though he twisted it in falling.

Still, he feels less pain than might have been anticipated; perhaps they have given him some sort of shot.

His mind is foggy. He is receiving some mental input from those about him in the ward, but everything is garbled, nothing is distinct; he picks up auras but no intelligible verbalizations. Trying to get his bearings, he asks passing nurses three times to tell him the time, for his wristwatch is gone; they go by, ignoring him. Finally a bulky, smiling black woman in a frilly pink dress looks over to him and says, "It's quarter to four, love." In the morning? In the afternoon? Probably the afternoon, he decides. Diagonally across from him, two nurses have begun to erect what perhaps is an intravenous feeding system, with a plastic tube snaking into the nostril of a huge unconscious bandage-swathed black. Selig's own stomach sends him no hunger signals. The chemical smell in the hospital air gives him nausea; he can barely salivate. Will they feed him this evening? How long will he be kept here? Who pays? Should he ask that Judith be notified? How badly has he been injured?

An intern enters the ward: a short dark man, concise and fine-boned of body, a Pakistani by the looks of him, moving with bouncy precision. A rumpled and soiled handkerchief jutting from his breast pocket spoils, though, the trig, smart effect of his tight white uniform. Surprisingly, he comes right to Selig. "The X-rays show no breakages," he says without preamble in a firm, unresonant voice. "Therefore your only injuries are minor abrasions, bruises, cuts, and an unimportant concussion. We are ready to authorize your release. Please get up."

"Wait," Selig says feebly. "I just came to. I don't know what's been going on. Who brought me here? How long have I been unconscious? What—"

"I know none of these things. Your discharge has been approved and the hospital has need of this bed. Please. On your feet, now. I have much to do."

"A concussion? Shouldn't I spend the night here, at least, if I had a concussion? Or did I spend the night here? What day is today?"

"You were brought in about noon today," says the intern, growing more fretful. "You were treated in the emergency room and given a thorough examination after having been beaten on the steps of Low Library." Once more the command to rise, given wordlessly this time, an imperious glare and a pointing forefinger. Selig probes the intern's mind and finds it accessible, but there is nothing apparent in it except impatience and irritation. Ponderously Selig climbs from the bed. His body seems to be held together with wire. His bones grind and scrape. There is still the sensation of broken rib-ends rubbing in his chest; can the X-ray have been in error? He starts to ask, but too late. The intern, making his rounds, has whirled off to another bed.

They bring him his clothing. He pulls the curtain around his bed and dresses. Yes, bloodstains on his shirt, as he had feared; also on his trousers. A mess. He checks his belongings: everything here, wallet, wristwatch, pocketcomb. What now? Just walk out? Nothing to sign? Selig edges uncertainly toward the door. He actually gets into the corridor unperceived. Then the intern materializes as if from ectoplasm and points to another room across the hall, saying, "You wait in there until the security man comes." Security man? *What* security man?

There are, as he had feared, papers to sign before he is free of the hospital's grasp. Just as he finishes with the red tape, a plump, gray-faced, sixtyish man in the uniform of the campus security force enters the room, puffing slightly, and says, "You Selig?"

He acknowledges that he is.

"The dean wants to see you. You able to walk by yourself or you want me to get you a wheelchair?"

"I'll walk," Selig says.

They go out of the hospital together, up Amsterdam Avenue to the 115th Street campus gate, and into Van Am Quad. The security man stays close beside him, saying nothing. Shortly Selig finds himself waiting outside the office of the Dean of Columbia College. The security man waits with him, arms folded placidly, wrapped in a cocoon of boredom. Selig begins to feel almost as though he is under some sort of arrest. Why is that? An odd thought. What does he have to fear from the dean? He probes the security man's dull mind but can find nothing in it but drifting, wispy masses of fog. He wonders who the dean is, these days. He remembers the deans of his own college era well enough: Lawrence Chamberlain, with the bow ties and the warm smile, was Dean of the College, and Dean McKnight, Nicholas McD. McKnight, a fraternity enthusiast (Sigma Chi?) with a formal, distinctly nineteenth-century manner, was Dean of Students. But that was twenty years ago. Chamberlain and McKnight must have had several successors by now, but he knows nothing about them; he has never been one for reading alumni newsletters.

A voice from within says, "Dean Cushing will see him now."

"Go on in," the security man says.

Cushing? A fine deanly name. Who is he? Selig limps in, awkward from his injuries, bothered by his sore knee. Facing him behind a glistening uncluttered desk sits a wide-shouldered, smooth-cheeked, youthful-looking man, junior-executive model, wearing a conservative dark suit. Selig's first thought is of the mutations worked by the passage of time: he had always looked upon deans as lofty symbols of authority, necessarily elderly or at least of middle years, but here is the Dean of the College and he seems to be a man of Selig's own age. Then he realizes that this dean is not merely an anonymous contemporary of his but actually a classmate, Ted Cushing '56, a campus figure of some repute back then, class president and football star and A-level scholar, whom Selig had known at least in a passing way. It always surprises Selig to be reminded that he is no longer young, that he has lived into a time when his generation has control of the mechanisms of power. "Ted?" he blurts. "Are you dean now, Ted? Christ, I wouldn't have guessed that. When—"

"Sit down, Dave," Cushing says, politely but with no great show of friendliness. "Did you get badly hurt?"

"The hospital says nothing's broken. I feel half ruined, though." As he eases into a chair he indicates the bloodstains on his clothing, the bruises on his face. Talking is an effort; his jaws creak at their hinges. "Hey, Ted, it's been a long time! Must be twenty years since I last saw you. Did you remember my name, or did they identify me from my wallet?"

"We've arranged to pay the hospital costs," Cushing says, not seeming to hear Selig's words. "If there are any further medical expenses, we'll take care of those too. You can have that in writing if you'd like."

"The verbal commitment is fine. And in case you're worrying that I'll press charges, or sue the University, well, I wouldn't do anything like that. Boys will be boys, they let their feelings run away with themselves a little bit, but—"

"We weren't greatly concerned about your pressing charges, Dave," Cushing says quietly. "The real question is whether we're going to press charges against *you*."

"Me? For what? For getting mauled by your basketball players? For damaging their expensive hands with my face?" He essays a painful grin. Cushing's face remains grave. There is a little moment of silence. Selig struggles to interpret Cushing's joke. Finding no rationale for it, he decides to venture a probe. But he runs into a wall. He is suddenly too timid to push, fearful that he will be unable to break through. "I don't understand what you mean," he says finally. "Press charges for what?"

"For these, Dave." For the first time Selig notices the stack of typewritten pages on the dean's desk. Cushing nudges them forward. "Do you recognize them? Here: take a look."

Selig leafs unhappily through them. They are term papers, all of them of his manufacture. *Odysseus as a Symbol of Society. The Novels of Kafka. Aeschylus and the Aristotelian Tragedy. Resignation and Acceptance in the Philosophy of Montaigne. Virgil as Dante's Mentor.* Some of them bear marks: A −, B +, A −, A and marginal comments, mainly favorable. Some are untouched except by smudges and smears; these are the ones he had been about to deliver when he was set upon by Lumumba. With immense care he tidies the stack, aligning the edges of the sheets precisely, and pushes them back toward Cushing. "All right," he says. "You've got me."

"Did you write those?"

"Yes."

"For a fee?"

"Yes."

"That's sad, Dave. That's awfully sad."

"I needed to earn a living. They don't give scholarships to alumni."

"What were you getting paid for these things?"

"Three or four bucks a typed page."

Cushing shakes his head. "You were good, I'll give you credit for that. There must be eight or ten guys working your racket here, but you're easily the best."

"Thank you."

"But you had one dissatisfied customer, at least. We asked Lumumba why he beat you up. He said he hired you to write a term paper for him and you did a lousy job, you ripped him off, and then you wouldn't refund his money. All right, we're dealing with him in our own way, but we have to deal with you, too. We've been trying to find you for a long time, Dave."

"Have you?"

"We've circulated xeroxes of your work through a dozen departments the last couple of semesters, warning people to be on the lookout for your typewriter and your style. There wasn't a great deal of cooperation. A lot of faculty members didn't seem to care whether the term papers they received were phony or not. But we cared, Dave. We cared very much." Cushing leans forward. His eyes, terribly earnest, seek Selig's. Selig looks away. He cannot abide the searching warmth of those eyes. "We started closing in a few weeks ago," Cushing continues. "We rounded up a couple of your clients and threatened them with expulsion. They gave us your name, but they didn't know where you lived, and we had no way of finding you. So we waited. We knew you'd show up again to deliver and solicit. Then we got this report of a disturbance on the steps of Low, basketball players beating somebody up, and we found you with a pile of undelivered papers clutched in your arm, and that was it. You're out of business, Dave."

"I should ask for a lawyer," Selig says. "I shouldn't admit anything more to you. I should have denied everything when you showed me those papers."

"No need to be so technical about your rights."

"I'll need to be when you take me to court, Ted."

"No," Cushing says. "We aren't going to prosecute, not unless we catch you ghosting more papers. We have no interest in putting you in jail, and in any case I'm not sure that what you've done is a criminal offense. What we really want to do is help you. You're sick, Dave. For a man of your intelligence, of your potential, to have fallen so low, to have ended up faking term papers for college kids—that's sad, Dave, that's awfully sad. We've discussed your case here, Dean Bellini and Dean Tompkins and I, and we've come up with a rehabilitation plan for you. We can find you work on campus, as a research assistant, maybe. There are always doctoral candidates who need assistants, and we have a small fund we could dip into to provide a salary for you, nothing much, but at least as much as you were making on these papers. And we'd admit you to the psychological counseling service here. It wasn't set up for alumni, but I don't see why we need to be inflexible about it, Dave. For myself I have to say that I find it embarrassing that a man of the Class of '56 is in the kind of trouble you're in, and if only out of a spirit of loyalty to our class I want to do everything possible to help you put yourself back together and begin to fulfill the promise that you showed when—"

Cushing rambles on, restating and embellishing his themes, offering pity without censure, promising aid to his suffering classmate. Selig, listening inattentively, discovers that Cushing's mind is beginning to open to him. The wall that earlier had separated their consciousnesses, a product perhaps of Selig's fear and fatigue, has started to dissolve, and Selig is able now to perceive a general image of Cushing's mind, which is energetic, strong, capable, but also conventional and limited, a stolid Republican mind, a prosaic Ivy League mind. Foremost in it is not his concern for Selig but rather his complacent satisfaction with himself: the brightest glow emanates from Cushing's awareness of his happy station in life, ornamented by a suburban split-level, a strapping blonde wife, three handsome children, a shaggy dog, a shining new Lincoln Continental. Pushing a bit deeper, Selig sees that Cushing's show of concern for him is fraudulent. Behind the earnest eyes and the sincere, heartfelt, sympathetic smile lies fierce contempt. Cushing despises him. Cushing thinks he is corrupt, useless, worthless, a disgrace to mankind in general and the Columbia College Class of '56 in particular. Cushing finds him physically as well as morally repugnant, seeing him as unwashed and unclean, possibly syphilitic. Cushing suspects him of being homosexual. Cushing has for him the scorn of the Rotarian for the junkie. It is impossible for Cushing to understand why anyone who has had the benefit of a Columbia education would let himself slide into the degradations Selig has accepted. Selig shrinks from Cushing's disgust. Am I so despicable, he wonders, am I such trash?

His hold on Cushing's mind strengthens and deepens. It ceases to trouble him that Cushing has such contempt for him. Selig drifts into a mode of abstraction in which he no longer identifies himself with the miserable churl Cushing sees. What does Cushing know? Can Cushing penetrate the mind of another? Can Cushing feel the ecstasy of real contact with a fellow human being? And there is ecstasy in it. Godlike he rides passenger in Cushing's mind, sinking past the external defenses, past the petty prides and snobberies, past the self-congratulatory smugness, into the realm of absolute values, into the kingdom of authentic self. Contact! Ecstasy! That stolid Cushing is the outer husk. Here is a Cushing that even Cushing does not know: but Selig does.

Selig has not been so happy in years. Light, golden and serene, floods his soul. An irresistible gaiety possesses him. He runs through misty groves at dawn, feeling the gentle lashing of moist green fern-fronds against his shins. Sunlight pierces the canopy of high foliage, and droplets of dew glitter with a cool inner fire. The birds awaken. Their song is tender and sweet, a distant cheebling, sleepy and soft. He runs through the forest, and he is not alone, for a hand grasps his hand; and he knows that he has never been alone and never will be alone. The forest floor is damp and spongy beneath his bare feet. He runs. He runs. An invisible choir strikes a harmonious note and holds it, holds it, holds it, swelling it in perfect crescendo, until, just as he breaks from the grove and sprints into a sun-bright meadow, that swell of tone fills all the cosmos, reverberating in magical fullness. He throws himself face-forward to the ground, hugging the earth, writhing against the fragrant grassy carpet, flattening his hands against the curve of the planet, and he is aware of the world's inner throbbing. This is ecstasy! This is contact! Other minds surround his. In whatever direction he moves, he feels their presence, welcoming him, supporting him, reaching toward him. Come, they say, join us, join us, be one with us, give up those tattered shreds of self, let go of all that holds you apart from us. Yes, Selig replies. Yes, I affirm the ecstasy of life. I affirm the joy of contact. I give myself to you. They touch him. He touches them. It was for this, he knows, that I received my gift, my blessing, my power. For this moment of affirmation and fulfillment. Join us. Join us. Yes! The birds! The invisible choir! The dew! The meadow! The sun! He laughs; he rises and breaks into an ecstatic dance; he throws back his head to sing, he who has never in his life dared to sing, and the tones that come from him are rich and full, pure, squarely striking the center of the pitch. Yes! Oh, the joining, the touching, the union, the oneness! No longer is he David Selig. He is a part of them, and they are a part of him, and in that joyous blending he experiences loss of self, he gives up all that is tired and worn and sour in him, he gives up his fears and uncertainties, he gives up everything that has separated himself from himself for so many years. He breaks through. He is fully open and the immense signal of the universe rushes freely into him. He receives. He transmits. He absorbs. He radiates. Yes. Yes. Yes. Yes.

He knows this ecstasy will last forever.

But in the moment of that knowledge, he feels it slipping from him. The choir's glad note diminishes. The sun drops toward the horizon. The distant sea, retreating, sucks at the shore. He struggles to hold to the joy, but the more he struggles the more of it he loses. Hold back the tide? How? Delay the fall of night? How? How? The birdsongs are faint now. The air has turned cold. Everything rushes away from him. He stands alone in the gathering darkness, remembering that ecstasy, recapturing it momentarily, reliving it—for it is already gone, and must be summoned back through an act of the will. Gone, yes. It is very quiet, suddenly. He hears one last sound, a stringed instrument in the distance, a cello, perhaps, being plucked, pizzicato, a beautiful melancholy sound. *Twang.* The plangent chord. *Twing.* The breaking string. *Twong.* The lyre untuned. Twang. Twing. Twong. And nothing more. Silence envelops him. A terminal silence, it is, that booms through the caverns of his skull, the silence that follows the shattering of the cello's strings, the silence that comes with the death of music. He can hear nothing. He can feel nothing. He is alone. He is alone.

He is alone.

"So quiet," he murmurs. "So private. It's—so—private—here."

"Selig?" a deep voice asks. "What's the matter with you, Selig?"

"I'm all right," Selig says. He tries to stand, but nothing has any solidity. He is tumbling through Cushing's desk, through the floor of the office, falling through the planet itself, seeking and not finding a stable platform. "So quiet. The silence, Ted, the silence!" Strong arms seize him. He is aware of several figures bustling about him. Someone is calling for a doctor. Selig shakes his head, protesting that nothing is wrong with him, nothing at all, except for the silence in his head, except for the silence, except for the silence.

Except for the silence.

26.

Winter is here. Sky and pavement form a seamless, inexorable band of gray. There will be snow soon. For some reason this neighborhood has gone without refuse pickups for three or four days, and bulging plastic sacks of trash are heaped in front of every building, yet there is no odor of garbage in the air. Not even smells can flourish in these temperatures: the cold drains away every stink, every sign of organic reality. Only concrete triumphs here. Silence reigns. Scrawny black and gray cats, motionless, statues of themselves, peer out of alleys. Traffic is light. Walking quickly through the streets from the subway station to Judith's place, I avert my eyes from the faces of the few people I pass. I feel shy and selfconscious among them, like a war veteran who has just been discharged from the rehabilitation center and is still embarrassed about his mutilations. Naturally I'm unable to tell what anybody is thinking; their minds are closed to me now and they go by me wearing shields of impenetrable ice; but, ironically, I have the illusion that they all have access to *me*. They can look right into me and see me for what I've become. There's David Selig, they must be thinking. How careless he was! What a poor custodian of his gift! He messed up and let it all slip away from him, the dope. I feel guilty for causing them this disappointment. Yet I don't feel as guilty as I thought I might. On some ultimate level I just don't give a damn at all. This is what I am, I tell myself. This is what I now shall be. If you don't like it, tough crap. Try to accept me. If you can't do that, just ignore me.

"As the truest society approaches always nearer to solitude, so the most excellent speech finally falls into silence. Silence is audible to all men, at all times, and in all places." So said Thoreau, in 1849, in *A Week on the Concord and Merrimack Rivers*. Of course, Thoreau was a misfit and an outsider with very serious neurotic problems. When he was a young man just out of college he fell in love with a girl named Ellen Sewall, but she turned him down, and he never married. I wonder if he ever made it with anybody. Probably not. I can't imagine Thoreau actually balling, can you? Oh, maybe he didn't die a virgin, but I bet his sex life was lousy. Perhaps he didn't even masturbate. Can you visualize him sitting next to that pond and whacking off? I can't. Poor Thoreau. Silence is audible, Henry.

I imagine, as I near Judith's building, that I meet Toni in the street. I seem to see a tall figure walking toward me from Riverside Drive, hatless, bundled up in a bulky orange coat. When we are half a block apart I recognize her. Strangely, I feel neither excitement nor apprehension over this unexpected reunion; I am quite calm, almost unmoved. At another time I might have crossed the street to avoid a possibly disturbing encounter, but not now: coolly I halt in her path, smile, hold up my hands in greeting. "Toni?" I say. "Don't you know me?"

She studies me, frowns, seems puzzled for a moment. But only a moment.

"David. Hello."

Her face looks more lean, the cheekbones higher and sharper. There are some strands of gray in her hair. In the days when I knew her she had one curious gray lock at her temple, very unusual; now the gray is scattered more randomly through the black. Well, of course she's in her middle thirties now. Not exactly a girl. As old now, in fact, as I was when I first met her. But in fact I know she has hardly changed at all, only matured a little. She seems as beautiful as ever. Yet desire is absent from me. All passion spent, Selig. All passion spent. And she too is mysteriously free of turbulence. I remember our last meeting, the look of pain on her face, her obsessive heap of cigarette butts. Now her expression is amiable and casual. We both have passed through the realm of storms.

"You're looking good," I say. "What is it, eight years, nine?"

I know the answer to that. I'm merely testing her. And she passes the test, saying, "The summer of '68." I'm relieved to see that she hasn't forgotten. I'm still a chapter of her autobiography, then. "How have you been, David?"

"Not bad." The conversational inanities. "What are you doing these days?"

"I'm with Random House now. And you?"

"Freelancing," I say. "Here and there." Is she married? Her gloved hands offer no data. I don't dare ask. I'm incapable of probing. I force a smile and shift my weight from foot to foot. The silence that has come between us suddenly seems unbridgeable. Have we exhausted all feasible topics so soon? Are there no areas of contact left except those too pain-filled to reopen?

She says, "You've changed."

"I'm older. Tireder. Balder."

"It isn't that. You've changed somewhere inside."

"I suppose I have."

"You used to make me feel uncomfortable. I'd get a sort of queasy feeling. I don't any more."

"You mean, after the trip?"

"Before and after both," she says.

"You were always uncomfortable with me?"

"Always. I never knew why. Even when we were really close, I felt—I don't know, on guard, off balance, ill at ease, when I was with you. And that's gone now. It's entirely gone. I wonder why."

"Time heals all wounds," I say. Oracular wisdom.

"I suppose you're right. God, it's cold! Do you think it'll snow?"

"It's bound to, before long."

"I hate the cold weather." She huddles into her coat. I never knew her in cold weather. Spring and summer, then goodbye, get out, goodbye, goodbye. Odd how little I feel for her now. If she invited me up to her apartment I'd probably say, No, thank you, I'm on my way to visit my sister. Of course she's imaginary; that may have something to do with it. But also I'm not getting an aura from her. She's not broadcasting, or rather I'm not receiving. She's only a statue of herself, like the cats in the alleys. Will I be incapable of feeling, now that I'm incapable of receiving? She says, "It's been good to see you, David. Let's get together some time, shall we?"

"By all means. We'll have a drink and talk about old times."

"I'd like that."

"So would I. Very much."

"Take care of yourself, David."

"You too, Toni."

We smile. I give her a little mock-salute of farewell. We move apart; I continue walking west, she hurries up the windy street toward Broadway. I feel a little warmer for having met her. Everything cool, friendly, unemotional between us. Everything dead, in fact. All passion spent. It's been good to see you, David. Let's get together some time, shall we? When I reach the corner I realize I have forgotten to ask for her phone number. Toni? Toni? But she is out of sight. As though she never was there at all.

It is the little rift within the lute,
    That by and by will make the music mute,
    And ever widening slowly silence all.

That's Tennyson: *Merlin and Vivien.* You've heard that line about the rift within the lute before, haven't you? But you never knew it was Tennyson. Neither did I. My lute is riven. Twang. Twing. Twong.
    Here's another little literary gem:

Every sound shall end in silence, but the silence never dies.

Samuel Miller Hageman wrote that, in 1876, in a poem called *Silence.* Have you ever heard of Samuel Miller Hageman before? I haven't. You were a wise old cat, Sam, whoever you were.

One summer when I was eight or nine—it was before they adopted Judith, anyway—I went with my parents to a resort in the Catskills for a few weeks. There was a daycamp for the kiddies, in which we received instruction in swimming, tennis, softball, arts & crafts, and other activities, thus leaving the older folks free for gin rummy and creative drinking. One afternoon the daycamp staged some boxing matches. I had never worn boxing gloves, and in the free-for-alls of boyhood I had found myself to be an incompetent fighter, so I was unenthusiastic. I watched the first five matches in much dismay. All that hitting! All those bloody noses!
    Then it was my turn. My opponent was a boy named Jimmy, a few months younger than I but taller and heavier and much more athletic. I think the counselors matched us deliberately, hoping Jimmy would kill me: I was not their favorite child. I started to shake even before they put the gloves on me. "Round One!" called a counselor, and we approached each other. I distinctly heard Jimmy thinking about hitting me on the chin, and as his glove came toward my face I ducked and hit him in the belly. That made him furious. He proposed now to clobber me on the back of the head, but I saw that coming too and stepped aside and hit him on the neck close to his adam's-apple. He gagged and turned away, half in tears. After a moment he returned to the attack, but I continued to anticipate his moves and he never touched me. For the first time in my life I felt tough, competent, aggressive. As I battered him I looked past the improvised ring and saw my father flushed with

pride, and Jimmy's father next to him looking angry and perplexed. End of round one. I was sweating, bouncy, grinning.

Round two: Jimmy came forth determined to knock me to pieces. Swinging wildly, frantically, still going for my head. I kept my head where he couldn't reach it and danced around to his side and hit him in the belly again, very hard, and when he folded up I hit him on the nose and he fell down, crying. The counselor in charge very quickly counted to ten and raised my hand. "Hey, Joe Louis!" my father yelled. "Hey, Willie Pep!" The counselor suggested I go over to Jimmy and help him up and shake his hand. As he got to his feet I very clearly detected him deciding to butt me in the teeth with his head, and I pretended to be paying no attention, except when he charged I stepped coolly to one side and banged my fists down on his lowered back. That shattered him. "David cheats!" he moaned. "David *cheats!*"

How they all hated me for my cleverness! What they interpreted as my cleverness, that is. My sly knack of always guessing what was going to happen. Well, that wouldn't be a problem now. They'd all love me. Loving me, they'd beat me to a pulp.

Judith answers the door. She wears an old gray sweater and blue slacks with a hole in the knee. She holds her arms out to me and I embrace her warmly, pulling her tight against my body for perhaps half a minute. I hear music from within: the *Siegfried Idyll*, I think. Sweet, loving, accepting music.

"Is it snowing yet?" she asks.

"Not yet. Gray and cold, that's all."

"I'll get you a drink. Go into the livingroom."

I stand by the window. A few snowflakes blow by. My nephew appears and studies me at a distance of thirty feet. To my amazement he smiles. He says warmly, "Hi, Uncle David!"

Judith must have put him up to it. Be nice to Uncle David, she must have said. He isn't feeling well, he's had a lot of trouble lately. So there the kid stands, being nice to Uncle David. I don't think he's ever smiled at me before. He didn't even gurgle and coo at me out of his cradle. Hi, Uncle David. All right, kid. I can dig it.

"Hello, Pauly. How have you been?"

"Fine," he says. With that his social graces are exhausted; he does not inquire in return about the state of my health, but picks up one of his toys and absorbs himself in its intricacies. Yet his large dark glossy eyes continue to examine me every few moments, and there does not seem to be any hostility in his glance.

Wagner ends. I prowl through the record racks, select one, put it on the turntable. Schoenberg. *Verklaerte Nacht*. Music of tempestuous anguish followed by calmness and resignation. The theme of acceptance again. Fine. Fine. The swirling strings enfold me. Rich, lush chords. Judith appears, bringing me a glass of rum. She has something mild for herself, sherry or vermouth. She looks a little peaked but very friendly, very open.

"Cheers," she says.

"Cheers."

"That's good music you put on. A lot of people won't believe Schoenberg could be sensuous and tender. Of course, it's very early Schoenberg."

"Yes," I say. "The romantic juices tend to dry up as you get older, eh? What have you been up to lately, Jude?"

"Nothing much. A lot of the same old."

"How's Karl?"

"I don't see Karl any more."

"Oh."

"Didn't I tell you that?"

"No," I say. "It's the first I've heard of it."

"I'm not accustomed to needing to *tell* you things, Duv."

"You'd better get accustomed to it. You and Karl—"

"He became very insistent about marrying me. I told him it was too soon, that I didn't know him well enough, that I was afraid of structuring my life again when it might possibly be the wrong structure for me. He was hurt. He began lecturing me about retreats from involvement and commitment, about self-destructiveness, a lot of stuff like that. I looked right at him in the middle of it and I flashed on him as a kind of father-figure; you know, big and pompous and stern, not a lover but a mentor, a professor, and I didn't want that. And I started thinking about what he'd be like in another ten or twelve years. He'd be in his sixties and I'd still be young. And I realized there was no future for us together. I told him that as gently as I could. He hasn't called in ten days or so. I suppose he won't."

"I'm sorry."

"No need to be, Duv. I did the smart thing. I'm sure of it. Karl was good for me, but it couldn't have been permanent. My Karl phase. A very healthy phase. The thing is not to let a phase go on too long after you know it's really over."

"Yes," I say. "Certainly."

"Would you like some more rum?"

"In a little while."

"What about you?" she asks. "Tell me about yourself. How you're making out, now that—now that—"

"Now that my superman phase is over?"

"Yes," she says. "It's really gone, eh?"

"Really. All gone. No doubt."

"And so, Duv? How has it been for you since it happened?"

Justice. You hear a lot about justice, God's justice. He looketh after the righteous. He doeth dirt to the ungodly. Justice? Where's justice? Where's God, for that matter? Is He really dead, or merely on vacation, or only absent-minded? Look at His justice. He sends a flood to Pakistan. Zap, a million people dead, the adulterer and the virgin both. Justice? Maybe. Maybe the supposedly innocent victims weren't so innocent after all. Zap, the dedicated nun at the leprosarium gets leprosy and her lips fall off overnight. Justice. Zap, the cathedral that the congregation has been building for the past two hundred years is reduced to rubble by an earthquake the day before Easter. Zap. Zap. God laughs in our faces. This is justice? Where? How? I mean, consider my case. I'm not trying to wring some pity from you now; I'm being purely objective. Listen, I didn't *ask* to be a superman. It was handed to me at the moment of my conception. God's incomprehensible whim. A whim that defined me, shaped me, malformed me, dislocated me, and it was unearned, unasked for, entirely undesired, unless you want to think of my genetic heritage in terms of somebody else's bad karma, and crap on that. It was a random twitch. God said, Let this kid be a superman, and Lo! young Selig was a superman, in one limited sense of the word. For a time, anyhow. God set me up for everything that happened: the isolation, the suffering, the loneliness, even the self-pity. Justice? Where? The Lord giveth, who the hell knoweth why, and the Lord taketh away. Which He has now done. The power's gone. I'm just plain folks, even as you and you and you. Don't misunderstand: I accept my fate, I'm completely reconciled to it, I am NOT asking you to feel sorry for me. I simply want to make a little sense out of this. Now that the power's gone, who am I? How do I define myself now? I've lost my special thing, my power, my wound, my reason for apartness. All I have left now is the memory of having been different. The scars of it. What am I supposed to do now? How do I relate to mankind, now that the difference is gone and I'm still here? *It* died. I live on. What a strange thing you did to me, God. I'm not protesting, you understand. I'm just asking things, in a quiet, reasonable tone of voice. I'm inquiring into the nature of divine justice. I think Goethe's old harpist had the right slant on you, God. You lead us forth into life, you let the poor man fall

into guilt, and then you leave him to his misery. For all guilt is revenged
on earth. That's a reasonable complaint. You have ultimate power, God,
but you refuse to take ultimate responsibility. Is that fair? I think I have
a reasonable complaint too. If there's justice, why does so much of life
seem unjust? If you're really on our side, God, why do you hand us a
life of pain? Where's justice for the baby born without eyes? The baby
born with two heads? The baby born with a power men weren't meant
to have? Just asking, God. I accept your decree, believe me, I bow to
your will, because I might as well—what choice do I have, after all?—
but I'm still entitled to ask. Right?

   Hey, God? God? Are you listening, God?

   I don't think you are. I don't think you give a crap. God, I think
you've been fucking me.

Dee-dah-de-doo-dah-dee-da. The music is ending. Celestial harmonies
filling the room. Everything merging into oneness. Snowflakes swirling
beyond the windowpane. Right on, Schoenberg. You understood, at least
when you were young. You caught truth and put it on paper. I hear
what you're saying, man. Don't ask questions, you say. Accept. Only
accept, that's the motto. Accept. Accept. Whatever comes to you, accept.

Judith says, "Claude Guermantes has invited me to go skiing with him
in Switzerland over Christmas. I can leave the baby with a friend in
Connecticut. But I won't go if you need me, Duv. Are you okay? Can
you manage?"

   "Sure I can. I'm not paralyzed, Jude. I haven't lost my sight. Go to
Switzerland, if that's what you want."

   "I'll only be gone eight days."

   "I'll survive."

   "When I come back, I hope you'll move out of that housing project.
You ought to live down here close to me. We should see more of each
other."

   "Maybe."

   "I might even introduce you to some girlfriends of mine. If you're
interested."

   "Wonderful, Jude."

   "You don't sound enthusiastic about it."

   "Go easy with me," I tell her. "Don't rush me with a million things.
I need time to sort things out."

   "All right. It's like a new life, isn't it, Duv?"

   "A new life. Yes. A new life, that's what it is, Jude."

*   *   *

The storm is intense, now. Cars are vanishing under the first layers of whiteness. At dinner time the radio weather forecaster talked of an accumulation of eight to ten inches before morning Judith has invited me to spend the night here, in the maid's room. Well, why not? Now of all times, why should I spurn her? I'll stay. In the morning we'll take Pauly out to the park, with his sled, into the new snow. It's really coming down, now. The snow is so beautiful. Covering everything, cleansing everything, briefly purifying this tired eroded city and its tired eroded people. I can't take my eyes from it. My face is close to the window. I hold a brandy snifter in one hand, but I don't remember to drink from it, because the snow has caught me in its hypnotic spell.

"Boo!" someone cries behind me.

I jump so violently that the cognac leaps from the snifter and splashes the window. In terror I whirl, crouching, ready to defend myself; then the instinctive fear subsides and I laugh. Judith laughs too.

"That's the first time I've ever surprised you," she says. "In 31 years, the first time!"

"You gave me one hell of a jolt."

"I've been standing here for three or four minutes *thinking* things at you. Trying to get a rise out of you, but no, no, you didn't react, you just went on staring at the snow. So I sneaked up and yelled in your ear. You were really startled, Duv. You weren't faking at all."

"Did you think I was lying to you about what had happened to me?"

"No, of course not."

"Then why'd you think I'd be faking?"

"I don't know. I guess I doubted you just a little. I don't any more. Oh, Duv, Duv, I feel so sad for you!"

"Don't," I say. "Please, Jude."

She is crying softly. How strange that is, to watch Judith cry. For love of me, no less. For love of me.

It's very quiet now.

The world is white outside and gray within. I accept that. I think life will be more peaceful. Silence will become my mother tongue. There will be discoveries and revelations, but no upheavals. Perhaps some color will come back into the world for me, later on. Perhaps.

Living, we fret. Dying, we live. I'll keep that in mind. I'll be of good cheer. Twang. Twing. Twong. Until I die again, hello, hello, hello, hello.